"Let me ask you a question. Have you slept with Admiral Stanley yet?" Ben James asked.

Melanie shook her head. "You told me not to."

"Excellent. Here's what I want you to do. The meeting's not until later this afternoon. I want you to get on the horn to the Pentagon and see if he can make a little time for you. Tell him you're dying to be with him on this important day, that you know he needs a friend right now. Then get on over there and haul his ashes right there in his office. Really build his ego, make him feel like Tarzan before he goes in for that vote."

"Come on, BJ," she said. "I have a lot of self-confidence, but do you really believe that one roll in the hay with me is going to make him swing his vote on this?"

BJ leaned forward, resting his arms on his knees. "No. One roll in the hay may not swing the vote. But that plus a million telegrams, a demonstration, negative press, and a call from his ninety-five-year-old former commanding officer just might."

★ ★ ★ ★ ★ ★ ★ ★ ★ ★ ★ ★ ★ ★ ★ ★ ★

PUPPETMASTER

Mike McQuay

★ ★ ★ ★ ★ ★ ★ ★ ★ ★ ★ ★ ★ ★ ★ ★ ★

FALCON ™

BANTAM BOOKS

New York · Toronto · London · Sydney · Auckland

Accustom your children constantly to this; if a thing happened at one window and they, when relating it, say that it happened at another, do not let it pass, but instantly check them; you do not know where deviation from truth will end.

DR. SAMUEL JOHNSON

PUPPETMASTER

A Bantam Falcon Book / October 1991

FALCON and the portrayal of a boxed "f" are trademarks of Bantam Books, a division of Bantam Doubleday Dell Publishing Group, Inc.

ISBN 0-553-29333-8

Published simultaneously in the United States and Canada

Bantam Books are published by Bantam Books, a division of Bantam Doubleday Dell Publishing Group, Inc. Its trademark, consisting of the words "Bantam Books" and the portrayal of a rooster, is Registered in U.S. Patent and Trademark Office and in other countries. Marca Registrada. Bantam Books, 666 Fifth Avenue, New York, New York 10103.

Printed in the United States of America

RAD   0 9 8 7 6 5 4 3 2 1

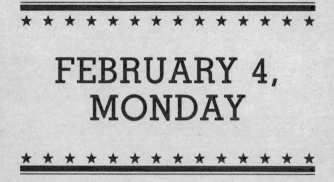

★ ★ ★ ★ ★ ★ ★ ★ ★ ★ ★ ★ ★ ★ ★ ★

FEBRUARY 4,
MONDAY

★ ★ ★ ★ ★ ★ ★ ★ ★ ★ ★ ★ ★ ★ ★ ★

▬▬▬ ■ NEWSBREAK ■ ▬▬▬

FTPO   copy #2, Sat. February 3

*Contains SCI enclosure—EYES ONLY—security present for reading

DATELINE: POBLADO, CARIBBEA

Early reports linking an American covert specialist with the assassination of Caribbean Foreign Minister Ramirez on 29 January seem to be accurate. Data from Tegucigalpa station indicates the presence of one Ken Breedlove in the area at the time of the termination. Breedlove is a free-lancer who has done work for DOD in past, but so far we have turned up nothing to indicate he was operating on anything save his own initiative in the attack. Russian Intel working upon same information. The search for Breedlove has so far turned out negative results, but sources place him still in country.

TO: White House Press Corps
FROM: The Office of the President
DATE: 4 February
RE: Intelligence reports from Caribbea

OFFICIAL NEWS RELEASE

The United States government forthrightly and categorically denies allegations that Caribbean Foreign Minister Ramirez was assassinated by a CIA-sponsored murder squad under the direct leadership of an American agent. Assassination and violence are not now, and will never be, weapons in the arsenal of democracy when fighting Communist oppression. American intelligence indicates that the assassination may have been the result of politics within the highest echelons of Caribbean rule and should be viewed, simply, as a normal power change within the structure of an unstable state.

". . . This is Tom Morrison, World Cable News, reporting from a balcony high atop the International Hotel in Poblado, Caribbea, overlooking the parade route taken by the state funeral of murdered Caribbean minister Miguel Ramirez. Below me you can see the streets jammed with people—one report puts it at over a million—who have come here to watch, to state their case, or simply to mourn the passing of a leader of world renown.

"I'm up here instead of being in the crowds because of the element of danger. All day long, a string of speakers has been leading the crowd in chants and tirades against America and what they call its 'puppet government' in Poblado. These people blame the U.S. directly for the assassination of Ramirez, a vocal leader of the opposition Companero party, saying that he was silenced because he spoke out vocally against the U.S.-backed government of Maria Madrina. This despite State Department assurances to the contrary. Anti-American sentiment has been growing steadily here since American promises of economic aid have fallen flat, the Communist-inspired Companeros making political hay of the worsening conditions in Central America, with today's demonstration standing as a high water mark of the movement's resurgence.

"Earlier, several of my colleagues from ABC News were severely beaten when they tried to interview people on the streets. Apparently the people of Caribbea have never heard of the freedom of the press. . . ."

Georgetown, District of Columbia
4 February—3:14 A.M.

Joann Durbin sat in the casement window—frigid cold seeping through the leaded glass to chill her naked body—and stared out into the deserted length of Dumbarton Street. The sky was slate-gray and still, the street lamp's harsh glare dividing the night into angular planes of light and darkness—nothing between. On or off, she thought, in and out. Like sex.

A light snow sputtered into the light's glare, turning the Victorian, high-walled splendor of Dumbarton into a Currier and Ives calendar without horse and sled. Dumbarton was a street of dreams, the high-tone resolution of the house of mirrors that was Washington. The houses were narrow, the gardens luxuriant. The power was here, the upward mobility, the old money. It was the legacy of Eleanor Roosevelt, who had renovated heavily on Dumbarton Street, reviving the splendor that in an earlier time had belonged to the river princes and land barons of the Port of Washington.

Joann Durbin thought a lot about earlier times these days, mostly her own, back when her life had been hers. Back when there had been options. Across the street, she could see a light still on in Henry Kissinger's house and wondered if he were watching the snow, too, and thinking about options.

She smiled at that. Maybe he had a pair of binoculars and was simply watching *her*. She stood, stretching,

thrusting out her famous breasts, just in case he *was*
watching. She felt a civic duty, after all. Some of the most
important hands and mouths in Washington had handled
her breasts in the previous five years, and as near as she
could understand, life and its importance pretty much
reduced itself to that for most of the men in the world.

BJ understood. The son of a bitch understood it all so
well he had cut her completely out of options—all except
one.

She walked away from the window after giving Kissinger enough time for a good show, but not enough time
to jerk off if he was so inclined. Joann had her limits. Let
him take it to his wife.

She tiptoed quietly past Jack Braedman who was sleeping fitfully atop the silk sheets of the ebony and chrome
framed bed near the open doorway, his penis semierect in
sleep, lying atop his stomach like a fleshy bludgeon. Jack
was a great guy for a senator and a fair sex partner, but
unfortunately she couldn't love the great guys. It was the
ones she couldn't have, the hard cases like Jerry, the
burn-outs, that she went for. Was it any wonder that she'd
gravitated to Washington from Ole Miss after graduation?
Like any good politician, she wanted *everyone* to love her.
And once she had them, it was time to move on.

Except with Jerry. Jerry had been different. He took the
sex casually and for granted, and she'd found a measure of
excitement in a life with someone she had to work at
pleasing. Giving could be better than getting, and if she'd
understood *that* five years ago, she wouldn't be getting
ready to exercise her last option as a free human being
tonight in the middle of the gloom of a February snowfall.

She moved into the dark bathroom, closing the door
quietly before turning on the lights. The room glared
harshly, the bright lights reflecting off the white wall and
floor tiles, dispelling all darkness—on and off, black and
white. Nothing between. It was a lesson she'd taken years
to learn, and now it was too late to make use of the
knowledge.

The full-length mirror was attached to the back of the
bathroom door. She stared at her own reflection clinically,
trying to see what it was about the arrangement of flesh

and bone that could make men do what they normally wouldn't dream of doing.

She turned to the washstand and the mirror that filled *that* wall. She'd always been pretty and had somehow felt the responsibility to stay that way, an occupation of sorts. Her face was childlike, green eyes wide, her stare open, trusting, framed by the willowy tumble of natural blond hair that she worked at fixing up hard enough to make it look like she hadn't worked hard. Her breast muscles were still several years away from sag. She'd kept her stomach hard through exercise, her buttocks and hips tight, shimmery with muscle. BJ would call her good horseflesh, and God, how far off was he really? Men had uttered oaths, revealed secrets, made pledges, and cried like babies, all for the chance to run their hands over her body and put a part of themselves into her for a couple of minutes.

She wasn't procreating the species or engaging in any sort of meaningful exchange with other human beings. She'd been fucking. For years, fucking. And try as she might, she had lost sight of the value of any of it. She looked at her body, shrugged at the incongruence of it all, and turned to the task at hand—teaching BJ the value of options.

She opened the medicine cabinet and took out the package of disposable razors. She smiled at the package.

"Even if you know, right now, what I'm doing," she said in clipped, even tones, "it's too late to stop me."

She smiled at her assertion, reveling in the control that she, for once, was exercising. The feeling was liberating, exciting, and she found herself smiling spontaneously for the first time in months.

"J-Joann?" came Braedman's groggy voice from the bed. "Were you just talking?"

"Go back to sleep, honey," she called cheerily, exaggerating her mild southern accent the way the men liked. "I'll be there in a minute."

"Hurry up . . . the bed's lonely."

She shook her head as she pulled one of the plastic razors out of the pack, twisting it this way and that in her fingers. Four years of business administration and a valedictorian speech so that she could screw politicians and pretend to like it. The two acting classes she'd taken in

college had served her in far better stead. The trouble with
being smart is that you can't get on the cattle car with
everybody else and think it's okay. It was like being able to
see the bones move under the skin.

She held the razor in her palm and brought it down
hard on the edge of the sink, breaking up the plastic,
cutting her palm deeply in the process.

"Joann. . . ."

"Coming!"

She held her hand up to her face and studied the blood
dripping down her hand onto her arm, smiling in satisfaction at the lack of pain. Then she held her palm up and
turned a full circle, as if showing it off. The excitement
surged through her. Coming to decisions was hard. But
once made, they took on their own kind of life, their own
momentum. She was caught in it now, anxious to push
ahead. Pieces of the razor lay on the floor and in the sink,
the shiny steel blade gleaming in the harsh glare. She
reached in and gingerly picked it up, kissing it lightly.

"Are you okay in there?" Braedman asked. He was at
the door.

"Now you just go on back and get under those covers,"
she said. "I'll be out in a few minutes to give you a big
surprise."

"What kind of surprise?" he asked, almost boyish.

"You know . . ." she said seductively, then smiled as
he war-whooped and jumped back onto the bed. What odd
childlike creatures men were, simple domination the
guiding force in their lives. She'd spent years trying to
understand that before realizing there was nothing to
understand.

Blood was dripping all over the meticulous washstand
now, and that made her happy, too. She took a long breath,
winked once to the beauty who stared back at her from the
mirror, then drew the razor blade in a long line down her
left arm, the meandering pale blue vein her stenciled
course.

The blood came quickly, unbelievably quickly, washing
out over her arm from wrist to elbow, bubbling out,
splashing everywhere. She hadn't realized it would go so
quickly. She needed to hurry.

She dipped her right pointer finger into the blood on

her arm and tried to write on the mirror, but her long, clear-polished nail kept getting in the way; so she bit it off and began forming the letters on the glass.

It wasn't easy. She'd become light-headed almost immediately. She kept forgetting where she was, what she was writing. It seemed to take so long.

Finally she finished, leaning heavily against the washstand for support. Everything around her was foggy and she was getting so tired. Sleep, peaceful sleep, had eluded her for months. It wouldn't tonight.

"Joann . . . Joann!"

He was at the door again, calling her name, and his voice seemed far away, like he was shouting down a tunnel. She tried to turn to the door, but lost her grip on the stand and slid to the floor instead. Sleep was overcoming her now, the glare of the bathroom just a pleasant summer day under a mimosa tree.

From a distance she heard a noise, like thunder, and just barely caught a glimpse of the door crashing open. A man was bending down to her. What man? She might have known him, but everything was so confused now. He was naked. Did he want to screw her one last time? She wouldn't have denied him that.

He was lifting her, but he seemed elongated, distorted. He was cradling her in his arms, but she didn't feel anything, and there seemed to be something—tears?—rolling down his distant face.

He seemed to be moving in slower and slower motion, and finally, the motion stopped. He became a freeze frame in her vision and she no longer felt anything at all.

The last image her brain could hold was stark and frightening. The freeze frame of Jack slowly metamorphosed into BJ's face, rosy-cheeked, cherubic. He was shaking his head, his vacant blue eyes tearing at her mind. Then he began to laugh, a deep and malignant rumble.

And she knew, then, that using her last remaining option simply meant that she wouldn't get to play anymore.

Central America 3:27 A.M.

Jerry Delany eased the servo forward slightly, nosing the C-130 down even closer to the dark black waters of the Caribbean barely a hundred feet below. To the west, just beyond the lifeless body of the pilot still strapped to his seat, the lights of Cauquira twinkled dimly off the far northeast coast of Honduras, the area they called the Mosquito Coast. He adjusted the yaw, turning slightly to hug the coast. Next stop Caribbea.

He took a drag off his cigarette, the tip glowing brightly in the blue-green haze of the instruments. The tricky part was coming up. He'd made this run a hundred times when he'd been with Southern Air, but this was his first time to announce the arrival.

Outside, in the black night, static electric lightning chained wildly across the sky, deep rumbling like angry voices bellowing as the night strobed black to blinding bright—on and off, on and off. The plane cried loudly in his ears and the continual vibration of the hull rattled his teeth. But that was the 130. They didn't call her the Herky Bird for nothing. He'd flown them for the government in jungles from Nam to Poblado, and now he was flying one for himself.

He was off the instruments now, watching the shadow of the Caribbean coast through the blood-splattered window on the starboard side. And as they pitched and rolled with the violent weather, the body of Murphy jerked around like a puppet in the next seat. It was a shame about Murphy. He'd seemed like an okay guy. But a million bucks cuts a lot of ties, and if he still felt badly about it he could always chalk it up to another casualty in the unending war against Communist aggression. Delany smiled and spit out a loose sprig of tobacco. That was it. Murphy'd been a victim of Communist aggression.

Delany's stomach tightened up when he saw the next set of lights at Cabo Gracias a Dios on the Caribbean side. The next few minutes would tell the story. He'd either be dead or on his way to the biggest payday he would ever know in his life. From there, Rio called—rum; dark women with bloodred lips; and a quick exit from that clingy bitch Joann. What a thought—no ties and enough cash money to last him the rest of his life. He turned and looked at Murphy again, the side of the man's head shimmering dark ooze where the .45 had taken half his face off. Sorry, pal. Luck of the draw.

Delany took one last pull off the cigarette, crushed it out on the floor, then pulled back hard on the servo, the flaps creaking up, angling the bird into a steep climb. It was all mechanical now. He knew what he had to do and simply put himself on autopilot, just the way he'd flown combat. If you don't think, you can't be afraid.

He took it up to ten thousand feet, leveling off quickly and pulling the microphone off the hot spur. He reached out and juiced the transmitter, speaking with the practiced nonchalance of a fighter pilot. "This is EquAir Flight 322 calling any station. EquAir Flight 322 calling any station. I believe I've got instrument problems and am seriously off course. Repeat off course, instruments screwy. Hey! Can anybody out there tell me where I am? Over."

He waited a moment, then repeated the message, a response crackling back immediately. "Flight 322, this is Holmes Field in the Canal Zone. Do you read? Over."

"Canal Zone?" Delany said with mock horror. "Where am I? I'm supposed to be on my way to Florida. Over."

"We're picking up an unidentified blip to our northwest. Can you give us a heading, 322? And what is your flight plan. Over."

"Negative. My instruments are shorted out, Holmes," he said, keeping the edge to his voice. "I'm traveling under government authorization 2Q2-1719 without flight plan and carry sensitive cargo. Over."

"How's your fuel, 322? Over."

"No problem. Get me out of here. Over."

"Can you give us a visual, 322? Over."

"I'm in the middle of a storm, Holmes," Delany said, lightly overamping the radio to static just to make his point. "There's a large land mass to my right. I thought it was Cuba at first, but . . . my God . . . my God!"

"322, do you copy? Do you copy? Come in. Over."

He sat back for half a minute, letting the controller at

Holmes wonder. Then he took a deep breath and leaned forward. "Mayday! Mayday! We're being fired upon from the ground!" he yelled, his voice keyed to hysteria. "We've been hit!"

"322 . . . 322!"

Delany began gagging loudly into the mike. "S-smoke filling the cabin! Something wrong w-with pilot. Direct me left or right . . . left or right . . . no controls. It's missiles! They're firing missiles! We're going down . . . we're—"

He reached out and shut down the radio, dropping the flaps and going into a dive to get below radar lest he become a self-fulfilling prophecy.

It would have to happen quickly now. He took it down to wave level, hugging the coast tightly, searching for the lagoon just south of Cabo Gracias. That fucking Breedlove better be there or he was done for. Flying into Caribbea would be a hell of a lot easier than flying back out now that he'd given away his position. The damned Companeros still controlled the army.

He flew the coast nervously, time hanging heavily on him as unnamed fishing villages flashed by the wingtips on the heavily wooded shoreline. It was Delany's fate to spend his life in the hothouse confusion of the jungle, any jungle, anywhere. It matched his spirit and it matched the darkness of his own nature. Where was the fucking lagoon? He should have reached it by—there, yawning wide beneath him.

He hit the controls hard to starboard, kicking the rudder pedals to control the yaw as he banked sharply, heading straight at the lagoon, diving at the inscrutable tangle of the jungle. As he did, torches flared brightly at lagoon's end, a small landing strip defining itself with a border of fire. Reaching out, he toggled the gear, listening to it snap into place with a hydraulic whoosh.

He cut the engines dead, the bird dropping as he flapped up to keep the nose. The languid waters of the lagoon were barely twenty feet below him as he fought for stability without the equalizing pull of the fan jets. He had no time for fear now as the mechanics of a landing he'd made so many times in the last ten years culled his senses to concentration.

The controls shook crazily, Murphy's body dancing in his harness as they hit uneven ground, bouncing hard, then coming down again, torches blurring past, easier this time as he came on full with the brakes. The heavy beast skidded, then held, the tires screaming loudly as they dragged the great bulk to a stop just at the end of the line of torches. He was sitting, in total silence for the first time in hours, the wall of the jungle barely ten feet before him. The torches began winking out immediately. And it wasn't until he heard his own rapid breathing in his ears that he knew how scared he'd been.

But it was over now. His part of it through and done. He still had to get out of country with the money, but that figured to be a piece of cake after this. All he needed to do now was deal with Breedlove.

He unstrapped and slid open the side window to a blast of hot, humid air—almost stifling. His hand was shaking as he lit another cigarette, but he wasn't sure if it was the residue of fear or simply excitement. Dark figures were running toward the plane down the distance of the now-dark dirt runway. He'd never put anything as big as the 130 in here before and would hate to have to try to take it out again—but he would, if Breedlove didn't come through as promised.

The men reached the Herky, and he looked down to see the big man with the red face and the red hair glaring up at him. "Pretty good landing for an asshole!" the man called up, Delany smiling and shaking his head.

"I see you haven't gotten any better-looking since the last time I saw you, Breed," he called back. "They ought to make your kind of ugly against the law."

"You did good." Breedlove smiled. "I knew you were right for this one. Come on down here and have a drink."

Delany looked at the others with the red man. Most he recognized from the old *libre uso* days, American mercs defending the borders and making a buck besides. Callera was with him, too. The remnants of the *libre* army were so hard up that they sent one of their leaders as a guide. Things really had fallen on hard times. He felt relatively safe, but wanted to keep control of things. "I'll come on out," he said, "just as soon as you show me a little something."

"Sure," Breedlove called, then turned to the camouflage-suited man beside him. "Jamie, get the suitcase." He stared back up at Delany, delight still showing on his face. "You got the ducks?"

"Yeah," Delany said, blowing out a long streamer of smoke that disappeared into the darkness immediately. "And you're welcome to them, just as soon as we've done some business."

Breedlove bowed low. "Just ask and you shall receive, buddy," he said, the man in camouflage hurrying back from a jeep parked nearby, carrying a streamer-sized aluminum suitcase in both arms. Delany craned his head farther out the small window as the man held his arms out with the suitcase.

"You're a lucky man," Breedlove said, unsnapping the lid of the suitcase. "As Shakespeare would say, 'Early retirement is a consummation devoutly to be wished in these hard economic times.'"

Now Delany knew why he was trembling. It was excitement, pure and simple. Breedlove lifted the lid on the suitcase. Stacks upon stacks of hundred-dollar bills filled the thing to overflow. "Is it all there?" he called down.

"Come count it yourself," Breedlove said. Something in his voice bothered Delany, but not enough to keep him from the money.

He dropped the cigarette out the window and squeezed past Murphy's body to move to the cargo bay. The bay was huge and cavernous, like an empty warehouse. He grunted as he moved into it, the sound echoing back to him. Except for the two wooden crates marked fragile tied up in the center of the bay, the cargo carrier was empty.

The hydraulic panel operated from the wall separated cabin from bay. He switched on the controls, the bay hinging open like a gaping mouth from the tail section, screaming with a piercing whine and a rush of air. The silhouettes of Breedlove's men rushed up the gangway and into the guts of the plane, twenty-foot poles with attached slings bouncing upon their shoulders.

It had begun.

NEWSBREAK

JOINT CHIEFS TO VOTE

(AP)—In an unprecedented Pentagon budget-balancing move, the Joint Chiefs of Staff are expected to vote today to cut their own spending of already allocated funds an extra 15 percent by eliminating the least cost-efficient programs from the service rosters. This budget recision is the first ever for DOD. The GAO has targeted twenty-three Pentagon projects as being cost prohibitive or unworkable, and sources close to the Pentagon confirm that the Chiefs will be voting to put them off stream, a move that will cut an extra sixty billion dollars from the defense budget. "This in no way will effect defense capabilities," a Pentagon spokesman said. "These are basically R and D programs that have worked their way into the system and need to be eliminated. In these hard economic times, and in response to lowered threat levels worldwide, every branch of government is striving to become more cost efficient. We are simply bringing things in line with the way the world exists today."

". . . merely because the Pentagon has never given back already appropriated money before, it's difficult to believe that the Joint Chiefs will roll over and let the Democratic weak sisters of Congress gut the very programs we need to take America strongly into the twenty-first century. It's a sad day for this country and its future if we allow the cowards and one-world liberals in our midst to cut the heart out of the military that has kept America and its allies free and strong for over two hundred years and take us down the path of expedience and placation. FDR

put this country in the red sixty years ago, not the
Pentagon."

—Knight-Ridder Syndicate

Arlington, Virginia 4 February—3:44 A.M.

Charles Merchant walked around the battle of Waterloo
and checked the field again from the south, from just
above the tiny Christmas garden shrubbery that was passing as the Forest of Soignes. The field stretched out before
him, just the size of the rec-room pool table upon which it
rested, the light over the table hanging low, illuminating
only the battle in the darkened room.

Merchant removed the straight-stemmed Algerian briar
pipe from his mouth and held it under the light, checking
the tobacco. Satisfied, he clamped it back between his
teeth and relit it with the disposable lighter, the air
immediately alive with the stale/sweet odor of Borkum
Riff. Waterloo was it, Napoleon's last, and in some ways
his most controversial, battle. The tiny hand-painted soldiers stood at attention on the highly detailed field of
honor: the Allies under Wellington in a three-and-a-half-
mile flank along the Wavre Road, the right flank, properly,
the heaviest concentration under Chasse's Dutch-Belgian
Division; the French less than a half mile to the north,
ready for the attack. Napoleon had understood the value of
publicity. He had gotten close enough to let them feel his
power—trumpets and drums could be clearly heard from
the Allied lines, while shouts of *Vive l'Empereur* added
thrilling accompaniment. Cuirasses glinted in the sun,
plumed helmets, bearskin caps, jackets of scarlet faced
with greens and purples, and crowned with gold epau-
lettes, caught the eye.

Splendor and power—the mental game.

For Merchant, it was a moment of high drama and
higher expectations. It was the last battle for him, too, the
culmination of a long-held dream. Dutifully he had con-
structed and relived each of the little Corsican's battles,

from his grapeshot defense of the Tuilleries against the anarchists in 1795 to the climax at Waterloo, some twenty years later. War, to Charlie Merchant, was a question of not only military options, but personalities as well. Events couldn't be put into perspective until the personalities were understood. And so he hoped that his re-creation of Napoleon's wars through the focus of personality could bring an insight that other strategists had missed to history's most misunderstood warrior and statesman. Merchant wanted to bring order to the process. And through studying battle, he felt he was studying the ordered mind in its most pristine state.

He wanted to close the book on the emperor with class and, in the process, leave something of himself behind. Something grand. He'd given his life and his dreams to the United States Army, and the army, in turn, had abandoned him because of a past mistake. For nearly forty years he had been fighting the ghost of his past, the specter of a young Intelligence lieutenant in Korea who'd made a wrong decision, passed along inaccurate troop strengths with disastrous consequences. For forty years he'd dreamed of the blood on his hands and worked feverishly to wash it off through total dedication and loyalty to those he served, only to be reminded, time and again in a thousand different ways, that he had failed to measure up.

As good as he was, as hard as he'd worked, the army had never forgotten or forgiven. He'd climbed the rungs of power the hard way, by being better and tougher and smarter than everyone around him. But in the final analysis, it had come to naught. He'd been disdained and passed over too many times, his self-recriminations just as brutal as the rejection of those around him. All he'd ever wanted was to serve his country with honor, to live the Code of Conduct as a guide for life.

Instead, he'd taken early retirement.

He'd tried to go on from there, to build another life for himself through a desk job with the General Services Administration. It had brought him some success, but had never slayed the demons. He'd quit again after ten years spent in a bureaucratic tug-of-war where there are no winners or losers, only survivors.

Charles Merchant still found himself trying to measure up as he lived in the pedantic hazy twilight of a life over before it had reached its sixth decade. He still wanted to give, to prove himself worthy. Where everyone else at his age was slowing down to reflect on life, he was still trying to build one. Maybe the book would do it.

Maybe.

The phone rang, loud, piercing. He turned and stared once at the unit hanging on the wall, then leaned over the table to look at his watch. No one would call this late unless it was urgent. He hurried across the length of the room and grabbed the receiver just as it was beginning its second ring.

"Merchant," he said.

"Charlie?" came a distant, strained voice he couldn't quite place. "It's m-me."

"I can't—"

"Hello?"

Linda had picked up the phone. "I've got it," Merchant said. "Go back to sleep."

"But what's—"

"I've got it," he said again, the extension clicking loudly in his ear. "Who is this?"

"It's me . . . Jack."

"Jack? God, you sound awful. What's wrong?" He turned on the switch behind the bar, lighting that area of the large room, and stretched the phone cord so he could sit on one of the bar stools.

"I—I don't . . . exactly know," the man said, his voice distant, disoriented. "I'm in Georgetown. I'm . . . c-covered with blood. I don't . . . don't . . ."

"Take a second," Merchant said gently. "Get yourself together first. Then just tell me what the problem is."

He could hear Braedman sobbing on the other end. Finally the man took a long breath and spoke. "There's a girl here with me," he said without inflection. "She's d-dead. She killed herself with a razor."

"You're sure she's dead?" he asked, his mind immediately alert, reeling through the scenarios of a married, big-time senator being found with a body.

"I didn't know a person could bleed so much," Braedman answered. "G-God, Charlie. What am I going to do? I was going to announce for the presidency next month. This could ruin me."

The man's voice had become stronger as he dwelled on the problems to himself. Merchant knew that the steps taken in the next few hours would write the climactic chapter in the book of Jack Braedman and decide its denouement, and he knew why his friend had called him, too. But he had to know something else before he'd offer that help. "You've got to tell me the truth on something, Jack," Merchant said. "No bullshit."

"You're the best friend I've got," Braedman said. "Believe me I wouldn't . . ."

"Did you do anything to the girl," Merchant said, his tone flat and professional.

"Charlie . . . !"

"Just answer me, Jack," Merchant said in a low voice. "Just tell me the truth. Did you hurt her . . . even accidentally? Or maybe she provoked you."

"God no," Braedman replied, his voice choking again. "You know me better than that. I loved her, Charlie. You've got to help me."

"I'll do what I can," Merchant said, wondering how quickly the contacts dry up once the power's gone.

"Thank God," Braedman said, breaking down again.

"Just hold on to it for another minute," Merchant said, massaging his tired eyes. "I'll need an address."

The track lighting on the rec-room ceiling flared brightly, Linda Merchant walking in, lost in the folds of an oversize robe. She took a faltering step toward him, but he put a hand up to keep her away. She turned from him then, moving past the battlefield to straighten a stack of drawings lying on the sofa.

"Let me get a pencil," he said, leaning across the bar for the cup of miscellaneous pens he kept back there. He put a hand over the mouthpiece and called to his wife. "Get me some paper, would you?"

She brought him one of his preliminary drawings for the Waterloo battlefield. He turned it over and took down the number on the back side. "That's quite a neighborhood, buddy. What did this girl do for a living?"

"I'm not sure," he said, confused. "I . . ."

"Never mind. Look, we're going to have to call the D.C. police . . ."

"No . . . isn't there something . . ."

"No, Jack," Merchant said harshly. "We can't compound this problem by illegal activities. It will only backfire on you. You sit tight. I know the police chief very well. I'll give him a call and see if there's anything we can do to keep this relatively quiet."

"Is it possible?"

"If it's simple, my friend," Merchant said. "If everything falls just right and everybody says the right things . . . who knows? I'm coming over there now. I'm only fifteen minutes away."

"Thank you . . . oh, God. I won't forget this, Charlie. You don't know how grateful . . ."

"We'll talk about it after it's over. Fifteen minutes. And Jack?"

"Yeah?"

"Don't touch anything."

He hung up and put his glasses back on. Linda was staring at Waterloo. "It was Jack Braedman," he said. "He's having a . . . problem and needs my help."

"What kind of a problem needs the cooperation of the D.C. police?" she asked, bending over to pick up a block of Hanoverian riflemen that guarded the chateau of Hougoumont between the opposing armies.

"Don't worry about it right now," he said, moving to take the riflemen from her and place them back on the battlefield. "This is business."

"You retired," she replied. "If there's a problem with Jack, I want to know about it. Is Eve all right? Maybe I should call her, I . . ."

"Don't call Eve," he said, glaring at her. "Please. Don't mention this to anyone."

She stared hard at him, her sleep-puffy eyes searching his. "I'm your wife," she said. "If there's a problem, you can trust me to keep my mouth shut."

He looked at his watch. Every second was precious. "We don't have time for this right now," he said, unwilling to start back in on the tune that had been the theme song of their marriage since his retirement. He put his hands on her shoulders and tried to look understanding. "Go back to bed. We'll talk about this later."

"Right," she said, pulling herself from his grasp and turning to stare at the emperor's last hurrah.

He started to say something, but stopped himself, knowing that discussions with Linda more often than not led him into the relentless clutching grasp of the tar-baby syndrome. He tightened his lips and walked toward the door.

"Does it ever end, Charlie?" she said, her voice softening.

He turned to her at the door. "Does what end?"

She looked at him with a kind of sadness that almost seemed condescending. "You don't have to be the one everybody calls. You don't have to be the one to run out in the middle of the night. They don't care anymore about you. Why do you care about them?"

"Jack's my friend," he replied.

"Yeah," she said, looking at the floor. "Be careful. The roads . . ."

"I know," he said, glancing quickly at his watch. He moved through the door. "Be home as soon as I can."

Cabo Gracias, Caribbea 3:47 A.M.

Ken Breedlove stood playing the beam of the flashlight over the rough wooden packing crates as his men hefted them gently up and into the slings to be carried down into the waiting trucks. "You have any problems?" he asked the man who stood in the dark beside him.

"You wouldn't believe how easy it was," Delany answered. "What a screwy world. I went in and signed off on a GS-20 and they smiled and said, 'Have a nice day.' Hell, they even loaded them for me."

"Easy!" Breedlove barked as his men tried to raise one of the crates, the weight of the thing bringing them back almost to their knees before they were able to straighten up and walk cautiously back down the gangway, their cargo undulating pregnantly in the slings as they moved.

"I saw Callera here," Delany said. "Have things gotten that bad?"

Breedlove grunted. "Hell, we probably didn't even need him. I already knew where the field was. It was just a kind of courtesy to use them at all. They did help with the torches."

"Well, this is for their benefit," Delany said. "But if the organization has disintegrated, how are they going to capitalize?"

Breedlove turned the beam on Delany, the man putting up his hand to block the light from his face. "You ask too damned many questions, Jerry," he said. "Let's go up front." He turned to the men who had stayed behind when the others had taken the first crate. "Jamie . . . Wee Willie. Come up front with us."

"I'd really rather not," Delany said. "I'm kind of trying to put Murphy behind me."

Breedlove nodded. Now or later. It didn't matter to him. "Sure," he said amiably. "Go on down with Callera and have a drink. I'll join you in a minute."

Breedlove and the others walked to the cabin. He moved with a slow deliberateness that could seem almost casual, but it wasn't. It was precision. The clock was ticking madly right now, Companeros undoubtedly blanketing the area searching for the blip that had mysteriously appeared, then disappeared on their coastal radar. They had twenty minutes at best to complete their business and get the hell back over the border.

He squeezed into the cabin to look at the pilot. Messy. It had apparently never occurred to Delany to offer the man a cut of the money instead of this. Wee Willie stuck his shaved head into the compartment. He was a huge man, a former Marine DI, his skin the color of deep walnut, his eyes hard and cold as ball bearings.

Breedlove pointed to the body. "We're going to have to lose this one's head," he said.

Willie nodded and slid his machete out of the scabbard as Jamie, a former Cuban colonel under Batista, squeezed past him to take the pilot's seat.

"Can you taxi this thing back to the water?" Breedlove asked.

"No sweat," Jamie said, dark eyes glinting under Breed-love's flashlight before turning to inspect the instrument panel. "Where do you want the charges?"

"I want everything concentrated under the port wing forward," Breedlove said as he watched Willie sawing off the copilot's head. "That way, we'll get the forward cabin and the fuel, but won't lose much in the blow. Okay?"

"Sure, Breed."

"And, Willie," Breedlove said, turning to the big man. "Don't make that cut too clean. We want it to look like the head blew off."

"Right, Cap'n," Willie grunted.

The heat was unbearable in the confined space. Breed-love was sweating profusely, his hair matted under the green fatigue cap he wore. "See you guys on the outside," he said. "I want everything done in ten minutes."

He moved out of the cabin, walking back down the bay. The second crate was already being lifted onto the sling. He checked his watch again. So far so good.

He moved down the gangway and into the night. A hard rain was falling now, turning the landing strip into a field of mud. The air was thick and still. He took the cap off and wiped his forehead on his sleeve. His boots disappeared ankle deep in mud as he trudged toward the covered jeep parked on the edge of the jungle beside an old, beat-up Ford wagon containing Callera's ragtag *libre* escort. He felt as if he were walking on a wet sponge in an oven.

Callera sat behind the wheel of the unmarked, olive jeep, passing a bottle of Jack Daniel's between him and Delany. The smell of marijuana drifted heavily from the interior of the Ford, the remnants of the revolution sliding headlong into forgetful decay. They were getting soft. Breedlove moved around to the passenger side, intercepting the bottle and taking a long drink. "Been a while, hasn't it?" he said, handing the bottle back to Delany, who was already half-drunk with excitement.

"We been talking over old times," the man said, taking a drink and passing the bottle to Callera again. "Jose and me used to meet on the download side over here when we were keeping the revolution going."

"It's still going," Callera said in heavily accented English, his pockmarked face dark, brooding. "America let us down, financed us and then told us to disband, even though the Companeros still control the hearts and minds of the people. Madrina will soon be finished and our country will need us again. No, my friends, the freedom still burns within us."

"Getting a little damp, though," Breedlove said, watching eight men walking carefully in step down the gangway, Jamie already firing up the fan jets in preparation for turning the plane around.

"What are you unloading?" Callera asked. "When you called on us, we assumed you were bringing weapons . . . but I only see two crates."

"You mean you don't know?" Delany said, incredulous.

Breedlove put a hand on the man's shoulder, applying pressure, silencing him. "Don't worry, *mi amigo*," he told Callera. "You'll be satisfied."

Over the roof of the canvas-covered jeep, Breedlove watched Jamie taxi the C-130 around 180 degrees and slosh slowly through the mud, heading back toward the lagoon at the end of the clearing. He was soaked through, drenched, but he was glad for the rain. This would hurt the search party far more than it would him. He'd learned, just as Lee Christmas had learned so many years ago when he'd turned Central America into United Fruit's private empire, that surviving the jungle meant accepting its tangled darkness into your own soul. He celebrated the rain; at least it was keeping away the mosquitoes.

"Well, I hate to drink and run," Delany said happily, "but if it's all the same to you, I believe I'll take my hard-earned pay and make my way out of here. I assume the jeep is for me?"

"With my compliments," Breedlove said, smiling. "But we'll have to wait for Jamie to bring the truck around. The suitcase is in the back."

The two covered deuce-and-a-halfs were following the plane down the clearing two hundred feet distant, stopping behind it as men jumped from the trucks and swarmed around the wings, several of them rushing to the water's edge where a number of fishing boats had clustered in the last several minutes. Breedlove checked the time again. They needed to hurry.

"What's left of your forces?" Delany was asking Callera as Breedlove continued to watch the unwinding of the operation. "This bunch here don't look like much."

Callera spit out the window; the khakis he wore were dirty and threadbare, saying more than words ever could. "Some went home," he said sadly. "It was either that or become bandits. Many left with the *coyotes*, paid them to sneak like dogs into the U.S." He motioned toward the men in the Ford, who were stumbling out of the car, searching for relief from the oppressive humidity out in the open air. "Some stay with us. We're not welcome anywhere. We keep moving, keep . . . hoping." He looked up at Breedlove. "Right now we're hoping that the U.S. government is wanting to help us again, huh?"

"I told you," Breedlove said low, "you'll be satisfied."

"If you ask me," Delany said, "the whole damned country's gone soft. We got Commies banging on the back door and all we can talk about are their rights. I fought this war for six years down here for nothing."

"Winning sides don't hire mercs," Breedlove said, and watched as one of the trucks started up in the distance and turned in their direction.

"We won't lose!" Callera said in frustration. "I've given my life for my people. When they get angry enough, they'll fight for a government without Companeros."

"Where the hell is that truck?" Delany said, nervous now.

"Right here," Breedlove said. "And right on time."

The mud-splattered yellow and blue truck pulled up at an angle to the other two vehicles. Breedlove immediately jogged over to it and opened the passenger door, Jamie climbing out while Willie jumped down from behind the wheel.

"Everything set?" Breedlove asked as he pulled the aluminum suitcase out from behind the seat.

Jamie nodded curtly, his lips tight. "Ready when you are."

Breedlove smiled. "I'll be ready quickly."

He moved back to the passenger side, holding the suitcase up, grinning broadly.

"All right!" Delany said, climbing out of the vehicle and reaching for the bag.

Breedlove handed it to the man, but as Delany turned to place it in the back of the jeep, Breedlove reached back a beefy fist and swung out hard, taking Delany at the base of the skull, slamming him forward into the side of the vehicle. Breedlove came up quickly, tangling his fingers into the wet mass of Delany's long hair and jerking back hard, the neck snapping.

Delany dropped into the mud like someone had cut the string, the suitcase tumbling loose as Callera's men shouldered their M-16s and aimed at Breedlove in a tight circle. Everyone froze in place, and for several seconds the only sound was the relentless pounding of the rain.

"Keep cool," Breedlove whispered, his arms flung wide in surrender. Wee Willie and Jamie stood like statues.

Callera was out of the jeep, a .45 shaking in his hand as he charged around the jeep to Breedlove. "What are you doing?" he demanded loudly. "What treachery is this?"

"Easy, partner," Breedlove said casually. "I had to do Jerry. He was standing in the way."

"In the way of what?" Callera said loudly, his eyes dark fire.

"Of giving you this," Breedlove replied, bending down to the suitcase and holding it out to the man. "You've seen the contents. I figured that the . . . revolution could use this a little more than it could use guns right now."

The fires of rage in the man's eyes quickly turned to the sharp-edged glint of greed. He began to smile, stifled it. "Perhaps you're right," he said, taking the suitcase and lowering his weapon.

"Want to count it?" Breedlove asked innocently.

Callera's eyes flicked just once toward his men before returning to Breedlove. "I already saw it," he said. "I trust that you're an honorable man."

"You may even want to . . . take the jeep," Breedlove said.

Callera immediately turned and set the suitcase on the front passenger seat. Then he turned again, motioning for his men to lower their weapons. "It's okay," he said happily. "Everything's okay."

"Thought you'd see it that way," Breedlove said, waving his own men beside him. On the ground by his feet lay Delany, his eyes open wide in horror, body twitching. Breedlove turned his eyes to Willie. "We want water in his lungs."

The big man nodded and bent to Delany, flopping him on his stomach and holding his head down in the deep mud. Within a minute, the body lay still.

"'Down, down to hell,'" Breedlove said, quoting from *Henry VI*, "'and say I sent thee thither.'" He kicked the body once to no movement, then nodded to Willie. "Get him back into the cockpit and blow the bird. We've got to get out of here."

The men lugged the body to the truck, tossing it like cordwood into the covered back. Then they climbed into the thing and fired it up, driving off, a shower of mud slinging up from behind the wheels as they dug for traction.

Breedlove turned and extended his hand to Callera. "Well, Colonel," he said. "I believe we've brought our business tonight to a successful conclusion."

Callera took his hand. "I'm not sure, my friend, what we've done. But I agree that the results are satisfactory. The contents of this case will ensure that the war can continue."

"Right," Breedlove replied, not believing the man for a second. "Why don't we split up getting out of here? I don't mind risking the main road to the Coco if you want the old mestizo trail."

The man brightened. "I thank you," he said. "And I believe that we will make, as you Yankees call it, a hasty retreat before you draw more attention to yourself." He turned to his men and whipped his arm around in a circle. "Amigos! Apurate!"

The man rushed to the driver's side and jumped behind the wheel, the excitement that Breedlove had seen in Delany transferred over to Callera. Greed. Callera waved once, then drove quickly off, Breedlove jumping out of the plume of mud kicked up by the tires. The Ford coughed several times before starting, the dope smoke a thick haze in the passenger compartment as the thing chugged away.

It was happening quickly now. Breedlove walked slowly in the downpour toward the 130, just as both trucks geared up and moved toward him. The jungle was lush and impenetrable all around him—deadly to its enemies, a safe haven to its friends. He was getting itchy to melt into that friendship, his intuition telling him that he had to go now.

At that exact instant, the 130 went up in a blinding ball of white fire that rose fifty feet into the air and lit the darkness around them to bright daylight. It was accompanied by a loud thump that rattled his teeth, and quieted all sound for miles around.

The trucks reached Breedlove, backlit by monstrous fire. He crossed the glare of the headlights and climbed into the vehicle driven by Willie. "Take the main road out," he said.

"The *main* road?" the man replied. "What we want to be doin' that for?"

"I gave the colonel the back road," he replied, unbuttoning his shirt.

The man looked at him, but didn't speak. With a grunt, he put the creaky old truck in gear and drove the fringe of the jungle until he found the nearly washed-out roadway, Jamie bringing the other truck up in line behind.

Breedlove removed his shirt and wrung it out the window, sticking his head out to look behind at the plane. The fire had already been extinguished, plunging the area into darkness again as the rest of his men hurried to drag the more manageable pieces onto the tow rafts waiting in the lagoon.

"They know to take it out three miles?" he asked, hanging the wet shirt on the rearview mirror.

"Yeah," Willie replied, his eyes glued to the bite of the headlights where they defined the pitted excuse for a road. "They're to cut the raft lashings at three miles and meet us back at the rendezvous in the morning."

"Good," Breedlove said, sliding down in the seat and putting his feet up on the dash. He pulled the hat down over his eyes. "Think I'll try and grab a little sleep."

"I want to ask you somethin' first, Cap'n," Willie said.

"Shoot."

"That suitcase you gave the colonel," the man said. "Didn't that have our pay in there, too?"

Breedlove lifted the cap from over his eyes and stared at the man. "I didn't give Callera any money," he said.

"But I saw . . ."

"You saw me give the colonel a suitcase." Breedlove jerked a thumb over his shoulder. "Don't worry. Our money is safe and sound behind the seat."

"If our money's behind the seat," the man said, "then what did you give Callera?"

At that moment the sound of a distant explosion reached their hearing, and Breedlove smiled at Willie. "Guess he just had to take a look inside," he said.

"And the back trail's gonna be swarming with Companeros," Willie returned.

"Yeah," Breedlove said, settling back and pulling the cap down again. "Lucky thing we decided to take this road."

"Yeah," the man returned. "Lucky."

Breedlove closed his eyes and pretended to sleep, but his mind stayed alive, jumping with the possibilities that the acquisition of two nuclear bombs had just given him. He was about to become one of the most famous men in the history of the world.

■■■■■■ NEWSBREAK ■■■■■■

INTERAGENCY MEMO

FROM: Covert Research
TO: Director, Overseas Stations
RE: Breedlove, Kenneth T.
CLEARANCE: Top Secret, jurisdiction of National
    Security Act, 1971.

Stan:

Here's the brief on Psychological Profile of Ken Breedlove as per request. The entire file is currently "missing" from Company records for security reasons. Read it and weep.

BREEDLOVE, KENNETH TYLER

AGE: 39
HT: 6'2"
WT: 200
EYES: green
HAIR: red, sometimes wears beard
DISTINGUISHING CHARACTERISTICS: tattoo on left forearm (mythological creature, Puck, from Shakespeare; words "What fools these mortals be" written beneath); bullet scars—right chest, right shoulder, left leg above knee.

Breedlove fits the typical pattern of most mercenaries: ideologically motivated, previous uniformed service, insubordinate, inexpensive.
POSITIVES: articulate, intelligent, imaginative, directed, dependable.
NEGATIVES: resentful and distrustful of authority; tendency to unauthorized improvisation; prone to violent solutions; suspicious of coworkers and conspiracies involving himself; brief but intense periods of depression followed by rapid mood swings.
CONCLUSION: Breedlove, while accumulating an enviable record during five years of free-lance work in Caribbea, had acquired the title of "Psycho" among his coworkers. Used in low-level or termination work only, and then sporadically because of personal deportment and chain-of-command problems. Barely controllable, Breedlove has been suspected in the murders of Company personnel in Central America, accusations never substantiated. He may be a bor-

derline schizophrenic. Finally dropped from Company free-lance for instability.

Breedlove is a dangerously creative, potentially unbalanced individual who is very capable of following his own covert agenda without authorization of any kind.

P.S. Stan: Recommend you get this man out of the picture—and quickly. Perhaps start revocation of citizenship status? Suggest you tone this down before further transmission. Damage control begins at home!—Tom

Arlington, Virginia 4:03 A.M.

Charlie Merchant drove his white Cadillac onto the eerie, deserted expanse of the Francis Scott Key Bridge, the telephone receiver jangling in his ear. Light snow swirled chaotically out of the black sky to dance before his headlights and die on the windshield, his wipers setting up a steady heartbeat rhythm to clear the debris. The night city still slept and dreamed of sunshine. Charlie Merchant never dreamed of anything he couldn't control.

He'd spent all the years since Korea being perfect, being in control, taking the indefinable out of his life. It had driven Linda half-crazy, but had brought a kind of sublime orderliness to his life. In the absence of happiness, orderliness had sufficed. It was enough for him.

He heard someone pick up the phone on the other end, the thing rattling in his ear as it was fumbled around on the night table.

"Bignell," came a voice heavy with sleep. "This better be good."

"Malcolm . . . it's Charlie Merchant. I'm sorry to bother you, I . . ."

"Charlie?" The voice had cleared somewhat. "What the hell's wrong?"

"We've got a problem," Merchant said, getting across the Potomac to drive under the overpass of Whitehurst Freeway. "I need your help."

"I thought you'd retired," Bignell returned suspiciously. "Couldn't keep away?"

"A favor," Merchant replied. "Like I'm asking you. You awake?"

"Yeah . . . what the hell. Should I stay sitting down?"

"You tell me. I got a call from Jack Braedman in Georgetown."

"Majority whip?"

"One of my oldest friends, Malcolm. Please remember that." Merchant shifted the phone to his other ear and pulled up to the light on M Street, paper trash whistling under the highway along with the snow, burying the city, sealing it up. He turned right, only a couple of minutes away now. "Listen. A girl he was with committed suicide just a few minutes ago."

"How the hell do you know?"

"He called me, hoping I could . . . do something."

There were several seconds of dead air on the other end before Bignell's gravelly voice came back. "Like what?" he answered, clipped.

"Don't dummy up on me, Malcolm," Merchant said, spindly trees, now white and skeletal, lining the C&O Canal to his right. "You know what I want. Just a little discretion when you check it out."

"You're talking about interfering with a police investigation, Charlie," the man replied, wide awake now.

"I don't want to interfere with anything," Merchant said, having the answer to his question about dissipating power. "I'm just asking if it's possible to investigate this without making a circus out of it. At least check everything out before throwing Jack to the wolves. He didn't do anything. I've known him for over forty years."

"You realize that this man has been talked about as presidential material," Bignell said. "How am I supposed to bottle it up? Whenever it does come out, the press will start screaming cover-up, and then whose head do you think the ax will fall on?"

The old canal towpath and its reconstructed revolutionary period houses filled up the corner at M and Thirty-

first, Merchant turning north, into the stately elegance of
Georgetown proper. He frowned at the phone, then pulled
out his chit. "You owe me, Malcolm," he said.

The man breathed heavily into the phone. "You're a
shithead for saying so."

"I'd do the same for you if you were in Jack's place."

"Which is the only reason I'm even thinking about it,"
Bignell said, his voice hard-edged. Merchant had just lost
a friend.

"Then you'll do it?"

"I can't promise much. But maybe we can hold off on
any announcements until after the coroner gets a look at
her and we're ready to make an official statement."

"That's all I ask," Merchant said, relieved. "If we can
turn this over to the press already opened and closed,
maybe they won't think it's such hot news."

"Don't count on it. What's the address?"

Merchant gave it, the man whistling into the phone on
the other end.

"God, who was he with, the Queen Mother? Do you
know what neighborhood you're talking about?"

"I'm just turning onto it now," Merchant replied, the
dark, multi-eaved mansions of Dumbarton rising into
the maelstrom on either side of him. He pulled over to the
curb, under a streetlight a distance from the house. "I
know this isn't easy for you. I really appreciate it."

"I think I'm a fool," Bignell said. "You've always been
fair and straight up with me, and like you said, I owe you.
But this evens it, Charlie. This clears the board between us."

The man hung up, Merchant staring at the dead receiver
for a minute before hanging it up. Reaching out, he shut off
the engine, snowflakes immediately hitting the windshield and sticking, trying to close him in, trying to seal up
everything under a forgetful layer of cold white.

He climbed out of the car, the wind whistling in his
ears, stinging his face. He buttoned up his thick wool
overcoat, turning the collar up around his ears, and bent
his head into the wind to move farther down the street.
He'd worked with Bignell for nearly a decade, the man
probably owing Merchant his promotion to chief.

He'd spent that time running the FPS, the Federal
Protection Services, for GSA, providing security to public

buildings. As such, he was the nexus between government and civilian police authority when trouble occurred. He'd covered Bignell's ass more than once in those days, rightly figuring that friendship and cooperation were the necessary requisites for success in joint ventures. Once, when a demonstration had gotten out of hand in front of the Lincoln Memorial and turned into a near riot, he'd personally stood up in front of the policy review board and defended Bignell's handling of the situation, bringing the weight of government to bear in the man's protection. Instead of a summary dismissal, Bignell had come away with a commendation and a raise. Amazing how little that ultimately counted for when the chips were down.

He fought the wind, powdered snow boiling around his feet as he walked, trying to pull him down. It wasn't difficult to find the house. Every light in the place was blazing. It sat in the center of the block, three stories tall, dormered windows on the top floor glowing yellow like piercing eyes glaring down at him. He pulled his collar tighter around his neck and pushed through the wrought-iron gate, the only breach in the seven-foot wall.

Other footprints had come up this walk, a man's boots defining themselves in the powder, only to break off and disappear into the thick brambles and thorny rosebush vines that made up the wide garden inside the wall. He turned in that direction, saw nothing, then continued to the front door, the thing flying open as he reached it.

Jack Braedman stood, a shadow hunched over in the doorway, dressed in a pair of tuxedo pants and nothing else. His hair was wild, his eyes wilder. His face, chest, and arms were covered in dried blood.

"Oh, God, Charlie," he said, throwing his arms around Merchant as he walked in the door. He was shaking, nearly out of control.

Merchant pulled away from him, searching the man's face. Since Korea, he'd seen Jack Braedman in many different situations. Drunk, angry, or excited, he was always in control, in command of the situation. But now an edge of hysteria lingered around his wide eyes, the look of a cornered animal. "You've got to get yourself together, Jack," he said, moving past him into the house. "The police will be here in a few minutes."

"I can't believe this is happening," he said, running bloody hands through his tangled gray hair. "Are you sure I should stay here? I mean, I didn't do anything, for God's sake. You know what's going to happen when this gets out?"

"Listen," Merchant said, taking him by the shoulders. "You called me because you knew I'd take the straight path on this. You didn't do anything, so everything will be all right. If you take a powder now, you screw yourself and the system."

Braedman jerked away from his grasp, looking up toward the upper floors. "Easy for you to say," he replied, his voice strung up tight. "I think about Joann lying up there, and I want to go crazy with it. But there's a bell ringing inside my head telling me to save my own ass while I've got the chance. I didn't *do* anything, Charlie! They're going to crucify me."

Merchant walked past him to look around the first floor. It was quite a place, polished wood floors with low-riding, oriental-style ebony tables and furniture. Everything was overstuffed and screamed a kind of elegance obviously out of the reach of most people. "The police chief promised to keep this under wraps until they've finished investigating." He turned to Braedman, the man following close behind him. "Where is she?"

"U-upstairs," he said, and Merchant couldn't shake the man's image. Confusion filled the strong face, a kind of numbing shock. "Oh, Jesus, Charlie. I still can't believe it. She was so alive just an hour ago. I—I was g-going to ask her to marry me."

"You're already married, Jack," Merchant said, walking to the black iron spiral staircase in the corner of the long living room. "Get yourself cleaned up while I see what's what."

He moved up the stairs. He didn't want to be terse with Jack, but at this point everything had to be handled just right if the man was going to salvage anything of his own life out of this. Braedman's attitude wasn't helping. If the son of a bitch was going to go falling in love and getting married, he needed to get rid of the first one before bringing in the second.

He reached the second floor, bedrooms to his right, a large sitting room to his left. Here, as below, the place was luxurious and meticulously clean, too clean. He stood staring at the sitting room. The furniture was oxblood leather, the tables mahogany. Several magazines were arranged just so on the coffee table. He moved to the table and picked up the magazines, looking at the covers. There wasn't a magazine any newer than three years old on the table.

It seemed so odd. If he were to walk into this place sight unseen, he'd guess that it was some kind of model home, fixed up just right, than laid with plastic runners on the floor and a rope barricade beside the runners to keep people out of the living area. It looked like a house nobody lived in. There were no personal items anywhere, no photos on the wall, no fresh flowers in the porcelain vases, no shoes or jackets strewn across the floor or furniture.

"It's not going to work," Braedman said from behind. Merchant turned. The man stood on the steps, the staircase coiled around him like a metal serpent. His hands were shaking before him. "If they want me, they'll get me."

"What are you talking about?" Merchant said. "If who wants you?"

"People . . . nothing," the man said, defeated, head hanging. "I've got to get out of here."

Merchant tightened up. "You'll do no such thing," he said. "You're going to do this right. Look, I promise you you'll get a fair shake. Now get upstairs and clean yourself up."

Braedman looked slowly up the spiral. "Up there?" he said shakily. "I don't think I can . . ."

"Dammit, just do what I say!" Merchant commanded, realizing finally that the man was too disconnected to act on his own. He moved back to the stairs, shoving Braedman up ahead of him. And as they twisted upward, he could feel, almost smell, the death that awaited them. The stairs terminated in a vacant, lit hallway, a bedroom on either side. He moved to the one with the open door.

"Fix yourself up, Jack," he said harshly, walking into the room.

The man got as far as the door before wobbling and grabbing the frame for support. "I—I can't go in there," he said, his voice pitiful, pleading. "Don't make me, Charlie."

Merchant nodded, jolted by the man's demeanor. He looked around. The bedroom, at least, had been lived in. Clothes were strewn around; an empty champagne bottle with two glasses stood on a small, marble-topped table in a seated alcove to the left. He quickly gathered up the remnants of Braedman's clothes from the floor and tossed them out the doorway. "Get dressed," he said, his own voice dry, cracking.

To the right stood the open door to the bathroom, bright glare dazzling from within. He turned from the place, not wanting to go in there until he had looked at everything else. A career in military G-2, plus a decade with FPS, had taught him to be thorough. It wasn't that he doubted Jack's story about the suicide, it was just that something seemed off kilter to him. It just didn't feel right somehow.

"Who the hell *was* this girl . . . Joann did you say?"

"She was . . ." the man fumbled. "I don't know. We didn't talk much about her life, I . . . what difference does it make?"

"You wanted to marry her, but knew nothing about her life?"

"For God's sake, Charlie, she's dead and I'm screwed. What are all these questions?"

Merchant shrugged. "It's this house," he said. "Something . . ." He let the sentence trail off, unsure. He quickly went over the room, going through drawers in the triple dresser, poking through closets. There was an amount of blood everywhere that had undoubtedly dripped from Jack. Steuben Glass knickknacks sat all around. The place screamed of money, but here, just like in the rest of the house, he had the feeling that no one really lived in it. There were a few clothes in the closet and a small amount of accessories in the drawers, but no more than a woman would take for a few days at a hotel. It just didn't make sense.

He turned to see Jack still leaning against the door frame, his face slack and pale, streaks of blood lined down his cheeks. "We're running out of time," he said, looking at his watch. "Get dressed and cleaned up now, understand?"

Braedman nodded, leaning down to lethargically pick up his ruffled tuxedo shirt.

Merchant turned to the bathroom. Walking to the doorway, he could see naked legs, unmoving, on the floor. He took a couple of deep breaths and went in.

She lay flat on her back, arms outstretched, in a pool of her own blood. Her eyes were open, staring, and even in death she looked desperately unhappy. She was beautiful, one of the most beautiful women he'd ever seen, the kind of woman every woman envied. She was perfection of a kind he barely knew existed. Her pale body was perfectly proportioned, her unlined face studiously childlike and expertly cared for. For a man who'd spent his entire life in the pursuit of perfection and excellence, Merchant found himself devastated by the loss of it. Why? The concept of such order destroying itself was beyond him. He found himself touched deeply by her sadness.

The blood had gotten into her blond hair, turning it strawberry. He bent to her, tracing light fingers over the high cheekbones, half expecting her to turn her eyes to him. But that wouldn't happen. She had obviously bled out, her perfection now in transition to something else.

He straightened, slowly, on stiff knees and looked around at the carnage, smelling the death. Then he saw the mirror above the sink. She had written on it in her own blood, a message apparently of such great importance to her that she used her final minutes of life to convey it. Actually there seemed to be two messages. The first was a line rendering of a heart with the words JERRY + JOANN written within, a crude arrow going through the heart. Beneath that, an even stranger notation: YOUR MOVE, BJ.

"What the hell is this on the mirror, Jack?" he called back to the bedroom without response. "Jack!"

He rushed out of the bathroom, running to the bedroom door. The man's clothes still lay strewn in the hallway, but he was gone. Then he heard the screeching tires.

He hurried back into the bedroom in time to see out the window a D.C. police car, lights flashing wildly, pull up at an angle to the curb before the house. Two uniformed policemen jumped out and charged toward the front gate.

So much for discretion.

He rushed out of the room and made the staircase, looking down the spiral two floors to the living room. "Jack!" he yelled. "Damn." He looked at the room with the closed door and opened it, turning on the only light Jack had missed. "Jack!" He wasn't there.

It was a guest room done in another neuter style,

Merchant realizing that's what had bothered him about the rest of the house. You couldn't tell if a man or woman was supposed to live there. This one was done in early American, with a four-poster bed with canopy and oak-stained furnishings. But it was even stranger. He moved to a night table and ran his finger atop it, drawing a line through the thick dust that lay there. This room hadn't been cleaned in months.

Footsteps charging up the stairs. The cops? Why the hurry? He walked back to the bedroom door, taking one last look at the room before turning out the light.

He could hear the police rooting around in the master bedroom. Where was Jack? He went back to the bedroom and walked in. The two cops were in the bathroom. One seemed to be searching the room while the other was, incredibly, using a towel to wipe the blood message off the mirror.

"What the hell are you doing?" he demanded, both men flaring around to him, their young faces locked in surprise.

"Freeze!" the searcher yelled, his service .9mm automatic coming out of the patent leather holster and brought to bear on Merchant in a two-handed grip.

"That's evidence you're destroying," Merchant said, taking a step forward.

"Hands behind your head!" the cop yelled, going into a semicrouch and cocking the weapon.

The smell of death mixed with the tension in the air, Merchant falling back and following orders. The cop with the gun marched him slowly backward while the other finished wiping the mirror clean of its message.

"My name's Charles Merchant," he said, glaring. "I'm the one who called Malcolm Bignell about the suicide, I . . ."

"Shut up!" the gunman yelled, and his face was at war, Merchant finally realizing that he was trying to decide whether to shoot him or not.

"Hey, come on. . . ."

"That's it!" the other cop said from the bathroom, throwing the towel away and stepping casually over the dead girl's legs to come into the bedroom. "It's clean."

"What about him?" the gunman asked.

Merchant saw a young man with deep brown eyes and slick black hair turn condemnation toward him. This man's face bore no confusion, no uncertainty. This man's face was hard and set, and he was looking at Charlie as if he'd already done him.

"He's seen," the man said easily, and Merchant immediately looked down for the name tag so he could curse the son of a bitch as he died. WESTON was written on the silver tag on the man's breast pocket.

At that second, sirens gutted the night, both men turning toward the sound. A second round of sirens joined the first, then a third. What the hell was going on? They were close, too close to be going anywhere else.

The cops looked at each other and Weston said, "Sir, you are hampering the scene of a police investigation. If you don't vacate the premises immediately, we'll be forced to place you under arrest."

"I'm going," Merchant said, knowing an escape route when he was given one. He turned and took a quick look out the window. Four police cars had screeched up to join the first, along with ambulances, a fire truck, and three broadcast vans from local news stations. Lights were on all up and down the street, joining with the wild carnival atmosphere of all the flashing emergency lights.

He walked quickly out of the room and to the stairs. As he started down he saw Jack coming up. The man hadn't done anything to fix himself up. He looked like a wild animal after a kill, rust-colored blood thickly matted in his chest hair and on his stomach.

"What the fuck's going on?" he yelled, out of control. "You swore to me . . . you—"

"I don't know!" Merchant yelled back, his insides jangling. "Just get up here and fix yourself up."

Voices below in the living room, a black man's face appearing through the stair cutout a floor beneath Jack. "You on the steps! Identify yourselves . . . keep your hands where I can see them!"

"Motherfucker!" Braedman yelled like a madman. "Motherfucker! Motherfucker!"

Charlie ran down several more steps, yelling as he ran. "I'm Charles Merchant! I called Malcolm about this!"

"God, Charlie!" Braedman screamed, shaking his

bloody fists above his head on the narrow stairs. "What did you do to me?"

The black man was yelling something about hands as he charged up the stairs, followed by several uniformed police, Braedman screaming in a guttural frenzy, drowning everything out. Merchant looked up, the upstairs cops on the steps, too, coming down.

Merchant reached Braedman just before the police did, grabbing the man, wrapping him in a full nelson before he got slapped with resisting arrest, too. He had crossed the line and was thrashing wildly, crazily. Merchant wrestled him to a sitting position on the winding steps as the black man arrived, his face stiff with rage.

"What is this?" he demanded through clenched teeth.

"He's torn up with grief," Merchant said as he continued to wrestle the struggling, crying man. "His girlfriend killed herself upstairs."

"You're the one who called," the man said, his eyes unyielding, suspicious.

"Malcolm promised . . ."

"Other calls came in. Nothing I could do. You say suicide?"

"Maybe," came a voice from behind Merchant. He turned to see Weston staring down, a tiny smile on his face. The man continued. "The bathroom door's been kicked open and the woman's hand is slashed up, like maybe she was trying to fight off the blade."

The black man's jaw tightened. "Cuff this one and read him his rights," he told the uniform behind him, then stood, turning once again to Merchant. "I'm going to have to check you out."

"Why, Charlie?" Braedman screamed. "You were my friend!"

"C'mon, Hurley," came a voice from below. "Get out of the way!"

Merchant looked down the spiral. The bottom stairs were filled with photographers with juicing cameras on their shoulders.

"Get these people out of here!" the cop yelled back, his men hurrying back down the stairs to block off the press. "They're trampling all over a crime scene. Get the tape up!"

"You can't arrest me!" Braedman yelled as they roughly pulled his hands behind him on the narrow stairs. "I've got immunity!"

He tried to break free, twisting wildly in the confined space, then flinging himself at his captors. Hurley flattened himself against the wall, cursing, as Braedman and two uniforms tumbled down the steps, coming to a stop in a tangle somewhere between floors one and two, the cameras rolling tape even as they were shoved out the front door.

Merchant stood and watched in horror. Braedman was a proud and vain man. The death plus this humiliation were more than he could bear. He looked at Hurley, the man staring back at him. "We've got to get some kind of control over this," he said.

"What you've got to do," Hurley said, his voice low and menacing, "is get the fuck out of the way and not leave this house until I've confirmed you with the chief. Let's have your I.D."

Merchant drew himself up and made to respond, but thought better of it, getting out his wallet instead. The detective grabbed it from him, pulling out the Virginia license before handing it back.

"Do you know who that man is?" he asked Hurley as they dragged Braedman down the rest of the stairs and trussed him up facedown on the living room floor.

"Maybe a killer," Hurley replied. "And maybe you're an accessory." He shoved past Merchant and joined the smiling Weston farther up the stairs. "Okay, Weston, let's see what you've got."

Merchant walked slowly down the stairs, trying to figure out what the hell had just happened. He had come within an inch of being killed by the police after finding them destroying evidence. The investigation had become everything Malcolm swore to him it wouldn't become, the press screaming out on the front porch, a thin line of yellow crime-scene tape all that was keeping the cannibals at bay. He'd given his word, and this was the result.

He moved to Braedman, the man cuffed from behind and lying on his stomach, a cop kneeling on his back as he read him his rights. He squatted to the man, getting close to his red, straining face. "Jack," he said. "You've got to calm down, you've—"

"Fuck you!" Braedman yelled, spitting at him. "You're gaming me . . . just like the others. Just like them!"

"Jack—"

"Fuck you! Go to hell!"

He stood, moving past the open front door and the barely contained monster out there in the driving cold. He walked farther into the recesses of the house just to get away from it.

He walked through the Chinese living room and into a high-ceilinged French Provincial dining area, complete with crystal chandeliers and silver candelabra on a wormwood table that looked like it could seat twenty people easily. The dead girl had to be no older than twenty-five or -six. How did she afford all this? How could Jack have known her long enough to propose marriage, and yet not have a handle on her life? Curiosity drove him on.

The kitchen had been redone, probably within the last five years; the traditional Victorian house with its accent on the actual cooking area had given way to stainless-steel fixtures and large butcher-block tables that accented the electrical appliances that now seemed the mainstay of the modern house. The kitchen was equipped to feed large numbers, yet very little food was visible. There were cans in the pantry, mostly heat-and-eat meals. The freezer contained a small number of frozen foods, while the refrigerator itself was all but empty except for condiments.

His pipe was riding in his coat pocket. He took it out and clamped it between his teeth. He felt sick inside, responsible.

"There you are," came Hurley's voice from behind him.

He turned to the man. "You called Malcolm?"

The man nodded. His hard face a little softer. He stood with hands on hips, a shoulder holster evident beneath his jacket. "He confirmed what you told me," he said, reaching out to hand the license back, "then reamed me out. I should have recognized you and Senator Braedman. Sorry."

Merchant took the license. "A lot of people thought that man lying on the living room floor was going to be the next president of the United States," he said. "You say that someone else called it in?"

Hurley nodded. "They called in a murder," he replied, sighing. His face looked suddenly drained and tired. "And I'll tell you something else. Whoever called us called the newspeople first. That's the only way they could have gotten here this quickly."

"Odd," Merchant said. "Can I ask you a question?"

"Shoot."

"The two cops who showed up first . . ."

"Weston and Mills?"

"Yeah," Merchant said. "How come they got here before the rest of you?"

The man shrugged. "They're patrol cops," he said. "Probably picked up something on the radio. Why?"

Merchant nearly told him, but so many strange things had already happened that he thought that the entire episode needed to be thought through first. He frowned. "Nothing . . . just wondering."

Hurley narrowed his gaze for just a second, then shrugged. "You're free to go for now," he said. "But I want you to stop around headquarters in the afternoon so we can ask you some questions." He reached into his herringbone sports jacket and came out with a business card that he handed to Merchant. "I should be there between noon and three."

Merchant put the card in his pocket without looking at it. "I don't know what Weston showed you up in that bathroom," he said, "but I've known Jack Braedman for a long time. He didn't kill anybody. He's not capable of it."

"Everybody's capable of it, Mr. Merchant," Hurley said wearily. "It's all just a matter of the circumstances, isn't it?"

He turned then and walked from the kitchen, Merchant not sure how to take the man. Charlie Merchant believed in the system: the system of government, the system of law and order, the system of faith. God and country embodied in the American way of life that he still strove to be worthy of. Nothing he'd seen tonight had supported those beliefs or those systems. He'd have to think about all of it.

The kitchen seemed to be laughing at him, defying his logic. He walked out of it and headed to the front door. He needed to get Cal Daniels on the phone. Jack was apparently going to need a good lawyer and Daniels was the best. He'd make the call from the car, though. The atmosphere here was too disconcerting.

He moved through the house, back to the front door. It had been barely an hour since he'd gotten the call from Jack.

Merchant walked to the open front door, watching the amazing entourage moving down the walkway to the front gate. There were five cops dragging a screaming Braedman, still stripped to the waist and shoeless, still struggling. Clustered around them was a buzzing hive of newsmen, floodlights blazing the dark, microphones gouging like cattle prods amid the loud buzz of their voices.

He ducked under the tape and followed them down the walk at a slight distance. They disappeared through the gate and into the now-large street crowds, who gasped and yelled when they saw the hysterical man covered in blood. He shook his head. God, it was a photogenic sight. He pictured it on the cover of Newsweek where it could horrify children and make the men nod knowingly, confirming everything they'd ever thought about politicians.

He got through the gate himself, stepping into the crowds and the crazily flashing emergency lights and the fog-like carbon monoxide smoke drifting quickly on the swirling winds. He saw the faces of the crowd, excited, wide-eyed. They were dressed for bed. They'd all have something to tell their grandchildren, and if he were able to stand atop a car and convince them of Jack's innocence, they'd undoubtedly be disappointed. He thought of Ted Kennedy at Chappaquiddick and remembered Napoleon's words as he fled the ruins of Moscow after losing an army of nearly a million: "From the sublime to the ridiculous is but a small step."

He turned left out of the gate, the circus turning right, voices loud, Braedman's voice shrill above it all, cursing him as he walked away, blaming him. As he walked, he felt jittery, as if he'd had too many cups of coffee. The heat of the crowd dissipated as he drew away, the night turning black again. The light snow had stopped falling, its remnants now being borne on howling winds, slashing at the night like a grave dancer.

Across the street a car was parked, a new red Jaguar. A young man with a smooth face sat behind the wheel listening intently as Weston and his partner, Mills, spoke to him in a whisper. Merchant watched them as he walked by on the other side of the street and suddenly Weston was pointing at *him*. At that moment the two cops stood aside, the young man turning hard eyes on Merchant as he passed.

"Smile," the man called, his lips curling into a cruel grin. He brought up a small video camera, putting it to his face. "C'mon, smile!" He began filming.

Merchant, tightening up inside, hurried past them. He pulled the pipe out of his mouth lest he bite off the barrel. What the hell was going on? He turned and took a quick look at the front license of the car, committing it to memory.

He moved quickly to his car now, getting in, the cold suddenly overtaking him, making him shiver. At least he hoped it was the cold.

NEWSBREAK

Honduras (Reuters)—The U.S. Navy has confirmed that the wreckage of an American cargo plane has been spotted in neutral waters off the northern coast of Caribbea this morning. The plane, an EquAir C-130 Hercules, was traveling from Houston, Texas, to Coral Gables, Florida, and was apparently off course due to instrument failure late last night. Early reports indicate the pilot radioed the Canal Zone that he was under attack by Caribbean SAM missiles just before disappearing from radar, but the State Department has yet to confirm that report. The

Companero military in Poblado flatly denies any responsibility for the downed plane, labeling the reports a "political move." U.S. naval units from Panama are searching the area for survivors.

Pennsylvania Quarter, Washington, D.C.
8:37 A.M.

Ben James stood, coffee in hand, on the wide veranda that was the very top floor of his reflecting glass hotel/office complex and looked out over his city. The traffic on Ninth and D streets, ten floors below, crawled slowly through the cold, gray morning, the blowing snow making the sharp edge of the wind visible, deadly. There was no snow on the tenth floor, the tallest any building in the capital was allowed to be. There was only Ben James and his gut-busting enthusiasm and head-over-heels love for the city that danced like a Christmas garden below him. And if you asked him why, he'd smile a crooked grin, brush a hand through his sandy blond hair, and say, "Why, I'm just tickled to death to be here."

And he was, too.

To his right, across the street at equal height, stood the imposing tan sarcophagus that was the FBI Building, no crowds lined up for tours on this frigid day. Across Pennsylvania Avenue from there stood the Justice Department and the National Archives, a mile from the White House on the right and a mile from the Capitol on the left, the Capitol dome dirty as a fuzz ball in the faint gray morning.

He wore his silver satin Regardie's team racing jacket over his dress shirt to keep out the cold, with the words MONEY, POWER, GREED embroidered on the back. A telephone headset buzzed Rob Danton's nasal voice gently in his ear. He took a sip of coffee. It tasted metallic and stale, and that was just fine, too.

"I recommend the hair of the dog, buddy," he said into the small mike stem curving up near his mouth. "Either that or quit mixing your liquors."

"It's not that," the man replied, voice heavy. "That damned woman I met at your party last night kept me up till almost six."

"Mary Ellen," he returned. "Worthwhile?"

"I may never walk again."

"You're breaking my heart," James said. "You know, Mary Ellen has a friend who likes to—how do you say it—join in."

"A threesome?"

"You ought to mention it to her, boy," James said, setting his cup down on the polished cut-glass tabletop beside him and walking closer to the edge of the porch. "So, what's the good word?"

"The President wanted me to call and thank you for setting up that meeting today with the Senate whip. We couldn't even get a return phone call."

"Course you couldn't," James said, sitting on the retaining wall at the edge of the patio to watch the traffic below. The cement was cold. He stood again. "What do you expect? The kind of budget you guys are trying to force down his throat will just about kill reelection for anybody running next time. . . ."

"Good God, BJ," Danton said. "You think I don't know that? But over twenty percent of our yearly budget goes just to the interest payments on all the money the country owes. We're going to have to do something."

"Well, Rob," James cooed sweetly, "you do what every other swinging dick in the country does—pay the interest and hope your ship comes in before the next payment's due. That's deficit spending, my friend. Your boss didn't worry so much about it when he was running for that damned office. And by the way, when you meet with the senator, don't let anybody smoke around him. He's got lung rot and it really makes him mad, though he won't say it out front."

"Oh, shit . . . that's why the last time—"

"—he got up, walked out, and led the vote to kill the grain entitlement bill. The stock market fell twenty points that morning."

"Don't remind me . . . anything else?"

"Yeah . . . put that secretary of yours . . . what's her name?"

"Gloria?"

"Gloria. Get her in there for dictation or something. She's from his home state, I believe. If she's on your side, it might just make her a metaphor for his whole constituency."

"Brilliant!"

"Only if it works. Break a leg, Rob."

"Thanks, BJ," the man said, relief in his voice. "I'm great with the ledgers, but this personal stuff . . ."

"That's what I'm here for," James said. "Tell the President I said hello."

"Will do."

James clicked off from his end and chuckled softly. Gloria Cartwright had once worked for the Senate whip, George Nichols. They'd had a heavy affair when she was barely nineteen years old and he was fifty-two. He'd made a fool of himself over the young woman and had soon gotten dumped, unceremoniously, by her and at great expense by his wife, Vera. The woman's appearance at the compromise meeting would ensure its quick failure.

What a great morning. The sky rolled menacingly above him with more snow, worse snow, undoubtedly on the way. But it didn't matter to Ben James. Washington was always the Emerald City to him, the city that in 1974 miraculously transformed itself into his town. That was the year the federal courts made it legal for corporations to form their own PACs and monetarily support candidates friendly to their interests. What they'd been trying to do was reform election spending; what, in effect, they'd accomplished was the invention of Ben James. Democracy in action.

The vacant lots, seedy liquor stores, and souvenir shops of Pennsylvania Avenue that had disturbed President Kennedy on his inaugural ride in 1961 had become Camelot and more by the mid-seventies. Washington had always had the power. Now it had the money, too. All sorts of money—Texas money, Dutch money, Japanese money, British money, Arab money—all pouring into the capital by the billions, all hoping to buy a little influence. Scores of new luxury office buildings, top-of-the-line hotels, stylish restaurants, and art museums helped polish the image. Think tanks, consulting firms, lawyers, and lobbyists became the new power brokers and a whole new country was born—invisible to the majority of its citizens, but just as surely different as bedrock and sandstone.

The land of opportunity, that's how Ben James saw it. There were over five thousand different political action committees, spending nearly a billion dollars a year. He had opened his first small consulting firm in a storefront in 1981 with the thought of telling all those PACs how to best spend their money. Within three years, Legislative Services, Inc. had been born with its own suite of offices and several dozen professional lobbyists. Within another two years, Ben James owned the building. And he'd done it using only what he'd been born with. He was just a preacher's boy with grass-roots political savvy, animal charm, salesman wisdom, and prostitute morality. He believed in friends and in doing small favors for friendship's sake. He believed in making people happy and in giving them what they wanted—or thought they wanted. He believed in guaranteed satisfaction. He believed in democracy and especially free enterprise. But mostly he believed in Ben James. What was good for Ben James had to be good for the rest of America as well. It was only natural.

The headset buzzed in his ear. He touched the receiver. "Yeah, June?"

"Everybody's arrived for the morning briefing, BJ," the woman said in the sexy voice he had hired her for.

He frowned. "What's the mood?"

"It's hard to say," June replied. "They're all talking about Joann."

"I'll be right in, good lookin'."

He walked to the table and picked up his now-cold coffee, carrying it with him back through the sliding reflecting door and into his office.

The office was huge, large as a house, entry doorways on two sides. It was paneled in deep walnut, and polished to high luster. The office contained not only desk space, but a large conference area, a sitting area, and a three-hole putting green. Bookcases full of never-read volumes lined the walls, a big-screen television dominating the conference area. A large telescope sat on a tripod near the patio door, pointing vaguely in the direction of the Capitol.

And then there was the glass collection; hundreds of pieces of crystal figurines took up space everywhere. Binoculars hung on pegs on the walls, microscopes and magnifying glasses sitting on the bookcases in front of the books. It took two hours a night to dust the office, James inspecting every morning to make sure the job had been done right.

Office space in Washington came at an expensive premium. Ben James wanted everybody who walked into his place to know exactly how successful he was. A small sign hung on the wall behind the large desk amid a number of framed photos of him with famous people. It read LEGISLATIVE SERVICES, INC.—MORE BANG FOR THE BUCK.

He set the coffee on the desk and took off his jacket, trading it on the wooden coat rack for his Brooks Brothers suit coat. Pulling the headset down to wrap around his neck, he walked out of the office, his mind already locked into the events that would profoundly affect his day. It was going to be incredible. He was rolling the dice and taking chances, and the excitement was almost palpable.

Legislative Services was already jumping as he walked into the beehive of the outer offices. Secretaries, lobbyists, and vendors milled loudly amid the tangle of desks and computer mailing equipment. Somewhere a photocopy machine was humming out a stack of mailings with a steady cha-chink regularity. Somewhere the odor of fresh coffee worked its way through the still-strong morning perfumes and deodorants that filled the large room.

June Chan sat atop a five-foot platform that the other employees had labeled "the watchtower," near the double front doors, surrounded on three sides by communications equipment. She was a receptionist plus. An expert in electronics and communications systems, she was also James's scheduler and screener and prioritizer, the iron lady of LSI—all packaged in a four-foot seven-inch, ninety-three-pound Chinese frame.

"Morning, boss," she called down as he moved to her station, staring up. "You gotta be done with this meeting in fifteen minutes. Your schedule looks like the Bataan Death March."

He nodded, pointing to the headset. "Only if it's important," he said.

"Always."

"And get me some of that coffee."

She mock-saluted, swiveling around to a stem microphone. "We need a fresh pot of coffee in Con-3," she announced over the office speaker system in an airline terminal voice.

He walked through the outer office for a few minutes like an official greeter, shaking hands, cracking jokes, giving everyone personal attention. People liked that. Then he walked past the small TV studio where the representative from Iowa was taping a political message for satellite feed to the folks back home. He watched for a while in silence, then took the long, paneled hallway to conference room number three.

Con-3 was set up for comfort and atmosphere, a quiet place to talk. The center of the room was dominated by a huge round orange sofa, a round coffee table bull's-eyed within its center. Large leafy rubber plants grew like a mock rain forest everywhere. New Age music and its endless bland variations gently trilled through unseen speakers.

The most beautiful women in the world were sitting on the sofa. Four of them, dressed tastefully for the office in silk suits and low-heeled pumps. They formed part of the inner core of the operation. They had all come from backgrounds of wealth and breeding. Their hair smelled of gardens and exotic nights in foreign lands. Their smiles showed perfect teeth, their eyes clear and bright as coral reef seas. They were educated and intelligent, women so perfect that most men wouldn't even be creative enough to dream about them. And they all worked for Ben James.

"Good morning, ladies," James said, moving with outstretched arms into the room. "And you, Roderick," referring to the lone male of the enclave.

He hugged each in turn, including Roderick, then took his place on the sofa. "I suppose you've all heard about Joann," he said without preamble.

"Did Braedman really kill her?" Roderick asked, his young face strained slightly, James noticing where wrinkles would eventually develop around his lips and eyes.

James shrugged. "I don't know," he said sadly. "It's difficult to imagine. I don't really know much more than I've seen on television. What a tragedy."

Angie Litton, a raven-haired, lithe ex-model from L.A., loudly set her cup down. "How did they get TV cameras there so fast?" she asked, shaking her head. "It all seems so . . . contrived."

"I don't believe he killed her," Melanie Patterson said, and James worried over the tone of her voice. A natural redhead and the most overtly sexual of his consultants, she was also the smartest. The best gamer.

"Well, who then?" he asked.

The woman stared evenly across the table at him. "You're usually the man with all the answers," she said. "What do you think?"

James sat back on the sofa and smiled widely. "Why, Mel, I think that you appear to be putting on a little weight."

"Well, I think he killed her," Barbara Morton, the blonde beside Melanie Patterson, said. "Braedman was head over heels for her, and she was in love with some pilot she'd met at one of your parties, BJ. I think he found out and went crazy."

"What pilot?" James asked. "She met somebody at one of my parties?"

"I remember that," Patterson said. "You introduced them, BJ, practically threw them into each other's arms. What was that guy's name . . . ?"

"It was Jerry something," Rayda Coombs said, twisting a long strand of chestnut hair around her finger. "Joann talked about him quite a bit. She wasn't able to control him and I think that really intrigued her."

James frowned deeply. "Guess I don't know what's going on under my own nose," he said, shaking his head as if dismissing the matter. "Mixing business with pleasure is a capital sin, and all of you know it. If what Rayda says is true, then I hate to say it, but she brought it on herself. I feel real bad about it, but we've got to think about other matters now. Maybe I'll start a scholarship fund in her name at . . . what was that place?"

"University of Mississippi," Patterson said evenly.

He watched them carefully, not sure of Patterson's reaction. He'd pick up on it again later just to see. "Her body is being shipped back to Memphis for the funeral," he said. "Send flowers if you want, but we can't involve

LSI personally in a scandal of this kind for reasons I don't need to elaborate. So we'll leave the funeral off our travel itineraries. Agreed?"

There were nods around the table, the conversation interrupted for the delivery of a pot of coffee and glass mugs. James poured himself another cup and looked at his watch. Time was so short.

"I suggest," he said, after retaking his seat, "that we move on to the matter at hand." He sat back on the sofa, hands linked behind his head. "This is an exciting day for all of us, the culmination of a lot of work. Some of us have been on this project for two years, and today's going to tell the story of how successful our time has been. The Joint Chiefs vote today. If they vote for site specific elimination of materials and recision of already appropriated money like everybody wants them to, our defense industry clients alone stand to lose over sixty billion dollars in R and D and manufacturing capital, to say nothing of what then happens to them in the stock market. It could spell the end of an industry that has sustained this country for half a century. We can't let that happen. I don't have to tell you how I feel about a strong defense and its priority in the world we live in. But beyond that, we've got our asses to think about."

He looked hard at them, sincerely. "I hope I don't need to remind you of this, but we manage to charge as much as we do here because we guarantee success and we deliver. And I certainly don't need to remind you that your fortunes are tied directly to the fortunes of Legislative Services. So only give me good news, okay? Give me something to feel good about down in my heart."

"Drop back and regroup," Roderick said. "These guys are getting it from all sides—the President wants to cut, the Congress has to cut, the press is all over them."

"The fear," Rayda said, "is if they don't go along voluntarily with the cuts, that Appropriations is going to come in and make the cuts for them. And don't you think they won't. Worse cuts."

"Let's take up the Appropriations Committee at another meeting," James said, irritated. "We've got to deal with the vote today. One step at a time. If the Joint Chiefs vote against the cuts, it will bring public pressure on

Appropriations . . . a new ball game, plus we've bought some time. We've got to make a go of it here and now. Is the letter campaign having any effect?"

"Sure it is," Barbara Morton said, sitting stiffly, primly on the edge of the sofa, her long legs crossed severely at the knee. "Angie and Melanie will tell you . . . we were all at a party at Wallace's house the other night and the general talked about it with Wallace and Stanley."

James looked at Melanie, trusting her interpretation. "You were there?"

The woman nodded. "I won't say the Chiefs weren't affected," she replied, "but the general feeling was that the criticism will go away as soon as the vote is finished. They really can't afford to anger the powers that be."

"I've got some other stuff going," James said, smiling now, scheming. "I got a news story coming out of Central America on the afternoon news. You might see that your people watch it. Plus I got a couple million telegrams coming in from the Conservative Caucus signature lists, plus we've got a demonstration already going at the Pentagon. We scared up a couple of thousand extra bodies from the Caucus lists and the VFW phone trees. I want you guys to do the rest. We only need one solid vote. They've always voted unanimously . . . one good crack and the whole structure could fall apart."

"What's the point of the news story?" Roderick asked. "It's going to be tough to get Alec near a television today, but what's a story about Central America going to do for him?"

"Misdirection," Patterson said, looking at James. He nodded for her to go on. "Billions for defense spending are just numbers to the public at large, but give them one little human tragedy and they get all worked up. Then you can kind of shove them in the direction you want to go."

"What a cynic!" James cackled. "I swear, Mel. Sometimes I think you haven't got any heart at all. People have feelings, strong feelings. Those feelings tell them the truth, God bless them. That's what separates us from the beasts of the field. Now, I have discovered that if you address those feelings in people, you can then help those people to verbalize the feelings in a concrete way. I always trust the folks."

"And they've always lived down to that trust," Patterson said, taking a long drink of her coffee.

"Lighten up, darlin'," James said amiably, but flashed his eyes at her just the same.

She jerked slightly under the intensity of his gaze. "Sorry," she said. "I think I'm still at loose ends over Joann."

"It's okay," he said softly, reaching out to pat her on the hand. "I don't mean to be so pushy. I just get so . . . into things. Take all the *personal* time you want for your grief." He looked at his watch and took a breath. "Who's going to give me the solid no vote. Angie?"

Angie stared at nothing, her black hair shimmering against the burnished gold of her silk blouse. "The general has been waking up in the middle of the night," she said, shrugging at BJ. She smiled slightly. "I tell him it's because his conscience is bothering him. Last night he couldn't get it up . . . and I think it's because he feels less of a man letting himself get pushed around on this vote. At least that's what I work hard to make him think."

They all laughed. "Will this translate into a no vote?" BJ asked.

"I don't think so," she said. "He just feels . . . over a barrel, that's all. I don't believe he feels he has a choice."

"What about Dennison, Barb?" he asked.

"Same thing," she said. "Horrified . . . especially of site specific and weak sister program cuts. They've always cut spending across the board before, which never condemns any program to a death sentence. But he feels he's got no choice. You know, BJ, this isn't like convincing somebody of something. They already agree with us, but they feel caught. They're watching their lives unravel."

"So we'll make them feel caught in another direction," BJ said. "It's just a question of raising the stakes. The game hasn't changed. Rayda?"

The woman sat fidgeting, tugging at the knee-length hem of her cashmere skirt. "General Nivan would go along if somebody else cracked first," she said. "But I just don't see him being the one to buck the system."

"Roderick," BJ said, "what about the Chairman? Is he going to try and influence the vote if it goes for us?"

Roderick Burns sat, spindly and hunched like a mantis,

his dark, slick good looks dampened intentionally by the tortoise-shell glasses he wore but didn't need. "One thing I can guarantee you," he said, "is that Wintering doesn't want to have anything to do with this thing. As long as he can just preside and doesn't have to break any ties, he'll be satisfied for the vote to go the other way. But he's as tied to the administration as to the Pentagon. He'll have to argue the other side, even if he doesn't want to. None of these guys *wants* to vote against military spending, BJ."

"So, what you're all saying is quite simple," BJ replied, sinking back into the cushions again. "If we can crack one shell, everything else will fall into line." He turned to Patterson. "That's why I'm depending on you."

"Why me?" she asked. "You brought me in late to this thing. Angie's been with Wallace for over a year and a half. She's having to fight off marriage proposals, for God's sake. If anybody can do any convincing . . ."

"You've got a larger hammer right now," he said, then held up a hand to keep her from responding. "Let's continue this in private." He turned to the others. "Ladies . . . gentleman. With any luck we'll be celebrating a major victory tonight. You know what to do. And get your people to watch the news."

They all stood, Angie checking for runs in her black hose. As BJ said his good-byes, the receiver still hanging on his neck buzzed gently. He slipped the unit on over his head and connected. "Yeah?"

"Mr. Bomar is here for his nine o'clock," June trilled softly. "Should I put them in your office?"

"Them?" he asked, watching all but Patterson file out of Con-3.

"He's got Miss Cement Mixer of 1985 with him again," she replied.

"Great. I'll be there in a minute. Find out what they're drinking, then don't give it to them." He rung off and pulled the headset back down to his shoulders. He fixed Patterson with hard eyes. Her dress was of white silk, set off by a black crepe half jacket and matching belt. It showed off her deep red hair to good effect.

"What really happened to Joann?" she asked.

He smiled easily. "Come over here," he said, reaching out his arms.

"BJ . . ."

"Just come over here."

She stood, smoothing down the dress over slender hips. She walked to stand before him, the coffee table just behind her. Without a word, he reached out large hands and grabbed her breasts, squeezing tightly, enjoying the feel of the slick material and the slight tension in her eyes. Then he slowly slid his hands down her body, pushing hard, staring up at her the whole time. He dropped down, reaching under her skirt to move his hands up her legs to her buttocks. He grabbed again, pulling her slightly forward. "Four pounds," he said.

"Three," she returned, holding herself rigid in his grasp. "And it's all in my tits. Nobody complains. What really happened to Joann? I know that you know."

"You know all sorts of stuff, don't you, Mel?" he said, pinching her ass hard, making her jump.

"I'm going to have to explain bruises," she said.

He let her go. The back of her dress had gotten hooked in the waistband of her panty hose. He pulled it out, smoothing down the material. "She took herself out," he said. "Used a razor blade."

Patterson returned to her seat, the table between them. "Why?"

"Why does anybody commit suicide?" he asked. "We really don't have time for a therapy session here, Mel. This is a big day. Let me ask you a question. Have you slept with Admiral Stanley yet?"

She shook her head. "You told me not to."

He sat back and clapped his hands. "Good!" he said, feeling the cogs fall into place. "Has he been wanting it?"

She rolled her eyes. "The sight of a grown man begging is a pretty pitiful thing," she replied.

"Excellent. Here's what I want you to do. The meeting's not until later this afternoon. I want you to get on the horn to the Pentagon and see if he can make a little time for you. Tell him you're dying to be with him on this important day, that you know he needs a friend right now. Then get on over there and haul his ashes right there in his office. Maybe on the desk. Really build his ego, make him feel like Tarzan before he goes in for that vote."

"Come on, BJ," she said. "I have a lot of self-confidence,

but do you really believe that one roll in the hay with me is going to make him swing his vote on this?"

BJ leaned forward, resting his arms on his knees. "That's why I'm the teacher and you're the pupil," he said, putting his hands together in the praying posture. "No. One roll in the hay may not swing the vote. But that plus a million telegrams, a demonstration, negative press, and a call from his ninety-five-year-old former commanding officer just might. Are you with me, Mel? You know as well as I do that we can accomplish anything we want to in this world if we just put our minds to it. Take away the polished shoes and the uniform with the fruit salad and he's just a man, honey. Worlds turn all the time on the kind of schemes we're laying here."

She stood. "You make it sound so simple."

He showed her empty palms. "It is. You can use the phone in here to call. I've got somebody waiting in the office."

He stood, pouring another cup of coffee for the trip back to the office. He still felt uncomfortable about Patterson. She had gotten too good, too sure of herself. "And listen," he said. "Forget about Joann, would you? We all die. She was just in a bigger hurry than most. We've got a lot riding on our actions here. We can't bring any adverse publicity into the building right now."

"She was my best friend," the woman said.

He just stared at her. "I'm my own best friend," he replied. "A person needs to look out after his own welfare first, don't you think? How much money did you make last year?"

She picked up her small purse and tucked it under her arm. "You know damned well how much I made," she replied.

"Almost half a million dollars," he said. "Well, I'm prepared to authorize a bonus for each one of you to match that salary if we bring this thing off with the Joint Chiefs. You can buy a lot of best friends with that kind of money. Think about it."

"I am," she said, turning toward the wall phone concealed by a potted plant in the corner.

"And watch that weight," he said, moving across the

room to the door, opening it. He watched her pick up the phone. "Remember, I'm counting on you."

She waved obliquely and he moved on, getting back out into the rush of the central office. The vote was going to be tight and he knew it. The Joint Chiefs usually survived by their very invisibleness in the scheme of things. This business was bringing them out into the open, and the pressure, he was sure, would begin to show. Put a military man under pressure and he reverts to type. It was his intention to put each one of them on the hot seat and see what kind of man he was.

He crossed through the mayhem of rush mailings to his office, the door slightly ajar. Bomar had taken off his gray suit jacket and was bent over a putter in shirtsleeves and vest while his overdressed bleached blond girlfriend, Pam Williams, stood looking through the telescope.

"Jeremy," he called, setting down his coffee and hurrying across the room with outstretched hand. "I really appreciate your working so late last night."

The man straightened from his putter, reaching out to shake hands. "No problem, BJ," he said, his smooth face, as usual, betraying no emotion.

BJ turned to the woman to give her a hug. "Good morning, Pam," he said.

She curled her lip and turned back to the telescope. "Nothing physical," she said. "I bathed already this morning."

"Come on, cut the crap," Bomar said. "Show a little respect."

The woman looked at him, frowning. "Show me a little something to respect, and I will."

BJ just stared at her.

Bomar smiled wide at him. "I guess she just don't like you," he said.

"Maybe it's just that time of the month," BJ offered.

She took a long breath. "Think I'm going to go out to the break room and get a little fresh air," she said, moving quickly across the room.

BJ watched her all the way through the door. "Swear to God, Jeremy," he said jovially. "I don't know what it is you see in that girl."

The man bent to his putt, hit it too hard. It rolled off the

AstroTurf surface and disappeared under a Louis XIV chair half the length of the room away. He looked up at BJ. "I like her cause she's got good taste," he said, dropping the putter and picking up his jacket.

"Got the package?" BJ asked.

Bomar slid into his jacket as if he were sliding under a narrow gate. "Your desk," he said, inclining his head in that direction.

BJ walked to the desk and picked up the manila envelope, sliding the material out onto his desk: a file folder containing printouts and a videotape. Bomar joined him at the desk.

"I made the tape last night when he was leaving," the man said.

BJ nodded and moved around to sit at the desk, opening the folder in front of him. The service and professional record of one Charles Emmett Merchant sat before him. It was a record cast in sterling silver, the life history of a man of integrity and forthrightness. A well-respected idealist was Mr. Merchant, and a pragmatist. BJ smiled. He picked up the tape and turned to put it in the VCR on the shelf behind his desk, the big-screen TV jumping to life across the room.

A picture faded onto the screen of a lean, hard man bundled up against the cold. He turned to stare at the camera as he walked past in the dark, his eyes hard crystals in the shadows, his teeth clamped viselike on his pipe.

"What was your impression of him?" BJ asked as the tape played itself out.

"Seems like a hardass," Bomar said. "Reminds me of a warden I knew once down in Huntsville. I think he got my license number."

BJ grunted, the phone buzzing on his neck. He pulled up the headset. "Yeah."

"James Whitworth on the line," June said, "from . . ."

"I know where he's from," he returned. "Put him on."

There was a second of silence, then "Ben James?"

"Mr. Whitworth," BJ said into the mike. "So good to hear from you. Think we're making some progress here on the U-4 wheel assembly. We may be able to get Appropriations to lower the standards to—"

"I'm not concerned about that now," the man said, tense. "It's that Joint Chiefs vote I'm wanting to know about. I've been checking our vendor files and you're into Unitech for one hell of a lot of money. You know we hired you—"

"You hired me because I guarantee satisfaction, Mr. Whitworth," BJ said. "And I believe at this juncture I'm still prepared to stand behind my guarantee."

"I've been doing my own vote counting," Whitworth said, "and I personally think you're crazy to say such a thing."

"This afternoon will certainly tell the tale."

"You're serious, aren't you?" the man was exasperated. BJ couldn't help but smile. "You've got to be the only person in the country who thinks the vote is in doubt. It's a done deal, James."

"Call me BJ," James said. "And there ain't no such thing as a done deal until the paper's been signed and the money spent. You know that. Go back and tell your people that everything's going to be just fine."

"I . . . I don't know what to say."

"Say thanks, Mr. Whitworth. And count your blessings that you and the American people have Ben James on your side."

BJ rang off before the man could answer, always preferring to respond to domination attempts with indifference. He pulled off the headset and glanced once more at the file in front of him. He looked up. Bomar stood silently in front of the desk. "I want you to go to stage two on Mr. Merchant," he said, opening up the top desk drawer and sliding the file inside.

"The full treatment?" the man asked.

"I think so."

"You'd better watch this one. He's got connections and I don't think there's much we could offer him. He could make trouble."

Ben James leaned back in his chair and smiled. "No, Jeremy," he said. "It's Mr. Merchant who's going to have the trouble. More trouble than he ever knew possible."

Bomar leaned up close, his brows knit. "I don't understand," he said. "Why don't we just do this guy and be finished with it."

James looked hard at Bomar, his eyes alive and glowing. "Everything else for me is just business, Jeremy. But the dismantling of Mr. Charles Merchant is going to be pure pleasure."

■■■■ NEWSBREAK ■■■■

New York (AP)—The government of Caribbea has lodged a formal protest with the United Nations Security Council this morning, charging the United States with reckless and aggressive disregard for sovereign airspace in the incident of the EquAir cargo plane downed in the Caribbean Sea late last night. While denying shooting down the unarmed aircraft, the Companero-controlled military claimed the plane was on an illegal covert mission to aid *libre uso* rebels who have steadfastly refused to disarm, despite recent democratic elections. This drives another wedge into worsening U.S./Caribbean relations as economic conditions in the Central American republic continue to spiral downward, the Communist Companero opposition already calling for new elections.

The U.S., meanwhile, has directly accused the Companero opposition of shooting down an unarmed, off-course aircraft that was lost and broadcasting on emergency distress frequencies. While denying that the plane was in any way connected with covert government activities, a GSA spokesman this morning refused to divulge the purpose of the flight or what possible cargo it contained. EquAir is an independent operator under contract to the General Services Administration.

In related matters, the U.S. Navy has recovered

two bodies from the Caribbean Sea amid the wreckage of what appears to be the EquAir flight. The bodies and the wreckage are being flown to the Canal Zone for identification.

Arlington, Virginia 10:14 A.M.

Charles Merchant walked his wide backyard, his litter skewer balanced in his right hand, the trash sack slung over his left shoulder. Small drifts of powdery snow climbed his brick barbecue pit and clogged in the gables of his two-story frame Georgian house. The yard was perfectly flat and level except for the small lump near the back fence where the previous owner had built an air-raid shelter during the cold war paranoia of the fifties. Merchant had completely landscaped the place himself, pulling up the helter-skelter arrangements of trees and shrubs that had accumulated during a hundred and fifty years of constant occupancy and replacing them with neat military rows of crabapple and elm trees down the center of the yard and high, squared-off hedgerows against the six-foot stockade fences that separated him from his neighbors.

Modern Arlington was the recognizable offspring of a proper Scottish merchant village, a gem of a time capsule polished to luster by George Washington himself, and protected from even the ravages of Civil War because it had been so beloved by both sides. It was the perfect place for Merchant. He had moved here first in the late fifties when on a stint as a Pentagon action officer, then later, in 1969, upon taking command of Army Intelligence's research section at the headquarters at Arlington Station, and the moment he had driven through the controlled and thoughtful orderliness that was this preserved Colonial town, he knew where he'd spend the rest of his life.

A fast-food wrapper lay at his feet. He speared it with the skewer, picking it up to slide into the bag. Merchant's yard was his statement, his message to the world. He kept it always neat and orderly, tidy. It was meditative for him, a physical manifestation of his organized mind. He began every morning here, straightening things up, getting it all in order. He used to get up and mow every morning during the growing season, but the neighbors complained, so he put that part off until the end of the day.

He hadn't been to sleep yet, but he'd known that would be impossible the moment he'd walked into the horror of Dumbarton Street. He was cold and miserable, his nose numb, as the gray skies rolled angrily above, occasional snow spitting from the clouds to swirl in confusion around his head. He was too old for this shit, and too much of a friend to forget about it.

He'd known Braedman since Korea. They'd come up through Eighth Army Intelligence, the two of them, plus Gene Tillotson, drawn together through the horror of the Chongchon Valley campaign, America's worst defeat of the Korean War, a defeat blamed on failure of intelligence gathering in allowing a huge Red Army force to infiltrate the country unseen. They'd been young, and no one had ever dealt with the Chinese before; so when soldiers in the field had brought prisoners, Merchant and the others had interrogated those prisoners in good faith, never realizing they'd allowed themselves to be captured in order to plant misleading information, seriously underestimating troop strengths. It had led to absolute disaster and devastating defeat for America, the finger of guilt finally pointing to Merchant and the young intelligence unit that had been formed from scratch for the operation.

That failure had hardened the three men into a unit. Though the Chongchon disaster was to haunt them through the rest of their careers, they'd stood tall in the face of it, forging their alliance into friendships that had survived the upheavals of years and changing situations.

They'd been pegged as the best and the brightest in those days, despite the shadow of Chongchon, all of them realizing success in and out of the military. They'd worked that much harder to overcome the blame, Braedman turning to politics while Merchant and Tillotson opted to stay in the military. Merchant had worked himself up to head of Army Intelligence, with all the perks and power that went along with the job. It wasn't until he was passed over for the directorship of the newly formed Defense

Intelligence Agency that he realized that Korea still wasn't behind him. It had made those closest to him angry to see him denied what should have been his, but for Merchant it had simply been the final spotlight on his unworthy career. He had failed mightily and, try as he might, could not undo his failure.

His resolve broken by the loss of the DIA job, he'd finished his tour and quietly retired just short of an almost automatic promotion to general. It would have meant a larger pension and a measure of respect, but in his heart he didn't feel as if he deserved it and wasn't about to take it simply as a consolation prize.

Gene had stuck, however, had taken his promotions and now had the same DIA job that had been denied Merchant, thrown as a gift to the man in his later life. It might have been Merchant's had he chosen Gene's path of least resistance, but his pride had walked him away and kept him away. He would take only what he earned, what he deserved, be it respect or promotions or the knowledge down in his heart that he'd done right by himself and those who mattered. He may have failed the country, but by God, he wasn't going to fail himself. Gene had taken the other path, and had to drink himself to sleep every night.

Thinking of the old days reminded him that he needed to call Tillotson and fill him in on Jack's problem, though he had a feeling by now that the whole world knew about it.

What had happened back there? So little of what had occurred in the last few hours had made any sense to him that he felt as if he were living out some sort of strange nightmare where facts didn't match up and worst case scenarios were the only things that ever happened.

He'd been afraid to watch TV for fear of the reports. He couldn't get the vision of Braedman screaming as he was being dragged away out of his mind. He felt responsible, and worse, Braedman felt the same way. God, if he was going to let somebody down, why did it have to be his oldest friend? He couldn't leave it at this. Something had to be done. It just didn't set right.

He heard the back door slam, turning to see Linda walking barefoot toward him. She was wrapped up in her robe, her face a strained and red-eyed mask.

"It's cold out here!" he called as she walked right through a small drift on the cement patio and moved onto the lawn. "Get inside. I'll come in."

She ignored him and kept coming, her lips tightened to a hard slash, her eyes set rigid. He hurried to meet her. "What is it?"

She reached him in the center of the lawn. "You son of a bitch!" she said through clenched teeth, her hand flashing out to slap him hard across the face. "You lousy son of a bitch!"

She tried to hit him again, but he grabbed her arms, pinning them to her sides. "What the hell are you doing?"

"Why didn't you tell me?" she demanded, then collapsed against him, crying, sobbing loudly.

He tried to fold her in his arms, but she stiffened, pushing away from him, her face angry again. "You should have told me about Jack."

"I was keeping a confidence," he said, returning her anger, the frost like steam from his lips. "If you can't understand . . ."

"A confidence for whom?" she said, crying, guttural. "Jack's dead, you son of a bitch!"

Something jumped inside him as he frantically searched her face for a lie. "What are you talking about? What do you mean . . . dead?"

Her eyes narrowed and she stopped struggling against him. "Y-you didn't know?" She turned, pointing to the house. "The t-television . . . it said he murdered a woman and then k-killed himself."

"No," he said loudly. "Jack would never do anything like that, and he didn't kill that woman."

She was still pointing, her arm trembling wildly. "The TV . . . the TV . . ."

He looked hard at her. "For God's sake get inside," he said, then turned and ran for the house, his mind clearing, focusing. He made it through the door and into the laundry room. To the right, from the kitchen, he heard the sound of a television droning and ran for it.

The kitchen was nineteenth century huge with modern fixtures and endless cabinet space. The portable television sat on the washstand beside the stainless-steel double sink. He was watching the video of Jack being dragged away by the D.C. police as the crowds cheered. It was hot in the kitchen, sweltering. He pulled off the heavy topcoat and folded it over the back of a kitchen chair, his eyes riveted to the screen. The scene switched to a shot of a full body bag being carried out the back door of police head-quarters and loaded into an ambulance. He turned up the sound.

". . . apparently unable to stand the weight of what he'd done, he threw himself down the sixth-floor stair-well, dying almost immediately of massive internal inju-ries."

"No," Merchant said again, not believing it. This was totally insane. The announcer kept talking though, saying all the things that didn't add up.

"He had confessed the murder of the woman, Joann Durbin, just moments before his fatal jump, listing jeal-ousy of another male friend of the woman as his motiva-tion."

"Poor Eve," Linda said from the door. She stood small and passive, leaning against the door frame, her arms crossed at the waist, a hand grasping each elbow. Her face showed no emotion.

"Poor Eve?" he said, unable to keep the ungodly hurt out of his voice. "Poor Eve? She's not the one dead. Hell, they hadn't had any kind of relationship for years."

"She was still his wife," Linda replied, eyes flashing indignation. "Like it or not. How much different . . ."

"Don't say it," he told her and made a point of turning back to the TV.

The wall phone rang loudly, Merchant hurrying to answer it.

"God, have you seen the news?" came Gene Tillotson's shaky voice. "Did you see about Jack?"

"I was there when they took him away," he answered. "I meant to call you, I . . ."

"Jesus . . . after all these years," Tillotson said. "The three of us, I . . . why did he do it?"

"He didn't do it, Gene," Merchant answered without hesitation. "He didn't kill the girl and he would never commit suicide."

"But the TV . . . ?"

"The TV's wrong. Everybody's wrong." On the screen

were the two cops who'd accosted him at the death scene, the ones who'd wanted to kill him. He stretched the phone cord across the room to get closer to the screen.

"How do you know that?" Tillotson was demanding, his own voice frantic now.

"Wait!" Merchant said, straining to hear the TV. He balanced the phone on his shoulder and began digging through his pockets as he listened to the hard cop with the death's-head eyes named Weston.

"He had made a . . . what we call a spontaneous statement to us, said he wanted to get it off his chest." The man shrugged. "We listened, then took him up to seven to put him into a holding cell until we could get the stenographer and video guy out here for an official state-ment. We knew this was a big case and we wanted to do everything just right. But he broke away from us at the top of the stairs, cuffs and all, and jumped into the stairwell headfirst." Weston shook his head. "It was over in a couple seconds."

"What's going on, Charlie?" Tillotson asked. "Don't keep me in the dark."

Merchant couldn't find the card in his pocket. He moved over to the table and leaned down to reach into his coat pockets. "The two cops who were with Jack when he . . . died. . . ."

"Yeah?"

"I saw them destroying evidence at the scene," he said, pulling the bent white business card out of the left coat pocket. "Jack had called me after the girl killed herself."

"What kind of evidence?"

"I'm not sure." He looked at the card of Detective Lieutenant Leonard Hurley—Homicide Division. "It was some kind of message she'd left, like a suicide note."

"What did the police say when you told them?"

"I'm getting ready to tell them right now," Merchant said, angry at himself for staying out of it even this long. Maybe if he'd acted immediately, Jack would be alive right now. "Something's up, Gene. I'm sure of it."

"What can I do to help?"

"Pull the strings to get him buried in Arlington," Merchant said, the words catching in his throat. "It's the least we can do for him."

"That won't be easy," Tillotson said. "Given the nature of . . ."

"Just try and do it, okay?"

"My best shot, Charlie. Just like always."

Merchant pulled his coat off the chair and put it on. The screen had switched to some early movies of Jack when he'd first gone into the Senate as the announcer did a brief bio that did nothing to touch on the real goodness of the man. "Thanks, Gene," he said. "And hang tight. I have no idea in what direction this is going to take me and I might need your help later. I gotta go."

"I'll call Eve. Keep me posted. And, Charlie . . . don't blame yourself for this."

"Then who should I blame?" he asked, walking to the wall and hanging up.

"You're going again," Linda said, straightening, almost as if she were trying to block the door.

He moved to stand before her. "I've got to take care of this."

"I've been hearing that for twenty-five years," she said. "What are you getting ready to get mixed up in?"

He looked at her. The anger seemed so sharp in her eyes. "I'm really not sure," he said honestly.

"Tell me anyway."

He moved her out of the way. "There's nothing to tell. I'm just going to check on a few things."

She turned and watched him move through the laundry room. "Well, I'm going down to the Center. Don't expect me to sit here and worry. You can go to hell if you think I'll ever worry about you again."

He reached the door, turning to her halfway through. "What's wrong with you?" he asked.

"I'm tired, Charlie," she said, head down. "Tired of waiting for you, tired of putting my life on hold. I thought when you retired things would be different, but . . ."

"For God's sake," Merchant said. "He was my best friend."

"And I'm your wife!"

He took a long breath. "Look, we'll talk later."

She nodded in resignation. "Later," she repeated in a monotone, and he started through the door again.

"Charlie . . ." she said once more, a plea.

"Yeah?"

Their eyes met for just a second, a flash of something that had once been there. "I'm sorry I slapped you," she said. "Maybe it's menopause."

He nodded once and was gone. The joke wasn't funny.

White House Press Room 10:00 A.M.

Sheila Traynor stood in the entry hall in the back of the White House Press Room and went through the news release bin one more time, holding her breath, hoping her exclusive was still intact. The bin contained several releases concerning Breedlove, the out-of-control mercenary, and a couple bits on the plane shot down in Caribbea. Things were obviously hot in Central America. It could only be a matter of time before her news became public, too. Only she intended to break it first and break it hard. Shots like this didn't come along that often, vacation openings only once a year. Where the hell was Michael?

She finished going through the paper stacks with a loud sigh, then turned quickly around to see if anybody had heard her. Reporters mulled over their coffee and cigarettes in the hallway all around her, laughing and talking loudly, getting awake, the press room seating slowly filling for the morning briefing concerning the handouts in the bin. She felt like a marathon runner a half block ahead of the pack with a mile left in the race. If she could just hold on and keep up the pace, if she didn't stumble, if she didn't tire—she might have a shot at winning this time. It was a victory she desperately needed, for Sheila Traynor had been around just long enough to know that success and self-respect weren't the same thing. She had gotten what she'd always wanted and found it empty. She was ready to work at it now, to earn the rung up the ladder she occupied. Twinkie Newsreader was not the epitaph she wanted on her tombstone.

"Sheila!" came Michael's voice from just inside the entry doorway. His hand was up, waving, as he slowly pushed his way toward her. Michael Baroni was her New York–based producer, the last link in the chain of organization that would get the story on the air. She felt a surge of excitement when she saw him, the rush turning to ice when she caught sight of his companion.

The two men reached her, Baroni leaning down to give her a hug. He wore a blue suit and a big smile. The other man wore gray, and it seemed to match his attitude. She pushed away from Baroni and put her hand out.

"Not often we get the head of the news division all the way down here," she said suspiciously. "How are you, Don?"

He smiled and shook her hand, and she took that as a good sign. "Not often we get this kind of scoop down here," he said. "You've got the whole division buzzing."

"Hey," she said. "You don't want to be too free with—"

"Don't worry," Donald Merck said in his boardroom voice. "Everything's under control. Where can we talk?"

She looked around, then looked at her watch. There wasn't time to go anywhere before the briefing. "Well, we sure as hell can't sneak into the john together," she said. "How are your feelings about cloakrooms?"

Baroni smiled. "You sure Woodward and Bernstein got started this way?"

"Well, if nothing else," she said, leading them through the crowd back toward the door, "maybe we can find new coats."

She took them into the long narrow room just by the door, down past the double rows of coats. You could always tell the print journalists' coats from the TV people's. Where the TV people had new wool overcoats and London Fog trenchcoats to look good on the tube, the print journalists tended toward old Air Force flight jackets and beat-up raincoats. The bitter cold of the morning still rolled off the rows of coats, making her shiver.

They gathered in a close little knot at the end of the room, the confusion of the outer hallway now just the sound of distant drums. "So, what's the problem?" she asked immediately, wanting to get it all out before she burst.

"Maybe nothing," Merck said, his toupee hugging his skull like a helmet, the slightest odor of eggs coming with his words. "It's just that . . . well, this is quite a bombshell you've dropped on us. Are you really a hundred percent on all your sources."

She narrowed her eyes. "What the hell more do you want?" she said. "I gave you a videotape of Russian trawlers dropping the missiles off in Caribbea, photos and videotapes of the bombs themselves, plus photocopies of intelligence reports."

"We understand the nature of your documentation," Baroni said, working hard at holding eye contact with her. "It's just that . . . well, we wonder how it happened to fall to you, that's all."

She drew herself up, all five feet three inches of her, and stared at the two men who towered over her. "Has it crossed your minds that I got hold of the information because I'm a good journalist? Why not me? Look, you guys gave me a vacation shot to prove myself in hard news when everybody else just called me an 'aging twinkie newsreader.' Have you changed your minds now?"

"Damnit, Sheila," Merck said, crossing his arms. "It has nothing to do with that. We believed in you and we still do. It's just that all we've got on the truth of this information is your word. That's hardly good enough. If this information is true, it represents a major policy shift for the Soviet Union. If you haven't noticed, they don't do shit like this anymore. Where did the leak come from? Who was your source?"

She turned to Baroni. "I told you on the phone, Mike," she said. "My source gave me this information in strictest confidence. I gave my solemn word that nobody but me would ever know. Believe me. I'm telling you as one ethical human being to another, my source is highly placed and unimpeachable. This information is absolutely genuine. Can't that be enough for you?"

"I appreciate your position," Merck said, "but it's the news division's ass in the sling if it's wrong. How do I go tell *my* bosses that I ran information without checking the source?"

"You tell them what I just told you," Traynor said angrily, pointing to the crowds milling past the door at the end of the room. "Every one of those assholes out there would *love* to have my story. Hell, the last time something like this happened was in '62 and we almost went to war with the Russians. We're getting briefed on that same area in a few minutes. In case you haven't noticed, the whole damned world's coming apart over there. Something's going on, fellas, and if you guys don't get your heads out of your asses you're going to lose the story of the decade."

The two men shared a look. "Just tell us," Merck said, lowering his voice. "Just a name. We won't tell a soul. Give me just enough that I can tell my people I'm satisfied with the sources."

"I gave my word, Don," she said. "And I'm going to stand behind it. I couldn't last very long at all in this city if my sources knew they couldn't trust my word."

Merck closed his eyes, nodding slightly. "I know you're right," he said, and looked hard at her. "I just hope to God you know what you're doing, lady. We'll run it as a bulletin this afternoon, then give it the top of the nightly news with your commentary. Can you get something together that quick?"

"You just watch my dust," Traynor said. "You won't regret this."

"I hope not," Merck said. "I'm too old to start looking for another job."

Arlington, Virginia 10:32 A.M.

Jeremy Bomar sat on the passenger side of the beat-up Univision Cable Television truck and tooted a snort of coke up each nostril from the small vial he carried in his pocket. On the dashboard, his coffee sat steaming up the windshield and filling the cab with morning smells. The coffee was to keep him awake. The coke was to put an edge on it. Ritchie Mancini sat beside him, keeping time on the steering wheel to some tune in his head, while Ritchie's brother, Tony, did the phone hook-ups up on the pole.

"Looks like he's leavin'," Ritchie said, pointing to the target house.

Bomar watched the white Cadillac pull out of the

driveway of the big old frame house with the heavy shutters. "Good," he said. "I'm ready to get done with this shit today."

"Just the man," Ritchie said as Tony climbed back down the pole and gave the thumbs-up sign, his beer gut nearly busting through the snaps on the overalls he wore. "We gonna wait for the woman to leave?"

"Not if I can help it," Bomar said. "This waitin' around makes me nervous. Come on. Bring your tools."

They climbed out of the truck, looking around. Bomar turned a slow circle as he crossed the street, his eyes searching windows and lawns overlooking the house. It seemed all right. He moved right up the flagstone walk of the target, shaking his head at all the trees and shrubs on the front lawn. He'd never live in a house like this—too many places for people to hide. It was wide-open corner lots for him.

He moved right up to the door and rang the bell. "How many phones?" he asked Ritchie.

"Five extensions," the man answered, reading from a phone company printout. "You want all of them?"

"Yeah . . . and cameras in the kitchen, living room, and den. Bedroom if we can—"

The door opened, a middle-aged, washed-out blonde standing there, clutching a quilted robe up around her throat. She looked all tired and used up, with some sort of want hanging around her eyes. He knew the type and he knew the cure. He smiled, staring hard at her. "Morning, ma'am," he said. "Sorry to bother you."

"Yes?"

"We're going to be working on the cable lines around here for a while," he said. "Just wanted to make sure it was okay to have three strange men walking around in your yard."

"Is there a problem with the cable?" she asked.

"Weak signals up and down the line," he said. "How's yours working. We can check it if you—"

"Ours is fine," she said quickly, her hand now up on the door. He could tell she was ready to be through with them. "Do I need to be around for any of this?"

"No, ma'am," Bomar said. "Just wanted to warn you."

She nodded. "Well, I'll be up getting ready to leave for the day, so I won't hear you if you ring again."

"No problem," he said. "You just go on with your day. We won't bother you."

"Okay," she said, meeting his eyes for just a second, a fleeting something registering before she closed the door in his face.

He turned to Ritchie. "Back door," he said quietly, and they moved around the walk to go down the driveway to the back.

"This guy really keeps his place sharp," Ritchie said. "Jesus, it don't even need paintin'. Break into enough houses and you get to be an expert, you know?"

"Can it," Bomar said as they went through the stockade gate that led into the meticulous backyard. He moved from window to window around back, peering through to make sure she wasn't downstairs anymore before using one of his picks to open the heavy back door.

The three men moved quietly into the house, Bomar loving the intrusion onto the property of others. It was a powerful feeling, knowing he could enter other people's lives without consent, that no one could be safe or above him. It was a high beyond compare, an ego boost that made him as good as the people he victimized.

He turned to Tony, pointing to the right. "The kitchen's that way," he whispered. "Go."

He and Ritchie went left, into the den, Mancini walking immediately to the Waterloo battlefield set up on the pool table. "Hey, lookit this," he said, leaning down close to it. "They play with toy soldiers."

"Gimme a camera and a bug," Bomar said, walking up next to him. He heard a sound above, footsteps across the bedroom floor, then the sound of water gurgling down the drain pipes in the wall.

He took the instruments from Ritchie, both of them fitting easily in the palm of his hand. "Hurry," he said. "I'm gonna take the upstairs. I want you done down here in five minutes."

"Yeah," Ritchie said, reluctantly tearing himself away from the mock battle. "Have fun up there."

He hurried out of the den, moving through a large

formal dining room with breakfront and heavy-looking table, then found the stairs up just off the living room.

The carpets were thick pile, his feet not making a sound as he took the stairs up two at a time. He found himself in a long hallway, open doors lining both sides. He walked past the doors, two empty bedrooms and a bath. The master bedroom sat at the end of the hall.

He moved to it cautiously, a smile etched on his face. He really loved this, the excitement a physical thing, invigorating. He poked his head into the bedroom, the sounds of the shower running coming through the open door of the attached bath. He walked into the bedroom, moving quickly to the night table and the phone that rested there.

He picked up the receiver, unscrewing it to drop the device into the mouthpiece, then closing it back up— finished in twenty seconds. He looked around. The room was large, done in blues with dark wood furniture. Only one side of the king-size bed had been slept in. Hanging plants dangled from macramé ropes in front of the windows. He moved to one of the baskets and placed the transistorized camera within the confusion of stems of lush fern.

Finished, he looked at his watch, then moved around to the slept-in part of the bed and lay down, stretching out, listening to the shower running just a few feet away.

He heard a sound, like a soft moan, coming from the bathroom. Curious, he got up and walked to the door, poking his head into the steamy room.

The shower stall was frosted glass, the pink, fuzzy form of the woman just visible through it. She moaned again, louder. She was leaning against the back of the stall, partially leaning against the glass of the door. She had a hand-held shower nozzle trapped between her legs, two hands working the thing up and down as her breath came in gasps and sobs. Bomar knew that his first impression of her had been the right one.

She cried out loudly, a strangled squeal, and he took a bold step toward the shower, stopping barely six inches from her and raising his hand to trace her outline on the glass. She cried out the last of her release, slumping over as she quaked violently.

Bomar smiled. This was going to be more fun than he'd thought.

▬▬▬ NEWSBREAK ▬▬▬

". . . while on surface a decent family man, devoted to his wife, his children, and the nation he'd served for so long, a violent sexual monster apparently lived beneath the presidential skin of Jack Braedman that led him down a dark and twisted trail ending in gruesome horror and revulsion at one of posh Georgetown's trendiest addresses. What were the demons that drove one of America's most promising sons down the twisted alleys of murder and depravity? And what of the beautiful young woman who shared that journey and its horrifying conclusion with him? Don't miss tonight's edition of *Inside Scoop* and our headline story, 'Jack Braedman: Violence, Sex, and Politics.'"

Police Headquarters, Washington D.C. 12:10 P.M.

Merchant never complained about the cold. It was a given, the starting place. It never did any good to complain about things you couldn't do anything about. He parked the Caddie at the lot on Pennsylvania and Tenth and walked the two long blocks to the station, his collar turned against the needling stingers of dry, wind-lashed snow.

Network vans sprouting obscene-looking six-story transmitter poles from their tops jammed the entire block in front of the local government complex of jails, courts, and city offices, a large crowd gathered on the sidewalk despite the cold. They were drawn by the transmitters: the promise of recognition and eternity.

He made his way through the chattering crowd and up to the triple set of double doors leading into the building. A blue uniform stopped him at the doors. He was middle-aged and flabby, one of the desk boys from inside.

"You got business?" the man asked, Merchant pulling the business card out and showing it to him.

"I have an appointment with Lieutenant Hurley," he said. "Charles Merchant."

"Yeah . . . Mr. Merchant," the cop said, giving back the card. "Thought I recognized you. What brings you out in this lousy weather? You here for the show, huh?"

"The . . . show?"

"You know . . . Braedman. Man, he really made a mess in there."

Merchant took a long breath, then moved past the man without a word. Jack had already become a "show," part of the great American mythos machine.

He moved through the swinging doors and into the madhouse. The huge lobby was filled with newsmen and writhing coaxial cables. Their feet thundered on the fake marble floors and their voices slashed a ping-pong vibration off the cold stone walls. Lights flared brightly from a corner of the lobby, the place where everyone seemed to be trying to get to, as a police spokesman in the dazzling glare tried his best to answer overlapping volleys of questions.

Two desk sergeants sat behind a five-foot-high Formica counter at the other end of the lobby, laughing at the plainclothesman giving the news conference. Merchant moved through the fringes of the crowd, reaching up to lay the card on the countertop. "Name's Merchant. I'm here to see Lieutenant Hurley."

One of the cops stopped laughing long enough to pick up a receiver and punch up some numbers. He spoke softly into the phone, his voice drowned out in the echoing lobby sounds. After a moment the man put a beefy hand over the mouthpiece.

"He says he's kind of busy right now, and—"

"We have business," Merchant said coldly. Then nodded toward the receiver. "Tell him."

The cop glared at Merchant for a long second, getting it right back, then spoke softly into the phone again before nodding and hanging it up. He jerked his thumb toward a hallway stretching out behind the desk. "Homicide's just down—"

"I know where it is," Merchant said, sliding the card off the counter to pocket. He moved quickly down the familiar tiled hallways, taking the first fork left. Hurley's office was set off by itself halfway down the hall, totally removed from the barnyard of Homicide proper at hallway's end. If he'd been angry on the ride over, Hurley's attempt at putting him off stoked the fire to intensity. He turned the knob without knocking and walked in.

Hurley sat hunched over a computer typer wearing the same clothes Merchant had seen him in the night before. His sleeves were rolled up, the herringbone jacket slung on a love seat against the wall. His tie was at half mast. His face puddled, eyes downcast and tired. "The goddamned snow has already doubled our work load. The last thing I need is trouble from you right now," he said quietly.

"Then I'm your worst nightmare," Merchant said, carefully taking off his overcoat and neatly folding it atop the love seat before pulling a chair up to the desk. He sat, staring hard, his hands gripping the desktop. "You people have just murdered my best friend and I'm not going to let you get away with it."

Merchant watched Hurley's eyes carefully for reaction, getting nothing in return but a long, inscrutable look. "I have a difficult time," the man said calmly, "reconciling your enviable career record with the craziness I hear coming from you right now. I suggest, Mr. Merchant, that you are suffering from the effects of grief at the moment. Because you are truly talking like an idiot."

"Good," Merchant said, standing to glance around the room. "Good." A chessboard on its own small table with one chair pulled up before it sat on the wall opposite the love seat. It was flanked on either side by filing cabinets. He'd have a decision to make about Hurley in the next few minutes, and stepping wrong now could be fatal. He'd already made that mistake at Dumbarton Street.

"How could this have happened to Jack?" he asked the man, his eyes still on the chessboard across the room.

"I'm really sorry," Hurley said, genuine, heartfelt. Merchant sat again, watching him, as the man continued to talk. "I really think you got caught in the middle of something with your friend. We all get lied to, and we all believe lies. Nobody would have . . . could have thought he'd be suicidal." He shared Merchant's eyes. "I should have realized the state he was in and taken better precautions. He was distraught. . . ." The man laughed without humor. "*Obviously* distraught. Maybe a day or two in a cell . . ."

"So, is this an official version?" Merchant asked, taking the pipe out of his suit coat pocket and sticking it between his teeth without lighting it. "Is this going to go out as a murder/suicide?"

The man narrowed his eyes and held out empty palms. "What else?" he asked.

Merchant stood abruptly and walked to the chessboard, a game frozen in progress. He smiled down at the pieces. A Napoleonic set. The emperor himself stood proudly at attention beside Josephine, his queen. He picked up a bishop. Talleyrand? The closest the French Revolution got to parochialism.

"How else can it line out?" Hurley asked from across the room. "He killed the girl, then freaked out and took himself out. It wouldn't take too much realizing what the rest of his life was going to be to get in that kind of a state. All things being considered, how else can we peg it?"

Merchant held up the porcelain Napoleon, the piece painted in royal blue uniform. "How come there's only one chair at your table?" he asked.

Hurley smiled for the first time then, easing back in his chair to rub tired eyes with the heels of his hands. "Because," he said, "the only games that matter, the only ones that are truly meaningful, are the ones you play in your own head."

"Are you saying that man is his own worst enemy?"

"I'm saying that if we could control ourselves, we wouldn't need to control each other."

"Good way to put yourself out of a job."

"Yeah."

Merchant put the piece back in its place on the board

and returned to the desk. "Will you show me where it happened?"

Hurley pointed back out the door. "Just go out and—"

"I want you to show me," Merchant replied.

Hurley thought for a minute, then shrugged, standing to retrieve his jacket from the sofa. "I'm doing this because of what you've done for the department in the past and I'm doing it because Braedman was your friend. But I'm not going to be doing much else, no matter if I like you or not." He half knotted his tie and put the jacket on. "The word is to put this behind us quick and get on with things."

"No investigation?"

Hurley shook his head and opened the door. "What's to investigate?" he asked. "Open and shut. Come on, we'll take the elevator to six and look at it from up there."

As they moved back through the halls to the echoing lobby, Merchant filled his pipe from the leather pouch that Gene Tillotson had given him in Korea in 1951. Across the lobby, the two cops who'd nearly killed him, Mills and Weston, had been brought into the spotlight and stood answering questions before a large bank of microphones. "You get anything on the girl?" he asked.

Hurley frowned down at the pipe in Merchant's hands. He shook his head. "You can't smoke that in here," he said. "City ordinance."

"Sorry," Merchant replied, sticking it between his teeth without lighting it.

They skirted the crowd, a sergeant guarding the bank of elevators waving them past and into an island of calm. Hurley pushed the up button. "We've got nothing on the girl you haven't heard on the television," he said. "She came up here three years ago after graduating college and went right to work for a lobbying firm."

The stainless-steel doors to the first of three elevators slid open, the two men stepping in. Hurley pushed the sixth-floor button, then grunted and pushed it again when the door didn't shut fast enough to suit him.

"What was the name of the lobbying firm?" Merchant asked as they shuddered and began moving upward.

Hurley shrugged. "Don't remember . . . what difference does it make? What's important is that she quit her job six months ago when she started going with Braedman to avoid conflict of interest."

"How has she supported herself the last six months?" Merchant asked, taking the pipe out to tamp the tobacco with a forefinger.

The man sighed and put his hands on his hips. He faced forward, occasionally turning his head to Merchant. "I don't know . . . maybe her boyfriend gave her money."

"Jack didn't have that kind of money."

The elevator jerked to a stop, Hurley punching the open door button with his thumb when the doors stayed closed. "All Congressmen have that kind of money," he said, moving through the opening doors and into a hallway, Merchant right behind.

"What's that supposed to mean?"

"Read the papers," Hurley said, leading him down a wide, tiled hallway lined with local government offices. "They all do it—bribes, kickbacks, premiums, honorariums . . . whatever you want to call it. They all know how to get hold of some tax-free income."

"Not all of them," Merchant said. "Not Jack."

"You sound like a man who either knows his friend real well or not at all."

A red EXIT sign glowed at the end of the hallway, drawing them in. "Why are we down here?" Merchant asked. "The jails aren't on this floor."

They reached a doorway at the end of the hall and moved through it into the dark, bare cement sixth-floor landing. The landing and the stairs were bordered by a blue iron railing three feet high. Hurley pointed to the stairs up. "This started on seven," he said. "The way Weston tells it is that he broke away from them when someone opened the door, running and falling down the stairs between seven and six before throwing himself off . . . here."

Merchant moved slowly toward the railing and looked down.

"It was you who wanted to see it," Hurley told him.

"Yeah."

The stairs down continually folded in on themselves, making a vague box shape with the breezeway walls, with a large rectangular hole straight down the middle to ground level. Part of Braedman's head was slopped all over the railing and stairs of the next level down where he had apparently hit before completing the fall. From the looks of it, he'd probably died at that instant.

Several men in lab coats squatted around the muck of Jack's gray matter. They'd drawn chalk lines around the area and were poking at it with long metal rods. Merchant hated them for their coldness, but he forced down the dry-throated anger and tried to take in as much as he could.

His hands were shaking on the rail as he looked past them to the floor six stories below. Reporters pushed and shoved against a loose cordon of blues surrounding the chalk outline of a man drawn onto the floor, flash units blinking bright white like the popping synapses of his brain. The outline on the floor had no arms. He turned to look at a frowning Hurley. "He was still handcuffed, wasn't he?"

The man swallowed hard. "Maybe you ought to come away from there," he said. "You don't look good."

"What the fuck did you people do to him?" Merchant asked, low, intense.

"Come on." Hurley took his arm, pulling him gently back from the rail and against the metal door with the black six painted on it. The man got up close, pointing a finger in his face. "My patience with you is about up. Now, I'm sorry that your friend thought that bashing out his own brains was a good way to get out of a sticky situation, but you running around here accusing us of murder isn't going to bring him back or keep you out of trouble. Murder/suicide, Mr. Merchant. Get used to it; it happened."

Merchant pushed away the man's pointing finger. "Can I smoke out *here*?" he asked around the pipe stem.

Hurley looked quickly around, then shrugged broadly. "Sure. Why not? Now look—"

"It seems to me you've just got it backward," Merchant said, puffing under the flame of a disposable lighter. "Not murder/suicide, but suicide/murder."

Hurley leaned against the retaining rail and stared at him. "Okay, I'll play. Murder by whom?"

Merchant exhaled a long plume of blue-gray smoke. It was now or never. He could never keep this alive without help inside the police department. If they dropped the case, it was all but over. But who to trust? He'd watched Hurley since the beginning of their meeting, using every cold-read technique he'd ever known from eye blinks to dry lips, coming away with the conviction that if Hurley was a liar, he was one of the best Merchant had ever seen. That, in itself, deserved recompense. "I have some new information for you," he said, and quickly told the somber-faced man about the destruction of evidence and his near brush with death at the hands of Weston and Mills.

When he was finished, Hurley stared blankly at him. "I frankly don't want to believe this," he said.

Merchant relit the pipe. "You said before that you couldn't reconcile my record with the way I'm acting today. Does it reconcile now?"

Hurley pushed away from the rail and prowled the landing. "You really *mean* all this shit, don't you?" he asked loudly, his voice echoing down the breezeway, making the lab men below look up. He lowered his voice to a harsh rasp. "You are seriously telling me that two of my men altered the scene of a murder, then casually pushed a United States Senator over a sixth-floor railing headfirst."

"Think about it," Merchant said. "Why did these two, *these two*, arrive first at the 'murder' scene? Why were they the ones to bring him upstairs."

"Maybe they were the arresting officers."

"Then why were *they* the arresting officers? Why the sixth floor? Doesn't it seem odd to you that Jack would run down a flight of stairs and *then* decide to kill himself? Have you checked out that story? Who opened the door that he ran through?"

"This is crazy—"

"And who was the man in the red Jag running the camera?"

"Red Jag?"

"You got it," Merchant said, pulling a pen and small spiral notebook out of his blue suit coat. He began writing on the pad. "Weston and Mills pointed me out and he took my picture with a camcorder."

"Weston . . . and Mills pointed you out?" Hurley said, eyes narrowing.

Merchant ripped the small piece of paper out of the book and handed it to the detective. "Here's his license number. It's a good place to start with all this."

Hurley frowned down at the paper, then stuck it in his pocket. "Why me?" he asked. "Why not go to your friend Bignell with your theories?"

Merchant fixed him with a hard, even gaze. He had laid all his cards out on the table and had to roll with his choices now. "Somebody called the media," he said softly. "Somebody called Homicide and started the circus parade. Somebody called Mills and Weston. It wasn't me, and it sure as hell wasn't Jack. For the moment, Malcolm's my only other suspect. I don't know who to trust anymore."

"What makes you think you can trust me?" Hurley asked, face set.

Merchant pulled out the pipe and looked at the chars in the bole. "You work long hours," he said, tapping the pipe gently against the rail to clean it out. "Your hair's cut, not styled. Your clothes are nice, but well worn. I noticed that the sleeve on your sports jacket had been rewoven. Your shoes have been resoled. Pictures of your family on the wall, a commendation plaque from the Salvation Army, a couple of well-watered plants in the office. A messy desk, but not disarray—the sign of a good mind. You look at me when we speak, and you seem to mean what you say. I like the way you play chess. You seem to be my kind of man, Lt. Hurley, like it or not."

The detective nodded knowingly. "Also, you forgot the part about how if I was a part of this . . ."

"Is the word 'conspiracy' what you're thinking?"

"If I was a part of this conspiracy, I'd be trying to reel you in closer instead of trying to get rid of you where somebody might listen."

"That thought had crossed my mind," Merchant replied. "That is, of course, if I'm not simply insane."

Hurley shook his head quickly. "No," he said, "you're not crazy. I wish it were going to be that easy. Let's go back down to my office. I've got some thinking to do."

Merchant stuck his pipe back in the jacket pocket and

rode the elevators back to the monkey house on one, neither speaking until they were alone again in Hurley's office. Merchant picked up his overcoat, unfolding it carefully and putting it on. "Are you going to help me?" he asked.

Hurley walked past the chessboard, moved a rook on Wellington's side, and took a seat behind his desk. "I don't know what I'm going to do," he said. "What about you?"

"I'm going to pursue this on my own as far as I can," Merchant said, buttoning the overcoat. "If you won't help me, will you at least let me get a look at your files?"

"I don't know," Hurley replied. "We're talking about the department being tied into political murders, maybe even up as high as the chief. We're talking real organization here. If you're right . . ."

"If I'm right," Merchant said, his hand on the doorknob, "we may be seeing just a small part of this thing right now. Don't sit on the fence too long, Hurley. It's about a six-story fall to the ground."

"And what's your angle in all this?" Hurley asked, his eyes fixed hard on Merchant's.

"What do you mean?"

"Don't play stupid with me—you do us both a disservice. Why are you pushing this? What do you get out of it?"

Merchant turned from the door toward Hurley. "Jack was my friend, I . . ."

"No," Hurley said. "There's more. This is some sort of personal crusade for you and you're asking me to put my neck in the noose, too. I want to know why."

Merchant lowered his eyes. How could he explain that up until Jack's call he'd been drowning in a sea of Napoleonic lore and that this was the most alive he'd felt in years? It was a chance, maybe his last chance, to contribute, to do it right. "Because it's your job," he said, turning from Hurley's penetrating gaze and opening the door.

Merchant moved out the door, Hurley jumping slightly as it slammed behind the man. He settled back in his chair and looked at the computer screen, his mind moving back onto the problem that had been pricking at him when Charles Merchant had entered earlier. His problem also had to do with Weston and Mills. He scrolled through the screen again, reading the separate statements that the two men had made concerning the death of a Braedman. He'd been a cop for twenty-two years. The only times he'd ever known witness statements to duplicate one another word for word was when the witnesses had been coached in advance; yet here were Weston and Mills giving duplicate statements. Worse yet, he still hadn't found anyone to admit to being the mysterious door opener for Braedman's escape try.

He rocked back in his desk chair and reached out to shut off the computer. Instead, on impulse, he brought up the entire file and ran hard copy through his printer. The only way any of these things made sense was through Merchant's conspiracy explanation. He put the files in a file folder marked CRIME FIGURES and shoved the entire thing in his bottom desk drawer.

Merchant had already said it. Who to trust? God, it would be so simple to leave all this alone, to just put it out of his mind and live his life out as if he'd never known anything about it. At least Merchant had an emotional stake in all this. He had nothing. Except his job. Except doing the right thing.

He sat up straight and pulled the heavy black telephone off its cradle, punching up the overworked Auto Theft division. Armstead's nasal voice answered after eight rings. "Yeah?"

"Bobby," Hurley said, reaching into his pocket and bringing out the plate number Merchant had left with him. "Got something for you to run through the gizmo for me. D.C. plate . . . C—Charlie, K—killer, H—hall, 479."

"You want this soon?"

"Quick as you can," Hurley said, deciding that a little more information wouldn't be a bad thing to have at this point. "And, Bobby, when you've got it . . . don't go through regular channels. Maybe . . . just give me a call, okay?"

"Sure, Leonard. My mouth to God's ear."

Hurley hung up, staring at the phone. Damn Merchant for coming to his office. Damn Bignell for getting him involved in this at all.

He looked at his watch, wondering how long Bobby would be with the plate.

The Pentagon 1:18 P.M.

Melanie Patterson watched out the tinted glass of the Pentagon shuttle bus window as it inched its way through the huge, sluglike crowd that blocked the roadway. It was a massive demonstration complete with signs and buttons, leaders with bullhorns, American flags and an American Legion brass band to whip up the emotions. She'd never seen a pro–military spending demonstration before, but the DOD budget had never been cut this obviously before.

The crowd surged and chanted, thrusting fists and signs in the air as the demonstration leaders urged them on with fears of lost freedoms and death from foreign nationals. Funny. She'd always thought that freedom was something people were all too happy to give away if it could be traded for security. Unfortunately, the only real security she knew about resided in people like Joann. She frowned as they finally got through the demonstration and up to the south-side shuttle drop-off at what the denisions of the place affectionately called the Building. She needed to get Joann out of her head. There was more to that story than was healthy for her to know or care about.

The minibus jerked to a halt. Two Air Force colonels and three Beltway consultants in sharkskin suits moved to the front door, silently leaning down to watch the demonstrators outside. They were also watching her, but she'd have been disappointed otherwise. She stood as they moved past and walked out into the frigid cold.

The bullhorns staticked through the deadly cold, so distorted she couldn't understand what they were saying. They jammed the roadway and the large parking lot. Most of the demonstrators looked old and wore their former uniforms adorned with VFW and American Legion buttons and patches. Their breath rose in white anemic stringers as they shivered under red noses and red cheeks. They were singing "America the Beautiful."

Pro-defense. She couldn't get over it. And in such weather. BJ must be really working the streets, because she didn't see this happening without his organizational hand. He was the best networker she'd ever seen, drawing in ever-larger circles of connections and mailing lists to individuals keyed to his issues. It was a numbers game, the one game that really mattered in Washington.

She followed the signs to the visitors' entrance, an innocuous unmarked door set up a flight of stairs on the east side of the five-sided, rough cement structure—an inauspicious entry into a small city of six and a half million square feet and a population of twenty-eight thousand.

She moved into the place, enjoying her own ease in these corridors of vast power. She'd lobbied here in one form or another for the last several years, making BJ's connections for him as he wormed his way into every aspect of government activities. To her right stood a long line of businesses: gift shops, barbers, shoe shines, the corridor terminating at an in-building Metro subway stop and holding area for the large number of daily tourist groups that made their way through the nonclassified part of the Pentagon.

Before her stood a small kiosk manned by a young Marine lieutenant who was presently speaking with the consultants who'd been on the shuttle bus with her. Behind him, a large open archway led into an upsloping corridor, a huge ramp, that eased access to the higher levels of the place.

She moved up to the kiosk just as the contractors moved off to join the flow up the ramp. The Marine looked hard at her, and she smiled at the desperate sexual energy that oozed from his eyes. All men were the same. All of them.

"Help you, ma'am?" he asked, looking her up and down.

"My name's Patterson," she said. "Melanie Patterson. I have a two o'clock with Admiral Stanley."

At the mention of the name of the Chief of Naval Ops, the Marine dropped his eyes to the appointment printout, realizing he was out of his league. "Yes, ma'am," he said with solemnity, pulling out a temporary ID and handing it to her. "That's 2E143. You go up the ramp—"

"I know where it is," she replied sweetly, then moved around to his side of the booth. "Would you help me get this tag on?"

She moved right up to him, the man's hand shaking slightly as he clipped the tag to the lapel of her gray wool suit. She slid closer, letting her body rest against his in several places. A line of sweat had broken out on his forehead and she could feel something stirring in his pants. She bumped against him once more for good measure, then abruptly pulled away, turning from him and walking off without a word. The next time she came through, he'd remember her.

She moved quickly into the crowd going up, melding perfectly with the other women who worked the Building, yet standing out. They all dressed the same, severe suits set off by slinky silk and rayon blouses cut to the cleavage. Washington women never seemed to be especially pretty, but they all shared a certain feral quality, a guileless sexuality brought on by the sheer nearness and excitement of power. The power attracted them, giving them an electric edge, a kind of rut allure. Washington was a city of fucking, one kind or another, but Mel wanted to do more than simply fuck power. She wanted to control it. And the one thing that BJ had taught her was that you can have anything you want if you're willing to believe in yourself and work for it. She believed, and until the skin dried out and the muscles sagged, the dream was hers.

The ramp got her as far as the stairs to the second floor. The Pentagon contained seventeen and a half miles of corridor and to make traveling the place easier, it had been divided into a series of spokes and rings for faster access. So, the room number 2E143 meant: second floor, ring E, room 143.

She moved into the second-floor hallway and down corridor ten to the E ring, a seaman passing her pushing a shopping cart full of classified material to photocopy. She was in the Naval Operations corridor, its walls full of paintings of famous sea battles and boat models such as a small boy would construct. The doors were oak up here, like ship's doors, the fixtures brass. The only place in the

Building like it. As she passed the office of the secretary of
the navy, she heard the toll of six bells, another difference
in this corridor that told time by the navy system. She was
right on time. The admiral appreciated punctuality.

Stanley's waiting-room door was open to the corridor,
staffers hustling around like there was no tomorrow. She
moved right into the confusion. The room was narrow and
long, the furniture expensive, the wallpaper flocked—like
the lobby of a Marriott. She turned to the reception desk,
a hungry-looking WAVE petty officer with the name
Murdock tagged above her small left breast. "Good afternoon, Janine," she said, the WAVE not bothering to
disguise the jealousy in her eyes. "I believe the admiral is
expecting me."

"You realize he goes up to the Tank in thirty minutes?"
the woman returned coldly. "This isn't the best time to—"

"I'll just let myself in." Mel smiled, walking right past
her to the inner office door beyond. She tapped lightly.
"Stan?" she called gently. "Stan?"

She entered when no response was forthcoming. Admiral Armon Stanley's office was neat and clean, what
he'd call shipshape. It was his atmosphere and it was
controlled, absolutely and completely, from the dust-free
symmetrically hung photos and plaques on the walls to
the empty in basket on his walnut-stained desk bearing
the eagle and frigate emblem of the U.S. Navy on its false
front.

The man stood at parade rest, staring out his window to
the demonstration in the employee parking lot, the window to the outside in itself a sign of power. He was
wearing his dress blues, his lanky six-foot four-inch frame
stooped somewhat. He half turned to her and jerked his
thumb in the direction of the protestors. "I keep thinking
that I should be out there with them," he said.

She smiled, hurrying quickly across the room to fit
easily into his arms. "Sounds like you have had a rough
morning," she said, kissing him quickly, then pushing out
of his demanding embrace to sit in a black leather chair by
the window, where she pretended to watch the demonstrators with him. Stanley was an easy read, an aging
warrior shadow chasing his lost youth, unwilling to give
over to the gaping, inescapable maw of his years. He was

a good and intelligent man acting foolishly in the face of mortality, and she had become his symbol, the gossamer, unattainable metaphor for all that was now lost to him. It was almost too easy. "You want to talk about it?"

He laughed dryly and took a chair directly across from her. "Ten minutes ago," he said. "I got a call from Pappy Layton, my CO during the war." He narrowed his eyes. "And God, don't ask me which war."

"I'm not *that* young, Stan," she said as the man put a hand to the back of his neck, rubbing.

"Anyway, Pappy calls. You've got to understand, I'm not talking with this man for twenty, twenty-five years. He calls me out of the blue, all ninety-five years of him, and says I'll put him in a grave if I vote to cut spending. His *grave*, for God's sake."

"He's old," Patterson said. "Maybe he's . . ."

"He pulled me, unconscious, off the bridge of a sinking, burning destroyer in '42 in the Pacific," Stanley said, standing and walking away from the window, trying to deny its existence. "He saved my goddamned life. You just don't forget something like that."

She stared at the man, his face drained and tired, showing every one of his sixty-eight years for the first time since she'd known him. She tried to picture him in his twenties, couldn't. She could sense something of indecision in his eyes. With luck and the right angle, he could be moved.

"Well, you know how I feel about it," she said, watching him walk back to his desk to stare down at it. "They've put you in a position that no fighting man, no patriot, should ever be put in."

"It's not that simple," he said. "Nothing ever is." He abruptly turned from the desk to look at her. "Sorry I couldn't make lunch. I've had a lot of . . . thinking to do."

"I just wanted to see you for a few minutes before you went down," she said. "You've probably been inundated all morning."

"I've dodged a lot of it," he replied. "Contractors mostly, people like Pappy, a couple of congressmen with large projects in their districts. The hell of it is, all the desperation is real. Everything's been cut so much since the Ruskies gave up on Europe that there's just nowhere else to take it from without cutting throats." He shook his head. "It is nice to talk to someone who isn't trying to talk me into something."

She looked at her watch, timing BJ's surprise news bulletin. "Oh, my gosh," she said, standing. "There was some kind of news bulletin that I caught the tail end of on the radio on the way over." She moved to the portable TV set on the bottom level of the bookshelves facing his desk. "Do you mind if I . . ."

"Go ahead," he said as she turned on the small set. "What sort of bulletin?"

In response, the picture faded in to the sight of Russian trawlers docked at what looked to be a tropical port, the video too close in for good identification. A female voice was speaking over the pictures. ". . . revelations came from a highly placed, unnamed source within the government intelligence community. What you're looking at is classified videotape of a Russian delivery of ICBM missile parts to the Caribbean port of La Barra. . . ."

"What!?" Stanley said loudly, moving up to squat before the TV screen. "We've heard no information like—"

"Shhh," Patterson said, reaching out a hand to gently cover his mouth, the admiral kissing her palm. "I want to hear."

The voice continued: "There are also recon photos showing the development and building of missile launching sites." The picture was replaced by satellite photos of ground clearing and track building in the jungle, Patterson wondering just how the hell BJ got hold of this stuff as the voice droned on. ". . . have been following this buildup for the past two months. So far, the President and the State Department have had no comment on the release of the data, so anything we say is speculation, but it appears as if the Companero-controlled military now has the bomb, the Russian bomb, and it's pointing right at us. What this means to the future of Central American relations is uncertain. Stay tuned for more details as they develop. This is Sheila Tranor reporting."

Patterson shut off the set and stared down at the man who still squatted at her feet. "See?" she said, voice high-pitched. "This is the way the goddamned Russians act. Glad-hand us on one side while they load up against us on the other. Haven't I told you we can't trust them?"

The man stood, grimacing as his knees straightened. He looked tired. He looked old and used up. "This can't be real," he said. "The Russians don't do this sort of thing anymore. We would have heard something, for Christ's sake. I can't believe . . ."

"Well, you'd better start believing it," she returned, "because there's the evidence."

He moved to the door, opening it to stick his head out. "Somebody find out what you can on this damned news bulletin," he called to his staff. "Russian trawlers in Caribbea with missiles. Get somebody at DIA." He came back in and closed the door, shaking his head. "Something's screwy here."

"And you're still going to go in there and vote our country down the tubes," she said. "Don't you know the politburo is sitting back laughing themselves sick right now."

"Goddamnit, Mel," he said. "Everything's so black and white to you. We're been having this argument for a year. You know as well as I do that the country is rapidly going bankrupt, that we can't afford our own technology anymore. It's going to cost seventy billion dollars just to get a squadron of Stealth bombers in the air. And after the democratization of Eastern Europe, even I'm not hardheaded enough to think we need to continue to keep troops there. The administration's been moving toward these cutbacks for the last two years. A lot of thought has gone into the military recision. We've all agreed to scale down no matter how we feel about it personally."

"While the Soviets shove missiles up our rear end," she countered. "It is black and white. They're the black and we're the white. They're just setting us up for the Sunday punch, can't you see that? Don't you see how vulnerable you're going to be leaving the country?"

The man turned from her in frustration, walking toward the window until he remembered that thousands of people just like Mel were chanting out there. He came back to his desk and sat behind it. "We're not talking about cutting the military's throat here," he said, his voice slightly hoarse. "All we're doing is revamping to cut back on programs that aren't cost effective, just R and D money. A few base closings. A few old fighter wings. . . ."

"Destroyers . . . aircraft carriers."

"Damnit! What do you want me to say?"

"Research and development have been the heart and soul of the Pentagon," she said. "I lobbied enough in this building to know that since the future can't be predicted, you people never know what you have to prepare for, so you prepare for everything. Cut those programs, and you just might be cutting our throat."

He slammed his hand down hard on the desk. "I'm not going to dump what manpower I have to keep the research projects. This is just out of control. We can't afford to do it anymore, and we don't *need* to do it anymore," he said loudly.

She walked up to the desk and gave it back to him. "You can't afford not to!" she yelled, pointing to the television. "Just look what's happening!"

The door burst open, the WAVE moving tentatively inside. "Is everything all right?" she said. "I heard loud voices, I—"

"Get out!" the admiral yelled. "And don't ever come in here again without knocking."

"Yes, sir," the woman said, lips set hard. She left.

Stanley slumped back in his chair. "God, Mel. I . . . I just don't now what to do. I've given my entire life to the defense of this nation. This *is* God's country. You think I'd *want* to leave it vulnerable? The numbers are just so . . . devastating these days. Everything's so expensive."

The facade was beginning to crumble. Good. She moved up close to him, realizing what a true genius BJ really was. "I'm sorry, Stan," she said softly, walking around to stand beside him. She leaned down, pulling his head to her breast. He hugged her fiercely. "You're the greatest man I've ever met. I just hate to see what the politicians are doing to you and the country."

His gray eyes were liquid as he looked up at her, and even in his personal turmoil she could feel him sliding his hands down her back to rest on her buttocks, waiting for her to rebuke him as she'd done so many times in the past. When she didn't move away, the admiral began squeezing her ass, pulling her up closer to him. "Please try and understand my position," he said, sliding his face a little lower on her right breast, his cheek teasing the nipple as the wool jacket slid off her shoulders. He was trembling like a schoolboy as he pulled her down onto the chair with him, her skirt hiking up way past her knees.

"P-please . . . don't," she said, struggling only slightly as he cradled her on his lap, his face lost in the hollow of her throat. "We r-respect each other too much to . . ."

"I can't stand it," he said quietly. "I want you so bad, Mel. You've been putting me off for so long."

His hand slid up her thigh and along the shimmering length of her black hose, finally disappearing beneath her skirt. When she tried to protest, he silenced her with a long, hard kiss, his fingers scratching at her crotch, insistent now, a pleasant, liquid warmth spreading through her. Now was the time.

She broke the kiss. "Yesss," she rasped throatily. "God, I want you, too."

She kicked her shoes off and spread her legs wide, allowing his fingers free rein. He started lightly, then more deliberately, rubbing her clitoris right through hose and panties, not believing his good fortune. When she began to moan down low in response, he abruptly stopped.

"The door," he groaned, trying to rise. "I've got to lock it."

He attempted to stand, but she grabbed him tightly, letting him know just who was in charge here. "No," she said low. "Do it now. Now!"

"But, Mel . . ."

"Now or never," she said, harsh, reaching between them to grab his erection right through his pants. "Do it, old man!"

His eyes flashed, the fighting man coming to the fore. He grunted down deep in his throat, then bodily lifted her, dropping her on her back on his desktop. She threw her arms wide, knocking telephone, pen and pencil set, and photos of the admiral, Mrs. Stanley, and the President onto the blue-carpeted floor.

He fell atop her, pulling her blouse open, several buttons flying off. He started tugging at her French bra, but she stopped him, unclasping it in the front and opening it for him. He kissed her breasts, going from one to the other in wild abandon. She'd been building the relationship to this point for a year, always putting off the inevitable, always waiting for the moment of advantage, when it could mean more for her than it could for him. Finally, Stanley had gotten old enough that he was young and foolish again. It was her moment.

He moved from her breasts, reaching up under her skirt to pull off hose and panties, Mel holding up her legs to make it easier. She looked at his eyes. They were hard-edged now, animal eyes, staring at her widespread legs.

"Hurry," she urged, reaching for him. "Please hurry."

He used his arms to push her legs farther apart, then went to work on her with his mouth, the woman giving herself over to the feeling. He wasn't bad, not bad at all.

"Fuck me," she rasped. "Fuck me now."

He straightened, breathing hard, his face flushed as he struggled out of his uniform pants, letting them fall to the floor. His legs were pale and blue-veined, but the muscles were still firm. His erection vibrated from his loins, semen dripping from the bulging purple head. She reached for his cock, pulling him to her. "Hurry," she whispered.

He moved up to the desk, sliding her closer. She guided the head of his cock to her vaginal opening, then looked at him with want and fear. "Protect me," she said quietly. "Please don't l-let them d-destroy our country."

"Never," he said, shoving himself into her with a long sigh. "Oh, God! Oh, God. I've waited so long."

She closed her eyes then, giving over to the feelings, her job done as well as she could do it. But as he moved in and out of her, their grunts and groans mixing in animal cacophony, she couldn't help but think of BJ. What did the man have on his mind? The Joint Chiefs would be the easiest to convince. It was going to get a lot tougher from this point on.

It wasn't just a committee or a specific congressman that BJ was trying to turn on this, it was the entire machinery of the U.S. government. How did he hope to overcome that?

Stanley had begun to quicken his pace, a year of pent-up want seeking quick release. She pushed back hard against him, trying to hurry her own orgasm.

He half yelled, a garbled, strangled cry as he collapsed atop her, his hips still jerking. She pulled his ass tight, holding him in her as she kept grinding against him, the feeling tight and building tighter.

He tried to pull away, but she wouldn't let him, pushing, pushing until she felt his cock begin to go limp within her. At that moment she crested the peak and screamed out her release, loud—louder, until his hand came up to muffle her mouth. She bit down, hard, tasting his blood, then collapsed back atop the desk.

There was a knock on the door, a man's voice from without. "Admiral, are you all—"

"Go away!" Stanley yelled, pulling away from her to cradle his bleeding hand. "Just get the fuck away!"

She sat up, his semen running out of her to pool on his desktop. She half laughed, covering her own mouth this time. "Oops," she said softly. "I guess I got a little carried away. Are you all right?"

He bent down to bring his pants up, then pulled a handkerchief out of his pocket to wrap around his hand. "Jesus, we could have been caught."

She slid off the desk and hooked her bra. "Your fault," she said sweetly. "It wasn't my idea to fuck on your desk. And it certainly wasn't my fault that you were so good."

His eyes lit. "You liked it?"

"I loved it," she said, bending down to retrieve her underwear. "I just hope we didn't ruin a beautiful friendship."

They dressed hurriedly and cleaned up the mess she'd made of the desk, Stanley's phone ringing the second he picked it up from the floor and put it back on the cradle.

Patterson watched him carefully as he answered, the look on his face telling that their interlude had only budged his depression slightly. The fact that he'd been able to move at all on the issue was simply a testament to a lifetime of military service and concerns. It *was* a question of money, of drowning in the same sea of red ink that had forced the Russians in out of the cold. She again wondered what it was that BJ thought he was doing with all this.

"Yeah," Stanley was saying. "I'm on my way now." He hung up, frowning down at the phone.

"The Joint Chiefs?" she asked, tucking her blouse tightly into her skirt to hide the fact that most of the buttons were missing.

"It's time for the vote," he said, running both hands through his close-cropped gray hair. "Do I look okay?"

"Except for that big wet spot on the front of your trousers," she said, laughing when he jumped, frantically searching his pants. "Just kidding."

"You bitch." He smiled, moving to take her in his arms again. She molded against him, kissing him deeply. "When can I see you again?"

She smiled, catlike, then jerked out of his grasp. "Don't know," she said, putting her jacket back on and moving toward the door. "We'll talk again after we see how the voting goes. Ta."

She moved out the door without a backward glance, letting it close loudly behind her. Stanley watched her go, his entire psyche in turmoil. The woman had kept him on the ragged edge of sexual tension, reeling him in and out like a fish—making him feel awkward and gangly like a child. He hated the way he catered to her, but was as lost as a drowning man. But God, she was dynamic: sharp, intelligent, well read and well spoken, her throbbing sexuality a badge she wore proudly. He loved and hated her in equal measure, his very own bitch goddess. Being with her was like jumping out of an airplane with no parachute: ultimately deadly, but what a trip.

He gathered his notes together quickly, knowing even as he did that he might not be using them. His head and his heart were at war right now. He understood the need for cutbacks. No one had to explain that to him. But, unfortunately, Mel was right in one respect. Without the huge R and D unsupervised budget, it would be impossible to prepare for an uncertain future. Sure, it looked like the face of the world had changed and that the Soviets were no longer a real threat, but what would it look like next year, or in ten years? The thought that a decision he made today could inadvertently destroy the country in later years chilled him to the bone. Were the money problems really that bad, or was it, as Mel had hinted, simply a reaction to the Russian assertion that the cold war was over? If so, what of the news bulletin?

He shoved his papers in the black leather briefcase with the words "Chief of Naval Operations" debossed on the flap in gold letters.

He walked out of the office, his entire staff staring at him, then looking quickly away. God damn Mel. Why here, in front of his subordinates? Every one of them must know what had happened. He sometimes felt that she led him around by his dick, pushing him here and there by dispensing and withholding favors. He walked up to Murdock's desk, the WAVE typing, not paying attention to him.

"I'm . . . sorry I yelled at you before," he said.

"Your prerogative," she said coldly.

"I'm sorry anyway," he returned. "Is there anything on that news report?"

The woman shook her head, not meeting his eyes. "DIA doesn't know anything about it and the NSC doesn't know anything about it. The Langley office of the Company won't even return our calls."

"Son of a bitch!" he spat. "A goddamned national emergency and they give us the mushroom treatment." He jammed his briefcase up under his arm. "I'm going to the Tank."

"Yes, sir."

He moved out of the office, feeling their eyes on him and knowing he'd lowered several notches in their estimation. He'd try to make it up to them later with some one-on-one face time. He walked the long hall of ring E, moving in the direction of the north-side river entrance. Off the main halls, the Building was less well kept, with broken wall clocks and furniture piled up in the hallways. The windows facing out were washed on the average of once a year, making the daylight pale and gray-looking. Within minutes, he arrived at an innocuous door, unmarked except for its number, and got in line behind a number of morose-looking three-star deputies filing in.

The Tank itself was unimposing, a medium-sized conference room smaller than you'd find in any corporation. A large, long table dominated the center of the room, its floor down a step from the rest of the place. Chairs ringed the walls, all of them filling quickly with officers, members of the Chairman's group, and the secretary of the Joint Chiefs. The entire room was buzzing with talk of the news bulletin, no one admitting any prior knowledge of the events depicted.

He moved up to the table, nervous, excited, still unsure of what he was going to do and say. Shining at him from the shoulders and collars of the men around the table were over sixty stars divided among twelve flag officers, who everybody called purple suiters. This was the place where everything happened, where most of the major military decisions of the United States were made. And he was beginning to believe that they were getting ready to make a very bad decision, indeed.

He took his seat beside his operations deputy, Harv Deely, spending the few minutes before the meeting convened watching the faces of his colleagues. They were no happier than he was.

To his right, at the head of the table, the Chairman, Alec Wintering, sat talking quietly with his vice-chairman and deputy director.

"Have you heard about the Russian missiles?" Deely asked him as Stanley pulled his papers from his briefcase and spread them out on the oak table.

"Is there any confirmation from the White House?" he asked in return.

"Nothing," the man said. "It doesn't make any sense."

"Unless the administration is keeping it under wraps until after we vote," Stanley said.

The man's face was pockmarked, his skin leathery after years at sea. He narrowed his eyes when he looked at the admiral. "Would they do that?"

Stanley shook his head. "What do you think?"

Admiral Wintering was banging a gavel on the table, the room coming to grim order within seconds. The man looked gravely around the table. "I hereby convene our regular Monday meeting of the Joint Chiefs, February fourth," he said. "Our agenda today is a one-item vote— site specific cuts of fifteen bases, plus the elimination of Research and Development projects with cost overruns that have not met up to specifications, plus numbers of troop reductions, plus the deactivation of three fighter wings. Gentlemen, I'm open for any discussion before the vote." He pointed his gavel at the Marine commandant seated at the far end of the table, a prearranged signal. "The Chair recognizes General Marcus Dennison from the Department of the Navy."

Dennison stood, clearing his throat and speaking in the low, crisp cadence in which he delivered everything from the ordering of a hamburger and fries to the eulogy given on the death of two hundred Marines in Beirut. "Gentlemen," he said, referring to notes set before him on the table. "I know this isn't an easy time for any of us. The process by which we sit here and vote today is the culmination of over a year of intensive study and discussion between ourselves and the executive and legislative branches of the government regarding the necessity of keeping certain already funded projects that have outlived their usefulness. We've all agreed in kind and we've all agreed in principle. Before today, the Pentagon procurement procedure was in essence a marriage of convenience between ourselves, the industrial complex, and friendly members of Congress in whose states the defense dollars are spent. In past, we've always voted as a group, cutting spending across the board when necessary without deleting entire programs in order to keep that marriage of convenience alive. It's time for a divorce. The cost of technology has skyrocketed to the point where we can simply no longer afford this kind of luxury, and potential threat can no longer be a viable reason for continuing to do so. It's time to ask ourselves the tough questions and then act upon them. I'm asking here that we simply hold on to our fears, vote these cuts quickly, then get back to the job of getting the most out of what we have left."

"Mr. Chairman," Stanley said, raising his hand without realizing he was doing it.

"The Chair recognizes Admiral Armon Stanley of the Department of the Navy," Wintering said.

Stanley stood, Mel Patterson suddenly in his mind. She had asked him to protect her, to protect the country, and he realized there was a way to have his cake and eat it, too. "Gentlemen," he began, "they tell us the cold was is over. Every estimate we have tells us that it is time to scale down from class-A nuclear warfare and gear for low intensity, terrorist, and Third World conflicts such as our operations in Panama City and Iraq. In keeping with such changes, they say we must cut those 'useless' R and D programs 'for the good of the country.'

"I'll have to tell you that I feel that I've always operated 'for the good of the country' and I'm damned proud of it."

A few fists banged on the table, several, "hear, hears" coming from around the room. "All I can say," he continued, "is that they sure seem to like to tell us how things are and how badly we've messed them up. But then we see something like that news bulletin on the television and you have to wonder what it is that they know that we don't. Who was it who said that not with a bang, but with a whimper, the world would go out. Well, I'm beginning to think that we're the whimper, with the emphasis on wimp." A few chuckles. "If we vote these cuts, our budget will be down almost forty percent from '85 levels. Can we really defend the country on that?"

"Come on, Stan," Dennison said from across the table. "Programs like DIVAD and the Maverick missile have really made us look bad. Nobody did that to us. We did it ourselves because we couldn't stand to cut a program."

"Don't 'come on' me," Stanley replied. "For every DIVAD, there are three useful, necessary projects in development that could be vital to the future of this country. We can't predict war: the when, the where, the how. It is essential to the continued future of our nation that we keep our options open. Hell, if we don't, the fucking Companeros could bomb us out of existence."

"What's your point?" General Wallace, the Air Force Chief, asked from beside Dennison.

"My point, Harvey, is that we are experts, specialists in the art of warfare and protection. The people who are telling us we must change are not." He turned a full circle, speaking to everyone. "Why do we have no knowledge of the news bulletin we heard? Who has been keeping that under wraps? Maybe the same people who are telling us to cut back. Maybe they're keeping it from us . . . for our own good. Who really is running the action on this? Why don't we know about it?"

"Jesus, Stan," the Army Chief of Staff, General Nivan,

said from a seat near the Chairman. "We've already hashed all this out. We've already agreed."

"So, we can change our minds," Stanley said. "That's what this whole procedure is about, isn't it? Let me ask each one of you a question: Which of you is willing to say you have no qualms about what we're getting ready to do." No one spoke up. "Well, doesn't that prove something right there? Doesn't it tell you that, perhaps, you're being talked into making a terrible mistake?"

"It tells me there are no easy choices," Dennison said, his face hard. "After all this time, after all this work, you suddenly turn around and get hard-assed. Who the hell have you been talking to, Stan?"

He stared the man down. The Marines were the bastard stepchildren of the Navy Department. Dennison would barter his own mother away if he thought it could give him more power. "Are you making an accusation here?" he asked in a low voice.

The man's hands were hard fists at his side. "No, damnit," he said. "I'm just saying that we've made our own problems here. Through waste and territoriality we've dug ourselves into a deep hole."

"You're all looking at this the wrong way," Stanley returned. "It's not our place to worry about these things. Our traditional role is the pro-defense posture. That's what we're here for. And I'm certainly not going to apologize for being high on the military."

"You're being a fool, Stan," Dennison said, "a blind fool."

"Who's being the fool, gentlemen," Stanley said, the room deadly quiet around him. "There are thousands of demonstrators, our people, out in the parking lot burning us in effigy. The Russians are arming our enemies to the teeth in our own backyard and we haven't even been informed about it. Why should this onus be put on us when not a one of us really believes in what we're doing?"

"The choices are clear, though," General Nivan said.

"But the beauty here is that we don't have to make those choices," Stanley said. "Gentlemen, this is a golden moment. If it's the politicians who want these cuts, let them make them. We're nothing with the Appropriations Committee anyway. We can walk away from it right here and stick them with cutting off the funding. Let them be the ones responsible for America's vulnerability."

"Maybe," Wintering suggested, "we should talk to the secretary of defense on this."

"No," Stanley replied. "When we had our regular meeting with the secretary last week he refused to even talk further options besides cuts. He's one of them, committed to cuts before he even came into the Building. He doesn't have our concerns. Fuck him and the horse he rode in on."

"That's not fair," Wintering said.

"No," Stanley replied. "But it's accurate. I'll be honest, gentlemen. The more I talk, the more sense I'm making to myself. The damned politicians want us to make the cuts because then they won't have to take the heat from those people outside demonstrating and the millions like them all over the country."

The Chairman looked hard at him. "Is this just debate, Stan, or are you pushing to something. Because if you're pushing toward something, you'd better remember that to go against the flow on this thing will put us at odds not only with the secretary of defense, but with the President, his cabinet, and the entire Congress. We're talking about dropping a major bomb into the apparatus of this country. These people could make it extremely tough to—"

"I don't care," Stanley said. "I'm a man who's always followed his own conscience and the consequences be damned. Well, my conscience is screaming at me to do what I know in my heart is best."

"Which is?"

Stanley fixed Wintering, his close friend for eighteen years, with hard eyes. "I won't cut one program from my roster, not one program, not one dollar. If the sons of bitches want it, they'll have to come take it away from me. It's the only way I'll ever be able to sleep at night."

"But we've always voted as a body before," Dennison said, looking directly at him. "We've always agreed among ourselves."

Stanley leaned forward, bracing himself against the table to stare at the commandant. "This is a gut check, Marc," he said forcefully. "Vote your own conscience like I'm going to do."

"I'm not too much on this eleventh-hour conversion,"

Dennison replied, addressing the room. "If we stand together as a group, we can still vote out the majority of cuts."

"No," General Nivan said. "Stan is right. You saw the news flash. Why don't we know about it? Why? None of this makes any sense. Besides that, the army is always the first place they want to make cuts when it comes to modern warfare. We can dodge the bullet on this. I'll be damned if I'll voluntarily vote to cut my branch when his branch gets to keep its programs intact."

"Gentlemen . . ." Dennison said.

"I'm not voting to cut, either," Nivan said. "Let the Congress come and take it away from us. We'll see what kind of heart they have for the dismantling of our defenses. And I'll damn well sleep a lot better, too."

"The onus *doesn't* have to be on us," General Wallace agreed. "I've never seen a good reason for cutting the military dollar in the past, and I sure as hell don't see the need for doing it now."

All eyes turned to the Marine commandant, who was still standing. He looked around the table. "I think we're making a terrible mistake," he said, "but I'm surely not going to be the only one to cut. No way would I do that to the Corps."

"Is this a vote?" the Chairman demanded loudly. "Is this what we're walking out of this room with and taking to the Hill? Do you people understand the Pandora's box you're opening?"

"We're voting our consciences," Stanley said, feeling better about it every moment. "It's time to gin up and circle the wagons, my friends. The fight has just begun!"

From somewhere around the outer ring of chairs the applause started and within seconds was picked up by most of the room, surrounding Armon Stanley in a warm and protective cocoon of service camaraderie that was designed to sustain them all through the hard times to come. It made him feel good, a man again. He looked at his watch as the applause turned into a standing ovation. If he could get out and call Mel soon enough, maybe he'd get to see her again before making the drive back to Silver Springs and the never-ending duty tour with his wife.

NEWSBREAK

". . . Well, Mr. Secretary, I understand the needs of the military in these uncertain times; but surely, sir, you're not trying to tell me there isn't a spending problem connected with the Pentagon?"

"Of course there's a spending problem. The weapons systems are gold-plated, contractor costs are excessive, and for the last two decades defense industry profits have averaged nearly four times the norm of nongovernment profit. But this isn't the military's problem, it's Congress's. They're the ones funneling all that pork into their home districts."

"Do you agree with that, Congressman Rosen?"

"Of course I don't. The military bureaucracy is so fat that it contains more clerks than combat personnel, more generals and admirals than during World War II, with only one sixth as many troops to command. I can only sum it up in the words of Barry Goldwater: 'I am saddened that the services are unable to put the national interest above parochial interest.' Competition among the services is bankrupting the country."

—*The Newsmakers*
February 4

Arlington, Virginia 9:57 P.M.

Charles Merchant leaned down over the pool table, into the soft white bite of the hanging lamp, the only light on in the room as he reached out a gentle hand to move the lines of French Imperial Guard to the base of Mont Saint-Jean. He looked up slowly at the silent audience of blue and green uniforms that packed tightly around the table, outside of the light, the only sound the tinkling of the ice in their Scotches and gin and tonics. He felt out of place in his dark suit among so much brass.

"Wellington had taken up positions at the top of Saint-Jean," he said softly, nearly whispering the words. "He had withstood the pounding of the French guns by putting his troops on the reverse slopes of the hillsides, bringing them up fresh and in high spirits when the battle went to the infantry. Nothing had gone right for the little Corsican all day. The Prussians were tougher than he'd thought and had returned from a rout to strengthen Wellington's lines. The English soldiers had remained cool under fire, and worse, Wellington had studied Napoleon's techniques and had mastered them."

He moved Marshal Ney's horse to the head of the column, the problem of Napoleon's last battle taking over his mind and heart. "The Guard had never known defeat. They were Napoleon's last hope, as everyone else, including the heavy cavalry, had tried to take that hill and failed. Ney led the assault as the drums began to beat the *pas de charge* and the Grenadiers' band played Gebauer's 'Marche des Bonnets à poil.' The stage was set for the cosmic gears of history to mesh. The Guard began the slow charge up the hill, sixty men abreast, and the beauty of it turned to carnage."

He cast his eyes around the table, his audience transfixed, their eyes locked hard on the tabletop battle, fighting it in their own minds. "The Allied gunners poured Congreve rockets, canister, grape, and shot in the flank of the densely packed French ranks, men going down like wheat before the scythe. Ney had his fifth horse shot out from under him. And still the survivors climbed over the bodies of the fallen and continued upward to what still looked like a deserted ridge. And then it happened. As the surviving Frenchmen neared the ridge, Wellington yelled to his men, 'Stand up, Guards! Make ready! Fire!'

"Death rained from the sky upon Napoleon's finest and proudest, and when they lost their flank, still they fought on. Finally, as night fell heavily, Wellington gave the order to advance. The charge was met, too much for the best of troops, and the terrible and never-before-heard cry went up, *'La Garde recule!'*"

Merchant straightened, knocking over the lines of Guard with his finger. "The collapse of the Guard signaled the end of everything, as all the ranks broke into wild retreat. As Napoleon stood, confused perhaps as his men fled all around him, he could hear Blucher's troops singing the Lutheran hymn 'Herr Gott, Dich Loben Wir,' and the English bands playing 'God Save the King.' That night the Allied armies slept on the battlefield they'd fought so hard to win, sharing it with the bodies of forty thousand men. And the greatest military mind of the nineteenth century finally knew lasting defeat."

Someone laughed. "And the French haven't been for shit ever since!"

They all laughed, including Merchant. "So that's the battle," he said. "Napoleon, until his dying day, never was able to understand how he lost."

He looked at the densely packed row of fighting men, watching their faces as they watched the mock battlefield, knowing that they, more than any others, would understand the combination of guts, glory, and insanity that was the beautiful destruction of war. He could hear music and laughter from the rest of the house, where the birthday party for his son, Josh, was in full swing. But it seemed that no matter what else was going on, when his military friends came over, it was Napoleon's battles they fought. He had walked the Pentagon elite through every one of them, and this was the end, the last battle.

"He screwed up before he ever started," said Colonel Jeter, a compact whirlwind of a man, always moving, doing something. He'd taken over Army Intel after Charlie had left. The man leaned to the battlefield. "Your boy attacked his enemies separately and at less than full strength. Had he waited and taken up defensive positions, he could have fought off the attacking forces as they came at him, instead of stretching his own lines and his own men thin by going on the attack."

Charlie cocked his head. "That is what Wellington had thought Napoleon should have done, also, but I don't buy it. His attack was a good military and political gambit. The Allies weren't fully mustered yet and could have been routed by a swift and concentrated attack. Had it worked, the Netherlands could have declared for France, which would have had the effect of forcing the British to temporarily, at least, withdraw from the campaign. The battles would then be fought on non-French soil, which builds in-country morale and enhances further recruitment. It was a good gamble."

A major named Differing picked up the representation of Napoleon upon his white charger, Desirée. "I've heard he had hemorrhoids and couldn't concentrate on the battle."

Everyone laughed again, Charlie shrugging. "It's been a theory for a long time. All I can say is that I've seen the memos he wrote while in the field, and they're all done with a firm and readable hand, which was always an indication of the condition of the emperor."

"What kind of guns did the armies have?" someone asked.

"Smooth-bored, muzzle-loading muskets that fired three-quarter-inch iron balls. They could put out about two rounds a minute with a range of two hundred yards. The heavy French guns were twelve-pounders."

"Maybe it was his intel," Differing said. "Why didn't he know that the Prussians would come back to fight again after he'd beaten them once at Ligny?"

"He did know," Merchant said, picking up the piece representing Jerome Bonaparte and showing it around. "His own brother told him so at dinner the night before. He simply chose not to believe it."

"He ignored his own intelligence?" Differing said with surprise.

"Why not?" Jeter said from the eastern, Paris Wood section of the battlefield where he had squeezed his way up to the table. "Apparently that's what we're doing in Caribbea right now."

"I have a question," came a voice from outside the circle. "How come on the morning of the seventeenth of June Napoleon was visiting wounded Prussian prisoners instead of kicking Wellington's ass while he had him on the run?"

The crowd parted for the two-star general, Gene Tillotson, his face drawn and tired-looking, walking up to the mock battlefield. He pointed to Mont Saint-Jean. "Wellington wasn't able to solidify positions until the afternoon. A morning attack would have finished him."

He turned his eyes to Merchant. There was a question there, and an indefinable hollowness that he couldn't quite peg. "Hello, Charlie," he said. "It's been a while."

Merchant nodded, the men embracing, two thirds of a triangle of friends that was no more. "I'm glad you could come, Gene," he said softly. "God, it's good to see you."

"Do you agree with my assessment about Napoleon?" the man replied.

Merchant smiled. "I don't know. Why do you think he didn't attack?"

Tillotson winked at him, his pale blue eyes twinkling with a little of the old charisma that had impressed Merchant for so many years. "He'd gotten old and soft," he said, and Merchant didn't know if Tillotson was serious or not. "He was acting like a retired general being pressed back into service without his heart being in it."

"General," an Air Force captain on the opposite side of the pool table said. "What's the story on the Russian trawlers? Where's our intelligence on this?"

Tillotson smiled wide, turning to the whole crowd. "Gentlemen," he said, arms partially outstretched. "You know as much as I do, as much as anyone does. I'm sure that Colonel Jeter will tell you the same. We've had absolutely nothing come through our offices that even remotely suggests a nuclear buildup in Caribbea. My guess is that it's either a Company leak or something weird out of NSC. Whatever it is, I wouldn't put too much credence on it. Although, I'll have to say, things are jumping over at the Puzzle Palace right now. Anybody here with intelligence units better be prepared for a long night." A loud groan went up from the assembled. "Now, where the hell is a man supposed to get a drink around here?"

"Straight bourbon, right?" Merchant said, moving toward the kitchen as the officers turned their attention back to the problems of Waterloo.

"Nothing blended, though," Tillotson said, then walked after him. "Hell, I'll just go with you."

He caught up with Merchant at the laundry area separating the den and the kitchen. "How old's Josh?" the man asked as they moved into a kitchen awash with the discarded remnants of snack-food containers and paper trash. "He's looking pretty good."

"Thirty today," Merchant replied, moving to a kitchen table full of booze and mixers. "Makes you feel old." He held up a bottle of Jack Daniel's. "This okay?"

"Great," Tillotson said, looking around the brightly lit room. "I'm trying to remember the last time I was here."

Merchant filled a highball glass with ice and whiskey, handing it to the man. "1985," he replied. "It was another anniversary . . ."

"Oh, God," Tillotson said, real pain in his voice. "Martha and I had celebrated our thirtieth anniversary that night. Thirty years, just like Josh. It wasn't a month later that old Doc Withers diagnosed the cancer. . . ."

The man's words trailed off, Merchant watching his face as he tried to put his mind somewhere else. The loss of his wife had devastated Tillotson, gutted him in a way that Merchant could barely understand. They had fought the cancer together for years, but it had been a battle destined to be lost, and it was almost as if Gene had somehow emotionally died with her. Afterward, he'd closed himself in, turning down invitations and burying himself in their Silver Springs home. Merchant had tried to bring him out of the shell, but looking at him now, he wondered if he'd tried enough. He chastised himself, wondering if he, indeed, had simply not wanted to share such all-consuming pain.

The man took the bourbon and drained it in one swallow, putting it back on the table before the ice had even had a chance to melt. He was lean and gaunt, his bright white hair just a touch longer than regulation. Merchant looked closer, finding his tie knotted crookedly, his shoes not recently shined. This wouldn't mean much to the average person, but Tillotson lived by the details as much as Merchant did, and a change of routine bespoke something deeper.

"Things haven't been good for you, have they?" he asked, picking up the bourbon and refilling the man's glass.

"Not very," Tillotson said with a frown. "But it's my

own fault. I got lost in it, Charlie, you know? I fought so hard with her, I'd . . . I'd never lost before, never thought I could lose. When it fell apart, I fell apart with it because I kept thinking I was somehow responsible. Geez, it's been two years and I'm only just now beginning to get a handle on things." The man took another long drink.

"Still go fishin'?" Merchant asked, the man's eyes flashing for just a second before fixing on the ground. Tillotson had flirted with alcoholism for forty years. "Gone fishin'" was the term he politely used whenever he was going off on a long bender.

"Too much the last couple of years," Tillotson said, once again meeting Merchant's gaze. "Too damned much. By the way, I've managed to get Arlington for Jack's funeral."

Merchant felt it in his stomach, almost like a small punch. "When?" he asked, mixing himself a gin and tonic.

"Day after tomorrow. They kicked. I had to dig up my own honor guard. He's going to go out like the man he was. Let's hope he's remembered that way."

"Thanks, Gene."

"He was my friend, too," the man replied, then took a long breath. "Now, what's all this shit about the D.C. police?"

"Not completely sure," Merchant answered, cutting a lime wedge for his drink and dropping it in the tall glass. "I'm tied in with a Homicide lieutenant right now who may feed me some info, but it appears they're trying to close down any investigation."

"I can almost understand that," Tillotson said. "It's such a damned mess. You want me to exert some influence over there?"

Merchant shook his head. "Not yet. I'm not sure who we can trust."

The man looked hard at him. "You're not going to let it go, are you?"

Merchant returned the stare. "No fucking way."

"Good. I want in."

"This isn't going to be easy. It may be a lot stranger than we can imagine right now. You may not want—"

"Don't say it," Tillotson interrupted, draining his second drink. "I've been wallowing in self-pity so long that I don't know which way is up anymore. This means something to me. For God's sake, Charlie. Our friendship . . . the three of us . . . it was always somehow pure and good to me. I'm going to sound stupidly sentimental and say it was honorable—"

"That's not stupid or sentimental," Merchant replied, cutting him off. "The three of us stuck together . . . honorably, for a lot of years. I'm proud of our friendship and what we stood for. We survived hell together on the Kunari-Sunchon road, then hell of a different kind when we ate the flak. We were held back for years, yet stood strong—together."

"Then don't shut me out of this," Tillotson said. "I need it. I need something to make me feel . . . needed again. The DIA is at your disposal. If we can somehow right this wrong that's been done to Jack—well, it'll make me feel real again. It may be the only thing that can."

Merchant looked at Tillotson again, and this time was able to define the look in his eyes. It was fear: of getting old, of losing control. It was the look of a man caught in a whirlpool desperately looking for a branch to grab hold of. He felt awful, realizing he had left his closest friend alone during the time he was needed the most. He stuck out his hand. "We'll do this together," he said. "You and I, just like the old days."

Tillotson smiled, his eyes alight. He grabbed Merchant's hand and shook it vigorously. "God, Charlie. You may be saving my life here."

"No, Gene. You're saving your own life."

"Well, hello, stranger!" Linda called from the kitchen doorway, both men turning toward her. She wore a long black hostess gown with white blouse unbuttoned to the cleavage, the sleeves rolled up several turns. She carried a silver tray full of empty glasses.

"My Lord, you're a sight for sore eyes," the man said, moving to her and taking the tray away to set on a counter. "You never age!"

The two embraced, Tillotson, in his usual physical way, lifting her and turning a full circle before setting her down again. He moved his fingers to her ears. "What's this— peace symbol earrings?" He threw his head back and laughed loudly. "Glad to see he hasn't regimented you completely over the years."

"Enough of that," Merchant said, smiling, though the earrings did irk him somewhat. He'd asked her not to wear them. He looked at Linda. "How's everything in the living room?"

"Everyone's wondering where the host is," she returned, her smile full of invective.

"Oops," Tillotson said. "I believe that's my cue to go back out and visit with the fellas." He pointed a finger at Linda. "Save me a dance later."

She looked coquettish. "My card is empty, sir," she said, the man turning to mouth a silent "thank you" to Merchant before exiting back through the laundry room.

"Did you have to drag our problems out in front of Gene?" he asked as soon as they were alone. "For God's sake, we haven't seen the man in years and you're already involving him in our squabbles." He moved up to her, reaching out to her blouse. "I think a couple too many buttons got loosened here."

She jerked away from him. "I know how many buttons are undone," she said harshly. "I can dress myself, thank you."

"Obviously not very respectably," he returned.

She ignored him and moved to the makeshift bar to begin mixing drinks. "You really do need to mingle with the rest of the guests," she said. "You were the one who insisted we go on with the party despite Jack's death. The least you can do is help make it work."

He watched her pour grenadine into several tall half-filled glasses, then pick up a spoon to begin stirring. "What are you making there?" he asked.

She fixed him with suspicious eyes. "A tequila sunrise," she said. "Why?"

He showed her empty palms. "You don't stir a tequila sunrise," he said. "You just pour the grenadine on top and let it spill down into the drink."

She pulled out the spoon and dropped it to clang loudly on the table. "Okay, I'll play. What possible difference could it make?"

"That's where the name comes from," he said, voice

tight. "You know . . . sunrise. It's supposed to look like a sunrise."

"Jesus Christ, Charlie," she said. "The only thing those people out there care about is how much liquor is in the drinks. Do you have to make a big deal out of everything?"

He felt the anger rising in him even as he tried to control it. She really knew how to push his buttons. "I just like things to be right and proper, that's all."

"That's probably what the guards on Devil's Island say, too," she answered.

"Devil's Island was shut down years ago," he said. "Look. It's no big—"

"Yes it is! Everything's a big deal to you." She returned to the drinks, putting them back on the tray as she mixed them. "I've been putting on the proper front since the day you picked me like a pedigree dog out of the Radcliffe yearbook. I weigh exactly one hundred fifteen pounds, the optimum weight for my height, just like you demand. I don't wear eye shadow and I always defer to superiors' wives." She pointed toward the living room, her hand shaking. "Shit, the last time I ever had any choice in our relationship was thirty years and nine months ago!"

"Go to hell," he said quietly.

"I'm already there," she replied, picking up the tray of drinks and handing them to him. "Here. Make yourself useful." With that, she turned and strode from the room without a backward glance, leaving him with a silver tray full of booze and a hard residue of anger. His first impulse was to drop the tray to the floor, but Charlie Merchant very seldom went by his first impulses. He took several long breaths, put a fake smile on his face, and walked out into the living room.

Music hit him first, the piano, played with expertise by Phil Rosen. There wasn't a thing that Rosen did that wasn't perfect and professional. At forty-seven, he was the youngest speaker of the House ever elected to Congress, the respect he generated among colleagues and constituents alike a living testimonial to the man's commitment to the public trust. His sister, Della, had been married to Josh for five years and was admittedly the best thing that had ever happened to the younger Merchant.

He'd always felt a great affinity for Phil Rosen and his

sister. They'd remained unabashedly different and Jewish in an assimilated world, Phil's rise to power just as uphill as Merchant's had been after Chongchon. Suffering, if people didn't give in to it, made them stronger, made Phil and Della two of the strongest people he'd ever known.

The room smelled of perfume and after-shave, but not smoke, the talk high-pitched and enthusiastic, punctuated by spontaneous laughter as the gathered congressmen got to impress not only their own dates, but the wives of the military also, the reenactment of Waterloo just too much for all but the stoutest hearts. He wasn't exactly sure why he had gone on with the birthday party, except that somewhere in the back of his mind he thought it might be important to reestablish contact with the real world as he dove into the investigation of Jack's death. He'd been around long enough to know that his undertaking was going to border on the impossible without help—and big-time help at that—especially if Hurley let him down. Gene Tillotson had been his first duck. Now to line up a few from Jack's stomping ground.

"Hey! Drinks on the house!" he said loudly, moving into the conversation pit that formed a semicircle in front of the large fireplace in the wide-open Colonial style.

He set the drinks down on the table as Rosen played a fanfare from the baby grand Yamaha piano just off the pit. There was applause as everyone grabbed for drinks, no one remarking on the mudlike color of the sunrises. He hated the conversation pit. It had been built-in by a former tenant, a Pentagon action officer who apparently loved face time, its very existence dictating the type of furniture to go in the room. Early American was never designed for round areas, so they settled for long-slung modern, over-stuffed, for the entire room. He always thought of it as Linda's room, since it was the only one in which she'd picked the furniture.

"Well, now that the gang's all here . . ." Rosen announced loudly. He hit a strong chord and began to sing "Happy Birthday" to his own accompaniment.

They all joined in, singing loudly and standing. Della sat by a red-faced Josh, laughing at his embarrassment, putting an arm around him so that the cascade of her curly black hair spilled onto his shoulder. He tried to catch

Linda's eye, to smooth things over with a look, but she stood next to the senator from Ohio, never even looking in his direction.

Everyone applauded after singing, Josh, shy, standing to wave. Rosen, still at the piano, announced in a mock Georgie Jessel stage voice: "We will now return you to your regular schedule of prerecorded music."

"Play something else," Linda called, a chorus of voices shouting agreement, Rosen beaming.

"Unaccustomed as I am to public performance . . ." he began.

"C-Span's not here!" someone yelled. "Just play."

"Please," he said, a hand to his forehead. "I'm a sensitive artist."

He stared, smiling, down at the keyboard. Then he reached out slowly, Merchant noticing a change, like a cloud, passing over his face, altering him somehow. His fingers found the keys, tentatively at first, then with authority, playing the opening bars of "I'm Getting Sentimental Over You."

He heard Linda cry out softly, and this time their eyes found each other. She was frowning heavily, her look glazed. Both of them knew what Rosen was doing, the man speaking even as the images flashed through Merchant's mind, tumbling over themselves with stark rapidity.

"I spent a lot of years with Jack Braedman," Rosen said softly, with no small agony as he continued playing. "I've been with him in a lot of situations and places. Wherever we were, at that little piano bar off of Eighth Avenue or at a state affair at the Kennedy Center, if there was a band, Jack would ask them to play this song. Only this song."

Tears began to well up in Merchant's eyes and he forced them back. It was true. Braedman had been obsessive about that song since Korea, which was as long as he'd known him. He knew that it had something to do with Braedman's first wife, a young marriage that had ended badly. But beyond that there was nothing. It was the one part of his life that Jack Braedman had never talked about.

"I think it had something to do with a woman," Rosen said to small laughter, "but then doesn't everything? Jack never said. No one ever asked him. This was something specially his. Tonight I'll give it back to him."

He played then, his face hard and intense. He played better than Merchant had ever heard him play. He slowed the melody down somewhat and used a heavy foot on the pedal, making the minor chords sound hollow and ethereal, almost a funeral dirge. And when he was through, there wasn't a dry eye in the house. He stood and said quietly: "I really am finished now." Then he closed the keyboard cover and walked away from the piano.

Dead silence wrapped him in a cloak for several seconds, the mood rescued by Linda turning on the stereo to Sergio Mendez, the soft Latin rhythms easing everyone back into the conversation. Rosen walked up to Merchant, smiling softly, his dark eyes bursting with intelligence. "Sorry," he said. "Guess I could ruin a sunny day."

"God no," Merchant said, shaking his hand. "It was the best tribute Jack could ever have. I never knew you two were that close."

"You know how things are on the Hill," the man said, Della walking up to slip within the protective reach of her brother's arm. They had the same eyes, both of them the kind of people who couldn't be bullshitted successfully because they were actually listening to what was being said to them. "Life in the trenches and all that. We worked the same causes for a long time. I guess the feeling remained even after the ground rules changed."

"What do you mean?" Merchant asked.

Rosen looked puzzled. "Something, I don't know . . . changed in Jack a number of months ago. He began shedding his role in the liberal caucuses and taking on a more conservative slant."

"In what way?"

"The military, mostly," Rosen replied. "His defense of Pentagon issues became downright laughable. He was singing the praises of projects even the power bosses in the Building weren't interested in defending. His candidacy suffered, and he started falling in the polls. And the funniest part is that there's very little Pentagon money even spent in his district. Is that enough change for you?"

"This really surprises me," Merchant said. "Defense was the one issue he and I argued on. He was always wanting to cut back the military."

"You apparently hadn't seen him lately," Della said. "He'd changed completely in the last year."

"I wonder why," Merchant thought aloud.

"Hey, Charlie!" someone yelled from the pit. "You'd better get over here and straighten out this son of yours."

Merchant rolled his eyes at Rosen and walked back to the pit, several couples near the stereo beginning to dance without shoes on. "It's not my job anymore," he said, pulling Della with him. "That's what he's got a wife for."

A formidable group sat before Merchant's roaring fireplace, seasoned wood crackling as it consumed itself in the flames. Four senators and three congressmen filled the semicircle, most of them accompanied by their female aides or secretaries.

Josh Merchant sat on the hearth, looking slick in a silk suit, his tie still knotted firmly at his throat, his red hair, a genetic fluke not seen for three generations in Merchant's family, cut stylishly long. He'd grown up in the maelstrom of Washington politics, had done gofer work for most of the men here. The House and Senate chambers had been his playground, the changing cadre of young aides his playmates. When he'd grown up and gone to law school, everyone had thought it a shame he'd been born in D.C., the one impossible place to be from if you wanted to be a professional politician.

Gordon Hulett sat gingerly on the edge of the sofa, chuckling softly. He was a huge, ugly man, his very size the distinguishing characteristic that had gotten him elected in a backwoods North Carolina district thirty years ago and kept him there ever since. He was a good man, a man of integrity, and had been invited to the Merchants' house on many occasions, his insights into life and politics poured out with syrupy southern drawl a joy to listen to. He seemed fairly stuffed into his suit, as if one wrong move would split the pinstripes from stem to stern and leave him naked, "Your boy is tryin' to tell us that insider trading is all right and shouldn't be against the law."

Josh looked up at his father. "I'm just saying that all of life is insider trading, people taking advantage of friends, associates, and the breaks to make their lives work. If insider trading is a sin, tell me who it hurts? What's wrong with a guy finding out there's going to be a merger and dipping into the pot of gold by buying in. He's helped himself, but he hasn't hurt anybody."

Merchant grunted. "I'd better sit down for this one," he said, everyone laughing. He squeezed in between the senator from Oregon and the current sack mate of the congressman from Wisconsin, a post-pubescent aide named Wendy, long on baby fat and short on material in her skirt.

He watched Phil Rosen and Della grab seats before speaking. "You're talking in the wrong arena," he said, looking directly at Josh, who smiled at him, wisps of childhood freckles still evident on the bridge of his nose. "All these fellas here live their lives by checking the ethics of everything. If they give their sister a job, it'd better be because she's the most qualified or he's going to be in a world of hurt."

"I don't see anything wrong with that, either."

"It's the fairness of the thing, Josh," Merchant said. "You're an SEC lawyer, for God's sake. You know what I'm going to say. All this is a big game, every one of us knows that, but if you don't play it by the rules, then soon there are no rules left."

"Every millionaire on this planet would laugh in your face for saying that," Josh said. "Your attitudes are not only out-of-date, but childish. For every commodities broker we put in jail, there's another hundred so marginal in their lawfulness there's not a hair's worth of difference between them. It's just a fucking game, if you'll pardon my French."

"The federal courts don't think so," Phil Rosen said. "They prosecute every chance they get. Hell, the SEC exists because it's not a game."

"Which is where this discussion began," Josh replied. "Everybody cheats at everything. You can't prosecute the entire world."

"Speaking of cheating," Hulett said diplomatically, "what do y'all think about the Joint Chiefs' defection today?"

"They cut their own throats," Rosen said. "They're forcing the Budget and Appropriations committees to do their dirty work for them."

"Why?" Merchant asked. "I'm not exactly sure of what happened with that vote."

"Because their day is over," Rosen said quietly. "It's all changed around and it's going to shove them out. I don't know if any of you have ever read a philosopher named Hegel, but back in the early 1800s he predicted that western liberalism would eventually surplant all other political theories, and effectively end history as we know it. The cold war's over, folks. We've won. The question is: What now?"

"I don't know that I agree with that assessment," Merchant said, shaking his head. "With all due respect, the American fighting man is the only thing that has kept this country free for two hundred years. England disarmed after World War II and it destroyed them. They live on tourist dollars now. Believe me, when you get rid of cold wars, hot ones pop up. Look at the Persian Gulf. . . ."

"These budget cuts," Rosen said, "they're the beginning of the dismantling of the military establishment whether you like it or not, Charlie. I don't know if it's quite as black and white as Hegel's *Critique of Liberalism* paints it, but the changes are happening. The sad part here is that this flushes a year and a half of hard work by both the Congress and the Pentagon down the toilet. This city's full of angry people right now. This had already been agreed to. Apparently the military has decided that it doesn't want to convert to low-intensity warfare." He shook his head. "Guess they're not going to go down without a fight."

"Neither will the armament people," said a young woman sitting next to Congressman McCready from Oklahoma.

"Touché," said Rosen, who was still looking at Merchant. "The world is changing rapidly. We're standing at the crossroads of the most momentous time in the history of civilization. We've finally managed to, in a very real sense, bankrupt ourselves out of war, finally managed to technologize ourselves into the ground. The Joint Chiefs can vote any way they want to, but we're going to ax them in the Appropriations Committee."

"You can take that one to the bank," Hulett said in his hard drawl. "That's my committee, and as soon as we get everybody else back in town, we're gonna deal with it.

Most everybody's gone on for the weekend, but our regular meetin' day is Wednesday, and believe me, we're gonna be takin' a vote on this bullshit. What with the situation in Caribbea, I'm not sure I'm trusting our military just now."

"Are you saying that information is being purposefully kept from you on this issue?" Merchant asked, angry at Hulett.

"Well, somebody's got it," Hulett said, "and it ain't nobody on the Hill. Nobody up there can keep a secret this long."

"Well, the President must know," Merchant said, sick of the way civilians were always ready to trash the military—until they needed it. "And maybe it's precisely because you boys can't keep a secret that he hasn't told you."

"Charlie," Rosen said, shaking his head. "I met with the President not three hours ago. He's absolutely shocked over this thing. I'm convinced he doesn't know."

"Somebody has to," Merchant said.

"Maybe they don't want to say for ethical reasons." Josh snickered into his drink.

"Stow it, honey," Della Merchant said sweetly, "before you make a fool of yourself."

He smiled sweetly back at her, raising his drink. "It's my birthday, remember? It's okay to make a fool of yourself on your birthday."

"Well, I resent what I'm hearing," said Colonel Jeter from outside the circle. The military was returning, moving through the dancers, an Air Force captain taking his wife from the arms of a congressman and pulling her toward the door. "You automatically assume that we're keeping things from you because you don't know everything."

"I'm sure he didn't mean . . ." Merchant began, but it was already too late.

"All of us here have devoted our lives to the defense of this country," Jeter continued with the Pentagon party line, walking right up to the sofa and pointing at Rosen. "How dare you infer that we would withhold pertinent info for our own devices. Who do you think you are, anyway?"

Rosen smiled at the man, unperturbed. "Sorry, Colonel," he said easily, "but I'm not playing. Congress and the

Pentagon have been hassling this issue out for more years than either of us have put in to it. We keep things from you, you from us. Since the Congress doesn't have intelligence-gathering units, I must assume that the leak didn't come from us. Whoever it did come from, however, had better quickly own up. You guys don't run the country. We do."

"Right," said the young captain, his wife still in tow. "All we do is die for it, and I don't mean while getting a piece of ass somewhere like your—"

"That's enough," Merchant said, standing. "That's quite enough from all of us. Jack Braedman loved this country as much as anyone. And he served it with more distinction than most. I don't intend to stand here and have him smeared in my own house."

The front doorbell rang, the young captain, dragging his wife by the wrist, went to open it. A whole squad of MPs moved into the front room along with a frigid gust of outside air, heavy with portent. "I'm sorry, sirs," a large, blond MP announced loudly, his hands behind his back at parade rest. "We've been sent to bring all intelligence officers back for briefings. I have a list of names and will check you off as you leave. There are cars waiting. This is a priority wakeup call, gentlemen. Let's move!"

"What about our wives?" asked the captain.

"Our orders are to bring you back, sir," came the clipped reply.

"I'll make sure everybody gets home, son," Merchant said, the captain frowning in the direction of his wife, who had turned and was smiling at the representative she'd been dancing with.

"Whew," Rosen breathed low. "Saved by the bell."

The military men gathered at the door, asking questions that weren't to be answered, Tillotson seeking out Merchant in the confusion. "Can we talk for a minute?" the man asked.

"Sure," Merchant said. "Let's try the kitchen."

They walked off through the tangle of military, Merchant noticing Linda dancing, too closely, to the senator from Ohio. She was trying to make him mad and it was working. He swallowed the anger whole and moved into the kitchen with Tillotson.

Linda watched him go, angry that she hadn't gotten a rise out of him. She heard his laugh rumble back from the kitchen and stiffened involuntarily in her partner's arms, the man turning her face to his with a gentle index finger. "Something wrong?" he asked.

She looked into his eyes, softened. "No, Lowell," she said, pulling closer and resting her cheek against his so he wouldn't see the hard edge that still glinted her eyes. "Everything's great. You're a good dancer."

"Everybody's good with the right partner," he said, bumping against her with his hip. His voice was soft as puppies and a touch gravelly, what Charlie would call a "radio voice," and indeed, Lowell Joiner had once been a radio announcer on a Gospel station. But the words he was saying into her ear were some he'd never used on the radio.

"You're a beautiful woman, Linda," he said. "That old curmudgeon of a husband you've got better realize that before I come and steal you away from him."

He was using his put-on, just-pretend voice, but she knew he wasn't kidding. He'd been looking at her with sweet eyes for years. "Well, if anybody could do it, Lowell, it'd be you," she said, just to see what would happen.

"Yes, sir," he said, still in the same voice. "All woman." He held on tighter and bent into the song, dancing in an exaggerated fashion, almost as if he were on stage. In his own odd, semi-shy way, he was building to something. Within seconds, she understood.

The man dipped with her, her legs going on either side of his. He shoved at the base of her spine, jamming her against him, an erection pushing insistently against her pelvis. She was paralyzed with surprise as he pulled his head back and looked into her eyes, not saying a word.

She could have extricated herself gracefully; she'd done it before, but for reasons she couldn't put her finger on, she didn't. He pulled her up out of the dip and danced close, humping against her slowly, in rhythm to the music. At first she simply let him, her mind spinning, realizing that she was enjoying the attention; then gently, imperceptibly to anyone watching them, she began to return his motion. And there, in the center of a boisterous party, she had the closest thing to enjoyable sex that she'd had in nearly ten years.

Tillotson tipped the quart bottle of Jack Daniel's to his lips and drank long and slow, Merchant watching his Adam's apple rise and fall and he swallowed.

"It doesn't make sense that the Russians would put missiles into Caribbea," Merchant said, Tillotson pulling the bottle away from his mouth and handing it to him. "Not now. They've moved too far in the other direction."

"'Less it's a trick," Tillotson said, "all this *glasnost* shit. We used to have détente, too. Whatever happened to that?"

Merchant took a drink from the bottle, swallowing hard. "But their empire has crumbled, their economy . . ."

"Yeah, I know. But they still got plenty of bombs, though, and what if they decided to pull one big trick so they could whip us *before* they went broke. Universal disarmament would be one helluva trick."

Merchant handed him the bottle back. "Do you really believe that's possible?"

Tillotson started to drink, stopped, and pointed at Merchant with the bottle. "The only thing I know for sure is that those motherfuckers lie more than we do, and that it's not wise to believe everything they say. We thought we'd shut them down with the Madrina election, but the damn Commies retained control of the military. What a public relations coup that would be, putting missiles into Caribbea right under our noses. The Caribs aren't our friends. They just wanted us for our money, and when we didn't give them enough, they hated us again. The last polls I saw showed that the Companeros would win if they held the elections again. So there we go, back to square one. Does anything really ever change?"

"General Tillotson!" came the MP's voice from the living room. "Is General Tillotson here?"

"Comin', son!" Tillotson called, chuckling, bringing the bottle to his lips again. He brought it down, the amusement solidifying to something harder as he looked at Merchant. "I'm really sorry how we've lost touch, Charlie."

"Couldn't be helped," Merchant said, knowing that it

could've. "Life changes. We've always been close in our hearts."

"Have we?"

"What do you mean by that?"

The man put the bottle down on the table. "When you got passed over for the DIA job, it was like you hardened even more. You had the guts to say, 'Fuck everybody,' and walk away from it all."

"Was it guts, Gene," Merchant said, "or am I just a quitter?"

"Quitter, shit!" Tillotson said loudly. "Hell, you built a whole new career for yourself. Jesus, Charlie . . . ten years out of uniform and you can still get half the Pentagon over here with a phone call. You were born to command. I've had to juice myself into it."

"Linda says I just can't cut the ties," Merchant said, "that I'm still trying to fit in even though nobody wants me."

"You don't believe that and I don't believe that," Tillotson said with finality.

Merchant hesitated. "Gene, I . . ."

"You just listen for a minute," Tillotson said, his eyes murky, unfocused. "You were always the strongest, the best of us. You made us hold our heads up and stick together when everybody else was screaming court-martial back in '51. When they offered me that DIA job years later, I felt at first like I should have turned it down, as a show of solidarity with you, I guess. But I didn't have the willpower, I've . . . never had the willpower. I wanted it, and I wanted the prestige that went along with it. I always wondered at how much our losing touch had to do with you thinking the same thing. We ate a lot of fire back in them old days and for years after, but every fire eventually consumes itself. You ultimately jump in and move with the current."

"I never could," Merchant replied, taking a long breath. "And I'd be lying if I told you I didn't have some bad moments when you took the job." He was suddenly very tired. "But we all have to make our own lives. I've never had any expectations for you beyond friendship."

"Do you really mean that? I know how much the army meant to you. You were born to be a military man."

"I was born to come up short," Merchant said, angry at his own self-pity. "I was born to wonder what might have been."

Tillotson, glass in hand, pointed to him. "That DIA job should have been yours." He brushed at the stars on his shoulders as if they were dandruff. "These should have been yours. Your ghost sits in that office every day I go into work. I can't shake it. That's why I don't want to be cut out of this investigation. Maybe Jack's death can bring us close again, get those fires stoked up again."

"Believe me, I need it as much as you do," Merchant said, and meant it. In truth, neither of them had recovered from Korea. They both still lived on the outside, Tillotson taking scraps of charity while Merchant dug through the garbage cans. Maybe this investigation was what they both needed.

"General Tillotson!" the MP called.

"You're being too hard on yourself," Merchant said, though he didn't believe it. Tillotson straightened a bit, gathering himself for the cold and the briefings. "I've made my own life and learned to live with it, just as you have done with yours." He moved to the man, embracing him for just a second. "We're going to do this thing together, just like the old days. You'll see. We haven't lost the edge at all."

"That's the best thing I've heard in years," Tillotson said, straightening his tie. "Oh, well. Time to go in search of the heart of the envelope."

"Good luck," Merchant said just as the kitchen phone rang. "I'll keep you posted, and probably have some work for you."

Tillotson smiled, saluted with one finger, and was gone, Merchant moving to pull the phone off the wall hook, his eyes drifting to the television on the washstand that had been switched to CNN all day. "Merchant," he said into the receiver.

"This is Hurley," came a distracted voice on the other end. "I want to talk."

"Is there something . . . ?"

"Let's just meet and talk," the man answered, clipped. "Tomorrow."

On the TV screen was newsreel footage of plane wreckage floating on the ocean, a score of small boats, some military, forming a loose cordon around the area. "I can be out to headquarters first thing in—"

"No," Hurley interrupted. "Let's meet on neutral ground, somewhere away from the Metro."

"How about lunch," Merchant replied, "in George-town."

"Fine."

"Do you know the Vietnamese place on Thirty-first and M?"

"Yeah. Meet you there at twelve-thirty."

The line went dead. On the small TV screen he could see bodies being recovered from the water. He hung up the phone and walked over to turn up the TV.

". . . released the names of the dead," the announcer was saying. "They are, pilot Harrison Murphy of Erie, Pennsylvania, and copilot Jerry Delany of Seattle, Washington. It was Delaney's first day on the job with EquAir."

He watched for a moment, not really listening, just letting the visuals flow over him. One of the bodies had no head.

Odd. Hearing the name Jerry Delany had made the hair on his forearm stand. Jerry had been the name Joann had written on the mirror in her own blood. It was a common name, no doubt millions of Jerrys in the United States.

Then why did it bother him? Why?

FEBRUARY 5,
TUESDAY

⬛⬛⬛ NEWSBREAK ⬛⬛⬛

". . . And still the questions concerning the down-ing of EquAir flight 322 persist. Listen to this last extraordinary message from the copilot of that flight, Jerry Delany. This transmission between flight 322 and Holmes Air Base was picked up by a ham radio operator in the Florida keys. The government has refused to comment on the information contained herein."

"I'm in the middle of a storm, Holmes . . . (static) . . . There's a large land mass to my right. I thought it was Cuba at first, but . . . my God . . . my God!"

"322, do you copy? Do you copy? Come in. Over."
(long static)

"Mayday! Mayday! We're being fired upon from the ground! We've been hit!"

"322 . . . 322!"

"S-smoke filling the cabin! Something wrong w-with pilot. Direct me left or right . . . left or right . . . no controls. It's missiles! They're firing missiles! We're going down . . . we're—"

"At that point the transmission abruptly ended, leaving only the questions. Flight 322 was supposed to be on a routine, but unexplained, mission for the GSA to Florida. How did it get so far off course? Why was the copilot flying the plane? More importantly, why was it shot down—an act denied by the Caribbean military even in the face of the evidence? And does this action in any way connect to the rumors of Russian missiles in that Central American country or to last week's assassination of the Caribbean foreign minister? So far, the State Department refuses to comment."

—*CBS Morning News*
February 5

White House Press Room 10:33 A.M.

Sheila Traynor could feel the eyes turn on her as she moved out of the Canadian cold front and into the heat of the governmental kitchen. She was the center of attention, the subject of the back-of-the-hand murmurs that arced through the room like static electricity, and to Sheila Traynor that was the way it was supposed to be. She had it all now, the best of both worlds. She'd brought in the hard news story of the seasoned journalist, and now was ready to handle the feedback like the trained model and actress she was. She wore her best Rodeo Drive gray suit with a bright white cotton blouse set off with a wide, red power tie.

She moved into the confusion of television cameras, microphones, and her peers, not even stopping at the release basket before moving up to the banks of folding chairs to take a seat, people who'd never given her the time of day before mouthing encouragement and patting her on the back as she passed.

"Sheila!" came a voice from the midst of the seating, people still milling around. "Over here!"

It was the Washington reporter and sometimes anchor for ABC, his incisive eyes cutting right through her. She smiled, waving. "Hello, Sam." *You've never had time for me before, you motherfucker.* She moved up and took the seat beside him. "It's started snowing out."

He sat back, shifting his steno pad on his lap. "Great. The best story to come along since Iran Amuck and we're going to have to slog through snowdrifts to get it." He stared at her again, and she could tell that he was trying to size her up.

"Want a photograph?" she asked.

"What?"

"Nothing. Do you think they'll brief us about the Caribbean situation."

He smiled. "What choice have they got? You spilled all the beans and now they're going to have to pick them back up. Where'd you get that shit anyway? I've been pulling my strings in since last night and still come away empty. Is your source dependable?"

"Totally. And there'll be more."

He shook his head, a quick jerk. "Lady, I believe you've just made your fortune. Uh-oh. Here we go."

Several Secret Service agents moved out onto the small stage at the end of the room, preparatory to the entry of the President of the United States. The room hushed immediately, reporters hurrying to get their seats as a camera operator called, "Stand by. Thirty seconds."

The White House Press Secretary hurried to the podium. "Ladies and gentlemen," he said tiredly. "Please maintain good order. The President will try and get to as many questions as possible. Please raise your hands if you have a question, and don't call out unless you are called on." He gazed out into the audience, his eyes fixing hard on Traynor. "There will be a brief statement before the President begins to answer questions."

"Five seconds!" the cameraman called.

The secretary turned to the wings, nodding once, and announced: "Ladies and gentlemen, the President of the United States."

The President moved out toward the podium, leading another contingent of Secret Service as he went. Traynor watched him carefully, his demeanor wary but surprisingly light. President Jefferson Macklin was a man who ate up publicity the way most people gulped air. A man not known for being especially issue-oriented, he seemed less upset about having to deal with a real issue in a public forum than she would have thought. He looked up once from the podium, frowning, she thought, in her direction. But there was something else going on here, she was certain of it.

"Yesterday afternoon," the President began without preamble, "a news bulletin was released to the American public concerning the placement of Russian offensive missiles into Central America—a leak, as it were." He stopped reading and looked meaningfully out at the audience, the same sincere, heartfelt look that had gotten him elected to begin with. "I'm here to tell you, there is no leak," he continued. "There is no leak, there are no Russian trawlers, there are no missiles in Caribbea. I don't know where this information has come from, but it is false information, completely wrong, and is an example of the kind of sleaze journalism that is hurting the credibility of legitimate news sources. This sort of vicious innuendo is unworthy of the news organization that put it out and the Justice Department is, at this moment, considering filing charges."

The ABC newsman leaned closer to Traynor and whispered, "You really did uncover something, didn't you? I've never seen him so on the defensive."

"In order to put these rumors completely to rest," Macklin continued, "I've instituted an extraordinary step"—he turned to the wings with an outstretched arm—"Mr. Ambassador. . . ."

A small, balding man in a gray suit buttoned up to his bulging midsection walked out onto the stage.

"My God," Traynor breathed. "It's the Russian ambassador."

The ABC man laughed, shaking his head. "My goodness," he said excitedly, and began writing furiously in his notebook, Traynor wondering why. "Curiouser and curiouser."

So this was Macklin's ace in the hole, an authentic Russian in the woodshed. She watched him walk up to stand, uncomfortably, next to the President.

"This is Mr. Yuri Petrovich," Macklin said, "the official Russian ambassador to the United States. He'd also like to make a statement. Mr. Ambassador?"

Petrovich cleared his throat and leaned toward the huge bank of microphones on the podium. "Ladies and gentlemen . . . and reporters," he began to light laughter. "I was asked to come here today to address the subject of yesterday's news bulletin. In response to that, I can only say there is nothing to address. The Soviet Union has put no missiles into the democratic nation of Caribbea. The Soviet Union is dedicated to peace and to disarmament in this hemisphere and globally; a path we've chosen jointly with the United States of America. Such news reports are not only wrong, but dangerous to the delicate process of peace that has been undertaken by our two nations. I hope that a retraction is forthcoming soon, so that we may get back to business."

The man smiled, though it didn't look easy for him, and stepped back from the mikes. As if that were a cue of some kind, the room burst into a chorus of "Mr. President" shouts, the newsmen frantically waving their arms for attention. Traynor was right up there with them, shouting for recognition. She was angry now, really hurt. Denying the leak was one thing, but attacking her integrity and that of her network was unforgivable. If they wanted a press war over this thing, she was more than ready to give it to them.

Helen McConnell of the AP got the first question, which was traditional. "Mr. President," she said, "are you denying the video and film footage that all of us saw on this issue? The pictures don't lie."

Macklin frowned and leaned to the mikes. "I don't know where the pictures came from," he said, and it sounded idiotic coming from his lips, and for the first time, Traynor was beginning to wonder if he did know about it. Maybe he was being kept in the dark, too. The Reagan Syndrome.

"Nobody in any of our intelligence units knows where they came from," Macklin continued. "Perhaps you'd better ask the woman who released the info."

"Mr. President!" she shouted, unable to take the continuing references to her nonprofessionalism. "Mr. President!"

His eyes met hers, then passed on to another newsman. "Mr. President," the man said. "Other administrations have kept secrets from the press, have denied the truth."

"Is this a question?" Macklin returned angrily. "I called this press conference to deal with the lies that you people have let slip out. I will not have you stand there and call this administration one of lies. Next question."

He passed Traynor over again, and she realized that he'd never call on her. A woman with a Spanish accent near the back of the room was called upon. Her black eyes flashed as she spoke. "Was the assassination of the Caribbean foreign minister by an American mercenary tied in with this issue, perhaps in retaliation for the missiles?"

Macklin's eyes had begun to take on a hard glint and Traynor could see that this wasn't going as he'd expected it to.

"First of all," he said, "no one knows who assassinated Mr. Ramirez. If it was an American, he wasn't working for us. All of these events are simply sad coincidences. I know that sounds strange. . . ."

"Mr. President," the next questioner said. "What about the EquAir shoot-down yesterday? That plane was on a U.S. government mission. What was it doing over the coast of Caribbea?"

"It was off course . . ." the President began, the questioner interrupting him for a follow-up.

"And why are the Navy planes and divers still in the area after the bodies and wreckage have already been removed?"

"We're still trying to recover the plane's black box," Macklin replied uneasily, "to see what sort of info—"

Petrovich, his eyes drawn hard, moved up beside the President, shoving him aside slightly as he took the mike. "There was no shoot-down," he said. "The Caribbean government couldn't shoot it down because it was beneath radar cover over open seas."

The questioner turned, smiling to the rest of the audience. "Pretty soon they're going to tell us that we're not here."

"That's quite enough," Macklin said angrily, shoving the Russian back away from the mike again, no doubt regretting ever bringing him on to begin with. He was losing control of his own press conference. "We must maintain order here. Another question?"

He frowned again at Traynor's upraised hand, and called on the man beside her. "Yes, Mr. Danasson?"

The man winked at Traynor, then said, "I'd like to

relinquish my question to Sheila Traynor of NCC News."

Macklin's eyes widened noticeably, but being the public man that he was, he bottled his rage and looked at Traynor, the press conference now way out of hand.

She stood, knowing this was her territory. Macklin had blundered into giving her an emotional forum, and she dredged up every ounce of training and feeling she had to pull it off. "I have stood here and listened to you impugn my credibility and my veracity simply because I spoke the truth, then refuse to call upon me to defend myself. You have the Justice Department file all the suits you want to because every bit of this will come home to this administration. My source is unimpeachable, the videotapes self-explanatory. You may say whatever you wish, but I will continue to bring the truth to the people of America."

"If your source is so unimpeachable," the President returned, leveling a devastating gaze, "then drag him out here. Let's question him now and get to the bottom of this."

He'd walked right into it. She could barely believe it as she delivered the coup de grace. "My source has requested anonymity for his own safety, and I intend to honor that request. I will gladly go to jail to protect my source. The First Amendment protects the free press and its sources."

The room burst into spontaneous applause, Macklin turning, red-faced, from the podium, dragging the Russian ambassador with him.

"Way to go," said Danasson from beside her. "You handled him."

"Thanks for giving me the question," she said.

"Oh, I don't know if you should thank me," he said, arching an eyebrow. "They may never let you in here again."

"Yeah, they will," she said confidently, riding the crest of her self-generated wave. "You just watch."

She stood and turned then, heading through the cacophony of excited voices that filled the room to bursting. As she made the hall leading to the cloakroom, she saw the two nondescript men in the black suits and knew immediately they had come for her. She pretended they weren't there and tried to walk past them to get her coat.

"Miss Traynor," one of them said, stressing the Miss.

"You're blocking the door," she returned, the man reaching into his breast pocket and extracting a small wallet. He flipped it open to an ID card and a badge.

"FBI," the man said simply. "You're going to have to come with us."

Georgetown Noon

Charlie Merchant sat in his car for a moment, watching the heavy snow fall onto the vehicle, melting on the hood, congealing on the windshield. M Street was all but shut down, the Canadian air mass choking the narrow Georgetown streets with frigid, swirling snow, six inches deep already and no predicted end in sight. At least he'd been able to get a good parking space.

He was anxious for the meet with Hurley, starved for any information. As Braedman's death passed more and more quickly into the public domain, it was becoming urgent to him to nose things in another direction, to clear Jack's name before it became a literal impossibility. More and more, his own sense of self-worth was getting tied into the investigation, almost as if Jack had died so that he could redeem himself. He couldn't let it all fall apart now.

His home life had all but crashed and burned, Linda unwilling or unable to understand how important this was to him. He couldn't blame her really, he'd never been much of a husband, promising her and himself that it would all be different when he retired. But it wasn't different. If anything, the emptiness of his life had grown to cavernous proportions when there was no job, no busy work, to occupy his mind. He spent his time dwelling on the past and playing with toy soldiers. It couldn't go on like that for much longer before he ended up like Gene, or worse—like Jack.

As the windshield iced over, he cracked the door and stepped out, his car parked directly before the front window of the restaurant called Vietnam Georgetown. He moved to the door of the place, a coating of snow already turning his overcoat white as his feet sank past the ankles in the sidewalk covering. He stopped to brush off his coat in the entryway. It was miserable.

A late-model Ford, covered with snow, pulled up to the curb across the street, heading the other direction. He watched Hurley get out, look suspiciously both ways, then trudge across the nearly deserted street that was usually jammed with tourist shoppers. He had a large manila envelope tucked under his arm. His face was grave.

"You're punctual," Charlie called to him as he reached the sidewalk, snow building up in the man's short-cropped hair. "I appreciate a man who's on time."

"Have you been inside yet?" Hurley returned, brushing the blizzard off his hair and coat.

"No . . . why?"

"Go in," Hurley said, frowning. "Make sure there's no one inside who knows you."

Charlie tightened his lips and turned to the door, letting himself in. Vietnam Georgetown was barely more than a large, open square dining area, very minimal in both furnishings and atmosphere—wooden tables with white linen tablecloths and tall, fluted water glasses. There was a young couple, sitting close together, toward the back of the room. Other than that, it was deserted.

Merchant turned back to the door, giving Hurley the high sign through its glass front. A stairway downward occupied the entire right side of the place. A Vietnamese waiter in black slacks and white, starched shirt came slowly up the stairs. Merchant wondered if, in time, our only legacy of the Asian wars would be a number of very good restaurants.

"Two for lunch?" the man asked as the watched Hurley walking in.

"Give us a seat in the window," Hurley said, and Merchant couldn't quite put a finger on the man's mood, although deeply troubled seemed to be the starting place. God only knew where his head went from there.

They hung up their coats and got a two-seater by the picture window that defined the entire front of the dining room, looking out at the pre-mall, small townlike rows of shops and restaurants across the street. Merchant was angled to where he could see part of the length of 31st

Street where it crossed M. They were a block and a half away from the house on Dumbarton where Joann Durbin had killed herself. There was traffic moving in that direction. Even with the cold and the blizzard, the hot blood of death could bring out the crowds.

Both men ordered quickly and glibly, and both asked for chopsticks with the meal. Merchant didn't need to ask to know that Hurley had been in 'Nam, too.

"You've really fucked up my life, you know it?" Hurley asked as soon as the waiter had left. "I shouldn't be here. I know I shouldn't be here."

"Then why are you?"

The man looked at him, working his lips, his jaw muscles tightening. "You know why," he said.

Merchant smiled. "I knew you were the right man to go to with this," he said. "What's happened?"

"Too many . . . coincidences," Hurley replied, then stopped, his eyes drifting away from the table, the waiter returning with a pot of green tea. The man wouldn't speak until after the waiter left the table again.

"Let me tell you what I've got," he continued, "and you tell me what it means."

"Fair enough."

"First of all, the case has been officially closed, which probably doesn't come as a real surprise."

Merchant poured them both a cup of steaming tea as the snow piled up against the window outside and the traffic continued to move along Thirty-first to Dumbarton. "How did you get the news?" he asked.

"Bignell called me," Hurley said, picking up his handleless teacup, trying unsuccessfully to take a sip. He grimaced and set the cup back down. "Hot. Bignell said that a long investigation would only drag things out and be bad for everyone when it was obvious what had happened. He also alluded to a call from the Justice Department asking for speedy resolution."

"God, that pisses me off," Merchant said. "Consigning Jack's life and career to the ashes for the sake of expedience. . . ." He shook his head. "Do you think the order originated from Bignell?"

Hurley shook his head. "I honestly don't know."

"What else?"

The man frowned deeply. Leonard Hurley was a man of loyalty and integrity, none of this easy for him. "Weston and Mills," he said at last, "their stories . . . match."

"You mean, match *exactly*?" Merchant asked, immediately grasping the implications.

"Almost word for word," Hurley said, trying his tea again. This time he got a sip before setting it down, Merchant using that as the cue to try his own. "And there's something else. I never did find anyone to corroborate their story about Braedman's escape on seven."

Merchant pointed at the man. "Word for word . . . . that is what you said?"

Hurley nodded grimly, and Merchant knew he hadn't heard it all.

"There's more, isn't there?"

"Last night," Hurley began slowly, then stopping again as the waiter brought the food: prawn and bean sprouts in a curry sauce, with steamed rice.

Merchant had developed a taste for South China Sea cooking while he'd been in 'Nam helping set up American Intel in the early sixties, and ate lunch here often. Vietnam had been a pleasant experience to Merchant with none of the connotations of horror and loss that the soldiers in the field had experienced. Saigon had been, in those days, the essence of a slow-paced French colonial town with wide verandas and polite waiters serving gin and tonics. He'd been long gone before the tragedy of Tet changed everything in 1968.

"Last night . . ." Merchant prompted when it seemed that Hurley had suddenly become extremely interested in his lunch.

The man took a long breath and ate some rice. "Last night I pulled a hard copy of the Braedman file. I don't know why." He shrugged at Merchant. "This morning I tried to get into the file to see what had been added."

"And?"

"It wasn't there," the man said. "It was gone, vanished, as if there'd never been a file at all. I asked somebody over in operations about it and they said that the Justice Department had dumped it into their computers and killed it in ours for 'national security reasons.'"

"Jesus Christ!" Merchant exclaimed, dropping his chopsticks. "This is nuts. Does it make sense to you?"

Hurley put down his chopsticks and laughed. "That the D.C. police would turn over all the pertinent info on a big shit murder case without at least a court hearing on the issue?" He shook his head. "No, it doesn't make any sense at all."

"It doesn't to me, either," Merchant replied. "From the government's end, that would look like a cover-up."

"Unless national security really is involved."

"Anything's possible, I guess. Did you get the registration on that Jag?"

"Yeah, I did," Hurley returned, bending once more to the plate. "Only it's not a Jag, it's a Chevrolet."

"Oh, really?" Merchant replied, knowing the difference between the two and knowing it was no General Motors product he'd seen at the murder. "Who does it belong to?"

"It's a lease job," the man said, going for the tea again. "Belongs to a company called Legislative Services, the people Joann Durbin had worked for until six months ago."

"Interesting," Merchant said, filing the information in the back of his mind. "So, where do we go from here?"

"Maybe we play it your way," Hurley said. "Do you have any outside info-gathering capabilities?"

"I think I have an arrangement with someone in the DIA," he returned honestly, wanting the trust to be complete between them. "Although I don't think I should give you any names."

"Believe me, I don't want any," Hurley said around a mouthful of shrimp. "I'm only doing this because I think the only thing that'll help the department and me in the long run is the truth."

"You say you were able to pull hard copy?"

Hurley looked around again before bringing up the envelope from the vacant chair beside him and sliding it across the table to Merchant. "Everything we had up until last night is in that file, and I'm putting my career on the line to give it to you."

"I'll honor it as a trust," Merchant said without hesitation, his fingers itching to tear open the flap. "But I'm not going to thank you for doing the right thing."

"*If* this is the right thing." Hurley idly picked up a shrimp with the chopsticks, then let it drop back to the plate. "I also went to the property room and went through his stuff. We found his address in his wallet and his keys in his pocket. He had an apartment in the embassy section. We never even sent anybody over there. I put the key in the envelope, too. I can't officially work on this case anymore, but I'll do what I can on the sly and funnel information to you, if that's okay?"

"You're a good cop," Merchant said.

"Yeah, Mr. Merchant. . . ."

"Charlie."

"Yeah, Charlie. I'm a good cop, maybe too good. That's what my old lady says, anyhow. She warned me not to have anything to do with you."

"Probably good advice."

"Right. Only I'm a really simple guy." The man pushed his food away and rocked his chair back on two legs. "Something has to matter to me. So, it's my job. I don't want easy answers and closed files, Charlie. I want the truth. And if I have to get to it by using you and the DIA, then so be it. Something stinks here. Now let me ask you: What the hell is this all about?"

Merchant took out his pipe and stuck it in his mouth without lighting it. He looked Hurley in the eye and said, "I'm totally mystified."

"You mean that, don't you?"

Merchant removed his pipe, tapping it on the plate as the waiter brought them the check, Hurley grabbing it immediately. "All I know, Leonard," he said, "is that Jack Braedman could not have killed that girl or himself. If it turns out to have been Mills and Weston, I'll want to find out who they work for. Do you have any suspicions?"

"Bignell, for starts," Hurley replied, turning to look out at the still-piling snow, a drift already moving up the window from sidewalk level. "But beyond that, I've got nothing."

"Do me a favor," Merchant said. "Poke around a bit on the sixth floor, see if anyone remembers that day. Also, see what else you can dig up on Mills and Weston, but don't go through your regular channels, try other sources."

Hurley nodded, dropping a twenty on top of the check.

He stood. "I've got to get back," he said. "Where do you go from here?"

Merchant, standing also, held up the large envelope. "Start with Jack's apartment," he said. "Then I've got some researching to do."

Hurley tried to smile, reaching out a hand that Merchant shook. "I'll leave first," the man said. "Give me a minute, then follow."

He watched Hurley leave, the detective's whole body bending at a severe angle into the wind as he crossed the street, his car already lost in a snowdrift. He wondered what the man was really thinking, because the thing, the one thing that they had tiptoed around, was the fact that two of his cops were cold-blooded killers and that something was going to have to be done about it.

Something was wrong with the system that allowed animals like Mills and Weston to slip through the cracks. Merchant figured that it was the system that needed fine-tuning to the point that it would squeeze in on those two by itself. This was America, a benignly integrated system of values, social systems, politics, and bureaucracy designed to allow maximum freedom for its citizens. And he knew that if he just kicked it the right way, the system would triumph. It had to. If it didn't, his whole life would have been a lie. He would have fought all these years for nothing.

He walked out into the snow and the razored air, making a mental note to pick up the tab next time he met with Hurley. He resisted the urge to open the envelope until he got into the car and locked the doors, snow covering all the windows as if he were in a cave, secure.

Jack's key fell out into his lap first thing. He picked it up and stared at its irregular pattern of teeth and grooves. His hand was shaking slightly as he mulled over the contradictory feelings its power gave him. His years with Jack had been straightforward and honest. Now he was going to search the man's apartment like a common thief, almost an insult to their previous life together. Nastiness breeds nastiness.

He turned on the engine and tried the wipers. They were already stuck, frozen and mired in the shit on the windshield. He turned the heater/defroster up full and sat

back for a moment to go through the rest of the envelope.
There wasn't a whole lot: a background computer check
on Joann Durbin, Weston's and Mill's statements, the
original arrest report—and photos.

There were a number of eight-by-ten glossies that
Hurley had slipped into the file. Several of them were of
Joann, her death played from every angle, with close-ups
of her arms. They were suicide marks, no doubt. No
attacker would so carefully draw the blade down the vein.
It couldn't happen that slickly without cooperation. Then
there were several photos of Jack, crumpled in a wide pool
of his own blood at the bottom of the stairwell, his hands,
indeed, cuffed behind him. Merchant had seen death
before, knew its meatlike inhuman posture, but this was
almost more than he could bear. So much good the man
had done over the years, so much love and devotion he'd
given his country and his friendships. Braedman had
freedom marched in Selma, held Bobby Kennedy's
hand as he lay dying in L.A., and fought convoys of food
through rebel-held lands in Chad and Ethiopia. All to lie
drowned in a thick flood of red with his hands tied behind
him like a Lebanese hostage. Merchant could feel his
temples throbbing with the inanity of it all as human
pettiness stripped this great man of his dignity and good
works, all for a dirty joke. He couldn't allow this to
happen; it flew in the face of everything he honored and
believed in. He may have retired, but he still commanded
some respect. Every bit of clout he could muster would go
into this thing.

He looked up, the windshield practically cleared from
the defrost. Throwing the car in gear, he pulled out into no
traffic, heading east on M Street. He drove through a bleak,
white world of howling wind and swirling confusion, the
storefronts homogenized like a frosted gingerbread city,
stalled and skidding cars making the road itself a treacherous obstacle course. He centered his mind on the movement, the tracking. Braedman had once been his best
friend. In the space of a day, he had become a puzzle to
solve. Rosen had said that he'd changed. How? Why? And
did the change somehow tie in with his death? Hopefully,
the apartment would begin a chain of answers to the list of
questions that got longer by the minute. Just like Hurley,

who was willing to use Merchant to get at the truth, he was more than willing to put his best friend's life under the microscope to achieve the same end, accepting without question the notion that the truth would set everyone free. That feeling had always been the cornerstone of his life philosophy, and he was unafraid to put it to the test now.

He would save Jack's name with the truth. It was that simple and that complicated.

He stayed with M Street all the way to Thomas Circle, then made the turn onto Massachusetts Avenue, heading toward the old section of crumbling mansions commonly known as Embassy Row near Whitehaven Street. He'd been to Braedman's apartment before, but it had been years. Again he tried to figure out why they had gotten out of touch and how much changes with time.

He half drove, half skidded past the antebellum splendor of the British, Brazilian, and Iranian embassies before pulling into the basement garage of the nine-story highrise called Washington Heights that had been a home away from home for Jack Braedman for almost fifteen years. He parked in the dark underground catacomb of concrete, feeling the cold more here than he had outside.

He locked the car, his breath frosting bright white as he walked, footsteps echoing hollowly, toward the elevator. The inside of the elevator was warm, its pale yellow walls marred by high-tone graffiti: MEAT IS MURDER and FUR IS DEAD.

Braedman had lived on nine. He clutched the key hard as he climbed out of the elevator and moved down the hallway of polished wood parquet, door numbers lining out on either side of him.

He felt a rush of excitement as he found Jack's door and slid the key into the lock. The excitement turned to horror, then rage as he pushed the door open.

The place was a shambles. All the furniture was overturned, cushions slashed, stuffing everywhere. Every drawer in the place had been dumped upside down. His first thought was of vandals, but then he thought again.

He waded into the room, leaving the door ajar behind him. He was ankle deep in junk, as he had been in snow. The TV and VCR were still intact, the television actually turned on to CNN. He moved to the small kitchen, silverware and broken plates now littering the floor, the drawers tossed aside. A microwave oven sat untouched on a countertop. There had been no vandals or thieves here, nothing of value had been taken. Whoever had done this had duplicated Merchant's thoughts. They had been looking for something—but what?

He walked back out of the kitchen. The dinette table had been overturned, the curtain pulled down from the patio door, the rod separated. Someone had, indeed, been searching for something.

The bedroom was just off the living room. He moved through its open doorway to see more of the same in there. The mattress had been slashed and pulled from the bed, dresser drawers lay upside down on the carpet, even the linings of Jack's suits in the closet had been ripped out. The depersonalized invasion of Jack Braedman's life continued even after his death. Merchant stared all around him, the cold fire building within him the more of it he swallowed.

He walked slowly around the room, hands on hips, seeing no point in searching anymore, since obviously more thorough hands than his had already done it. Weston and Mills again, or someone else, perhaps the man with the "Chevy" registered to the lobbying firm?

A small desk was overturned near the window, its view of the Capitol dome hampered by driving snow. The desk drawers lay in a pile, their contents scattered expertly. He bent to the debris, extracting a photo from the mess of paper clips and U.S. government pens.

He held it up, studying it. The snapshot was of a young blond woman in color. The shot was posed, the woman smiling catlike against an outdoor scene. She wore a tight yellow sweater with a bright red scarf and matching lipstick. From the fading of the picture and the woman's long, looping curls, he estimated the photo to have been taken in the late forties or early fifties. He turned it over. On the back, in faded maroon ink, were the words ALL MY LOVE . . . MAGGIE.

A noise at the front door startled him, then voices, then a woman's scream. He jammed the photo in his overcoat pocket and hurried into the living room. Eve Braedman stood, face slack and eyes wide, staring at the devastation.

Her daughter, Mindy, was arguing loudly with someone at the door.

"Eve?" he said, feeling like a caught thief.

The woman met his eyes, stared for a second until recognition set in. "My God, Charlie," she said, her voice on the edge of hysteria. "What's going on here?"

"No!" Mindy practically shouted out the door. "We have no statement!"

Merchant got a peek at a microphone pole through the door space, and it was all he needed. He strode resolutely through the mess, hugged Eve briefly, then moved to the doorway, gently shoving Mindy out of the way. "I'll handle this," he whispered.

"Thanks," the girl sighed.

Merchant winked at her. "My pleasure," he said. "Believe me."

He flung open the door and met the press—a young woman as tall as him wearing too much makeup and a scruffy cameraman with a three-day growth of beard. "My name is Charles Merchant," he said. "I'm acting as spokesman for the Braedman family."

The woman nodded to the man who began to roll tape, Merchant smiling congenially. "We'd like a statement from Mrs. Braedman about Joann Durbin's murder. Did she know about her husband's tendencies toward violence? How does she feel about what happened? What's she going to do now?"

Merchant held up a hand, smiling. "Here's Mrs. Braedman's statement to you," he said sweetly. "You people are monsters, vampires sucking the lifeblood of dignity from decent people for a cheap thrill on television. You take advantage of people at their lowest ebb and exploit their misery just for fun—one more scene of the crying woman; one last look at the baby's casket; ask 'em how bad it feels; make 'em really tell you, in close-up, how horrible it was. You got enough? Want more?"

The woman was frowning, the cameraman long finished rolling tape. She looked hard at Merchant. "We have a right to do this," she said.

He met her gaze fully. "And I have the right to be disgusted by it. Now, if there's nothing else. . . ." He slammed the door in the woman's face and turned to Eve, who had righted an overturned kitchen chair and was sitting down, her face buried in her hands.

"I can't believe this," Mindy was saying, her voice strung up in the manner of young people. She was twenty, attending, he thought, Harvard, and he tried to remember what it was like to be so young and so outraged. "Who could have done this?"

"That's what I intend to find out," Merchant replied, and moved another chair through the mess to sit beside Eve. "Don't believe everything you hear."

Eve looked up at him, her bright, intelligent face now slack, her eyes hollow. She had been a pretty woman once, but hadn't aged well. A worrier, he thought, her brow overwrinkled, hard frown lines etched permanently around her lips. "What are you trying to tell me?" she asked, somewhat standoffish.

"I don't think Jack . . . I don't think it happened the way the police say. He didn't kill that girl and he certainly didn't kill himself."

"How do you know?" she asked. "You haven't been really close to Jack in several years. You have no idea of what he'd become."

Mindy hurried to her mother's side. "Don't get worked up over it again," she said, leaning down to put an arm around Eve's shoulder. The girl looked at Merchant. "My father put my mother through hell the last year. He deserved everything he got!"

"Mindy!" Eve said. "Please. . . ."

"Well, it's true," the girl returned. "He was no father to me and no husband to you. I'll be damned if I'm going to make a martyr out of him."

"I'm not trying to make a martyr out of him," Merchant said, addressing himself to Eve, away from the girl and her young emotions. "I'm just trying to arrive at the truth."

Eve stared at him, her eyes red-rimmed and glistening. "You want the truth?" she asked. "All right, here it is. Jack Braedman asked me for a divorce several months ago. When I wouldn't give it to him, he told me he was going to carry on without one. He said he's been living a lie. . . ."

"A lie?" he asked. "What does that mean?"

"Who knows," she said. "What it meant to his family

was that he abandoned us to spend time with that—that—"

"Whore," Mindy said from beside her. "It's as if we'd stopped existing for him. I could never even reach him on the phone, even when it was to offer him a speaking engagement at school."

"That doesn't sound like Jack," Merchant said.

"Like I said, Charlie," Eve replied. "How would you know?"

Merchant fixed his eyes on the floor. "I guess it would be foolish to ask you about anything odd happening in the last several months, anything to do with money or politics?"

Eve wiped at her eyes, a deadly calm seeming to come over her. "Just leave it alone," she said. "The last time I saw my husband was Christmas a year ago. He's dead, Charlie, which means that my pain is finally ending, too. Don't stir it up anymore. What good could it do?"

"But the truth . . ."

"The truth hurts. The truth is nothing but pain and remorse." The woman pointed toward the door. "The truth is what those newspeople wanted, what you wouldn't let them have. Don't tell me about the truth. Give me ignorance and peace every time."

He stood, gesturing around the room. "What about all this?"

"I don't care about it," she said in deadly calm. "Tomorrow I pay someone to come in and two hours later this doesn't exist anymore. I just can't take any more pain, Charlie."

"I understand," he said, but he really didn't. He reached into his pocket, fingering the photograph, deciding not to show it to her even though it was probably harmless. He moved through the mess toward the door. "We've got Arlington for the funeral."

"I know," she said coldly. "I suppose I have you to thank for that dandy little extravaganza, too. The press should love it."

"I just thought—"

"I know," she said, cutting him off. "If you really want to help me, please, just stay out of this. Let it, let Jack, die. Promise me that."

"I can't," he said.

"Then you have become my enemy."

He looked once at Eve, then at Mindy, who was glaring pure hatred at him. "I'm sorry," he said quietly, then disappeared out the door.

◼◼◼◼ NEWSBREAK ◼◼◼◼

MOST THINK PRESIDENT LIED

Washington (AP)—In a CNN/*Time* magazine poll taken after President Macklin's news conference in which he denied any knowledge of offensive missiles in Caribbea, 68 percent of those polled felt that the President did, indeed, have prior knowledge of the events depicted in news broadcasts of the last two days. Only 15 percent of those polled thought the President was telling the truth, with the remaining percentage either undecided or having no opinion on the issue. In an interesting sidebar, in the same poll, fully 60 percent of respondents thought that the news media was overstepping its authority in reporting the touchy international issue at all, citing "liberal bias" of the press as its reason.

Rayburn Office Building, Washington, D.C.
1:15 P.M.

Ben James walked the cavernous halls of the House office building, "Gucci Gulch" as it was called because of the steady stream of resident denizen lobbyists always on the prowl in its confines. James never got there much himself anymore, preferring to leave the legwork to his people. But this was different—special.

He wore a dark suit and red power tie, sinking into the milieu, loving it as he nodded to the surprised faces he passed in the hall, stopping to shake the occasional hand as the tall office doors, mostly open and affixed with the seals of the various states, slid quickly by him.

The North Carolina door hung open, the state flag in a heavy iron base acting as a doorstop. This was the place. He could barely contain his excitement as he walked in. He was ready to change the world this afternoon, and all it depended upon was his ability to sell. Piece of cake.

The outer office was narrow, containing a leather sofa down one wall, the receptionist's desk set at the far end. A young woman sat behind the desk, a small TV in front of her, tuned to C-Span, a listing of the events of the day. The wall was filled with photographs and plaques, most from Wildlife Federations and Peanut Growers' Associations, extolling a quarter century of service by the man who'd occupied the office so long he'd probably take it with him when he retired.

"Pretty girl," he said, the woman looking up, flushing a bit, but smiling. She couldn't be over twenty. He wondered if Hulett was fucking her. He needed to get a fix on that.

"Can I help you?" she asked, green eyes sparkling.

"Well, you can begin by quitting this job and coming to work for me," he said, reaching out to shake her hand. "I'll double whatever Gordon pays you."

The girl giggled and looked down at the desk. "I could never leave the congressman," she said. Maybe he *was* fucking her. He made a mental note to check into it.

He pointed a finger. "Never's a long time," he said, pulling a card out of his pocket and handing it to her. "I'm serious about the offer. Just call. Now, is the congressman in?"

She set the card down and used a pencil to turn the pages of the appointment book. "I don't seem to see your name here, Mr. James."

"Call me BJ," he said, smiling. "And I really appreciate your efficiency, Ms. . . . ?"

"Joiner," she replied. "Cheryl Joiner."

"She's mine," came a hard drawl from the inner office doorway, BJ turning to see Gordon Hulett's immense form filling the door space. They'd have to trim him down somehow. Pork may play well in North Carolina, but was a sign of weakness everywhere else. "There's a whole city full of women for you to pick from, BJ. Leave this one alone."

"What did I do?" James said, exaggerating, shrugging broadly. He winked at Joiner. "I can't even say hello to a pretty girl without somebody making a federal case out of it."

"What brings you all the way over here?" Hulett asked, his bushy eyebrows bunched hard together. "Haven't seen you out this way in months."

"I came by to talk with you, of course. Only I'm told that I don't have an appointment, is that right?"

Hulett smiled, but it held an edge. "My office is always open to you," he said, and BJ could tell that it wasn't easy for him to get the words out. They'd done just enough business together that Hulett couldn't ignore him and both of them knew it. The man stepped out of the door space and motioned BJ within. Then he looked at Cheryl Joiner. "Don't disturb us."

Hulett's office was filled with the same kind of rough wood and leather furniture that jammed up the reception area. Bookcases filled with law books and fishing trophies covered all the walls. Outside the widow, snow came down in blinding sheets. BJ picked an easy chair near the window and sat, pretending to stare out, Hulett pulling a hard-backed chair up before him. "How are you, Gordon?" he asked, not looking at the man.

"In wonderment," Hulett replied, rubbing a beefy hand across his chin. "I believe I'm about to hear something interesting and astounding."

James cocked his head. "Well, I hope you find it to be," he said. "You know, these are interesting and astounding times with crumbling ivory towers and news of war from across the sea. This age of mass communication. Things change . . . rapidly. A man really has to be on his toes to keep up with it all."

Hulett sat back. "I have a committee meeting in fifteen minutes," he said.

"Appropriations Committee?" BJ asked.

"That's tomorrow and you know it," Hulett said. "Let's get on with it, BJ."

"You know, I think the Joint Chiefs did the right thing yesterday . . . voting the way they did, I mean."

Hulett frowned, looking out the window. "The Joint Chiefs fucked us all, the whole damned country. We don't have the money to—"

"We have the money to do whatever we want," James said, his eyes getting harder. "The Joint Chiefs voted to keep jobs for Americans, a lot of them in your district. They voted to keep this country safe, just as they've always done. I've been checking polls this morning, Gordon. Over half the population of this country is against cuts to our military, especially given the nature of the Russian threat in Caribbea."

"The Pentagon tells me that it's just some kind of mistake," Hulett said.

"Right," James replied. "You can take that to the bank. If it was a mistake, how come they didn't vote the cuts then?"

"I don't know that they connected the two subjects."

"Can you be absolutely sure of that?" BJ asked, sitting up on the edge of his chair. "Because if you can't, your Appropriations Committee could go down in history as making the mistake that cost us our freedom."

Hulett stood, walking to the window, his large frame bunched up tight. "You're making too big a thing out of this. It's just budget shit, that's all."

"How's your war chest doing?" James asked.

Hulett flared around to him. "What do you mean by that?" he said, angry.

"Just wondering," BJ said lightly, knowing how touchy politicians could be when reminded of their puppet strings. "I know how much we've put in there. It's your other sources I was wondering about. Running for national office takes a lot of cash these days. Too bad about Jack Braedman."

Hulett narrowed his eyes again and walked slowly past BJ to the other end of the office, prowling like a cat. He finally perched on the edge of his desk. BJ could almost watch the wheels turning in his head. "You're gonna have to slow it down to light speed," he said. "You're movin' in too many directions for me now. What about Jack?"

"Going to the funeral tomorrow?"

"No."

BJ stood, smiling broadly, arms outstretched. "I was just saying that it's too bad about Jack because he would have made a hell of a chief executive. A lot of people expected a lot out of Jack. Hell, I expected a lot. It would have been great to get a Democrat in the White House again. Now they've got to pick up their chips and find a new game. Any suggestions?"

"Yeah . . . drop back and punt."

"Can't do it, Gordon," BJ said, moving right up to the man, cornering him finally and sticking an index finger in his chest. "Elections come right on schedule, like it or not. Nope, we can't punt, but we can try and consolidate our losses by picking a man to run whose integrity and qualifications are beyond reproach, a man of grass-roots sensibilities and universal vision."

Hulett applauded quietly. "Good speech. Where you gonna find Sir Galahad?"

BJ looked around the room. "I don't see anybody else but me and you in here, pardner."

"Wait a minute, wait a minute," the man said, laughing, putting his hands in the air. "I'd like about a pound of whatever dope you're on right now."

"A natural high, my friend," BJ said, slapping the man on the shoulder. "Your name has been coming up with alarming consistency ever since Jack took the big leap."

Hulett moved away from him and slumped into the chair behind his desk, flustered for the first time in BJ's memory. His lips were sputtering soundlessly, but his eyes—his eyes—they were the giveaway. His eyes were glazed, out there somewhere. "I'm just an ole tar heel, crackerbarrel, fat boy. Why'd anybody be interested in runnin' me for president?"

"Besides the fact that you're one of the greatest statesmen this country has ever produced," BJ said, getting into it, "I'll give you the short list. You're a fiscally conservative Democrat, which means you could appeal to crossover vote. You've got the Deep South locked up going in. You're not a party boy, which will come in handy when what Jack did really sinks in. You've got a level head about the importance of our military, our present disagreement notwithstanding. You've always been fair with industry and the industrialized states. You've got a nice smile."

"Naw," the man said. "None of that shit means anything these days. A man's got to have a platform, some forum on which to launch his rocket as it were. I don't—"

"Before you say it," BJ interrupted. "I want you to think about the fact that you *do* have a platform. Your committee has the eyes of the world on it right now. You are sitting in a historic position, the future of this country's military in your hands. Judging from the polls I've been seeing, and from the news from Caribbea, I'd say that you are in a position to launch that rocket of yours tomorrow, right from your committee room. You can be the man who injected reason back into the process by not bartering away our military might. For my part, I can guarantee you the financing and the political backing and the publicity to get you the nomination . . . if you want it, of course."

Hulett stared at him. "Any man would be a fool to want to be president," he said, frowning. "But, then, any man would be a fool to run for office at all."

James stood. "You think about it, Gordon," he said. "The moving finger has settled square on you. It's the call of history and you don't have the right to ignore it. The country needs you, just as much as they need the strong defense you'll be voting on tomorrow." He moved to the door, opening it. "There's worse issues than national defense to build your career on. Not a soul could hold it against you."

"Sure would make my grandkids proud," the man said.

BJ was out the door, then, making a mental note to try and get to Hulett's grandchildren, maybe they could make a call or something before the committee vote. Grandchildren were good—wholesome, innocent—a family man like Hulett could never resist rosy cheeks and puppy-dog eyes.

"BJ," came Hulett's voice from behind. He turned to see him frowning and shaking his head from the doorway. "Damn you for coming to me with this."

BJ smiled. "Get used to it, Gordon. The country needs you." He looked once at Cheryl Joiner, fixing her with deep eyes. The girl was an interesting wild card in all this. He couldn't wait to shuffle her into the deck.

He was out the door, moving down the hall as he looked at his watch. Hulett wasn't the only one with a one-thirty meeting. He took the elevator down with a bunch of local crackers from Iowa or someplace who were wearing red vests, cowboy hats, and big buttons that proclaimed the value of methane gas. By the time they'd reached the first floor he had managed to give business cards to everybody in the elevator and had promised them undying support of anything they could come up with as a by-product of corn.

The cold outside was stupefying, arctic air hovering deadly over the city, but BJ hardly noticed as he floated in a euphoric cloud to his limo with the fake diplomatic card in the window that was parked on Constitution, right in front of the Rayburn Building. BJ had met Rayburn once, years before, quickly concluding that the man's slow, sonorous drawl was far more suited to radio than television, and had dismissed him out of hand.

Constitution was jammed with beat-up silver cars, methane slogans, and giant ears of corn painted all over the things. "Shitkickers," BJ mumbled as he saw his driver waving to him from the far lane.

He moved between two of the parked methane cars, sticking a business card into the wipers of one. Constitution was up to his midcalfs as he crossed it and climbed into the back of his gray stretch limo with the illegally dark-tinted windows, immediately putting on his headset as he brushed snow from his wool suit pants.

His driver, dressed in the full uniform of a capital policeman, turned to smile at him from behind dark glasses. "How'd it go, BJ?" he asked.

"There's only one way it could go, Freddie," he said, punching up June Chan on the number pad. "My way." He pulled the headphones over his ears. "Get me back to the Quarter."

The driver turned and started off immediately as Chan's voice came through on the private line. "Things are jumping here, boss," she said, sounding tinny.

He adjusted the tone with a small knob. "The war council in place?" he asked.

"Just about all of them, though the lobbyists are none too happy about it."

"I know what lobbyists like," he said. "They're no problem. You gotten hold of Barbara yet?"

"She's here."

"I want her out on the Hill today. Tell her to push all the buttons she knows with Hugh McWilliams."

"Budget Committee?"

"I'm counting on her. Also, pull up the files on the other Democrats on the committee for one, two, and three access. I think we might be able to pull the chairman."

"Hulett?" the woman replied, surprised. "You must have offered him the moon."

"It's not what you offer 'em, darlin'," he answered. "It's how you do it. Go in and tell the assembled that I'll be there in five minutes."

He cut communication, sinking back in the seat, letting the warm air from the heater wash over him as they picked their way slowly down snow-clogged Constitution toward Third Street. He'd been building his three-level access points ever since he'd come to Washington, cataloguing and recording the three main vices of human beings— chemicals, sex, and money. He could supply or withhold all of them, and such dispensation brought power. The equation was simple enough. The trick was in convincing people that they were doing the right thing, no matter what it was. He had grown up a preacher's boy, learning just the opposite—how to convince people they were doing the wrong thing. This approach was a lot easier and achieved the same ends.

They turned from Third onto Pennsylvania, BJ getting out at the front entrance, the tall, fake Ionic columns of the Quarter looking oddly imposing under the weight of snowdrifts. He slogged through the mess, the doorman recognizing him and opening the handicapped door beside the revolving one for entrance.

"Thank you, Steve," he said cheerfully as he walked into the lobby of the hotel that comprised the first five floors of the Quarter. Knowing the names of everyone he'd ever met was the keystone of the Ben James philosophy. Remembering people made them feel special, beholden somehow, especially if they perceived the person remembering them to be their superior in station.

The man followed him to the bank of elevators using the key he wore around his neck to open BJ's private elevator. James stepped in, pushed nine, and was off.

It was magic time, time to make everyone realize that reality simply awaited the proper form, and that he was the architect. Life didn't happen; it was made to happen. There were only two kinds of people in the world, those who created and those who lived that creation. What was the defense industry but the creation of a paranoid reality? He wanted to move it from the realm of paranoia into the realm of the mercantile, the economy of staying free and keeping jobs. It was a very small shift with large consequences.

He walked to the end of the hall, the small theater. Several men stood outside the door, smoking cigarettes and talking quietly. "Gentlemen!" he said, smiling wide. "Hope I haven't kept you waiting. Shall we go in?"

He swept past them without eye contact, not wanting to talk to anyone until he'd made his presentation. Some of this was going to go down hard, and he wanted to get it all out before taking the flak.

The theater was full, one hundred fifty seats of crushed purple velour in a semidark, soundproof space. The back of the room was occupied with tables full of coffee urns, orange juice, and pastries. The small stage sat in the front of the room, the covered easel in its place. The noise levels were harsh as he moved down the center aisle and took the stage, infusing himself with confidence and control, making him want to take charge immediately and hold it.

He climbed the stairs to the stage, everything scaled down to three-quarter size to make BJ look bigger and more imposing. "No fights yet, huh?" he said loudly as he stood before the small wooden podium, shoving the microphone aside to speak directly to the group.

His eyes drifted across the crowd as he waited for the noise to die down. "This is the first time all of you have ever occupied the same room together," he began, "a sure sign of how scared all of you are right now."

"Damn right!" somebody called from the center of the crowd.

"In case you don't know one another," he continued, "I want to tell you that corporate executives of General Electric, Northrop Corporation, Boeing, Kamen, Bell, General Dynamics, Lockheed, North American Rockwell, Unitech, Philco-Ford and all its avionics and weapons divisions, Raytheon, and Hughes are here today. There are many others. I just haven't seen all of you yet. Your regular lobbyists are here also. I recognize all of them; they're glaring at me."

There was general laughter, a trifle on the nervous side. "Get on with it," came the same voice from before.

" 'Get on with it,' the man says," James returned. "Okay. I will. I'm here to save your asses. End of speech."

He stood, smiling out at them. The roomful of people stared back at him in dead silence.

"So," he said loudly. "The man told me to get on with it and I did. Why are you still here?"

A man in a black pin-striped suit rose from his seat in the front and glared at BJ. "Is this what you called us here for today?"

"No," BJ said innocently. "I came here to explain to you how you can not only save your businesses, but maybe even improve them. But I refuse to be insulted. Why should I care if you guys go broke or not?" He glared right back at the man, letting them all know who was boss. They really *were* scared or they would have hooted him off the stage. Good. They needed him and knew it. "Should I continue at my own pace?" he asked quietly.

The room quieted immediately, the heckler not heard from again. BJ continued, totally in command. "I promised you the Joint Chiefs vote yesterday," he said. "I delivered. Not one penny was cut from one program. We'll have two more hurdles, the Appropriations Committee tomorrow, and then, most probably, a full House vote. On a recision vote, we only need the House side voting with us because recision must be approved by both houses. It'll be close, but I believe we can win. If we don't, we have another shot in the senate."

The door in the back opened, Melanie Patterson coming slowly in and taking a seat in the back. Nosy. He didn't like that at all. He never wanted any one person to see too much of his operation.

"You see," he said. "America has got to be the greatest country in the world. Our politicians need no other qualifications than the ability to make people like them. Politics therefore attracts people with a sick need for approval at all costs. So, we take these emotionally retarded individuals and give them absolute power over us and tell them they can keep the job only as long as people continue to like them. And so, they perform constantly, jumping through the hoops of public opinion like a cheap dog act. National policy is dictated by the emotional demands of the moment. In a system like this, anything is possible. All we have to do is show the Congress that *public* opinion agrees with *our* opinion."

He moved to the easel, pulling the sheet from it to reveal a list of names printed in large black letters. "Starting with the committee," he said. "There are fifty-eight members in the House Appropriations Committee. Thirty-five of them are Democrats, twenty-three Republicans." He pointed to a block of names. "The ones with the check marks are solid votes in our favor. These are people whose own districts are targeted for massive cuts and they have to vote against them to get reelected next time. No sweat. The Repubs on the committee will be easier to turn than the Democrats. My count gives us twenty-five solid votes at the moment. We only need five more to take the committee, and I can deliver them by morning."

"You'll never get it past Hulett," a woman in the front dressed in red called out. "He's totally committed."

"He's totally committed to me." BJ smiled, picking up the Magic Marker on the easel ledge and putting a slightly premature check mark next to the chairman's name. "I already got him."

There were loud murmurs from the crowd, BJ deciding to show them the good old boy. "Come on, fellas," he called. "You think I'd go to all this here trouble if I was gonna let you down?"

"You're really serious, aren't you?" the man in black said after rising.

"Ladies and gentlemen," BJ said. "This is Mr. Whitworth from Unitech, the firm that designs the triggering mechanisms for our atomic bombs and the guidance systems on our rockets. To answer your question—yes, sir,

I am quite serious, just as I was when I promised you the Joint Chiefs yesterday. I recall you didn't believe me then, either."

The man shrugged broadly, sitting again.

BJ looked around the room. He had them now. He could feel the room turning to his point of view. His smile broadened. "I've got deep files," he said, "and the good Lord has endowed me with a considerable gift of gab. We can pull this off. Even now the polls are showing signs of American restlessness in the face of the news from Caribbea, and the people know what they're talking about. Always trust the folks. The pressure of the citizens of this great country, plus all the hard work we can muster, will certainly put us over the top.

"We're even now saturating mailing lists to deliver our strong defense message to the people, putting a great deal of pressure on the legislators themselves. Groups sympathetic to our patriotic message of freedom through strength have been using their permission cards to deluge the Congress with cables and letters. I'm going to need to concentrate myself, though, and that's why I asked you here today.

"I need to get you guys together, all of you. I need your information, every bit of it, on the men whose minds we will be changing. I need to not be duplicating efforts, either. That's why I'm asking you to forgo your usual ways and means, and let me handle everything for all of you."

"What do we do with our lobbyists?" came a voice from the back.

"Fire 'em," James said with a smile.

The room erupted into turmoil, people jumping up and screaming, shaking their fists. BJ smiled through it all, giving them the opportunity to vent their rage and frustration before stepping in.

The lobbyists had left their seats and were moving toward the stage. When they were within striking distance, BJ put up his hands and yelled for quiet. Then he said, "Oh, I forgot to mention. I will be happy to hire all the lobbyists in this room to come and work for me, at say . . . a fifty percent increase in wages and benefits."

The room quieted again, James unable to keep the grin off his face. He loved moving the emotions back and forth.

The angry faces were suddenly slack and wide-eyed. "The reason I'm doing this," he said, "is to better coordinate our efforts. We're fighting a war here, and missed or faulty communication is a great reason for failure on the battlefield, as most of you already know. We're all going to work together instead of at cross-purposes. Together we're strong. Together we're unstoppable. I guarantee it, and I've never lost yet!"

Melanie Patterson sat in the back of the little theater in stunned disbelief as she watched the leaders of major corporations fall all over themselves to turn their autonomy over to BJ. They crowded around the stage now, firing questions that were glibly answered, the crowd totally in his constantly shifting hands.

Didn't they realize that once they turned everything over to him that he'd have them forevermore? Didn't they understand that without their own lobbyists they were totally at his mercy? She shook her head over the thought of all the information BJ would glean when they opened their files to him. And through it all, she couldn't help but notice his continual references to Caribbea, the one fixed area of activity that he could point to as a reason for change.

His fingers were in this and his fingers were dirty. Jerry Delany, Joann, and Jack Braedman had already died because of this, along with a pilot whose name she couldn't even remember. BJ had gone from playing king to playing God.

She stood, moving back toward the door. She turned back once to see BJ looking above the sea of heads surrounding the stage to stare daggers at her. He smiled when she caught his eye, and the smile chilled her. The games were getting out of hand. She had to figure a way to play it all in her favor before everything fell to pieces.

If it wasn't too late already.

Arlington 2:49 P.M.

Charles Merchant stood beside his pool table, staring down intently at the black and white photos of Joann

Durbin's body spread out before him, stark in the white light. Waterloo lay beneath his pile of evidence on the Braedman case, the woman's body where the Paris Wood used to be. He'd come back to the photos again and again, always freshly astounded by the milk-white perfection of the woman, always freshly stunned by the fact that the lifeforce had been so casually left to slip away. Her eyes were open, staring. There was no peace to those eyes; only a deep pain showed through.

He forced himself to straighten up, out of the bite of the overhead table light. He picked up the disposable lighter left on the table's edge and lit the pipe that was clenched tightly between his teeth, inhaling only lightly. Why would she have done it? What troubles could possibly have overtaken this woman—beautiful, well-to-do, connected—to make her end it all? Nothing happened without reasons. Nothing.

He blew out a long streamer of smoke to swirl above the table, caught in the light, showing the photos through a glossy haze. He picked up a full-length shot, his eyes slowly roving the woman's delicate curves, her legs slightly spread. Every muscle had been toned and developed. He told himself it was only professional curiosity that brought him to the photos again and again.

The woman's life had been even more perfect than her body. From the evidence in the report, Joann Durbin was a real human being only in the most casual of senses, as if her life had been written by a Hollywood press agent. As a teenager she'd won beauty pageants with her looks and academic recognition with her brain. She'd had no steady boyfriends when she'd lived with her parents, no formal ties to anything. And when she'd left Memphis for Washington, she'd never returned, only calling her parents on special occasions. They hadn't seen her for five years. She'd kept in contact with none of her college friends, and had been close to no one.

He took the pipe out and lay it in the ashtray that balanced precariously on the corner pocket, leaning down into the light again to stare at the photos. He remembered her still, there on the bathroom floor, the rustlike blood thick and wet on her arms. Her skin had been so clear, like a human canvas waiting for the right artist to etch his masterpiece.

She'd gone to work in Washington for a firm called Legislative Services, a lobbying outfit that seemingly specialized in nothing. Her job description had been "consultant," whatever that meant, and the metro police investigator had been told that she'd had very little connection to the actual operation of the place. There were no friends to question, no coworkers to share stories about her. She'd quit her job six months before, presumably to avoid conflict of interest in her relationship with Braedman. She'd leased the townhouse in Georgetown from a group called Landmark Investments, who said she paid on time and in cash. Her neighbors were surprised to find that anyone had lived there at all.

That was it, the whole book on Joann Durbin. She'd lived a secret her entire life, then took it to the grave with her. He wanted to crack it, to get inside that secret place just as much as he wanted to save Jack's human soul before it was stripped from him. A spiral notebook lay atop the mound of Mont Saint-Jean, squashing a battalion of Englishmen. He moved around the table to it, writing on the notebook: Landmark Investment—call Josh; Legislative Services, nature of business.

He moved back to his station, taking up the pipe again. The jigsaw puzzle lay before him, and the way to crack any jigsaw was in organization. He took the info on Durbin and put it into a small pile. Then he took the scant, nearly nonexistent info on Braedman and put it beside that pile. Atop Braedman's pile he placed the photo he'd found in the wreck of the apartment. Atop that he placed the newspaper clippings he'd gleaned that featured quotes and stories involving the killer cops, Mills and Weston. And then, just for a kicker, he placed a laserphoto of Jerry Delany, the downed pilot, atop Durbin's pile and made a note in the spiral to get Gene Tillotson to check into the man. That left one piece of evidence—the writing on the mirror. On a piece of paper, he did the best he could in approximating the way the words looked on the mirror:

JERRY + JOANN (in a heart shape);
YOUR MOVE, BJ

Why that particular message—YOUR MOVE? It was almost as if she were issuing a challenge. But to whom? Who or what was BJ? Ben James had those initials, the head of LSI. . . .

He placed the message atop Joann's stack. When finished, he had two piles of knowns and unknowns—knowledge and ignorance. The trick was to become educated in the ignorant areas, and the phone was the best place to begin.

He dug through the Joann Durbin stack until coming up with the phone number of Legislative Services. He moved to the wall phone by the bar and dialed it, setting his pipe on the bar top. A pleasant-sounding woman's voice answered after the second ring.

"Legislative Services, may I help you?" the voice asked.

"This is Charles Merchant with the Justice Department," he said. "We've moved into the investigation of the deaths of Jack Braedman and Joann Durbin, and wondered if I might make an appointment for some follow-up questions."

"We were informed earlier today that the investigation was closed," the voice, still pleasant, returned.

"That's the police investigation," he answered. The woman was sharp. "The government has several areas still working here, Miss . . ."

"Chan," the woman answered. "We'd be more than happy to cooperate fully with a government investigation, Mr. Merchant, although I believe that it would be a waste of time. No one here knows anything about the Durbin woman."

"Well, let us be the judge of that, Miss Chan," he said. "Would this afternoon be all right to come in and—"

"No," she said. "This afternoon is impossible. We'll need time to check out your credentials, of course, and then to notify our counsel and get him here, easier said than done, sir."

"I just want to ask a few questions."

"Of whom, Mr. Merchant? Of whom do you wish to ask these questions?"

"Of whoever . . . knew anything about the woman."

"I've already told you that no one did," she returned,

voice ever cheerful. "Believe me, it would be a waste of your time to come out here."

"Let me be the judge of—"

"You've already said that," she interrupted. "Tell you what we'll do. I'll make copies of our personnel files on Joann Durbin and send them to you at Justice. I'll inquire if anyone has anything to add."

"Then you won't make an appointment for me?"

"Our time is too valuable," she said. "If your credentials check out, and if you read the personnel files and find something there that means something, we'll make an appointment. Good day, Mr. Merchant."

The phone clicked in his ear, dead air quickly replaced by the persistent dial tone. He stood there dumbly. He'd been put in his place, and quite handily, too. So much for the direct approach. He dialed again, this time the congressional switchboard. "Could I have Phil Rosen's office?" he said, picking up the pipe again, sticking it between his teeth cold.

"Speaker Rosen's office," came a tired-sounding male voice, a job that Josh had once occupied.

"Is the congressman in?" he said, hoping to catch him before the one-thirty committees. "It's Charles Merchant calling."

"Hold please."

He waited, Rosen's ebullient voice coming on within a minute. "Charlie," he said. "Good party last night."

"Thanks. You sound chipper today."

"The damage control's going well," the man replied. "Despite the telegrams, most everybody's holding firm on the defense spending thing."

"Telegrams?" He removed the pipe and set it back on the bar, not wanting to get into a political debate with someone he was asking a favor of.

"In the hundreds of thousands," Rosen said. "Somebody's organized a hell of an effort to stop us from making the budget cuts. They're hitting the people with military bases or defense contractors in their districts." The man stopped talking, chuckling instead. "I don't guess you called me to listen to my problems, though. What's up?"

"What do you know about a company called Legislative

Services?" Merchant asked. "I think they're some kind of lobbying firm."

"Some kind is right," Rosen replied. "They're what's become known as a superlobbyist."

"What the hell is that?"

"Where you been, Charlie? The superlobbyists are umbrella groups for other lobbys. In other words, when a lot of clout is needed somewhere, the superlobbyist represents the interests, and the power, of many special interests. PACs limit the amount any one lobby is able to spend on a particular congressman. But a superlobby, representing many, has the combined resources of all."

"That doesn't seem right," Merchant said, turning to stare at the piles of evidence on the pool table. "Financing for entire campaigns could theoretically come from one person."

"Can and does," Rosen answered. "Where the hell do you think Jack Braedman got the war chest to run for president?"

"Legislative Services was financing his campaign?"

"Their motto is 'More bang for the buck' and they mean it."

"The dead girl worked for them."

"Not surprised. Look, if you want to learn some more about these guys, why don't you come around tomorrow and I'll introduce you to some people who really know about LSI. Meanwhile, we'll hit the Budget Committee and watch them fuck the Pentagon. What do you think?"

"I think it's been too long since I came out to the Hill," Merchant said. "You want to do lunch first?"

"Sure, how about noon at my office?"

"Thanks, Phil. So long."

He hung up, hearing Linda coming in the front door. So Jack was in tight with the lobbyists Joann Durbin worked for, the same people who, apparently, filmed him from Dumbarton Street. And the two cops were also tied to LSI through the photographer . . . and how else? Finally a string to grab hold of.

"Charlie?" came Linda's voice from the living room.

"Back here," he called, wishing she'd have waited another hour or so to come home. Things were slotting together a bit and Linda represented a division of intellect and emotion. God, he wished he had an office to go to.

"We're going to be buried before morning," Linda Merchant said, walking into the den as she unwound a long scarf designed to look like a piano keyboard. Her hair and overcoat were dusted white. "I haven't seen it snow so much in years."

"Hmm," Merchant replied as he drifted back to the table. "The weatherman says it's going to get worse. How was your day?"

It didn't make any sense. If Braedman was LSI's boy, then why would they kill him? And what did the suicide have to do with that?

"A lot of cancellations," she said. "Tomorrow we'll be lucky to get into the parking lot. Only four showed up for Group today. We had a new kid there. Very odd."

"Odd?" he echoed, using the old technique of repeating the last word to keep someone talking. That way he could listen without really listening. Linda worked part-time at a catch-all therapy and rehab place called the Wellness Center. She had been able to qualify as a counselor with a minimum of training to deal with substance abusers and other unsociable types. He thought it was all a bunch of nonsense, just catering to people too weak to practice self-control; but it seemed to fulfill Linda somehow, so he didn't attempt to stand in her way. Besides, something down inside told him she wouldn't allow him to stand in her way on this.

"There's something . . . strange about his manner," she answered, shrugging out of the heavy coat and laying it across a chair, Charlie making a mental note to hang it up in a few minutes. "I don't believe I've ever seen anyone so despondent, yet he refuses to talk about his problem. I'm really afraid he's suicidal."

"Suicidal?" he repeated, trying to figure out where the police fit into the scheme of things. And Bignell. What was his role? Why was this so far-reaching?

"It's scary. We've talked him into coming back tomorrow. Maybe we'll have better luck then." She moved up to the table, wrapping her arms around his neck, forcing him to turn to face her. He let his arms slip around her waist, pulling her close so she wouldn't see his irritation.

"I'm sorry that we fought last night," she said. "Guess I'm getting touchy in my old age."

"It's not you," he said, pulling back now to look at her. "I'm just a control addict, that's all. Don't pay any attention."

They kissed, but it was perfunctory, Charlie afraid that it would lead to some strung-out reconciliation that he didn't have the time for. She felt dumpy in his arms, her muscles gone soft from years of inactivity; her face, while still pretty, seemed also to be falling victim to gravity. She should keep herself up, work at her appearance. People judged by what they saw.

He searched for her eyes, but they were looking past him, down at the evidence on the table. "What's this?" she said, pulling away from him to begin thumbing through the material. She came up with one of the photos of the dead woman.

"Oh, how horrible!" she said, staring transfixed at the picture. "Is this . . . this . . . ?"

"Joann Durbin," he said, snatching the picture away from her, wishing she'd leave his stuff alone.

"Where'd you get all this?"

"Honey," he said, leading her away from the table, "this just business. I'm going to be doing a little checking on my own, that's all."

"Despite Eve Braedman?"

He jerked, staring hard at her. "What's Eve got to do with anything?"

"You talked to her today, didn't you?" There was an accusation in her voice.

"Yes, but . . ."

"Well, so did I." Linda moved several paces from him. "She called me, nearly hysterical. She said the police have closed the investigation into Jack's death, but that you're pursuing it on your own."

"Yes, that's true," he said, watching her face harden. "There are still a lot of unanswered questions."

"Not to the police," she returned. "Look. Your friend screwed it up in a big way. Why can't you just leave it alone, let him have peace. Let Eve have peace, for God's sake."

"Somebody murdered Jack," he said. "I can't leave that alone."

"Why can't you? You left *him* alone for years." She had it, that exasperated look again. The one she always got when she came up against his ideals. "It's over. We've got to care about the living, and right now, you're driving Eve Braedman into a nervous breakdown."

"You're oversimplifying," he returned, moving back to the bar to retrieve his pipe. He put it in his mouth, clamping down hard, angry. "People drive themselves into nervous breakdowns. That's a lot of bullsh—"

"Don't say it," she warned. "Don't start attacking my job."

"I'm not attacking anything," he said, walking back for the lighter at the pool table. "I'm just looking for the truth, that's all."

"Why?" she asked loudly. "What's so all-fired hot about the truth. Look around you. We live in a city of lies, a world of lies."

"I can't believe you're even asking that question," he said, lighting the pipe and drawing deeply, his eyes drifting to the photo of Joann that his wife had left on the table. He gently set it back in its place in the stack of evidence. "The truth is the only thing that matters to me."

"No," she said, shaking her head wildly. "All that matters to you is controlling your little world and everybody in it. Give it up, Charlie. Stop trying to be everyone's father. I've spent my whole life as an army widow while you chased after your own shadow, trying to make the world love you. I'm too old and worn out to keep playing this stupid game with you."

"It's not a game," he said harshly.

She pointed to the pool table. "Then why is all that stuff up there with your toys?"

"Toys . . ."

"It's me or your pipe dreams," she said, crossing her arms across her chest, head high. "I'm not going to chase your wild geese anymore. I didn't screw your career up, you did, and I'll be damned if I'm going to continue to suffer with it. Look in the mirror, Charlie. You're getting old. Nobody cares. You're through, retired. They've taken the brass ring off the carousel. Give it up or give me up."

"If that's all you think of me—"

Her scream cut him off. His eyes caught hers, but they were staring past him, out the window. One hand was at her mouth, the other was pointing. "Outside!" she said. "Someone was looking in the window!"

He turned and bolted for the door immediately, the pipe dropping from his mouth, his fingers fumbling for a second with the back-door lock before getting it open. He charged into the three-foot snowdrift piled up against the back of his house.

His head jerked in the direction of the back window, a set of footprints leading up to it and away. He turned, picking up the prints before him and running with them. They curved around the back of the house and down the driveway to the street. He never even noticed the cold as he charged, coatless, down the driveway, just in time to see the taillights of a red Jaguar disappearing into the snow swirls a block distant.

His whole body was shaking as the rage and the cold made themselves known. "I'm going to get you, you son of a bitch," he said, breathing heavy frost, but it was lost in the roar of the storm.

■■■■■■■ NEWSBREAK ■■■■■■■

FROM THE DESK OF DONALD MERCK
PRESIDENT, NATIONAL COMMUNICATIONS
CORPORATION, NEWS DIVISION

To: All producers: Latin American, Washington,
    General Investigative Divisions
Date: 6 February
Re: Operation Hot Potato (confidential)

Dear troops,

We're going to have to carry the ball ourselves with
the Sheila Traynor story. The government's holding
fast to denial and no other leaks have appeared to
corroborate our evidence. We must lean on Central
America. Work the off-roads on this thing. Get me a
feature on the death of that Caribbean Foreign
Minister Ramirez, and keep juicing the dead pilots
from yesterday. Also, try and track down something
on that mercenary, Ken Breedlove, who's been tied
in with the Caribbean situation.

  If we keep doing sidebars from the region,
Traynor's story will appear to fit right in. It will lend
credence while we dig up some more poop. I'm
going to make this a priority. Sorry about any other
assignments you may have been working on, but
the Network's credibility is on the line here and we
cannot appear to the viewers to be dropping the
ball. Hopefully this will straighten itself out in a
couple of days. Good luck.

                                             —Don

Tegucigalpa, Honduras 7:35 P.M.

It was the most wondrous of nights. As Ken Breedlove sat
on the narrow veranda of the Hotel Alameda, listening to
the annoying drone of the voices within the adjoining
room, he felt the center of a magnificent spectacle put on
just for him.

Seven stories below the twinkling splendor of the
Honduran capital spread itself wide before him like a
woman giving herself fully to a waiting lover, its treasures
bursting forth in unashamed abandon.

He put his feet up on the fluted iron railing and took a
long drag from his cigar. "'In nature's infinite book of
secrecy,'" he whispered reverently, quoting Shakespeare,
"'a little I can read.'"

It was the middle of the eight-day religious feast Feria de Suyapa, the streets and the hotels filled with a heroic and pathetic lot of supplicants from all over the world: cripples, the deformed, the terminally ill, and the poor. They were all lining up in desperation to beg miracles from the Virgin of Suyapa, the patron saint of Honduras, through her representation—a tiny statue only a few inches tall.

They had formed a candlelight procession beginning at the Church of the Virgin of Sorrows three blocks from his vantage point, an imposing Spanish adobe Cathedral built in the seventeenth century, and wound through the city of half a million that had never lost its colonial small-town look and feel. The procession, one hundred thirty thousand moving pinpricks of light, snaked through the narrow, winding streets and brightly colored houses clustered in barrios built directly into the hillsides, then finally made its way four miles out of town to the unfinished basilica of Suyapa, where the Virgin resided. The pilgrims sang Spanish hymns, the sounds drifting in small pulsing waves up to his hearing, beating like angel wings against his consciousness.

"I don't understand," came the American ambassador's voice form the attached room, "why I had to come out here alone. If we have to talk, why not talk through regular channels?"

"It's not that simple," Molina responded. "This talk cannot go through regular channels."

Breedlove smiled, wiping an ash off his bright white suit pants. He loved stirring up the pot. If the ambassador was freaked out now, just wait until he got to talking to the man.

He watched the line of moving light as it inched inexorably toward the horizon, the foothills of the Agalta Mountains farther in the distance adding their own sparkle to the diamond as hundreds of small fires burned away at the flesh of the mountainsides, the *campesinos* preparing the ground for cultivation through slash-and-burn techniques. It made for a extraordinary sunset, the carcinogens swelling the air, refracting the visible light spectrum even more, the entire evening sky seemingly on fire in reds and purples. And he couldn't help but feel, as he sat upon his lofty aerie, that all of it had been done just for him.

It was all so perfect, as if the universe were a giant set of gears ready to mesh into place. He was in Honduras, man. *Honduras!* This was the original banana republic, a land wrested from the primitive for United States fruit companies by Lee Christmas. Through most of this century, export taxes paid by Americans for bananas offset the entire cost of Honduran government. It was only fitting that his career go into high gear in these same magical lands. It was still possible for one man to make himself heard in today's world and Honduras was the place to prove it. His nukes were going to make him the new Lee Christmas, a man capable of changing the world on a whim. When those babies went up, it would be as if two new suns were rising, illuminating his name for everyone to see. He loved Honduras as he'd never love a woman.

". . . don't deny that there's a problem on the border," the ambassador was saying. "I just question the wisdom of a secret meeting to discuss it."

"Because it must be."

"But why?"

"Please . . . Mr. Jurgenson. Just hear me out, then you will see."

Breedlove chuckled again, a waft of warm air, carrying music, blew over him. Tegucigalpa was a paradise weather-wise, a seven-month rainy season give or take, and temperatures never reaching much above the mid-seventies. Maybe he'd make his home here sometime.

He set down his cigar and picked up the highball glass full of Jack Daniel's, taking a small sip. He wondered what BJ was doing right now. He enjoyed thinking about BJ, enjoyed on the one hand the fact that a high roller would care to associate with him, and on the other hand he enjoyed the notion that he was, by far, James's superior. The man had a good head, no doubt about that. They had dialed each other in almost immediately. The thing he had over Ben James, however, was a working knowledge of the beautifully pristine cunning of the jungle—and not just the physical jungle.

James was a man who used money and people selfishly

and relentlessly while Breed simply considered himself a visionary. While James could plot, Breed could breathe life into the plotting, which was how he was able to scope BJ out from day one. This may all have been BJ's idea, but he was the one who made it fly. It would cost the man. It would cost him more than the extra million in the suitcase. It would cost him everything by the time Breed was finished with him. He had been too good a pupil. When BJ had said to him, "When you dream, dream big," he had taken it to heart. The bard had understood. "The hind that would be mated with the lion must die for love." So would go the alliance between Ben James and Ken Breedlove.

He heard the rasp of the sliding screen patio door and turned his body just slightly, so that he could keep it in his vision. Molina's head poked through to frown into the night, his face fat, a fleshy piñata. "He's going to leave," the man said in heavily accented English. "He's uncomfortable. I told you that. . . ."

Breedlove raised a hand for silence. "Bring him on out, then," he said. "I'll do the talking."

Molina nodded, relief flooding his face. He disappeared back into the room. Breedlove stood, straightening out the creases in his silk suit. He was a man of action in a world of inaction. His philosophy was to be found in the ancients, in Musashi's *Book of Five Rings*, the ultimate in situational ethics. He reduced life to systems, ways of naming conflict in everyday life and determining strategies to beat them. He certainly had a system for the American ambassador—it was called masturbation.

He watched the ambassador walk out onto the veranda, his eyes, at first, caught up in the spectacle of Feria de Suyapa. Molina followed him out, sliding the door closed loudly.

"Beautiful night," Breedlove said, the ambassador jerking in his direction.

The man looked at him hard for several seconds, his face a mask. Breed thought he'd like to play poker with him sometime. Then Jurgenson turned without a word and strode for the sliding door, cursing under his breath when he discovered he couldn't open it.

"Mr. Ambassador," Breedlove said, holding the keys up to rattle in the breeze.

"I demand—" the ambassador began, Breedlove cutting him off.

"I understand all that," he said. "We just don't have time for it. I promise I'll let you out after we've finished talking."

The man stared at him for a long moment, then walked to the rail, leaning on it on stiff arms, his eyes hard as ball bearings as he fixed them on the city. Breedlove motioned Molina to the far side of the patio and joined Jurgenson at the rail, affecting the same stiff-armed posture.

"Don't know if I've ever seen anything prettier," he said.

"A terrible security problem," the ambassador replied. "Too many people coming into the city too fast: libres trying to move all the way inland, Companeros following them. Honduran undercover. American intel. Everybody with guns."

"Do you know who I am?"

"No," the man answered without hesitation.

"Now you see," Breedlove replied. "We need to begin this relationship on an honest basis. As American ambassador, you are also CIA Tegucigalpa Station Chief, and probably know my face at this point better than your own."

"I don't believe we're going to have a relationship, Mr. Breedlove," Jurgenson said, admitting what both of them already knew.

"Call me Ken," Breedlove replied. "Can I call you Mark?"

The man pissed off Breedlove with a look that he must reserve for his mestizo pool boy and said, "I want you to let me out of here right now, you fucking traitor."

Breedlove took a breath, swallowing hard. "Whatever else you might think of me," he said, a slight quiver to his voice, "believe that I'm a patriot. I've given my life and my heart to the defense of freedom in this region, which is more than I can say for our own Congress. I would die for the American flag, Mark. I'd do it in a minute and without question." He turned the man to face him, eye to eye, nose to nose. "Would you?"

Jurgenson tried to turn away, but Breedlove grabbed him by the lapels of his dark blue serge suit and held him steady, leaving the man with nowhere to look but the bottomless pools of his captor's eyes. "Would you?" he repeated.

Breedlove burned fire into him. Jurgenson, bludgeoned by the intensity, sagged physically in Breed's grasp, his eyes now darting, afraid to light.

"I'm sorry if I offended you," the ambassador said, and Breedlove knew that no matter what, at this point the man would at least listen to him.

He freed Jurgenson, straightening the man's tie. "The Companeros are getting ready to make a big, final push to wipe out the *libre unos*," he said conversationally. "They intend to insinuate themselves across the border and destroy the refugee bases and all supply towns or settlement towns. They intend to do it soon, within days. You and I, Mark, have got to stop it."

"I really don't want to hear any of this," Jurgenson said, tightening his lips. "Especially from you."

"'The nature of bad news infects the teller,'" Breed answered, and the man looked at him in surprise.

"*Antony and Cleopatra*," the ambassador said, smiling. "You're well read."

"I'm a fucking Renaissance man," Breed answered.

Jurgenson turned from the cityscape, leaning with his back against the rail. He took a long breath, spying Breed's drink perched on the wooden table. "You got any more of that?"

"Sure," Breedlove replied, looking at Molina. "Carlos, get the ambassador some whiskey."

The man nodded, smiling, hurrying his large, squat frame off the patio. As Honduran interior minister, Molina carried just enough clout to sound important, and had just little enough power to not be dangerous. He'd always been good blood chit to Breedlove.

"Where do you get your information?" Jurgenson asked. "We've seen nothing come through that would suggest what you've just told me."

"I get my information the way I've always gotten my information," Breed answered, moving back to the table to pick up his own drink. "From border peasants, from *libre* recon, from Companero army informers. I've been working this region for ten years, Mark. We may have put our puppet in the president's chair, but nothing else has changed. The reason that you haven't heard any of this is that the United States of America has made Central America a nonpriority area, and so you hardly bother with good intel anymore. Tell me I'm lying about the downgrade in status."

The man sucked air through his teeth, his eyes finding the veranda floor suddenly interesting. He didn't answer. He didn't have to. Breedlove hated the way politics changed things. One day the freedom fighters are the heroes of the world. The next day they're a destabilizing influence and everybody dutifully shifts their feelings.

"Carlos has, independently, come across the same information," Breed continued. "He fears, I believe, that the Companeros won't stop at the border cities. He believes that once they incur and encounter resistance, it will give them an excuse to retake some old disputed border territory. Bingo! A major war in Central America and the potential of dangerous destabilization."

Molina reappeared on the patio, two tumblers full of Jack Daniel's in his hand. He gave one to the ambassador, then drank greedily from his own.

"How does your government react to the news you've just given me?" Jurgenson asked Molina. "I've heard nothing."

"Unfortunately," Molina said, "my country is a—what do you call it—subsidiary of American business interests and, by extension, the American government. The American government doesn't want to hear about the libres and Companeros right now, not while they're cutting back on military spending. They say it's 'bad timing.'"

Jurgenson smiled and took a long drink. "Fair enough," he said. "If that is, indeed, the case, then what can you possibly hope to accomplish by coming to me?"

"I've studied you," Breedlove said, the strains of "Ave Maria" blowing in on a stiff breeze. "Through your days at Harvard, through your business career and the diplomatic services, you've always proved yourself a decent man and a loyal American. You're an old college friend of the President, and have his ear. Nobody wants to lose Honduras,

Mark. They just don't want to have to deal with its problems."

"And you do want to," the ambassador said, taking a long drink, loosening up.

"Ken has been our most loyal friend," Molina interrupted. "He has always worked shoulder to shoulder with us. Listen to his words. They are true."

Jurgenson shrugged, his still young-looking face fixed in amusement. "I still don't see how I can help you?"

Below, at ground level, hotel management was running off a group of beggars at the hotel doors, cursing and screaming as they dumped pots of dirty dishwater on the interlopers. Breedlove leaned way over the rail to watch the show.

"You can get on a telephone," he said, not looking at Jurgenson, "and call the President. You can tell him that this country is in danger of going down the pump if he doesn't send some troops over here right away to discourage the Caribbean incursion." He looked at Jurgenson. The man was smiling. "At the very least he can save the *libre* cause. When Madrina falls, we'll need them again."

"And should I tell him," Jurgenson said, "that I got all my information from the man wanted in connection with the assassination of the Caribbean foreign minister, the man who, even now, is being stripped of his citizenship at the State Department level?"

Breedlove straightened, draining his glass and dropping it to break on the veranda floor. "You're not taking me seriously," he said.

"Show him," Molina said quietly. "Just show him."

Breedlove moved from the rail to the far edge of the porch. "I represent a number of American business interests who believe very strongly that this region should remain free." He picked up the aluminum suitcase and put it on the wooden table, knocking off the ashtray containing his cigar. "These business interests believe in an aggressive defense of freedom and feel that it is a good investment to retain people in this region who believe the same way. Mr. Ambassador. . . ."

The man walked quizzically up to the table, Breedlove opening the suitcase to reveal the million dollars within. "Half of this goes to Carlos for his part," he said. "The other five hundred thousand is yours if you make that phone call. That's all I'll ask you to do."

The man stared at the money, then looked up, the tension now a physical thing, charging the air as Molina made small whimpering noises.

"I see your point," the ambassador said.

"Then you'll do it?"

The man frowned for a long moment, his eyes narrowed in concentration. "Not quite yet," he answered after a moment. "I'll need a little more than your word to go on here."

"More?" Breedlove said, listening carefully.

The man nodded, rubbing a hand across his face, his eyes never leaving the money. "We'll need an . . . event of some sort, an incident that I can point to as part of the conspiracy."

He looked at Breedlove then, and Breed knew they were on the same side. "How large an event are you talking about?" he replied.

"Large enough to be of international significance," Jurgenson answered without hesitation.

"I understand," Breedlove said, nodding slightly. "And then, of course, there are the nukes."

The man's eyes widened. "You know something about that?" he said.

"I might," Breedlove said. "If and when you make that phone call, I just might give you all the details."

Jurgenson took a long look at the money. "Gentlemen," he said, "I believe we might be able to do some good business together."

"That's what Honduras is for," Molina said, beaming. "Business."

And the men all shook hands, sealing the bargain.

FBI Headquarters 7:23 P.M.

As Sheila Traynor watched the female FBI agent knock her coffee all over the table, her male counterparts jumping up to avoid the spill, she reflected that the problem, the actual problem here, was that the FBI didn't really understand show business. Or politics, for that matter.

She'd been made to sit in this god-awful conference room for most of the day and part of the evening, the deep walnut paneling and indirect lighting wearing on her nerves and her patience, closing her in. It had been almost dark before they'd let her call her lawyer, and by the time she'd arrived, Traynor wanted nothing more than a good show to fuck all of them.

She was getting it.

The agent they'd brought in, Madelline Tennyson, had apparently become some feminist groundbreaker years before by cracking the all-male buddy club and working her way up to agent. Maybe they thought that would make some sort of difference, since Traynor realized finally that the reason she'd been put on ice for so long was to have Ms. Hot Ass flown in from the boonies somewhere especially for the interview. But all the woman had found when she'd shown up was that she was dealing with real professionals, women who outclassed her in looks and in political knowledge and clout. She looked mousy and unimportant in a gray rayon suit. And anybody who thought that looks didn't make a difference was insane.

And so they got their party. Sheila sat at the big table with her show-business lawyer, Alicia Brown-Williams, a sultry black lady, dressed to devastate in bright red wool offset by a string of the most incredible black pearls Traynor had ever seen. Ms. Hot Ass sat at the other end of the table with her two male flunkies who did nothing more than watch, listen, and scribble little notes to each other and the woman. The peanut gallery was the real laugh, though. A group of absolutely solemn men sat on hard-backed chairs or stood, ringing the small conference-room walls. Their pedigree was deserving of a Russian spy.

The President's domestic adviser, Rob Danton, sat whispering to the under secretary of defense, a middle-aged Jewish lawyer named Feldstein. Danton was young, early thirties, and had been the architect of the military budget recision plan to return already Appropriated money to the government coffers. Both men sat in deadly concentration, legs crossed at the knee, hunched over somewhat, heads close together. An unnamed NSC representative, a Marine colonel in full dress uniform, stood, unmoving, just as he had for the last two hours, his cap under his arm, his eyes fixed on the small spiral notebook he continually wrote on with a mechanical pencil. Finally the FBI director himself, William Sutter, paced nervously back and forth across the room. He was dressed in a three-piece suit of the darkest black, his thumbs hitched in his vest pockets, his thinning hair slicked down hard across the crown of his head. He never spoke. A practically invisible stenographer sat in a corner before her small machine, her fingers rummaging the keys to a steady clack-clack rhythm. No one smoked.

"All we're saying," Alicia told the agent, "is that you're either going to have to charge my client with something or let her go."

"And I've told you already," the Tennyson woman replied with undisguised distaste, "that this is simply an interview, that so far no charges are being contemplated."

Tennyson stood looking down at the coffee she had spilled in the heat of anger. As her helpers hurried to clean it up with paper towels from the lavatory, everyone in the room knew it was the badge of her inability to handle her situation. She couldn't get beyond her adversaries' natural superiority in this arena to make any headway.

"Then I request that you let my client leave for the night," the lawyer said. "You've kept her locked up here for an entire day, denying her constitutional rights to representation. Incarceration without filing charges is against the law, as I assumed you already knew."

The woman turned and winked at Sheila, both of them enjoying their turn at bat. These were the moments Sheila lived for.

"Can't we get beyond this?" Tennyson asked, walking partway down the length of the table, metaphorically entering her opponent's territory. "We just want a hint of the documentation of this thing. We want to get a line on it, that's all."

"Then why don't you just call me up," Traynor said. "We'll chat."

Tennyson, always on the edge, slammed a hand down hard on the tabletop, the other agents grabbing their paper cups of coffee before they spilled. "Damnit! We can't just 'chat' over matters of national security."

"Then you admit," Brown-Williams said quickly, "that this information is true and valid, and that it is a matter of national security?"

Ms. Hot Ass looked at Rob Danton. It was subtle, but Traynor caught it. The man shook his head just slightly.

"No," Tennyson said. "We're not admitting anything of the kind."

"Which brings us right back to where we've spent the last two hours," Brown-Williams said in fake exasperation. "If this is not a matter of national security, if my client's story is not true, then you are holding her in violation of the law, since only a national security matter would give you the right to hold her at all. This is the United States of America, Miss Tennyson. I suggest you read your Constitution."

The woman leaned down, jaw muscles so tight they stood out like mumps on her chin. "I have read the Constitution," she said through clenched teeth. "Perhaps you should read the Alien and Sedition Act."

"Sedition." Brown-Williams smiled, her teeth bright white and perfect. "Now we're getting somewhere. Are you saying that my client is inciting a riot?"

Tennyson took a scrap of paper from her flunky, looking at it quickly before wadding it up. "If, indeed," she said, "your client is making up her information, a federal sedition case could be made."

"I assure you," Traynor said, "that I didn't make up my information."

"Then where did you get it?" Tennyson demanded.

"My source wishes to remain anonymous," Traynor replied for the fiftieth time. They were trapped in a conundrum, a verbal puzzle that continually fed back into itself with no clear avenues out. "Why don't you guys just admit the truth of my allegations. Stop lying to the American people."

"We're not lying," Tennyson said, turning and walking back down to her own end of the table. She whirled back around, her face softening somewhat. "Maybe you're being duped. Tell us your source and we can double-check."

"You've seen my evidence," Traynor replied. "I'd

hardly call that duped." She laughed. "If you knew my source, you'd believe it, too. From my standpoint, Miss Tennyson, you're the one being duped. The government has set you up here to defend an indefensible position and trick me into giving up my constitutional rights at the same time. And, honey, it ain't gonna work."

Tennyson just stared at her, the light draining completely from her eyes. To Traynor, it seemed the first time in the entire meeting that the woman was beginning to realize the already foregone conclusion—that she was being asked to make very large determinations with precious little to go on. For Tennyson, it was a no-win situation.

"This is your country," she practically whispered, all pretense of superiority gone, and with it the vaunted policeman image. "Can't we just work this out . . . you know, talk about it? We need your knowledge."

"Why?" Traynor asked.

Once again, Tennyson looked at the President's man, Danton. Once again, the man shook his head. Tennyson slumped into her chair, all but beaten.

"It's over," Alicia whispered to her.

"Miss Tennyson," Danton said quietly, curling a finger toward her as he caught a glimpse of his watch. It had interested Traynor that the man had spent the entire evening with an eye on his watch. She wondered where it was he had to go.

Tennyson glared in jealous anger at Traynor, then stood quietly, walking over to the man, the two of them conferring in hushed tones.

"How do I look?" Brown-Williams asked Traynor. "We're going to be out on the streets in about five minutes, and on national news in five minutes after that."

"You look great, of course," Traynor said. "Are they really going to let me go?"

"They've got no choice, sweetheart. They tried to fuck us, but now all they've got is a handful of dick. You could use a touch of lipstick, by the way."

Traynor smiled. "Hell with the lipstick," she said. "The only cameras this face looks good before are my own. You think I'm going to let somebody else have my story? That's what you're here for."

"No!" Tennyson said loudly, walking away several paces from Danton. "You can't do that yet. Give me until tomorrow, I . . ."

"Madelline," the FBI director said, staring evenly at her, Traynor realizing now why he was here. "There's no choice. Forget it."

Tennyson looked all around the room, taking more failure upon herself than seemed proper to Traynor. The woman's eyes finally settled on her and Traynor read the sense of loss there. Madelline Tennyson had been washed and hung out to dry, and Sheila wondered if this whole thing had been somebody's idea of a payback.

Without a word, Tennyson turned and walked from the room, head down. That's the big leagues for you.

Rob Danton cleared his throat, standing. "Miss Traynor," he said. "Miss, ah, Brown-Williams. You're free to go. We may want to bring you back for more questioning later, though."

"And we may file a false arrest and imprisonment charge against you," Alicia said, standing and picking up her Gucci briefcase. "The least you owe my client is an apology."

Danton smiled and looked at his watch again. "We are certainly sorry that we held you here for so long, Miss Traynor. We will take steps to avoid such inconvenience in the future. And, Miss Traynor . . . there will be a future. This isn't finished yet."

"Is that a threat?" Brown-Williams asked.

The man shook his head. "No," he said. "Not a threat. Perhaps more of a grim inevitability. All I can tell you is this: You'd better be damned sure of your source material on this matter."

"I am," Sheila said, standing also. "Gentlemen, it's been real."

Both she and the lawyer moved out of the room without a backward glance, Traynor wondering how all of them felt being frozen out by a woman. For all the lip service to the contrary, politics was still a man's game.

One of the agents trailed out after them, their coats on his arm, following at a discreet distance just to make sure they found their way out of the building. He joined them at the elevator, giving them their coats, Brown-Williams slinking into a jet-black cape of virgin wool to match her outfit.

"Get off at one," the innocuous agent said. "The door's right in front of you."

He turned and walked off as the elevator doors slid open, the women remaining silent until they'd climbed in and started down.

"Now what?" Traynor asked.

"Just who is your source?" Alicia asked.

"A little knowledge can be a dangerous thing," Traynor replied. "I don't believe I'll tell you."

"The government doesn't know," the lawyer returned. "They were shooting completely in the dark."

Traynor looked at her in surprise. "You really think so?"

Brown-Williams let out a long breath. "Honey, ain't no way we would have waltzed out of there if they'd had anything. They'd have held you for a hearing, at least. The only possibility going is that they had nothing and were just hoping you'd let some information slip. This source of yours must be God himself."

"Yeah," Traynor said, dejected. "I was supposed to meet with him this afternoon. Hope it doesn't queer anything."

The elevator settled on one with a slight quiver, the doors wheezing open to the sight of Donald Merck in sunglasses and a snap-brimmed hat that had knocked his toupee asunder.

"Thank God you're free," he said, grabbing her up in his arms and squeezing her tightly. What the hell was wrong with him? "I can't believe those sons of bitches kept you locked up so long."

"I was in a conference room, Don," she said, extricating herself from his grasp. "Don't worry about it."

"Here, put these on." He shoved a pair of sunglasses at her, fitting them crookedly on the bridge of her nose. "I've got a limo waiting."

"A limo," Alicia said, fluttering her eyelids. "You must have done something right. Let me go first to run interference."

They moved off across the semidark, blandly efficient lobby that led to the Eighth Street entrance, Brown-

Williams ten paces in front of them. Traynor wasn't
surprised to see the huge number of newspeople waiting
outside. After all, this was the news of the decade. But the
snow . . . the snow surprised her. It had not stopped
falling and lay hugging everything in deep pile, like a huge
comforter upon a small bed. Washington, through the
windows, looked more like a cemetery, its slab-stone
public buildings like quiet headstones and mausoleums.

Alicia went out first, the reporters and cameras and
pole mikes surrounding her immediately, sucking her into
their vortex.

"You ready?" Merck asked. "We'll make a run for it." He
smiled. "All lady reporters can run in high heels, right?"

Traynor nodded. "Whoever said I was a lady."

They hit the push-bar doors at a jog, the arctic air taking
her breath away at first. The snow was knee-deep and still
swirling crazily out of the black night sky as they skirted
the beehive of reporters, their combined breath a cloud of
steam hanging in the bite of their mini-kleigs.

Traynor couldn't keep the grin from splitting her face as
she slogged through the deepening field of white toward
the gray stretch limo by the curb. This was all for her, all
the attention, all the excitement. Sheila Traynor had
found her way into hard news the only way she could—
she became it.

As she reached the car, her feet already numbing, she
heard people calling her name from behind, the news
recognizing her too late. The back door opened from
within and she all but dove through, Merck behind,
pushing her.

"Good evening, Ms. Traynor," came a gentle, pastoral
voice. She looked at kindly blue eyes and luminescent
white hair beside her, her heart leaping as she fought to
keep the surprise off her face.

"M-Mr. Lehman," she said, looking in shock at the
network president. "I certainly wasn't expecting to see you
here tonight."

"Go!" Merck ordered as the newsmen waded toward
them, cursing, cameras above their heads on stiff arms,
like soldiers in a war movie crossing a river. The limo
rolled slowly away from the curb, complaining as its
wheels spun wildly, trying to get a bite on the ice.

"And why not, my dear?" the man said, reaching out a bloodless white hand to shake. She took it, and the return grip was weak, sickly. "You are the one to bring me out on a night like this. Your story is beginning to smell like the new Watergate. Congratulations."

She looked at him in puzzlement.

"The new footage you had sent over was nuclear, it was so hot," Merck said excitedly, stroking her arm, and Traynor realized that his newfound affection was in direct proportion to her value to him.

"The new footage," she repeated, wondering what the hell the man was talking about.

"Yeah," Merck said. "How did you manage to get it smuggled over to us while you were in custody?"

Traynor smiled, easing out of her high heels to rub her cold feet. "A woman's got to have some secrets," she replied. "Where are we going, by the way?"

"Airport," Lehman said. "They're holding the shuttle for us back to Manhattan. We're giving you live air tonight."

Her heart was in her throat. "How much?" she asked.

"How's forty-five minutes sound?" Merck asked. "We'll go on at eleven-thirty. That'll give you time to write your copy to go with the tape, and time for us to come up with segues to work in the sidebars we've put together. After you go on tonight, there'll be absolutely no doubt that you're presenting the truth to the public. We can bring the administration to its knees."

"Was there ever any doubt?" she asked, wondering just what the hell was going on.

Pennsylvania Quarter 11:13 P.M.

Melanie Patterson stared at the Cadillac's upholstered ceiling and smelled the heady perfume of the leather interior as Sam Mooney, the representative from Alabama, dry humped her on its wide backseat. Her black crepe Christian Dior after-five was pushed up above her hips, her bare skin tingling under the air generated by the backseat heaters as he gently pulled her breasts out of the gown's bodice, all the while groaning down deep in his throat.

"You've got a Boeing plant in Tuscaloosa," she whispered, her black three-quarter gloved hands holding his lips to her left breast. "It employs over five hundred people."

He pulled himself fully atop her, his penis the size of a brick within his tuxedo pants. They were face-to-face, his breath husky with Scotch and lust. He was a powerful man; it emanated in waves from his eyes. Those eyes at the moment, though, were glazed slightly. "Everybody's got a Boeing plant," he said. "B-1 strategy. Worked, too. And it employs three hundred forty-seven people, not five hundred. God, honey. You sure you don't want to go somewhere else? I haven't have sex in a car since I was seventeen."

She reached between them, grabbing his penis to stroke right through his pants. "Then pretend you're seventeen again," she said. "And the plant employs exactly five hundred and eleven people, counting the part-time help. Things so good you can take those folks off the payroll and put them on unemployment?"

He rolled half off her to unzip his pants, his erection plopping out. Even in the pale outer lighting of the Pennsylvania Quarter's underground car park she could see the blue veins and bulging purple head of his grotesquely large penis, thinking of how fast she would have run if she'd seen that thing at age seventeen. Word was that Mooney had the third biggest cock in Congress, just behind the Senate minority leader and a page from New York City.

"I don't want to see anybody out of work," he said, breathing hard. "We're having to make some tough choices here for the good of the country."

She slid partway down the seat to take him in her mouth, her hand gently massaging the whole time. He moaned low, a continuous, kittenish wail, his hands coming to her head to push her up and down.

This had been a good deal for Mel. She'd found that BJ was working late tonight and figured there was a reason. Taking care of business with the senator here, at the

Quarter, meant that she could keep an eye on comings and goings, also. Although it looked like "comings" was the problem at the moment.

Mooney was bucking his hips slightly, rising to meet her lips. His face was strained, red and sweating. She'd learned a simply fact about sex when she was very young and it had always stood her well: The longer you can keep a man from orgasm, the more intense the orgasm when it does come, the better lover he'll think you are.

She pulled her mouth away from Mooney's dick and grabbed it hard with her right hand, holding him back, stopping the surge. "Not yet," she cooed, his bucking hips settling down somewhat. "You don't get away that easily."

"G-God . . . Mel," he strained through clenched teeth. "You m-make me crazy. I want to fuck you. Please . . . now."

"Not without protection," she said.

"I don't have—"

"I'm like the Boy Scouts, lover." She smiled, sliding up to kiss him hard on the lips. "I always come prepared."

She swung away from him, sitting on the edge of the seat to go through her purse. She came out with a prophylactic, unwrapping it carefully to dangle before him. "Now, while I put this on you," she said, hoping the thing was big enough to fit, "you explain to me how destroying so many jobs and taking away so much manufacturing revenue and weakening the military that much in a government that simply prints up as much money as it wants anyway is a good thing for the country."

"The international monetary system is a little more complex than 'printing up as much money as it wants,'" he said as she bent to his penis, flicking her tongue quickly over the sensitive spot beneath the bulbous head. "We have to maintain a certain position in the . . . oooh."

She was masturbating him with two hands, blurring over his arguments in a fundamental way. Perhaps he'd never be able to think about these issues again without remembering. Most men thought that the prophylactic was a comedown to sex, a mechanical act amid real passion. But to the Japanese, the putting on of the rubber was an erotic part of foreplay. As she slowly unsheathed the thing over his penis, she stroked and licked and kissed in the Japanese way, his hips jerking crazily by the time she was finished. She grabbed him again until he subsided.

"Sit up," she said low, never letting go of his penis.

As he sat up, she pulled his pants down and over his shoes, his legs muscled and thick with black hair. Mooney was a handsome man, early forties, who'd made his money in lumber before running for office. Like many in the South, he was a name-only Democrat, a Republican in Democrat's clothing. The legacy of the carpetbagger. She was beginning to look forward to the, how would BJ say it, consummation of the contract.

She moved to straddle him, the man taking his penis in hand to guide it into her. "I want it slow," she said, just poised above him.

Impatiently, he jerked upward, impaling her. "And I just want it," he said, both of them laughing as she sank all the way down upon him, amazed that he could fit.

The squeal of tires made them jerk, headlights swinging quickly across their position, the two of them in unspoken cooperation falling sideways as the light swept above them, a car passing behind.

"Sit up," she said, still astride him. "I want to see who's here."

"Hotel guests," he said, trying to pull her back. "What dif—"

"Sit up," she said, baring her long-nailed fangs and growling. "I'm nosy."

"Okay . . . okay," he said, the two of them rocking back and forth to try to sit again without breaking contact. They'd been at a dinner given by North American Rockwell earlier that evening, Mel suggesting an early night, maneuvering Mooney into position by asking to be brought to her car at the Quarter. As they got upright, the senator's dick buried inside her to the hilt, she stared out into the stark angles and shadows of the underground concrete building, long, flickering fluorescent lights bathing the place in an eerie glow—a washed-out half-light.

She heard echoing laughter, but hadn't seen anyone yet. She had gotten Mooney to park just near the elevator, though. Anyone wanting access to the building would have to come by them.

"C'mon, baby," Mooney cooed, trying to get a rhythm going. "I can't stand to wait much longer."

She smiled down at him, moving her hips fluidly back and forth for several seconds, then stopping. "Your district's not going to understand your unwillingness to support our military, especially in light of the problems in Caribbea."

"Fuck Caribbea," he said, trying to get her moving with his large hands.

"No." She smiled, rising partway off him. "Fuck me."

She rode him for a moment, watching his face, stopping when it looked at if he were going to come. He tried to force her to get moving again, but she clamped her thighs hard on his buttocks, and refused to budge.

"Damn you," he swore.

"Wait," she said. "Listen."

He stopped, face straining, as the sound of footsteps thunking hollowly on the cement floor drew near.

"There." She pointed, two men emerging, talking and laughing, from between several parked cars and walking toward the elevators.

They were in civilian clothes, but she recognized them immediately. It was the two cops who'd been with Braedman when he died—Weston and Mills.

As they passed her position, she leaned forward, pulling herself against Mooney, the man wrapping his arms around her and physically lifting her off his erection and dropping her back down again, grunting like a pig the entire time.

The two cops passed within a foot of the back of the car, and would have seen everything had they cared to look. But they passed, moving right to the elevator.

"Yeah," Mooney was saying. "Oh, yeah."

There was no stopping him now as he pushed quickly toward the long delayed orgasm, Mel giving herself over to the convenient fantasy of her high-school senior prom and the sex she'd had with her chemistry teacher that night in the back of his car. It was a favorite memory and heated her up quickly.

When the cops disappeared into the elevator, she began to ride Mooney hard, determined to be right there with him on the roller coaster. As she lost herself in the fantasy, she watched the numbers climb on the chrome board beside the elevator—three . . . four . . . five . . . they weren't going to the hotel.

"Oh, God!" Mooney groaned. "I'm going to come."

"Yesss," she rasped, her well-conditioned hips moving viciously now, grinding hard. Floor six . . . seven . . . eight.

Mooney jerked wildly, screaming so loud that Mel feared he had hurt himself and that in itself was enough to push her also, quivering wildly, over the edge. Floor nine . . . ten.

She collapsed, sobbing loudly against him, the man lying back, arms outstretched, his mouth open, jaw slack as his head lolled from side to side on the seat back.

"Oh, my," she whispered, kissing him wetly on the neck.

So, they'd gone all the way to ten, nothing up there this time of night except Ben James. That iced it completely for her. She was convinced of it now. Ben James had committed murder. Or was assassination the proper term?

"Jesus, honey," Mooney said, sliding her off him, his dick large even as it deflated. "You liked to kill me just then. I swear I've never met anybody like you in my life."

"It's you," she said, looking him deeply in the eyes. "You bring this out in me. No one else does."

He sat up finally, sliding the limp rubber off and pulling his pants on. He shook his head. "I may never walk again."

She laughed. "Tomorrow morning you'll be walking . . . and fucking again."

He buckled his pants and looked at her. "Tomorrow morning I'll be wanting you again," he replied. "What do you say?"

She smoothed her dress down, stuffing her panties and hose into her purse. "Don't know," she said, opening the car door to frigid air. She stepped out, grabbing her coat, winking at him. "Give me a call tomorrow . . . after the Appropriations vote. Bye now."

She pushed the door closed without another word and turned, walking away, her own Mercedes 380 SL on the other side of the garage. She reached her car, listening as Mooney's drove out into the night.

The heater came on immediately when she started the

engine, warming her up again. Reaching into her handbag, she pulled out a pin-sized joint and lit it, toking casually as she waited. It didn't take long.

Mills and Weston were back out within ten minutes, both of them acting as if they'd just won the lottery. She slid down in the seat as they moved across the garage, the blond one carrying an attaché case he hadn't brought in with him.

The payoff. She knew it. At this point, she had two choices, either run or stick. It was that simple. If she ran, it would mean safety and the possibility of immune testimony if they caught on to BJ's little coup d'état. If she stuck, there was blackmail and the possibility of a much improved position if he could pull this off. But more than all that was the kind of deadly fascination with the game that pilots called target fixation. How far could BJ push this? Where, exactly, did he think he could go with it? And, most importantly, what could she get out of it?

She stubbed out the roach in her ashtray and put the car in gear. She was going to see how close to the fire she could get without getting burned.

Arlington 11:49 P.M.

Charlie Merchant sat in pale blue pajamas at the foot of the bed in the guest room, staring in stunned disbelief at the visuals he saw playing before him on the nineteen-inch TV screen. His area survey books sat opened beside him, along with a still-classified DOD weapons' master list. This had once been Josh's room, though no traces of his life there remained. It was a section of the house Charlie hadn't seen close up in three years, since he'd last had the room painted. Two hours previously, Linda had informed him that it was to be his sleeping quarters until further notice. He thought about that as he scribbled barely coherent notes on a yellow legal pad in the washed-out flickering light of the television.

It was a news special, hosted by the female newscaster

who'd broken the Caribbean missile story. He found her presentation uninformed and overly dramatic, the same reason he never watched her nightly news show, but the story content was incredible. Moving apparently by Braille, the network seemed to be putting together a picture that looked remarkably like the one he'd been building with his small chain of evidence.

There'd been a story on Jerry Delany, the dead pilot, showing a history of arrests and broken lives. Charged with fragging an officer in Vietnam at age nineteen, he'd spent the next twenty years of his life proving over and over again that the innocent verdict reached in that case had been seriously in error. He'd smuggled and sold everything from guns to drugs to illegal aliens to women. He'd spent ten of those last twenty years in seven different prisons both here and abroad. How the hell could he get a sensitive government job? One thing for sure, Delany was dirty enough to have been tied up with the people who killed Jack. That, in itself, was enough to keep Mr. Delany's name in the hopper. This was where Gene's DIA resources would really come in handy.

There'd been two feature stories that had tied together dealing with a mercenary soldier named Breedlove and his possible connection to the death of the Caribbean foreign minister a week ago. The only connection that led to Delany was small, but intensely interesting. The Companero military was now saying that Breedlove had been spotted in the area of Cabo Gracias a Dios the night of the plane downing, a place barely five miles from the crash site.

But they'd saved the best for last, and it had gotten the blood pounding in his head just to see it. There was videotape footage of the delivery of two nuclear missiles to an under-construction missile base, with a small warehouse, railroad tracks, and camouflage netting covering construction areas, the entire operation supervised by a god-almighty *Russian* lieutenant colonel. Shit was going to fly over these shots. It looked to him like the world was getting ready to come apart. These were good, crisp shots, showing much detail, even managing to get a fairly good look at the weapons themselves. And the incredible part of it was—he recognized the terrain.

He'd spent two 3-year tours in Central America back in the mid-fifties, and as was his custom, he'd vacationed a great deal in country, trying to learn about the land he inhabited. Those missiles were in Central America, all right. They were in a huge section of rain forest shared by Caribbea and Honduras called the Mosquito Coast, in the section named Gracias a Dios, by Christopher Columbus's crew when they'd survived a vicious storm there in 1495. He'd camped there for a week in 1958. It was dense, impenetrable, and easy to lose yourself in. He'd recognize it anywhere.

And there were the missiles themselves. He wasn't sure of Russian configurations, but as he sat staring down at the DOD book, it sure seemed to him that the picture of the Raytheon/Martin XMIM-104B Bearcat looked a whole lot like the missiles being unloaded into the warehouse onscreen.

He looked down again at the book, straining in the flickering light to read. The Bearcat carried a two-megaton nuclear warhead with a Unitech trigger. He closed the book and stared at the screen as the missiles finally disappeared into the corrugated tin warehouse, the picture ending. It made no sense that Russia would have access to Bearcat missiles. They probably have their own birds that look like it.

He tossed the book aside. Then why did all this make him feel so uneasy? He reached out and pulled the DOD book back closer to the others. Something weird was going on, and the closer he got to it, the more confused it became.

What could Jack Braedman's death possibly have to do with missiles in Central America? If Jack and Joann Durbin had ties to Legislative Services, and Joann had ties to Jerry Delany, was it logical to assume that Delany had ties to Legislative Services? All three of them were dead. Legislative Services was still alive.

It was the key ingredient. He had to crack it.

He went to bed, but sleep eluded him. Something incredible was going on right under all of their noses and somehow *he* was a part of it. He could feel the excitement of it coursing through his body, physically throbbing. It was heady and frightening all at the same time and at the bottom end he couldn't help but feel that Fate had taken a hand in his life. Linda had given him an ultimatum—her or the investigation. There was no way that she could possibly understand that he had been waiting for this his entire life and nothing could keep him from it. Nothing.

It was the call to greatness, and no matter what the cost, he couldn't help but follow.

FEBRUARY 6,
WEDNESDAY

▰▰▰▰▰▰ NEWSBREAK ▰▰▰▰▰▰

DOWN AND DIRTY

In this week's issue of the *National Inquisitor*, learn the frightening untold story of sex addiction and murder in the highest seats of power as we reveal the sordid, deadly past of the man who would be king, Jack Braedman. For the first time anywhere, we explore the well-hidden past of the man who'd fooled an entire nation, from the wartime atrocities to his charter membership in John Kennedy's infamous "rat pack." Revealed here for the first time is Braedman's role as go-between in the Kennedy brothers' liaisons with Marilyn Monroe and the suspicions surrounding his actions during the hours of her untimely death. Don't miss JACK BRAEDMAN, DOWN AND DIRTY . . . THE MONROE CONNECTION in the next issue of the *Inquisitor*, on sale February 12.

—press release, February 6

SOVIETS TO PROTEST

Washington (AP) — The Soviet Union is expected to lodge a formal protest in the United Nations this morning over what it calls "a flagrant and unethical misuse of its media to spread lies and propaganda—disinformation of the worst sort," in the showing of videotapes alleging the introduction of nuclear missiles into Caribbea.

"There is no truth in any of these pictures or stories," Soviet ambassador to the United States, Yuri Petrovich, said in a hastily called news conference this morning. "They are counterproductive to the continuing process of world peace and must be stopped. The days of lies and propaganda must end."

The Republic of Caribbea is also continuing to protest the assertion by the United States that its coastal installations shot down an American cargo plane over international waters, an alleged action they categorically deny. In a startling news conference, Caribbean President Maria Madrina accused the U.S. of "provocations" against the people of Caribbean, implicating her once-solid allies in the assassination of Foreign Minister Ramirez. Latin American experts see this as an indication of how slim her hold on power has become as she tries to placate the Companero majority and lessen tensions in her own country. What this will do to U.S./Caribbean relations is not clear at this time.

In an angry reply, State Department spokesman Norman Wortham said that the Soviets simply "don't understand" the concept of a free press and accused them of "shamelessly grandstanding for publicity" in filing the largely toothless protest. And in a startling addendum, the official statement added what might be the initial crack in the armor of secrecy that has covered the issue until now. "The Soviet Union needs to understand," Wortham said, reading directly from the statement, "that the United States of America will not tolerate the presence of offensive nuclear weapons anywhere in this hemisphere. Just because we're silent, doesn't mean we're not watching. If a shoe fits, one should wear it."

". . . You've reached the Smithson residence. No one can come to the phone right now. We're having to stay away from the house and the television so we won't have to watch those pictures about those nonexistent missiles that are not being put into Caribbea. So, at the tone please leave your name, number, and a brief message. Thank you."

—answering machine message

Auasbila, Honduras Daybreak

Ken Breedlove sat in the uppermost branches of the pine tree and reconnoitered the area around the sleepy border city through his field glasses. He felt good about this mission, its accomplishment the last unknown component to the forward momentum of his plans. Everything else he'd leave to human nature. The intellectual Tupamaro terrorists of Uruguay had invented a word for it—*coyuntura*—coming together, the merging of diverse elements to make a unified whole. Precise timing. Careful adaptation of tactics to a situation. That was the purpose of his visit to Auasbila this morning, to merge the elements.

The smell of coffee drifted lazily up to him as his people grunted through their wake-up ritual below, preparing themselves for a long morning. They were all good men, but too much time spent living off the rain forest would wear them down. It was imperative that things be made to move swiftly in this, swiftly enough for everyone to hold together as a unit.

The small Indian city was just beginning to come awake in the distance, scattered roosters crowing, the old priest hobbling his way down the dusty main street, a ragamuffin altar boy in short pants dragging his feet behind. The damned place, a few dirt streets of rough adobe shacks with thatch or corrugated tin roofs, sat out in the middle of fucking nowhere, just on the edge of the rain forests, no more than a mile from the Coco River—the Caribbean border. The city had spent its existence serving *compasenio* farmers from the grasslands and a bit of river traffic.

But Breed's reason for being here had nothing to do with that.

Since 1985, Auasbila had been a stopover checkpoint for *libre* guerrillas escaping to Honduran refugee camps. They'd move through, register, perhaps stay for a few days awaiting assignment. He'd been there a great many times himself, leading small bands of refugees to safety in the manner of a *coyote*, and for the same reason—money. People who choose to flee their home country usually do so after reaching the realization that escape is more important than anything else. Property, diamonds, vehicles, and even sexual favors are all up for grabs at times like that. Had the flow of refugees not trickled out eight months earlier, he would have been content to operate indefinitely in that netherworld. But life has its little exigencies, and he was forced to move on. It was while he was in Washington trying to drum up *libre* aid that he met Ben James.

He started back down the tree, his binoculars bouncing against his chest. It was time to move, before outside traffic came in, before those inside went out. He could feel the excitement building within him. Before the next hour was finished, life would have moved inexorably forward, dropping into a new groove of his creation.

When he got to within ten feet of the ground, he dropped, coming up in a crouch in the middle of the makeshift camp, a hundred feet from the dirt roadway and out of sight on the edge of the pine forest, their two deuce-and-a-halfs parked on the perimeter. They'd been there only long enough to grab a couple hours sleep, for they'd had business that took them far into the night.

Ten men in various stages of multinational fatigue dress stood or squatted around the small campfire, cleaning the humidity from their weapons, drinking coffee out of the tin cups of their mess kits. Loners mostly, they kept to themselves, psyching up as best they knew how to face the morning. They were men who could kill without thought or compassion. Sure, they killed for ideology, or thought they did, but Breed knew they really did it because it was the most exciting way they knew to make a living. In the real or concrete jungles of the world they lived as they chose beyond law, beyond reason—an insane and glorious existence. And usually a short one.

He pulled off his fatigue cap and wiped the sweat from the already hot sun from his forehead, the tattoo of cherubic Puck glowing in rosy, subdued colors on his left arm. "Gentlemen," he said, smiling as he turned a complete circle to look at all of them. "Welcome to the focal point of world politics. Willie. Break out the Russian guns."

"Fuck that," said a small, squat blondie named Mulroy, holding up his American automatic. "I told you last night, I use nothing but my M-16. I ain't never seen an AK-47 didn't jam before the clip was gone."

"Don't worry about it, Joe," Breed returned. "We're not giving up any marksmanship medals this trip. You agreed—"

"I use nothing but my own weapon," the man said adamantly, standing slowly to stare Breed down.

"The gun's just a tool, you fuck," Breedlove said, anger beginning to seep in. He didn't have time for this. "Don't get attached to it."

"I'm using the M-16."

Wee Willie came walking up to Breed, his arms loaded down with the Russian assault rifles. He took one, tossing it hard to Mulroy, the man having to drop his own gun to grab it.

"You'll use the Kalishnikov and like it," he said coldly, "or we can share up and you can walk right now."

The man studied him, agonizing for several long seconds. He couldn't have been over five feet four, a little guy who'd gotten a chip on his shoulder and toughened up to survive. His kind never knew how to back off. He looked around the group. "You'd shoot me before I got ten feet," he said.

"'Good Hamlet,'" Breed said, bolting another Kalishnikov and pointing it at the man, "'cast thy nighted color off, and let thine eye look like a friend on Denmark.'"

"Stop it, Breed," Mulroy said, his adrenal juices lost somewhere in the juncture between fear and anger. "I'll use the fucking gun."

Breedlove smiled. "'Distilled almost to jelly with the act of fear,'" he said, throwing his arms wide to the camp.

"My friends. We're all in the process of becoming independently wealthy. We're in the process of having as much fun as we've had in months. Let's not ruin it with pettiness." He nodded to Willie. "Pass 'em out."

As the weapons moved around the group, Breed made as much explanation as was necessary. One thing he'd learned from Ben James was the art of never telling more than anyone needed to know at any given moment.

"As you know," he said, "plunder is the reward of the merc and is his domain. Today, we plunder in order to save democracy. Jamie, I want you and your squad to set up perimeter watch . . . surround the whole damned place and kill anything that tries to get out."

"Will we meet with resistance, Captain?" a long-haired young one with passionless eyes and a Marlboro dangling from his lips asked.

"A few *libres* hanging around perhaps," Breedlove answered. "We'll need a bit to make this look right. Those of you going into town . . . be methodical. Work from the edges toward the middle. Anything you want there is yours. Anything. The only imperative here is that no one leaves alive. Kill everything, and be back out in thirty minutes. Questions?"

A massacre leaves little to question or supplement. With muted laughter and a few whoops the men stood, eyes alight, and moved toward the trucks.

"Business first!" Breedlove called to their backs. "Fun second."

He walked the pine-needled ground toward his truck, the smells fresh and invigorating after the smothering cloak of rain forest decay they'd been living in. He reached the truck, swinging up into the passenger seat as Willie climbed behind the wheel. "Give Jamie a minute to get into position," he told the man. "We can't afford any fuckups on this one."

"Yeah," Willie said, settling back with a groan into the seat. "Getting too old for this shit."

"What the hell else would you do?" Breed replied. "Buddy, there isn't anything but a cold slab in the meat freezer waiting for you from here."

"What you gonna do about Mulroy?" Willie asked, starting the engine.

"Things have a way of working themselves out." Breed-love smiled. "Let's get it."

The truck whined painfully into gear, starting off with a jerk. Willie skirted the clearing and rode the tall grasses on the edge of the forest until they refound the road into town. Once on the road, Auasbila stood out in bold relief a mile distant against the brown fields that surrounded it.

He could see the other truck reach the edge of the city, disgorging men who charged off in two directions. The smile involuntarily spread across his face as he anticipated the kill. "Willie. See that telephone pole on the east edge of town? Drop me off there."

"Sure thing, Cap'n."

They bounced on, gears straining and crying under Willie's aggressive hand until Auasbila filled the windshield. They passed Jamie's now-empty truck and rolled on, the phone pole connected up to what looked like a general store and bait shop of some kind, a Coca-Cola sign, in Spanish, tacked up on the door. "Here's fine," Breed said, opening his door and jumping out before the truck could even stop rolling. He clutched an AK-47 in his right hand. He moved past an old, rusted gas pump toward the door, not even looking back at the truck as it continued on. Willie knew his job and would attend to it.

A few people were out on the streets now, moving erratically as poor people tend to do. He'd made a study of how people moved, one of Musashi's systems he'd developed to survive hostile environments by blending in. Americans tended to move quickly, in a straight line, toward their destination. Poor people tended to walk slowly and zigzag a lot. The really poor seemed to move almost in circles. Odd.

He walked to the slatted wooden door of the *abacería* and tried the handle. Locked. Bringing up a jungle-booted foot, he kicked out viciously, the door exploding inward in a shower of splinters. He moved inside the small building, dust hanging thickly in the morning light, dancing across a counterful of candies and cigarettes, canned and dry goods stacked on shelves behind. A heavy black telephone that looked fifty years old rested on the countertop.

"*Que es?*" came a voice from the back of the place. "*Que es?*"

Breed primed the bolt and walked toward the telephone just as a withered, white-haired old man dressed in his underwear came charging in, stopping with wide eyes at the sight of the red-haired man with the gun.

"Good night, sweet prince," Breed said cheerily, giving the old man a full second burst on full auto, the man's stomach exploding blood and intestines as he went down with a loud wheeze, almost a sigh.

His wife, much younger and grossly fat, ran into the room with a dirty sheet wrapped around her. When she saw the dead man on the floor, she shrieked, piercing like a siren, falling to her knees to clutch at the body. Her sheet fell away, revealing acres of bulging flesh. Breed, disgusted, took her out with a single shot to the head.

Turning back to the counter, he lay his smoking weapon on the countertop and grabbed a handful of Hershey bars, sticking all but one in the breast pocket of his unbuttoned fatigue shirt. Shooting and screaming had begun outside, the sounds like Rio at carnival time. He unwrapped the candy bar and took a bite, going into his back pocket to take out the sheet of folded-up paper with the phone numbers on it.

He dialed up the distant-sounding operator, eventually reaching the Honduras Maya, the one truly five-star hotel in Tegucigalpa.

"Honey," he told the receptionist, "don't cut me off here. I want you to ring all the rooms with American television people in them. When I cut off from one, ring me another. Got that?"

"Yes, sir."

Jerry Delany's timely demise had been good business in a variety of ways, not the least of which being that his worthless carcass brought a shit load of American television people down here to snoop. Delany had been worth far more dead than alive.

The phone rang seven times before a sleepy American male voice garbled something that sounded like hello.

"Listen to me," Breedlove said. "Listen carefully, there's no time to waste. Caribbean Companeros have crossed the border into Honduras and are even now attacking the *libre* village of Auasbila, on the Coco River."

"What the fu—"

"There's no time," Breed interrupted. "Get there. It's war."

He jiggled the connection, getting the receptionist again, the woman punching up another number. As Breedlove spoke, one at a time, to the media, he went through the cabinets and drawers behind the counter in disgust. Nothing worth taking. What a useless existence these people led.

When he'd finished with the media, he put a call in to regional Honduran Army command at Catacamas and told them the same story, tearing the phone out of the wall when he'd finished. He looked at his watch. Twenty minutes had passed. It was time to get things moving along.

The rotted floor creaked beneath him as he grabbed the weapon and came back around the counter, stepping over the bodies, to make his way into the already blistering morning sunshine. Shooting had subsided to the occasional volley and perhaps thirty bodies lay scattered like litter around the stark white streets. His men were laughing, running from house to house, some of them with burlap sacks, Breed wondering just what it was they thought worth taking. Women moaning and screaming, unseen, filled the brisk air, and a breeze blowing in from the river carried just the slightest odor of rotting fish.

He walked to the old gas pump and pulled the nozzle out of the holster. The damned thing was still operational. He squeezed on the flow and hooked the flange to make it work automatically. Then he set the hose on the ground and walked toward Willie's truck at the end of the block, stepping on bodies that were in his way.

Fifty feet from the gas pump, he stopped and called through cupped hands, "Let's wrap it up! Honduran Army on the way!" He looked behind him, a stream of gas licking toward his feet. The matches were deep in his pocket. He pulled them out and lit one, tossing it onto the gas stream, the trail of fire igniting with a whoosh, rushing back to the gas pump, the underground tanks going up with a loud, hollow boom and a beautiful orange flower that rose fifty feet in the brightening sky. A thick column of black smoke followed the blast, drifting gently westward. Good. Give them something to home in on.

Willie was house-to-housing, scaring up his men, as Breed reached the truck parked before an unpainted wooden church with a flat roof. The priest lay dead in the entryway, the altar boy nowhere to be seen.

He walked to the back of the truck. The tailgate was down, Mulroy atop a naked teenage Indian girl, pounding away, her head hanging down out of the truck. She was screaming wildly, eyes bulging, but no sound came out. Her jet-black hair reached almost to the dirty ground.

"Let's go," Breed told the man. "We're flat out of time."

"In a minute," Mulroy said, straining against the struggling girl. "Just a—"

"Now!" Breed shouted, and placing the barrel of the AK-47 against the girl's temple, he pulled the trigger and blew her brains all over Mulroy.

"Damn!" Mulroy yelled, jumping off the body as it fell out of the truck. He wiped at the grue on his face as he tried to pull up his camouflage pants. "I said in a minute."

"Unload the truck," Breed said through clenched teeth. "Do it now."

He turned away from the truck as the others came hurrying up in twos and threes. "Willie, have your squad unload a few bodies from the truck. Not too many. Be creative with it. Any resistance?"

"Couple kids with M-2s," Willie said, moving to the truck back, his granite face and shaved head glistening perspiration as he hefted himself up and into the truck. Within seconds, the body of one of the Companero regulars they'd killed at the forward outpost near Sang-Sang earlier that night came flying out of the truck to fall heavily on the road, a cloud of dust rising like a spirit from around the body.

Breed turned to Jamie's squad. "You guys hoof it back to the other truck and get out of here. We'll meet back at the checkpoint. Anybody slip away?"

Jamie smiled with tight lips. "No one got past me," he said.

"Great," Breed said. "Thank you, gentlemen. You've earned your pay today." He looked again at his watch. "Take off." The squad turned and jogged in the direction of the pillar of fire still rising from the gas tanks, the sky above now cloudy with smoke.

Willie and his people had removed from the truck four bodies that they were, even then, dragging to various parts of the city. Breed loved punctuality, and today's little scenario was right on schedule. The gears were still meshing. He turned a circle, smiling at the devastation all around him. This was his reality. He had built it, and now everybody was going to have to live in it.

He walked to the passenger side of the truck and hoisted himself up, Willie's squad returning on the run at that moment. The big man climbed up behind the wheel, the entire truck settling a bit on that side. "Checkpoint?" he asked.

"Drop me by last night's camp," he said. "Then you go on."

"What do you want to stay here for?"

"I've got to watch," Breed replied.

"What for?"

"I'm an artist, my friend," he said, leaning back in the seat. "I've got to see people appreciate my work."

"You're crazy. That's what you are."

Breed turned his head lazily on the seat back to look at the man's squat, quizzical face. "Everybody's crazy," he said. "Everybody." He leaned up close and whispered, "I just harness it."

NCC Tower, New York City 8:04 A.M.

"This is America, isn't it?" Sheila Traynor said, pumping the exercise bike harder, getting the speedometer up to forty mph. "They can't just cut us off from vital information."

"They can and they have," Donald Merck replied from his perch on the edge of her always-clear desk. He took a bite of the banana he held in his left hand. "National security's a huge umbrella."

"Can't we take it to court?" Traynor asked, her breath coming faster the harder she pedaled. She hated exercise, but at her age missing even one day made a difference on the scale and in the mirror. She hated getting older more than she hated exercise, so the battle raged on.

"Certainly we could take it to court," Mari Bendorff, the capital producer, said. "And by the time we moved it through the hell the government would create, the issue would be as dead as the hula hoop. The audience really can't hold interest in any story more than a week or so. The government would love us to take it to court."

Traynor turned to look out the window as she continued to pedal. As anchor, she had a choice office with a view of the Hudson, at least what the World Trade Center's bulk didn't block off. It was snowing lightly in Manhattan, large flakes drifting lazily past her thirtieth-floor view, nothing like the blizzard that had engulfed D.C.

She had everything: the largest office in News, a personal hairdresser, even seven figures in salary, which was probably two figures higher than she deserved. All she had to do to hold it was not get old, and not demand Baroni's title of news editor along with anchor. "How much did we get before they cut off the flow?" she asked.

"Enough to tantalize," came the response from John Demeter, their Dartmouth graduate news writer.

The room was alive with the unspoken tension that only a really big story can generate. It was palpable.

The large, modern office with the bookcases full of knickknacks had divided itself, as usual, into two groups—the hard cases and the dilettantes. It was easy to tell them apart. The hard cases—Mike Baroni, Sheila's newscast producer and overall program editor, and old-time writer Joanie Silver—occupied the small sitting area just inside the door. Baroni was leaning over the coffee table, dripping the pineapple out of a large Danish that he would eventually wash down with twenty cups of coffee before the morning was over. Silver, white-haired and withered like a prune, nervously chain-smoked, holding the whirring, smokeless ashtray the rest of the newsroom had gotten her when she'd refused to acquiesce to the no-smoking ordinance they had voted on earlier in the year.

The dilettantes clustered around Sheila's desk on straight-backed chairs as she continued pumping away, dressed in sweats and a terrycloth headband. They wanted to seem *in control*, worthy somehow of their lofty status of information disseminators. They felt they had a responsibility to be what they thought people expected them to be—scions and defenders of American culture. Merck with his fresh fruit and horrible-looking gloppy brown health mixture he drank from a thermos every morning. Demeter, all razored hair, uncertain sexuality, and holier-than-thou attitude about anything other than accepted values. And Mari Bendorff, pristine and aloof, who delicately sipped tea from a hand-painted porcelain cup *with* saucer and who thought that heaven would be getting locked into Saks Fifth for the night.

The group this morning was rounded out by a strange old man named Derek Willough, a Brit, who was somehow vaguely connected up with the Jane's military evaluation people. Willough occasionally worked with NCC on military matters as a consultant. He wore a tweed sports jacket and glasses so thick they made his eyes as big as Bendorff's saucer. Not aware of the class divisions in the group, he had picked a comfortable seat in the hardcore area, relatively close to Joan Silver, who he kept uselessly trying to engage in conversation.

"What does . . . tantalize mean?" Traynor asked, breathing deep, beginning to tire. "Anything we . . . can use?"

Demeter shifted in his chair, crinkling his nose in distaste as a whiff of cigarette drifted over from Silver's spot on the sofa. "They admit that Delany worked for EquAir, that this was his first flight for GSA under standard charter work, and that his security clearance was pending. The clearance, they said, was subsequently denied, but he was already in the air. It would have been his first and last flight under those conditions. Beyond that, they screamed 'classified.'"

"What about EquAir?" Merck asked, sipping brown glop from his thermos lid.

Demeter shrugged. "They read me the government statement, then told me that they survived on government contract work and would tell me nothing more. National security."

"What do . . . you . . . think . . . Mike?" Traynor panted, getting the speed up to fifty.

"Umm," Baroni said, straightening and wiping his lip with an index finger, the Danish drooping in his grasp. "I think we should run what we got, then dead-end the son of a bitch. There's enough going on at this point that all the answers are going to come eventually. Anything new on that missile identification?"

Bendorff frowned at Baroni's loosened tie and plaid sports jacket. "How can you put that . . . stuff into your body?" she asked.

"What . . . this?" Baroni said, holding up the sagging pastry. "Hell, my granddad lived to be ninety-three on very little but buns and coffee, Mari. If I wanted to hear that shit, I'd hire my wife to come in here to work, you know? Now what about those reports that the missiles in the tape looked American?"

Bendorff took a long breath, then set her teacup into the saucer she held up with her left hand. "DOD released a statement about an hour ago saying that the missiles were Russian, Dobrin class, light intercontinental ballistics, and that they were definitely not American made."

Willough sat up, chuckling softly, then hacking. "Missiles tend to look a lot alike," he said, settling down. "It's probably impossible to come up with a positive ID based on the videotape. We just never do see the whole blasted thing all at once. They do resemble the Raytheon Bearcat, and they also bear a striking resemblance to several other classes of missile, including the Dobrin series. Although the Dobrin would have to grow an extra fin to be the bird in that tape."

"Is that possible?" Baroni asked.

"To upgrade their specs?" the man said, raising bushy eyebrows. "Most certainly."

"Which leaves us nowhere," Baroni said.

"Wait a minute," Traynor said, stopping the bike and climbing off. A towel lay on her narrow windowsill. She picked it up and wiped at the perspiration on her face. "You're missing the boat here. It doesn't matter whether we can identify those missiles or not."

"What do you mean?" Merck asked.

She wrapped the towel around her neck. "Don't you get

it?" she asked. "The Department of Defense has just *told* us what they are. They have just officially stated the position of the United States government: that there are *Russian* missiles in Caribbea."

"My God, she's right," Baroni said. "That's damned close to an actual admission of the entire story." He turned to Willough, a section of sugar glaze sliding off the pastry to fall into his coffee. "What kind of range do those, whoozit . . . Dobrin missiles have?"

The old man smiled. "Oh, it's a nice one," he said, and Traynor could see real joy in his features. "The Dobrin A-14 carries a three-megaton warhead as far as two thousand miles, accurate to within twenty miles at that distance. Enough firepower to vaporize any large city within the continental limits of the U.S. Some of them also have burrowing capacities that would enable them to be launched, targeted, then detonated weeks or months later."

"What's the President doing today?" Baroni asked.

"He's canceled all his appointments," Bendorff replied, eyebrows arched. "And called an NSC meeting."

Baroni set down his Danish. "This is downright scary."

"It's all bullshit," Joan Silver replied, her voice morning husky. "What happened to the end of the cold war, people?" Her hand inscribed the air wildly as she talked, the cigarette that dangled between her fingers writing her gibberish in the air with smoke. "I can't figure out why the Russians would do something like this. They can't afford, literally or figuratively, to involve themselves here. It makes absolutely no sense. Those guys aren't any stupider over there in the Kremlin than we are. If they did it, they'd have to think we'd find out. In case you haven't noticed, they've got a ton of other problems eating them alive right now. No way they'd blow it on something dumb like this."

"Don't underestimate the savagery of the Russian machine," Willough said, drawing himself up, his quiet voice trembling with righteousness. "Military might is still its stock in trade, especially today as they lag further behind us techno—"

"Yeah, yeah," Silver said, waving him off. "I've heard it all before."

"It's not our place," Merck said, "to interpret the news. All we can do is present it."

"My point exactly," Silver said, waving her cigarette at him. "And don't tell me how to do my job. Here's our news: The Caribbean military may or may not have shot down a plane that may or may not have been on a secret spy mission; the United States government denies that it has knowledge that the Russians have put missiles into Caribbea, then proceeds to identify the nonexistent missiles as Russian, which, according to our expert, would mean they'd have to grow new fins; the Caribbean foreign minister may or may not have been assassinated by an American mercenary soldier who may or may not be tied into the missiles and the alleged shoot-down. This isn't news, it's speculation. We ought to call this thing, Rumor-gate." She shook her head and took a long drag, her hand shaking. "And now the other networks are coming to us for news."

"Aren't you forgetting a few things?" Traynor said coldly. She'd always had trouble with Silver. The woman had resented her lack of hard news background from day one and took every opportunity to dig at her. But she wasn't going to rain on this parade. "Aren't you forgetting the hard news we do have? Like Jerry Delany's last radio transmission where he identified the SAMs that took him out of the air as they shot him down? Or like my source and his guarantee that the Russians are, indeed, arming the Companeros and that our government is, for some reason, covering it up?"

Silver smiled, catlike, sitting forward with her forearms resting on her legs, the ashtray on the coffee table sucking her cigarette smoke in at nearly a right angle. "Ah yes," she said. "Your source. The font from which all wisdom springs."

"What are you getting at?" Traynor replied, jerking off her headband and pulling back her short hair.

"Nothing personal, my dear," the woman replied, "but I feel at this juncture that we are putting the credibility of this news department . . . the entire network, into the hands of a, for lack of a better word, nonprofessional."

"You have no right to attack my credibility," Sheila said, trying to retain control. She had known it would come to this. "I've put ten hard years into this network and I know my job. My source is one hundred percent solid gold. Above reproach on any level."

"Let us be the judge of that," Silver replied without hesitation.

"Now wait just a minute!" Merck said, standing, his cheeks flushing slightly. "The network stands behind Sheila and her story to the max. How could any rational human being deny what's happening out there, Joan? The whole country's coming apart."

"And I'm trying to figure out right now," Silver replied in soft tones, the fight out of her already, "whether or not we bear any responsibility for that circumstance."

"That's enough," Merck said with unhappy resignation. "You're off this one. Get back to your other stuff and send Price in here."

"With pleasure," the woman replied, standing immediately and walking out of the room, Demeter waving his hand in front of his face to clear away real or imagined smoke.

A messenger from production passed her on his way in, a videotape in his hand. He walked immediately to Merck and gave him the tape. "Mr. Grimes said to hand this directly to you," the young man said. "He said you'll want to see it right away."

Merck examined the tape at arm's length, with distaste, as if it were a dead frog. "Where did it come from?"

"We pulled it off the satellite feed . . . from Honduras."

Traynor grabbed it from Merck and hurried to the television in the middle of the bookcase. She turned on the set and slipped the tape into the VCR playback unit atop it.

After several seconds of static, a picture came up on the screen. It was a shot of Anne Dalton, one of their Central American people, dressed in camouflage clothing. Her face was drained completely of color. She spoke:

"This is Anne Dalton for NCC news," the woman said, voice hoarse. "I'm standing in what remains of the Honduran village of Auasbila. The story here is one of unbelievable savagery. . . ."

The scene switched to a shot down a dusty Indian village street, a large, bright orange fire raging in the distance. Bodies lay all over the streets as Honduran Army personnel moved through the carnage with stretchers. "The medics are merely gathering the dead," Dalton's voice rasped over the tape, "for there was no one left alive in this once-peaceful fishing town of fifty residents."

The picture switched to a shot of a Honduran civilian, a large man with a fleshy face. Dalton's voice: "Honduran Interior Minister Carlos Molina arrived here with the first wave of troops."

The man spoke: "We have found the bodies of several Companero regulars among our own dead. It appears the village was attacked at dawn. There was some small resistance to the massacre, but it was fruitless. Then our troops showed up and the Caribbeans ran away. This is a tragedy for my whole country. Our machismo will not let this go unavenged."

More scenes of the carnage: a family of six children butchered in their one-room shack; an old priest dead in the entry to his adobe church; a man slaughtered in his field beside his dead cow. Dalton's voice: "No one can speculate as to exactly why this inhuman incident took place, though Minister Molina suggested that it might have been in retaliation for Auasbila's close connection with former *libre* refugees. For now, all we can do is wait, wonder . . . and bury the dead. This is Anne Dalton, speaking from the war-torn border of Caribbea and Honduras."

"My God," Traynor whispered, shaken and excited at the same instant. "Everything's falling apart."

"Speculation?" Baroni asked loudly. "Mr. Willough?"

Willough cleared his throat. "Well," he wheezed. "There does seem to be a pattern developing."

"What do you mean?" Traynor pressed, feeling the crush of history now and knowing herself a part of it.

"The U.S. Congress has shown a great deal of weakness when it comes to Central America," the man said, almost sneering. "It has shown itself time and again unwilling to get involved in the fights that really matter. Consider this: The Companeros intend to retaliate against Honduras for years of affiliation with the *libre* cause, maybe even take back that border territory that's been in dispute for so long. They put some missile placements in, knowing that the news will leak out, and figure that the Congress will fear that kind of confrontation and back away, allowing them to ride roughshod over Honduras and at the same time have some punch to use against America or its own immediate neighbors. One thing at least now is certain. The Companeros are on the move. They're getting ready to pull *something*. It's now undeniable."

"That's it then," Traynor said. "We've been handed the ball and we have to run with it. We've got to sell this hard, Mike."

Baroni picked up his coffee and took a long drink. "Okay," he said, draining the cup. "World War III it is. We'll devote everything to this, tonight's entire newscast. We'll push the story and the government so hard they'll have to take a stand."

The phone on Traynor's desk rang, everybody turning to stare at it. Merck picked it up angrily. "I told you, no calls . . . what?" He turned to Traynor. "For you . . . somebody named Froggy."

"That's *him*," she whispered harshly, hurrying to the phone.

"What kind of name is Froggy?"

She took the phone from Merck, holding it against her chest. "When I asked him why he was leaking the info, he said he jumped because he got froggy. We've used it ever since. Everybody out, okay? He's not only froggy, but antsy, too."

They all trooped dutifully out, Traynor mouthing a silent thank you to Baroni for not fighting her on pushing her story to the max. To Sheila, at this point, the journalistic Emmy Award was hers and only awaited her successful completion of the whole affair. She really was going to show them all.

She brought the phone to her lips. "This is Sheila Traynor," she said, her voice strung up high with the excitement.

"It's me," came the response. "I want to thank you for the job you've done getting this out . . . and in keeping me removed from it. I took the liberty of sending more tape to NCC in your name. I hope that's all right. And I'm so sorry about the FBI, if I'd have known . . ."

"This is more important than my comfort," Sheila said.

"I'm just doing my job. And of course it was all right to send the tapes. Will you have more for me?"

"Perhaps," Froggy replied. "But things have tightened up at the Pentagon. Everyone is watching everyone else."

"We need to bring this all the way home," Traynor said.

The man chuckled softly. "From what I'm seeing around me now," he said, "I believe there's no way to stop the issue from resolving itself. The administration can't continue to deny the truth for much longer. I think you've already done your country a great service, Ms. Traynor."

"I'm just a newswoman, sir," she said, turning the compliment back onto her source, but even as she spoke a realization was beginning to sink in. The action was already shifting away from snowed-in Washington to the Honduran tropics, and if she didn't shift with it, she'd be left behind, her story becoming someone else's story, her Emmy on someone else's mantel.

It was time to get really creative.

██████ NEWSBREAK ██████

FTPO   copy #1 of 7, Wed., Feb. 6

*Contains SCI enclosure—EYES ONLY—security present for reading

OVERNIGHTS

Following is a compendium of overnight public opinion surveys. Drawn from thirty-seven polling services, it represents every major geographical and economic breakdown in the country, reflecting an accurate portrait of the feelings of the American public.

1. Feels the President is lying about the events
   in Caribbea   **Yes—82%   No—11%**

2. Feels that missiles in Caribbea pose a physical threat to America   **Yes—79%   No—4%**

3. Feels that the President should take deci-
   sive action, including use of American
   forces, to eliminate offensive missiles from
   region   **Yes—68%   No—17%**

As evidenced by these figures, the administration's
deniability factor is negligible as regards this issue.
Though corroborating evidence is not forthcoming
from the loop of the Intelligence community, denial
of the issue seems counterproductive at this time. A
different course of action based on published reports
is, perhaps, warranted and is not without historical
precedent.

Pennsylvania Quarter, The Vault 8:27 A.M.

Ben James sat smiling at the picture of Charlie Merchant
that was juicing on the sixty-inch TV screen at the far end
of the vault, thirty feet distant. Merchant stood at his pool
table, staring at the photos of Joann that he'd gotten from
that nigger cop Hurley. These were the distillations, the
"good parts" from the lives of Charlie and Linda Merchant, taken the previous day. Their home life was boring,
but filled with fascinating anthropological detail.

"I'm dialing you in, Charlie," he called, raising his
coffee cup to the screen in salute.

The video, taken from one of the cameras Jeremy had
planted at the Merchant house, was somewhat dark and
fuzzy, but the large screen and the total access more than
made up for it.

The vault was long and narrow, running right beside his

office behind a locked steel door to which only he had the key. The walls were filled with floor-to-ceiling bookcases, the top two shelves of which contained his rarer glass pieces: Egyptian vases from the 18th Dynasty, first-century Roman cameo cups, and Venetian *latticinio* circa seventeenth century. The rest of the long shelves were crammed with closed file boxes marked only with a code number. The tan clapboard boxes contained his documentation, tapes, and written records. He rarely ever used his evidence, preferring to simply buy or talk people into things, but his "little persuasion" was always there when needed. Research was the key when trying to get ahead. There was simply no substitute for it.

On screen, Charlie's wife had come home from the Wellness Center and was complaining about the snow. He shook his head as she and Charlie childishly tried to apologize for their growing distance. He'd seen in a report that they'd moved into separate bedrooms. If they'd wanted to patch up their lives, their first shot should have been to get back in the same bed again. Not that it mattered now.

BJ's end of the vault was set up like a small den, with an overstuffed beige love seat from wall to wall and a walnut coffee table, which, at the moment, was covered with a stack of files and videos pertaining to Charlie Merchant.

On the TV, Linda and Charlie had slid easy as an old sock into another argument, BJ enjoying the way Linda's voice would begin climbing a ladder in pitch and timbre whenever she got mad. This one was about Eve Braedman. "Somebody murdered Jack," Charlie was saying. "I can't leave that alone."

"Good boy!" BJ called. "Stand your ground. Don't let that anemic bitch kick you around."

He nodded his head vigorously, clapping, as Linda's voice trilled up the ladder, culminating in the line ". . . you're driving Eve Braedman into a nervous breakdown."

"You're driving Eve Braedman into a nervous breakdown," he mimicked to the television, his voice a harsh falsetto.

He reached down and picked up the remote control,

turning it up a touch. The best part was about to come. Whenever Linda would get emotional, Charlie's response was always self-righteous and memorable.

"The truth is the only thing that matters to me," the television Charlie said.

"Yes!" BJ yelled, pushing the button to freeze frame the video, Charlie's face set rock solid and indomitable on the screen.

He stood and walked the length of the room to stare at Charlie's face. "You arrogant, self-centered motherfucker," he said, lips curled in a tight smile. "Don't you know I'm purely going to love takin' you down."

The headset around his neck buzzed. He pulled it up to cover his ears, moving the mouthpiece into position. "Yeah, June."

"CNN, bossman. You'll want to watch."

"Love you, sweets."

He used the remote to shut down the VCR; the television, already tuned to CNN, replaced Charlie's face. It was news footage taken in Honduras and zapped over by satellite. A pile of bodies lay on a dusty street, a good crop of flies already zoning the area in. It was a massacre, the newsman said. But more specifically, a Carribbean massacre of Honduran citizens.

The adrenaline was squirting now, really pumping out. BJ stood, once more saluting the TV screen with his coffee. "Thank you, Ken," he said loudly. "For a dumb so-and-so you've sure got yourself a good work ethic."

He shut down the TV, feeling like he was rushing on a methadrine fix. The world was an exciting and malleable place, and as near as he could figure, he was the only one to realize it.

He touched the control pad to buzz June. She came on seconds later. "Talk to me."

"Listen, beautiful," he said, moving down the length of the vault to exit the door beside the love seat. "Line all my ducks up for today. Let's go forced march with the meetings. Cut me off halfway through each one."

"You're going to burn yourself out, BJ."

"Not this week I'm not. Hop to it, girl. We've got a legislature to control. And while you're at it, give yourself a raise."

He moved into the office proper, the vault entry nearly invisible in a small alcove by the sliding veranda doors.

"You've got an eight forty-five with the head of the California VFW to talk about Congressman Nash."

"Good," BJ said, moving to check his hair in the mirror behind his desk. "Send him in here and give me eight minutes with him."

"Got it." She paused for several seconds, BJ smiling. "Boss? Did you really mean it about the raise?"

"You're my right hand and this is my big day," BJ returned. "Give yourself an extra grand a month. When Ben James wins, he shares it with the world. I'm what they call a philanthropist, honey. A dyed-in-the-wool bleeding heart. Now, send the veterans in."

He cut communication and pulled the headset down off his ears, his mind turning once more to Merchant. For all his bullshit, the man was a real threat and one who would have to be dealt with. But until then, he had other plans for Colonel Merchant, more interesting plans. And today, for the first time, they would meet. Merchant didn't know it yet, but it would be the moment of his life—the one he'd be able to talk about forever after and say, "Everything changed here."

Arlington National Cemetery 9:19 A.M.

Merchant sat in the back of the hearse as it slowly plowed its way through a nightmare of frigid white, the devil's own entourage snaking in a line behind. Arlington National Cemetery, four hundred acres large, lined out all around them a solid rolling field of snow, every one of its hundred thousand headstones hidden, burying the past, burying memory.

"I wish there were some way to keep the damned reporters away," Gene Tillotson said from his facing seat across from Charlie, Braedman's casket on a stand between them.

"It's a national cemetery," Phil Rosen said from beside

him. "You can't keep them out." He turned and craned his neck out the back window to look at the line of fifteen cars and news vans stretched out like a conga line behind. "I just wish that somebody *besides* reporters were here."

"It's a cruel town," Tillotson said, wearing a deep depression on his sleeve like another epaulet. "It eats people alive and shits out their remains. I hate the cowardice of it all. None of Jack's friends had the guts to show themselves."

Merchant sat and listened to them, a sense of melancholy overtaking him. Their anger was justified. They couldn't even muster enough sympathy to come up with pallbearers. Josh sat beside him, the two Army corporals who Gene had commandeered into service to help with the casket sitting across from each other. Four other Army noncoms, pressed into service by Tillotson as an "unofficial" color guard, followed directly behind in an army jeep. The procession was being led by another hearse, white as the snow it was slogging through, carrying Jack's family, Linda, and Josh's wife, Della. That was it for the mourners. Everyone else was a vulture.

Nothing had gone right. The Department of the Army ran Arlington. Even with the interference of two-star General Tillotson, the army had only allowed the funeral because they couldn't deny it. Braedman qualified for burial on several points, being a decorated veteran and a member of Congress. But even with the army's reluctant acceptance of the inevitable, they had refused to supply an honor guard and had flatly refused to allow Jack to be shrouded with the flag. It just wasn't right.

"It's hard to blame the no-shows too much," Josh said. "Washington's fueled on image. Without image you can't survive. Only you guys loved Jack enough to cut your own throats for him. Besides, there are a few other problems going on right now . . . like war in Central America."

"There's not going to be a war in Central America," Rosen said wearily.

"You don't think so?" Tillotson replied. "With what I saw on the early bird this morning, it looks like, missiles or no, Caribbea is encroaching Honduran territory. How could they turn on us like that? I can't believe that

Macklin would deny the use of our troops to protect that region."

"Then why is he denying the missiles?" Josh persisted. "It seems—"

"He's denying the missiles because we've seen no intelligence on it," Tillotson answered. "We still have no confirmation of those videotapes. Madrina swears it didn't happen."

"I can't believe that," Josh said. "It makes no sense."

Rosen showed empty palms. "Forty-one branches of our government have intelligence-gathering agencies of one sort or another. I've talked with each one of them in the last two days. Everyone admits that the area shown in the tapes appears to be the Mosquito Coast. But no one has any sort of confirmation of any kind."

"Oh, it's the Mosquito Coast all right," Merchant said, his eyes turned to the window, to the numbing, blank waste surrounding them. "I think the missiles are Bearcats, too."

"Come on," Tillotson said. "You and I both spent our years on the imaging teams. There's no way you can positively ID those missiles. How could American missiles get down there anyway?"

Merchant turned, finally, to stare at him. "I don't know," he said. "I'm working on instinct right now. By the way, I've got a job for you if you want it."

Tillotson straightened, his eyes lighting up. "I'm all ears."

"It's a name: Ben James, founder and sole owner of Legislative Services, Inc. I want everything you can find on him."

Rosen laughed from beside Tillotson. "You really do have it in for Mr. James, don't you?"

Tillotson turned to look at him, then returned his gaze to Merchant. "Does this have something to do with Jack?" he asked.

"Yes," Merchant said easily. "I think it does."

"I'll do everything I can," Tillotson replied, sitting back then, his eyes resting for a long moment on the casket before he settled into the seat cushion to look at the ceiling. "God, I hate all this."

"How does all this missile shit affect your Appropriations vote, Phil?" Josh asked. "Della told me things are tightening up on the Hill."

"We've got the momentum going right now," Rosen answered. "I think that anger will sustain us. All of Congress is committed to fiscal responsibility. It's crucial. We're getting inundated with letters, telegrams, and phone calls from veterans and other affected groups. Somebody has organized the hell out of this. I've never seen the computer mailing lists used to such advantage before. But we'll hold. Budget is meeting right now to kick the changes to Appropriations over the Joint Chiefs' heads. Appropriations will vote them in this afternoon."

"Has it occurred to you, Phil," Merchant said, "that the American people might simply be speaking their minds right now, that maybe they've finally realized that they don't want America to be without the solid anchor of a strong defense? Maybe you should start listening to them."

"Who's going to foot the bill, Charlie?" Rosen countered, then shrugged broadly. "Lord knows, I love you like a brother, but arguing defense with a military man is like arguing religion with a preacher."

Merchant winked at Josh. "So, where do you go from here, Mr. Disarmament?"

The man smiled thinly. "I've moved our calendar around in the House," he said. "We'll vote on this tomorrow before weekend recess. The President has already withheld the sixty billion in budget allocations to defense. All we have to do is vote to make the recision legal."

"What if you don't have the recision votes?" Josh asked.

"I have them," Rosen said, clipped.

"But, theoretically, what if you don't?"

"I do," Rosen said. "But for the sake of argument, if both houses don't vote for recision, the money has to go back to DOD."

Just then, a muffled curse came from the driver, the hearse fishtailing slightly, then stopping with a jerk. They were leaning heavily to one side.

"Shit . . . we're stuck," Josh said, the driver confirming the statement with more curses as he gunned the engine to a whine, the hearse rocking, but not making forward progress.

"Let's get out and take a look," Merchant said, bumping his door open and stepping out into knee-deep snow that immediately soaked into his pants, numbing his legs. He was standing in a wasteland, a place he'd been to dozens of times that was now entirely different. Snow still sputtered out of the low gray sky, wind swirling it like frozen dust devils. The hearse had fallen off the edge of the roadway, its back right wheel spinning uselessly in a deep crevasse.

"Should we try to push it out?" Josh asked as all of them exited the vehicle.

Merchant looked around to get his bearings. Everything was so altered in the confusion. Before them, Eve's limo had stopped, waiting for the train to continue. Behind, reporters were climbing out of their cars, dragging cameramen with them ready to roll tape. In the far distance sat the restored home of Robert E. Lee, on whose land the cemetery stood. Closer, to the west, stood the huge neoclassical amphitheater, suitably mausoleumlike. The burial spot was fifty yards in front of them, a blue and white striped awning, half covered in driving snow, the landmark. A lone priest paced nervously at the gravesite. The grave diggers sat in the covered cab of a bulldozer smoking cigarettes just beside the awning.

"I think we should walk it from here," Merchant said, turning to stare daggers at the approaching media.

"Yeah . . . and quickly," Tillotson replied, understanding immediately. He pulled open the side doors of the hearse, the driver moving around to kick the back wheelwell of the buried tire.

Movement was difficult, the six men trying to maneuver in the deep snow as they lined up on either side of the open doors, the rest of the phony honor guard conscripted by Tillotson moving up to get in the way while trying to assist.

"Smile!" one of the reporters called. "You guys look like you're going to a funeral!"

"You bastard," Tillotson growled back, moving a step in that direction.

"Let it go," Merchant said. "They're just trying to fluster you. Come on, let's move."

The corporals in their dress blues with braid and white

gloves reached into the hearse, sliding the casket slowly out, the pallbearers grabbing at brass rails on the highly polished ash.

"Got it?" Merchant called softly, everyone nodding in the affirmative. "Okay. Let's move on three. One . . . two . . . three."

They started out all right, but on ground that was barely traversible anyway, the extra cumbersome weight of the casket was more than they could fight. Rosen, in the lead, had his right foot go out from under him and crumpled to the ground, dropping the casket. Everybody on that side went down like a row of dominoes, the casket falling into deep snow, nearly turning upside down.

The newspeople surrounded the scene like ants on a picnic lunch, laughing and rolling tape while they shouted out mock encouragement.

"Stop it!" Tillotson yelled, his face strained and deep crimson. "What kind of animals are you?"

"Gene," Charlie said. "Just pick it up again. Just keep moving."

The man stared at him, his shortened breath puffing out bright white as he talked. "What the hell is going on here, Charlie?"

Merchant could only shake his head.

The limo ahead was disgorging passengers, Linda comforting Eve as she leaned, crying, against the vehicle.

"On three," Merchant said, all of them bending, again taking the brass rails, cameras grinding soundlessly. "One . . . two . . . three."

Once more they hefted, Merchant not even noticing the weight of the thing, so focused was his anger and indignation. "Move slowly," he said. "Take half steps. Ready?"

Once more they nodded. Merchant, forcing stoicism, said, "Go."

They procession moved, slowly, up onto the roadway again where there were no surprises. They closed the distance between themselves and the limo, no one talking, the only sounds an occasional labored breath. Eve Braedman and her children stood together at the rear of the limo, staring with vacant eyes. Mindy Braedman's lips were tightened, still, in anger—an emotion so total for the young. Randy Braedman, over six feet, wearing a bushy

beard and long hair was just the opposite. Nothing but
sadness and loss shone from his pale green eyes as he kept
a protective arm wrapped around his mother's shoulder.
Randy had always been a simple and compassionate kid,
a bit of a loner. He was a park ranger at Yosemite, a job that
fit his personality to a tee.

They reached the limo, then passed it, Merchant's eyes
touching Eve's for just a second, the woman looking away
immediately. He'd have to talk to her about the photo
today. She was leaving for home after the funeral, and he
would have lost his chance.

Linda and Della pressed themselves against the side of
the limo, giving way, as the bier passed them. Linda was
staring at the coffin. She had forced Charlie to sleep in the
guest bedroom last night for the first time in their entire
marriage, and what bothered him most about it was that it
didn't bother him at all. He was too eaten up with the
investigation to worry about anything else right now.

As they approached the awning and the gaping wound
of a hole in the ground that it covered, the trailing
reporters quieted somewhat, all of them realizing the
approaching finality of their activity. Perhaps it sobered
them to understand that no matter what they said about
Jack now, none of it could touch him in the cold bosom of
the earth.

"This is starting to get h-heavy," Josh said from behind
him. "My arm's cramping."

"Another thirty feet," Merchant whispered harshly, his
tone telling Josh to gut up and take it like a man.

Mercifully, they reached the awning without another
mishap, all of them coated with a fine, pale white dusting.
Merchant's nose, ears, and feet were completely numb, his
eyebrows crinkling as he shifted his gaze.

A blue felt covering surrounded the grave area, the
naked dark earth somehow vibrant and obscene amid the
bleakness. A smattering of flowers were grouped together
by a corner post of the portable awning to look like more.
There were no chairs set up for the mourners.

The pallbearers shuffled to position themselves on
either side of the grave, then moving up to set the coffin
down upon the slings that would lower it into the ground.

The slightest sound of rock and roll music, muffled, drifted toward them from the bulldozer cab.

Merchant released the brass rail, his left hand coming up to rub his own cramping arm, his thoughts inexplicably turning to Jerry Delany. The man was some kind of a key; he was sure of it. So many questions surrounded him. Why were the Companeros denying the shoot-down still in spite of the evidence? They would normally jump to take credit for an American shoot-down by calling it a spy plane as they had done in the Hasenfaus case. They could easily claim justification and probably make it stick. And why was Delany so far off course to begin with? More importantly, what was his cargo? That great, unnamed cargo manifesto that was being kept quiet because of national security reasons. But if national security was involved, how come the job was left to GSA, a nongovernment industry. He'd worked for GSA for ten years and saw very little of a confidential nature going on within its ranks. Maybe all that time, however, could stand him in good stead when he tried to get a few hard answers.

The service was embarrassingly brief, and then was simply embarrassing. Linda refused to make eye contact with him or stand beside him as the Catholic priest made veiled references to mortal sins and unhallowed ground as he prayed for Jack's less-than-perfect soul. When he was finished, Tillotson inadvertently added the coup de grace. Unable to get a bugler, he played a cassette of Taps on a small distorting tape player as his honor guard went through the poorest rendition of an armed salute Charlie had ever seen, the men totally out of sync and at sea, firing their carbines into the air individually and at the wrong times. The press was loving it, and it was with the greatest sense of relief that he saw the coffin finally lowered into the cold ground.

The group broke up quickly then, even the reporters unwilling to stretch things out in the horrid cold. Everyone began to tromp slowly back to the vehicles, Linda hurrying off to accompany Eve. Charlie, walking with Tillotson, stayed close behind them, fingering the photograph in his overcoat pocket, dreading what would come next.

"What do you know about the EquAir shoot-down?" he

asked Tillotson as they walked, the man shrugging with his face.

"Enough," he said. "It really was a legitimate charter on a scheduled flight and it really was off course."

"Any idea of the cargo?"

The man stopped walking, Merchant stopping with him. "Funny you should say that," he replied. "I can't seem to find out. GSA defers to the State Department who've put a lid on it."

"Did they say why?"

Tillotson smiled. "You know what they said."

"But you *are* national security, Gene. They'd keep things from you?"

The man slapped him on the back and they began walking again. He smiled. "When you ran Army Intelligence," he said, "how much info did you share with Navy Intelligence or Air Force Intelligence? You know what competition within the system is like."

"But DIA was created to be above all that."

"Nobody's immune, brother," Tillotson said. "I'll keep trying and see what I can come up with. You think it's important?"

"I honestly don't know," Merchant answered, noticing Eve getting back into the limo twenty feet ahead. "I've got to talk to Eve a minute."

He hurried himself through the drifting snow, fighting it all the way to the limo, Eve getting in just behind Mindy, Linda still standing outside.

"Eve," he said, slightly out of breath.

"Not now," Linda said as Eve turned to stare at him.

"What could you possibly have to say to me?" she asked. "We've already lived through this fiasco, so there's no reason to apologize."

He started. An apology had never been on his mind. "I just wanted to offer my condolences," he said, knowing there was no graceful way of getting into the real discussion, "and to ask you about . . . this."

He pulled out the weathered photo, holding it out in a red, chapped hand. She took the photo, her face bunched up, questioning. "What?" she asked.

"Have you ever seen this picture before?" he asked.

She shook her head, eyes suspicious. "Never," she said. "Should I have?"

"I found it at the apartment yesterday, I—"

"Is this her?" Eve asked loudly, Charlie noticing the cameras being drawn magnetically toward them again. "Is this the woman who—"

"No," Merchant said, taking the picture again. "It's not the dead girl. It's . . . it's . . ."

"Somebody else?" she nearly screamed. "Another one? Is that what you're saying? You've got another one?" Her eyes widened in horror and revulsion. "What are you trying to do to me? Why do you want to destroy me?"

"No, I—"

"Leave her alone!" Linda shouted, pulling the woman toward the open doorway of the car, reporters now asking a thousand questions all around them.

Linda got Eve into the car, then flared back around to Merchant. "You asshole!" she said, balling up her fists. "I hate you!"

She came at him with both fists, Merchant reflexively stepping back a pace, Linda slipping then, falling face-down in a snowdrift.

"The picture," reporters were calling. "Let's see the picture."

He tried to help Linda up, but she slapped at him and stood on her own. Her face, hair, and clothes were encased in snow. "That's it," she said, voice low with suppressed anger. "For years I've been putting up with your arrogance and abuse, and made excuses for it. But you've finally done it, Charlie. You've gone too far. Leave Eve alone and leave me alone."

She climbed into the limo then and slammed the door, the thing immediately taking off, leaving him standing, staring at open space. He turned, emptied out, only to face a ring of electronic eyes prodding him, examining, dissecting. "Let's see the picture," they called, mocking. "Show us the picture."

He spun in a slow circle. They surrounded him totally now, sucking him into their vortex of invented realities, re-creating him in their own image.

Nothing seemed real anymore. Nothing made sense. Nothing mattered. He jammed the picture back into his pocket. "No comment," he said, running on autopilot as he elbowed his way through the crowd, escape now his only thought.

The Wellness Center 11:39 A.M.

Linda Merchant stood, shrugging out of her wet overcoat in front of the two-way mirror overlooking the group therapy room, the director's office warm and homey all around her. The Hispanic kid's voice was grating harshly through the office speaker.

". . . a bunch of whiny babies," he was saying. "Oooh, my mama don't love me . . . oooh, Daddy beats me up."

"Well . . . he does!" the little brown-haired girl, Gina, said loudly, voice cracking.

"Fuck you," the Hispanic boy said.

Linda turned to the director, who was watering her plethora of green plants with a spritzer. "Been like that the whole time?" she asked.

"Let's just say," Doley Green replied, moving her rex begonia farther from the touch of the dieffenbachia, "that you've got your work cut out for you." Doley was that rarest of human beings, energetic and always positive. She bustled around in quick bursts of movement, her round, cherubic face always radiant, ambulatory sunshine. She was the most caring person Linda had ever known.

Linda turned to the glass again. The other kids were jumping to Gina's defense; Jorge Mendel, the new one, smiling wider the more they attacked him. "What have you got on him?" she asked.

"Not a whole lot," Green replied, setting the spritzer on her desk and picking up a slim file to read: "Seventeen years old; city school system; low achiever; antisocial; suspended for the fifth time for fighting." She closed the file. "The last suspension had enforced therapy connected to reentry. He's all yours." She handed Merchant the file. "If anybody can reach him, you can."

Linda sighed, sticking the file under her arm. "Any trouble with weapons?"

"So far, no."

"Drugs?"

"That's what I think you might watch for."

Merchant nodded. In the next room, Jorge had punched a boy a foot taller than him in the nose and the two of them were mixing it up on the floor as Barry Farris, the counselor, tried to break them up. Ferris liked to stay out of things unless they got out of hand. "He may not be ready for group yet."

Doley smiled. "An understatement."

Merchant shook her head. "He wasn't that bad yesterday." She took a lab coat off the wooden rack next to the dark-stained office door and slipped it over her funeral clothes, buttoning it to the sternum. The funeral had been horrible and emotionally draining, its aftermath depressing. Work was the last thing she wanted right now, which was precisely why she'd come. She smiled in trepidation. "Wish me luck."

Green returned the smile. "You don't need luck, Lin. You're a professional and you're"—she looked at her watch—"thirty minutes late for work."

"Yeah, boss," Linda said, opening the office door to step out into the hall.

She walked the fifteen feet of bright carpeted hall to the therapy-room door. She could hear Barry's voice droning from within as he tried to gently restore order without destroying the ambience of the group. She stood for a moment, breathing deeply, psyching herself up.

The Center was her salvation, the only thing that made her feel like a worthwhile, contributing human being. The fact that she was somehow able to help others while saving her own life was nothing short of miraculous to her. Here she was wanted. Here she had worth. She had heard once that our laws were based on English Common Law, and that women, by law, were looked upon as possessions. It was certainly true enough of Charlie. She sometimes felt like his little trained dog, made to jump the hoops again and again before getting a treat.

Thank God for the Center.

Divorce was probably the next logical step for her, cut away the cancer that constantly ate at her. But the word itself struck fear into her, as if the word carried all the connotations of loneliness and emptiness that formed the core of her premonitions of divorce. She could barely broach the subject in her own mind without numbing pain. So she stayed, stayed on with her own little policeman on her own little devil's island—damned by reality on the one hand and by expectations on the other. Compared to her own demons, the ones being experienced by the kids in the next room seemed almost compelling. She took a deep breath, opened the door, and walked in.

The new kid was physically struggling with Ferris, the others yelling as the session threatened to get completely out of hand.

"That's enough," Linda said. Then louder. "That's enough."

The boy's eyes met hers and softened immediately, surprising her. He stopped struggling with the counselor and stood, sheepish. There was something about this boy that was different, deeper somehow, than the others. His jet-black hair fell in long strands in front of his dark eyes. He snapped his head, fast, like a whip, the hair flying back away from his face, back into place.

"My goodness," Ferris said, his Mickey Mouse T-shirt soaked through with sweat. Linda didn't approve of the therapist getting so close to the group that he became a part of it as Ferris had done. She would never dress like her charges. "It appears mother has arrived."

Everyone laughed, all of them except Jorge, old veterans of group who understood that the male and female counselors took on father and mother group transference roles.

Jorge turned angrily to the others. "What are you laughing at?" he demanded.

"I'll explain it in a minute, Jorge," Linda said. "Once we've all resumed our seats."

"Think I'll, ah, find a medic," Barry said, faking a limp to the still-open doorway. "Wonder if I can get hazardous duty pay." He turned from the doorway and waved at everyone, Linda mouthing a silent thank you for his taking over the first half of her session.

Everyone except Jorge sat. The boy, still defiant, jammed his hands into his pockets and slumped slightly.

"You don't want to sit, Jorge?" Linda said, indicating an empty folding chair in the midst of the circle. The room was bare, nothing breakable, anything allowed. Groups were kept at an arbitrary limit of ten people. Linda specialized in juveniles. She had ten here, five of each sex, who had any number of alcohol- and drug-related problems, complicated by family lives that the Borgias would have been proud of. The group was primarily black and Hispanic, the Wellness Center a county-financed facility that tended to be a dumping ground and halfway house for welfare recipients and their children.

"I don't know if I'm stayin'," Jorge answered.

"Why not?" she returned.

"What's it matter . . . nobody here likes me anyway."

"Because you've acted like a prick," said a large, young black man named Luper.

"I'm just what I am, that's all."

"Yeah, a prick," Luper said, everyone laughing.

"See?" Jorge said. "They all make fun of me because I don't want to play their stupid little let's-pretend game."

"Let's pretend?" Linda replied, confused.

Jorge looked hard at her, his dark eyes fiery and intense in a way that was almost frightening. He spoke firmly, pointing at her the entire time. "The let's-pretend game that our lives are important and mean something in all the crap we have to live with. The let's-pretend game that we're all special because we get hooked on dope and booze as if everybody in the fucking world didn't get hooked on something. All we are here is a bunch of piss-ant babies who get to cry on some guilty damned white woman's shoulder while somebody else pays for it." He turned to the others. "Wise up. The only thing wrong with us is that we're weak, all of us . . . just weak . . . that's all."

Then, inexplicably, he broke down, sobbing into his hands, his whole body vibrating, shaking wildly as he tried unsuccessfully to hold back the tears. The group quieted immediately, all of them knowing and sharing Jorge's fears.

Fifteen-year-old Denise Waller moved cautiously toward the boy to touch him on the shoulder. Linda shook her off. "And you, Jorge," she said softly. "What's your own personal let's-pretend game?"

He took his hands away slowly, his entire face wet, his eyes a distant, desperate plea for help. "It don't matter what mine is," he said hoarsely, the agony in his voice heartbreaking. "I ain't gonna be on this planet long enough to worry about it."

With that he charged from the circle and out the door, Linda right on his heels, her heart pounding in her chest. As she got through the doorway, he was already down the hall. "Jorge!" she called, the boy waving her off. "Jorge!"

He stopped then, hunched over, his back still to her. She slowly closed the distance between them and put an arm around his shoulder. "Do you want to talk?" she asked.

He looked at her, the confused desperation in his face an unignorable plea for help. "Not now," he said sadly. "Not . . . anymore . . . now."

"Come back tomorrow," she said, wiping at the tears on his face with a tissue from her lab-coat pocket. "We'll talk, just you and me."

"Yeah . . . maybe," he said, dejected.

She grabbed his chin, forcing him to look into her eyes. "Promise me," she said. "I respect your feelings, Jorge. I'm just asking you to promise me you'll come talk to me before you do . . . anything." She hated to use the word "suicide" directly, preferring to let the patient bring her into that world himself.

He nodded after a moment. "Tomorrow," he said. "I promise."

He turned then, moving down the hallway to the reception area fifty feet distant. He turned once to stare at her, hauntingly, and he was gone.

She looked down at her hands. They were shaking. She had never stood so close to that all-consuming fire before, had never had to literally confront the life and the death of it. A seventeen-year-old voice was screaming for help. She'd have to listen, to try to save a life.

United States Capitol Building 1:18 P.M.

The elevator doors opened to madness in the Capitol basement. In all the years that Merchant had spent in D.C., working in and around the Hill, he'd never seen the like. It seemed like thousands of people were jamming the subway system connecting the Capitol to the House and Senate office buildings, and all of them were keyed up.

"My God," Phil Rosen said, backing up slightly farther into the elevator. "We'll never get across this way."

"There's a cop," said Sherman Tate. "Maybe he'll wade us through."

Tate was a staunch conservative from Arizona, and chairman of the Budget Committee over on the Senate side. He was a fortyish, handsome man, a constitutional lawyer and former Rhodes Scholar, who used the orator's tongue to do more than simply tell people what they wanted to hear. He dove out of the elevator and disappeared into the confusion as Charlie and Rosen slipped out themselves, a part of the rowdy crowd surging in to take their places, ignoring the REPRESENTATIVES ONLY sign above the sliding doors.

Merchant had always taken pride and comfort in the Capitol Building. It was the lasting testimonial to a government by and for the people. It was totally open to the public, even to the deepest workings of the system. Anyone could come here, participate in the process if they chose, approach those whom they elected to make the laws if they chose.

But things were changing, getting somehow stranger. Lunch in the Capitol cafeteria had been as he remembered it—heavy and greasy, but other than that, things were somehow different. One of his favorite places, the Document Room, the dusty, moldy-smelling hall of memory and permanence just off the rotunda, was gone now, jettisoned in favor of a brand-new Radio and TV Gallery where senators could go and pitch themselves to the folks back home, the sign over the glass and aluminum doors reading MEDIA, SENATORS, AND PRESS SECRETARIES ONLY!

And the people here today, the people lobbying, seemed more interested in running roughshod over the process than in participating in it. Loud and angry, they were of one stripe only—pro-defense. As if the impending votes were somehow magically calling to an entire segment of the population like lemmings drawn to the sea. There were American Legionnaires and Veterans of Foreign Wars, all in uniforms and ribbons. There were Right-to-Lifers and a number of Moral Majority clone groups. There were farm groups and there were business groups who stood to lose an amount of local revenue with projects cut, all wearing the particular garb and using the particular lingo of their persuasion. But all of them were there, loudly sharing the same purpose. None of them wanted defense budget cuts on any level. One of the groups began singing the "Battle Hymn of the Republic," the entire basement within seconds resounding with the swell of a thousand voices joined in song, as all of them waited for a pitiful few aluminum trains to take them under Constitution Avenue to the Appropriations Committee vote in the Rayburn Building.

"This is downright scary," Rosen said loudly, above the din, as they flattened themselves against the wall to avoid getting crushed.

"There's no one here representing the other side," Merchant duly noted. "Why?"

Rosen smiled at him. "What is the other side, Charlie?" he said. "There's no pro-budget-cutting group that I know of. There's only common sense, and it's obviously in short supply here today."

Magically, Tate appeared out of the crowd, a capital policeman in tow. "They're holding the House-only train for us," he said loudly. "We've got to hurry!"

The uniformed cop leading the way, they plunged into the mob, Charlie running into a huge woman wearing a flower-printed dress, a straw hat with a plastic fetus on the front, and a large button with the single word "Caribbea" on it contained within a red circle, with a line through the circle. She was singing so loudly her face was strained red. He excused himself and moved on, the determination he saw on her face giving him pause. For the very first time he realized that this defense business, within a very few days, had become an *issue*, perhaps *the* issue. Why? Three days ago, nobody seemed to care.

For a minute they were swallowed up, drowning in a sea of too-small uniforms and bobbing heads; then suddenly, they had broken free and were standing on the House-only platform of dark concrete, an island of relative calm. An open train was waiting. Five cars long, only the last car was unoccupied.

He and Rosen sat together on the bench seat facing forward, Tate taking the seat opposite and shaking his head. "You ever seen anything like it?" he asked in a combination of giddy wonder and fear. "The post office upstairs is flooded with millions of pieces of mail and the switchboards are so tied up you can't get out to order coffee."

"Is this . . . spontaneous?" Merchant asked.

Rosen showed him empty palms. "I don't know," he said. "When we tried to get that pay raise back in '88, people rose up from the heartland to send us teabags and spank our bottoms, but this . . ." He shook his head. "It's so large, so . . . directed."

The train started off with a shudder, Tate falling forward just a touch before regaining form.

"The crazy part about this," Rosen said, "is that last week's polls showed the country behind the military budget cuts by almost two-thirds. Hell, in any election that would be a major landslide."

Merchant turned to him, the man's face somewhat downcast. The numbers of people seemingly settling a pall over his confidence. On the one hand Merchant was overjoyed to see the public rising up in defense of its military establishment, but there was something sinister about the way it was happening that bothered him a great deal. He couldn't put his finger on it, but it was there, lurking in the shadows just out of reach. "Could it be fear?" he asked, knowing even as he said it that the solution was too simple.

Rosen returned his look. "Fear of the Caribbean thing?" he asked. Merchant nodded slightly. "Could be. We've spent most of this century convincing the American people that Russians are all animals. It's difficult to turn around now and say, 'Well, folks, we were mistaken. Imagine our surprise to find that people on the other side of the ocean may not be that much different from us.'" He shook his head. "I hope to God nobody's hiding anything on us."

Merchant narrowed his gaze. "But you said—"

"I know what I said," Rosen interrupted. "That I was convinced we knew nothing about the missiles. But I'll tell you, the last twenty-four hours have set me thinking about Nixon's secret war in Laos and about Iran-contra. We wouldn't be the first Congress lied to by a president."

The volume of the crowd faded behind them as they entered the concrete tunnels, passing two other trains going the other way. The genesis of this crowd wouldn't leave Merchant's mind. He looked at Tate. "Do you think it could be spontaneous?"

The man thought for a moment, then let his eyes drift from Merchant to Rosen and back again. "No, I don't," he said, waiting for reaction before continuing. "It's too organized. They're all wearing the same buttons, for Christ's sake."

Merchant pressed harder. "But who could have organized it . . . and why?"

"Our lunch wasn't that long ago," Tate replied. "We were talking about the superlobbyists and Ben James."

Rosen started. "James could have done this?"

"I watch him closer than you do, Phil," Tate replied, his eyes flashing. "Because I'm more afraid of him than you are. James convinced a large segment of the armament industry that they were doomed unless they put him on retainer with an eye toward organizing as a group against further budget cuts. I'm sure he's got access to the computer lists of every one of those groups back there. Good organized phone trees within already existing structures, automatic computer calls to action, preprinted petition letters with pre-agreed signatures on them . . . people like James have access to all of that and much more."

"I don't want to believe the armament deal," Rosen said. "That's too much power for one man to wield."

"That's what I've been trying to tell both of you," Tate replied. "Listen. I've personally seen AIPAC and AARP lobbyists *writing* legislation for senators to introduce. Do you understand what I'm saying? We've made running for office so damned expensive that anybody who can build us a good war chest will get to call the tune for us. An overwhelming percentage of incumbents get reelected because they are so well financed as to discourage anyone who'd want to run against them. We've managed to institute job security in elected office, and we can thank people like Ben James."

"If what you're saying is right," Rosen told him, "then this entire issue may boil down to the Congress fighting against a single lobbyist for control of the United States government."

Tate nodded knowingly. "It's just a theory," he said, sitting back and staring out of the car as they arrived at the basement terminal on the office building side, just as jammed up with demonstrators as the other side. Tate had to speak loudly to get over the noise. "The crazy part is, I'm not sure who would win such a fight. I believe it'd be a toss-up at this point."

They stood and exited the car as the automatic doors slid open. Things were more organized at this terminal, with several policemen forming a line to clear a pathway for the congressmen to approach their private elevator, which was also guarded by a House aide.

They hurried past the cordon, and into an elevator already half full of congressmen. "There's no key to centralized power anymore," Tate said as the doors slid closed. "Congress had been chopped up like bait into subcommittees. When you walk into a hall and call 'Mr. Chairman,' seventy-five heads turn. It's natural for human beings to move toward a power base for unity."

Rosen looked around the innards of the moving elevator before speaking. "It's all so simple, I guess," he said. "We in Congress can't stop thinking about what we're doing as a job, and jobs are something we all want to keep. Likewise, we can't help but think that the people who support us financially are our bosses. I hate to say it . . ." He looked at Merchant. "I've taken as much money as the next fella from Ben James and people like him."

"So have I," Tate said. "And if he came to me specifically with an issue, I'd have to think pretty hard about turning him down."

The elevator had gotten suddenly very quiet, Merchant able to hear the raspy breathing of the man behind him. "This is all such a logical progression," he said.

"So far," Rosen said, "all of us have wanted the same thing."

"So far," Tate echoed. "I'd venture that a lot of people are interested in hearing the fate of today's Appropriations vote."

The elevator had stopped on one, everyone exiting into more crowds. Merchant felt himself tensing as they made their way through the jammed-up hallway toward the committee room. He loved the process of government, but he wished that petitioners would dress a bit more appropriately. It didn't help his feelings about the solemn nature of things to see surroundings that reminded him of the audience on *Let's Make a Deal*.

The flow came to a standstill at the committee-room door, the crowd packed tightly here. Every time the door itself opened, tantalizing bits of oratory would drift out into the hall. Tate, always undaunted, fought his way into the jam-up and cleared them a path to the door, the guard there letting them into an already-packed house on visual recognition.

Committees and their rooms came in all shapes and sizes, but Appropriations was the largest and most influential. It contained four tiers of blond oak jurist boxes with attached microphones and swivel rockers for the fifty-eight committee members. All seating on the panel itself and in the thousand-square-foot gallery was filled, the French Provincial wall space occupied two deep in standing room. Merchant and his party could do little but just get inside the door. Gordon Hulett, the chair, was busy throttling a freshman rep from California.

"You're out of order, Ms. Bainbridge," he said, an edge to his voice. "The representative from Alabama still has two minutes."

"Will the representative yield one minute," Bainbridge said, her face red with anger.

"No, ma'am, I will not," Sam Mooney from Alabama said.

"Sounds like the show has started without us," Tate whispered. "And I think we've missed something."

"I don't like it," Rosen said. "This shouldn't be happening."

"Mr. Chairman," Bainbridge said, trying to maintain control. "I'd like to know what's going on in this committee. These are not the things we discussed yesterday in—"

"You are out of order, Ms. Bainbridge," Hulett said again. "If you can't control yourself, please vacate the committee room."

"I can control myself just fine," Bainbridge said, breathing deeply. "I just wonder who controls you."

The entire room erupted in shouts of encouragement and disbelief. Merchant was astounded. He'd never seen this sort of open hostility in the genteel old boys club of Congress before. He looked at Rosen who was shaking his head, mouthing a silent no.

"Ms. Bainbridge!" Hulett shouted, hoisting his large frame up out of the chair to intimidate the woman. Bainbridge rose also, feisty, taking a tentative step toward the chairman.

"Don't walk," Rosen whispered. "Don't walk, Gail. We need the vote."

"What's going on?" Merchant said.

"Hulett's just defected," Tate said, raising his eyebrows to his hairline. "The shit has hit the fan."

As the shouts and murmurs continued in the gallery, Hulett and Bainbridge faced off on the dais, other representatives rising also to try to dam up the emotional flow. Finally, Bainbridge broke the eye contact with an audible sigh, the woman falling heavily back into her chair, her vote, as Rosen had noted, too important to screw off at this juncture.

Hulett sat as soon as Bainbridge sat. He picked up his gavel and banged it loudly. "We will have order in this committee room or I will have it cleared by the federal marshals." He banded the gavel again. "I will have order."

"Mr. Chairman," Bainbridge said.

Hulett pointed the gavel at her. "Yes, Ms. Bainbridge?"

She closed his eyes and took a deep breath. "I would like to apologize to the chair and to all here present for my previous outburst. Emotions are running high."

"Your apology is noted and we thank you for it," Hulett replied, bringing the altercation back full circle and reestablishing the process. "I believe that Mr. Mooney from Alabama still has two minutes."

The hearing picked up again, representatives from both sides of the issue dutifully taking their turns at the mike. There were witnesses from Budget and several of the Joint Chiefs in attendance, but they were never called or acknowledged. This was all just a show, a public display. Merchant turned to his left and watched the C-Span cameraman zoom in close for remarks from the chair. The whole country was playing out this charade.

Finally, Hulett himself took the microphone, and the words that came from his lips were like a slap in the face to Merchant, so foreign they seemed to the Gordon Hulett who had expressed diametric opposition to them barely a day and a half ago at Josh's party.

"My friends," he said, eyes fixed somewhere above the camera in the back of the room, "these are troubling times for the United States of America. Our technology has gotten expensive; our deficit continues to increase. Soon we may no longer be able to compete at all with the foreign businesses that have such a large market share of the world right now. I fear this problem, this growing malaise of economy because it will eventually make America a second-rate power, a second-rate country.

"We have come here today to discuss ways of helping that economy. We thought we had a way—taking sixty billion dollars from our military budget. But I have come to accept the fact over the last several days that cutting the defense budget could be the first step toward the military annihilation of this country. . . ."

"God, he did it," Rosen said. "Until I heard it with my own ears, I wouldn't have believed it. Hulett sold out."

"The cold war is not over," Hulett said. "The Soviet military machine is still rolling the dice, trying to outflank us. They've put missiles into Central America, missiles trained at us. What is our president doing during these trying times—he's practicing denial on a massive scale, denial of a threat that has been our uppermost concern for nearly half a century. Well, I cannot ignore the threat. When the Joint Chiefs voted on Monday to not accept the cuts, they did it because they are professionals at this horrid game of war, and as professionals they were of the opinion that the threat was real, the dangers not exaggerated.

"What is mere money when put up against the lives of our citizens? We can worry about the ledger books another day. Today, we must concern ourselves with staying alive, with keeping active the ideals of democracy in the greatest country on the face of this planet. We owe it to the world, if not just to ourselves."

"Sounds like a campaign speech," Tate said with a half smile.

The speech went on for ten full minutes, nobody calling the time rule on the chairman, ten full minutes of paranoia aimed directly at the heart of the American dream. It hurt Merchant to hear the words, most of them meaningful to him, coming from a man he knew didn't really share the sentiment.

"That is why," Hulett finished at last, "I have decided to sustain the military on this vote and send a message to the entire Congress not to uphold the President's recision of allocations. I want a peaceful, safe world, but peace through strength, not through the totalitarian boot in our face. God bless America!"

The room broke into uproarious applause, Hulett smiling, pleased with the results. "Our debate time is up," the man said. "If you all will quietly file out of the room and leave us to vote."

The doors opened, Merchant and his party the first ones out since they were the closest to them. They moved directly across the hall to lean against the beige wall. Rosen was dejected, as if he'd been diagnosed with incurable cancer.

"What now?" Merchant asked him.

The man shook his head, a kind of fright creeping into the corners of his eyes. "We may lose this vote," he said low. "Last night we had a two-thirds majority on our side. I was listening to patriotic speeches in there from people who swore to me last night that they wouldn't do that."

"How important is the vote?" Merchant asked.

"The recision vote must be taken in both houses of Congress," Tate answered. "Both houses must accept it or the money goes back where it came from. A negative vote in Appropriations isn't the end of the world . . . but it could be the next closest thing. The committee carries a lot of weight."

"Fuck Appropriations," Rosen said. "When we take this onto the House floor, I'll pull every favor, every chit I've been saving for The Big One. I'm going to twist so many arms they'll want to put me on the professional wrestling circuit. This thing is not going to beat us!"

"Speak of the devil," Tate said, pointing to the door to the committee room, people still filing out. "It's the man himself, Ben James."

Merchant knew who Tate was talking about immediately. James stood out from the rest of the crowd. He was tall and dressed to the teeth, his blond-haired, cherubic face almost glowed with light. Merchant had seen real charisma only a few times in his life—MacArthur had had it, and Kennedy, and Reagan; it oozed from Ben James like hot lava. The man commanded the crowd that surrounded him through natural superiority. As he studied James, the man turned and fixed him with a stare. Then he smiled and walked right up to Merchant.

"Charles Merchant," he said, extending his hand. "We meet at last. I'm Ben James."

Charlie took the offered hand, shook it. "You know who I am," he said.

"I make it a point to know everybody in my town, Mr. Merchant," James said. "I hear you've been asking around a bit about me, too."

"Well, your name keeps poking up in the strangest places. Though your secretary wouldn't allow me to speak with you."

"June's very protective of me." James smiled as he unabashedly sized Merchant up. "How's your wife Linda?" he asked. "Did she go to the Center this morning?"

Merchant frowned heavily, realizing there was a deadly serious confrontation going on amid the smiles and laughter. If the man wanted to play, he was certainly ready to give a little back. "You're quite the little encyclopedia, aren't you? You been getting all your information from that goon who took my video the other night?"

"You must mean Jeremy," James said. "A good worker,

but not a very nice man. What did you want to talk to me about?"

"About the death of Joann Durbin and Jack Braedman."

The man frowned, but it didn't seem sincere. "Oh, the tragedy," he said. "How sad when life is taken from someone so young. I feel that justice was left to languish when Braedman took his own life. What do you think?"

"You tell me," Merchant said, reaching into his pocket to take out his pipe to stick in his mouth cold. "You seem to know so much about me."

James looked hard at him, and it was as if the rest of the world were suddenly fading away, leaving only those two. The intensity of it ground in his ears like a buzz saw, and Merchant felt as if he could see the man's skeleton right through the skin. Something major was happening between them and he couldn't, for the life of him, figure out why. So he responded with his gut, tightening up, just as he would to any threat. "You're a good man, Charlie," James said. "I knew I'd like matching brains with you. There's so little amount of brains out there these days, Charlie. You don't mind if I call you Charlie?"

"Are you behind all these demonstrations?" Merchant asked point-blank, taking the offensive. The man's mock innocence was calculatedly maddening.

"Me?" James put an incredulous index finger to his chest. "You talking about me? I'm just a poor country boy trying to make a living, that's all. You know, Charlie. If you want to talk things over, why don't you and Linda come by the house tonight. I'm giving a little dinner party. We'll talk about the tragedy if you want to, and I believe I've got a proposition for you that you might find interesting."

At that moment the doors to the committee room burst open, congressmen storming out with the bad news. The committee had voted to stick with the Joint Chiefs, and it hadn't even been close.

James smiled at Merchant. "My, my," he said. "It looks as if common sense has won out again."

Merchant felt his insides jerk. Under other circumstances, he would have loved to see the vote come out this way. But not if James was behind it, not in a million years if James was behind it. He struck out irrationally and emotionally. He couldn't help himself. "You know," he said. "You should have a talk with that friend of yours, Jeremy," he said. "His license plate doesn't match up with his car. That usually means that the car is stolen."

"You don't say," James replied. "How very observant of you." He waved into the crowd of departing representatives. "There's someone I need to see. If you'll excuse me."

The man started off, Merchant throwing in the rest. "And if I see him anywhere around my house again, I'll kill him. I mean that."

James smiled, his teeth almost sparkling. "I believe you do," he said, then put on a fake frown. "I guess this round goes to you, Charlie."

"I didn't know we were sparring."

James took several steps away from him, the smile never leaving his face. "Don't be mawkish. We were doing so well with our honesty. I expect the good fight from you. The most dangerous game and all that. See you around eight, champ."

With that he turned, picking out Hulett from the crowd and moving right up to him, the man shaking hands vigorously. Merchant turned to look at Rosen, whose face was set hard as he watched the exchange between Hulett and the lobbyist.

The crowds had begun to drift away, the pro-defense people shouting and laughing loudly, their voices drifting back haunting and ethereal, a sound borne on a vagrant breeze, disjointed, unreal.

"It won't end here," Rosen called to James, both he and Hulett turning to stare for just a second before moving off together down the hall, their heads close together. Rosen raised his voice as they departed. "You're in my ballpark now!" he called, but to Merchant it seemed hollow and filled with dark cynicism. And he somehow knew that it was he, not Rosen, who would have to carry the weight of responsibility for Ben James.

Tonight would tell a story.

Hotel Alameda, Tegucigalpa 4:38 P.M.

Ken Breedlove sat, savoring the whiskey in small sips, letting the continual flush of warm air from the overhead fan wash over him like millions of tiny dancing fingers. The heat of the day had settled, finally, onto the city just in time to begin its retreat from the impending night. Outside the heat vied with the beggars for possession of the streets, as everyone else retreated indoors. Feria de Suyapa was winding down, leaving its usual residue of tons of garbage, both natural and human. After the festival there was always a huge contingent of supplicants who'd decide they liked the city and wanted to stay. The morning after the festival, the state militia would run them off at gunpoint.

Inside, a far more interesting spectacle was taking place. The ambassador to Honduras was in the process of remaking the world with the assistance of the President of the United States. Jurgenson, in rolled-up shirtsleeves and no jacket, stood talking into a telephone on a coffee table in the sitting-room area of the suite, the furniture heavy wood with brocaded upholstery. Carlos Molina sat on the low-slung couch not three feet from Jurgenson, the open suitcase full of money sitting next to him so he could always turn and stare at it when his knees got weak.

Jurgenson's phone was hooked up to a black box the size of a briefcase, the encoder. The ambassador would speak, his voice going into the code box for scramble, coming out uncoded on the Washington end through a similar box. The response voice was hollow, flat, and tinny, President Macklin as a mechanical man. Breedlove thought that funny and dwelled on it for a moment.

"I'm telling you, Jeff," Jurgenson was saying, "things are coming apart down here. There's action all along the border, bodies coming through all the time. We've got to take some sort of action down here."

He pulled the receiver away from his face and shrugged in Breedlove's direction. It would take just under a minute to get the response. "You may be overreacting," the mechanical voice intoned through the speaker. "Border disputes have been common down there since the mid–nineteenth century. Are you sure this is worth intervention?"

"Yes," Jurgenson said without hesitation. "They're gearing for civil war down here. Come on, Jeff, old buddy. I wouldn't pull your chain on this."

"I didn't say that you were," came the delayed reply from the robot president. "It's just that committing troops is a big step, one not to be taken lightly."

"Isn't my word enough?" Jurgenson said, looking to Breedlove for moral support, the man giving him the thumbs-up sign. Funny how half a million dollars could make fast friends.

"God, it's almost enough, Mark," came the reply, then a shift. "What have you heard on that mercenary, Breedlove? Anything on that?"

Jurgenson smiled wide. "Haven't heard a word," he said. "Is it that important?"

"Yes . . . no . . . I don't know. We're trying to catch flies with a fishing net here. I'm looking for something solid, something . . ." The voice trailed off and didn't resume.

"You really need to think seriously about helping these people out," Jurgenson said, taking the initiative again. Breedlove liked that, the indomitable American spirit in action. "We could fuck around and lose this whole region."

"Is that your professional opinion?"

"Yes. Most definitely."

"This isn't something to rush in to, Mark. I'm going to have to think on this one for a while."

Breedlove watched Jurgenson's shoulders slump in resignation. "I hope you decide before it's too late," he said. "My best to Gertie. Cutting contact now. Out."

He dropped the phone delicately onto the cradle, the encoder flashing and whistling off the line like a steam calliope before settling down with a vibrating groan. Jurgenson slumped heavily into an easy chair across from Breedlove. "I did the best I could," he said, his eyes drifting to the suitcase. "Guess I didn't have as much pull as I thought."

"Don't worry about it," Breedlove said, finishing the drink he'd been teasing with one gulp. "I got what I needed."

Jurgenson nodded, sat up straighter, and looked at his watch. "Well," he said with a tone of finality. "It was nearly impossible for me to slip out by myself again, especially with the encoder. My people are probably tearing up the city looking for me. I'd better get back." He stood. Molina, excitement showing on his face, stood also.

"We will need to transport the cash," the Honduran minister said.

"Indeed," Breedlove replied. "What have you got in mind?"

The man frowned broadly. "One of us can take the suitcase, the other . . . I don't know. Do you have—?"

Breedlove shook his head. "Sure don't. All I supply is the cash." He stood and moved to the suitcase, closing it and latching it.

Molina looked at Jurgenson. "Perhaps we can take the suitcase together and go to a place where we can share up."

"Yeah," Jurgenson said, and an amount of concern was beginning to show on his face, as if he'd only just really thought about the situation for the first time. A smart man. He turned once more to Breedlove. "I really am sorry about how things turned out."

"I told you, Mark," Breedlove said, "that I got what I wanted. In your case, what I wanted was credibility."

"Credibility?"

"Sure," Breedlove said, smiling widely as the man's eyes narrowed. "You didn't really think that Macklin would send troops just on your say-so, did you?"

"Then what—?"

"Come on out here," Breedlove called, the suite's bedroom double doors slamming open, Wee Willie and Jamie hurrying in, silenced .22s in their hands, evil leers plastered on their faces.

"What the hell!" Jurgenson yelled. "What—"

"Ice them," Breedlove said.

Both Molina and Jurgenson bolted in opposite directions, Willie firing face high at the Honduran, the man yelling and falling against an end table, hands covering his face as both Willie and Jamie turned and fired at a fleeing Jurgenson.

"Come on," Breedlove called. "Take it like a man."

A silenced hit caught Jurgenson in the lower back, the man stumbling, but still moving for the door as another took him in the buttocks, knocking him to the ground fifteen feet from them.

"Damn you!" he yelled through clenched teeth as he tried to rise again, Molina screaming like a baby as he knelt on the floor, his hands covering his face, blood running in thick, syrupy globs onto the beige carpet.

Willie and Jamie moved closer and hit Jurgenson again as he got to his feet, his left shoulder and upper back exploding, running thick dark blood, and still he moved, cursing low, his hand making the door handle. Willie caught up to him then, put the .22 to the back of his head, and fired, the man standing, shaking wildly, vibrating for several seconds before falling like a rock to the floor, a large smear of blood on the door and handle.

Breedlove turned to a sobbing, whimpering Molina, still kneeling on the floor. "Please, Breed," he whined, blood still oozing thickly between fat fingers. "Please . . . don't. Please don't k-kill me. Please . . . don't."

Breedlove, disgusted, took Jamie's automatic and moved right up to Molina, leveling the weapon at the top of his head. He pulled the trigger to a loud pop. The man slumped, quiet finally, his head lolling, his body locked in the position of supplication.

Breedlove looked around the room. "Good," he said, and moved to the sofa, reaching behind it to pull out the flags. They were Caribbean. He tossed them on the floor. "Wrap the meat up in these," he told the men.

He watched Willie and Jamie drag the bodies together and wrap them in the flags. Then he sat down and penned a note in Spanish, giving the Companeros full credit for the murders and blaming the President of the United States for "acts of provocation." He tacked the note onto the chest of Mark Jurgenson, then stood back to appreciate the beauty of his work.

It had been a productive day, and it was still early. Good. He moved to the sofa and picked up the suitcase.

He looked at Willie, smiling at the perspiration that glistened on the man's bald head. "'Give me my robe,'" he said, "'put on my crown; I have Immortal longings in me.'"

Chevy Chase, Maryland 8:14 P.M.

Charles Merchant couldn't miss the house belonging to Ben James as he slowly maneuvered the Ford wagon down the wide, well-plowed, old-money street. It sat a hundred yards deep on its lot atop a rolling hill. Right now, for some reason, it sparkled like a diamond under the dazzling glare of a large number of high-intensity floodlights. It was huge, three-story red brick latticed with brown ivy vines that threw black shadows under the brilliant lights, making the vines look like a spiderweb covering the entire house. The deep-piled snow glowed brightly, the whole area standing out in bold relief against the darkness of night, making it seem more a monument than a residence.

"What kind of party is this?" Linda asked from beside Charlie as they pulled in behind a black limo at a police checkpoint at the walled entry to the house's long, pine-lined driveway. "You didn't tell me it was anything fancy."

"You didn't give me the chance to tell you much of anything," he replied, mood dark despite the promise of the evening. "I couldn't stop you bitching long enough to listen to me."

They were driving Linda's car because somebody had sneaked into the garage while they'd been getting ready for the party and slit the tires of the Cadillac. He couldn't help but wonder if it was a friendly greeting from Ben James and his pal Jeremy.

She turned to glare at him in the pale green light of the dashboard, her arms wrapped protectively around her chest for warmth, the collar of her black wool coat turned up to her ears. "You did everything but force me here at gunpoint," she said flatly. "How do you expect me to act? I had a board meeting at the Center tonight."

"This is important."

"So is my board meeting!" she said loudly, turning to stare out the windshield again, her body held rigid. "And you won't even tell me what's so important about this stupid party tonight. I'm just expected to go along like the good little army wife. Is that why you've put on the uniform tonight, Colonel? Should I salute when I speak to you."

"Stop it," he said. "You are my wife. This is important. And I want you to be here. That should be enough."

He wasn't sure exactly why he'd put on he old uniform tonight of all nights. He hadn't worn it for ten years, hadn't even thought to. Until tonight. Until Ben James.

"Believe it or not, Colonel," Linda said, "I sometimes think about myself as something other than your appendage."

"I don't mean it that way."

"How do you mean it, then?"

He briefly considered telling her about Ben James and his connection to Jack, but that would only make her angry for Eve's sake. Better to just let her blow off steam. "Never mind," he said, and pulled up to the checkpoint, rolling down his window to be greeted by a Maryland State policeman and a blast of arctic air.

"Name, please," the man said mechanically, his face pale white with red splotches from the cold. He held a clipboard in his gloved hands, a small flashlight taped to the clip, shining down on the pad.

"Mr. and Mrs. Charles Merchant," Charlie said.

The man ran his finger down the list of names. "Is that . . . Linda Merchant?"

"Yes," Linda said.

The cop straightened and waved them through. "They'll show you where to park," he said, pointing up the drive, his voice emphasizing the word "they'll," giving it portent.

Merchant rolled up the window and drove slowly on, the driveway scraped nearly clean of snow. The drive over had been a mess, the inadequacy of the D.C. snowplows nearly legendary. It wasn't snowing at the moment, but well over a foot and a half lay on the ground, many roads impassable.

"I'm not going to do this for you again, Charlie," Linda said, making him start.

"What?"

She didn't turn to him. "I'm not ever going to go anywhere else with you unless I want to go."

"You're overamping on this thing," he replied. "It isn't that big of a deal. Most wives would love getting to go to a Washington party."

"That's me—ungrateful. I—my God!" She had jumped back in the seat, a hand to her mouth. Charlie looked through her window. Fifty-foot pines lined the drive on both sides. A man in a white parka covering him from head to foot, black goggles where eyes should be, stood leaning against a tree trunk, an M-16 held in his grasp.

Charlie drove past, the man turning his head to watch them but making no other movements.

"What's going on?" she asked loudly.

"Look around the lawn," he said, scanning out the windshield, more gunmen in white blending into the lawn in a number of places. "Look for a white step-van."

"There," she said, pointing to the south corner of the house. "What is it?"

"Communications truck," he said. "I don't believe it, but I think the President is here."

"*Our* President?" she said. "With me dressed like I'm going to the PTA?"

"Looks like," he said, feeling a gnawing pain eating at his gut. He automatically reached into his side pocket and took out the pipe, clamping it between his teeth. What would the President be doing here? Merchant's conversation with Ben James was beginning to come into sharper focus. The man wanted him here for a reason. It was as if the two of them were involved in some sort of war game, like his tabletop Waterloo, and James was busy defining the rules.

The presence of the President obviously showed exactly how much clout James had at this moment in time. It wasn't an unusual situation to put the entire machinery of government into action just so that Macklin could attend a party, otherwise the man would remain a prisoner in the White House; but it galled Merchant to no end to think that his taxpayer dollars were providing protection to someone like Ben James.

Light spilled out into the driveway from the open front door as they pulled up behind the limo, the front of the house a half rotunda of wood, supported by antebellum columns. White-gloved Marine MPs hurried to open car doors and help passengers out before climbing in themselves and driving to the back parking lot. They took their turn in the gate, the Marine saluting Charlie as he got out, reminding him again that he was wearing the uniform.

Linda walked around to join him. He took her by the elbow and gently guided her up the three flaring steps to the porch. "Did you see the formal on the woman who went in ahead of us?" she asked in a low voice.

"No," he whispered back.

"You've really managed to embarrass me this time."

They moved through the doorway to find themselves in a small entry hall, an archway to the left leading to a large, crowded party. Male and female Secret Service were stationed just inside the door, wearing surgical gloves and holding the looping coils of portable metal detectors. Two of them took the Merchants' overcoats, while two others approached with the detectors.

"We're going to have to search you, Colonel," an innocuous male agent said. "Sorry for the inconvenience. Would you raise your arms please."

Charlie did as he was told; Linda was given a similar treatment from one of the females. As the coil search began, a butler in full livery asked for their names and checked them off another list. The butler then went to a small phone set in an alcove and spoke softly over the receiver. After the coil search, the agents patted them down in the classic police fashion, even taking Charlie's pipe apart and checking inside.

The butler hung up the phone and spoke to Charlie. "Mr. James wants me to tell you that he'll be with you momentarily. Meanwhile, please join the other guests in the ballroom."

"Everybody's going to be looking at me," Linda said, staring down at her burgundy, double-knit suit. "I'm not going to be able to stay here."

"Would you stop worrying," he said, guiding her to the archway. "It doesn't matter. Nobody cares."

"Thanks, Charlie. You always know the right thing to say."

They walked through the archway and into the most glamor Merchant had ever seen. James's "little get-together" was something quite a bit more. The ballroom itself was two stories tall and half the size of a football field. Blazing crystal chandeliers hung on long chains from the cathedral ceiling. Huge fireplaces roared at either end of the long room, casting dancing light sabers across the length of the highly polished tongue-and-groove mahogany floor. The walls were wood panel, fitted with intricately carved balusters of filigree, stained-glass rose windows fifteen feet high lodged between the panels. The czars must have had hunting lodges that looked like this.

There were several bars manned by black men in white starched jackets and a fifteen-piece dance band occupied its own bandstand set in the side center of the room before a roped-off dance floor. Much to Merchant's dismay, the band was playing "Getting Sentimental Over You."

"I can't believe this," Linda whispered, grabbing his arm. "Do you see who's here? God, there's Bob Hope . . . and David Brinkley."

The pain in his gut was getting worse by the minute. Merchant bit down harder on the pipe stem. He hated the waiting. He was more than ready for movement.

The guest list was something out of the contents page of *People* magazine. Not just pols, either. Military superstars, business leaders, entertainment celebrities, anybody who was at the moment getting his fifteen minutes of Andy Warhol's sunshine was there, talking and laughing and drinking and dancing just like ordinary people. He knew everyone in the room, yet had never met any of them—alone amid a sea of familiar faces.

"There's Paul Newman," Linda said, hitting him on the arm. "Paul Newman is here."

"Here?" Merchant replied, using his tune-out talk while he let the guest list sink in. This man was connected to the max and beyond. And he wanted Charlie to understand it. Why? What was it that James wanted from him? What was the game?

He felt Linda pull away from him and begin to walk off. "Where are you going?" he asked.

She turned hard eyes on him, the sounds of the party nearly drowning out her words. "I'm going to go to the bar and get drunk enough to talk to Paul Newman," she said, then turned and walked off.

He started after her, then stopped. If they weren't together, they weren't fighting. It seemed a reasonable compromise, one they had made quite often lately. He turned from her retreat and moved through the thick crowd to a freestanding bar on the other side of the room, ordering Scotch and water, neat, from an embarrassingly obsequious black bartender who seemed to think that everybody had shown up at the party to make small talk with him. He turned his back on the man first chance and watched the dance floor, one elbow still resting on the bar.

"Can't get there from here, Charlie," came a voice from beside him. "Gotta learn to swim first."

He turned, startled, and found himself staring into the eyes of a man he'd only seen at reunions since they'd joked about swimming the Yalu to get the Chinese Communists—Korea in 1951. "Tuck Tucker," he said, doing a fake recoil from the general's star on his shoulder. "Who'd you have to kill to get that?"

Robert "Tuck" Tucker, small, no bigger than five feet four inches, and built like a barrel, smiled around his big unlit cigar and his regulation mustache, his hand thrusting out to shake Merchant's. He seemed perfectly natural this way; this was how Charlie would have pictured him as a general. He hadn't changed in forty years. His skin had just gotten more leathery, his youthful pigheadedness giving way over the years to the hard-nosed officer hiding within—the normal progression. "They got tired of my bellyaching about discipline in the ranks and kicked me out of the Joint to let me do something about it," he said, the handshake turning into an embrace. Finally, the man pulled away from him and narrowed his eyes at the uniform. "I'm down running the 82nd Airborne out of Fort Bragg. I'd heard you'd retired."

"Ten years ago," Merchant said, removing the pipe and taking a sip of his scotch.

"God, am I that out of touch?" the man replied. "What have you been doing all these years?"

"Ran the Federal Protection Service after I severed," Merchant answered, watching Linda down a tequila sunrise in one long pull at a bar on the other side of the dance floor. "The last five or six months, I haven't been doing anything."

The man shook his head around his drink. "Shit, Charlie. You could have been Chairman of the Joint Chiefs by now. Why'd you get out?"

"Got sick of apologizing for Korea," Merchant said, "and got tired of swimming uphill."

The man snorted in return. "Thank God I was just a flunky back then," Tucker said, narrowing his eyes. "You know, I was telling some of the recruits last week about how we trained Korean spies to jump behind enemy lines."

"I seem to recall that we didn't have any parachutes for training."

Tucker pointed at him. "We'd put 'em in a jeep, get it up to about forty, and shove them out of the back yelling, 'Tuck and roll. Tuck and roll.'"

"And that's how you got your name," Merchant dutifully said, knowing the man expected it.

"Bingo!"

North Carolina sure seemed a long drive from Chevy Chase just for a party. There had to be some reason for Tuck's appearance. "Quite a shindig here tonight."

"Yeah," Tucker answered, looking around as if noticing for the first time. "This guy really knows how to put on the dog, all right."

"You a friend of Ben James?"

"Never met him," Tucker said, turning and ordering bourbon from the chatty bartender, ignoring the man when he tried to make conversation.

"Then how'd you get the invite?"

Tucker took his drink, stuffed a dollar in the bartender's tip jar to shut him up, then leaned back against it the same way Merchant was doing, his eyes continually scanning the women on the dance floor as they grunted through a loud rumba, skirts flying. "We get a lot of LSI invitations over at the Building," he said, sipping the whiskey. "James has been good to us over there. He kept things together when they wanted to fall apart."

"Fall apart, how?" Merchant said, ignoring the fact that the man hadn't really answered his question.

"You know, the cuts," Tucker answered. "The damned civilians are trying to dismantle the military. If it wasn't for Ben James and his influence, they might have done it already. The man's got his finger on the pulse beat of the whole fucking nation right now. Hell, you think Macklin'd be here tonight if James wasn't the man of the hour? I tell you, he could save it all."

"Then you don't buy the government's reading of the budget problem?"

"Hell no!" the man said loudly. "What military man would? Especially with the Central American thing active."

It was a good point. Merchant had no answer for it. No bureaucracy wants to make itself smaller. The nature of all things is to grow and thrive. He was finding the conversation with Tucker unsettling. He was beginning to judge the budget affair from the outside, instead of from the trenches with Tuck where he belonged. Damn Ben James for turning his world upside down, for making him view everything with suspicion, even the values and systems he held most dear.

"What about Central America?" Charlie asked.

The man looked suspiciously all around, then drew Merchant by the arm slightly away from the bar. "We're mobilizing," he said, his eyes unmistakably alive with the knowledge, "ready to move at a moment's notice. I don't think we're going to take those motherfuckers lying down this time. Do you know our ambassador to Honduras is missing?"

"What do you mean, missing?" Merchant asked, finishing his drink, turning back and leaving the empty glass on the bar top. One was enough for him tonight. He wanted to stay sharp on enemy territory. He resettled the cold pipe between his teeth, neither man lighting his smoke.

"Missing, missing," the man said. "Nobody knows where he is." Tucker removed his cigar and pulled Merchant down somewhat to get his mouth near Charlie's ear. "If it's go on a mission to Caribbea . . . I'm up in the rotation to get command. Imagine, our first real jungle action since 'Nam."

"You're forgetting Grenada and Panama City."

"No I'm not."

Both men laughed, though Charlie figured that if the 82nd was involved in the invasion, its scenario would be exactly like Grenada. He took a long breath and watched all the civilians drift by in their expensive clothes and their put-on ethics. The band had inexplicably switched to a polka, tuxes and formals dutifully oomp-pa-pa-ing to the steady rhythm. In Washington, everyone watched everyone, just to make sure they were doing okay themselves. Imitation was a survival tactic in a city where your importance was measured by your place in the continually changing power loop. You were either on the bus or you were nothing.

"Nope," Tuck said, clucking his tongue. "It'll be real troops this time . . . none of these pork pies in short pants and no shoes. We're talkin' about the real thing . . . kick 'em in the ass like in the Gulf."

Merchant watched a man in a dark suit and black frame glasses winding his way through the crowd, searching for someone. He wore an earpiece, a tiny wire descending from the thing to disappear within his collar somewhere. His jacket was a touch too big, Merchant realizing he was Secret Service, the jacket designed to cover the 9mm automatic he no doubt wore beneath. The man moved closer to him, finally zeroing him in.

"Charles Merchant?" he asked, and looked at his watch.

"Yes."

"I've been asked to take you upstairs to Mr. James," the man said, his tie a faint pattern of American eagles, his breath smelling slightly of decay. He seemed a man totally made of faint and slight impulses, a company player.

"Wow," Tucker said, jamming the cigar back in his mouth. "You've made it upstairs."

"We need to find my wife," Merchant said.

"I'm sorry, sir," the man replied in a monotone. "I was only told to bring you along."

That was fine with Merchant. He didn't want to drag their problems out in public anyway. He didn't really trust

Linda to do the right thing anymore. He turned and shook
Tucker's hand. "Good seeing you again, Tuck," he said.
"Maybe you'll still be around when I come back down. If
you see Linda, will you tell her I went up?"

Tucker winked at him. "Call me sometime, pard," he
said, and Merchant wondered if the invitation had to do
with the man's perceiving him as rating higher in the
power structure.

He walked off then, grateful for action, finally. He took
the pipe out of his mouth and stuck it in the side pocket of
his dress blue jacket. The Secret Service man, unnamed,
walked briskly ahead of him, as if trying to hurry him
along. Merchant deliberately slowed his pace.

They left the ballroom by a side door, then took a back
staircase that wound upward for two stories, its banister
highly polished brass. More Secret Service, armed for
show, guarded the second-floor landing. The President
was apparently up here, too. And as they walked into the
thickly carpeted hallway, he knew what Tucker had meant
when he had commented on Merchant's invitation.

The hallway was jammed with senators, representatives, cabinet members, and advisers. In that rarified
world of Access, Merchant had just skipped the loop
entirely and ended up close to the inner circle. All the
people who were downstairs were down there because
they weren't allowed to be up here. He was getting close to
the fires of state, close enough to get a burn. They began to
move down the hallway, all eyes turning to them as they
walked soundlessly, all eyes asking the question: Where'd
this one come from and whom does he threaten?

They kept walking, past the hallway insiders to another
set of guards at the door on the hall's far end.

"Charles Merchant," his guide said, then turned and
walked off.

Charlie was checked off another list, then physically
searched again before the wooden, antiqued door was
opened and he was ushered into the master bedroom, the
juncture of Access. The room was very large, expensively
furnished French Provincial, with an attached dressing
room and a bath leading off from there.

Expensive glass figurines were placed everywhere, on
dressers and night tables, on shelves built especially to

hold them, in small, lighted cases. James was apparently a serious collector.

The room, however, had been turned into a portable communications center; the President of the United States never traveled light. A large bank of phones, including the red "hot line," manned by technicians, filled the king-size bed. A continual murmur of low voices vibrated the room as phones rang, were answered, instructions given before the next phone rang. The briefcase-sized encoder sat silently on a dresser, one man assigned just to that. There were computers and printers, some of them operating quietly, jammed on card tables and affixed with movable signs with the presidential seal. In Merchant's years with the Federal Protection Service, he'd seen similar setups dozens of times.

Interestingly enough, people he didn't recognize filled these rooms—nameless technicians, a few Secret Service and Langley types. The First Lady, Gertie Macklin, sat on the edge of the bed with a gray-haired woman he didn't recognize watching Wheel of Fortune on a big-screen TV mounted into the side wall. Not seeing James in the bedroom proper, he ambled toward the attached dressing room, feeling somewhat giddy at his sudden thrust into the corridors of real power. His two rotations at the Building had naturally given him a nose for smelling out the real thing and an unavoidable urge to be a part of it. Even when he'd reached the height of his own personal power with Army Intelligence, he'd never gotten within ten miles of anything like this. It aggravated and elated him that Ben James should be the instrument of his wish fulfillment.

He moved through the archway and into the dressing room, surprised that no one stopped him. This part of the bedroom was large and square with walk-in closets branching off from it and a small sitting area done in frail-looking Louis XIV brocaded furniture. And here, more glass, different kinds of goblets arranged on wall-length shelves, dazzling under track spotlighting. Here, another group, those close to the President. The secretary of defense stood talking to Macklin's adviser on foreign affairs, Ben Fenwick. Several other cabinet members sat talking heatedly on the fragile furniture, tall drinks in their hands, their voices full of authority. And there were the women. Two young women mixed easily with the group. They were more than beautiful. Like Joann, they were perfect—women no one ever really meets, women you see on the television or sometimes on the street and you wonder who the hell they belong to. Merchant felt a kind of stabbing pain deep inside himself, a nameless longing he tried to ignore. Ben James was not to be seen.

He stood for a moment, looking around and listening. The talk was of Central America, the possibility of military action. It gave a high pitch to everyone's voice. Nuclear war hadn't been discussed with such immediacy in America for thirty years and it filled the guests with a fearful excitement, as if they were talking of cabalistic and arcane phenomena. Perhaps they were.

One of the women, a redhead, turned and smiled at him, and he realized that he'd been staring. Embarrassed, he looked away and examined the shelves containing the glass. He picked up a long-stemmed goblet, thin and delicate. When he held it up to the light, the entire spectrum of color prismed through the crystal curves.

"It's Tiffany favrile," came a voice from beside him. Ben James stood, smiling, two drinks in his hands. He and Charlie were eye to eye, the two largest men in the room. "Late nineteenth century. It was a part of the art nouveau movement. Quite delicate, don't you think? Worth five grand on the open market."

"It's beautiful," Charlie replied, gently replacing the goblet.

"I believe you take Scotch and water neat," James said, holding a drink out to him.

"No thanks," Charlie said, looking him in the eye. "Already had one. You really like glass, don't you?"

James set down both drinks, and picked up a hunk of Steuben Glass that doubled as a paperweight. It was the size of a large rock and topped by inch-high gold figures of David preparing to loose his slingshot on an ugly, lunging Goliath—drama frozen at perpetual climax. "Glass reminds me of reality, Charlie," James said, handing the thick chunk to Merchant. "Playful, malleable. It's a solid with the properties of a liquid. It can bend light, dissect it, change it. Yet it can be tamed, controlled." Merchant watched the man's eyes light as he spoke, his voice getting low and reverential. "Ground properly, it can show us the majesty of the cosmos or the crowded universe of a drop of water. It hides and reveals everything . . . everything. Do you know that we have evidence that prehistoric man was working with glass as long ago as ten thousand B.C.? And, Charlie, that fragile piece of glass you hold in your hand will stop a bullet better than a solid steel wall. Glass, you see, can be all things to all people."

"Just like you?" Merchant replied.

The man's eyes seemed to glow unnaturally. "I'm a mirror," he said. "People look at me and see themselves in glorious perspective. Perhaps I am all things to all men— the heart of the envelope as our friends in the Building say. I reflect the circumstance."

"So does a chameleon," Merchant said, uneasy around the man's fantasy. He'd seen a lot of ego in his life, but nothing short of Napoleon's approached Ben James. "But a chameleon is cold-blooded and leathery."

"And has no conscience," James said, eyes snapping, his jaw muscles clenching and unclenching. Then he smiled widely. "I'm so glad you could come to my party. You look good in uniform, too. Let me introduce you to a couple of my employees. Mary Ellen . . . Mel . . . come over here for a minute."

The two women he noticed coming in withdrew from a conversation with the HUD secretary and walked toward them. One was platinum blond and wore a shimmery blue silk dress with a low neckline, maddeningly set off by a large scarf of blue gradations worn around the shoulders and pulled down to just cover cleavage. The other one, the redhead who'd been studying him earlier, wore lime-green chiffon, layered, the hem just above her knees, and held to the shoulders by spaghetti straps. She was voluptuous, a word Merchant had never thought to use before. Her eyes were vibrant green. He could feel them pulsing all the way across the room.

"Pretty girls, aren't they?" James asked as the women joined them.

"Beautiful," Merchant said, looking at the redhead, the woman's eyes flashing in return, the contact jolting.

"Mary Ellen Colby . . . Melanie Patterson, I'd like you to meet Mr. Charlie Merchant, U.S. Army, retired. Girls, Charlie was once an important man in the intelligence loop."

The women shook hands with Merchant, Patterson holding on for several seconds before releasing him. "You seem awfully young to be retired," she said.

"Well, I—" Charlie began, but James cut him off.

"Charlie's a writer. He's writing a book about Napoleon. Isn't that right?"

"Well—"

"Napoleon," Patterson said, cocking her head slightly and picking up the Scotch that Merchant had refused. "Pro or con?"

"Pardon?" he asked. "Pro or con . . . what?"

She took a sip of the drink. "Every book I've ever seen on Napoleon either thinks he's a monster or a savior. What's your opinion, Mr. Merchant? Or should I call you Colonel?"

"Charlie's fine," Merchant answered, flustered. "The viewpoint on Napoleon in history books depends on where the book was published. And I'm basically trying to get past all the propaganda. That's why I'm writing solely from the truth of his battles."

"History was written by the winners of wars," James said.

The women smelled vaguely of Giorgio and fresh flowers. Up close, their unblemished, unlined skin shone with an inner luster, and Merchant realized that except for a little eyeliner and lipstick, they weren't even wearing any makeup. Where did women like this come from? He forced his attention back to James. He needed to keep his guard up here. "There's consensus on events, simply differences of interpretation. The trick, always, is to get to the source." He looked at the redhead again. "Are you a student of the little Corsican, Ms. Patterson?"

"Call me Mel," she said, nearly smiling but pulling it back and hiding it. "More a student of history, I suppose. That period in France had some very interesting parallels to the world in which we live today."

"Charlie has other areas of interest, also," James said, breaking up the conversation as if he couldn't stand to have people talking about things he didn't know about. "He is right now attempting to investigate more thoroughly the deaths of Jack Braedman and poor Joann."

"So, that's what brings you out here tonight," Patterson said, brightening.

"It was such a terrible tragedy," Mary Ellen said, her thick lashes fluttering wildly. "She had so much to live for. Why did he kill her, Colonel Merchant?"

"What makes you think he did?" Merchant replied.

James chuckled. "The colonel is a friend of Jack Braedman's," he said, picking up his own drink and taking a sip. "He's trying to find evidence to clear him."

"Oh?" Mary Ellen said, crinkling up her nose and shivering slightly. "I don't know how we could help you. I hadn't seen Joann for months."

"Maybe you can just tell me a bit about her life-style," he said. "Throw some light on her character. I haven't been able to get a handle on it. Tell me, just what do you people do? What was her job description?"

"I can answer that," James said, loud voices drifting from behind the closed bathroom door. President Macklin, with his top two or three advisers, must be behind that door. Merchant was within five feet of total access to the most important human being on the face of the earth. "I hire personable, intelligent, attractive people to help me make contacts. I'm very egalitarian myself, you understand, but the truth of the matter is that a young, pretty girl or guy can get listened to when nobody else can. They lobby issues. They mix well at the parties. You know how it works."

"And we wait a lot," Mary Ellen said. "I'm with Rob Danton tonight . . ."

"The domestic affairs adviser?" Charlie said, incredulous.

She answered him with just a flick of the eyebrow. "And he's been locked up with the president for thirty minutes. Never thought the day would come when I'd be waiting for some *man* to come out of the powder room."

"It's your karma," Patterson said.

"Does part of your job include . . . dating contacts?" he asked, deciding to be direct.

Both women laughed. "Sounds like you're accusing us

of being prostitutes, Colonel," Patterson said, her smile revealing an even row of white teeth. "I assure you that our sex lives are on our own time. Any more information than that gets a little too personal for my tastes."

"I didn't mean it that way," Merchant said, but that was exactly how he'd meant it and they all knew it. "When did she last work at LSI?"

The women looked at each other, thinking. Finally Mary Ellen said, "I believe it was early last fall when she went on semipermanent leave," she said.

"Last September," James said. "We'd discussed her growing relationship with Jack Braedman and decided that it would be best all the way around if Joann would close out her contact with LSI while the relationship ran its course to avoid any embarrassment to Braedman, or any conflict-of-interest charges."

"Did Braedman take any money from your PACs?"

James fixed him with bright eyes, the man's face jovial, eager-looking. "Charlie . . . everybody takes money from my PACs. That's what they're designed for."

The bathroom door opened up directly in Merchant's line of vision. Jefferson Macklin in rolled-up shirtsleeves and opened tie stepped into the dressing room followed by a large plume of cigarette smoke, the first Merchant had seen here tonight. Rob Danton, short and energetic-looking, followed him out, with the White House chief of staff, John "Goody" Goodrich, walking glumly behind. Merchant felt his breath catch.

The President walked directly up to them, coming between the women to put arms around both their shoulders. "I swear to God," he said, "you could bronze these ladies and put them in an art museum." He looked tired, frazzled. His short gray hair was disheveled, the skin on his face sallow and loose. Only his eyes held power, the absolute presence of his eyes.

"Then who would do my lobbying for me?" James replied. "Sorry things are going so rough right now, Mr. President."

The man shrugged. "How's the old story go . . . her nymphomania never bothered me before we were married? Guess this just comes with the job." He looked directly at Charlie. "I don't believe we've met, Colonel."

He pulled away from the women and took a step closer to Charlie, sticking out his hand.

Merchant shook hands with the President. "My name's Merchant, sir. Charles Merchant."

"Charlie used to run Army Intelligence," James said, always playing the good press agent.

The President nodded. "Then you tell me," he said. "What the hell are we going to do about Central America? The more we rattle our damned sabers over here, the more I hear the Russians and Cubans rattle theirs. What's your opinion, Colonel?"

Merchant was somewhat taken aback. "Should we be discussing these things here, Mr. President?" he asked, looking around nervously.

Macklin laughed, but it was a tired laugh. "Typical Intelligence officer," he replied, taking a long breath. "Unfortunately, I've been discussing these things twenty-four hours a day, everywhere I've been. There's no time clock in the Oval Office I can punch. Security's the same here as it is there at this point, and BJ has knowledge I can use. I assume that you wouldn't be here if you didn't have knowledge I could use, too. This would be a hell of a job to have to face all by yourself."

"But ultimately you, sir, have to stand on that mountaintop alone."

"Indeed," Macklin said, "but I need all the help I can get climbing up. What do you think, Colonel?"

"My opinion is that you are in a far better position to make a judgment than I am, sir," Merchant answered, still uneasy.

"Not fair," Macklin said, managing another weary smile. "Here's the deal: the border to Honduras has been incurred by Companero troops, invoking mixed response from the Honduran government and a plea for military aid from the American ambassador. The Companeros may have Russian missiles trained on us right now. Maria Madrina continues to deny that anything is happening, despite the evidence to the contrary, which tells me she may have sold out to the Communists and can't be trusted any longer. Now Rob Danton tells me that we need to sweep in with troops, secure the border, and go into the Mosquito Coast looking for the missiles."

"I second that advice," BJ said, holding up his drink.

"But," Macklin continued, "Goody tells me, and I tend to agree, that none of our other intelligence sources back up the hypothesis that intervention is essential now. . . ."

"Even if the missiles are there?" BJ asked.

Macklin smiled, running a hand through his hair, straightening. "Ah, the missiles," he said, then shook his head. "The goddamned missiles."

"The Raytheon Bearcats," Merchant said, drawing a sharp look from Macklin.

"Anyway," the President said, "if the crisis isn't imminent at the border, perhaps I could wait a few more days to get better confirmation on the missiles, then take the case through diplomatic channels. That could save us an unpopular war that just might make them decide to use those missiles if they lose . . . and they will." He put an arm on Merchant's shoulder and smiled at the insanity of it all. "And I have to make a decision on this. Jurgenson is missing, so I can't question him further. If I fail to move, we could lose Honduras. So, you sit on the hot seat, Colonel. I'm ordering you, as your Commander in Chief, to tell me what's happening in Central America."

"All right, I'll tell you," Merchant said. "But first you have to tell me something: What was the cargo of that C-130 downed off Caribbea?"

Macklin looked at him for a long moment, and in that time Merchant realized that he had inadvertently touched an exposed nerve. The President narrowed his eyes and leaned closer. "What would make you ask that?" Macklin said, eyes rock hard.

"I don't like to make judgments without all the evidence," Merchant replied. "There are still hidden pieces, hidden players. I will say this, Mr. President. This issue is far more complex than the television would have us believe. Perhaps even more complex than you would have us believe. I don't mean to be blunt, sir, but you did order me to tell you what I thought."

"So I did," Macklin replied, immediately changing the subject. "BJ, you seem to be our resident expert at the moment on the effective range of the Kamen Seasprite helicopter. You got a few minutes?"

"Sure," James replied, looking at Charlie. "If you'll excuse us?"

Merchant nodded slowly at the President, the two men walking off. Macklin had called James BJ. Then he'd been right. There was no more room for doubt. It had to be the same BJ Joann had called upon as the life force was slipping away from her. BJ! Like the hub of a giant wheel, Ben James seemed to be the revolving center point just now.

He watched the two men disappear into the bathroom, along with the chief of staff. He felt gutted. This whole night had been ass showing so far. James was rubbing his nose in it, daring him to try to prove something. And how far wrong could he be? The man had direct access to the President. Kings and prime ministers wouldn't be allowed in that bathroom right now, but Ben James, expert on the machineries of war, was invited in.

Rob Danton walked over to join them, slipping in beside Mary Ellen to wrap an arm around her waist. After introductions were made, Mary Ellen said, "We're hearing out here that you boys are thinking about sending in the troops to deal with the Companeros. It'll make for an exciting few days."

"It's just an idea," Danton said. "There's a lot to think about before committing troops."

The woman reached out and tapped him on the nose with an index finger. "Sounds like you've been talking with that old coward Goody Goodrich," she said. "You know as well as I do what happens to that region if we don't help the Hondurans." She took Danton's arm and looked at Merchant. "You have to excuse Rob, Colonel Merchant. He's one of the enemy, the man who wrote the book on useless military budgets."

"My theory is sound," Danton said.

"Your theory is based on a declining Soviet threat, darlin'. Which we ain't got!"

"That remains to be seen."

"How many democracies are you going to let sink before you understand that the threat is still real. Honey, you can't afford not to send troops. Now, how about you and me going and getting some refreshments." She looked up at Merchant. "Unless you've got some more questions for me."

Merchant shook his head. "There's nothing that Mel can't handle . . . that is if she wants to."

Patterson smiled broadly and took Charlie's arm, snuggling her breasts up close to him. He hadn't flirted for years, but was enjoying it now. "I'd be pleased to help you out if I can," she said.

He looked down at her, dwelling on the implicit suggestions in her words and in her eyes. At some point Danton and Mary Ellen walked off, but he failed to notice.

"If you're trying to get the truth about Joann," Mel said, "you're going up against BJ."

"I've already figured that one out," he said. "Tell me something I don't know."

"You can't beat him," she said. "You must not know that or you wouldn't be here. BJ's a thunderstorm moving across the face of the land. You can't stop a thunderstorm."

"Why are you telling me this?"

"Because you look like a good and honest kind of guy," she said. "Because this game already has enough players. Don't mix in, Charlie. Stay retired."

"Jack Braedman was my best friend."

"So what?"

"I owe it to him to do what I can to find the truth."

"The truth," she said, eyes brightening. She took another sip of Merchant's Scotch. "Now I understand."

"Understand what?"

"The game, Charlie. The game that BJ's playing with you."

"If it's a game, what are the stakes?"

"I honestly don't know. Maybe I'll tell you when I find out."

"And what game are you playing with me?" he asked. "What's your angle?"

"Interested bystander," she said, eyes narrowing. "I'm sitting on top of the fence, Charlie, trying to decide which way to jump."

"A dangerous game if BJ's into illegal activities," he said. "You know, even the things you're telling me now could get you in legal trouble later on."

She laughed, genuine and heartfelt, then she set the drink down and hugged him quickly.

"What was that for?" he asked.

"I haven't met an honest man in years," she said. "Look, you're a nice guy, but you still haven't figured it out. This is far beyond legal and illegal at this point. What are you going to do, run and tell the police that Ben James is busy creating a reality for us all to live in?

"There are no rules here, no laws. There's nothing I could tell you that would get me in trouble. You're doomed from the start." She smiled sadly, then backed away and looked him hard in the eyes. "You like me, don't you?"

"Well, I suppose. I don't know you very well, I—"

"No, no," she said, putting a finger to his lips. "I mean, you're attracted to me."

"What makes you say that?" he replied, his voice a trifle husky, betraying him.

"You think you were the only one to feel that electric jolt when we met?" She laughed. "You're turning red. Don't be embarrassed. You've set my clock to going, too."

"Maybe we should change the subject," he said.

She seemed surprised. "You're not attracted to me?"

"I didn't say that," he replied, forcing his eyes away from the sucking vortex of her look. "I'm not allowed to be attracted to you. I'm a married man, Ms. Pat—"

"Mel," she interrupted, shaking her head in amusement. "You're a true original, Charlie. Okay . . . we'll change the subject. What would you like to talk about? I really am thinking about helping you."

"Well," he said, his throat suddenly dry. He picked up the Scotch and took a sip himself since BJ wasn't around to see it. He had no idea of what her tirade about reality had to do with anything, but if he could keep her talking perhaps he could learn something. "We could go back to talking about Joann. What, exactly, was her relationship to Jack?"

The woman shrugged, disappointment lining her face. "She liked him okay, but she was never as crazy about him as he was about her. The world is full of relationships, most of them silly. This one may have been a little more silly and one-sided than most."

A loud beeping came from the bedroom interior, a young man with wire glasses and a dark suit jumping to answer the red telephone that sat in the middle of the bed.

"Then why did she quit her job for him?"

"We make good money at what we do," she answered, a gentle hand coming up to plaintively touch his face. "Strong," she whispered, then pulled her hand away, Charlie's face on fire where she'd touched him. "Joann understood the implications of what she did for a living affecting a man running for president, so she took the time off. More of a vacation than anything. She could afford to do it, so she did. That's all."

The man talking on the red phone moved around the bed to tap Gertie Macklin on the shoulder and speak to her in whispers. As he watched, the woman buried her face in her hands and wept softly.

"Did she have a lot of boyfriends?" he asked, drinking again.

"You saw her body, right?" Mel asked. "You tell me."

"She was a beautiful woman," he said, unable to stop himself from adding, "like you."

Her face brightened. "You *are* attracted," she said, moving up close to him again.

The First Lady stood, her face now stoic, and moved into the dressing room, passing Charlie's position as she walked to the bathroom and lightly tapped on the door. Merchant wondered what would happen here if someone actually had to use the facilities for their intended purpose. The door opened and she slipped inside.

"Did Joann have any serious boyfriends or lovers besides Jack?"

She shrugged and took the drink out of his hand, finishing it. "Not really. She was still young, still looking. It's a free country, you know. She wasn't serious with anybody."

He tried a blind shot. "Not even with Jerry Delany?"

She jumped slightly, eyes widening. "You know about Jerry?" she asked, incredulous.

It was his turn at superiority. "Perhaps I'm not as unarmed in this thing as you believe. Tell me about Joann and Delany."

His revelation had cracked some sort of armor in her,

forcing her off a game plan and into honesty. He'd seen similar changes in a hundred interrogations. "How does that old song go?" she said. "Everybody's somebody's fool? I guess that Jack was Joann's fool and Joann was Jerry's. For his part, he just used her. Probably deserved—"

Her words were cut off by a shriek coming from within the bathroom, followed seconds later by the door slamming open and Macklin charging out, his face dark and twisted with anger. "My friends," he said loudly, his voice resonating deep, righteous anger. "Mark Jurgenson has been murdered by a Caribbean assassination squad. The time of decision is at hand." He hurried through the dressing room and into the bedroom proper. "Pack it all up. It's going to be a long night!"

The room broke into furious activity, Merchant feeling like a distant outsider as he watched, having nothing to participate in. He glanced at the bathroom door, James walking slowly out, a large smile consuming his face. As he moved toward Merchant and Patterson, she grabbed Charlie's arm and whispered urgently, "He never loses," just as the man arrived.

"Miss me?" James asked as if nothing else were going on. "What were we discussing?"

Patterson gave Merchant a quick look, then said, "I was just telling Charlie how Joann didn't date much, that she and Jack Braedman were just about it."

"That's the way I see it, too," BJ replied, shaking his head, feigning sadness. "What a tragedy." He looked at Merchant. "Are we answering all your questions, pardner?"

Merchant just stared at him, BJ turning his perpetual smile in the woman's direction. She hadn't told the man of his knowledge of Jerry Delany. Perhaps she *was* intending to help him. But that raised the question, why?

James clapped the woman familiarly on the ass, a game of ownership. "Mel," he said, "why don't you go freshen up or something. Colonel Merchant and I have a little business to discuss."

"Sure, BJ," she said, giving Merchant's arm another squeeze. "It was great meeting you. Perhaps we'll . . . get together sometime."

Merchant nodded. "It was good meeting you, too."

Patterson walked off as techs hurried around the rooms wrapping wires and pulling phones, the President and his entourage already long gone. He and BJ stood alone amid a sea of activity.

"I guess it's just you and me, Charlie," BJ said, eyes twinkling. "Let's really talk."

"Fine," Merchant replied. "You said earlier that we have something to discuss."

"Yes, we do. You know, I've been thinking that you are far too young to be retired. You're a nice man: strong, intelligent, personable. Why don't you come to work for me? I'll give you the kind of money the army never envisioned. And don't say a damned thing about your book. Book writing is for anemics, people who never do anything with their lives. Nobody really makes any money at it. Come on, you're still aggressive and vital. I can use you at the Pentagon."

Merchant looked hard at him, and hoped the man could see the disgust in which he held him. "You're an influence peddler, BJ," he said, "and from what I've put together so far, you could also be a briber, a strongarm, and a murderer. I'd honestly like to see you in prison. What in the world would make you think that I'd be interested in working for someone like you?"

The man clapped his hands together. "Yes!" he said loudly. "I love your forthrightness."

"Why don't you can that shit before I jam it back down your throat?" Merchant said. "I'm sick of the charade."

The man put a hand on Merchant's arm. It was shrugged off. "You don't understand yet how much alike we are, Charlie," he said. "We come from similar backgrounds. I'm a preacher's kid, you an English professor's. Two sides of the same coin. Both of us fled home at an early age and made our own place in the world. Both of us know the difference between right and wrong, and both of us have made our choices. We both know there's more to life than what we see on the surface."

"Why would you want me to work for you?"

"I told you, I can use you at the Pentagon."

Merchant finally caught on to what the Patterson woman had suggested earlier. "That's not it," he replied. "I think it's deeper than that. I believe that you're trying, for some reason, to corrupt me, to make me accept your values. Why?"

James jumped back a step, forcing an exaggerated frown before letting the natural smile return. "You're getting a little deep for me, Colonel. I'm just a salesman moving product."

"Bullshit. Why did you bring me here tonight?"

"To show you." BJ smiled.

"To show me what?"

"You tell me."

"All right. You wanted to show me your power, the depth of your connections. Maybe you want to frighten me off the investigation."

"Frighten you off?" BJ said loudly. "My dear friend, that's the last thing I'd want to do. I don't have any power. I just introduce people to one another. I get people together through favors and friendship. I wanted you to see my reality." He gestured around the room. "I wanted you to see my world, that's all."

"Your world is phony, full of lies and deceptions," Merchant said, and decided to play a few of his cards. "You play a weird game, but it doesn't matter. I believe that you're up to your neck in illegal maneuvers that lead all the way to the D.C. Police Department and Jack Braedman's murder . . . and it was murder. I believe you're somehow responsible for the events that are transpiring in Central America. I'm putting together my chain of evidence on you, and when I get done, I'm going to nail you to the wall."

James sighed deeply and rolled his eyes like a child. "Charlie, my friend, you just don't understand anything. Don't you see that this is my town? Don't you see that truth, at the moment, is what I say it is?"

"God, you may be insane, too."

The man laughed loudly. Then, "Society's norms determine what insanity is," he said. "We'll see who's judged insane when this is all through."

"I'm going to nail you," Merchant said. "Both you and Jeremy, your little friend who slashed my tires this evening."

"Here you are," BJ said, "the whole world in motion and flux, and you're worried about the tires on your car.

Really. Can't you get with the program? You know, from where I sit, there're only two kinds of people in the world, friends and enemies. You pick the wrong side just once, and you'll see the meaning of reality. It's that simple. I eat clowns like you for breakfast."

"Then do your worst," Merchant said.

James just smiled, catlike, in return. "You're good, Charlie, solid as a rock. We're gonna have us a time, boy." He reached into his pocket and pulled out a business card and pen. He turned the card over and began to write on the back. "I'm giving you a number," he said, then finished writing and handed it to Merchant. "You can reach me anytime of the day or night on this line."

"Why would I want to call you?" Merchant replied, but took the card anyway.

James's eyes were unashamedly deep as he looked at Merchant. The words purred from his lips. "Oh, you'll want to call me all right," he said, then winked lewdly and turned away, walking out of the dressing room.

And suddenly, Merchant was alone. He stood for a moment and stared at the open bathroom door that moments before had been the scene of a major foreign policy discussion. Ben James had gotten to Merchant more than he cared to admit. It hurt him—deeply—that the President, his President, sought out the confidence and advice of someone like Ben James.

Technicians were still tearing down phones in the bedroom proper, but everyone else was gone. He wandered into the hall, which was now empty, and back down the stairs he had come up.

The ballroom was still going strong, the party in full swing as more and more people made it up to dance. He looked around for Linda, finally seeing her on the dance floor in the arms of Paul Newman. He waited patiently for the song to end, then retrieved her, dead drunk, after she had given the actor a long, lingering kiss. Tanned and athletic, Newman was gracious enough, shrugging sympathetically at Charlie with his famous pale blue eyes as Merchant led his stumbling wife off the floor.

"I have to hand it to you, Charlie old boy," she slurred as he practically dragged her back to the cloakroom. "Thish time you did all right. Thish is a wonderful party!"

She tried to whirl around, but lost her footing and fell, Charlie grabbing her and supporting her as he silently kept moving, wanting out of this place desperately.

"What's the hurry?" she asked as he got their coats and pulled her toward the door.

"I want to get you out of here before you make a bigger fool out of both of us," he said, and knew when he said it that it was BJ he was mad at, not Linda.

"Fuck you very much," she told Merchant as the butler opened the door for them.

They moved into the night, the floodlights now off, the communications van gone. A light freezing mist was falling, matching the cold darkness of Merchant's heart.

The stairs and sidewalk leading to the house were cleared of snow, but the rain was icing everything over again. Merchant put an arm around Linda, the two of them gingerly making their way down the front steps, Merchant silent, brooding; Linda humming "Raindrops Keep Falling on My Head."

They reached the bottom of the stairs and took one step along the walk, Charlie's legs going out from under him on the ice, he and Linda both falling heavily to the ground. He lay there for a second, pain shooting from several places, Linda giggling as she tried unsuccessfully to regain her feet. It was all falling apart, everything going to pieces.

And now doubt had been injected into the scenario. Killing, maddening doubt.

★ ★ ★ ★ ★ ★ ★ ★ ★ ★ ★ ★ ★ ★ ★ ★

FEBRUARY 7,
THURSDAY

★ ★ ★ ★ ★ ★ ★ ★ ★ ★ ★ ★ ★ ★ ★ ★

▰▰▰▰ NEWSBREAK ▰▰▰▰

". . . with the assassinations of Mark Jurgenson and Interior Minister Molina, the Honduran military has gone on full alert down here, Bryant. As we drove through the capital this morning, we could see signs of preparation everywhere, with National Guard vehicles patrolling the streets and the reinforcement of government buildings. It's still business as usual down here . . . but we don't know for how long."

"How much of an effect have the reports of more border attacks during the night had on the attitude there, Leslie?"

"There's an almost-visible tension in the air in Tegucigalpa, as if everyone's waiting for the other shoe to drop."

"The other shoe being the United States government?"

"Right. The current feeling is that the death of Mark Jurgenson, longtime friend of President Macklin, is bound to involve the United States in any conflict with the Companeros, although Honduran governmental feelings are mixed."

"How so?"

"Bryant, Honduran military officials tend to discount the idea of a massive Companero surge across the border. They say it makes no sense for them to directly affront the United States govern-

ment, which is how all of this plays. At the moment,
however, emotions are running extremely high, the
Central American machismo giving full vent. If I
were a betting woman, I'd say we'll be seeing an
American expeditionary force down here within the
next few days. . . ."

—the *Today* show

". . . and button it up, Washingtonians, it's going to
get worse before it gets any better. The National
Weather Bureau has just issued another blizzard
forecast for the D.C. metropolitan region. It seems
we're caught in a pressure bowl in the jet stream,
arctic air masses moving slowly in and staying
around. It will be frigid and overcast all day today,
an official seventeen inches of snow already on the
ground. Tonight, look for increasing winds and the
possibility of as much as another foot of new snow.
Nobody ever said that winter was easy."

—WBAP Radio 900

NSC, Threat Evaluation Division
Washington, D.C. 6:43 A.M.

Rob Danton sat, bleary-eyed, trying to focus on the mammoth wall-sized TV screen that was juicing silent CNN
pictures of Mark Jurgenson's body being brought out of the
Alameda Hotel. Nearly all of Headline News's output for
the last three hours had revolved around the problems in
Honduras, constantly tying every event of the last four
days visually together, over and over, as if they were trying
to build some sort of case for something. The news was
always trying to build a case. They just never knew what
case they were building.

"What I don't understand," President Macklin was
saying to the DIA chief, Gene Tillotson, "is how come we

know from the videos where the missiles are, but still can't pinpoint them."

The room had begun crowded about midnight, but one by one, Macklin had excused extraneous personnel, tying the knot tighter and tighter, trying to pare his analysis down to the bare bones. At present, all that remained were a Langley rep named Warren, Tillotson from DIA, Foreign Affairs Adviser Ben Fenwick, and, of course, Goody Goodrich.

The room wasn't overly large, and seemed even smaller because every bit of wall space was covered with maps, projections, and aerial photographs of the Mosquito Coast. A large round table sat in the room's center, its top covered with scribbled pieces of paper and the silent Styrofoam tombstones of myriad cups of harsh black coffee. It had been a long night.

"I don't have an answer for you, Mr. President," Tillotson said, his face pale and drawn, a cup of coffee shaking in his hand. The man had been looking anxious for several hours and Danton couldn't help but wonder if the shaking could possibly be the d.t.'s. "Since viewing the videos we've sent outer envelope surveillance, including satellites, all over that region. On the Honduran side we've used choppers at tree level and extended search parties and village intelligence. The damned Caribbeans have cut us off from searches in country so they won't look bad in front of their people. They're even talking about throwing our ambassador out of the country. We've photographed with thermogram and radioactive sensitive film and found nothing."

"I understand that," Macklin said, rubbing a hand across his slack-looking face. "What I don't understand is how is it possible?"

Danton sank back farther in the padded chair and closed his eyes. They'd been through this already, over and over, Macklin wanting all the numbers to add up before making a commitment, even though this time they simply weren't going to.

Danton hated all-nighters like this. Missed sleep devastated him for days afterward. His constitution was delicately balanced. His health would make for a great series of articles for the *New England Journal of Medicine*.

Being a world-famous Harvard economist had been a breeze compared to being a yes-man in the White House. His constitution vented peptic ulcers, a redundant colon, and symptoms of pancreatitis, and that was on good days. On the bad days he wandered around smiling like a normal human being as volcanic plasma burned through his intestines and noxious gases bloated him like a weather balloon. Besides that, last night was to have been the big night with Mary Ellen and her friend, the one who liked threesomes. Instead, he'd spent the night here, eating Rolaids like candy, then stoking the uncontrollable fire with more coffee.

On top of everything else, he'd found the reality of having to protect a country far different from the theories he'd predicated from the safety of his office at Harvard. It was beginning to make sense to him that if you flexed a little muscle, you could buy yourself some room to operate. It was a Ben James philosophy, but it was a sound philosophy and one that made rational sense in this instance.

He'd been patient, but he was beginning to wonder why. It seemed so simple at this point: they kicked us, we kick back. BJ could have tied this meeting up in five minutes flat.

"Mr. President," he said finally. "This doesn't seem as difficult to me as it is to you. . . ."

"Maybe because you don't have to make the decision," Macklin countered, but it wasn't heartfelt.

"But, sir," Danton replied. "A decision must be made. Let's simplify things. Take the missile thing out of it. Take the 130 shoot-down out of it. Just dwell on the actions of the last two days. Companero troops have incurred the borders of a country with which we have a mutual defense pact, and have killed our ambassador to that region. Isn't that, in itself, an act of war? We keep trying to draw in the larger issues. Hell, Reagan sent in men with simply the threat of border incursions imminent. We've got the by God real thing. Let's not worry about the missiles. Let's deal with this border thing, then look for the missiles once we get down there. Sending troops doesn't necessarily mean you have to use them. Besides, public opinion—"

"I don't want to talk about public opinion," Macklin interrupted.

"How can you not, Mr. President?" Danton said, a stomach cramp nearly doubling him over.

"He's right," Fenwick, the foreign affairs adviser, said. "The American public is making its desires known about defense and the Communist threat in this hemisphere. Can we do anything but listen?"

"What you're telling us," Goodrich said, "is that the polls aren't in our favor anymore, so we should change our plans." His red bow tie bobbed with his words. Goodrich was always neat and perfect, as if he'd stepped out of a fashion ad, his hair always in place, just so, his suits always pressed. "That's a cowardly attitude."

"Come on, Goody," Macklin said, swiveling his chair to face the man beside him. "We represent the will of the people. We can't ignore them completely. They're scared and angry right now, and I'll have to say, so am I."

"If you put it to a vote right now," Danton said, "we'd already have troops there."

"If we put it to a vote," Goodrich replied, "we'd have had major wars with everyone from the Libyans to the Lebanese in the last five years. The day they put the voting button in everybody's house is the day I move out of the country. This is a sensitive issue with worldwide ramifications the average American could never understand. That's why we're here, to ferret out the truth and act upon it intelligently. And I'm telling you, to the world it looks like we've set up the Caribbeans because we don't like the political turn they've taken. We put troops over there, and we'll have Cuban nationals on the border within a day. They've already offered."

"Good," Tillotson said. "We'll take care of them, too."

Goodrich pointed at the man. "That's just the kind of attitude that's going to get us in so deep, we'll be fighting Vietnam all over again."

"And maybe we'll win this time," Tillotson replied, jaw muscles tight. "For God's sake, we're going to have to stand up and act like men at some point here!"

Macklin looked at Fenwick. "What *will* the Russians and Cubans do?" he asked. "I mean, for real."

The man cleared his throat and sat up straighter. He

was an intelligent man, a considered man. He pursed his lips, thinking his response all the way through before speaking. Finally, he took off his black frame glasses and laid them on the table. "The Russians are acting as if they didn't put missiles over there, which means that they're acting as if we are aggressors in the region. It's a dangerous game for them to play, since all we need to do is locate the missiles to show them up for what they are. They will agitate in the U.N. and try to stir up public opinion against us while the Cubans will mobilize troops. The Cubans and Companeros have been extremely chummy lately. Our intelligence says they are already mobilizing, just as theirs says that we are doing the same. If we, indeed, fight in Central America over this issue, we will most likely be fighting Cubans as well as Companeros."

"What is your recommendation?" Macklin said, the first time he'd actually asked anyone point-blank to commit.

"Send in the troops or we lose the entire region," the man said, then sat back in his chair, looking at his watch.

"And you, Mr. Warren," Macklin said. "What's your recommendation?"

The Company man leaned up close, his elbows on the table. His face was an expressionless blank, his hands folded in a tight knot before him. "Image is everything in politics, especially global politics. We are perceived as weak by our friends right now and warmongers by our enemies. But our enemies always think we're warmongers, so we must work on our allies. Globally, we can't afford to show such weakness in our own backyard. We have enough trade and prestige problems as it is. Send in the troops. We really don't have much to lose if we do. If it comes out all right, it will be the public relations coup of the century. As far as the missiles are concerned, I agree with Mr. Danton: things have gone beyond that now. In reading the polls, I see a disillusioned American public. They perceive you as ineffectual. Your administration cannot survive a massive downturn of opinion. It moves mountains nowadays."

Macklin turned to stare at Goodrich. "Goody?" he said.

The man shook his head. "Mr. Warren would crucify you on the cross of public opinion," he said. "Doesn't doing the right thing here count for anything at all? You know, the dire predictions only come true if you're wrong. Suppose you sit tight a few days and everything blows over? Public opinion blows over with it. Even Reagan survived with his public confidence intact after Iran-contra. General Tillotson can talk all day about standing up and acting like men, but look at his own evaluation procedures. If we are to look at our intelligence on the region, the facts we have, we'd rate the thing an F6: reliability of source cannot be judged; accuracy of information cannot be judged. It's our lowest evaluation, guys. You're talking about sending troops in on F6 information. It's unheard of."

"But they killed Mark," Macklin said, standing and walking up before the giant TV screen. Everything ultimately came down to that. The TV dwarfed him as videos of a burning village swirled crazily around, Macklin turning back to stare at the table with a background of black smoke and orange bursting fire. "They killed my best friend just to show what little regard they hold us in. I've listened all night, tried to let my own mind, my own feelings, settle down so I could make a rational decision. But here, in the cold, clear light of morning, I'm beginning to realize that this is no time for rationality. It's time, for once, to listen to my heart, and my heart tells me that we've got to draw the line somewhere. And I'm drawing it, right here, right now." He looked at Tillotson. "What kind of troops could we get down there and how soon?"

The man smiled and extracted a bright white sheet of typing paper from a stack of papers and folders, sliding it across the table toward Macklin. "The Joint Chiefs took the liberty of drawing up some possibilities," he said, "all of which can be accomplished within a day."

"I'll hold you to that," Macklin said, raising his eyebrows.

"Units of the 82nd Airborne from Fort Bragg can be airlifted quickly, plus the 7th Infantry from Fort Ord and the 5th Infantry from Fort Polk. We can quickly move over the 24th Tactical Air Supply and 24th Composite Wing permanently stationed in Panama. We can get refueling squadrons from SAC and AC-130 gunships from Eglin, Florida. The navy has promised us the 6th Mechanized and the 5th Battalion of Navy SEALS. We've even lined up a carrier load of Seasprites to search for the missiles once we get there. My estimate is that we can have well over twenty thousand troops in country within the next twenty-four hours without leaving us up short anywhere else."

The President looked at Goodrich, frowning deeply. "I'm sorry, Goody," he said, "but this time I've got to act. I've got the power and I've got the will. The people want it and I want it. It's time to strike a blow for freedom." He turned to Tillotson. "Get the ball rolling, Gene, Red Alert. I want this on priority and I want it now."

"You won't regret this," Tillotson said, standing. He looked almost grateful to Danton, the man probably contemplating a breakfast Bloody Mary. Alcoholism, the scourge of writers and warriors. Occupational hazard.

Tillotson gathered up his paperwork and hurried from the room without a word. The TV had switched to a close-up of the President of Caribbea, Maria Madrina, attired in a severe khaki dress that could have almost looked like a uniform. She'd been put in power by the United States and its promises of financial aid. But the promised aid had never been enough and now she looked like nothing so much as the puppet that she was. Desperately trying to hold on to power, she postured mightily, denying the C-130 shoot-down while warning the U.S. that Caribbea was a free and independent nation that would tolerate no interference in its internal politics. A Cuban general stood by her side to emphasize the point, but Danton knew that it was to no avail. Central American machismo had been offended mightily and a female leader, plus democracy, could last only until the next election. Or the next coup.

The room was still quiet, although everyone had to be pleased after so much indecision to at least have a game plan. Everyone but Goodrich, who sat staring hard at the walnut tabletop, strain lines etched on his face.

The President looked at him as he gathered his own paperwork. "This doesn't mean we're going to fight, Goody," he said. "We'll just send them down, that's all, a show of force."

"Kill for peace, right?" Goodrich said, standing. "That's

what they used to say back in the sixties." He gazed at all of them, then faced the man he'd been calling Mr. President for three years. "You've made a desperate mistake and I can't, in all conscience, go any further with you on it. My resignation will be on your desk this afternoon. Gentlemen."

He walked from the room then, head held high with dignity, Danton amazed that he could walk away from the power that easily. As for himself, he'd found he enjoyed the spotlight despite its affect on his stomach, and now that Macklin had come to his senses about Caribbea, he had the feeling that Mary Ellen would forgive him for his early departure last evening and be glad to rearrange their tryst for tonight. The little perks make life worthwhile.

"Let's go, people!" Macklin said loudly, bolstered with new energy after making the decision. "We've got a world to save."

1600 Pennsylvania Avenue 7:14 A.M.

Ben James had sunk back into the deep leather cushions of the limo's backseat, letting the warm air from the heater lull him as he talked about friendship with the representative from Nevada. "We've had a good relationship over the years, Randy," he cooed into the headset mouthpiece. "When you were up on those silly old ethics charges two years ago, who gave you the satellite access and the money to broadcast your side of the story to the folks back home? And who helped you to swing those committee votes on the ethics panel to kill the thing right there? And what about the increase in the war chest when the ex-governor decided to run against you right after that?"

"You've been a good friend," the man responded tiredly, BJ having awakened him for the chat. "But we're talking about saving the country from financial ruin here."

"That's what I'm talking about, too!" James laughed. "This country's economy has been based on government spending in the armament sector for fifty years, you know that. They're now saying that we need to base the economy on something else, something apparently new. But with this thing in Caribbea . . . did you know the President has ordered troops in there?"

"N-no," Randy Johnson said in surprise. "When did you hear that?"

"It'll be announced soon. Look, Randy. Have I ever asked you to do anything but vote your own conscience?"

"No, you haven't," the man replied flatly.

"Well, I'm telling you, my friend, that if your conscience isn't in the defense of this great land in its time of need, then I've overestimated you right along and made a terrible mistake about supporting you."

There was a slight hesitation on the line. "The troop commitment puts a new spin on all of this," the man said at last. "A man would be a fool to vote with the Communists and against our national defense."

"That's what I've been trying to tell you, pard," James said, opening his eyes and pointing to Jeremy Bomar, who was at that moment snorting cocaine from the flat surface of a clipboard containing a complete list of representatives and which side they'd probably vote on the recision question. James gave Bomar the thumbs-up sign, the man marking an X next to Johnson's name before sitting back and putting a finger to each nostril, drawing the white powder farther back into his sinuses.

"I always try to do the right thing, BJ," Johnson replied happily. "And I really appreciate the talk."

"Good man," James said, sitting up straighter. "And I've got June already working out the details on that fund-raiser for you next month."

"Thanks, BJ."

"My pleasure."

James cut contact, pushing the mike stem away from his mouth and leaning over to check Bomar's list. Outside of the warm car, clogging further the already clogged streets, were several hundred demonstrators chanting and carrying placards decrying the death of the military and cowardice in Central America. Given the cold and the snow, the crowd was especially enthusiastic. And well they should be. BJ had picked them all up from Central Casting and was paying them double the usual rate for extras. It had been expensive, but well worth it as the network cameras ground away, reporters standing before the White House fence to do live stories for the morning news shows.

"What's the count, Jeremy?" he asked, one of the demonstrators outside throwing himself against the White House fence for the ABC cameras, screaming for the President to protect the country. Capital police quickly dragged the man off to a waiting paddy wagon. Nice touch, but he wasn't paying them to get arrested. He made a mental note to dock the man who took the easy way out of the cold.

"You got about a hundred ninety solid," Bomar said, running his finger down the list. "You need thirty more to make it close, forty to give yourself a cushion. That's a long haul."

"Maybe not so long. How many Repubs we got?"

"A hundred and fourteen."

"There's what, a hundred and fifty-seven?" BJ asked, doing some mental calculations. "I have a feeling that after the news of the troops goes out, all the Republicans will switch over to our side. They're too oriented in that direction and have been looking for an excuse to jump ship. This should do it. But just in case . . ."

He reached down into the briefcase that leaned against his leg on the car floor and extracted a thick handful of manila envelopes, which he gave to Bomar. Each envelope had the name of a high-ranking congressman written in pencil on the outside.

"Documentation," he told Bomar as the man whistled at the names he saw on the envelopes. "Photos, transcripts. . . ."

"A little juice," Bomar said, smiling. He reached into the first envelope and pulled out a photo of the man whose name appeared on the outside. He was lying naked on a bed while a young teenage boy serviced him with his mouth. "What's that they say—don't get caught with a dead girl or a live boy?"

"That's what they say." James smiled. "These men all have influence. I don't want to use the documentation unless the count is too close. But if you do use it, stress the necessity of convincing others to vote our way, also. We may as well milk this."

"It's still gonna be pretty damned close," Bomar said.

"That fucking Rosen is working overtime trying to fuck us."

"Yeah," BJ smiled. "We get to go up against the hard ass. Do you see me shaking in my shoes? Hell, Jeremy, I've got friends everywhere on the Hill. Ain't no fucking egghead lawyer going to get in our way here."

"What about Merchant?"

BJ smiled widely. He loved Charlie Merchant and his self-righteous anger. The man was providing him with more fun than he'd had in quite some time. "The colonel is my dessert," he said. "You let me worry about him. You just make sure that when you lower the boom on those boys in the envelopes that you don't drag me into it. While we're at it, we need to tidy up at DCPD. I've got Hurley in motion, but we need to pink slip the two cops who aced Braedman. Think you can handle it?"

"I don't know," Bomar said. "You got a little something for me?"

"Maybe," BJ said, then reached into his inner suit-coat pocket and pulled out a long white envelope. He held it up for Bomar to see. "Doesn't look like much, does it?"

Bomar snatched the envelope out of his hand and tore it open to reveal a small stack of money, a number of sheets of paper, and a key. The man looked at BJ, his eyes alight. "It's mine?"

BJ nodded. "We closed the deal with the Justice Department last night," he said. "They signed off on the consignment to my disposal company and I am subcontracting to your toxic chemical disposal company and paying you a thousand dollars to get rid of this stuff."

Bomar laughed and held up the key.

"A warehouse on the Houston docks," BJ said. "Thirty million illegal abortion pills, prepackaged, with a three-year shelf life. Direct from a legitimate supplier in Paris to you, with a small Customs bust in between."

Ben James loved connections. When Bomar had told him that abortion pills were going to be smuggled into the country, he'd simply arranged with his friends in Justice to notify Customs of the time and place. Once the pills were confiscated, he simply went back to Justice and put in a ridiculously low bid to provide for their disposal, writing off the loss and using them to pay off Bomar. It was a simple transfer and cost him relatively little. "How you going to move this shit?" he asked.

"I got a partner with a pharmaceutical company," Bomar said, shuffling through the paperwork as he talked. "We'll put it out on the sly through doctors, clinics, and women's groups. I think I got a half billion dollars here."

"Tax free," BJ said.

"Yeah," Bomar said, pocketing the thousand. "It was my lucky day when Joe Vanacorri bragged about bringing this in." He laughed loudly. "Fuck you, Joe!"

"Now," BJ said, pointing to the stack of envelopes. "Can you handle my problem?"

"Are you kidding?" Bomar said. "I cut my teeth on shit like this. Now you're starting to do business my way. I like that. Bomar and James. It has a ring to it."

"Don't fuck around," BJ said, surprised that it had taken the punk so long to start putting his possibilities out front. That was okay. He'd expected it. "You work for me, remember? And while I'm clearing things out, you need to dump the Jag."

"Fuck you," Bomar said. "That's my car and I intend to keep it."

"It's stolen and chopped. We don't need to get busted on something stupid like that."

"Thought you weren't afraid of Merchant?"

"He's a worthy opponent," James said. "He's going to give me a good run. I respect him and I'm not an idiot. Dump the car. Put the plate back on the one it belongs to."

"I want another Jag," Bomar said. "Legit. You buy it for me."

"Sure," BJ said, noticing the definite change in tone. The man was a South Chicago gangster, one of the new breed of mafia who drank the blood wine with no code of honor or territory. The new gangs survived on double-dealing, extortion, and turning one another in to the police as a means of advancement. It was only natural that the man would hint at extortion once he had the goods on BJ. That was okay, too. Life was a series of challenges.

Through the side window, BJ watched the TV people packing up their cameras and cables. This particular show was over. "Jeremy," he said. "Would you, on your way out, talk to the straw boss with the bullhorn and tell him everybody can go home."

"You gonna need him again?" Bomar asked.

BJ sat back again, smiling wide. "No, Jeremy," he said. "With this morning's poll results plus the troop announcement, I think we've already effectively put the good folks at home on the right side of the issue. The next step will be to keep them there."

"How you gonna do that?" Bomar asked.

"I figure to blow up a couple nuclear bombs in Caribbea," he replied, then joined Bomar as the man broke into a big laugh.

Jeremy thought he was kidding.

D.C. Police Headquarters 8:13 A.M.

Hurley stared down at the small woman, trying to keep the urgency out of his voice as he asked her again: "You're absolutely sure of what you're telling me?"

She cocked her head like a dog, her hand resting protectively on the door frame of the Municipal Water Works billing department. "Of course I'm sure," she said, an unspoken question in her words, as if she'd become aware of something significant without knowing what it was. She wore a semitransparent white blouse, a hint of lace showing beneath. Her lips had a permanent wrinkled pucker, a face used to disapproval. "They've never brought prisoners down our floor before, especially one half-naked and covered with dried blood. Oh, I'll never forget that."

Hurley was standing in the hall, the office behind the woman a bustle of break activity, people charging everywhere with coffee and doughnuts, the fastest any of them ever moved. He turned and stared both ways. The hallway was a long series of city offices, some with glass doors, some wood, with PRIVATE written across them. It stretched for thirty or forty feet on either side of him. The red EXIT sign above the stairwell entrance drew him like a beacon, Jack Braedman's exit from the land of the living.

"You'd be willing to swear to that," he asked, "under oath?"

She nodded, then asked, "What's this all about?"

"I can't tell you right now, Ms. Hollister," he said, reaching out impulsively and taking her by the arms. "Just know that you are doing the law, and perhaps your country, a great service. Please, don't tell your story to anyone else before clearing it with me first."

"All right," she said. "But I don't understand."

"I don't know if I do, either," he said, releasing her arms. "Thank you very much."

He turned and moved down the hallway toward the EXIT sign, a glowing red tombstone. Leonard Hurley was a simple man. He believed that the call to civilization was the birthright and the duty of all human beings. Defending that civilization from those who would deny its existence had always struck him as a cause so noble as to be almost religious. That Weston and Mills could use the badge to cover murder and destabilization didn't so much make him angry as it hurt him emotionally. He felt personally betrayed.

He walked through the metal stairwell door, the number 6 written in black paint on the dirty white cinder-block wall of the landing. It had been completely cleaned off, all trace of the mayhem that had occurred here consigned to forgetfulness. But he wouldn't forget. He'd hoped to be wrong. He'd prayed that he'd be wrong, but he wasn't. Weston and Mills had brought a United States Senator onto the sixth-floor landing and thrown him, headfirst and handcuffed, to his death. And now he had the evidence to prove it.

He slowly walked back into the hallway and moved to the elevator near the Water Department door, the place where Ms. Hollister had seen them. She'd been on her way, herself, to the elevator to use the photocopy machine on five because hers was broken. They'd apparently been quiet. He'd interviewed the entire floor, and the Hollister woman was the only one who'd seen anything.

He climbed into the elevator, its innards reflective aluminum, and took the ride down to his office on one. It was time to marshal his evidence and get Charlie Merchant on the phone so they could plot their next move.

Who to trust, though? He needed Merchant's expertise and knowledge.

When he entered the office, Malcolm Bignell sat before his chessboard, moving pieces. He looked up at Hurley without smiling. "Been looking for you," he said. "Where you been?"

"Here and there," Hurley answered, moving to the chessboard to see what the man had moved. "What's up?"

Bignell was dressed in a three-piece black suit that effectively covered his large belly. His totally white, longish hair stood out bright in contrast to his clothing. He held a chess piece in his hand, Hurley looking at the man's well-manicured nails and wondering how Merchant would assess him.

"You use your knight to excess," Bignell said, holding up a French cavalryman with upraised saber.

"How so?" Hurley said, taking the piece from him and putting it back on its square.

"The knights can do damage, but they're not team players . . . always moving erratically, jumping over other pieces. Overuse of the single, gallant knight will always result in a game plan not fully executed."

Hurley moved to sit behind his desk. "So, you came down here to talk chess?" he asked, opening his top desk drawer to see some disarrangement, as if someone had made a quick perusal of its contents. He closed the drawer and looked hard at the man.

"Not at all," Bignell said, turning from the board. "I've come with some great news. You and me are going to do a little TDY, a bit of easy duty for a change."

"What are you talking about?"

"About this," the man said, standing and moving quickly to the desk. He leaned way across it, an airline folder in his hand, which he shoved in Hurley's face. "You and I are out of here."

Incredulous, he took the ticket from Bignell and opened the airline folder. "Frankfurt, Germany?" he said.

"The International Symposium on Terrorism," Bignell said. "Commissioner Thompson thought that you and I ought to go and bone up a little bit."

"This leaves this afternoon," Hurley said loudly. "I can't—"

Bignell put up a hand for silence. "I knew you'd say that," he said, smiling. "But it's already taken care of. I called your wife a little while ago to tell her and she's all excited and is packing your bags for you right now."

"You called Rita?"

"Sure, why not?"

"Well, I don't know if I can go," he said. "There's no use getting Rita all—"

"This isn't a request, Leonard," Bignell said, the smile draining from his face. "You and I have been assigned to duty in Frankfurt and we're going to go." He straightened, the smile returning. "Come on . . . it'll be fun. The weather sure can't be any worse than it is here. We've got a slight break in the clouds. No telling when that will happen again. So you go on home and get your gear and I'll be over to pick you up around noon."

"You can't assign somebody else?"

The man's face darkened. "No, I can't. Don't make me put it in the form of an ultimatum."

Hurley returned his glare. "You already have."

Bignell winked at him. "You just do your job, Leonard. And give that little wife of yours a kiss for me, you hear?"

Without waiting for a response, the man walked out of the office, closing the door loudly. Hurley stared at the closed door, wondering if Bignell's words about Rita were meant as an implied threat. Merchant had been right not to trust the son of a bitch.

He sat for a moment, breathing deeply. He'd been in Vietnam working embassy compound protection as a Marine MP during Tet of 1968 when the whole world came apart and the streets of Saigon ran dark with confusion and blood, but never had he felt as closed-in as he felt now, never had the chill run so hard up his spine— not on drug stakeouts, not in apartment-to-apartment manhunts. Before, he'd always known who the enemy was.

He picked up the phone and dialed Merchant's number. When no one answered, he dialed the car phone number, the man answering hollowly on the first ring.

"Charlie, it's Leonard," Hurley said, speaking low. "Can you hear me all right?"

"Yeah . . . what's up?"

"Got some information for you," he said, the loyalties shifting even as they talked. "Can I . . . speak freely?"

"I'm taping . . . go ahead."

"You were right about Weston and Mills. I've got an eyewitness who puts them on the sixth floor with Braedman just before the murder. That plus no corroboration on seven and the similarity of statements—false statements—from both of them would give a prosecutor enough to act on."

"Good," Merchant said.

"Is it?" Hurley replied. "Listen. I've been thinking about this. For the case to have gotten dropped the way it did, there has to be collusion higher up than at Bignell's level. We're talking the commissioner . . . perhaps even the mayor's office. I've done some local checking on LSI and found that it puts an awful lot of money into the city of D.C., something that most other Washington businesses never even consider because that's not why they're in town."

"What are you saying?" Merchant asked.

"I'm saying that we'd better feel people out before giving them this information. Hell, who can we trust? LSI puts money in local politicians just as they do national. It may be tough to even find a judge who'll swear out arrest warrants on this, and if we do find one, it stands the chance of being thrown out immediately by the powers-that-be."

"You sure you're not overreacting?" Merchant replied. "After all—"

"Charlie," the man says. "I've been reassigned."

"What?"

"TDY in Frankfurt, Germany, for a symposium. They're sending me and Bignell."

"Both of you."

"Yeah. And my job was put on the line for it. I said yes . . . I didn't know what else to do."

"There was nothing else you could have done," Merchant said. "You're being officially muzzled. When do you go?"

"This afternoon if the planes are flying and the runways clear."

"Jesus . . . they don't waste time."

"What are you going to do?"

"Muddle through, I guess," Merchant answered, his voice now sounding faraway and preoccupied. "Weston and Mills can probably keep until you get back. Is there any evidence you need to squirrel away?"

"I've kept it all in my head," Hurley said, the words sounding stupid to him when he got them out. "I've been afraid to write anything down. I think they're searching my desk."

"Is there anything else I need to know?"

"No, I . . . wait. There is something else. I did some checking on Joann Durbin's bank accounts. Not only did she have over a million dollars in savings, but she was still receiving checks from LSI to the tune of forty thousand dollars a month."

"Forty *thousand*?" Merchant returned, then whistled low. "Not bad severance pay."

"Nice work if you can get it. But I've got a question: If I'm being put out to pasture here, how is it that they caught on to me? I mean . . . our contact has been slight and controlled. I haven't talked to anyone else. So, what's the deal?"

"I've been wondering about that myself," Merchant said. "That's why I'm glad you're going. Take you out of the line of fire for a while."

"And that leaves you, Charlie. All by yourself."

"Yeah . . . I know."

Merchant wished Hurley well and hung up the car phone. His allies were so few. He hated to lose another one. He was driving fifteen mph right behind the snowplow as its wide, slanted blade scraped the concrete ribbon, shoving large mounds of dirty black snow onto the already mountainous pile on the shoulder. The Pentagon was usually a ten-minute trip from his house. This morning, he'd already been in the car over forty minutes and they still had a distance to cover. He hoped that Gene's news was worth the trip. Blowing snow billowed up around the plow in a shifting white haze, ethereal and mesmerizing.

"Who was on the phone?" Josh asked from beside him, his son bundled in a wool coat similar to his own, his red hair vibrant against the backdrop of unending white that totally surrounded the Cadillac with the new tires.

"D.C. police with another angle," he said, looking at his watch. It was time for the other call. He picked up the phone. "I might have the evidence to at least prove Jack's death was murder."

"You're kidding," Josh replied, and in that instant, Merchant realized that his son had not really believed him 100 percent. He dialed up the GSA Headquarters number in downtown D.C. and waited for the ring. If Hurley's news had been so good, how come it all felt wrong to him? He needed to—

"GSA," came the mechanical female voice on the sixth ring. "Which department, please?"

"Internal Security," Merchant said.

"Thank you."

"Who's that?" Josh asked.

"I'm trying to get Ned Bramley," Merchant answered.

"Uncle Ned?" Josh asked, and Merchant turned, startled, to glance at him. He sounded almost childlike, invoking the name he'd used for Bramley since he'd been three. Bramley had been a permanent fixture in the old days, a constant guest of no-invitation-needed status.

"Yeah," Merchant answered. "Your uncle Ned has been ducking me for three days."

"Internal . . . this is Jenkins."

"Ned Bramley please," Merchant said, deciding to pull a rabbit out of the hat. "This is the data center with a question about his W-4."

"Please hold."

The phone hummed lightly in his ear, silence better than elevator music, or the endless varieties of "Sukiyaki" he'd had to listen to during a three-year tour in Japan.

"Why's he been avoiding you?" Josh asked.

"That's what I hope to find—"

"This is Bramley," came a tired-sounding voice.

"Ned," Merchant said. "It's me . . . Charlie Merchant."

His voice sounded high-pitched, suspicious. "Charlie, what the hell are you—"

"Sorry to use the ruse," Merchant interrupted, "but I haven't been able to get you any other way. Even your answering machine at home is off and nobody answers anymore."

"I'm really up to my eyeballs right now, Charlie."

"Are you blowing me off, Ned?"

"No, of course not, I . . . oh, hell, pard. What's up?"

"A couple of questions, then I'll leave you alone. Guess you heard about Braedman?"

"That was strange. Why did he do it? He didn't seem the type, I guess."

"Yeah," Merchant said, unwilling to drag his suspicions out every time someone mentioned Jack's name. He took a breath and changed the subject. "I've been watching the reports about that GSA charter shot down over Caribbea and I was wondering about that pilot . . . Delany?"

"We shouldn't be talking about this," the man said, his voice strung up tight. "Why did you call me about it?"

"You're Internal Security chief," Merchant said. "Who, but you, would know about it?"

"Nobody asked you to call me?"

"Of course not."

Something was wrong. Merchant turned to Josh, his son staring hard, quizzically.

"Is something wrong, Ned?" Charlie said.

"I can't say right . . . Jesus, I shouldn't even be talking to you. Why did you call me?" he asked for the second time.

Bramley sounded close to the edge, and he was not the kind of man who lost control easily. Merchant turned his mind toward providing safe haven. "Meet me, Ned," he said. "Get yourself out of there and meet me somewhere. We can talk about it."

"You may not want to know this," Bramley said, and his voice had reduced to a whisper.

"You sound like you need someone to talk to . . . advice perhaps. A sympathetic ear."

There was a silence on the line, Merchant noticing the Pentagon turnoff, its formerly green sign above the roadway now simply a convenient surface for driving snow to stick to. He made the turn slowly, noticing a van turned upside down just off the ramp, its bottom covered with a foot of snow.

"Maybe you *can* help," Bramley said at last. "I need

advice with this thing bad. You've got contacts. Maybe you can help."

Merchant looked at his watch. "Look," he said. "Meet me at one o'clock . . . where?"

"The Air and Space Museum is near here," Ned answered, still whispering. "Meet me at the *Spirit of St. Louis.*"

"You got it, Ned. Hang in there."

"I might say the same to you, Charlie. You won't thank me when this is over."

The man cut contact then, Merchant hanging up and turning to Josh. "Wonder what that was all about?" he asked. "Ned sounded as if the Devil himself were chasing him."

Josh tightened his lips, his brows furrowed in concentration like they used to get as a kid watching Saturday morning cartoons. "Dad," he said after a moment. "It begins to occur to me at this juncture that perhaps you've bitten off more than you can chew here. Murders, high-level cover-ups, classified materials . . . you're not equipped to deal with things like this."

"What are you saying . . . that I should just walk away from it?"

Josh raised his arms in exasperation, then let them fall into his lap again. "You're retired, Dad, out of the loop. There are probably a lot of good reasons for the things we see going on right now. You're just not privy to them anymore."

"I'm old, right?" Merchant said, getting angry. "I'm too old to carry the ball anymore. Is that it?"

"You're fishing," Josh said, "exaggerating to get my goat. I'm a lawyer; it won't work. In fact, I'll give it back to you. In a sense, you are too old, not in years, not in mind . . . but in attitudes. You came up in a different world with different values—friendship, trust, loyalty— those things are not the components of modern politics. Politics now is a media game. Alliances are always temporary. Holding power is more important than its application."

"I don't believe that, and I won't believe that," Merchant said. His son's ability to infuriate him legendary over the years. "There are values. They are important.

God, how did you live with me for all those years and not take any of my feelings away with you?"

Josh looked hard at him. "I did at first," he said. "Then I grew up. You're an old soldier in a world that doesn't care about old soldiers. You're getting ready to make a monumental fool out of yourself."

"Does that mean you won't help me?"

Josh tightened his jaw muscles and stared hard for a moment, then he sighed, relaxing. "I didn't say that," he replied softly, then turned and looked out the window at a line of cars on the shoulder that had been buried under a snowplowed mountain of dirty white.

The Wellness Center 9:15 A.M.

"I'm glad we could get together this morning," Linda Merchant said, trying to sound concerned and sympathetic without being condescending. Maintaining professional detachment while seeming open and accessible was the most difficult part of the job. "I worried about you all last night."

"We got a snow day today," Jorge Mendel replied, his dark eyes smoldering with a deadly kind of passion. The boy laughed dryly. "I'da cut anyhow."

She smiled. "You don't like school much," she said.

He sat staring around the room, swiveling the thick, padded executive chair in a complete circle. "The counselors at school told me . . . they said I think school is ex-traneous, whatever the fuck that is."

She shifted her weight on the folding hard-backed chair, trying to get comfortable. Little had she suspected when she'd given him the option of where to sit that he would have chosen her chair. "What else did the counselors say about you?" she asked.

"That I was a borderline," he answered, suddenly swiveling the chair to face her, jerking it to a halt. "What's that?"

"Something they shouldn't have said," she replied, once again having to curb her anger at school counselors and their pathetic botched attempts at therapy. "I don't think you're a borderline anything, and I don't think that school is necessarily a problem to you. You scored very highly on the tests we gave you when you came to us. I believe that if you have a problem fitting in, it has to do with something else, something . . . personal."

He jerked slightly then, and swiveled away from her, staring around her office, probably responding negatively to the too-perfect demeanor of the place. Linda had furnished stylishly, as was her custom. Charlie had taught her to be neat and tidy. But here, in this place, her office looked like nothing so much as enemy territory to the impoverished who visited there. She really needed to change it.

"You called everyone weak yesterday," she continued when no response was forthcoming. "You included yourself in that group. Yet your attendance here was forced by the school district, hardly a weakness on your part."

"I get sick of everybody whining like babies," he said. "Life's rough. You got to gut up."

"They why did you call yourself weak?" she replied.

He looked hard at her then, gave her the full measure of his pain. And it was intense. There was a tremor there, in those eyes, in that hard-edged psyche, something beginning to crack. She tried to exude encouragement in return, tried to make him feel at ease. Yesterday's implied threat of suicide had yet to be mentioned.

He looked down at the floor. "I'm a-ashamed to say," he told her, and the fact that he was willing to admit anything at all made her think the problem was so all-encompassing that he'd even share it with a stranger.

"You want to tell me, don't you?" she said quietly, reaching out and taking his hand when he still wouldn't look up. "Why did you calm down so quickly when I came into Group yesterday?"

He looked up in confusion, his eyes darting at first, looking for escape. She could see a terrible war being waged within him.

"You know there's nothing you could tell me that I haven't heard before," she said. "There's no problem you can have that's unique."

"You mean that?"

"Trust me," she returned and gently pulled her hand from his, putting both hands on either side of his face. "There's nothing mentally or emotionally wrong with you, Jorge. You're just having a problem of some kind right now that may need a little help. We all need help from time to time. Reach out to me. Please."

She almost added, before you do something irreversible. But she didn't. She waited for him to do it for himself.

He stood then, pacing the room for several long minutes before returning to the seat. His stare was even as he watched her. Whatever his private battle, he had apparently won it.

"Promise you won't . . . laugh at me or think I'm a . . . freak or something," he said earnestly.

"Of course not, Jorge," she said. "I'd never do anything to hurt you."

"You mean that?"

"Absolutely."

He sat quietly for another moment, Linda letting him get around to things in his own way and time. When he started, finally, it was slowly, unsteadily, his voice picking up speed and volume as he got everything out.

"It's girls, Ms. Merchant," he said. "I got a problem with girls."

"Every man has a problem with girls," she said, then added, "Please . . . call me Linda."

"I ain't no man, Linda," he said flatly.

"You mean . . . sexually?"

"Yeah," he said, then angrily spat out, "sexually. It ain't like there's something wrong with it down there. Man, I wake up with a boner every morning. But it's like . . . I don't know, when I'm with a girl, it just kind of . . . shrivels up. Am I some kind of fag or something?"

"Are you attracted to boys?" she asked.

"Fuck no!"

"Then we can safely rule out homosexuality," she said in what she hoped was a casual voice. At this point it seemed to her that her job was to begin making Jorge think of himself as something other than a freak of nature. "You know, Jorge, most all men have trouble with impotence from time to time, perhaps—"

"I have trouble all the time," he said, his voice a cry. "It's like, I really like girls. They come around and we strike something up. Everything will be fine, but when we get right down to things, it's no good." His voice caught, almost a sob. "I want to do good. I want to do the right thing."

"Maybe you want too much to do the right thing," she said, wondering how in the world a seemingly dynamic and self-assured kid like Jorge could ever have a problem with sex. But at his age, given the drive of young hormones, she could understand why he thought it a life-and-death matter.

"What do you mean?"

"Sex is give and take, Jorge," she said, the boy on the edge of his seat, hanging on every word. "We all want to give pleasure, but at the same time, the drive is a selfish one. The term for what you're suffering is a common one and barely medical. It's called performance anxiety. Let me ask you a question: When you're with a woman, is pleasing her the uppermost thing in your mind? And if it is, do you fear taking in return?"

He thought for a minute. "For women," he said, drawing himself up, "I have respect. Men kick them around, get them knocked up . . . they take it. Not all men are assholes like that, not all men treat their women like trash, do they? I try to show that, to be—I don't know—gentle. But when we're doing it, I worry that they don't really want to, or that I'm not doing something right, or even sometimes when they talk and, you know, encourage you, that maybe they're really just pretending and laughing at you on the inside. Then, when you can't do it, they laugh at you on the outside." He began pounding his leg with a balled-up fist, harder and harder. "They call you a fag . . . or some kind of wimp and they tell all their friends . . . all their friends."

He broke down completely then, Linda jettisoning the professionalism and moving to hug the boy, who sobbed loudly into her shoulder.

"Oh, Jorge," she said, stroking his thick black hair. "Not all women are like that. Most women I know would cut off an arm to have a man as sensitive and caring as you."

"S-sure," he said, sobbing, his body proximity having

an effect on her, his closeness rousing feelings, making her flush. There was a tension there between them, a physical tightness. The longer she held him, the more her brain screamed "unprofessional" in her head.

"I mean that," she said, taking the opportunity to pull back from him and regain her composure. She sat back in her chair and took a breath. "Men tend to be very selfish sexually, more interested in scratching their own itch, as it were, than in satisfying a partner. Your concern shows your sensitivity. Unfortunately, sensitivity is what is leading to your impotence."

"So, I can't ever do it . . . right?" he demanded.

"Don't put words in my mouth," she said. "You've just got to learn that women want to be really close as much as you do. Sex isn't a game with winners and losers. It's not a contest. It's just a mutual sharing. You're just taking it too seriously, that's all."

"If you couldn't do it, lady," he said, eyes flashing a touch, "it would be serious to you, too."

She nodded. "Yes, I guess it would." She screamed inwardly, wishing she could tell him just how little sex had meant to her in the last ten years, just how little anything had meant to her.

"Can you help me?" he asked her point-blank.

"Nothing's that easy," she replied.

"Can you help me?" he demanded.

"Yes . . . if you're willing to give it some time."

He stood, moving partway toward the door. "I ain't got no more time," he said. "Word's gettin' around that I'm some kind of fag. Man, in my neighborhood that's the same as bein' dead."

"Jorge," she said, trying to find the words to explain it. "The problem is in your mind, nowhere else. But you can't force your mind to make your body perform just because you feel you have to. That's a stress you won't be able to overcome."

"I won't be able to overcome being a fag, either, Linda," he said. "I wish the girls I knew were like you, but they ain't. They whisper about me when I go by. I seen them before."

"Don't you understand the kind of pressure you're

putting on yourself?" she asked, standing also, closing the distance between them.

"I don't know about no pressure," he replied. "I just know that if I can't get it up, I'm gonna take my brother's gun and blow my fuckin' brains out."

There, he'd said it. It was out in the open now and she could talk about it. "This isn't worth killing yourself over," she said. "There's nothing really wrong with you."

"Easy for you to say," he replied, and walked to the door, opening it.

"What are you going to do?" she said, putting a hand on his arm.

Just as suddenly as it had come, the fire had gone out of his eyes. "I got a date tonight with Joey Umberto's cousin," he said. "If I fuck this one up, everybody will know."

"Cancel the date," she said.

"I've got to work this out," he said. "I can't stand it no more."

"You can't expect to come up with answers in one day," she said. "Don't be a fool."

His eyes devastated her. "Is that what you think I am?"

"Promise you'll come back tomorrow," she said, ignoring his attempt at cheap sympathy.

He shook his head. "I can't," he said.

"Please, Jorge." She touched his face, her fingers trembling. "Please . . . for me."

He just looked blankly at her for several beats, then turned and moved quickly out of the room, his face an unreadable mask as he hurried down the hall and disappeared through the waiting-room doorway, saying goodbye to what he considered his last chance.

She stood in the hallway, breathing shallowly, quickly, her heart beating like a jackhammer. She was losing this one, just as surely as if he were going to the electric chair. She couldn't let that happen. She just couldn't.

The Pentagon 10:34 A.M.

The DIA had been created during the Kennedy administration in response to the fact that each intelligence branch of the individual services had a different count on the number of Soviet missiles being deployed worldwide. It was thought that a centralized intelligence-gathering unit that pooled the efforts of each branch, then coordinated through the secretary of defense, would smooth over such inconsistencies and at the same time form a bridge to the executive branch of government. What it in fact accomplished was simply the addition of another intelligence-gathering operation amid a sea of intelligence-gathering operations. But at least they could come up with one missile count and stick to it.

It was probably natural that leadership of such a group would come, for the most part, from Army Intelligence, and the years had proven that to be the case with one notable exception. Charlie Merchant had never been considered for the job, even when he was the most likely candidate as head of Army Intel and it was his turn in the rotation. That had been 1976. His evaluation at the time had been devastating, branding him "too outspoken" and "not a team player."

But that wasn't the real reason and everybody knew it. Merchant had been passed over, pure and simple, because of a lost battle on the Chongchon River on Thanksgiving Day in 1950. The army had a long memory when it came to failure, and even though everyone up the chain of command who'd had any sense had never really blamed Merchant for the defeat, the stigma had hung on for years. It had paid benefits in some ways, had made him mentally tough and forced him to consolidate his own power bases, so much so that he still commanded the respect and devotion of those who'd served under him. Including Bramley, who he expected to be a key piece in the puzzle. But the insult, ultimately, had proven to be more than he could take.

As he approached the office suite, however, he wondered if his pride had been his undoing. Memory persists, but ultimately fades through death and changing circumstance. There was no doubt in his mind that when they'd ultimately given the job to Gene, it was really *him* they were trying to honor. It was almost like a posthumous apology, and as he entered the office with its beautiful oak paneling and the five-foot frieze of the United States seal greeting him, he knew that Tillotson had been right the other night when he'd said that the promotion had come between them. He loved Gene, but had felt that his acceptance of a job meant for someone else had been selfish and weak. And to Charles Merchant, weakness was a capital sin.

Uniformed and civilian personnel scurried around the offices, pulling info from a large bank of teletypes and computer terminals as phones rang like trilling birds and lifeblood coffee perked from five different sources. The atmosphere was happy, almost festive, an attitude mirrored in the entire building.

"Man, you'd think it was Christmas Eve," Josh said as they made their way across the royal blue carpeting to the large reception desk and the dark-haired Amazon who sat behind it. A small clay statue sat on the desk. It showed a military man, a captain in dress uniform, half sticking out of a toilet, his hand on the flusher. A small card attached to the thing read IT AIN'T OVER TILL IT'S OVER.

"Charles and Josh Merchant to see General Tillotson," he told the woman. Her name was Lucy Adams and she'd been with Gene for ten years. She had to be six feet five at least, Gene referring to her affectionately as "my mutant."

"Good morning, Colonel," she said, eyeing Josh. "Is this your son?"

"Only on the good days," Josh responded, and though all of them laughed, Charlie felt as if there had been no joke intended.

The woman gestured toward the big double doors behind her. "The general said to send you in as soon as you arrived."

"Thanks, Lucy," Merchant said, the two men skirting the desk and moving to the big doors to push inside.

The room was monstrously large and plush in a way that could never help but make Merchant a touch jealous. The furniture was all heavy, dark wood, reclaimed from century-old three-masted schooners and reupholstered in the same royal blue as the carpets. The walls were filled with hundreds of pictures: signed photos of America's more legendary warriors from MacArthur to Blackjack Pershing, interspersed with more personal photos of

Gene's career, Charlie himself figuring prominently in many of them.

"What a glorious day!" Tillotson said, standing as they came in, the top of his mammoth wooden desk looking more like the deck of an aircraft carrier. Despite his enthusiasm, the man was obviously tired, drawn-out, and Merchant figured that he'd been present for last night's briefings. His tie was off, shirt open to the sternum, and his sleeves were rolled up past the elbow.

Tillotson moved around the desk and shook hands with both of them. "Have you noticed the blue skies and sunshine?" he asked.

"Be hard to miss," Josh said. "What the hell's going on around here?"

Tillotson led them to a sitting area in an alcove off the main room, coffee and ashtrays handy along with electronic gear, a television, and a computer.

They all sat, pulling their chairs close. Tillotson carried a large file folder under his arm, which he set on the circular coffee table that separated them. "We were dying men," he said, "and now we've been given a reprieve."

Josh looked around, shaking his head. "I'm not sure I understand."

"What he's saying," Merchant replied, "is that a few days ago the American military felt it was looking at the end of the trail, the beginning of the slow dismantling process that would ultimately mean death."

"But now," Tillotson said happily, "we've got troops getting ready to go into Central America and a good chance of winning the recision vote in the House. Happy days are here again."

"For how long, Gene?" Merchant asked, watching the man turn and open the bottom part of the computer table and pull out a bottle of Jack Daniel's. "What happens when this passes? The money problems will still be there. All Panama and the Gulf war did for us was dig the money hole deeper."

"You've been around Rosen too long," Tillotson said, pulling three shot glasses out with the whiskey and setting them all on the coffee table. "Like they say in AA: We'll just have to take it one day at a time."

"One day at a time," Merchant repeated, wishing it

could still look as simple to him as it did to Gene. His association with Ben James had soured him to everything. "I don't know. I'm beginning to think that everything is . . . changing around us. Maybe we have to change, too."

Tillotson looked at him then, his blue eyes crackling amusement. With a barely suppressed smile, he said, "Turning into quite the little socialist, aren't you?"

"Okay," Merchant said, hands up in surrender. "So my heart is bleeding today. But I haven't changed my voter registration to Democrat, and I'm not off base. War as we know it is a thing of the past. No one can afford a massive arms or technology buildup. Period. These offices will eventually have to reflect that reality."

Tillotson poured a shot of Jack Daniel's for each of them, then set the bottle aside uncapped. "Retirement's made your brain mushy," he said, picking up a shot and handing it to Josh, waving him off when the man tried to protest. "I disagree with your assessment of the change. Nothing changes. Ever. We disband our military and our enemies disband us. It's that simple." He handed a shot to Charlie.

The man picked up his own shot and held it up. "I'd like to propose a toast," he said.

"It's pretty early for me," Merchant said.

Tillotson glared at him. "Shhh." He cleared his throat. "To the spirit and heart of America," he said, face getting serious. "To the selflessness of the fighting man. To friendships that mean something." He looked at Merchant. "Anything else?"

"To honor," Merchant said, the words choking in his throat. That toast had first been made in a foxhole on the Naktong Line in the midst of an artillery barrage that lasted for thirty-six straight hours. Braedman had been there then. They'd all been so young. So young.

They drank the shots down, Tillotson trying to refill the glasses, but only getting as far as his own. The man repeated his theme. "One day at a time," he said again, and cranked down the second shot, hesitating only slightly before pouring a third.

"Rosen's gone ballistic. He's been running around here this morning like a crazy man, trying to convince everyone not to lobby against the recision, telling us it's ultimately in our best interests. There's a nonstarter for you. Kind of like asking rivers not to run."

The man tossed back the third shot, setting the glass back hard on the coffee table and shoving the large file folder toward Merchant. "The goods on Ben James," he said, shaking his head. "He's quite the boy."

Merchant opened the folder to a stack of printouts. "Give me the high points," he said, sliding the folder to Josh.

"He's a preacher's boy from Podunk, Kansas . . . somewhere. Was a little preacher himself at five years old. Got ahold of some old clippings. James used to really pack them in when he was young."

"What changed?" Merchant asked.

"His daddy went and got a thirteen-year-old girl pregnant . . . the police chief's daughter." Tillotson shrugged. "They ran the whole family out of town. James left home at seventeen, knocked around for a while, then put himself through college selling Bibles door-to-door."

"What's any of this got to do with his political career?" Josh asked, his eyes narrowing as he looked over the lists of holdings in the folder.

"No idea," Gene replied. "After college he disappeared for a time, maybe to avoid the draft . . . it was 1968. His trail picks up several years later. He went through a succession of sales jobs: cars, above-ground pools, Club Med, you name it. Then one day, he just turned up in a storefront on Constitution Avenue as a lobbying consultant."

"Jesus," Josh said. "He's worth over a billion dollars."

"Only on paper." Tillotson smiled, his eyes turning to look at the bottle. He started to reach for it, stopped, and turned deliberately to Charlie. "He seems to love moving cash. It's all ebb and flow to him, everything fluid, though we haven't been able to pin down any illegalities. Josh has got his list of holdings. They go on for twenty pages."

"Can I make some calls on this?" Josh asked, curiosity finally piqued. "This cash flow is almost too interesting. I'll bet we've got something on this guy in our SEC files."

"Go for it," Tillotson said, Josh standing and walking back toward Gene's desk. "The green phone on the desk is an outside line. James takes very little for himself. LSI owns all of his holdings corporately. His personal tax returns show him drawing only about twenty thousand dollars a year."

Merchant shook his head. "And he paid Joann Durbin forty thousand dollars a month when she wasn't working for him. Any criminal background?"

"Not that we could find, though we're still checking those missing years in the late sixties. You really think this guy had something to do with Jack's death?"

"I know he does," Merchant said. "I believe he hired it done through the D.C. police."

Tillotson's eyes widened. "You got proof?"

"Close."

Tillotson recapped the bourbon bottle and put it away, his brows knit in concentration. "Why would he do it, Charlie?" the man asked, and Merchant realized that even Tillotson had doubts about the story.

Merchant shook his head. "Not sure. I do know that LSI was Jack's main source of contributions for his presidential campaign. Maybe he wouldn't play ball. Maybe he knew too much."

"Too much about what?"

"I don't know!" Merchant said, too loud. He put up his hands. "I—I'm sorry, Gene. This thing is so complicated. I really don't have all the pieces yet."

Gene looked at him with concern. "Do you have any of the pieces? This begins to make less and less sense to me."

"Here's what I'm sure of," Merchant said, sitting up straighter, his elbows resting on his knees. "I'm sure that Joann Durbin committed suicide. I'm sure that Jack was wrongfully accused of murder and taken into custody. I'm sure that he was waltzed down the sixth floor of the city government building and thrown down a stairwell by two cops named Weston and Mills. I know that Joann Durbin had a relationship with Jerry Delany—"

"Jerry Delany!" Tillotson said. "You mean the guy who got shot down over Caribbea?"

"He's the one."

"Are you trying to tell me that Ben James ties in somehow to the shoot-down?"

"Yes. The shoot-down. Perhaps the missiles. Perhaps

the assassinations. Did you ever find out what cargo that EquAir flight carried?"

The man shook his head and slowly stood. "Me and you go back a long way," he said. "And I don't mind telling you that this story of yours gets weirder by the minute. You start spewing this in front of the wrong people and they might just pack you off to the Old Soldier's Home."

The breath went out of Merchant as if he'd been punched. There was the same old soldier crap he'd heard from Josh. "You don't believe me?"

"I believe in our friendship, Charlie," the man said. "It's kept me going. I believe in you. I'm not sure what I think about this deal you're laying out for me. I'll help you as much as I can, but I believe that it's possible that Jack's death is making you see spooks behind every bush. Consider carefully the steps you take and the accusations you toss around."

"I'm not a child, Gene."

"Then stop acting like one. Washington lobbyists don't shoot planes out of the sky. They take people to dinner, that's all."

"We're on the trail!" Josh called from the desk. "We're running some of the holdings through our computers. The worst that will happen is that I'll find some new ways to make money. This James guy knows his stuff!"

Merchant stood, realizing that Tillotson was looking at him differently now, a kind of rough pity around the man's eyes. God, if he couldn't convince Gene, who could he convince? "Can I run another name through you?" he asked.

"Sure," Gene said, voice kindly, but the eyes the same.

"Jeremy . . . somebody," Merchant said. "Sorry I don't have a last name. He works for James and will probably be listed on his employment records. Check criminal records first."

"Got it," Tillotson said, reaching out a hand to shake. Merchant took the hand. Was he being dismissed? Tillotson sighed loudly. "I'd better get back to work. I've got a stack of imaging to go through. We're still trying to track down those Russian missiles."

Merchant started to correct him, but stopped himself. He'd already made a large fool of himself here today. It wasn't time to compound it now. He'd been too cocky, too sure of his friendship. He realized he'd have to keep most of this to himself from here out. Until he could prove it, nobody would believe or even listen to him. Something else, too. It had been on his mind since his conversation with Josh in the car on the way over. He carried no authority anymore. He ran no agency, had no job. He was a retired colonel and as such commanded absolutely no one. Not working for a living tended to make his viewpoints, also, worthless. If this was, indeed, his call to greatness, he'd have to accomplish it alone. He felt himself being slowly deserted by everyone he'd ever depended upon. It wasn't just the army anymore—no one thought he could measure up.

Josh moved up to them. "I'm going down to one and take the Metro back to work," he said, walking toward the door. "I'll let you know as soon as I have something."

"Thank you, Josh," Merchant said, his son, at least, not deserting him. He looked at Tillotson. "I appreciate the talk . . . and the advice. Thanks for all the poop on James."

He picked up the file folder and tucked it under his arm, a large black DECLASSIFIED stamped on the outside. "Are we really going to send troops down to Honduras?" he asked.

Tillotson smiled. "The worst-kept secret of the decade," he said. "I think the President will be making an announcement this afternoon."

"It seems like something like this would go against his grain," Merchant said.

"Normally," Gene replied, "but remember, they killed his best friend. That severs a lot of connections, doesn't it?"

"Yeah, I guess so," Merchant answered, his mind on Jack Braedman and how quickly the connections sever. "See you."

He was out the office door then, excited and depressed at the same time. Big things were happening, but no one seemed to relate to any of it. He really had to be careful what he said . . . and to whom. Maybe he was just being a wet blanket, but the only thing worse than questioning the motivations of the military was *not* questioning them. It all carried an air of unreality to him.

As he walked, he quickly glanced through the file on the life of Ben James, reaffirming for himself the information that Gene had given him. Oddly, there seemed to be a page missing from the dossier that corresponded to the missing years in BJ's life.

He ran into Rosen in the halls. The man was, indeed, wild-eyed—the Pentagon's chimera—as he continued his lonely quest to keep the military out of the afternoon's vote. At least here was a man who finally feared the kind of power Ben James was wielding. They commiserated in the hallway, Merchant promising to be present for the afternoon vote.

He left then, feeling odd and disjointed. The river entrance parking lot was swirling with confusion as he carefully picked his way over the ice to his car, his hip still sore from the fall he'd taken last night. All the parking lines were covered with last night's new coating of frozen rain and blowing sleet, the area around the lot now mounded with huge piles of already-plowed snow. Cars were parked everywhere helter-skelter, and all of them were trying to get out for lunch at the same time. Exhaust rose like palsied fog and roiled in thick heaves through the lot as horns blared and cars bumped one another or spun wheels uselessly attempting traction. He hated disorder, the parking lot simply a harsh metaphor for the condition of the city and the government that resided there.

"We've got to stop meeting this way," came a female voice behind him, Merchant losing his balance as he turned to see Melanie Patterson standing there. As he slipped, the woman reached out and steadied him, their bodies so close he thought he could feel her heat right through her heavy, oxblood leather overcoat. They stood that way, close together, the frost of their breath intermingling as they talked.

"Didn't think I'd see you again so soon," he said. "It's a nice surprise."

She smiled. "I lobby out here," she said. "It's my job. But what are you doing here?"

He decided to try honesty on her the way she had on him last night. "I'm checking up on your boss," he said.

She smiled, nipping at her lower lip with white teeth. "You're really going to go ahead with this," she said. "You got guts, Charlie. Nobody can take that away from you."

"If I recall," he said. "We were talking about Joann and Jerry Delany last night."

"That was last night," she said, her face barely six inches from his. "Are you going to kiss me or am I freezing my ass off out here for nothing?"

He leaned down without thought and took her lips for his own, her cheeks cold against his nose, their tongues gliding effortlessly together. He was overwhelmed by her smell and by her taste, and found himself immediately turned on, the woman making small cat sounds down in her throat as she snuggled closer to him, her pelvis zeroing in on his erection even through the heavy clothing.

He pulled away, finally, reluctantly, and looked into her half-lidded eyes.

"You like the games, too," she said, her eyes opening slowly after the extended kiss. "That's why you're still in. By the way, Colonel, you're a hell of a kisser."

They were still close together, clinging lightly, Merchant not knowing if it was for business or pleasure on either of their parts. He didn't know whether to feel guilty or conspiratorial, though he did admit that if this was business, it was the nicest work he'd ever had.

"Have you decided which side of the fence you're on yet?" he asked, pulling her closer, smelling her hair.

She backed away from him, a large smile consuming her face. "It'll take more than a kiss to get me to choose up sides," she said. "If I went your way, it'd be because I thought you had a shot at winning. At the moment I don't believe you do."

"Why not?"

"You've hobbled yourself with ethics," she said. "You've limited your thinking. You'll have to open your eyes wider if you want to see BJ."

"I don't know what that means," he said.

She nodded, the smile leaving her face. "I know," she replied, putting up a finger. "By the way, I decided that you were just fishing with that talk about Jerry last night. You were good, though. You really had me going for a few minutes."

He reached out a hand to touch her face. For the first time, a kind of sadness had come into her green eyes. "There's right and there's wrong, Mel," he said. "That's where your decision should lie."

She turned her head and kissed his fingertips, then took hold of them. "We all make our own right," she said, drawing his fingers back and placing them on his temple, "up here. In our own heads."

"You're wrong."

She sighed and looked at her watch. "Gotta go, lover," she said, blowing him a perfunctory kiss and wheeling around quickly to walk off.

He stood and watched her move off and get into a blue Mercedes twenty feet distant. The car roared to life and skidded off, fishtailing wildly into the flow of traffic, Merchant left with slightly shaking hands and the knowledge that in a world of inscrutability, Melanie Patterson was more inscrutable than most.

He didn't trust her. He found that her most appealing point. She'd been right. He *did* like the games.

Pennsylvania Quarter 12:17 P.M.

Melanie Patterson rode the private elevator up to nine, her body still cold from the walk through the crowded parking garage, her mind desperately trying to rid itself of thoughts of Charlie Merchant. He was like a child, all ideals and heavy-handed morality, but there was something about him, some aura he wore as casually as his ubiquitous wool overcoat that got all tangled up with her brain and kept him, nagging, right at the forefront of her consciousness.

She'd already made too many mistakes with the man and didn't really know how to stop herself from doing it. It was as if she wanted to somehow reward him for surviving until late in life with his values still intact. But it was more than that. She was drawn to him for a number of reasons, all of which had to do with his commitment to life and its purposes; for Charles Merchant had survived

without encumbrances. He was a man who answered no
call save his own conscience. He was a man beholden to
no one.

He was free.

She was rich. She had knowledge. She had power. But
freedom she would never know, not in this lifetime. How
could she not be drawn to the man? He'd struggled and
survived whole and intact. She'd merely survived.

The elevator deposited her on nine and she moved
tiredly toward the Pit, halfway down the hall from the
little theater. It had been a long night and a long morning.
She'd spent the evening working her best licks on a
spend-it-at-home liberal Democrat from Oregon who had
no defense money in his home district and no desire to
relight the cold war. There were no wiles to work on this
one, no intelligent arguments other than the paranoid fear
of surprise attack from Caribbea, which he didn't buy
anyway. She'd simply gone at him with the most athletic
and erotic sex she knew how to conjure, then told him he
could have it again if he voted right. Whether or not it
worked depended upon the amount of sexual tension
inherent in the man's life-style: how often he saw his wife;
how hot and willing his aides and secretary were.

She'd worked that one till nearly four A.M., then was up
at the crack of dawn, negotiating treacherous roads to the
Pentagon to try to dilute the thrust of Rosen's visit to the
Building by suggesting to Admiral Stanley and other top
brass that they needed to drop all their invasion of
Caribbea work and concentrate for a few hours on phoning
congressmen who had marginal defense work in their
districts and promising them that future defense money
spending would go to the congressman who voted properly on the recision question.

She was drained and tired, and was still looking at a
long day, since the vote wouldn't be taken until late
afternoon. She knew that one long day wouldn't spoil her
looks to the casual observer, but she *felt* ugly right now
and needed a confidence booster—Doctor Jonah.

The door to the Pit was always kept locked and unmarked, like a harem. The room had no regular title, had
always simply been called the Pit because of the pain and

the groaning and sweating that went on there. It was the secret of BJ's success.

She pushed the buzzer beside the red metal door, a high-pitched male voice answering immediately. "Name, rank, and serial number," the swishy voice said.

"Paul, is that you?" she answered, smiling. All the men who worked in the Pit were homosexual. Like the eunuchs in the harem their job was to administer to the women without entangling them. "It's me . . . Mel."

"Mel-an-ie," he said, drawing out the name as usual, playing with the cadence. "Mel-an-ie Pat-ter-son."

The door buzzed in return, the locks clicking open. She pushed the handleless door inward and entered, the door swinging closed, to lock, behind her.

She was amazed at the crowd within. BJ never said, but she'd figured once that he had almost fifty women working for him and a handful of men. Three fourths of them had to be here right now, everyone, apparently, having had the same sort of night that she'd had.

They called the entry the Hall of Mirrors because floor-to-ceiling reflecting glass covered the walls, giving everyone a good look at themselves and what they had to work on. From there, the Pit divided three large rooms fanning out from the mirror hall, the rooms themselves divided into smaller units. The first room was called PHYSICAL and contained aerobics and ballet floors and a fully equipped Nautilus exercise area where BJ's people grunted and groaned through toning and tightening rituals. Most everyone was in here, sweating themselves to perfection. The next room was called VISUAL, and it contained beauty shops, massage tables, makeup areas, saunas, steam rooms, and a huge wardrobe kept continually up-to-date with the latest trends in fashion. The third room was MEDICAL, and it was here that Mel was headed. Medical was the place of plastic surgery, the nip and tuck, as they liked to call it. Here was the nutritional regimen forced upon them by BJ, the vitamins, the minerals . . . the sexually transmitted disease testing and treatments. Dental work was done here, caps and braces and artificial whitening. Everyone who ever came to work for BJ had to undergo complete makeover in the Pit before going public. The place was fully staffed twenty-four hours a day by

serious professionals who were the top people in their
fields and it was probably the largest and most complete physical hygiene establishment extant in the entire
world.

Yet very few outside of this building even knew of its
existence.

She entered to the smell of heavy vanilla incense to
cover the sterile alcohol odor common to hospitals and
clinics. There were eight sterile surgery areas encased in
floor-to-ceiling glass walls, each one containing operating
table, bed, and barber chair. Stainless-steel lights hung
low, the walls and floors carpeted. Instrument cases and
bottled gases waited at each station.

Once, several years earlier, Doc Jonah had dug two .38
bullets fired by a D.C. prostitute out of the chairman of the
Senate Budget subcommittee on one of these tables, the
man recuperating right there in the Pit. He was the only
straight male to ever spend any amount of time there. He'd
been especially grateful to BJ for keeping the incident
totally private. Of course that gratitude had, of necessity,
converted itself to proper voting on crucial bills. It was the
nature of the game.

Several women lay behind the glass walls on operating
tables, the lights intense on their faces and bodies as
white-clad surgeons worked on their lips, plumping them
with collagen, or on their breasts—either augmenting or
reducing. BJ demanded that his women hone to a certain
ideal of beauty.

She saw Rayda Coombs at the far end of the clinic in a
barber chair, a fat man with long hair and short-sleeved lab
coat bent over her, working on her face. Doctor Jonah,
small and stooped, hovered like a dark angel nearby.

She closed the distance, shrugging out of her heavy
overcoat as she walked, a simple blue cashmere dress
beneath. The dress showed off her full breasts and hips to
best advantage. They liked that in the Building. Bass
heavy disco music drifted thinly through the walls from
the aerobics class two rooms away.

Arriving at the barber chair, she laid her coat across the
unused bed and looked down into the brilliant egg of light
that encased Rayda's face. She had her eyes closed, her left
eye covered with an ice pack as the man worked on her

right. The man was bent over her, bracing his arm on the
back of the chair, the three-pronged tattooing pen humming continually in his hand as he slowly, painfully,
tattooed her eyelid between the lashes—permanent eyeliner. A small metal aperture kept the lid clamped closed.
He'd already applied a small beauty mark on her left
cheekbone, highlighting her best feature.

"Looking good, hon," Mel whispered into Rayda's ear,
the woman smiling and pulling the ice pack from the eye
that wasn't being worked on.

"Feels like he's burning my eye out," Rayda answered.
"I think the doc's being stingy with the local. Glad I don't
want a battleship on my chest."

"I don't know," the tattooist said, his own body a
veritable color catalog of the possibilities of his art.
"You've already got the torpedoes."

Both women laughed.

"Don't touch the ice!" Doctor Jonah said, moving up to
shake his head and secure the ice pack back on Rayda's
eye. "She's had anesthetic. This eye will swell and we
won't be able to work on it."

The doctor was an intense little man of indeterminate
age who took his job very seriously. He was an artist, a
sculptor of flesh, who seemed to equate inner and outer
beauty on the same rung of the metaphysical ladder. He
looked up at Patterson. "Do we have an appointment for
you, Mel?"

"Just need a little B-12, Doc," she said. "It's going to be
a long one."

He looked at her then, studying her face as if he had
forgotten something when he was building it. "Bend a
little more into the light," he said.

She did, and while Jonah studied her, she looked
through the long window opening into the beauty shop
next door. A young girl she'd never seen was lying back in
another barber chair, getting the full beauty treatment from
four men at once.

"You're not getting enough sleep," the doctor said.
"You're puffy."

"Thanks," she said. "You made my day. Why don't you
give Rayda a valium. She's in pain."

"Because Mr. James wants everyone in full possession of their faculties today," he answered, frowning.

He moved even closer, examining with a magnifying glass behind her ears, the tiny scars where he'd taken a small tuck. "The acid peel came out all right; you're a good piece of work," he said after a moment. "Don't muck yourself up."

He walked off to the cabinet, Mel leaning down to Rayda. Through the window, the girl was smiling, beaming as they worked on her, her hair being done even as she was getting the full steam treatment on her face. One man huddled around her feet, softening them, working them with a pumice stone.

"Who's the new blood?" Mel asked.

"Oh . . . yeah," Rayda said, hand coming up to scratch around the ice pack. "BJ brought her in with a lot of fanfare earlier, told them to give her the works. What's her name . . . Cheryl. Cheryl something. I think she's Hulett's secretary."

"Appropriations chair," Mel said. "Wonder what he's up to with all this? He's cashing in all his favors and I can't figure out where it's supposed to lead."

"Don't worry about it," Rayda said. "Just do your business, collect your money, and go about your life. It's BJ's lookout, not yours."

"Aren't you even curious?"

"Bend over," Doc Jonah said to Mel, a large syringe in his hand.

"No, I'm not," Rayda said, eyes still closed, jumping slightly as the large man put the pen to her eyelid again, the thing humming louder as he worked, Mel briefly considering, then rejecting the idea of a small rose tattoo on her hip. Rayda continued speaking: "Look. In the last three years I've managed to get six figures worth of capital into the system working for me. I've got a part interest in three businesses and sole interest in two others. I've a top D and B rating and property in seven states. If BJ goes out of business tomorrow, I've got no more worries for the rest of my life. Why should I care how he runs his business as long as I get mine?"

"Bend over, Mel," Jonah said again.

Mel turned and leaned over the operating table, her

back to Rayda and the humming tattoo pen. She hiked her skirt up her right thigh, the doctor rolling down the top of her panty hose enough to stick her in the hip. "I want you getting more sleep," he said. "When the facial muscles sag, you have to work twice as hard to bring them around again."

"I think after tomorrow, we'll all be able to get more sleep," Mel said, straightening and dropping the hem of her dress. She felt the warm rush of fluid through her system, waking her immediately and totally. She turned back to Rayda. "And what makes you think that if BJ went down, he wouldn't find some way to take you with him?"

"Why do you say that?" the woman asked, pulling off the ice and opening an eye wide.

"I think Joann knew something that the rest of us haven't figured out yet," Mel replied. "When you sell your soul to the Devil, he keeps it forever."

Rayda laughed as if it were a joke, Mel smiling along with her, then taking another look at the teenage girl in the beauty shop. Two men were lightly massaging her face with cleansing oils, the girl smiling dreamily as they worked their velvet magic, making her feel different, special somehow. Mel knew the feeling well. Another one lost. She gave it three days tops before BJ had her in bed with her boss, the magical event preserved for future generations through the wonder of videotape.

She walked off then, past another woman getting her nipples tattooed to enhance the color, and out of the Pit. She felt better now, surer of herself with the B-12 pumping her system up. It was difficult to get angry at Rayda for her feelings on the matter of BJ. All of them to some extent or another were forced to live in his fantasy. And it was a pleasant enough fantasy, even if, for Mel, the seams were beginning to show.

She took the elevator up to ten, unprepared for the madness that would greet her up there. Telephones by the hundreds had been moved into LSI, phones everywhere: in the hallways, the waiting rooms, and probably the rest rooms as well. The phones were all manned by men and women who sat with maps of specific congressional districts in their laps and who called specific representatives over and over again, changing their voices and their names and addresses each time they called and punching the redial as soon as they were finished. This way, they monopolized the phone systems, insuring that only one kind of information would get through. Their voices rose in confusion, filling the offices with a loud, machinelike drone.

She skirted the phone banks in the main hallway and moved toward the doors leading to the hub of activity, June Chan's tower. The doors opened before her, several workmen dragging mail sacks full of telegrams passing her as she entered. The noise within was even louder than out in the hall as every machine in the place operated at maximum output: teletypes, printers, phones—machines that carried the messages of BJ's reality to the world.

June worked the tower like a mad scientist, swiveling back and forth, answering phones, directing activities, giving orders. It was June who worked the duty rosters, the prioritized cogs in LSI's wheel.

"Hey, boss!" Mel called from the base of the platform. "How about the rest of the day off!"

June swiveled to her, face set hard until she realized that Patterson had been joking. "You're a funny girl, Mel," she called down. "Maybe you should go to clown school."

"What have you got for me today?"

The woman looked briefly down at her circular desktop, answering a phone call as she searched. Chan was a plain woman, everything about her, on the surface, dull and listless, from her flat, sallow face to the dime-store clothes she wore. But her mind was the most beautiful thing Mel had ever seen. It danced continually, spinning, scheming, dialing things in. If knowledge was power, she feared June Chan only second to BJ himself.

The woman got off the call and frowned down at her. "There is a folder," she said, "with your name on it sitting on BJ's desk."

"Is he there?"

The woman shook her head, still frowning. "On the Hill," she said simply. "I'm kind of busy here now, I . . ."

"I'll get it myself," Mel replied. "The doors unlocked?"

"I can do it from here," June said, turning to her control board and punching a button. "Go for it."

She turned and walked off through the clamor and

confusion, a childish elation washing over her. Silly as it seemed, she'd never been in BJ's office alone before. She was experiencing the same rush she'd gotten as a teenage baby-sitter at a new house, rifling drawers and cabinets, trying to piece together the private lives of the people who lived there.

The hall leading to the double office doors was quiet, the noise of the rest of the floor receding as she got closer, focusing her attention. BJ's door was cracked just a touch from the unlocking. She pushed in without hesitation and entered the lion's den.

As she closed the distance to the desk, several thoughts were running through her mind. First of all, was her entry here mere coincidence? Ben James survived by keeping his plans to himself. No one was ever allowed to enter his office alone. Why, all of a sudden, did she have such easy access? Secondly, she needed to make a decision, and for that she needed more information. Here was her best source of that information. Everything that BJ didn't keep in his head, he kept in here. The man had cameras everywhere, recording everyone's personal and professional lives, but not here, not in his own office. The watcher never wants to be the watchee. Besides, she'd checked already, slowly, discreetly, over a period of years. She was safe here.

Her folder lay in the center of the huge desk with her name on it in large letters. She walked around to the business end of the thing and picked it up, opening it quickly to a list of phone calls she had to make, a list far larger than she could hope to accomplish in one day.

She lay the folder back down and gazed around the office, her heartbeat picking up pace. Dropping quickly to her knees, she looked carefully at the desk drawers, checking the edges to make sure nothing had been put across them, like a hair, to give away entry to the drawer. Finding nothing, she quietly slid open the top desk drawer, staring down hard at its contents: office supplies, a couple of stacks of banded cash, a gun, a telephone pad—nothing to provide insight into BJ's ultimate goals.

She checked the other drawers to similar effect except for one thing: In the bottom desk drawer she found a file with the name Charles Merchant written atop it in red. She stood and looked through it quickly, a background check and class-A current surveillance on Merchant and his family. She shook her head. BJ was really pulling out the stops on this guy. The file was deep, deeper than she'd ever seen. It would probably make wonderful reading if she had the time.

She didn't.

She placed the file back into the drawer and shut it quickly, her eyes traveling to the far wall and the vault door out of sight near the sliding glass of the veranda. She stuck her own file back under her arm and moved quickly across the room to stand before the ordinary-looking door that held all the secrets. She'd never been in the vault before, could only imagine what he kept there; but since blackmail was their line of last resort she figured that the documentation had to reside within the vault.

She smiled, her mind roving back several years to the only time BJ had ever had sex with her after her hiring. Not surprisingly, he wasn't much of a bedmate—too selfish, too much in a hurry to get on with it, to keep it moving. When he'd fallen asleep, she'd liberated his ring of keys from his pants pocket and, having nothing to work with except candles, proceeded to take impressions of all his keys in soft, hot wax for reasons that had truly escaped her until this minute.

She needed his knowledge and she needed it soon. Sometime last year he'd changed over the lock on his office door to a punch pad system. But the vault was still the same, and she had a key for it.

The sliding glass door stood beside her, driven snow piled halfway up its height. She hurried back to the desk and pulled a length of cellophane tape out of the dispenser. Moving back to the outside door, she unlocked it and slid it slowly open a few inches, the snowdrift remaining stationary, not caving into the office. The door had a spring lock, which she taped down, holding it in place before shutting the thing again, keeping it unlocked.

She straightened.

"Did you find everything all right," came a voice from the front door.

She jumped, startled, turning to see June Chan standing just inside the door, staring hard at her. "Sure did," she said, trying to sound casual. She pointed out the sliding doors. "It's really piled up out there. Have you seen?"

"No," Chan said, inflectionless. "I'm too busy."

"Yeah," Mel said. "Guess I'd better get to work, too."

She walked toward Chan's position, her file folder locked securely under her arm. June held the door open for her, and as she passed the small woman, Mel looked deeply into her bottomless eyes, searching desperately for some kind of sign, some notion of what the woman had seen and what she intended to do about it.

June Chan half smiled at her, her face totally blank otherwise, dark and inscrutable. Melanie Patterson was beginning to feel very closed-in and intuitively she understood that it was the claustrophobia that had driven Joann to suicide.

National Aeronautics and Space Museum
Washington D.C. 1:15 P.M.

The Spirit of St. Louis had always looked to Merchant exactly as it was supposed to look, and as he gazed up at it now, suspended from the ceiling, tilted at a jaunty angle. He could still picture Jimmy Stewart jammed into the small cockpit of a plane that was nothing more than a flying gas tank. Sleek silver with paunched cowling, squat, heavy wing directly atop the fuselage, struts supporting it like Atlas holding up the world. It was a single engine with exposed pistons and did no better than eighty mph flat out. But it was the size of the thing that was important to him. The size was just right. Everything else in the museum's twenty-four covered buildings and acres of outside exhibits was too small. From the Wright Brothers' plane to the B-17 Flying Fortresses of WWII, to Gemini capsules and Atlas rockets, all seemed too small to have supported the great deeds that had occurred in them. In imagination only did they loom huge. But the Spirit, that was something else. The Spirit was just about the right size for a twenty-five-year-old man to sit in to challenge the world and conquer the skies.

He'd first seen the plane in 1947, the year he'd entered the University of Ohio, obtaining an ROTC scholarship by telling the dean that his parents had abandoned his education and that he was his own sole support. He'd been too much his own man to let anyone finance his education even if his parents had wanted to, which they hadn't, given his stated goal of becoming a career serviceman.

He'd driven to D.C. that late spring. His love affair with things military and political was already so full blown at that age as to keep him at constant odds with his professor father, who'd felt his son had made some sort of pact with the dark side, abandoning his intellectual heritage to associate with, in his words, "the deviates and animals of the world." But the truth of the matter was that Charlie chose the services because he desperately wanted an identity of his own, one he could be proud of. His father had been a man of great intellectual prowess, personal magnetism, and all-encompassing ego who had to control everything around him. No one could measure up to his estimation, especially his own son. His father's favorite phrase, one that he repeated quite often, had come from Salvador Dali: "The children of geniuses are usually mediocre." Charlie had gone off in search of a new father, had thought he'd found one in the army.

The war was still close then, his high-school graduating class only missing it by a year and a half. He'd spent his most formative years preparing to go into combat. It seemed to put an exciting edge on things that was lacking when life returned to normal after the war. He'd gone to the Smithsonian to see the fighters and bombers that had won the war, trying to recapture that feeling, only to come away disappointed at how small they were. Then he saw the Spirit and got hooked by the sheer spit and vinegar of its bold intent and by the image of a small, soft-spoken man riding a two-ton gasoline can across a vast and bottomless ocean to glory in a foreign land. Merchant dutifully and consciously tracked that edge of excitement from that day on, not understanding why, just knowing that it was important to his psychological and emotional makeup. Then, mercifully, came the Korean War, answering his prayers.

Even as he looked up at the plane, he could hear Bramley's approach, the man's uneven cadence as he walked, the differences in footfall as clear to him as a good fingerprint. Funny how things stick with you. He lowered his eyes, the man approaching twenty feet distant through sparse crowds because of the weather, a canopy of vintage aircraft dangling above his hatless head. He wore a camel's-hair coat and a large white scarf pulled up around his ears. His ebony cane's rubber stopper made no sound on the parquet floor as it supported his bad right leg with each frail, faltering step he made. Bramley had gotten his Purple Heart in a barracks in Seoul. He'd been sitting on a cot, changing his pants, when a guy two bunks down accidentally discovered a bullet still in the chamber of his M-1 as he was cleaning it. The thing discharged, taking Ned's kneecap completely off and getting him a ticket home a returning hero. The fortunes of war. It was the same week that MacArthur had gotten canned by Truman, the two men getting drunk together on the plane ride back to the Z.I.

Ned Bramley had always been a quiet, intense man, his regular features as hard and lean as Charlie figured his mind to be. Even at a distance now, however, he could see something different around the eyes, an uncertainty that seemed as foreign to him as ice to a Samoan.

Charlie's smile of greeting wasn't returned as the man reached him, their handshake perfunctory, lost in Bramley's preoccupation. He'd gotten grayer since the last time Charlie had seen him—grayer all over.

"God, Charlie . . . God. You're a sight for sore eyes."

"Are you okay?" Merchant asked, Bramley's usual serenity lost to the shakes. "What can I do for you?"

"I can't believe I'm here," the man said, shaking his head. "I . . . guess I just feel that maybe you can help me."

"Help you, Ned?"

"Yeah . . . with influence, knowledge . . . something. I think that this is too hot for me to handle alone."

"You're talking about Jerry Delany, aren't you?" Merchant asked, recalling their phone conversation.

Bramley stepped back a pace, looking around quickly,

head darting. "Let's walk," he said. "I'll feel better if we keep moving."

"Sure," Ned," Merchant answered, the two of them turning and moving beneath the hanging lines of aircraft, a Fokker triplane diving at a Neuport, the building nearly deserted given the nature of the weather. "I assumed that Delany's security clearance came through your office."

"Yeah, it did," Bramely answered, fidgeting a dispenser of nose spray out of his deep coat pocket and unscrewing the cap. "The damned thing came back from the FBI with red flags all over it. The son of a bitch not only had a record as long as the Vietnam Memorial, but he was still *wanted* in several places."

"From the news reports," Charlie said, "it said that the clearance had been denied too late."

Bramley nodded, injecting the nasal spray into each nostril as he closed off the other with an index finger. "I was on the phone within thirty seconds of the FBI's warning, only to be told that Delany was copiloting a stockpile shift and had already been out for two hours."

"You double-checked then?"

The man breathed deeply, wetly through his nose a time or two. "You bet your ass," he said, then blew his nose on a bright white handkerchief. "The whole point of security clearances is that you're supposed to get the clearance *before* going on the payroll."

"And how did they justify it?" Merchant asked, desperate to find out about the cargo, but not wanting to push the man too hard, too fast. If things were as strange as Bramley was saying, he needed all the background.

The man took a breath and looked Merchant in the eyes. "You really want me to tell you?" he asked. "You may not really want to—"

"Ned," Merchant said, cutting him off. "I'm here. Unburden. You'll feel better. I want to help you."

Bramley looked at him for a long moment, then seemed to relax, the man Merchant knew coming to the fore. "I'm sorry, Charlie," he said, managing a smile. "I'm so cranked up I can't even think straight. Just bear with me a minute and listen. GSA's in charge of government stockpiles. We warehouse, protect, and . . . move things around. A larger than expected stockpile shift order came through channels, the usual assignments made through GSA subcontractors. Apparently EquAir had no one available for this one flight except for Delany and the interchange officer at our stockpile routing headquarters in Indianapolis went ahead, as per SOP, and cleared Delany for this one flight."

"All of which sounds reasonable," Merchant said, "unless something goes wrong. What stockpile was being shifted?"

Merchant realized that what had bothered him about Bramley's eyes was that the light had gone out of them. Now as he looked, they darkened physically, like Photogray lenses. He knew what was coming, but it shook him anyway.

"It was nukes, Charlie," the man said, almost a whisper. "Two Raytheon Bearcats, missiles and warheads."

Merchant stopped walking, grabbing Bramley's arm to make him stop, too. "We *gave* two nuclear missiles to a convicted felon?"

Bramley took a breath as if he wanted to respond, but then he shrugged, exhaling. "Yeah, I guess we did."

Merchant looked up. They were standing beneath the *Enola Gay,* the painted bathing beauty on the nose of the thing smiling down at him, mocking. This particular B-29 sat in the Smithsonian because it had carried a nuke, too. Only one bomb, however, to drop on a city. Hiroshima had been leveled by the *Enola Gay,* killing a hundred fifty thousand noncombatants. The bomb dropped there, however, was far weaker than either of the Raytheon Bearcats given to Jerry Delany by the United States government. "How could something like this happen?" he asked. "Can't we keep better control of our arsenal?"

"Channels get set up over the years," Bramley said, breathing deeply through his nose again. "The government has a lot of stockpiles of all sorts of things from office supplies to nerve gas. We move around the warheads to keep anyone from getting an accurate count. You know, just keep the flow going." He shrugged again. "We move them in trucks. We move them by air and by rail. In the twenty-five years that GSA has been involved in this business, we haven't had so much as one problem with it."

"Isn't it dangerous to fly them around?" Charlie asked. "What if the plane should crash?"

"Triggering mechanisms are never flown with the warheads," Bramley said. "A crash wouldn't detonate the bombs. Only a major explosion would have any chance of setting off the nukes."

"Like a surface-to-air missile?" Charlie returned.

Bramley lowered his head, a hand coming up to wipe across his face. "You're thinking the same thing I am," he said. "If Delany was shot down over Caribbea by a missile, even a conventional one, chances are we would have had a four-megaton explosion at five thousand feet right smack in the middle of the trade winds."

"You saw the films of the so-called Russian missiles?"

Bramley nodded. "The divers logged hundreds of hours searching the waters around the debris and never found even the hint of a missile. When I tried to go upstairs with it, I was told that it was a national security matter, that the State Department knew what was what, and that I needed to keep my mouth shut . . . but all of a sudden, we've pulled the divers, stopped denying the missiles, and are talking about sending troops. I think something's desperately wrong here, Charlie. I don't know what's going to happen with it. Things just don't add up. Who's got those birds, for Christ's sake . . . and why? I . . . tried to call the FBI anonymously, just to get something going, but they had too many questions about me. I had to get off. Go figure. Delany's dead and somebody has those missiles."

"And you said the order came down bigger than usual?"

"Yeah . . . kind of forcing us to abandon the game plans."

Merchant nodded. "Have you considered the fact that this came down from the inside?"

Bramley nodded vigorously. "That's what's eating at me. That order was entered in the computer system from somewhere within GSA. Hell, we don't have that many checks on the stockpile system. I mean, who would care, you know? So somebody entered that information and they probably know about me by now. I—"

Bramley froze, his eyes locked hard somewhere over Merchant's left shoulder, his mouth forming a silent no.

"What?" Charlie said, turning to see three men in suits and overcoats striding quickly in their direction a hundred feet farther down the hall beneath a canopy of Japanese Zeros and German Stukas painted in winter camouflage.

"I recognize two of them," Bramley said quickly. "One's the division head, the guy I called with my info. The other's one of the federal marshals who've been hanging around since Delany went down."

Merchant looked hard at the man who was still staring past him. "Why would they—"

"They're here for me," Bramley said, his voice quaking. "I've been afraid of this. I don't think they trusted me. They somehow must know that you and I . . . that you . . ." He leveled Merchant with a withering gaze. "You didn't tell them, I—"

"No," Merchant said, taking the man's arm. "I swear. This is probably just a misunderstanding."

Bramley's eyes were darting again. "That gun on that man's hip isn't a misunderstanding," he said, Merchant turning to see a man in a blue suit and earphones reaching inside his inner jacket. Bramley shoved Merchant behind him, placing himself between Merchant and the oncoming problems. "Get out of here," he said. "Quick. I'll try and hold them back. Tell people. Tell them what's happened."

"What are you talking about?" Charlie said. "We'll just explain to them, we'll—"

"You there!" boomed the marshal's voice from twenty feet. "Freeze!"

Bramley turned and shoved Merchant in the opposite direction. "Run!" he yelled. "You've got to be free. You've got to—"

The man was suddenly scuffling with the marshal, Merchant's momentum carrying him another ten feet the other way. The marshal had brought his gun out, but Bramley hit the gunhand with his cane, the thing firing, popping loudly, echoing.

"Run!" Bramley screamed again, the marshal cursing loudly, yelling to the other men.

"Get the other one! Get him!"

Hesitantly, the others started for Merchant, who stood

frozen on the perimeter of the now-violent struggle between Bramley and the marshal, the man's .45 automatic
gleaming as they fought for control of it. He wanted to step
in, to explain, to make them understand. Instead, he
turned and ran, just as he had from the television cameras
at Jack's funeral, his instincts suddenly more like a rabbit's
in a brushfire.

What was happening? Another shot went off, Merchant
twirling to see the weapon skittering across the floor, his
assailants lagging back, none of the hero in them.

He was off again, the museum blurring past like a finger
painting. Bramley had been right to send him on. One of
them had to be on the outside to keep pushing.

He distanced his pursuers to the outer doors easily,
slowing down to walk stoically past the door guard, an
FPS employee. He exited onto Seventh and Independence,
the weather providing instant cover. Blown and scraped
snow piled everywhere, the bumper to bumper traffic
bleeding thick fogs of carbon monoxide vapor white as
radioactive steam.

He hurried across Seventh Street, dodging the slow
moving traffic, bobbing and weaving, then headed north,
using the snow piled beside the sidewalk as cover. He
turned once to see an impromptu posse being put together
at the museum entrance, several men charging off in
different directions. It was time to pick up the pace.

Seventh Street cut directly through the Capitol mall at
Jefferson Drive, the mall itself steeped in frigid white, the
lines of trees giant snow cones. A small army of perhaps
thirty children was having a snowball fight, their laughs
and squeals ringing loudly above the sounds of grumbling
vehicles.

Merchant plunged into the mall area, the Capitol Building looming large behind the U. S. Grant Memorial at the
end of the mall. His car was parked at a lot just off Sixth
and Indiana, several blocks distant.

His mind was a jumble as he jumped, gazellelike, over
drifts, errant snowballs from the mini-war flying all
around him. The possibilities were staggering. If they'd
come and arrested Ned, if arresting was what they were
doing to him, it had to be because he was talking about the

Delany business. That meant the earlier conversation between him and Bramley had been eavesdropped on. It also meant that Bramley could be accused of passing national security secrets.

My God . . . what does that make me?

He hurried across Madison Drive at the far end of the mall, stopping in front of the Natural History Museum to check his pursuit. He saw no one coming, so continued north on Seventh, his nose and ears numbing quickly. Looked at in a certain way, the conversation between him and Bramley could be construed to be in violation of federal laws, state secrets violations among the harshest on record. But that wasn't what was bothering him the most at that moment. What worried him was *how* they knew.

Bramley's phone or office could have been bugged by the division head, worried about a security leak from an obviously shaken man. Hurley'd had the same problem with others anticipating his movements. It was possible he, also, had been bugged by Bignell. Possible, but not likely. Merchant had to consider the fact that both men were professionals in their fields and both probably took precautions for fear of bugging. He, however, hadn't taken precautions. Had he lost it that much? Was he the old soldier who figured himself a paragon, like Napoleon with the Prussian wounded, who failed to take even the simplest things into consideration?

The corner of Constitution and Seventh was a jumble of military and tourist crowds on foot and crawling traffic in the streets. He crossed with a gaggle of Japanese travelers, passing the National Archives before entering the mixmaster of Pennsylvania Avenue, Seventh, Indiana, and C Streets. Traffic was totally snarled here, angry horns blaring continually from all directions. Ignoring the signal lights, he simply jogged into the maelstrom and made his way across, arriving at the parking lot, numb and upset, within a few minutes.

His Cadillac sat in the middle of the lot, surrounded completely by other cars. He got in, started the motor to warm himself up, then began a methodical search of the vehicle. The phone conversation with Bramley had taken place in here. The night his tires had been slashed would have given anyone ample time to do anything he wanted to the car.

The phone was modular, impossible to bug for the most part. He began feeling around the bottom of the dash and the back side of the steering column. Meeting with failure, he started working upward with sensitive hands, finally finding something tucked within the lighted vanity mirror on the back side of the sun visor.

He pulled it out of the visor. It looked like a small hatpin with a rounded head. As transmitters went it was of a Japanese design familiar to him, and not especially powerful. If somebody had picked him up in the vehicle, it meant they'd have to be . . . following him!

He groaned, angry, mostly at himself and climbed out of the car, back into the cold. He walked casually to the Sixth Street side of the lot, looking around for the scout vehicle that must surely be parked nearby. Not seeing it, he walked to the curb and checked the slowly passing traffic. A D.C. police cruiser caught the light at Sixth and E, stopping ten feet from him.

Moving casually, he walked the sidewalk until he stood beside the cruiser, then reached out and stuck the transmitter into the crack where the trunk meets the back quarter panel.

The cruiser pulled away within seconds, Merchant easing back to stand partially behind a mailbox on the corner. He waited.

Within a minute, two nondescript men in a black van pulled up to the intersection, arguing. The driver was pointing toward the west, the passenger holding up a small black box and pointing in the direction of the police car.

Finally the passenger won and they slid through a turn, moving eastward, Merchant memorizing their back license plate as they fishtailed along E Street, dutifully following the D.C. police. He had no doubt in his mind that the car would be registered to Legislative Services.

He slunk all the way back to the car feeling old and worthless. Jack was dead. Hurley had been sent to Germany. Ned Bramley was probably in a federal jail by now.

And it was his fault. He'd been playing a new game with old tricks, letting his ego call all the shots.

He climbed into the car, groaned again as he settled in. This was BJ's game. Merchant had seriously underestimated the man—or perhaps he'd overestimated people in general. Whatever the case, he'd screwed up big time. As he started the Cadillac and pulled back into the Sixth Street traffic, he couldn't shake the nagging feeling that Ben James was just getting warmed up with him, that there was much more to come.

He reached the intersection of Sixth and E and turned right, in the opposite direction of his assailants. Shaking the tail had been a small gesture, but he'd even take a little victory right now. "Your move, BJ," he said.

The Mosquito Coast Early Afternoon

The Unitech trigger for the Raytheon Bearcat warhead was of the simple impact variety. Dense aluminum, a cylinder the size of a beer can, it formed a broken electrical connection with the ring of explosives in the warhead whose detonation would trigger the massive release of potential energy in the unstable mass of plutonium that formed the missile's core. An impact of sufficient strength would send a small conducting plunger through a ceramic nonconducting block into the base of the trigger to complete the electrical loop.

Bingo! Annihilation.

Ken Breedlove sat hunched over the small wooden table in the underground hootch, his self-contained arc light casting brilliant opalescence over the workbench and the jeweler's tools that lay spread out on a small length of black velvet. All around, his men sat cursing the rain that sheeted hot and steamy outside the hootch, the dark confinement and earthen smells of the place too intense and claustrophobic for them. They weren't really happy sharing space with two atomic missiles, either.

They'd made the shelter the day before yesterday in one

afternoon with the help of a dozer in the same clearing in which they'd set up the phony missile installation for the videotapes—camouflage netting over empty boxes, rail tracks to nowhere, a fake front of corrugated tin to pass as a warehouse. It had been easy to set up and easy to knock down again.

The shelter had been dug to hide the missiles, with a thin lead covering as their roof to deny the satellite probes that were undoubtedly zeroing in on the area in flocks. The shelter was merely a hole in the ground with a roof over it, the earthen walls now damp and running mud, bugs, and snakes an inch thick onto the floor. They usually made camp outside, but the rain had driven them, complaining, down here.

He pulled the lighted magnifying glasses back down off his forehead to cover his eyes and continued to examine the Unitech trigger that BJ had given him in November. Where the man had gotten it he had no idea, though he figured that it had to have come directly from the manufacturer. These things were watched over too closely once they made their way into the system to allow for much hanky-panky. Of course, that's what he had thought about the missiles, too.

"Willie, come here," he said, picking up the electric screwdriver, turning it on to a light static hum.

Willie, frowning and morose, skirted the large bulk of the missiles to move up next to Breedlove. "I can't take much more of this shit down here," he said low. "I don't like bein' closed in this way."

"Good," Breedlove replied as he set the trigger upright on the table and began removing the screws in the top that held the casing together. "I've got an outside job for you."

The casing came loose when the last bolt was removed, Breedlove sliding the assembly out of its thick, scored shell, exposing its innards, the tight spring-loaded plunger held in place only by the ceramic mass blocking it from the open connection.

"Gather up anything incriminating down here," he told Willie. "Start with the video gear and the Russian uniform. Burn what will burn, dump the rest in the river. Food scraps, latrines . . . I want everything covered."

"That mean we're about done with all this?" the man asked.

"Maybe," Breedlove answered, not looking up from his work. There was absolutely nothing he wanted to tell his cohorts. He remembered the line from *Macbeth*: "That in the captain's but a choleric word, which in the soldier is flat blasphemy." They all told themselves that they killed for all the right reasons. It's what they needed to get through the night. Best to leave it at that. He glanced reflexively at the suitcase full of money. "I want it done before nightfall. We're going hunting again tonight."

"Should I take help?" Willie asked, a good man because he questioned nothing.

"Sure," Breed answered, smiling. "As long as it's Mulroy."

"My pleasure," Willie said, grunting affirmation as he walked away, the closest thing to emotion the man ever expressed.

Using a pair of channel locks, Breedlove wrestled the nonconductor out of the trigger, the plunger snapping into place immediately. Had a bomb been connected, it would have exploded. A small pacemakerlike battery formed the back end of the plunger. Setting down the screwdriver, he picked up the small drill and put on rubber electrical gloves. Leaning down low, he hit the battery pack with the drill, the thing rending loudly, then sparking to black smoke before it died.

Mulroy, a bitter complainer, was walking around the hootch with Willie gathering evidence. Somebody had a field radio picking up the news that the United States was contemplating a field operation in Honduras. His men smoked and made small talk and played cards, not one of them realizing they were engaged in anything more meaningful than the shit work they had done in dozens of other jungles over the past twenty years. Nobody with a real chance ever hired mercs. They were grunts, plain and simple, and if Breed had a problem with the operation it was that he was unable to tell even one of them of the beauty and wonder of what they were doing.

Now that he had destroyed the electrical connection within the trigger, it was necessary for him to make another, one that he controlled. He set the small timer next to the trigger, trailing the two fragile-looking lead wires into the cylinder itself. He then soldered the leads to the plunger and put the thing carefully back together, filing two tiny notches at the join of the casing with the inner assembly, with the side of the drill, forcing the wires into the notches when replacing the cover. When the time came, he would set twenty-four hours onto the digital timer, the new electrical connection forming after he'd had ample time to put thousands of miles between himself and his success.

He felt the power flow through him, the control elevate him. It was all he could do to keep himself calm and stoic as he stood away from the bench, his back sore from being hunched over, and carried the trigger to the front of the missiles.

The forty-foot-long birds were mud-splattered, but still shiny and deadly looking. Something about engineered and tooled metal made human sense to Breedlove, a true creation formed in man's imagination, taken directly from the raw earth and forged by fire to do his will. It was like nothing that existed in nature and was nearly transcendental to him.

With slightly shaking hands he guided the cylinder toward a hole in the nose of the warhead, the trailing wires and timer held in his other hand. He screwed the trigger into its opening, holding his breath as it locked into place with an audible snap. He then set the watertight timer against the bulbous head of the missile, magnetic jaws clamping tightly. Happiness flooded through him, though no emotion escaped his sullen demeanor. He had grasped the moment, and would change history by his own hand.

He fought an irrational notion to make the contact right then, to see if this monstrous bird of destruction was really his to command. Instead, he quoted *Macbeth* again, a play much on his mind today. "'Where we are, there's daggers in men's smiles,'" he whispered to the bombs, "'the near in blood, the nearer bloody.'"

■■■■■■ NEWSBREAK ■■■■■■

". . . cannot let civilization falter under the dicta-
tor's boot in Central America. We cannot tolerate
such aggression in our own hemisphere, and
against our own friends. So, it is with deepest
regrets but firm resolve that I am ordering American
troops onto foreign soil once more. We will defend
democracy in this region. We will stand toe to toe
with our Honduran brother to expel the viper from
his midst. And with God's help, we will prevail. The
horrors of the last two days will not be allowed to
continue."

—Presidential address
February 7

CUBANS TO MOBILIZE

Poblado, Caribbea (AP)—In a press conference this
morning, Caribbean Defense Minister Joachim
Otello announced that two battalions of Cuban
Revolutionary Guard will be participating in joint
exercises with the Caribbean People's Army, commonly called the Companeros, over the next week.
The exercises are said to involve as many as fifteen
thousand troops and are the largest of their kind
ever on Caribbean soil.

This follows closely the announcement that the
United States Embassy in Poblado has been surrounded by Companero tanks, its diplomats and
their families ordered to leave the country. Caribbean President Maria Madrina has also severed all
ties with the U.S. in an effort to hold together her
faltering government in the face of increasing public
opposition since the alleged assassination of Foreign Minister Ramirez by an American mercenary.

Questioned as to the timing of the exercises, Otello denied that it was connected with the Honduran border problem or the fear of U.S. intervention, but added that the people of Caribbea will defend their lands to the death whether threatened by "Honduran nationals or Yankee killers."

The operation is scheduled to take place at an unspecified location near the Honduran border.

". . . as we still sit in amazement at the scoop that TV news femme fatale Sheila Traynor pulled on all of us old Washington watchers. No one had given Traynor a second thought when it came to hard journalism, and she left us all with egg on our faces.

"Where did she get her info? How did it fall together so perfectly while the rest of us were still chasing down end-of-the-cold-war stories? This reporter, for one, is not even going to try and answer, except to say that, perhaps, we all underestimated a journalistic talent of extreme value because of our own prejudices and misconceptions. *Mea culpa, mea culpa, mea maxima culpa.* Sheila, wherever you are, let me be the first to apologize for all the B words—bimbo, broad, brassy—that I've been throwing around about you, and as I watch the entire tone of our city change before my eyes, I suggest that it may not be too early to begin thinking about the Emmy Award. You'll get my vote."

—*Washington Insider*
February 7

NCC Tower 3:14 P.M.

Sheila Traynor sat at her desk piled high with telegrams and turned off the ringer of the telephone that kept calling to her. The TV set into her bookcase was turned on to a live broadcast from Fort Bragg, as 82nd Airborne Rangers prepared to board a fleet of C-141 aircraft bound for Honduras.

This was her doing—hers! The feelings that flowed through her were indescribable. Always before, upward mobility had been a long, slow, only partly successful climb. It had taken two EEOC lawsuits, ten years in local news, five years of extra night school courses in diction and journalism, and a parade of men, as long as the Buffalo telephone directory, who "helped" her with her career, just to get this far. Suddenly, with one story, she had become the most well-known newsman in the world. Yes, newsman. She could mix it up with any of them now, and thought of herself in the masculine since she'd beaten them at their own game. She still wasn't sure what had gone right, but she had sojourned well beyond questioning the good fortune at this point. She had to think ahead, to continue to solidify her gains by following the story to its conclusion. Her career may have had its ups and downs— from commercial model in lingerie ads to investigative reporter—but she was smart enough to know that she had to hold on to the raging bull until the buzzer went off. It wasn't over till it was over. They couldn't blast her off this motherfucker with dynamite.

There was a tap at her door, Don Merck poking his toupeed head in a second later, his eyes twinkling. "How's my superstar?" he asked cloyingly.

"You're just the man I wanted to see," she replied, wiggling her fingers. "Come into my parlor . . ."

"Said the spider to the fly," he finished, walking in dragging a mail sack stuffed full behind him. "You've reinvented journalism, sweetheart. Somebody told me there was even a cable from Walter Cronkite in there."

"Just put them in the corner," she said, distracted, pointing a long-nailed finger in the direction of two other mail sacks. "Then peel yourself off the ceiling long enough to talk to me for a minute."

His eyes narrowed as he pulled a chair over to her desk, the window overlooking Manhattan steamed over with humidity, hazing them in. "Lighten up," he said, reaching out always busy hands to play with her magnetic paper clip trap. "You've made it. The world has been appropri-

ately set on its ear and turned inside out. Of course, a lot
of thanks goes to the guy who gave you the shot. . . ."

"And I am grateful," she said, looking at him with a
small smile. "You had enough sense to know talent when
you saw it."

He took the top off the clear plastic container and
dumped the paper clips all over the desk. "Baroni came up
with a great idea a few minutes ago," he said, putting the
clips in one at a time, trying to see how many he could
stick to the magnet in the lid before they fell in. "He
thought that tomorrow might be a good day to do a feature
on you. You know . . . how you got the story, what
happened to you at the FBI—"

"No," she said flatly.

He froze, his hand hanging in midair, a clip poised
between thumb and index finger. "What do you mean?" he
asked in a small voice, like a child's.

"I can't do it because I won't be here."

He left the paper clips alone then, concern etching his
features as he leaned in close. "I'll bite. Where will you
be?"

She gave him the kind of smile that she had used in the
lingerie ads. "On an airplane bound for Honduras," she
said.

The man sat back hard, his arms waving at her as his
breath choked out of him in a low groan. He had the look
of an organ grinder who'd just lost his monkey. "No way,"
he said loudly. "You're our fucking meal ticket. No way
I'm letting you go down there to get yourself killed. You
know our ratings have jumped ten points in the last two
days. Do you have any idea how many people that
represents?"

"Eighteen million," she said, standing to turn her back
on him. She went to the window and began writing on the
frosted glass just as she'd done as a kid on the car
windows. She was not going to be denied this. She'd
waited too many years for the real break. "The story's
finished here. It's my story. I want to go where everything's
happening." She spun around to stare ice at him. "God
damn it, Don. I'm forty-one years old and have already had
two face-lifts. I can't sell my body anymore. I'm going to

make my mark one way or the other, and from where I stand, this is the only game in town."

"You want an early negotiation on a new contract?" he asked, standing to get eye to eye with her, the desk separating them. The good humor was gone from his face. "You want a bonus? It'll piss me off, Sheila, but I'll do it if you want to get hard-nosed."

"What I want has nothing to do with money," she said, exasperated. "It's self-respect I need, to know that I did something well and followed through with it. I want to be thought of as the same kind of professional as my colleagues are. They all had wars to make them famous. Edward R. Murrow had a war. Walter Cronkite had Vietnam. I want a war, too, Don. God, I want to contribute. Doesn't that make sense?"

"How about some specials?" he asked, moving around the desk to get feely with her. He put an arm around her shoulders and spoke low. "Just between the two of us. I could get you four or five specials next year . . . any topic of your choice: celebrity interviews, think pieces, investigative—"

"Either you put me on a plane for Honduras or I walk right now," she said evenly, slipping out of his grasp and walking around to his side of the desk, changing places.

His face looked as if it were melting as he fell heavily into her desk chair. "You really mean that?"

She pointed to the window, the man swiveling the desk chair to see the words "I Quit!" written there. She sat. "I do," she said, sweeping a small pile of paper clips off the desk and into her left hand. She fed them back into the container. "Think about this for a minute. How big are the chances that I'll die? All things being equal, I'm not going to want to be directly in the line of fire or anything. Now, given that, think of how you could milk the public—"

"My God!" he said, brightening, a kind of angelic light coming to his eyes. He was looking *out there* somewhere, at the giant TV screen of the mind. "Yes. The woman who broke the story now facing death to follow it through."

"The *reporter* who broke the story," she corrected. "This is really the solution for both of us. I mean, if the story moves out of my hands now, how long will we keep that ratings gain?"

That seemed to have the desired effect. Merck's face began another meltdown. "You're right," he said. A good dose of paranoia the best way to bring Don in line. "We'll send you, with your own crew, Saturday night."

"Why wait that long?"

"It'll take them most of the day just to get the troops and the chain-of-command going," he said. "I was down there when Reagan sent in the National Guard and it takes them most of their time just figuring out who's in charge. The longer we wait to send you down, the more we can build it up before you go. We'll film everything. We'll make you the Lone Ranger going in to clean up the Old West single-handedly.

"Yesss," she said low, loving the image. Now he was on her wavelength. This time next week she'd be a bright, shining square in the crazy quilt of American history. A legend in her own time.

United States Capitol Building 4:17 P.M.

The terrible, swirling north wind rolled into the Capitol Building along with a near-frozen Charles Merchant. Snow was flurrying again, the sky bursting gray-white, a monstrous deadly cloud hanging over the city and the lives of its inhabitants. He'd had to park in one of the public lots two blocks away on Maryland and the walk through the frigid wasteland that bore no resemblance to a major city was something straight out of a Jack London story, just like the Pawhatan Indians, who'd once used the Hill as their campground. His feet were totally numb, as were nose and cheeks, the wind whistling with him into the gingerbread halls of the high Roman architectural melange, the result of a Design-the-Capitol contest in 1792, that housed the nation's leaders.

He'd come in through the west-side visitors' doorway, the sandstone facade side, where George Washington had created the first conflict-of-interest debate by insisting that the Capitol Building be made of sandstone from his Aquia Creek quarries. Sandstone, with its tendency to decompose, had been a problem for capitol architects ever since.

Merchants moved through the metal detectors with a contingent of Navy midshipmen in pea coats and dress hats. Once in, the entire building seemed to be filled with uniformed military, surplanting the radical right of the early part of the week. He moved through the semidark halls to the elevators, only to discover that they were all reserved for representatives. Rosen must have demanded a roll-call vote. He went back down the hall and took up one of the curving staircases leading to the representatives' entrance. He showed the capital policeman the floor pass Rosen had given him earlier, half expecting the man to arrest him for violating the Official Secrets Act.

He had no idea of what was going to happen at this point. If Bramley had been picked up because of their phone conversation, there would be nothing to hold him on. He'd replayed the conversation twenty times in his head, trying desperately to remember if anything of a sensitive nature had been said. There'd been hints, but nothing concrete, and unless Bramley had been wired in the Smithsonian, they really had no reason to arrest him, and certainly no evidence. Despite that, when he'd stopped at a pay phone and made a call to Cal Daniels, his lawyer, he'd found out that Ned was being held but hadn't been charged yet, the lawyer now engaged in trying to get a federal judge to issue the writ to get him out.

He felt safe enough at the moment. With no proof that any information had changed hands, the entire episode fell apart. It was probably just BJ pulling his chain a bit, flexing his muscles. He couldn't—*wouldn't*—concede that the country he had served for so long could turn against him so quickly and completely. It simply defied everything he believed in. The entire incident with Bramley had to be some strange mistake.

The elevator was disgorging congressmen as he topped the stairs, the red-carpeted halls buzzing with conversation. Wide-eyed pages piled up in front of the swinging doors leading to the House floor, listening to the debate, their silence a witness to the high drama of the proceedings.

"Excuse me," he said, slipping around a group of them and moving into the chamber itself. Like the Smithsonian, the Congress seemed smaller than it was supposed to be, like a miniature version of the real thing, the Senate side even worse. But it was compact and intense, and he could feel pulsating waves of excitement ripple through him as he watched the battleground define itself like Waterloo.

The gallery was filled with armed forces personnel, watching down stoically. They almost seemed to be at attention. He knew what they were thinking, too, the same thing he would have thought a week ago. Who are these people to define our lives and duties? Rightness of intent was a sharp dividing line among the military between their outlook and those who disagreed. Disagreement in the service was equatable with aiding the enemy. There was no middle ground, no informed dissent. The gallery was filled with men and women venting primal hatred against their opponents on the floor. It was so thick he could taste it.

A man he didn't recognize was making an impassioned speech in favor of the military from the roving podium in the fore of the chamber, just in front of the building-block conglomeration of risers and desks that dominated the center of the room. The rostrum for the speaker and his deputies. Session was being presided over by another man he didn't know. Bench seating for the representatives fanned out around the rostrum, the decor suitably drab in the 1949 style, the last remodeling. A Congressional Record stenographer walked around up front, typing away as the speech proceeded, her machine sitting atop a small platform with strap that wound around her neck, like a cigarette girl's in the old movies. Pages sat on the stairs around the rostrum, listening to the speeches, hunched over for comfort. Congressmen moved at will through their sections, talking in small groups, working the issue in seeming disregard for the words of the man speaking.

He saw Rosen, haggard-looking, walking through the crowd. He moved from group to group, shaking hands, speaking with obvious passion, though Merchant couldn't hear the words.

He saw Della waving at him from across the chamber, from a door on the other side. It was then that he realized he'd come in on the speaker's left, the Republican side. A natural enough mistake for him.

He waved, then held up a finger for her to stay put. He moved back into the hall and around behind the rostrum to the other side, the woman meeting him just on the chamber side of the door.

"How's it going?" he asked, his voice low.

She shrugged. "It's tough. With the announcement of the troops today, everybody has a reason to vote against the recision."

"Phil looks worn out."

She looked up at him with inquisitive eyes, her brown, curly hair framing her face in softness. "If I wasn't following him around sticking food into his mouth from time to time, he wouldn't even be eating."

"This has really had an effect on him," Merchant replied. "He seemed to be in a whole different gear over at the Pentagon today."

She looked at the floor before turning her brown eyes back on him. They had misted over. "He's afraid," she said, and he put an arm around her because she was shaking slightly. "Chilly in here, huh?"

He smiled with a confidence he didn't feel. "I have faith in Phil and I have faith in the system," he said, squeezing her shoulder, then releasing her. "A man like Ben James will not get control of this Congress. Hell, your husband is, at the very moment, digging up all financial poop on our friend BJ."

She managed a half smile and brushed at her tears with the back of her hand. "I talked to him a little bit ago," she said, then opened her purse to pull out a compact, unsnapping it to look at her eyes in the mirror. "He seemed pretty excited and said he was zeroing in on what he called 'a financial wizard.' I do believe my husband thinks he can further his own career by untangling some of it. Are my eyes red?"

"You look beautiful," he said, playfully touching the

end of her nose with his index finger. His feet were thawing somewhat, helping his mood slightly. Things *were* going to work out. Phil Rosen, for all his self-effacement, was one of the most powerful politicians in the country. He could handle this. BJ had flash and money, but Rosen had working, continuing friendships and associations with these people on a day-to-day basis. There was feeling there, and understanding. "Here comes Phil."

Rosen was moving toward them, weaving through the standing clumps of humanity, eyes continually checking down at his watch. The man speaking was in the process of yielding two minutes to one of Montana's two representatives when Phil reached them. His face read like Shakespearean tragedy.

"What's it look like?" Della asked, her brother frowning at her, then turning to shake Merchant's hand without enthusiasm.

"Charlie," he said, lackluster. "Good to see a friendly face."

"Is it that bad?" Merchant replied.

"If you mean do the bad guys have more votes than we do—yes, it's horrible. Even the President's backed off on supporting this, and it was his doing. I can't even get him on the phone. Danton, the man who wrote the damned recision, is now out actively campaigning against it." He fixed Merchant with an unwavering gaze that told him volumes.

"How many votes?" Della asked, taking his arm, her eyes filled with a kind of wary concern that Merchant found fascinating. There was a strength to her that he'd never even imagined.

Rosen worked his shoulders, loosening them. He reached into his dark suit pocket and withdrew a list, handing it to Della. "There're ten names on here," he said, straightening his tie, trying to rebuild his confidence. "Swing votes. They call themselves uncommitted—"

"Uncommitted?" Merchant said, too loud. He looked around and lowered his voice. "This seems simple enough to me. You're either for it or against it."

"At any rate, whatever they are, I've got to get eight of the ten or . . . we . . . lose."

He stretched the last words out, staring hard at each of them in turn. It was really that close. Merchant couldn't believe it.

"Listen," Della said. "Do you finish with a speech?"

He shrugged, then ran hands through his thick black hair, pushing it back in place. "Could, I guess," he replied. "But what's the point? There's nothing I could say in a speech that I couldn't and didn't say to them in private. I can't tell you the promises I've—"

"Never mind that," she said, her face set hard. "You've got to go out there and make a speech that sets them on their ear. I know you, Phil. You enjoy working behind the scenes, getting things done quietly. But a speech . . . read into the record . . . can move people. You've got to give yourself that extra shot."

He folded his arms across his chest and narrowed his eyes. "Sis, we don't get points for good speeches. This isn't high-school debate."

"No, it's not," she replied quickly. "It's our lives. Have you forgotten who you are and where you came from? Come on, Phil. Do I have to spell it out for you? For two thousand years Jews have wandered from pogrom to pogrom in a world where no one wants us to be alive. If the rule of law can be trampled this way, how long before the next witch hunt? We cannot lose our Congress to that man." She took him by the shoulders and stared fire at him. "Too much depends on this. You will not stand by and watch America get joked and bartered away without doing everything you can to stop it. Do you understand me?"

"Yes, Mama," he said through a tiny smile, the two of them embracing quickly, meaningfully. "A speech it will be."

Della wiped her eyes again and made a face at Merchant. "He's so shy . . . hates to make a spectacle of himself."

Rosen looked at Merchant. "Do you think a speech will do any good?"

Merchant put a hand on his shoulder. "You go for every bit of it. Shove it down that motherfucker's throat. If you lose it won't be because you didn't do all you could."

Rosen smiled and wiggled his eyebrows, then flared around to face the chamber. "Will the gentleman yield for five minutes?" he called loudly.

The answer returned quickly from the representative from Georgia. "I will gladly yield five minutes to you, Mr. Rosen, leader of this great assembly and a fine gentleman."

Rosen walked slowly toward the podium, most of the activity ceasing in the room as everyone turned to him in apparent surprise, people quietly shuffling back to their seats. Merchant watched him as he bent to speak to a small group around the portable podium, undoubtedly working out the end of debate. Merchant leaned toward his daughter-in-law. "Don't think I've ever seen this many of them vote before."

She nodded. "Phil made it a roll-call vote. He wanted to see exactly who his friends and enemies were."

"Seems to me," he said, pointing up into the gallery, "that there's a few empty seats up there in reserved seating that have a good view of the tote board and give us a better angle on reactions. I think I'd like to watch from there."

"I'll go with you," she said. "I don't want to be alone for this."

They left the floor quickly, taking another set of stairs up, using their floor passes to avoid the various lines that had queued up waiting for the few seats that would come open. They moved into the gallery, a semicircular bowl overlooking the House floor with a highly polished brass rail running around it that no one was allowed to touch, a testament to the destructive powers of ten million visitors a year.

They moved right down to the rail in the small, mostly vacant reserved seating. The uniforms that filled the gallery were grouped by service, which told Merchant that they'd been bused in from close bases or even the Pentagon, with the midshipmen being brought in from the Naval Academy in Annapolis, just down the beltway. It was intimidation time.

The theater seating was comfortable as they leaned forward, avoiding the rail, and peered down into the chamber. Rosen was standing at the podium, the carpet a vibrant blue beneath his feet. He was looking up into the gallery, taking the full measure of the hate that flowed from there. Finally, he took a deep breath and moved up to the microphone.

"Here we go," Della whispered, taking Merchant's right hand in both of hers, squeezing tightly.

"It's going to be fine," he said, and wondered why he felt as if he'd spent his entire life saying that phrase.

"My fellow citizens of planet Earth," Rosen began, a slight titter trilling through the floor and gallery.

"Good," Della whispered, and seemed to relax a touch, Merchant realizing that Rosen was taking the real high road on this one. A gamble for sure.

"You laugh at that phrase," Rosen continued, gazing all around the chamber. "I wonder why. We share economics with most of the nations of this globe. Our television programs are changing its face, even as foreign business practices have all but ended our hegemonic control over the flow of goods and materials.

"It is a new world. Foreign ownership of American businesses is a fact of life. American business interests in other countries determine our political connections to those countries. The world no longer operates under the spin of military imperialism. The new world is one of business—"

"No. No. No." A chorus of midshipmen began chanting loudly, banging their feet, drowning out the speaker. The representative running the session that day banged the gavel loudly until the commotion died down.

"We will have silence in this chamber or I will clear it!" he called, pointing the gavel into the gallery. "One more outburst and all of you are gone."

Rosen stood with his head up, his face stoic, waiting for quiet. If the outburst upset him, he didn't let it show. "I'd like to ask the young men in the gallery a question," Rosen said, smiling up at them. "Do you gentlemen know how long America has been the premier military power on the planet, for how long our so-called military-industrial complex has been in control of our economy? Well, let me tell you. Only since World War II. A recent development. Until that time, we were a country of farmers mostly, agrarians just moving heavily into the industrial age. Now our military budget eclipses everything in our lives, threatening to squash us under its weight."

There was murmuring in the gallery, but no demonstration.

"We've discovered that the planet is really just a small island in which *all* of us have got to live together, because we not only fear the cost of our technology, we fear its power. We have the means at hand to destroy ourselves. We are now looking down into the valley of our past from a new mountaintop, and from that vantage point, it appears that we've all been blind, insane fools. War as we know it is finished. The new wars are fought with economics, with good trading partners and tariffs. All the arms race ever did for us was to make us the greatest debtor nation on earth, and to what end—enough bombs to destroy us all four hundred times over?

"If we want to survive as a nation in the new order, we must look ahead, not backward. This dollar recision can do a great deal toward putting our government on its feet and our citizens on the road to self-sufficiency once more. Think of all the people we could feed with all that money. Doesn't that fill you with hope?

"You must think of these things not as politicians, but as human beings. We can no longer afford to be a world military power. We can no longer go leapfrogging from one confrontation to the next simply to keep the defense spending high. It's time for real change. It doesn't matter whether the invasion of Panama or the war with Iraq was right or wrong, what matters is that fighting those wars has helped to break our back economically.

"We cannot be the world's policemen, not if we want to be able to feed ourselves. We should have been spending our time designing Honda automobiles these last thirty years instead of bigger, more expensive bombs. It's that simple. The new world is economic, not military. To survive as a nation we must radically alter our industrial base. We must loosen our grip on the saber and let it clatter to the floor. The ages demand that we do no less. Our children deserve that . . . and more. Please don't let them down."

Rosen turned then, nodding to the speaker pro tem,

who announced, "This here'll be a roll-call vote on Joint House and Senate bill HS-1437. When your name is called, please respond with yea or nay or abstention. Ackerman, Gary!"

As the slow roll call went out, Merchant leaned back and thought about Rosen's speech. It was good, for sure, honest. He feared that it may have been too honest, too high-handed. As he watched the lined faces of the military around him, he was conscious of how hard the truth can go down sometimes.

Della leaned back with him. "What do you think?" she asked.

"I flinched a few times," he said, "but Phil said nothing that wasn't true."

"You think he should have jacked them off a little instead?" she said, smiling through even teeth.

He shrugged slightly. "I wouldn't have last week," he said. "Today I'm not sure about anything, least of all honesty. You got that list of names?"

She pulled the list out of her coat pocket, making sure she kept it partway hidden in the sleeve or the seating ushers would take it away, as reading materials were not allowed in the gallery.

The voting proceeded slowly, the 435 names clicking out about ten to the minute, the numbers adding up slowly on the tote board, each man's name followed by three small light bulbs, the one lit denoting the vote.

As Rosen had predicted, it was extremely close, with the lead changing hands more than ten times, both Charlie and Della glued to the list of names. Rosen walked the floor, back and forth beneath the big board, watching, watching. . . .

"Panetta's just swung," Della announced excitedly. "He was the seventh on the list."

"So close," Charlie said as the name Parris was called out.

"We just need one of the remaining three swing votes," she replied, pointing into the chamber. Rosen was looking up, giving them a toothy grin. "Now all we need to do is get this thing wrapped up and get on with life."

All at once, a silence seemed to descend onto the floor

and the gallery, Merchant watching the grin melt away from Rosen's face.

"Oh, no," Della said.

Merchant looked up, directly across the chamber to the other edge of the horseshoe. A man in a bright white suit with a red rose in the lapel had walked into the gallery, a large smile on his face. Charlie watched with growing anger and concern as Ben James walked down the gallery stairs and directly to the rail, bracing his hands on the brass to lean with stiff arms. He fixed his gaze on the voting below and joked with a group of young airmen. No capital cops or ushers moved down to tell him to sit or leave the rail alone. He simply stood there, arrogantly, as if he owned the place.

Merchant felt a sudden and unreasoning anger wash over him. He kept failing to give James enough credit for perversion. By what right did this man stand in these sacred halls, amid this assembly that he so desperately wanted to destroy?

Everything had stopped, the entire room quieting to eerie silence. Every eye on the floor was looking up at BJ, Rosen standing with his fists clenching and unclenching as James's intense gaze swept slowly across the chamber like the discharge of a water cannon.

The voting continued, Merchant's teeth on edge as he watched James watching the action. The minutes got longer, the silence in the chamber growing more intense until it was almost physical. The next swing vote was a Representative from California named Richter. He voted against the recision.

Below, Rosen was running around the chamber, talking frantically with the remaining voters, his posture one of defeat as he moved from one to the other.

"We're losing it, Charlie," Della said, voice husky.

"Don't give up yet," Merchant said, trying to will the right thing to happen.

The vote was dead even when the name Simmons was called, the ninth name on Rosen's list.

"I vote, no, Mr. Speaker," the man said loudly, his eyes traveling immediately up to Ben James at the gallery rail.

Merchant stared fire across the expanse of fifty feet of air separating him from BJ. As if responding to the call,

Ben James looked up and winked at Charlie, then cocked his finger like a gun, firing across the gallery at him.

Below, Rosen had turned from the board, his hands covering his face, his head shaking a steady no.

The rest of the vote was a nightmare. Ray Ulmer, the swing vote from Vermont, voted enthusiastically with Ben James. From that moment on, the conclusion was foregone. Charlie watched the count, not giving up hope until the name Don Young had been called out and the recision had lost by three votes that may have well been three hundred.

He felt James's eyes on him and fought their pull, keeping his own downcast, his jaw muscles tight. Finally he could stand it no longer. He looked up. James smiled at him and raised his eyebrows. He mouthed the words "your move," then turned and walked out of the gallery.

"No!" came the scream from Rosen below, his voice primal and given over to uncontrolled fury. Seeing James's departure, he raised his hands in front of his face, clenching them into fists, and went charging out of the chamber.

"He's going for BJ," Merchant said, already on his feet and moving toward the entry, all the midshipmen cheering loudly and throwing their caps in the air as if they'd just won the Army/Navy game.

Merchant fought his way up the stairs and through the door, running the length of the formal hall, the shouts of capital policemen behind him. His rage was nearly overpowering and it was only a question as to whether he or Rosen got to James first. He hurried down the stairs to the second floor, racing the length of the hallway to reach the Statuary Hall ten seconds too late.

Rosen was screaming at a laughing Ben James. The men stood at the center of a loose circle of spectators on the alternating black and white tiled floor. Roman columns hung with heavy red drapes originally installed to discourage eavesdropping defined the edges of the large hall and gave backdrop to the unsympathetic stares of the life-size statues of past American greats that stood amid them.

"Phil!" Merchant shouted, shoving his way through the onlookers, arriving at the scene just as Rosen took a wild punch at James, the man sidestepping easily and coming through with a well-cocked right hand, snapping in stiff-armed impact with Rosen's face.

It was a hell of a punch, the crowd gasping and drawing back as Rosen was lifted off his feet to collapse, unconscious, on the ground right next to the plaque commemorating the spot where John Quincy Adams had died of a stroke in 1848. Della was pushing her way through the crowd. She screamed, dropping to cradle her brother's face in her hands.

Merchant stepped right up to James and grabbed him by the lapels, only to find himself jerked back by several capital police.

BJ just grinned, showing him empty palms. "Charlie," he said proprietarily. "I don't want to fight anybody. I was just defending myself. You saw how he came at me. I didn't even *do* anything, for crying out loud."

Merchant tried to break free, the cops jerking him several steps back. "Give it up," one of them said. "Don't make us cuff you." Merchant sagged in the hands of his captors, the men tentatively releasing him. He straightened his suit jacket, staring at the spectators, who were smiling and pointing. BJ made no move to leave, instead he seemed to be savoring the moment. "Let Bramley go," Merchant told him. "This is between me and you."

"Bramley . . . Bramley. Not sure if I recollect that name."

"Let the man go," Merchant repeated, his eyes locked to James's.

Very quickly, fleetingly, the smile left BJ's face and it turned dark as a moonless night. "It's not that kind of a game," he said. "No compromise." All at once, the smile was back, parting the clouds again. "Besides, we're just gettin' started."

Rosen groaned on the floor beside them, consciousness returning slowly. Blood flowed freely from his badly broken nose, as Della helped him to a sitting position. The cops began dispersing the crowd, two of them bending to speak to Rosen.

"You can't win, you know," Merchant said.

"How so?" BJ asked, cocking his head.

"I'm going to stop you. I guarantee that. Nothing will keep me from stopping you whatever you do."

BJ made a small punching motion in the air. "Now there's the spirit of the fighting man that made this country great," he said. "I commend you, Colonel. You've got a lot of spunk. I keep rubbing your nose in it and you keep coming back for more. Hell of a guy. You sure you don't want to come to work for me?"

"I'd kill myself and you first."

BJ nodded and narrowed his eyes a touch. "Yeah, that's what I figured. It's only the good that die young. But, my friend, I've already won. This vote gives me everything I need."

"No," Merchant said immediately. "It's not over yet. You've got a game plan bigger than Dallas cooking now. There's too many loose ends. No. You're not finished and neither am I. I'm going to claim your ass."

"Good for you," BJ said, moving closer to pat him on the shoulder, Merchant holding still for it rather than risk the police again. "Although I have to wonder at this juncture just exactly what means you're gonna use to do it."

"I'm going to use the truth," Merchant said, wanting to strangle BJ as the man's eyes got large like saucers and he began to laugh.

"The truth." He giggled. "God, you're a card." He turned and started walking away, then stopped and turned back.

"There's no such thing as truth, Charlie," he called, taking the rose out of his lapel and smelling it. "There's only you and me, brain to brain, dialing each other in." He tossed the rose to Merchant and shook his head. "It's silk. Can't tell the difference from the real thing."

The capital police had Rosen by the arms, helping the speaker to his feet. BJ sauntered over and bent down slightly to speak to the man as they got him up. "Thanks for the sixty billion, pal," he said, straightening and winking at Merchant. "I'll try not to spend it all in one place." Then he lowered his voice in concern. "That nose looks pretty shitty. Send him around to the Quarter later. I've got a great reconstructive surgeon named Jonah who'll fix him up like new."

"You're all heart." Merchant replied.

"Least I can do," the man said, turning and walking

away from the devastation he had done to both Rosen and the constitutional process.

Pennsylvania Quarter 11:00 P.M.

Ben James sat on his sofa in the vault, his large TV juicing a grid of live pictures from the hidden cameras in his offices, twelve in all, as VCRs located in June's tower dutifully recorded it for the ages. In his hand was a prism the size of a baseball that he rolled around in his palms, watching the light refracting through it in multicolored sabers, always new, always changing.

His success with the vote had been inevitable, no contest really. The representative system was too geared toward knee-jerk reaction to have responded any differently. No, he'd never even been especially worried about this part. It was the rest that had bothered him. Another day would tell that particular tale.

He wore a glen plaid suit, the last thing he'd bought at Brooks Brothers before they'd trashed themselves with women's fashions. His wine-colored silk tie was opened all the way, two red streamers hanging down the front of his pale blue shirt. On one of the twelve minimovies unfolding before him on the screen, the young one, Cheryl Joiner, was sitting atop a naked Gordon Hulett on the sofa in Con-3, a champagne bottle in her hand, acres of the man's pale white flab bouncing wildly as she rode him with all the enthusiasm of youth, Hulett with a death grip on her high round breasts as he grunted and snorted like an old nag. The girl was good, naturally talented, and might have been the only woman Hulett would have trusted to have sex with in BJ's offices. Funny thing, trust.

He normally would have had the victory party at his home, where the cameras were always rolling in the many bedrooms. But the weather had forced them here, close to the Capitol and the parking lots, and they'd had to improvise. Still, things were going well.

In Con-2 Rob Danton was finally getting his three-way

with Mary Ellen and Rayda Coombs. They were all on the
floor, rolling in the thick pile gold carpet, Rayda fellating
the man, who was wildly bucking his hips, as Mary Ellen
dangled her pendulous breasts into his face, his hands
roving all over her body. Danton had been a whiz kid at
Harvard who'd just written a best-seller on the economics
of the military when Macklin had tagged him as an adviser
and brought him into the real world. He hadn't taken to the
James style of politics at first, but BJ wore him down with
Mary Ellen. Danton's basic problem was that he was too
young and inexperienced to realize that everything had a
price tag. Strange for an economist. He should have
listened to Milton Friedman's free lunch speech.

Swing votes were getting their rewards in many of the
other offices, kind of like a sweet dessert after a fancy
meal. But there were other things going on that were just
as worthwhile—for instance, Unitech and G.E. corporate
officers and members of the Budget Committee drunk on
their asses, tooting lines of coke and playing a game of
Twister on the floor of the accounting department. Things
like that looked horrible in ethics hearings.

But the screen that was most interesting to him was
relatively calm. It was filmed in the small TV studio with
the satellite feed. Mel Patterson sat on a director's chair, a
fake Capitol Building backdrop behind her, holding open
court, mesmerizing a group of ten military brass, all
involved in the operation in Honduras. Closest to her right
hand was Bob "Tuck" Tucker, the general in charge of the
82nd Airborne and cochief of the Honduran expedition
along with SouthCom. She was explaining the threat of
peace to them.

Interested, he picked up the remote and brought Mel's
session up to full screen. He pulled the headset up over his
ears and buzzed the pad for June.

"Hey," she said. "When we go home, boss? I'm beat."

"Not yet," he replied into the stem mike. "All the sheep
haven't come back to the pen yet."

"You still think Jeremy's going to show?"

"He'll show," BJ replied, smiling. "He'll show all right.
When he does, buzz me and send him into the office."

"Check."

He pulled down the headset and brought the sound up

on Mel, holding the glass ball up in front of his face, Patterson multiplied a hundred times through the prism's facets. He found that notion particularly depressing and set the prism down on the coffee table in front of him.

"It's a sickness," the woman was telling the assembled men. "A kind of mass hysteria that makes people forget five thousand years of history and go off half cocked behind the Pied Piper of Hamlin. Let's face it: we may walk upright and live in brick houses, but we're still animals." She smiled with bright white teeth at them. "When you see a good-looking woman, that stirring you feel down in your pants . . ."

"Like now?" Tucker said from beside her, a beer in his hand, the other men laughing.

She reached over and patted his crotch. "Down, boy," she said, to even more laughter. "You've made my point. That stirring is natural, not something we could or would breed out of the species. Our bent toward violence is also natural. It's what enables us to protect ourselves and stay alive. If it went, so would go the human species. In fact, I'd be willing to make a very serious connection between that sexual urge and the urge to violence—I know what you military men are like in bed!"

A hoot went up from the entire group, Tucker standing and proposing a toast to "the most beautiful woman I've ever seen," Mel taking the compliment demurely, with downcast eyes.

"Thanks," she said, faking shyness. "You're either too nice or too drunk."

More laughter, everyone but Tucker sitting down. "Now about this stirring in my pants," he said.

"Ah," Mel returned, with a broad shrug to the audience. "If you're willing to get it out here in front of all your friends, I'd be willing to help you do something about it."

She made a quick grab for his zipper, Tucker, red-faced, sitting again and making a real show of crossing his legs and hunching over, the whole group breaking up with laughter.

BJ turned down the sound and stared at the woman right through the screen. Damn, she was good. She'd been his best pupil from the start because she never believed it or took it seriously. BJ felt that every good preacher was essentially an atheist, because only an atheist can stand back coldly and truly work the theater of religion. National defense was just another kind of religion, and the woman was reeling it like a prize bass on a ten-pound line.

He didn't trust her anymore, though. After all he'd done for the bitch, she was turning, he could feel it, conspiring against him. Even now, in his office on the other side of the vault door, one of his techs was dusting his desk for fingerprints. He'd set her up yesterday and June had caught her fucking around the vault door. It was a tribute to his feelings for Mel that he was willing to give her the benefit of the doubt even now, when it was obvious she had turned. He hated traitors. He'd done everything for her, been everything to her. She'd repaid him with treachery and disloyalty. He'd have to make an example of Melanie Patterson, to show the others that nobody could turn on him and stay alive. Suddenly, he found the thought of his retribution exciting. . . .

The headset buzzed quietly on his neck. He pulled it up and touched the pad. "They here?"

"On their way back to you," June said. "Can I go home now?"

"Yeah . . . and thanks. Leave the tapes running, okay?"

"Okay. Looks like some pretty hot stuff."

The woman cut off the phone, BJ shutting down the television and standing. Time to meet the mob. Bomar was one of the most predictable people he'd ever met. The man was always looking for the big easy score. The concepts of restraint and patience were beyond him. He was a light bulb. Once the juice was put to him, he'd light up like a Christmas tree and stay that way until the plug was pulled.

He walked out of the vault and into the office, the door closing behind him, its ten electronic locks sliding soundlessly into place, bonding the door to the steel beam that ran up the length of the door frame.

A thin man in a gray suit was kneeling in front of his desk, using a wide brush to put fingerprint powder on the top and front. A portable computer sat on the desk, the receiver of his phone resting on pads atop the thing.

"How's it going?" BJ asked the man.

"There're prints, all right," the tech said, not glancing up from his work. He stood, finally, and looked at BJ. "All one person's. I'll be ready to run it through the computer in a minute."

"Good," BJ replied as Bomar and his appendage, Pam Williams, walked into the office, the woman looking like a hooker with a thigh-tight leather skirt and spiked hair. The rest of her was bundled into a huge down-filled, quilted jacket in brown that made her look like a hand grenade with hair, the exact antithesis of his idea of femininity. He shook his head at the woman. "I see the circus parade has arrived."

She smiled sweetly at him. "Fuck you, too," she said, Bomar laughing and pulling a bottle of cheap wine out of his London Fog overcoat and holding it up.

"I hear that congratulations are in order," he said.

"We got lucky," BJ said, escorting them past the tech at the desk to the small sitting area back by the patio door, new snow falling dreamily outside, large fat flakes piling atop two- and three-foot drifts already clogging the wide veranda.

"Lucky . . . right," Bomar said, putting the bottle on a small marble coffee table and moving to the shelves containing the thousands of glass figurines, finding several cut-crystal glasses and bringing them back while BJ and Pam Williams glared at each other from opposing love seats. "You use the same kind of luck as I do . . . sure things."

Bomar sat beside Williams, the woman slinking out of her coat to reveal a nearly see-through blouse as she kittened up with the man, bringing a leg up to rest on his thigh. It was quite a show, Williams's eyes flashing at BJ the entire time, Bomar reveling in the attention.

BJ sat up straight and stared at the wine bottle's twist-off cap that Jeremy had made no move at unscrewing. "I wonder what brings you out here on such a cold night," he said, smiling. "Did we have business?"

"I told you," Bomar replied, putting an arm around the woman's shoulder, his hand casually draped over her left breast, fondling gently, almost unconsciously, "I wanted to congratulate you on the way you muscled the House today. I really didn't think you could pull it off."

"O ye of little faith," BJ said, reaching for the bottle. "Well, let's just—"

"Not yet," Bomar said, putting up a hand to stop BJ from taking the bottle. "We do need to talk about a little something first."

BJ nodded. "I had a feeling," he said.

Bomar craned his neck toward the tech at the desk twenty feet distant. "Do we really need him here?"

BJ smiled thinly. "If you keep your voice down, he won't hear you. What's the problem?"

Bomar's face darkened and he lowered his voice. "I been thinking," he said, just above a whisper. "I been doing your shit work for you for a long time now, taking your handouts while you get all the gravy."

"Seems you were talking about making a half billion dollars earlier today. That not enough?"

"It's too much if the IRS gets hold of me," the man replied. "Or if someone else tells them about me."

BJ turned his gaze to the woman and the sneer that she was trying to keep off her face. "Is this your doing?" he asked her.

"Hey!" Bomar said, then lowered his voice again. "I make my own decisions, get it? You leave Pamela out of it."

BJ sat back on the love seat again, laughing softly. "So, it's Pamela now, is it? Does the little lady have visions of sugarplums dancing in her head? You know, Christmas is already past."

"Look," Pam said. "I don't trust the way people have been getting ground under your wheels, Mr. Hotshot. What would keep you from fucking Jeremy off when you've got what you want?"

"Such a foul mouth on a woman," BJ replied, shaking his head. "It's unseemly."

Pamela rolled her eyes.

"You're talkin' to me," Bomar said angrily, "and I'm telling you that we're going to have to make another arrangement that's more . . . equitable for me."

"Where'd you learn that big word, Jeremy?" BJ asked, then got serious. "What sort of arrangement are you talking about?"

"I was thinking that a full partnership might be in

order," the man replied, eyes flashing. "That'll get me some legitimacy, you know? Kind of bring me out of the closet, as it were."

"No," BJ said simply. "I won't roll over for you. You want to fuck somebody, stick with Pamela here."

"What are you going to do to stop me?"

BJ just stared at him.

"Tell him the rest," Pam urged. "Go on."

Bomar stared for a long moment before speaking. "I've already made a contact on the organized crime strike force," he said. "If you don't work me into the legitimate end of things, I go to him and break open the abortion pill deal and turn state's evidence for immunity. I'll still sell most of the pills, but you, my friend, will be staring straight at a shit pile of Rico statutes, which will open everything up to government scrutiny. Racketeering covers a lot of territory, and the government has extreme latitude when they're prosecuting under Rico. *Capiesh?*"

"You'd do that to me after all I've done for you?" BJ asked.

"In a heartbeat," the man replied, the woman's face lighting up with a triumphant stare. "Before you do it to me."

BJ looked at the floor for a long moment.

"I've never seen you speechless before," Williams said. "I like you better when your mouth's closed."

When BJ finally looked up, he was smiling. "Well, what the hell, eh?" he said expansively. "Look, there's plenty here for everyone, and truth be known, I *was* using you for all the dirty work. You probably deserve the partnership. Besides, crooks usually make great straight businessmen when they put their minds to it. There's too much for me to handle alone anyway."

"You'll do it?" Bomar replied, and he seemed surprised.

"I've always been a pragmatist," BJ said, using the voice of sincerity that had been his father's stock-in-trade in the pulpit. "It seems you and your little friend have covered all my exits. Half of a fortune seems better than all of a jail term. I'm not going to tell you I'm happy about it . . . but what choice have I got?"

"Yeah," Bomar said, beaming. "What choice? But I want

this to happen now, today, before you think of some other choices."

"Sure," BJ said. "Have your lawyer get in touch with mine in the morning. We'll divide everything fifty-fifty, straight down the line." He reached out a hand to the man. "Welcome to your new home."

Jeremy Bomar was lit up like a floodlight when he shook BJ's hand. "I'll be damned," he said. "I've just gone straight."

"Not too straight, I hope." BJ smiled, always amazed at just how predictable the man was. He reached for the bottle again. "Now, we've got something to drink about."

As he uncapped the cheap rosé, BJ watched Pam Williams plaster herself to Bomar for a victory kiss. The male-female relationship was so symbiotic to BJ, in ways that people never thought about. In most respects, men were the vehicles driven by the dreams of their women. He smiled. Bomar was more like an ox pulling Pam Williams plow. Whatever. He poured them each a glass of wine, an obvious bulge in Bomar's pants as he leaned forward to pick up his glass.

"Not yet," Jeremy said as BJ brought the glass to his lips. "That's not the way my people do it."

BJ set down his glass, watching in amusement as Bomar pulled a Swiss Army knife out of his suit pants pocket. He'd certainly heard about this, but hadn't really thought he'd be expected to do it. The blood wine was typical mafioso ritual, dating back to a time when oaths had meant something. Bomar did it because even scum had to believe that something mattered, and BJ was all too happy to accommodate him in that regard.

"Give me your right hand," Jeremy said. BJ did as he was told.

Bomar quickly drew the blade across BJ's index finger. It was so sharp he didn't even feel the cut. Blood welled out of the finger, Bomar turning it upside down to drip into his wineglass. He spoke with more solemnity than BJ knew he was capable of. "When we drink the blood wine," he said, "you and I will be bound by the will of *la còsa nòstra*, this thing of ours. We will respect each other to the death, as brothers, just as surely as we are mixing our fluids. Our lives are one, our secrets . . . one."

He gave BJ back his finger, the woman pulling a BandAid out of her coat pocket and handing it to him. How thoughtful. Bomar then did the same to his own finger, reenacting a ritual with its roots in Sicily, a land and a people far beyond the punk's experience or understanding.

Bomar lifted the wineglass as Williams put a BandAid on his finger. "To politics . . . the greatest racket in the world," he said, taking a long drink and handing the glass to BJ.

"To partnerships," BJ said. "May everyone get what he wants."

He drained the glass, then set it down on the table.

"We're bound by blood now," Bomar said, as if the silly game meant anything. "Bound for life."

"Then long may we live," BJ said, smiling intensely at Pam Williams, Bomar's plowman. If there was a throne, then she was the brains behind it.

"Mr. James!" came the tech's voice from the desk. "I think we're on to something here."

"Excuse me . . . partner." BJ smiled, getting up to walk to the desk, his finger beginning to throb a bit beneath the bandage.

The tech was staring down at the portable CRT screen he'd set up on the desk. BJ watched in fascination as a long series of faces flashed upon the screen in half-second intervals, the word SCANNING flashing at the bottom of the display.

"I got a real clear print off the bottom drawer," the man said, shoving his black frame glasses a little higher on his nose. The man had a prominent Adam's apple that bobbed every time he spoke, driving BJ crazy. He concentrated on the screen instead. "The drawers and that file folder you showed me were all showing the same prints. The desk must have been polished up just before the prints were made."

"Indeed it was," BJ answered. All at once, a buzzer sounded from somewhere within the bowels of the small CRT, a face freezing on the screen with the word MATCH locked in solid beneath two sets of identical prints.

He stared at the face on the screen. Melanie Patterson even looked beautiful on an ID picture, though this one had been made before her nose job. He shook his head. Options had just run out on the woman's contract with the world of the living.

Arlington 11:44 P.M.

Charles Merchant unscrewed the mouthpiece of the kitchen wall phone and stared at the quarter-size, paper-thin transmitter lying within. It was pale blue and looked like the Necco wafers he'd eaten as a kid and that they'd used at Our Lady of Fatima School to practice for first holy communion.

"Well, who's doing it?" Linda asked from behind him. "Why us?"

He glanced at her for just a second. She seemed more angry than frightened, the training of the good army wife, as she stood in curlers, her white, quilted robe emblazoned with bright red roses wrapped tightly around her.

"I think it's the people who killed Jack," he said, reaching to the mosaic-tiled counter, a remnant of the fifties, to pick up the small can of compressed air. "They're doing it because they want to know what I know. They want to know how close I'm getting."

"Then why don't we call the police?" Her tone was insistent as she hammered away at him. There'd been a time, not too long ago, when she would have accepted his explanations dutifully and without elaboration. He longed for the past.

"I . . . can't really trust the police right now," he replied, knowing how stupid that sounded, "at least not all of them. Cover your ears."

She put her hands up over her ears as Charlie laid the receiver on the table and stuck a finger in his own left ear. Holding the can of compressed air at arm's length, he put it up to the disassembled mouthpiece and pushed the yellow flange sticking out of the top of the can. The result was a peal of noise every bit as loud and piercing as a semi's air horns. Had anyone been listening, they'd have just lost an eardrum.

He set down the can and reached for the phone box itself, jerking the cord out of the wall. "You really need to be upstairs packing. I want you out of here tonight."

"And why do we have to do that?" she asked loudly, pointing to the phone, totally ignoring his order.

He turned to her, jaw tight. Why *now* did she have to decide he was full of shit. "There's a machine," he said, "called an eternity transmitter. They dial your number. The phone doesn't ring, but the connection opens and they can hear every word being said in the room." He picked up the mouthpiece and turned it upside down, dropping the transmitter into the palm of his hand. "Our phones simply become open mikes. I'm pulling all of them except for the bathroom phone upstairs. Now will you please go pack?"

"No," she said, walking with him to the large wooden kitchen table set against the wall. He laid the transmitter amid a growing pile of electronic bugging devices that he'd discovered in the last hour. "If it was dangerous, you'd call the police or the government or . . . somebody. If you can stay here, so can I."

"Damnit, it is that dangerous," he said angrily. "It's so dangerous that I don't know who I can trust with it."

"You're bullshitting me, Charlie," she said. "You're building some stupid conspiracy up in your head."

He pointed to the pile. "I didn't invent *this* shit," he said.

Suddenly the doorbell rang, both of them starting and looking at each other. "You stay back here," he said. "Listen for trouble."

"What sort of trouble?" she asked, still showing no fear.

"I don't know," he replied, and walked out of the kitchen, turning toward the front door. He peeked out the security spy hole in the door to see what looked like a woman and children on the porch, a yellow cab driving slowly away through deep snow, a good deal more falling through the bite of its headlights.

He reached out and turned on the switch. A black woman in a long gray coat stood on the porch. She held a baby in her left arm, her right buried in her coat pocket. Beside her stood a boy of about five.

"What is it?" Linda called from the kitchen doorway.

"I don't know," he said, and opened the door.

The woman looked at him with deep, painful eyes. She seemed distracted, her concentration elsewhere.

"Can I help you?" he asked.

Her eyes met his, but didn't seem to be really looking at him. "Are you Charles Merchant?" she asked.

"Yes, I am. What can I do for you?"

She answered immediately. "You can die," she said, her right hand coming out of her coat pocket with a long-barreled .38.

Merchant swung the door at her even as she pulled the trigger, knocking her arm. The shot, loud, going wild, the entry light exploding, showering down as Merchant fell back into the house.

The woman shouldered in, her children screaming, Linda crying loudly.

"You son of a bitch!" the woman yelled, firing again, wildly, hitting the piano, discordant notes swelling and vibrating as the five-year-old ran around the entry, hands over his ears, crying loudly.

"Lady, I—"

She fired again, glass breaking somewhere. "Who's going to raise my children? Who's going . . ."

She fired again, Merchant diving into the conversation pit, banshee wails all around. She tracked him to the pit to stand, looking down at him over the barrel.

"I don't know what you're talking about!" he said loudly, from his knees in the pit.

"I'm talking about my . . . about my . . . h-husband," she said, breaking down herself, her gun hand dropping to her side as she began crying, her face straining hard with lines of grief. "Oh, Leonard," she cried. "What am I going to do now?"

"Leonard?" he said, his own voice hoarse, Linda's curiosity overcoming her fear as she edged into the room. "Mrs. . . . Hurley?"

He stood, inching toward her slowly, not wanting to make any sudden moves. "He's d-dead," she said, her cheeks wet with tears, as he bent to take the gun from her loose grip.

"Are you all right?" Linda asked him, concern flooding her eyes, then racing away when he nodded.

"See to Mrs. Hurley," he said, feeling hollowed out, empty inside. Everything he touched seemed to wither and die.

Linda walked up beside the woman and put an arm around her. She was now concerned about the baby, holding it tightly to her while the little boy hid behind a chair, crying loudly, his hands over his ears.

"He went to Germany because of you," she said accusingly to Merchant. "I hoped it would get him away from your trouble. . . ." She shook her head, her words difficult to understand through her sobs. "He never even made it to the hotel."

"Oh, no," Merchant said. "What happened?"

"Car wreck," the woman said. "A dump truck. The whole car was demolished."

"Bignell?" Charlie asked.

"Dead," she said. "All dead. God, why did you have to drag him into this?"

Linda looked at Charlie. "Not another one," she said, hugging Rita Hurley close. Then to the woman, "I'm so very sorry."

The little boy had stopped crying and had run back to hide in the folds of his mother's coat as Merchant freed the cylinder on the .38 and dumped the bullets onto the floor. "He was such a good man," the woman said to Linda. "Such a good . . . f-father."

She broke down again, Linda patting her gently on the back and speaking softly, Merchant wondering if she'd learned the technique at the Center. Perhaps it wasn't such a bad place after all. As the shock subsided, he found that he was seething inside, residue of the fright and the indignity. BJ had reached halfway around the world to take care of this one. Was there no limit to the man's power?

Linda looked at him. "What the hell's wrong with you, Charlie?"

"Me?" Merchant said. "Jesus. She comes running in here shooting up the place and you ask what's wrong with me?"

Linda was ignoring him as she spoke to Rita Hurley, one old army wife to another. "You poor woman," she said quietly.

"I d-don't know what I'm going to do now, I . . ."

"Well, you're going to start by spending the rest of the night here," Linda said. "You'll get some sleep. We'll talk this out together, try and understand it."

"Wish you'd do that with me sometime," Merchant said, Linda glaring at him as she led the woman away, toward the stairs. Charlie stuck the empty gun in his waistband, determined that Rita Hurley wouldn't get another shot at him, at least while she was under his roof. He called to the woman as she went up the stairs. "Mrs. Hurley, when you want to know the whole story, come down and visit with me. I'll be up."

He moved to shut the front door as they disappeared up the steps. He'd worry about the damage to the house tomorrow. Tonight there were other things on his mind, like the fact that the entire world was falling all around his head.

The kitchen was bright and too cheerful as he walked into it and turned on the local news, pouring himself a cup of coffee from the Mr. Coffee on the counter. BJ's move tonight had been housekeeping, pure and simple. He still couldn't believe that Leonard was gone, that BJ dealt with life and death this easily. He figured, interestingly enough, that the killings in Germany had been made more to get Bignell than Hurley. This was a big operation and the only possible logical way to handle it was by getting rid of anyone who was involved in it in any way. That explained the elaborate death of Jerry Delany, too. A pattern was emerging.

This was no small game to Ben James. He was playing for keeps and beyond.

He wondered if James thought him enough of a threat to take him permanently out of the game. And God, perhaps anyone else working with him—Tillotson, Bramley, maybe even Josh. James had said, "No compromises." For the first time Merchant was beginning to realize just exactly how large the stakes were for him. He was in the game, locked in. He couldn't get out now if he wanted to.

He sat down at the kitchen table, his pipe sitting in an ashtray beside the small pile of electronic equipment. He picked up the pipe and clamped it cold between his teeth, idly handling one of the miniature cameras that had been planted around the house. It was the first time in his sixty years of life that *his* home, *his* property, had suffered the indignity of a personal invasion. He'd even found a camera in his bedroom. His life and problems had probably been that asshole's nightly entertainment. The thought made him feel cheap, dirty somehow. He threw the tiny camera down in disgust, the story about the deaths of Hurley and Bignell coming up on the local news on the small TV.

The deaths were going down as an accident, the satellite pictures from the crash scene an unremitting horror. The car had been caught between thousands of pounds of loaded dump truck and a thick security wall. Very little of the cab was left, none of it recognizable as a car. Even the driver had died, but then, what were a few bystanders to BJ? Horrible.

Then the wild card. Just as the announcer finished with the story on Hurley, he frowned and continued. "This has been a night of horror and sadness within the ranks of the D.C. police," he said. "Not one hour after receiving the news about our police chief and head of homicide, the department was struck with another blow. Two officers were gunned down at an alleged crack house on the city's east side tonight, their bodies found by the backup units who arrived apparently moments after the shooting. A large quantity of drugs, plus the body of a third, unidentified man who may have been involved in the shoot-out, were also discovered inside the house. The names of the dead officers are Patrolman Frank Weston and Sergeant Julian Mills. You may also remember them as the arresting officers in the Jack Braedman case earlier this week. Both suffered multiple gunshot wounds fired at close range from an automatic weapon."

Merchant felt numb. He set his coffee down and stood slowly. He needed help on this. James was too good, too connected, for him to take on alone. He'd try the Justice Department tomorrow after a morning meeting with Josh and Gene, hoping they'd have more information for him to take higher up, because his own theories sounded like little more than the ramblings of an insane man.

He walked through the laundry room to the den, to the

cabinet that sat beneath the bar. It was a long cedar chest, the kind that women called "hope chests." He took his key ring out of his slacks pocket and used the key that fit the chest's lock.

The thing hinged open, revealing all the stuff he'd brought with him into retirement, from old manuals to samples of the latest high-tech electronics gear that had made its way in his direction. But that wasn't what he was looking for.

Reaching down to the bottom of the chest, he withdrew the oilcloth bundle and walked back to the kitchen with it. He sat back down at the table, untied the knot on the dark cloth, the smell of gun oil strong and sweet. Within lay his old service-issue .45 automatic in pieces, the pieces heavily oiled and ready for reassembly.

He put the gun together by rote, his mind working on the possibilities. Staying alive was now his number one priority, staying alive long enough to take Ben James down hard.

He slid the gun barrel slowly into the chamber, the thing snapping into place. He'd have to make another pot of coffee.

Sometime in the middle of the night, Rita Hurley came quietly down the stairs and sat across from him at the table. He told her everything he knew about why her husband died. She took it stoically, like a soldier's wife.

FEBRUARY 8,
FRIDAY

". . . watching a line of helicopters we see coming in low, from the destroyer. General Tucker—are these gunships?"

"No, Tony, they're SouthCom troop carriers bringing in Navy SEAL units from Panama. We'll be coordinating with Canal Zone forces, paratroopers from Ft. Ord, along with my 82nd Rangers from Bragg."

"How many troops involved in the operation, General?"

"I'm really not at liberty to say, except that it's the largest United States expeditionary force ever sent to Central America."

"Larger than Panama?"

"Larger and tougher."

"Word from Poblado puts the strength of the Cuban troops airlifted into Caribbea at over twenty thousand."

"Well . . . you've got some pretty good bean counters there, son. That's pretty close to our figure. They're crack troops, too."

"Where does the task force go from here?"

"There's only one major road connecting the two countries, the Pan American Highway, and it goes right from Poblado to Tegucigalpa. We'll rendezvous with Honduran forces in Tegucigalpa, then divide into three task forces. One will march straight down

the Pan Am, another down Highway 4 a little farther
north, and another will split the difference and go
overland between the two forces. We will go to the
border and secure it along a fifty-mile line against
terrorist attacks, a right given to us by treaty with
Honduras and the OAS. We are acting in good faith
and in accordance with international law."

"What about the possibility of engaging Cuban
troops if it comes down to a fight?"

"I don't guess we'll be able to tell the difference
between them and the Companeros if shooting
starts."

"Do you expect to encounter resistance at the
border?"

"We have our job to do. The army is always
prepared for resistance. Now, I've got a task force to
coordinate if there's nothing—"

"One more question. Our sources tell us that an
aircraft carrier loaded with Seasprites is sitting on
the northern border to search the Mosquito Coast for
the Caribbean missiles, is that correct?"

"You have all the answers, Tony. You tell me."

—*CNN Morning Report*
February 8

". . . hard to believe that I stood on this same
balcony in Poblado just a week ago and watched an
enormous anti-American rally after the death of
Foreign Minister Ramirez. Now, today, the demonstration is larger, more vocal, more frightening. The
Cuban forces under General Antonio Gomez, the
aging hero of the Bay of Pigs, are marching below
us in incredible numbers. The entire city must have
turned out to cheer them on and demonstrate
against what is termed 'United States Imperialism' in
Central America.

"Below me, a large effigy of President Macklin is
being burned, the straw man being held up on
poles for our cameras to photograph. Watching the

enthusiasm and hysteria below, one begins to believe that a major confrontation between these two ideological powers is not only possible, but inevitable.

"It's kind of frightening and bit enervating. This will not be a cakewalk for the United States, not a mopping-up operation. We're looking at strength versus strength. We could be looking at fighting, close up, like we haven't seen in a generation."

—*CNN Morning Report*
February 8

Arlington 8:37 A.M.

Merchant stood at the kitchen window, watching Gene Tillotson plunging through knee-deep snow to get to the back door, an army jeep complete with driver sitting in the drive with the motor running. Merchant reached out and knocked on the glass, getting Gene's attention and pointing to the back door to let the man know it was open.

"You look like hell, Dad," Josh said from the Mr. Coffee as he scooped Danish grounds into the basket. "You can't go without sleep like you used to."

Merchant ignored the old soldier comment from his son and turned from the window, listening to Gene open the door at the end of the laundry room. It didn't help that Josh had been right. He *felt* like hell, his face numb, eyes puffy, his brain gearing slowly. Too much coffee had left a gnawing cramp in his gut and he was almost thankful for it; it reminded him he was awake and kept him that way.

"It's a bitch out there!" Tillotson said as he stamped into the kitchen, snow falling from his legs and green wool dress overcoat. The man was in his complete dress uniform, including all the fruit salad he'd ever accumulated.

He took off the coat and smiled at the Mr. Coffee. "Good," he said. "I need it." He turned to Charlie. "Couldn't even get off my fucking block this morning. Had to get a driver. I believe I'm beginning to envy all those troops down there in the tropics."

"Should we send something out to your driver?" Merchant asked as Hurley's five-year-old son came charging into the kitchen to get into the refrigerator.

"Got his own thermos," Tillotson said, his eyes fixed in fascination on the child, who grabbed an apple from the refrigerator and charged back out of the room. He looked up quizzically at Charlie.

"Long story," Merchant replied to the unspoken question. "Have a seat. I'll show you what we've got so far."

"Fair enough," Gene said, sliding out of his dress overcoat to fold it neatly over the back of a kitchen chair. He took a seat at the table. "Couldn't find anything on your boy Jeremy. You sure he works for Legislative Services?"

"Yeah, I'm sure," Merchant said as he stood at the counter waiting on the coffee. "Though I guess it doesn't surprise me that they wouldn't admit it. Tell the man what you've found, Josh."

The kitchen table was filled with papers and notebooks, the younger Merchant, tired-looking, reaching into the stack to pull out several typed sheets of paper, which he read over before talking.

"Well, to begin with," Josh said, setting the papers down and looking directly at Tillotson, "Ben James is a billionaire . . . but only on paper. He is the master of cash flow. Everything stays fluid with James, money never lights anyplace for any too long. Next, his list of holdings is somewhat erroneous."

"You mean he doesn't own the corporations we dug up?" Tillotson asked, stiffening, staring intently at Josh.

"Quite the contrary," Josh returned. "He owns them, but in and of themselves, they have no value. They're simply holding companies, corporations set up as umbrellas to buy other things and keep James out of it." He reached back into the stack, extracting another sheet of paper, which he read from. "Here's one holding company's roster. The place is called Landmark Investments. Landmark produces no goods, provides no services . . . but it owns a great deal, including two newspapers, a polling service, a television production company, and various properties in residential D.C., including the house on Dumbarton where Joann Durbin and Jack Braedman used to shack up.

Tillotson took the paper from Josh and studied it for a moment, his face intent. Merchant walked up to stare down at him. "Through James's investments," he said, "the man owns five newspapers outright and maintains majority stock in three others. He has TV stations, several polling services. He also owns EquAir, the charter transport that went down in Caribbea. And which, incidentally, was carrying two Raytheon Bearcat missiles in the cargo hold."

Tillotson looked up at him. "How do you know that?" he asked.

Merchant began to speak, felt hesitation for reasons he couldn't understand except to think that he feared an inability to truly convince his old friend. "Bramley told me," he said directly to stop the doubts.

"The man arrested yesterday?" Tillotson said low.

Merchant nodded. "He came to me because they were covering it up."

"That's an Official Secrets Act violation, Charlie," the man returned. "Of course they were covering it up. Would you want our enemies to know that two nuclear missiles are lost in the waters of the Caribbean?"

"They're not lost," Merchant said, stiffening. "They're sitting in the goddamned jungle."

The two men stared at each other for a moment, then the coffee maker gurgled deep from within, shoving out the last of the dark brew into the glass carafe. Tillotson rose and moved to the machine, taking a mug familiarly out of the cabinet and pouring himself a cupful. "What does any of this have to do with Jack?" he asked as the mug came to his lips. "You keep telling me everything but what I need to hear."

"Okay," Merchant said, taking Tillotson's seat at the table, the man looking out the back window toward the jeep parked near the garage. "I believe that Ben James ordered Jack's death and that it was accomplished by the two cops who were killed last night."

"Fine . . . what proof do you have?"

"Besides these holdings and some speculation . . . I don't know. Hurley said he had the proof. He's dead, too."

Tillotson grimaced. "So all the principles are dead."

"Except for Ben James," Merchant said harshly. "He's still alive, you can bet on that."

"James was the chief supporter of Jack's campaign. Wouldn't he be the last person to want harm to come to him?"

"I think that Joann Durbin's suicide made him a liability," Merchant answered. "Ben James is a manipulator who understands the value of controlling mental attitudes. Knowing that the public would never accept Jack after Joann's death, he decided to cut his losses and find a new game. When they were taking Jack away the last time I ever saw him alive, he said that someone was 'gaming' him. I think he realized what was going on, that the politics had changed, that BJ didn't need him anymore."

Tillotson came back to the table and pulled up another chair, getting up close to Merchant and looking at him sadly. "Don't you realize how stupid that sounds?" he asked. "The leading candidate for president was assassinated because he'd become socially unacceptable, a liability to a particular lobbyist. You're attributing godlike attributes to Mr. James, Charlie. For heaven's sake, he's just a salesman, a middleman."

Merchant slammed his palm on the tabletop so hard its generated breeze rearranged the papers. "I watched him control the recision vote in the House yesterday. And I'm here to tell you it *was* very godlike."

"History controlled that vote yesterday," Tillotson said, anger rising in his voice. "Everybody finally realized that peace only comes about through strength. We're having to go down to Central America right now to keep the wolf away from our door!"

Merchant sighed deeply. The farther he walked into the vortex, the harder it sucked him down. Through most of his years, life had been a simple matter of upholding the basic values of God, home, and country. But now, it was as if the solid ground of values was a wildly shifting thing simply awaiting someone to come along and imprint it with stability and meaning. He couldn't really blame Gene, either. It was all so comfortable right now, the path of least resistance and greatest familiarity.

"You know, I've just thought of something," Josh said

from his stack of paperwork. "You guys talked about this man Jeremy who works for James but isn't on his payroll?"

"And?" Merchant urged.

"Well . . . it just seems that a little extrapolation from the paperwork shows Mr. James could have a large amount of laundered cash that wouldn't come under government scrutiny."

"Bribe money," Charlie said. "Of course he'd need unreported cash. That would explain his low salary, too. Tell me how."

Josh showed him several sheets of paper marked CONSULTANTS, then read out a list of names from all over the country. "It appears that Ben James pays inordinately high amounts of cash money for consultant work. Cash money. Thirty-five million last year alone. Suppose, in exchange for paying well, those vendors kick back a sizable portion of the cash, leaving themselves enough for their fee and the taxes. Theoretically, James could pay out a million bucks and get nearly half of it back without anyone being the wiser."

"The speculation is getting wilder by the minute," Tillotson said, chuckling around his coffee cup.

"I think it's quite a bit more than speculation," Merchant replied, tight-lipped. "The son of a bitch even bugged my house. My house, Gene."

Tillotson set his coffee cup down hard, the smile leaving his face. "Okay, Charlie. Let's be honest with one another. Suppose I believe you, and I'm not saying that I do or I don't. But just suppose I do for a moment. Our next step is to take this higher up. So, what do we take higher up? Your word that two dead cops killed Jack Braedman on someone's orders. Your word that the same man has bugged your house. Your word that this man has not only totally controlled a congressional vote, but also has diverted nuclear missiles to Caribbea for his own purposes, whatever they may be. You haven't been out of the loop for that long, my friend. If someone were to come to you with this, you'd laugh them out of the house."

"He's killing people connected with this," Merchant said. "For all I know, all of us might be on the list, too."

Tillotson looked at him for a long moment, the steel of his eyes melting rapidly. "If he's only killing people who know something . . . then he's got no reason to kill any of us because we're as ignorant as the day we walked into this. I want to believe you, but even if I did, we've nowhere else to go unless you can get the information Hurley left behind."

"The SEC would sure be interested in this," Josh said. "With James's involvement in the manipulative mediums, we might have some Taft-Hartley violations for the Justice Department . . . maybe even some income-tax evasion if we can prove money laundering."

"No," Merchant said, standing and walking away from the table. "It's not quick enough, not sure enough. James is up to something in Central America, I'm convinced of it. We need to nail him soon."

"What about going to the press?" Josh asked. "They love a good conspiracy theory."

Merchant flared around to him. "No!" he said too loudly. "I will not deal with the press. They don't have any ethical or moral sense. They'd just confuse things even more."

"Then I don't know what else you want from us," Tillotson replied. "Without the evidence of criminal intent, we've nowhere else to take this. Don't you see that?"

Merchant walked back to the table, fighting to control his tone of voice. He needed Gene right now. "Listen to me," he said, taking the seat beside Tillotson. "I'm telling you that all of this is real. James admits it to me when we're alone. I don't lie, Gene. You've got to believe me."

Tillotson took a long breath, sighed it out while nodding slowly. "Maybe someone in the attorney general's office. . . ."

"Good," Merchant said, slapping him on the arm. "We'll start there. All you have to do is make the contact. I'll be happy to do all the talking."

"I might suggest that you stick with just a part of your theory," Josh added. "One aspect. They won't be able to swallow much as it is."

"But it's the truth," Merchant replied, exasperated.

Josh smiled. "But it's just one method of approach."

Merchant sagged in his chair, his son's words intentionally like a slap in the face. The truth had always been enough for him. Expediency of approach was Josh's way of doing business. He turned to Tillotson. "Do you agree with that?"

The man nodded immediately. "Maybe pick out the vote last night if you think you can make the point. That kind of fraud would be right up their alley. But remember, while accusing James, you are also accusing the entire House of Representatives of unethical activity. Good luck getting any of them to back you."

"Rosen will back me," Merchant said.

"Don't count on it," Josh replied. "He lost a lot of power last night that he's going to have to work really hard to get back. Going against his colleagues is a counterproductive way of achieving that goal."

Merchant picked up his coffee cup, set it down again. "What happened to truth?" he asked, the words sounding stupid once he got them out.

"It went away," Tillotson said, picking the photo of the mysterious woman out of the Jack Braedman pile and studying it. "Went away with the invention of television. Everything's sound bites and photo ops now." He showed Merchant the photo. "So, you know about Maggie."

"You know who this is?" Merchant asked.

The man shrugged. "Sure," he said. "Guess with Jack dead and all it doesn't matter now. She was his first wife. Pretty little thing, wasn't she?"

"What happened to her?" Merchant asked.

Tillotson shook his head, his eyes staring at the wall. "Must have been '51. They'd sent you out to help set up communications at the peace negotiations in Seoul. Jack and I stayed back and drank a lot. One night, I found him dead drunk with an M-1 stuck in his mouth. He was trying to reach the trigger when I pulled it away from him. That's when he showed me the picture and told me about Maggie, making me promise never to say anything. Guess she was what they call a depressive personality, afraid of most things. They'd only been married about six months when she blew out her brains right in front of him, splattered herself all over the wall for no reason. Her daddy'd done the same thing. Guess he never got over it, not really. You know Jack, always trying to help people. It destroyed him that he could never help Maggie. It was why he went into the service."

Merchant brought fingers up to massage tired eyes.
"God, no wonder Joann's death unhinged him so. Have
you noticed the resemblance between photos of the two
women."

"No," Tillotson said, tossing the photo back on the
table. "Can't say that I have." The man looked at his watch.
"I'm going to have to go in a minute here," he said. "If
we're going to make that phone call . . ."

"Right," Merchant said. "But we'll have to do it in the
upstairs bathroom."

Linda Merchant sat on the closed toilet seat, the phone
clutched to her ear in a death grip as Rita Hurley bathed
her children in the tub beside. The children splashed
happily in the large tub as the woman grumbled at no one,
the anger that still boiled in her wanting to scream out.

"Still have to get a funeral home out to claim Leonard
when he comes in," she said, staring down at LaToya, the
baby, as she ran the bar of soap around the small body.
"Gotta find a place to put all the family . . . like to get
my hands on the son of a bitch who did this . . . maybe
I'll move in with Mama for a while, she never . . .
never . . . I'll kill him, honey. I'll tear his fucking eyes
out . . . Oh, God!"

The woman sobbed, Linda reaching out a hand to lay on
her shoulder as she waited for Doley to come on the line
from the Center. Rita Hurley looked up, teeth clenched
through a veil of tears. "It's not right," she said, eyes
blazing. "He was too good a man to go down that way."

"Yeah . . . Linda?" came the director's perpetually
cheerful voice through the earpiece.

"They told me Jorge Mendel called this morning,"
Linda began without preliminaries, hearing the concern in
her own voice.

The woman's voice fell slightly in pitch. "Yes, he did,"
she said. "He wouldn't talk to anyone but you. Lin, he was
really upset."

"Did he say anything . . . anything at all?"

"Only that he had to talk to you right away."

"Why didn't you give him my home number?"

"You know our rules about that."

"But this . . ." She was practically screaming. She

fought to control her voice, lowering it to a stage whisper. "This is a special case, I . . . how did he . . . seem?"

"Distant," Doley answered. "Wired up. Distraught. Preoccupied."

"Damn." Linda's mind was turning a thousand miles an hour. "We had an appointment today. Did he say anything about that?"

"We've canceled all appointments," the woman answered. "The weather's too bad for anyone to get here. I'm getting ready to leave myself."

"I'm coming in," Linda said. "He may keep the appointment."

"I don't think—"

"I'm coming in," Linda repeated slowly. "Leave the lights on. I'll take the responsibility. Just leave his file on my desk."

"All right," Doley said, her voice softer. She was silent for a moment, but Linda knew there was something more. She waited. Finally the woman spoke. "I know I probably don't need to say this, but I'm going to anyway. Don't get too involved with this boy. Retain your professional distance. We can't help them if we're part of the problem."

"What are you implying?" Linda asked. Cold.

"Only that if you take his problems too much on yourself, you won't have the objectivity to help him."

It was good advice, only a day too late. "I'll keep that in mind, Doley," Linda said, hands shaking. "And thanks."

"Sure. Don't forget to lock up when you're through."

She hung up the phone, her hands still shaking. Rita Hurley had turned and was watching her. "You've got troubles, too, don't you?" she asked.

"A young boy," she replied, feeling the desperate need to talk to someone. "A patient. I'm afraid he's suicidal."

There was a loud knock on the door. "Linda?" came Charlie's voice, and it had an impatient edge to it that made her angry. "Linda. I really need to use the phone." "Just a minute," Linda shouted back. She looked at Hurley. "I'm afraid he's going to kill himself today unless I get to him first."

"Oh, you poor woman." Hurley leaned to her, hugging her fiercely while keeping one hand on the baby in the tub.

"You got so much love in you and . . ." She looked quickly at the door. "Nowhere to take it."

He knocked again. "I really need the phone!"

"Fuck you!" she yelled, both women stifling a laugh behind their hands.

"Linda!"

"I need to go find him," Linda said. "If you can get ready pretty quick, I'll give you a lift wherever you need to go."

The woman stood, picking up a large bath towel and wrapping the baby in it right out of the water. "Come on, hotshot," she told the five-year-old, the boy, giggling, climbing out of the tub. She looked at Linda as she dried the baby. "I can't tell you how much I appreciate what you did for me last night. I had to talk to someone. And about the damage . . ."

Linda waved her off. "Don't give it another thought," she said. "As much as you've suffered because of this . . . well, it's the least of it. And don't ever feel guilty about the anger. You're entitled to it . . . and more. Don't hold it in. Do what you need to do."

"This is important!" Charlie said from the door.

Linda rolled her eyes. "I'm going to have to let him in," she said.

"I understand," the woman returned, putting the baby on her shoulder and taking the other by the hand. "We're ready whenever you are."

Linda rose from the toilet and moved to the door, unlocking it and jerking it open in midknock.

"Why wouldn't you answer me?" Charlie said, looking past her to frown at the mess in the bathroom.

"Because you never hear me anyway," she said, shoving past him, followed by Hurley and her fatherless children. Over her shoulder she added, "I'm going down to the Center."

"I'll be damned if you are," he said, turning to call to her as she and her small entourage moved down the hallway. "The roads are impassable."

"I'll be back . . . later," she said without even looking at him. She moved with the Hurleys into the master bedroom, slamming the door behind her.

Merchant looked at Tillotson, the man shrugging in

return. "You may have better luck with the attorney general," he said.

The three men moved into the bathroom, Josh closing the door. As Gene moved to the toilet to get the phone hanging on the wall there, Merchant couldn't help but understand that he'd made another amateur mistake. So overwhelmed with the rapid movement of events, he'd let Hurley go off to Germany without leaving his evidence in safe hands. Now it was too late, and he couldn't help but feel it was possible that he had already lost the chance of bringing Jack's murder to public light. Tillotson realized it, too, but was too much of a gentleman to say so.

"Well, here goes nothing," the general said, picking up the phone to punch in the switchboard at Justice.

And nothing was what they'd gotten. As he stood at the back door watching his son and Tillotson wade off through the deep snow, Merchant couldn't help but feel old and used up. The phone call had been worse than futile, the assistant attorney general informing them that without a congressman willing to step forward and claim that he'd been bribed on the vote, that it would take solid, undeniable evidence that Ben James had carried on anything more than the normal course of lobbying in the Capitol. They'd be happy to investigate, but it would take something more than the word of a ordinary citizen that fraud had been committed. They hadn't even treated him with deference, the assistant AG expressing irritation at having been bothered with what was obviously the rantings of a lunatic. The man had been so angry that he'd gotten Gene back on the phone after finishing with Charlie to chew him out, also.

He closed the door slowly, to a quiet house. Everyone was gone now. He was alone.

He walked slowly back into the kitchen, trying to figure out just what had happened to the world. Maybe it wasn't the world. Maybe it was just him.

He walked into the kitchen, looking down at his now-large stacks of documentation, all just so much garbage. Josh was interested enough to push an SEC investigation, but that would do no good in the short run. Whatever magic Ben James had wrought on the world had worked.

The man had won and his world, whatever it might be, would come to pass. Perhaps this was how nations fell. Perhaps the world was made by scoundrels, the good men merely there to keep that world intact.

He sat down at the table and paged through the useless paperwork. He had worked through all of his channels, all of them coming to naught. All that was left was the wild card. Her name was Melanie Patterson, and as a solution, she seemed nearly as dangerous as the problem.

Pennsylvania Quarter 9:00 A.M.

Melanie Patterson stepped out of the cab in front of the cleared section of pavement leading up to the Quarter's main entrance, paying the driver five dollars on a dollar and a half fare as she looked angrily up and down the snow-filled street. Apparently she had lost her tail, one of Bomar's goons who'd followed her from her Georgetown condo and had probably been waiting there all night, no doubt trying to sneak peeks through her windows. She'd left her car at a public lot several blocks away. She didn't want anyone to know where she was this morning.

The snow was piled waist high on either side of her as she negotiated the narrow trail cut through it, moving quickly out of the arctic chill and into the blowing warmth of the hotel lobby on the first floor. She wore blue jeans and leather boots, a bulky white wool sweater bunched up beneath her overcoat.

Barely acknowledging the doorman, she hurried to the elevators, using her key on the private lift that would take her to ten. Angry and scared all at the same time, she wanted to hurry upstairs and get her business done before she talked herself out of it.

She took the ride up, her insides jangling. If BJ was having her followed, it meant he didn't trust her. Lack of trust in the last couple of days seemed to be having fatal results on the people who knew Ben James. The two rogue cops had died last night in a typical Jeremy Bomar setup.

Put an ounce of coke in a dead man's pocket, and no more questions were ever asked. She wasn't going to go down like that, not without a fight anyway.

The halls were deserted when she climbed out of the elevator, the frantic pace of the last couple of days slowed to nothing now that the vote had been cast. Whatever else BJ had up his sleeve would apparently be done in the dark of night, preferably with no witnesses.

She reached the visitors' entrance without being seen, then peeked through the frosted glass to see June Chan, out of her tower, making coffee at the far end of accounting. Several essential personnel walked sleepily through the offices, mostly cleaning people taking care of last night's debacle.

She slipped quietly inside, hiding among the ferns and rubber plants until June had her back completely turned to her, then she hurried through the entryway and into the hall leading down to the executive offices. BJ's door was locked, access controlled through the tower. She moved to the office next to it, the executive vice president in charge of consultants, Len Barry. His door was open, the office empty.

The sliding veranda doors were situated at the far end of the office, done all in low-slung, tasteless modern. She ran to the sliding door, getting it open and moving onto the wide balcony.

The wind was a vicious, slashing thing up there, the snow piling against the side of the building in monstrous fifteen-foot drifts. Her arms wrapped reflexively around her chest as she fought her way through deep snow and blinding wind to BJ's sliding door, the one she'd left open the day before.

She pulled on the door. It didn't budge, her heart sinking. She pulled again, harder, the door giving all at once and sliding open full. It had been frozen shut.

She moved inside, a snowdrift following her in. She couldn't worry about that now. Moving with deliberateness, not daring to think, she walked up to the vault door and took the key out of her pocket. She'd seen BJ open this door twice in the last three years. The first time it had surprised her. The second time, she'd committed it to memory.

The game was for keeps now and she'd have to be prepared for anything. BJ kept cameras everywhere, and though she'd never been inside the vault before, she had to believe that he'd wired it, also, that it was a trap ready to spring. But it was a chance she had to take for she saw no hope for herself otherwise. She'd pushed too far and knew too much, and if the devil himself were waiting for her on the other side of that door, she'd have to fight him for the secrets he protected. She could either fight or roll over and die, and dying wasn't on her agenda. If she was going to fight, knowledge could be her only weapon.

Fitting the key in the ordinary-looking lock, she turned it first a half turn clockwise, the thing clicking. Then she turned it again, a half turn counter-clockwise to another click. Then she turned clockwise again—twice, on the second click the door cracking open. With shaking hands she pulled it wide and entered.

Never having been in there, she had no idea of what to expect. Files, she figured, paperwork that she could use to keep BJ at arm's length when things got dicey. She wasn't prepared for the wall-to-wall blackmail that greeted her.

She moved farther into the vault, astounded at the hundreds of individual files containing names that surprised and awed her. Ben James seemed to have a file on everyone in Washington, with videotape to back it up. The names glittered out at her, making her laugh—until she reached her own. He'd always said that there was no substitute for good intelligence. She figured that the CIA could probably learn a few things from him.

Where to start? She was a kid in a candy store with the owner away. She turned a full circle, smiling. Then she saw the camera that she'd prayed wasn't there.

It was mounted just above the door she'd come in, its red running light glowing like the fires of hell. It was pointed right at her, slowly tracking her movements like a cobra with a mongoose. She was caught.

And at that instant, Melanie Patterson's life became a pure, crystalline substance. She knew she was dead, and soon. She knew she only had one chance to survive, and less than a chance to come out on top. She looked at her watch, abstracting time into meaningful living units. She gave herself thirty seconds, no more.

Realization, decision, and action were simultaneous activities as she sprang at the shelves, grabbing files as she scanned them on autopilot, her mind already plotting her route back out of the office and away even as she grabbed.

It was to be the most important day of her entire life.

The Wellness Center 10:17 A.M.

Linda Merchant all but blew into the Center, a three-foot drift of dry, powdery snow by the door swirling under her coat and skirt and packing into her fur-lined boots as the opening door caused a cross-breeze that nearly kept her from getting the thing closed again.

She had parked somewhere near the curb, halfway into a street that had yet to see a snowplow. She'd barely been able to get her car door open. Despite all that, just walking into the Center calmed her, gave her renewed direction. Events had gotten crazier than her ability to assimilate them. Charlie was pulling phones out of the wall even as distraught wives shot up their home. Her husband was acting stranger and stranger, staring for hours at pictures of a naked dead woman and claiming the entire United States government had been taken over by a lobbyist. She feared that he had gone around the bend and she could almost understand it. For a long time Charlie had been an important link in the chain, a man who others depended upon and who never felt burdened by that dependency, who, in fact, welcomed it. Now he was nothing, a private citizen with no special stature save a cadre of friends who still had real power, real connections. He, apparently, wanted desperately to feel important again.

She felt sorry for him, but nothing beyond that. Her psychologist's instincts to help, she found, in no way extended to helping the man she had lived with for so many years. She was too close to his problem, and in a way was part of that problem. But for her it ended there. She'd lived under his thumb for too many years. Her newfound freedom was too liberating. She'd never go back again. Never play the dutiful army wife. She'd realized this morning, waking up to the sound of Rita Hurley's baby crying, that as soon as the arctic air blew out to sea and the snow ended, she'd blow out with it. As with most problems people are afraid to face, it wasn't a difficult or heartbreaking decision once faced. She would simply leave, and in the leaving, a new life would open up for her. Her own life this time. Where Charlie's life was ending, hers would begin.

The Center was absolutely still as she moved through its semidarkness, Doley only leaving lights on in the front of the building. The presence of people was what gave an environment its character. The Center was such a different place empty—dark, creaking—a little scary.

She moved into the receptionist's niche, the red running light on the phone recorder the only light in the room, a demon eye flashing out five calls. She played them back, heart in her mouth, and found herself sighing loudly when there was nothing from Jorge.

The boy had been the only thing on her mind for two days now, his problem more important than hers. His salvation was an all-consuming mission to her now, saving his life and his heart an imperative that would somehow free her from her own bonds and make her worthwhile. So afraid to face her own fears, she put all of her feelings into Jorge's, never even considering the possibility that she wanted something, too. Doley's warnings about getting too personal had fallen on totally deaf ears.

She moved through the darkened chambers to Doley's office, removing her heavy coat to reveal denim skirt and black wool cardigan over a white turtleneck. She turned on the light to find Jorge Mendel's file sitting atop a clean desk, Doley's sense of organization legendary. She opened it and found the boy's number, calling it immediately to no response.

This would never do. Sitting in Doley's office and calling a number every five minutes would drive her crazy within an hour, especially knowing that Jorge could at this very moment be contemplating an unsalvageable destruction of his consciousness, his life. She ran a red-nailed finger down the page until she found his address, surprised at the uptown neighborhood. Apparently the boy, a city charity case, was living in foster care and she hadn't even known about it.

She looked at her watch. Had Jorge been coming to their appointment, he would have already arrived. She'd have to go to his house. There was no other choice. No one else could save him.

Shutting down the building behind her as she went, Linda trudged back through thigh-deep snow to the station wagon parked in the middle of Nineteenth Street, the thing not wanting to start when she first got in. Once it cranked, she set the heater blowing down on the floor to help her cold legs and feet, then headed northwest, navigating the rolling sea of snow.

The ride took nearly forty-five minutes on barely passable streets, cars stalled and wrecked all over the roads. While she drove, the radio carried a never-ending stream of politics—censure votes in the OAS, debate about U.S. troops in Honduras in both the General Assembly and Security Council of the United Nations. Russia, taking the high moral ground, simply condemned the U.S. with sad commentaries about a warlike people in a peaceful world. None of it meant much to her, she'd been living with propaganda her entire life, her love of American values getting lost in the shuffle somehow as she rejected the values of her husband.

By the time she pulled up to the Georgetown address, her heart was thumping in her chest. The narrow, three-story house was quiet as she moved through the wrought-iron gate and up to the door, ringing the bell to no response. After trying the bell three times, she tentatively reached for the doorknob. The door was unlocked.

Linda walked partway into the house. "Jorge?" she called. "Jorge Mendel?"

Nothing. The house was quiet all around her except for the smallest sound coming from upstairs. She took the curving stairway up, calling his name the entire time. When she reached the second floor, she recognized the sound as music, a low, mournful tenor sax crying out the blues. She went back to the stairs and up. She'd stopped calling his name by this point and simply followed the music.

She found him in an upstairs bedroom amid a haze of

marijuana smoke and a cocoon of music on the radio. He was methodically loading and unloading a shiny silver gun, a .38. The kind that Charlie had forced her to learn to shoot on the practice range. He wore only a pair of cutoff jeans, the muscles in his brown chest tight and sinewy, his sleek black hair wild and hanging in stringers down his face.

"There's got to be a better way than that," she said, walking into the room to stare down at him.

He looked at her as if he were looking through her. "Go away," he said, listless. "It's all over."

"No, it's not," she said, taking off her coat and dropping it on the floor. She came and sat beside him on the edge of the bed, turning to look into his eyes. "You're alive, and I intend to keep you that way until you realize that your problem's not that bad."

The boy's eyes flashed with anger and he finished punching the bullets into the chamber of the .38, slamming it closed, and holding it up in front of her face. "This is the answer to my problem," he said. "Nice, long sleep. No more pain. Now, go away."

"I'm not going anywhere," she said.

"Fine," he spat. "Then you can sit here and watch me splatter myself on the nice walls, huh?" He stuck the barrel of the gun in his mouth, Linda jumping, then holding herself back.

"P-please . . . don't do that," she said, trying to calm her voice. "Let me h-help you."

He removed the gun from his mouth, his face angry shadows in the darkened room. "How you gonna help me, lady?" he said. "You gonna fuck me?"

"If I have to," she said quietly, the boy's eyes narrowing as his lips tightened into a sneer. Suddenly his left hand shot out and grabbed her breast through her sweater. He squeezed roughly, Linda not moving.

Their eyes met, Jorge's more confused than angry now. "If you didn't hold it so tight, it would feel a little better," she said, and looked down at his hand.

He pulled away then, dropping the gun and burying his face in his hands. "Can't you leave me alone?" he pleaded. "Don't make fun of me!"

"I'm not making fun of you, Jorge," she answered, voice

low, soothing. "I just want you to know that sex doesn't have to be some sort of battlefield. It's a mutual sharing of two people who care about each other, that's all."

He took his hands away; his eyes were moist. "Why would you care about me?" he asked.

"Because you're like me, maybe," she said, putting a hand on his leg just above the knee, "trapped in a world that's not of your own making. Caught in social games that control you, instead of the other way around. Your problem isn't really sex at all, Jorge, it's insecurity. I've got to show you that."

With a smooth motion, she pulled her sweater and turtleneck up over the top of her head and tossed them on the floor. Her bra followed. She put her hand back on Jorge's leg. She hadn't planned any of this, but as she began to slowly stroke his leg, it all seemed to make perfectly logical sense. Her hand moved slowly up his leg on his inner thigh.

"I want nothing from you, Jorge, except to give you pleasure," she said in a soft, almost whisper voice. "I don't need anything from you in return."

The incongruity of her position kept trying to worm its way into her mind, but she refused to acknowledge it, at the same time refusing to acknowledge that he was not the only one getting pleasure from the action.

"You can touch me if you want," she said.

Their eyes still locked tightly together, he reached out gentle hands this time and began to massage her breasts, teasing the nipples into hard knots. For the first time since she'd met him, his eyes were beginning to look childlike as he slid himself closer to her, their bodies touching in several places. The anger was gone, now. Only desire mixed with a touch of fear remained.

"We're going to make love, Jorge," she said. "We don't have to do everything at once, but can move slowly if you want, a little at a time until you're comfortable. This is all for you. I have no needs or wants."

How ironic, she was playing the woman who Charlie had wanted her to be all these years. How angry would he be if he could see her now, a moan involuntarily escaping from her lips as Jorge bent his head to her breast, taking a hard nipple between his lips.

"Yess," she whispered, her right hand holding his head to her as her left slid farther up his leg, finding and grasping his erection. He groaned loudly and pulled her down beside him on the bed, Linda unzipping his pants to bring his large dark penis out into the open. She moved both hands to it, massaging gently. "Close your eyes. Lie back. Just enjoy."

He was breathing heavily as he flopped back on the bed, Linda sliding him out of his pants, then bending to take his organ into her mouth. He made small sounds down in his throat, his hips bucking slightly as she ran her lips and tongue up and down his shaft, the wetness between her legs telling her, finally, that this wasn't simply altruistic on her part.

"Move so I can get to you," Jorge said, voice husky, as Linda kicked off her boots and slid onto the bed. The boy immediately grabbed her hips and pulled her toward his face.

He shoved her skirt up to her waist and buried his face in her crotch, licking her right through her panties, his erection losing none of its stiffness in her mouth.

His touch was an electric charge, and she couldn't control her loud sobs or the fact that she was grinding herself against his face like an animal. God, how she'd needed this!

All at once, he jerked himself away from her, Linda jumping with surprise and staring back at him. "I want to try . . . I want to try now," he said, and within seconds he had pulled off her pants and had buried himself within her with a loud groan of pleasure.

Her own brain was popping madly as he slid like a wild man in and out of her, Linda throwing herself up to him, an explosive orgasm wracking her even as he screamed through his own barely half a minute after entering her.

They collapsed together on the bed, Jorge on top and still inside of her, his breath coming in short gasps as Linda held him fiercely to her and waited for the inevitable guilt that, strangely, didn't come. Within another minute he had stiffened again within her and had begun to move.

But she stopped him and rolled herself on top. "I'll show you another way," she said and began to ride him, all thoughts of her husband and his problems completely gone.

Arlington, Virginia Early Evening

Charles Merchant sat, working his pipe furiously in his mouth, his half-eaten dinner spread out, forgotten, before him on the kitchen table. Linda stood at the sink, humming happily to herself as she cleaned up her own dishes. Humming. He hadn't seen her so happy in years. As the world collapsed around them, his wife decided it was time to rejoin the land of the happy. Something was wrong.

She'd been gone most of the day, saying things had been busy at the Center. He didn't tell her that he'd called the Center many times only to get the phone recording saying all appointments had been canceled. When she'd finally come in, whatever dark mood had settled over her in the last several weeks had lifted as she bustled through cooking a beef Stroganoff dinner, more effort than she'd put out in quite some time.

If she'd been happier, she'd also been more distant, as if she were physically prying herself away from him. He'd never realized how important, essential really, her support of him had been until it was gone. He felt he was living with a stranger now, albeit a happy one.

She reached a hand out to the running television beside the sink.

"Leave it," he snapped, then added more humbly, "please?"

"Sure, Charlie," she said, turning to smile at him, the kind of smile she usually reserved for the bag boy at the supermarket. "I didn't know you were still watching."

"I am," he answered simply, keeping himself from adding, *What else have I got to do?* He still wasn't ready to give in to that kind of self-pity, even though the day had been a great leveling experience. He'd divided it between watching the developments in Central America and calling different government agencies, trying to enlist their aid in stopping Ben James. He'd gotten nowhere. In fact, as word of his calls began circulating the agencies, he found that hardly any of the people on his list were currently "in the office." Someone cursing in his ear would have been far preferable to the anonymous shuffling of bureaucratic feet trying to avoid the loony. He'd been turning himself into a clown. He finally realized that at one point his explanations to the junior-junior assistant to the assistant FBI director were getting piped over the loudspeaker in the office for everyone's amusement. They'd been patronizing him.

The pipe had gone cold in his mouth and he relit it, managing one more good puff out of an empty bole. It was then he heard the phone ringing in the bathroom upstairs.

"I'll get it," he said, taking his pipe out and leaving it on the table as he charged through the formal dining room to the stairs.

The phone had rung perhaps ten times before he was able to get to it, something he hadn't really considered when ripping them out. "Merchant," he answered, his own voice sounding hoarse to him.

"Dad?" came a small, faraway-sounding voice.

"Josh . . . what's wrong?" Charlie hadn't heard his son sound like that since he was ten years old, asking to come home early from camp. Even then they'd indulged him.

"I'm s-sitting in my lawyer's office, Dad," Josh replied, his voice getting firmer, edgier. "I'm trying to decide what's going to happen to the rest of my life."

"What do you mean?"

Linda had appeared at the doorway, her arms folded across her chest. "Is that Josh?" she asked. "Charlie, is it—"

"Wait," Merchant said, putting his hand up for quiet. "Josh. . . ."

"I have to turn myself into the authorities Monday morning," Josh said. "Our section chief came with two FBI men just an hour ago."

"Is something wrong?" Linda asked, her own voice rising in pitch.

"The FBI?" Merchant said, mind reeling. "What's . . . what's the charge?"

Josh laughed dryly. "Insider trading," he said. "Can you believe it? God, the man I've been drinking with for three years has been investigating me."

"Did you do it?" Merchant asked.

"Fuck you," Josh said. "I call you with this and you start playing cop. Well, listen Joe Friday, I've got some news for you. When I asked Doug why he was doing this to me, he says—you're going to love this—he says, 'Ask your father.'"

"Oh, God, no," Merchant's left hand came up to his face, the phone falling to his side. Linda came up and grabbed it from him, talking quickly, hysterically, into the mouthpiece, words that slid right past him.

He felt numb, nearly defenseless. It never occurred to him that BJ would reach so far and with such deadly accuracy. Even the lesson of Hurley's death hadn't really taught him anything. And now the son of a bitch had taken his son, destroying him through his own weakness.

He was aware that Linda was staring at him and he looked up. "What the fuck have you done?" she asked, her eyes hard, pitiless.

He just stared up at her. There were no words, no way he could explain. She bent closer to him, nearly nose to nose.

"He wants to know if you can fix it, Charlie," she said softly. "Can you? Can you fix it?"

"I don't know," he said, reaching into his back pocket for his wallet. "I don't think so."

"But you can try," she said, straightening. "You have to try no matter what."

"Yes," he said from far away. He opened his wallet and removed the card bearing the phone number that BJ had given him.

The sound of the doorbell came from downstairs.

"I'll get that," Linda said, getting off with Josh and moving quickly to the door. "You do what you have to do. I'm not sure what all of this is about, but you've got to stop it right now."

She was gone. He mechanically took the phone from the hook and punched in the numbers. He felt rage, but it was turned inward. He felt indignant, except that Josh probably *was* guilty. He was beginning to feel like Job playing to BJ's Satan.

BJ answered, as Charlie knew he would, after the first ring. "Charlie," he said immediately, jovially. "I knew I'd be hearing from you sooner or later."

"Let my son go, you bastard," he replied. "This is between you and me."

"Now, Charlie, you had ample time to back out of the game before, I—"

"Let Josh go!" Merchant yelled, hating himself the whole time. He forced his voice lower. "Look . . . I'll walk away from this, I'll forget everything, I'll . . ."

"Charlie," BJ chided, laughing. "Look what you're reducing yourself to. Such an honest man. Such a good man. Are you really asking me to somehow interfere with the criminal justice system to free a felon?"

"You son of a bitch," Merchant rasped. "Just let Josh go."

"Wish I could, old chum, but it wouldn't be right. By the way, how's Linda? You guys still sleeping in separate beds?"

Merchant slammed the receiver down, his insides shaking madly. This was all about humiliation now. James didn't want to so much hurt him as tear him down a piece at a time until he was no better off than the geek at the freak show, biting off whatever chicken head Ben James provided. He hated himself for making that call. He hated Josh for his weakness. He hated Linda for walking away from all of it.

"It's a delivery man," Linda said from the bathroom door. "We both have to sign."

He shook his head. "Not right now, I—"

"It could be important," she said. "Come on."

He rose from the toilet seat and dutifully followed her downstairs. A man in street clothes stood at the door, his "delivery truck" an old beat-up Chevy. He obtained both of their signatures on what looked to be a stationery store blank receipt form and handed them a manila envelope containing something bulky.

Merchant stood staring at the envelope for a moment, not wanting under any circumstances to open it. There were no longer good surprises. But that wasn't to be. Linda grabbed it away from him and reached inside, pulling out an unmarked videotape.

"What th . . . ?"

"I think we're supposed to play it," he said, and followed her through the living and dining rooms to the television in the den.

By the time he'd reached the TV, she already had it going and was shoving the tape into the VCR atop the set. They backed up several paces and watched the video static into view.

It was an underlit scene of a teenage boy lying on a bed with black silk sheets. Linda started to say something, then clamped a hand over her own mouth, her eyes wide with horror.

Something about the scene was familiar to him, but he couldn't quite place it. "You know what this is?" he asked, but had his answer from the tape itself.

Within seconds, Linda Merchant had entered the video and taken off her coat. She sat on the bed with the boy.

"No," Linda said sharply. She reached for the machine, Charlie's hand snaking out to grab her wrist.

He looked her in the eyes. "Why do you want to stop it?" he demanded, but she only looked at him with horror on her face.

They both turned back to the video, Merchant watching in growing revulsion as his wife undressed and began to fellate the Hispanic boy, humping herself against him like a hooker. A moment later she was crying out, pulling him into her, acting like a crazy woman. He'd never seen her like this. He turned to stare at the woman he thought he knew. Her eyes were darting, her mouth working soundlessly.

"How could you do this?" he asked low, and he wanted to hurt her, to physically punish her, but he couldn't. "Why didn't you just take a gun and shoot me?"

She was backing away from him, her animal cries on the TV filling the room all around them. Her eyes were wide, barely human.

"What the hell is going on here?" she said. "I don't understan—"

"What's going on is my wife humiliating me by humping some black kid on television!" he screamed.

She started, her eyes narrowing in anger. "It's always you, isn't it?" she spat. "Everything always comes down to how I've treated you."

"You fucking whore," he said, walking toward her as she backed across the room. "Is that how you get your kicks, with little boys?"

Her face settled into a posture of disgust. "He was twice the man you are," she said, Merchant slapping her hard.

She put a hand to her face, then smiled sadly. "At least I've still got feelings left," she said. "Yeah, so I slept with that kid and I enjoyed it." Her eyes flashed at him. "I may even do it again!"

"Get out," he said, his hands involuntarily balling into fists. "Get out of my sight before I hurt you."

"I'll do better than that," she said, turning to walk out of the room. "I'll get out of your life."

He stood, shaking, staring at the empty door space, the sounds on the tape loud all around him as Linda had her legs locked around the teenager's ass, grinding against him. He reached out and turned off the tape, the sounds fading to nothing, the new reality hidden out of sight—but not out of mind.

He walked over to the pool table, the battle of Waterloo scattered all over the plywood game board. He'd always thought that he was so smart, that he understood how things worked and was on the side of right and truth. But it was just a game he played with himself, like his Napoleonic battlefields, just a child's secure perception of his world.

If this had been a battle between himself and BJ over what was real, he'd not only lost, but had never even been in the contest.

Linda came into the den, a small overnight bag in her hand. "I'll come get the rest of my stuff when I'm settled," she said, her eyes dark, unreachable, both of them knowing that things had gone too far to repair. She shook her head slightly. "In a way I feel sorry for you, Charlie. You've spent your whole life chasing shadows, trying to make the world love you. Self-respect comes from inside, not outside. Maybe if you had liked yourself a little better . . . oh, hell, what's the use." She turned from him and walked through the den.

Without words, he watched her leave through the back door, the sound of her station wagon starting up and driving off a moment later. He was alone, totally alone. Everything that had meant anything to him in his life had been ripped away, capriciously, by a man who didn't care about him one way or the other. To BJ, this had all just been a game. Linda had said that self-respect comes from inside. That's all he was left with now—himself. And that's what BJ was testing: his inner self, his true manhood. The thought frightened him, but not as much as it could have. He'd lost it all and was still on his feet with nothing left to lose. There was a kind of comfort in that.

He thought about his years of faithfulness to his marriage vows and how Linda could destroy that in a moment. Then he thought about black sheets and black ebony bedroom fixtures.

Ben James may have made his first mistake.

Merchant returned to the television, juicing up the tape again. Linda was sitting atop the boy, rocking rapidly back and forth. He turned down the sound and forced himself to look at everything except the action. Why hadn't he seen it immediately? This was the same house on Dumbarton where Joann had killed herself. BJ must wire these places up for blackmail tapes. Of course. That's exactly how he'd operate. That's also what Joann had meant when she'd written "your move" on the mirror. BJ had been, quite literally, watching the activity.

He needed to get over there fast. This was good physical evidence that some sort of foul play had been involved in Jack's death, at least enough to open an investigation at the federal level, maybe enough to scare Ben James out of whatever plans he had in Central America.

The phone was in the bathroom. He hurried upstairs, realizing at this point that he'd need all the help he could get. He tried Tillotson at home first to no avail. A moment later he reached him at the Pentagon.

"Gene," he said. "I've got some proof for you. Something solid on Jack."

"Thank God," Tillotson replied. "I knew you'd come through. What do you need from me?"

"Credibility," Merchant returned. "Meet me at the

house on Dumbarton where Joann died, and quickly. Can
you leave now?"

"Give me . . . ten minutes," Tillotson said. "I'll get
there as fast as I can."

"Good," Merchant said, hanging up. Tillotson was just
the man to bring into this now. If the DIA couldn't be at the
forefront of an investigation into covert activities, he
didn't know who could. With solid proof, Gene could get
Justice to seal off the house and begin tearing it apart.
Once authorization was accomplished, there'd be no telling what they could find.

He gave Gene a few minutes to get himself out of the
Building, then bundled up and hurried out to the Cadillac.
The ride to Dumbarton was a nightmare. Very few streets
were even partway passable; those that were glistened
with a slippery sheet of ice under the street lamps.

A water main had broken in the middle of Thirty-first
Street, rushing water cascading high into the night sky like
a fountain, freezing as it fell, building lacelike fragile
palaces of ice all over the street, an alien environment. He
had to skirt the mess by a block, coming up on Dumbarton
from the Thirty-second Street side, passing a late-model
Ford going off the street as he was going on.

Dumbarton was a solid sheet of ice as he made his way
carefully down its length to skid to a halt in front of the
townhouse. He climbed out of the car and stood staring up
for a moment at the silent, looming structure, feeling the
coldness emanating from it.

An army jeep approached from the other direction to
pull up nose to nose with the Caddy on Dumbarton. Both
Gene and his driver climbed out.

"What's here?" Tillotson asked after shaking hands
with Merchant.

"I'll show you," Merchant said, taking him by the arm
and leading him down the walk toward the door.

"Do we have a, ah, warrant to come in here?" Tillotson
asked.

"Don't ask," Merchant replied, starting up the porch
steps.

In remembering later, Merchant would realize that
there had been three separate explosions at that moment,
one right after the other. But at the time, as he and

Tillotson dove back down the stairs along with the heavy front door, it seemed that one cataclysmic act had blown the downstairs apart, the doors and window literally disintegrating behind huge streamers of bright orange fire, the sound so loud it knocked their hearing out momentarily.

He remembered reaching the porch and he remembered lying beneath large shards of wood at the bottom of the steps, looking up to tongues of fire and an MP dragging Tillotson away from the inferno. He remembered crawling, trying to get his mind back, for it kept slipping away, blinking in and out of consciousness. He remembered reaching the iron gate and looking up to see the MP on the car phone, Gene Tillotson sitting on the sidewalk, his back propped against the jeep. He was bleeding profusely from the face.

The mind came all the way back then. He stumbled to his feet, for the first time noticing how torn up his clothes were and the blood that ran freely from his own arms and hands. He got to Gene, kneeling beside the man.

"You okay?" he asked.

Tillotson nodded, grimacing. "I've had worse hangovers," he said weakly. "Help me up."

"Just take it easy—"

"Help me up."

The man put out his hand, Merchant standing painfully, then reaching out to help his friend. He turned then, facing the fire that was engulfing the downstairs.

"That's a fueled fire," Tillotson said.

Merchant nodded, the orange color of the flames about the right color for burning naphtha as it spewed obscenely through the windows. The heat was unbearable, forcing them across the street as the MP moved their cars farther away from the house. People were on the streets then, the rapidly darkening sky alight with cinders.

He heard the sound of the fire engine before he could see it, turning to watch its approach along Dumbarton. The engine, lumbering like a giant red beast around the corner of Thirty-second, never actually seemed to get any traction on Dumbarton and didn't survive the turn. Fishtailing wildly, it smashed into several parked cars, firemen flying off the side of the thing in all directions. For several

seconds it seemed to be coming down Dumbarton sideways, but that ended as the cab slammed into a parked
Volkswagen, flipping the entire engine. It landed upside
down. skidding amid sparks for ten more feet before
stopping with the loud groan of dying metal in the center
of the street.

The crowds rushed toward the fire truck, Merchant
turning instead to watch the flames in the house lick up
through the upper stories, engulfing the entire place like a
mammoth torch. He'd had proof. It had lasted for one
hour.

◼◼◼◼◼ ◼ NEWSBREAK ◼ ◼◼◼◼◼

MONTAGE—We see a kaleidoscope of modern jungle
warfare images: helicopters landing troops, men in
the bush, the outskirts of a firefight from the
trenches—stock images pulled from Iraq, Panama,
Grenada, and Vietnam. The sounds are marching
feet and grunts, all very loud. At the bottom of the
screen, SUPER the words: FROM THE NETWORK THAT BRINGS
YOU THE NEWS FIRST, COMES THE REPORTER WHO MAKES THE
NEWS.

CUT TO:

ANGLE—WHITE HOUSE PRESS ROOM—The Press Room is full
of reporters, the President of the United States at the
podium. Sheila Traynor is standing in the audience
and addressing the President.

CUT TO:

CLOSE-UP—SHEILA TRAYNOR

SHEILA: And I would be willing to go to jail to protect
those sources!

NITE—FBI HEADQUARTERS—We see Sheila coming out of the FBI Building, chased by reporters through deep snow.

NARRATOR (OS): Sheila Traynor, the reporter who faced down the President of the United States to break the story of the decade, is the backbone of the NCC news team of professional journalists with a combined 150 years of reporting experience.

CUT TO:

MONTAGE—Silent montage of events from Sheila's daily professional life: preparing copy, getting made-up, reading on-air, covering a location story.

NARRATOR (OS, CONT): Sheila Traynor is a tough, seasoned professional who knows that getting the job done right is the only thing that matters in the highly competitive business of news. And getting the job done right is what Sheila Traynor's all about!

CUT TO:

A CONFERENCE ROOM—Sheila Traynor sits at a production meeting, about ten people around a small table. She is jabbing the air with her finger, making a point.

SHEILA: The only way to get this thing done is for me to go down there and follow through with it. This is an important story, and I want it done right.

NARRATOR (OS): That's why Anchorwoman Sheila Traynor is following her story to Central America, so that you, the viewers, can know the truth. While other networks deal with the rumors, NCC gets the facts.

CUT TO:

CLOSE-UP—SHEILA TRAYNOR—She is looking directly at us, her face sincere.

SHEILA: I know that this border incident has more to do
with Russian missiles than Caribbean incursions.
Watch me prove it. See my special reports: *War in
Caribbe*, every hour beginning Saturday evening
on this NCC station.

CUT TO:

FREEZE FRAME—Sheila's face in close-up

NARRATOR (OS): The reporter who makes the news
brings it all the way home . . . just for you.
Sheila Traynor: tough, insightful, honest . . .
news.

Arlington, Virginia 10:15 P.M.

Charles Merchant sat in front of the den TV, saluting the
newswoman with his third Jack Daniel's. What a wild card
Sheila Traynor was! He smiled at her guileless face in
close up, wondering if she had any idea of the forces she'd
unleashed. It had all started with her revelation about
missiles in Caribbea. She'd never revealed her sources, yet
somehow seemed to have climbed to the top of the
information heap just the same. Just like everything else in
this crazy business, rumor had become truth and the truth
nothing but a vicious rumor that everyone felt obliged to
squelch.

He drank again and thought about his father. The
thought was hardly a transitory vagrant, though. He always thought about his father when he drank heavily.
Drink had finally been the undoing of old Tom Merchant,
or Doctor Tom as the students at Centenary had liked to
call him. Running an English Department could be a lot
like running a religion—decide what truth is, then control
it absolutely. In an English Department it could be decided
that literature began with the birth of Shakespeare and
ended with the death of Henry Fielding. All the dogma,
therefore, was unchanging, the individual professors the
priests with all the answers. Like the Mayans with math-

ematics. Old Tom had liked it that way. Like his son, he believed in controlling his world absolutely. College tenure and government service both provided the same ends: security.

But even that hadn't been enough for Tom Merchant, because he'd been smart enough to know that the control wasn't real or meaningful. He took to the bottle heavily, desperate for escape from the world he'd made. Eventually, even tenure hadn't been enough to protect him and he'd been forcibly retired, living out his remaining few years as a bitter and unrepentant drunk who never forgave his son.

Charlie had always managed to escape the pull to the bottle, maybe because he'd believed, really believed, that his life was right, honest, and honorable. What a farce. As he sat amid the devastation of a world he'd thought built on solid rock, he realized just how transitory all of life really was.

The phone was ringing upstairs. He briefly considered letting it wear itself out, but the habits of a lifetime couldn't be broken in a night and he'd never been able to ignore a ringing phone. He picked himself up and trudged back through the house. He didn't hurry. He'd learned that much.

His whole body was heavy as he sat on the closed toilet seat and picked up the receiver to BJ's voice.

"How does it feel, Charlie?" the man asked. "You're not such big shit anymore, are you?"

"No, I'm not," Merchant replied, then knee-jerked, "at least I'm still on my feet, you son of a bitch."

"For now," BJ said. "Hell, the party's just getting started."

"What have you got on your mind for Central America?" Merchant asked, determined not to let James see his emotional deterioration. "You've sure lined your ducks up down there."

"Good man," BJ replied. "You're still hanging in. As far as Central America goes, I'm just a citizen same as you. I do favors for people, that's all, and they do favors for me. It's not such a big thing. You're a military man. You should understand the absolute value of a strong defense. I'm just a cheerleader for the military, that's all. Same as you."

The last line was meant to be painful, Merchant grimacing, but keeping it inside. "Are you connected with Sheila Traynor?" he asked instead, coming out of the blue.

The silence on the other end of the line only lasted for a second, but it was a valuable second for Merchant. The woman had to be a major player. BJ replied quickly, "I hear that your wife has left with a suitcase," he said, chuckling. "Guess you didn't like watching her suck off the little minority kid, huh?"

"At least I have a wife," Merchant replied. "You may have destroyed my life, but at least I had a life to destroy. What do you do for friendship and companionship, Mr. James?"

There was no answer, the line had gone dead in his hand.

"I let myself in," came a voice from the doorway. He looked up to see his daughter-in-law standing just outside the open door. "I rang the bell, but no one answered."

He stood slowly, then moved to embrace her. "I'm so sorry about Josh," he said. "I wish . . . wish . . ."

"I'm not like my husband," Della Merchant said, breaking the embrace. "I don't blame you for what he's brought on himself. If he hadn't done it, BJ wouldn't have been able to pin him."

"They've really got him then?"

The woman nodded. "Eight ways from Sunday," she said. "Oh, he won't go to jail right away, they've already worked out an appearance and bail, but in the long haul . . . I don't know." Her face became fearful. "He's not strong, Charlie. Tell me the truth; you've known him longer than I have. Will he be able to make it?"

"He's my son," Merchant said. "He'll make it." He took a long breath, wanting to consign Josh to the back of his brain for now. He had more pressing problems at the moment. "Why are you here, anyway? Shouldn't you be at home lending moral support?"

"He's all locked up with Harvey talking lawyer bullshit," she said. "He doesn't need me. He needs Perry Mason. Besides, I was more worried about you right now. You're the one with the fight on your hands."

"So, you see Ben James's work in all this, too?"

"Indeed," she said, then pointed to the drink he still carried. "Got any more of that?"

He nodded, smiling sadly. "Downstairs," he said. "Come on."

As they walked down, he told Della about Linda's leaving, not mentioning the tape, but allowing that it was connected to BJ. They moved back down to the den, Merchant pouring both of them a highball glass filled with Jack Daniel's and rocks. They stood, leaning against the pool table, drinking silently for several minutes before Della spoke.

"Why don't people understand the kind of trouble Ben James is?" she asked.

"Nobody likes to look for trouble, Della," he answered, "and everyone wants to believe what they hear is the truth. Hell, my own wife doesn't even understand."

"I don't believe that," Della said. "Have you ever really tried explaining the whole thing to her? Be honest."

He stared down at his drink. "I'm used to not telling her, I guess," he answered. "The military code and all that. . . ."

"No." Della smiled, reaching out to touch his arm. "You're just a stiff-necked son of a bitch, that's all. I love you, Charlie, and I respect you, but I'd hate to be married to you. You want to swallow everything around you whole. No human being deserves that, especially Linda."

"Am I that bad?" he asked.

She nodded. "Worse," she replied, then smiled. "But you're also honest and dependable and even-handed. I'm proud to be related to you."

They embraced quickly, Charlie knowing that whatever BJ took away from him, he couldn't take away all the years of happiness his family had brought to him. "You make me feel like maybe we're not finished yet," he said, breaking the embrace.

"There's still a monster to vanquish. What are we going to do about it?" she asked.

He shook his head. "Don't know," he said. "Haven't much cared, I guess. Without someone saying they were bribed in the House vote, we can't stop him on that front. What are Phil's feelings?"

"Mixed," she said, taking a long drink. "He lost a lot of

face yesterday. He'll have to fight just to get even again. I don't think he's ready for another battle with James."

Merchant shrugged. "We're also at an impasse with the police. Leonard's evidence died with him. No one else cares. Obviously, we can't stop things in Central America. Troops are already committed. I guess Josh's SEC complaint is totally out the window now. The IRS and the Justice Department won't even talk to me."

"You don't intend to do anything?" she asked, her voice accusing as she watched him turn to the remnants of Waterloo and stare down at it.

"I'm an old man," he heard himself say, "an old soldier who's out of his element. It's not that I don't intend to do anything, it's just that I don't know what to do."

"We can't just give up," she said. "You know, Josh used to tell me that he thought you could do anything."

He turned to stare at her. "That's an odd thought," he returned. "All I ever get from Josh is his embarrassment over how old-fashioned I am."

She shook her head, smiling. "That's because he can't live up to your example, that's all. It's his self-defense mechanism when he's afraid he can't measure up. He thinks you're the greatest man he's ever known."

He felt tears well up in his eyes. He'd done the same thing to his son that his father had done to him, and Josh had turned his life at right angles to Charlie, just the same as Charlie had done to his father. "He doesn't hate me?"

"What's to hate?" Della said, smiling. "You're a good man . . . a caring man."

"I can't tell you what it means to me to hear that," he replied.

He wiped at his eyes. It was a night of many revelations—not all of them bad—and of understanding priorities. BJ could perhaps tell everyone what was real to their eyes, but he could never understand the reality of their hearts. The concept was beyond him, and could possibly prove his undoing.

"Touching scene, really touching."

Both of them turned to the doorway leading to the front of the house to see Melanie Patterson standing there, a suitcase dangling from her right hand. The woman was frowning, shaking her head. "You didn't even lock your fucking front door. Don't you know that *anybody* could walk in here?"

"Well, Mel," Merchant said, turning to Della, deciding that cordiality in the face of disaster was an extremely civilized action. "I'd like you to meet Della Merchant, my daughter-in-law. Your boss has just seen to putting her husband in jail."

"Charmed," the woman replied, dropping the suitcase and looking at her watch.

"My pleasure," Della said, turning to Charlie in perplexity.

"Far be it from me to break up old home week," Mel said, moving into the room and directly to the Waterloo field to stare down at it, "but we don't have much time. We need to get the noncombatants out of here before the show starts."

"P-pardon me?" Della said.

Merchant and Patterson were staring hard at each other, the charge from their eyes an electric jolt. "Ms. Patterson is suggesting you leave now before you get hurt," he told Della. "I think we'd better do what she says."

"You mean . . . ?"

"Go on home now," he said, his eyes still fixed on Patterson, the woman smiling wryly at him. "I'll let you know how things are going."

"Are you sure, I—"

"Do it, honey," Patterson said sharply. "It gets tough from here on out. Only the hardball players are allowed in the game now."

"I'm not going anywhere," Della said, and Charlie hardened, fearing for her safety.

"I can't deal with this and worry about protecting you at the same time," he said, narrowing his eyes. "The best thing you can do at this moment is to go hide out somewhere."

"Charlie?" she said, confusion on her face.

"Do what I tell you," he said in a voice used to command. "Do it now."

She lowered her eyes and nodded.

"I'll call," Charlie added as he watched Della gather up coat and gloves, leaving by the back door.

As soon as the door closed, Melanie Patterson quickly

closed the distance between herself and Merchant, fitting into his arms for a long kiss, Charlie responding to her as he had the last time.

She pulled away after a moment, eyes flashing. "We probably don't have much time," she said. "I've got to give you a crash course on surviving BJ and you won't be an easy subject. I've seen your file. It's got a change-of-status notice in it set for tonight. First thing we need to do is get you out of here."

"Change of status?"

"Yeah . . . like from living to dead, or something equally counterproductive."

"He won't kill me yet," Merchant replied, turning to stare at her suitcase. "He could have done that anytime. He's not finished humiliating me. What's in the bag?"

"My secret." She smiled, leaning up to kiss him quickly. "I got a hotel room under another name. We'll go there first, then plan the next move."

"I'm not running from anything," he said.

She narrowed her eyes and pointed to his drink, which was sitting on the pool table. "How many of those have you had?" she asked. "This isn't the battle of Gettysburg, lover boy. Nobody's trying to chop off your balls or anything. We're just going to make a strategic withdrawal to consider our options. Now come on."

She led him out of the den and into the darkness of the living room, Charlie realizing for the first time that with Patterson on his team, he at least had a fighting chance.

He saw the lights just as they were beginning to go up the stairs. Headlights sweeping silently across the entry, several pairs.

They looked at each other, then wordlessly hurried back through the living room to the front door to peer out into the snowscape. The entire block was filling with cars that slid up quickly, then killed their engines. There were D.C. black and whites, a paddy wagon, and a half-dozen nondescript General Motors products that undoubtedly had OFFICIAL USE license tags affixed to their bumpers.

It didn't even surprise him to see the vehicles, so much had he come to depend on Ben James's ability to deliver reality on demand. It was then that it began to occur to him that perhaps Mel was all part of some grand scheme herself. It was all just games, silly, childish games. He found himself, in absolute calm, watching a cadre of men carrying weapons move comically through the snowdrifts, trying with their guns and numbers to move surreptitiously to the house.

"Is there any way out of this?" she asked him, her hand grabbing his arm hard, the nails biting into his flesh.

"W-what?" he said, pulling himself out of the reverie, shaking his head.

"Out of here!" she said urgently. "Out of here."

He looked once more out the window. Whatever they thought he'd done must have been pretty terrible; there was enough hardware out there to rearm all the *libres* left in Caribbea. He turned to face Mel. She looked incredibly beautiful wrapped in the soft shadows. Underfoot was broken glass from Rita Hurley's entry the night before. He smiled at her as his own gears began churning. "Maybe my life hasn't been totally useless," he said. "Prepare to be astounded. Come on."

He took her by the hand and hustled her through the kitchen to the back door, grabbing her suitcase from the den before going out. Neither of them wore a coat. He'd acquired a broom that he was brandishing like a sword.

He looked at her with wide eyes. "Ready?" he said.

"Ready for what?" she said, and he threw open the door to a frigid blast and jerked her out into the night.

He charged headlong into the rolling snowfield of the backyard, pushing her ahead of him, dragging the broom behind to cover their footprints.

"You've gone nuts!" she called into the roar of the razored wind.

"Yes!" he called back, laughing, then throwing her down into the snow toward the back of the yard.

She watched as he scrabbled around on hands and knees amid snowdrifts that kept them hidden from the view of the house. They could hear voices then, shouts, and could see lights going on all over the house.

"What are you doing?" she whispered, crawling up beside him.

He looked at her, snow cascading down the length of her red hair, her green eyes vibrant even in the darkness. "My God, you look better than a calendar picture," he said, kissing her cold lips quickly. "You know your eyes, they remind me . . ."

"Of Joann's," Mel said. "I know. BJ always paired us up because of it. If you haven't noticed, BJ is into bright colors. Now what the hell are you doing?"

"Looking." He laughed. "Looking to justify myself. Here . . . here!"

His hand had grabbed something a couple of feet down in the snow. He pulled, the door to the fallout shelter opening slowly, a camouflage covering of snow rising with it. "For years people have been telling me I was nuts because I keep this thing in good shape." He gestured into the dark cavern opened up by the door. "Ms. Patterson . . . your boudoir awaits."

She hesitated only slighting before slithering through the shelter door, Merchant right behind her, going through as small a space as he could to keep from losing the snow cover on the door. The wind was up high. If their pursuers didn't find the remnants of their tracks within a few minutes, they had a better-than-even chance of staying hidden, at least until morning. And the morning would be another day, another reality.

For now, he had a million questions for Melanie Patterson and all night to ask them.

FEBRUARY 9, SATURDAY

AMERICANS SUPPORT INCURSION

New York (AP)—In the latest poll results, released
Friday evening, record numbers of the American
public favor the U.S. military operation in Honduras. When asked the question: DO YOU THINK
AMERICAN INTERVENTION IN HONDURAS IS JUS-
TIFIED? fully 83 percent of those polled responded
favorably as opposed to only 10 percent against. On
the larger issue of whether or not the missiles-in-
Caribbea question has spawned the intervention, a
slightly smaller, but still sizable, segment of the
population (75 percent) agreed the intervention was
really about missiles, not border incursions—a situation upon which the government has yet to extend
a viewpoint. Most insiders seem to feel that the
Macklin presidency intends to take care of the missiles quietly so as not to upset the delicate balance of
worldwide peace evident during the last decade.

". . . as you can see below us, Task Force Tango is
moving straight down Highway One, the Pan Am
Highway that connects all of Central America.
We're about fifty miles from the border right now.
General Lofton of SouthCom is leading this particu-
lar task force. There are two other task forces: Red

Man, the overland expedition led by General Jarra of the Honduran Army, and Thunder, led by General Tucker down Highway 4.

"There appears to be no game plan here, except for securing the border, but one has to wonder about the *John F. Kennedy*, anchored off the northern coast with all those Seasprites lashed down to its deck. It seems to be the consensus among reporters that the search for missiles may be the hidden agenda on this trip, but all that may soon get lost in the throes of battle if conditions here continue to degenerate. Both sides are claiming battle losses for last night. We personally saw the bodies of ten to fifteen Marines lined up for the TV cameras this morning that were killed by sniper fire during the night. Remarkably, the Cubans and Caribbeans are claiming similar casualty numbers, also through sniper fire.

"No longer does this appear to simply be an American show of force in another Central American republic. It's beginning to take on the ugly trappings of war, and from here, from the American end of it, they are preparing to do serious battle once they reach the border sometime this evening."

—*NCC Morning News*
February 9

The Coco River Daybreak

Ken Breedlove was anchored by the high, gnarled branch of the pine tree with Mulroy, the blond kid. The river rushed loudly a hundred feet below as his men prepared to raise the second warhead up the pulley wheel. Rain fell hard and straight, dripping from clothes that never had the opportunity to dry. The rain would last no longer than fifteen minutes—it never did—then the Caribbean sun would bake everything to a steam bath in preparation for the afternoon rain . . . which preceded the evening rain by a couple of hours. The usual.

He stood against the tree, held secure by his leather safety strap, the telephone lineman's contraption that he'd learned working on Air Force FLR-9 listening posts years before. It had been the only real lesson the air force had taught him. Mulroy lay on the fat branch, bouncing on it slightly, his own safety strap dangling from the leather belt. He was making sure the branch could hold the weight of the warhead while securing the small steel pulley tightly to the branch.

"How's it look, brother?" Breed called to the blondie, the nylon rope dangling in the pulley wheel, squeaking back and forth.

"Think we've got a go, Cap'n," the man said, shinnying back to where the branch joined the trunk to sit up, straddling the branch. He smiled widely with his surfer-boy teeth. "After we get out of here, I want to go to the desert for a year. If I never see another cloud, it'll be too soon."

"You just don't know when you're well off," Breed replied, leaning down to the others and yelling through cupped hands.

"Hoist away, mates!" he called, five of them picking up the rope and backing up, tugging. The warhead lifted with a strange wobble from the soaked ground and began its ascent to the branches above. The missile itself had been torched from the five-foot, six-hundred-pound warhead that now looked like a heavy blunt egg. Its brother was already hung in a matching pine on the other side of the sixty-foot-wide river.

The pulley wheel sang a violin song as the warhead creaked upward. "'Most friendship is feigning, most loving mere folly,'" Breedlove called. "'Then heigh-ho! the holly! This life is most jolly.'"

The warhead wobbled slowly upward, inching toward his position as the men below, their faces like fried eggs looking up, hoisted in unison whenever Wee Willie grunted, "Pull!"

"So, what's with all the Shakespeare crap?" Mulroy said as he sat a foot above Breedlove, who was hanging out from the trunk, a hand on the pulley rope, guiding gently.

"I thought you were fucked in the head when I first met you."

"Shakespeare understood human nature, my son," Breedlove replied, not even bothering to look up at Mulroy. The warhead was close enough now that he could see the rainwater beading up on it. "You could learn a lot by studying the great bard."

Mulroy grunted. "No book ever taught me how to kick somebody's ass," he said, a never-ending font of wisdom. "No book ever taught me how to hump pussy, either."

"That's right, Joe," Breedlove said, smiling up at him for just a second. "You can fight and fuck with the best of them. Just don't get into a talking contest."

"What's that supposed to mean?"

The bomb had moved up to touching distance, the readout dial for his timer was staring a black screen at him. He waved down at the men below, and heard Willie yell for them to stop, the bomb halting its upward journey to sway in an almost-circular motion. "It means," he said to Mulroy, "that there're two kinds of people in this world, those who make up the rules and those who do what they're told. Now, secure that wheel up there."

Mulroy frowned and leaned out on the branch to push the thumb lock on the spool, the pulley itself now taking all the weight.

"Secure up here!" Breedlove called below. "Tie her down."

The men below began running the rope around the trunk like a maypole. "If you're so much better than me," Mulroy said, "what is it that you're gettin' out of this deal that's different from me? What is it that you want?"

Breedlove leaned out as far as he could, his fingertips just reaching the timer. "Immortality, Joe," he said. "That's what I get. History will remember me and the world that I'm making. You take nothing from here but some money—"

"A lot of money," Mulroy corrected.

"Which you'll spend in a couple of years and be right back in the gutter where you started," Breedlove said. He punched the timer on, its face lighting up a digital countdown clock running backward from twenty-four hours. He felt the blood course through him when he turned on the timer, an exhilaration flushing him. They were all, from that moment forward, living under the reality of sudden death. "Just think," he told Mulroy. "Tomorrow morning at this time, this whole area will be naked wasteland, stripped of all life, the river boiled away, the atmosphere uninhabitable for decades."

"Yeah," the man answered. "Kind of gives me a soft spot . . . right here." He pointed to his head.

"You amaze me, Joe," Breedlove said, leaning back to the tree and sliding up a bit on the strap, getting head to head with Mulroy. "You seem to have no capacity at all for philosophical thought on any level. I mean, how do you live with yourself? You never give any real thought to the why or the how of things, never relate to the country you're abusing. You're bankrupt, man, morally bankrupt."

"Listen, you asshole," Mulroy said, pointing at him, sticking the finger right in his face. "I'm sick of you and your holier-than-thou bullshit. You're no different than me, no better, no smarter."

"Ah, but you're wrong," Breedlove said, smiling. "If you were as smart as me, it would have occurred to you that setting this here bomb up in this here tree was really only a one-man job, and that here we are, you and I, not exactly fast friends, up in the tree together, me with a safety strap on, and you . . . without. Bye, Joe."

Scissoring his thighs tightly on the trunk, Breedlove reached out with both hands and grabbed Mulroy by the front of his soaked Motley Crue T-shirt, pulling hard. The shirt ripped, but did its job, Mulroy tumbling headfirst off the limb without a sound. As he fell, coming out of the roll back first, he looked up at Breedlove as if he were still trying to interpret Breed's last speech, not yet realizing that he was dead. Dumb fuck.

"Whoa!" Breed yelled down, then skip-jumped the hundred feet down the tree like the lumberjacks in the Pacific Northwest, humping over the small stumps of branches they had cut on the way up, reaching Mulroy just as the others did. The body was broken up quite a bit, but still recognizably human. Mulroy still had that stupid look on his face as the hard rain pooled in his eye sockets and open mouth.

"The dumb motherfucker was playing around up in the

tree," he said, shrugging. "He was jumping around like a monkey or something . . . fell right off."

"Chopper!" Jamie yelled, the whump-whump sound of the rotors close and closing.

"Into the brush!" Breedlove yelled, he and Willie dragging Mulroy with them into the tangles of vine and fern growing on the riverbank.

The chopper was on them seconds later, riding the river. Breedlove, on hands and knees in the underbrush, watched the Huey pass quickly, almost at water level. It made him proud to see American military out on the job again, the Huey loaded with M-60s mounted in the open bays, men with long, heavy bandoliers ready to feed when the gunners needed. God, it'd been years since he'd seen the like.

The vision was gone in a second, all of them out of the trees and staring at the river, churned up from the chopper's passage.

"Obviously, gentlemen," Breedlove said loudly, "time is running short. But the good news: We have completed our mission, our success rate, one hundred percent." As the remaining members of the group applauded and whooped, he looked back at Mulroy's body, still in the bush. He said, "Through an unfortunate accident, we also have one less person to share up with. We have only to divide the goods at base camp, tear down the camp, and beat a hasty, strategic retreat. Since the prevailing winds are from west to east, I would suggest departing upwind if you wish to avoid some bit of nastiness. Questions?"

Willie pointed back toward the body. "What about him? What do we do with Joe?"

Breedlove shook his head sadly. "I have given it a little thought and realized that, even in death, poor Joe can be of use to us. We need to get the troops closer in to the river, the highway is too far, the winds could spare some lives. What we need is to get their attention, to focus them on the river."

"The satchels won't do that?" Jamie asked.

"The satchels will be more effective if the troops are already here," Breedlove said, then scratched his chin, waiting.

"Maybe if we planted him out in the open somewhere close to the river," Willie said, "we could—"

"Excellent idea," Breedlove said. "There're reasons why I love this man. Look, let's just plant him in the middle of the field where we've set up the satchels. If we were to leave old Joe here smack out in the middle of that field, I'll bet even those boys in the choppers could find him. Then they can invite everybody to the party!"

"Yeah!" Willie laughed. "Guess it's kind of good luck that Joe died."

"Yeah," Breedlove said. "The best."

Arlington, Virginia Daybreak

Merchant and Melanie Patterson sat on folding chairs staring at each other, knees nearly touching, in the cramped quarters of his fallout shelter. Merchant, in his usual fashion, had kept the shelter operational and fully stocked, reasoning that there was no reason to have one if it wasn't prepared. There were wooden shelves stocked with C rations and a great deal of canned fruit and potted meat. There were radios of different sizes and powers, plus a crate of batteries to keep them going. There were cots and blankets and pillows. There were lanterns and flashlights, five-gallon jugs of distilled water, plus a small stove for boiling more. There was a shelf of books, mostly survival guides and mysteries, plus a small tape library to play on the VCR that was hooked up to the portable television that Charlie was watching at the moment, tuned to local news. A small gas heater kept the place warm, and he even had a hot plate with a pot of coffee.

Merchant sat, quietly puffing on the extra pipe he kept in the shelter, dividing himself between news watches and picking Mel's brain. His mind and its patterns were altered and he knew it. Too little sleep and too much change had taken him dangerously close to crippling ennui or, worse, uncontrollable rage; but he had fallen back on his military training to control himself. He thanked that training, plus his own sense of self-control, for keeping him sane now.

"You've got to understand BJ's mind," Mel said as she ate a can of peaches with a fold-up Boy Scout fork. She turned slightly in the cramped space and banged her knee on a wooden box sticking out from the bookshelf next to her. "Ouch! Damnit. If you weren't so damned anal, we might be able to get comfortable in here."

"This is all necessary survival gear," he said.

"Yeah . . . right." She pulled out the offending wooden box and opened it to a flare gun and a half-dozen projectiles. "I can see where this is going to come in *real* handy."

He took the box from her, closing it up. "You never know," he said, replacing it on the shelf. "Now, I still don't understand about BJ."

She rubbed her knee, crossing her blue-jeaned legs. "He's simply a businessman, trying to do as much business as he possibly can. I guess he's the ultimate businessman, unfettered by normal conventions and possessing a free mind. He just applies the business ethic absolutely, that's all."

"You make him sound like a machine."

"Not a machine . . . just a man with a boundless imagination and no restraints. The Carnegies, the Trumps, and the Rockefellers of the planet are all doing the same thing, controlling their world and its politics."

"What's his deal in Central America?"

She shrugged, then slithered another peach quarter down her throat. "I don't know. He keeps most everything in his head, the ultimate plotter. When I was trying to find out, I got caught."

Charlie pointed to the open suitcase near her feet. "That's when you grabbed these?"

"Right. He keeps them in a vault. Blackmail material. Not that he needs it. BJ's strength is his patience. He does a lot of favors for people, small things, big things. Eventually he asks for small or big favors in return, that's all. He calls it networking. But he has the backup material just the same. I wouldn't be surprised if he had something on every member of Congress."

"At least the ones who perform extortable deeds."

She set the peaches on the bookcase, Charlie grabbing the can and tossing it in the wastebasket near his feet. "Charlie," she said, "everybody does things they don't want other people to know about."

"Not everybody," he said. "I don't."

She laughed loudly then. "So that's why your house is crawling with D.C. cops and federal pinheads . . . because you didn't do anything."

"I didn't!" he said angrily.

Her eyes narrowed and she leaned up to rest a hand on his leg. "Charlie . . . what's the problem? Whether you did or didn't—who cares? We're all human beings. We're entitled to screw up sometimes. You can drive yourself crazy worrying about things all the time."

He watched her reach down into the purse at her feet and pull out a cigarette case. "If people didn't live by ethical standards," he said, "we'd all still be animals in the jungle. Something has to matter."

"Well," she said, opening up the case and removing a hand-rolled cigarette, "at least you didn't drag heaven and hell into it."

"Because we've got to live here . . . together . . . our entire lives. We've got to make our lives like heaven, every day, or we risk losing the planet."

"So what?" she said, bringing out a lighter and starting her cigarette.

"So what?" he repeated sadly. "Have you no feeling for our past . . . our future . . . the future of our children and their children?"

"I don't have any children," she said, almost bitterly.

"Mel!"

"Look," she said. "I'm trying to show you how BJ operates, that's all. To him, there is no past, there is no future; there is only him and his success, right here and right now. It's how his mind works."

"He's evil," Charlie said, and Mel's cigarette smelled awfully strange.

"He's a businessman," she replied, and took a long drag on her cigarette, holding it in.

"What are you smoking there?" he asked, but she was pointing past him to the small television.

"It's your house," she said.

He spun around and turned up the sound, smiling when he realized that it was a live shot, that the reporter was speaking from his front yard at that very moment.

". . . quiet of this upscale Arlington bedroom community was shattered last night when units of the D.C. police and FBI descended upon this house, with arrest warrants for one Charles Merchant . . . the charge: conspiracy to obtain classified documents."

Charlie felt the breath go out of him. They'd just accused him of being a spy!

"Already charged in the case is one Ned Bramley, currently an employee with the GSA and longtime friend of Merchant's who, as head of Army Intelligence back in the seventies, led an active and highly decorated military career. What went wrong is anybody's guess.

"Merchant has escaped the dragnet, though his wife was picked up at a local motel and his daughter-in-law, the sister of House Speaker Phil Rosen, was detained leaving the house late last night. A team of federal investigators is now going over the house with a fine-tooth comb, searching for more evidence that would link Merchant to an ongoing spy operation. Speaking to neighbors this morning, they all say that Charles Merchant was a quiet man who kept to himself a lot, a man obsessed with appearances, a mystery man who never seemed to get into the swing of the neighborhood.

"Credit for breaking up the ring has been given to DIA chief, General Gene Tillotson, a onetime friend of Merchant's, who obtained firsthand evidence of the spy operation last night and turned it over to the FBI. General Tillotson could not be reached for comment this morning. We were told that he'd 'gone fishing.' Well, General, all I can say is that you've already caught a big one."

The pipe had dropped out of Merchant's mouth upon the mention of Tillotson's name. He bent down to pick it up. What a fool he'd been. No wonder they'd beaten him to the house on Dumbarton last night: Gene had bought them the time. No wonder every step of the way he'd been stymied. He'd trusted the wrong man, a man he'd trusted for all his adult life.

"Good old Gene," Mel said, shaking her head.

"You know him?" Merchant asked, his head spinning again. How much was he expected to take?

"Yeah. BJ's been using old Gene since his wife died a few years ago. A little sex, a lot of booze. He was really a pretty cheap buy-out considering his position."

"That's my best friend you're talking about."

"I think you need a new way of picking friends."

"This is foolish," Merchant said, standing, slightly stooped because of a low ceiling. "My wife's been arrested. My son's wife has been arrested. Jesus, there goes Phil's career. Everything has ramifications attached." He suddenly looked up at her. "Why are you here . . . really?"

"Because I'm dead if I'm not here."

"There's got to be more . . . what are you smoking?"

She held it out to him. "A joint, pardner. Want some?"

"Put that shit out," he said sternly. "That's against the—"

"Say it," she said, smiling. "Against the law. Maybe if they catch us here, they'll add misdemeanor possession to your espionage charge. Here, take it."

He grimaced, shoving her hand away. He turned and looked back up the small set of stairs to the hatch out. "I've got to give myself up now. Maybe they'll at least leave everybody else off the hook. It's just me they want."

"Sit down, asshole," she said sternly, staring hard fire at him. "All that happens if you give yourself up is that you're screwed beyond repair . . . your family, too."

He looked at her face and saw no bullshit. He sat. "Look," she said. "I've been trying to explain things to you but you don't want to understand. BJ has made the truth. In that truth, you are a traitor, your family . . . traitors. No one's going to believe your truth because BJ's papers and TV and polls will tell them that you're wrong and they'll believe it. I'm here because the truth must be changed again, and you are just the man to change it."

"Me . . . how? Look what's happened so far."

She took a drag and handed him the joint. He took it, holding it delicately between thumb and index finger as if it were a live bomb ready to go off. "You've got the mind for it, Charlie, and you've got the will for it. Between you and me, I believe we can whip him."

"But what about the things that have already happened?"

"Damnit . . . you're still acting as if reality were solid. It's not, it's fluid. All things change—or remain the same. It's minds that vary, attitudes. Believe me. The truth you've lived all these years isn't real truth, either. Wise up, buddy. You've been buying a crock all this time yourself. Look inside your heart and tell me that the military budget couldn't be cut in half without any compromise of American security. And remember. This is *your* truth. Now take a toke on that weed. It'll help you think, because I'm counting on you to carry the ball on this thing and you can't do it with your mind caught in the same rut. What do you want me to do, call you a pussy?"

"Why me?" he asked, taking a small puff in deference to his manhood.

"This is military shit and you know the military inside and out," she replied. "Plus, you still do have contacts that I could never approach. Hold that shit in longer. It's got to work on your lungs. You've got the mind to free yourself, and if you'd ever loosen up, you'd have the heart. You're a schemer just like me. Why do you think we're attracted to each other?"

He took another drag, holding it until his lungs burned. It came out as a cough. "You're telling me that I need to change reality," he said, handing the joint back, his mind lightening by slow degrees.

"And the way to change reality is to simply know that you're not married to it. You can make people believe anything you want them to believe." She handed back the joint, Merchant taking a big toke this time.

"You really think we can pull this off?" he said. "You know everybody else thinks I'm over the hill."

She pulled herself close to him, leaning up for a deep, long kiss. She tasted sweet, like peaches. "You've got greatness in you," she whispered as the kiss ended. "You've got all that BJ has, except you've also got something else. You care, really care about what you're doing. BJ only loves the game itself. You're looking at the outcome. It's called vision, Charlie. It's what's going to help us win this thing."

He took another toke, feeling his mind drift as he held

it in. "I busted a whole barracksful of men for smoking this once," he said. "Seems kind of stupid now that I think about it. I mean, this stuff grows wild, it—"

"Maybe we need to first work on getting out of here," she interrupted.

"Yeah," he replied, "and getting to Gene. If I can get my hands on him, I might be able to nip things in the bud right there. We go back too far together."

"Don't count on that," she said. "BJ's had him for a long time."

He sat back, feeling relaxed, disassociated somewhat from his body and his problems. "How about you," he said. "How long has BJ had you?"

She smiled. "Four years ago I was the weather girl on a local Des Moines TV station. I was stuck somewhere between greatness and suicide and moving in neither direction. One night after the late news, I went home to my apartment. No sooner had I arrived than there was a knock on the door. I opened it to find BJ standing there in one of his million-dollar suits with that nasty little-boy smile on his face. He held out a tall stack of banded money. 'There's five thousand dollars here,' he told me. 'It's all yours if you get down on your hands and knees and suck my dick. You've got ten seconds to decide.'"

Charlie grunted at the crassness. His mind, though, was enjoying envisioning the described scene. "So what happened then?" he asked.

She narrowed her eyes. "What?"

"What did you do then?" he asked.

She shrugged broadly. "I took the money," she said. "Who wouldn't?"

"I wouldn't," he said.

"Come on," she replied. "Five grand for a blowjob?"

"Five grand is a damned cheap price for a soul."

She jumped a bit, he thought, stirrings of morality; but she recovered quickly. "Whoa," she said. "Thought we were on the same side, General."

"You know my rank," he said. "And we're just establishing ground rules here."

"I have no ground rules," she answered. "Neither does BJ. Neither will you if you want to win."

"I don't care about winning," he said, his mind slipping

freely through channels he hadn't ridden in years. He thought of Josh as a kid, of the closeness he and Linda had known before things had gotten so complicated. "I just want life to be right again."

She shook her head, and he couldn't interpret the soft look in her eyes. "God, they broke the mold when they made you," she said. "It's no wonder that BJ wants to destroy you so badly. Your very existence defies him." A tear formed in the corner of her eye. She wiped at it angrily. "How come you never went to Des Moines?"

"I don't understand."

"Of course you don't."

He toked the joint again. Mel was beautiful. Even in the lantern light with sleep-puffy eyes, she was the most beautiful woman he'd ever seen, and her eyes, her eyes were just like Joann's: bright, intelligent . . . sexy. Funny, he'd always thought that he hated pushy women, of which Mel was one of the pushiest. But what he found was that he loved the sparks, loved the pressure of matching brains with someone so free and intelligent. Not that Linda wasn't intelligent, she was just too subservient. But whose fault was that?

He felt strange, as if he were standing back from his life for the first time and looking at it like the stage manager in Our Town. He did have a good mind. Why did he always use it to control?

There was something else, too. He'd been branded a traitor, the worst thing he could ever have imagined happening, yet it really didn't bother him that much. He could live with it as long as justice was done. Was that the self-respect that Linda had talked about last night? Maybe BJ had unwittingly provided him with the tools for his own salvation.

"How long could somebody live down in this shelter?" she asked, looking around and frowning.

"All right, all right, I'm thinking . . . okay?" he said, his mind freewheeling, jumping wildly from random thought to random thought. It occurred to him that it was Saturday and that the weather was lousy. Both factors that would affect the number of people assigned to him at that moment. He stood and turned to the ladder. "Kill the light for a minute," he said, and climbed the short ladder until his head bumped into the shelter door.

Mel turned down the flame on the Coleman lantern to a matchpoint, Merchant slowly butting his head against the door, the thing opening an inch at a time. Soon his entire head was poking out in the fuzzy morning light. He could just glimpse the house. No lights were turned on, and he could see yellow crime-scene tape roping the whole place off. He turned slightly to the right and could see the garage, a police car containing two uniformed cops parked in the drive right near it.

He came back down the ladder, Mel turning the light back up full. "Where are you parked?" he asked her.

"About a half a block away . . . on the street," she said. "Why?"

"I think that all we've got is a couple of cops to watch the place right now," he replied. "It strikes me that a little misdirection might free us up to get to your car."

"Great," she said. "What have you got in mind?"

"The world has collapsed around me," he said. "I'm now a traitor to the country I've given my life to and I don't even seem to care. I think it's time for a really grand gesture."

He moved to the bookshelf and removed the wooden box containing the flare gun that looked like an oversize derringer. The single chamber hinged open and he shoved a flare the size of a shotgun shell in and snapped the apparatus closed.

"What in the world are you going to do?" she asked, smiling slightly.

"You just follow me up the ladder and get ready to run," he said, winking at her.

With that, he moved back to the ladder and up again, cracking it open. "Come on," he whispered harshly, Mel climbing the ladder behind him to rest on the rung below, their bodies overlapping as she reached around his chest to hold herself on the ladder.

"You sure this isn't just a trick to grab a cheap feel?" she asked, Merchant responding by bringing a hand around behind him to grab her ass. What in God's name was he doing? He hadn't acted this way in years.

"Here goes nothing," he said, coming out of the shelter

chest high. He took quick aim at the garage window twenty feet distant and fired the flare gun without hesitation. It was time to turn on the heat.

The window broke with a small pop, then for several seconds a pretty lavender light glowed in pulses through the near darkness within the garage. A can of gasoline for the mower must have gone up, for a loud whump shook the structure, black smoke fairly billowed through the broken window, and all at once the garage itself was a monstrous orange torch.

He watched the police car. The cops jumped out, yelling and starting to charge the garage. Then the flames billowed out in huge, demanding licks, one of the cops yelling, "His car'll go!"

The two uniformed men hurried back to the black and white and, tires spraying snow showers, careened back out of the driveway just as the gas tank in the Cadillac exploded loudly, a Charlie Merchant vehicle always full of gasoline.

The blast literally vaporized half the garage. The car itself jumped up through the remnants of the roof and twisted over, dead, in midair, crashing into the neighbor's yard, probably the one who had told the reporter that Charlie "kept to himself."

"Let's move!" he yelled, scrambling out of the shelter, then turning to grab Mel by the hand and jerking her out behind him.

Her hand in a death grip, he charged back toward the house, the garage burning furiously behind him. They crashed through snowdrifts four feet high, jumping to move at all in the deep snow. When they reached the back of the house he dragged her around the side, both of them covered head to foot in white by the time they reached the front.

They threw themselves flush against the cold brick of the two-hundred-year-old chimney, Charlie inching around to see the cops in front. They'd pulled out halfway into the street, one of them running back up the driveway while the other stood outside the car, display lights now flashing, to talk on the radio. He was calling for fire department backup, the answers squawking loudly back on the outside speakers.

"Come on," Merchant whispered. "Move it."

The cop finished with the radio, leaned into the car to replace it on the spur, then turned and hurried back up the drive toward the fire.

"Now," Charlie said, grabbing her hand again and charging for the street just as soon as the cop had disappeared around the other side of the house. It wouldn't take them long to figure out what was going on.

They made the street, most of the neighbors now watching with wide eyes through their windows. Patterson was jerking her head wildly up and down the street.

"Where is it?" he yelled.

"I—I don't know!" she returned, her face already bright red from the stinging wind, her arms wrapped tightly around her body. "It was down there . . . they . . . they must have towed it away."

"Damn!" he yelled, then turned toward the police car: motor running, lights blazing, the driver's side door hanging open. The garage he'd destroyed had been his. The police car was official government property, its theft a federal offense. He thought about Josh and Linda and maybe even Della sitting in jail because of him, and he thought about Mel's words about reality. He had no time to bullshit himself anymore. He had to know truth, real truth.

He took her hand again and hurried her toward the black and white. "Here's our transportation," he said.

They made the police car just as the cops watching the burning garage saw them. Mel was still getting her door closed as he fishtailed off, the cops falling and sliding down the drive as they tried to catch up to them.

"Jesus," she said, breathing hard, then turning back to make sure no one was behind them. Then she looked around and smiled. "Don't guess I've ever driven in one of these before." She leaned back, relaxing. "Now what, General?"

"We find Gene," Merchant said, all of the concentration of his stoned mind going into keeping control of the car.

And the game.

NCC Tower 9:43 A.M.

Sheila Traynor hated Don Merck's office; it reminded her too much of the man. It was overwrought and facile, its just-so combination of stainless steel and symmetry some overpaid decorator's idea of an art deco wet dream. The room was huge, its space frivolously wasted with monstrous bushy green plants and statues of classically naked women holding up Sally Rand–size opaque spheres while pink and turquoise geometrical logos dominated every vertical and horizontal surface. Nothing worthwhile could happen in a phony room like this, and nothing worthwhile was happening now.

Macklin's man, Rob Danton, sat with the White House legal counsel on an overstuffed white Naugahyde love seat facing Merck and the NCC counsel, Ted Ames, on an identical seat. A series of miniature coffee tables of various heights separated them physically, though mentally they seemed to be on the same wavelength. An easy chair of the same design as the couches was set at an angle to the pit group for Sheila's use, but she couldn't sit down. The conversation angered her and kept her pacing.

"You're looking at this in the wrong way, Miss Traynor," Danton said, leaning around a tall green plant to watch her pace. "All things being equal, there's no reason for the administration to give you permission at all to go to Honduras. You haven't exactly been . . . sympathetic to our side of all this."

"What side?" Sheila said, moving near her chair to lean against it as she spoke. "We're newspeople, you're news. You do, we report. Nobody has any side here."

"What Mr. Danton means, Sheila . . ." Merck began, smiling, but she cut him off.

"I know what he means, Don," she said. "He means that because I wouldn't play their little game over the missiles, they want to take the ball and go home."

"Not at all," Danton said, smiling. "What I'm saying is that we'd be more than happy to bury the hatchet with you, but that you are going to have to observe certain conditions to insure our cooperation. It's the way the world works, Miss Traynor."

"This is nothing new," Merck said, and his eyes were harder than usual. "We've worked this way for a while. The administration wants security in a war zone, we want the story. We kind of . . . work together to achieve that aim. You haven't been out in the field, so I understand your not knowing."

"Are you telling me that I can't go to Honduras and do the stories I want to do?" she asked, leaning down and pointing at Danton.

"I'm not saying that at all," Danton replied. "I'm saying that everything you do will have to go through our censors before release, which is common practice. I'm saying that for security and safety reasons only certain areas will be open for your perusal, but they will be newsworthy areas. We guarantee good photo ops; it's part of the deal."

"What about the Seasprites?" she asked. "What about the missiles."

"There are no missiles," Danton said.

"Damnit!" Sheila said, banging her hand loudly on one of the small tables, the action nearly knocking it over. "You're still trying to box me in. The missiles are the story down there, not the damned—"

"Miss Traynor," Danton said, the smile leaving his face. "These are not debatable points. I've come here today in good faith to try and work out a deal that we all can live with. In a deal, everyone gives a little bit."

"And we really appreciate it," Merck said.

"The way the deal works is very simple," Danton said. "There is perceived a serious breach of . . . working relationship between you and the President. Now, you come forward and ask to be allowed access to a war zone. The President would like to grant you that favor. The President believes in a good relationship between press and public officials. Remember that when Reagan went into Grenada, the press wasn't allowed. Remember that when Bush went into Panama, only pool reporters, chosen by the administration, were allowed access. President Macklin has been gracious enough to extend the unnecessary courtesy of allowing the networks' own reporters access to this story and will be happy to extend that same courtesy to you. All he asks in return is that you follow the simple rules I've laid out, and that you use your airtime to bring harmony not dissension to the fore. This is a time when all Americans must pull together."

"Patriotic talk from the man who engineered the budget recision," she said.

"It's a time to put our partisan differences aside."

"In other words," she said, "make the press the propaganda arm of the administration."

Danton frowned and sat back, sinking into the seat cushions. "You are being purposefully argumentative while I'm trying to help you."

"Help me!" she said. "You come in here and tell me to drop the real story here and pursue your fantasy about making Central America safe for democracy. Explain to me how this can help anybody?"

"Okay," Danton said, sitting up again, looking at the lawyer next to him before speaking. "Tell you what I'll do. I've been authorized to go just a little bit further with you. If you go along with the deal here, I will promise you exclusives, at least one photo op a day that nobody else is getting. Best access, what do you say?"

Sheila stared fire at him. "You son of a b—"

"Great!" Merck yelled, cutting her off. "You are a jewel, Rob, I really mean that. You can depend on us. This is going to come out great!"

"Don!" Sheila said, the man turning smoldering eyes to her.

He kept the smile on his face, though, and said through clenched teeth, "Let me have a couple of minutes with Sheila on this, okay?"

Danton looked at his watch. "A couple of minutes," he repeated, his eyes drifting from Merck to Traynor and back again.

Merck stood, taking Sheila, hard, by the elbow and directing her away from the pit and into a small forest of rubber plants, complete with a babbling brook and tiny waterfall where a replica of the White Rock girl leaned out over a rock, watching water gushing from it to tumble to the pool below.

"Why are you letting him push you around?" she asked him as soon as they got there.

"You just shut up for a minute and listen to me," he said. "I'm telling you, Danton is about five minutes away from tearing your career into little pieces and tossing it out the window."

"What do you mean?"

"What good are you if they take away your White House credentials and bar you from overseas assignments? What happens if the government decides to sue us over your story, and tie us up in court for years? We can weather these things, but do we want to?"

"What about the story, Don?" she said. "Remember, this is the biggest thing since Watergate. What happened to our search for the truth?"

The man looked at her as if he were deciding on the best way to tell his teenage daughter about sex. "Sure . . . we search for the truth, that's right. But this deal, this Central American deal, that's something else. We're rolling on this now. Look at all we've already sunk into advertising. They promised us visuals, the best visuals—"

"But, Don," she interrupted. "I was going down there to solidify the missile story."

He made a tossaway gesture. "So, life is compromise. We give a little something away to get a little something."

"I was looking for the truth," she said, exasperated.

"Damnit, Sheila," he said, taking her hard by the shoulders. "Don't you get it? Television's not about truth— it's entertainment; it's good visuals—but it's not truth. The administration controls our access in war zones and they control our editorial output and that's all there is to it. We've got an opportunity here to get a leg up on everybody else, and by God, I'm going to take it."

She pulled out of his grasp. "What happened to yesterday's enthusiasm?" she asked, turning from him.

"Today's a new day," he said. "It was you who talked me into this little adventure to begin with. Well, okay. Now we're stuck with it, and if you value your job here you'll go along like a good little girl. The game has been fine up until now, but it's changing and we need to change with it." He took her by the shoulder again, this time gently, and turned her to face him. "Come on, Sheila," he said softly. "We're putting you right up there in the catbird seat. Play the game. You'll come out on top and we'll have smoothed over things with the administration so that you can stay on top."

She looked at him, realizing that there was no way she could explain how she felt. Don Merck was a man to whom truth meant ratings and to whom integrity was a brand-new Mercedes with a CD player and tinted windows. She wanted to fight him, to force him to understand how badly she wanted to do it right just once in her life, but she didn't know how. She lowered her head and said, "Okay, Don. You've got a deal."

"I knew it!" he said happily, grabbing her up in a big bear hug and spinning her around. "I knew you wouldn't let your old uncle Don down. The sky's the limit from here on."

He set her back on the ground and took her hand. "Let's go give them the good news," he said.

"No," she said, pulling her hand away, then smiling weakly up at him. "I—I want to start getting things together. You go on . . . I'll just see you later."

"You're the boss," he said, beaming. "And try to get some sleep. It won't do for our top newsman to have puffy eyes."

She nodded and walked across the long stretch of mauve carpet to the door, the voices behind her raised in laughter at some joke she never heard.

Wars were busy news times. Sheila walked out into halls filled with excited people, all hurrying toward destinations that undoubtedly seemed important to them. She watched them flow all around her, but she herself felt no connection.

It had all been a lie. The talk of the Emmy, her incredible rise to the top of the heap, all a game that had been comfortable until the rules had changed. Yesterday, she'd been designated martyr to the cause of the free press. Today, she was NCC's love gift to Jefferson Macklin to show that they really hadn't meant it. She should have realized it, of course. Had the integrity of the news business meant anything, Don Merck would have never been lured away from NCC's Entertainment Division to head up News and she would've never been hired to begin with.

She wandered through the maze of executive offices and ended up in production, having no idea of where she was going until she found herself standing before Joan Silver's partway open door.

"Come in or move on," came the throaty voice within. "I feel like Big Brother's watching."

Sheila moved uncertainly into the clutter of an office so small it wouldn't even hold Merck's desk. Books were jammed everywhere as well as full ashtrays and half-drunk cups of coffee with filter tips floating in them. Joan Silver sat at a small steel desk, her computer typer on a stand beside it, ubiquitous cigarette in her hand. The room was full of smoke. The woman stared curiously up at her, a pencil stuck behind her ear, her hair ruffled on the pencil side, sticking out.

"May I . . . talk to you for a few moments," Sheila asked.

"Slumming?" Silver answered. "Or did you just come to gloat?"

"I have nothing to gloat about. I think I've opened my eyes for the first time and don't like what I see."

Silver frowned hard, her lips tight. "Look," she said. "There's no love lost between us, lady. If you've got something to say, say it, or move along. You're technically my boss, so I can't throw you out."

"You hate me that much?"

"It's not you, Sheila. It's what you stand for, what you've done to what was once a noble profession."

Traynor stood and took it, feeling like she deserved every bit of the invective. "I never meant for it to be that way. I—I'm sorry. I guess I . . . oh, hell." She turned and started from the room.

"Wait," Silver said, concern softening her eyes somewhat. She indicated a folding chair containing a stack of old *Newsweek* magazines. "Move the stuff and sit down. Go ahead, tell me your worst."

Sheila picked up the stack of magazines and set them atop a stack of *New York Times* on the floor beneath a poster of H. L. Mencken with a bull's-eye painted on his forehead. She sat. "I hope I'm not interrupting anything, I . . ."

Silver smiled and shook it off. "Nothing important, believe me. I was working on my novel."

"You?" Sheila asked. "A novel?"

"Don't be so surprised," the woman said, reaching for her whirring ashtray on the outer perimeter of a garbage-strewn desk. "Every newswriter in the country has a partial novel hiding somewhere in the computer belly of the corporation that feeds him. It's the only thing that print and visual people actually agree on. It's our attempt at controlling the thing that controls us."

The woman turned on the ashtray to a low hum and moved her cigarette hand closer to it.

"Don't do that on my account," Sheila said, Silver narrowing her eyes and cocking her head. "Really. It doesn't actually bother me."

The woman shrugged gently. "Okay," she said, sticking the ashtray back out on the edge of the desk and flicking her cigarette ashes into a half cup of coffee set on the cluttered bookshelf behind her.

"So how is it?" Traynor asked.

"What?"

"The book . . . how is it coming?"

"Oh, terrible," Silver said. "Like all old newspapermen, I get six inches of copy and run out of things to say. Yep. Twelve hundred words is about it for me before I start looking for the next story. What about you . . . what's your story?"

Traynor laughed without humor. "I guess I just found out how things really work around here," she said. "I wanted to go over to Honduras to track down the story of the missiles, and Merck cuts a deal instead that'll have me down there kissing Macklin's ass."

"That bothered you?" the woman replied, taking a puff of the cigarette.

Traynor stiffened. "Is your opinion of me *that* low?" she asked.

Silver shrugged. "Everybody has to sell themselves off a piece at a time to work here. Over the years you try to maintain, you try to hold on to your dreams . . . but the numbers wear you down. The ratings decide your news for you. Without the ratings you die, and so rather than die, you give up your self-respect. Welcome to newsman's hell."

"Merck says that TV news is just entertainment."

Joan Silver trembled at that, shivered as if a cold hand had passed through her. "Lord help us," she said. "I don't want to believe that, but how far wrong could he be? It didn't start out that way, but I think that what happens now is that we try to read the national mood, then feed it. The better we feed it, the more we are rewarded with ratings. The better the ratings, the better, obviously, the quality of news we report. Right?"

The woman took a drag on the cigarette and coughed it out.

"I'm sorry about the other day," Sheila said. "I wouldn't have wanted you kicked off the project. I don't know. I guess I feel that you don't like me very much."

Silver looked apologetic. "Don't mind me," she said. "People accuse people of what they themselves are guilty. I looked at you as part of the 'other side,' whatever that is. Hell, if I wasn't part of the other side, I'd be sitting at home writing my lousy novel instead of on NCC's ticket."

"What am I going to do?" Traynor asked, voice shaky.

Silver stood, pointing. "Close the door," she said, Sheila complying.

When she'd returned to her seat, Silver told her, "A wise person once said that art is born of restraint and dies of freedom. Take that to heart. You want to do your story? Okay, find a way to do your story. Take all their constraint and all their censorship and find a way to get around it—subtlety, counterpoint, stealth—you can handle these people."

"Because I'm looking for the truth," Traynor said.

"And it will resonate through, loud and clear, every time. It's where the phrase 'the ring of truth' came from."

"What about Merck?"

Silver laughed and clapped her hands. "Fuck that motherfucker," she said. "He's too walled in to hurt you. You just do the best job that you can do under the circumstances and hold your head up. You want to be a real newsman? Here's your chance to act like one."

The ring of truth. Sheila Traynor knew it when she heard it.

Fourth Street, East Washington 10:23 A.M.

Having a police car provided infinite advantages. Merchant was able to listen to the scanner to make sure no one was closing in on him. He had a siren to help him get through tight intersections. There was even a riot gun hanging under the dash to replace the .45 that he'd left in the house when they'd fled to the shelter. He'd never stored guns in the shelter, determined that should nuclear war ever come to pass, he wouldn't spend his last days on earth fighting his neighbors to keep them out.

Twenty minutes ago they'd tried contacting him on the car radio, telling him to give himself up and that his wife wanted to speak with him. He hadn't responded, knowing that all they really wanted to find out was if he'd dumped the black and white or not.

Patterson sat sullenly beside him, her lips a tight slash. She was angry with him for "wasting time" searching out Tillotson when what they really needed to be doing was working on BJ. He'd tried to explain to her that the years had bonded him and Gene in ways that transcended anything BJ could come up with, but she didn't believe him.

"There it is," he said, pulling into the parking lot of a run-down motel called the Red Slipper that looked like it might have been quite a place in 1955. He drove slowly through the lot, searching for something familiar.

"Will this be the last shot?" she asked, looking at her watch. "You really are running out of time."

"Look," Merchant answered, coasting past the parked cars, checking out each one, hoping for a sign. "He's going to be in the worst shit hole he can find. Whenever Gene says he's 'gone fishing,' it means he's holed up in one of these places. I've fished him out of enough of them. The only problem right now is the car. Last time I spoke with

Gene, he hadn't been able to get off his bl . . . my God, there it is."

They were sitting behind a row of parked cars, Merchant staring angrily at the blue Lincoln with the government tag. "Shit, he had his car all the time."

"So what?"

"It means that the last few times I saw him, he wasn't traveling alone because he wanted backup."

"That's friendship for you," Mel said. "Now what?"

"Now I confront him."

"How do you know what room he's in?"

"Easy," he said, pulling the cruiser into an empty slot and pulling the riot gun off the rack. "Get down," he said while rolling down the window.

"What the fuck?" she said, and he pulled the trigger on the shotgun, firing through the window into the air.

He shoved her head down, hunkering down himself as doors all along the two-story structure opened and people peered into the parking lot. Tillotson's head came out of number twenty-three just long enough to see nothing happening, then quickly closed the door again.

"Okay," he said. "I know where he is."

"Love your subtle approach," Mel replied, and he thought he detected a bit of relaxation on her face, like maybe she wasn't so unhappy with her choice of partner after all.

"Stay here," he said, replacing the gun and climbing out of the car. "Keep it running. If something should happen to me, get the hell out of here. Get out of D.C. Hide."

She leaned toward him, Merchant bending back into the car for a lingering kiss.

"Be careful," she said. "I need your ass in one piece."

"I'd kind of like to hold on to it myself," he replied and straightened, closing the car door.

He walked toward number twenty-three. The parking lot had been scraped and was now hard-packed and slippery. He took mincing steps until he reached the orange door. He had no idea of what he was going to say to Gene, or how he was even going to react to him, but none of that mattered now. He had to look the man dead in the face. He had to ask him why.

He knocked lightly on the door to no response. He

knocked again. "Come on, Gene," he said. "It's me, Charlie. You might as well open it up. I know you're here."

There was ten seconds of silence, and just as Merchant had raised his hand to knock again, the door cracked open an inch.

"Come in," came Tillotson's shaky voice.

Merchant started through the door, a hand grabbing him and throwing him against the wall, hard. "Don't move, Charlie," Tillotson said as he pressed the barrel of a Glock-17 tight under his chin. "I'll kill you if I have to."

"I'm not going to do anything, Gene," Merchant said, leaning with his palms against the wall. Tillotson kicked his feet out, then quickly searched him to no avail.

"Happy?" Merchant asked, turning to face the man. "I'd never come after you with a gun."

Tillotson was dressed in slacks and a knit shirt and no shoes. His hair was a mess, his eyes red and bleary as he held the Glock stiff-armed out in front of him, directing Merchant to an easy chair that had been pulled up near the old-style mahogany desk.

Merchant sat, watching Tillotson's eyes. He could see the man wanted no part of what he was doing. The general took the desk chair, pulling it out to face Merchant at a distance of several feet. He also sat, seeming to relax somewhat, but keeping the gun trained on his best friend just the same.

"Why did you have to come look for me?" he asked, anguished, and Merchant could smell the alcohol on his breath even from that distance.

"You've accused me of high treason," Merchant replied easily. "What the hell did you think I'd do?"

"I had to, Charlie," the man said, his voice slurred, as Merchant saw a half-empty Jack Daniel's bottle on the desk, its already dead brother in the trash can. "You were close, trying to expose the whole operation. I couldn't allow you to do that."

"What operation is that?" Merchant asked.

"Central America," Tillotson said. "You know what I'm talking about. For God's sake, we're back on track, ready to take care of some Commies over there and remind people that the military is the only thing keeping us free. I couldn't allow you to stop that. BJ said that we could work you out of it later, but that we had to stop you now."

"BJ said," Merchant repeated sadly. "How did you get tied up with that son of a bitch?"

"He's a good guy, Charlie," Tillotson said, switching the gun to his right hand so that he could pick up the half-full bottle with his left. He took a long drink. "He's a patriot. While everybody else is trying to dismantle the military as fast as they can, BJ's the only one willing to stand up for it. He's a great American. The only man who understands."

"Was it Martha's illness that brought you together?" he asked, beginning to get a handle on BJ's methods.

"The government's wonderful," Tillotson said, "to a point. When the Army doctors said there was nothing else we could do for her, I started looking around at other treatments. I . . . just couldn't let her die without trying. What would you have done?"

Merchant shook his head. He had no answer. The man didn't really seem to want one. He continued: "We went to Mexico for treatments illegal in the U.S. We went to Europe . . . BJ covered it all and never asked for anything in return, almost a half million in debts, he covered."

Merchant felt shame. While he'd been busy trying to shut Gene's pain out of his life, BJ had been using that pain to gain a convert.

"After Martha died," Tillotson said, "BJ did everything he could to help me pick my life back up."

"Including sending women over," Merchant said.

"I'm over twenty-one," Gene replied, eyes flashing. "BJ's women are like goddesses. Show me a man who can turn one of them down and I'll show you a faggot."

Merchant thought about the woman waiting for him in the car right now. "You worked with this deal from the first, didn't you?" he asked, light finally dawning when he understood exactly how much of a schemer Ben James really was.

"What do you mean?"

Merchant pointed. "You," he said. "You're the source of the leaks about the missiles."

Tillotson shrugged. "We were getting ready to vote our military right down the toilet," he said. "BJ and I spoke about it a lot and finally put the plan together to try and save the country. At first I dug through our old files and came up with some usable film and photos from the old Cuban missile crisis days, and covert film of other tropical installations. As it went along, BJ began providing me with film."

"Where does the woman—Sheila Traynor—fit into all this."

"She was BJ's idea. Somebody new who wouldn't think of too many personal questions to ask. She really was perfect. I'd call her, using the name Froggy, and she'd dutifully take down everything I'd say. . . ."

"Well, you are head of the DIA," Merchant said, "a top government agency. Anybody would believe the things you say."

Tillotson smiled. "Well, she did. And now we've got American troops defending democracy down on the Caribbean border. With any luck, by tomorrow night, Caribbea herself will be free of the fucking Commie Companeros and the American people will once again realize the value of a strong, prepared military."

"While me and my family rot in jail," Merchant said.

"BJ's a whiz. He'd have thought of a way to get you out. But even if he hadn't, Charlie, the price would still be worth it. You're military . . . expendable in a just cause. And this is the most just."

"No," Merchant said simply. "It's not a just cause and you should be ashamed of yourself for saying it is. Regardless of your feelings about the military, it's the people of this country who run it, not you . . . and certainly not a maniac like Ben James."

"No," Tillotson said loudly. "You're wrong. BJ is good. We're doing the right thing here, the only thing."

"Good? For God's sake, he's a murderer. He almost killed you when he blew up the house on Dumbarton. Shut up, Gene, and listen to me. Somewhere in that sotted brain of yours you must realize that truth is something that exists outside of yourself. You've trashed the entire system. You have put yourself above the country you've sworn to defend."

Tillotson stiffened, his lips trembling. "You have no right to accuse me of things like this."

Merchant looked hard at him, tried to lock him in to

something besides the gospel according to Ben James. "This madness must be stopped now. You've got to go to the attorney general or the President and tell them what you've done. We've got to stop whatever has been set in motion before it's too late."

"I was hoping you'd understand," Tillotson said sadly, tilting the bottle to his mouth again. He drank. "This is bigger than you or me. We fucked it up at Chongchon, but not this time."

"Chongchon was forty years ago, Gene. We've all paid our dues for that. Not you or anybody else is going to bog me down in Chongchon again. I let it eat me alive for forty years, but no more. We made a mistake, that's all. Everybody makes mistakes." Merchant felt a great and terrible burden lifting from his shoulders. For the first time in his life he felt free.

"What are you going to do, Gene, shoot me?"

Tillotson just stared at him, his eyes lost. There was little that anyone could say to him at this point. He'd bought a program to justify his actions and wasn't about to accept that he could be so horribly, terribly wrong.

"Think about it, Gene," Merchant said. "Ask yourself what he's really up to. You saw the reports. BJ conspired to shoot down that 130. Ask yourself what he's going to do with two nukes."

"BJ doesn't have the nukes," Tillotson said, his voice lowering, his speech more scattered. "That's all just a coincidence. The missiles were just a trick to get troops down there so they'd fight, that's all."

"BJ owned the plane. The man shot down was one of his people."

"Coincidence. BJ owns a lot of things. Forget about it. Everything's going to work out all right."

"My wife's sitting in a jail cell because of you," Merchant said. "My good name has been trashed and dragged through the mud, just like Jack's. Ask me to forget that." A wild thought struck Merchant. "You told me about Jack's first wife. Did you ever tell BJ about her?"

"Well . . . BJ was looking around to support a presidential candidate and asked me some questions about Jack's past, you know, to see if there was anything that would keep him from being elected. I just—"

"Don't you see," Merchant interrupted. "BJ went out and found a girl for Jack who was just like his dead wife. God, she even ended up the same."

"You're reading into this," Tillotson said loudly, his armor cracking slightly. "Just making things up. BJ's a good man . . . a friend."

"Like me? Like Jack?"

"Where were you when I needed you?"

Merchant stared at him for a long moment. At his weakest, Gene Tillotson had found another star to hitch his wagon to, something else to believe in when his own life got too painful. Mel was right. BJ could be all things to all men. BJ's vision was the American reality of thirty years ago, before the world changed. It was comfortable—especially to an old soldier.

But it was dangerous now.

Merchant stood, Tillotson stiffening, wagging the gun at him. "So I ask you again," Merchant said, not moving. "Do you shoot me?"

"Charlie," the man said, passion choking his voice. "Listen to me. Work with me. When this is all over, everything will be fine."

"How many people have to die in Central America for Ben James before everything's all right again?" Merchant asked.

Tillotson just shook his head, tightening his lips, his eyes were darting, the mental equivalent of putting his fingers in his ears so as not to hear. Merchant was really wasting his time. He was looking at a stranger.

"Please, Charlie," he said softly. "Please."

"I'm sorry for you, I really am," Merchant said, shaking his head. "But I'm not going to make it easy for you." He moved to the telephone. "The first thing I'm going to do is call the FBI and get them here with us. Then we'll take our chances—together—with the truth. If you're going to shoot me, you'd better do it now."

Merchant picked up the receiver to the motel's grating dial tone.

"I can't shoot you," Tillotson said, Merchant turning to him. "I knew that when you walked in the door."

Merchant put down the phone. "Come with me to the

FBI," he said. "We'll go together. We'll just tell the truth. It won't hurt anybody."

"I can't do that, either," Tillotson said, standing, bringing himself up to his full height. "It would ruin everything. I told BJ that you wouldn't tumble, that you were too goddamned hardheaded to come with us."

"And what did BJ say?" Merchant asked.

"He said I should . . . buy time," Tillotson said, and Merchant's mouth went dry. He was seeing a kind of determination blooming in Gene's eyes that hadn't been there before, a sublime kind of insanity. Merchant knew what the man had come here to do. It was the act that a true soldier would equate with true sacrifice.

"Don't do it, Gene," Merchant said, taking a step toward him, Tillotson stepping back a pace and sticking the barrel of the Glock into his mouth. Anger tore through him as he envisioned BJ talking Gene into the grand sacrifice for the good of the cause, a cause he'd invented to make a few bucks.

Merchant took another step, Tillotson cocking the gun.

The two men froze in position for several seconds, both of them realizing the actions in the room had walked as far to the end of the road as they could. Push had come to shove.

"Gene," Charlie said sadly, his voice one of friendships lost, emotions withered, youth spent and wasted.

Tillotson pulled the trigger.

Gene's jaws clamped down on the barrel as he fired, the cavern of his mouth deadening the Glock's single report, barely any sound coming out. The man fell backward over his chair, going straight down, the gun popping out when he hit the carpeted floor, eyes darting, no wound visible at all. A second of hope flashed through Merchant as Gene jumped back to his feet. Then he saw the mess of skull and meat and blood oozing on the carpet where he'd fallen.

Merchant looked up. Gene, eyes now wild, tried to walk toward him, arms outstretched. His hands went to his throat as he threw up, an incredible amount of blood gushing like a fountain out of his mouth. The shot must have ricocheted off bone to take out his jugular. For several horrible seconds he stood gagging out his lifeblood before falling to his knees, then forward on his chest.

Merchant ran, bending to him, his pants from the knees down soaked immediately in blood. Tillotson's legs kicked wildly, quickly, for several seconds before they stopped and he lay still. Merchant began to roll him over, then stopped himself. Gene was dead. There could be no doubt. Did he really want to stare it in the face? Did he want to have to answer for it?

He stood, backing away. He bumped into his chair, stopping to stare down at it. Merchant took a handkerchief out of his pocket and leaned down, wiping at the chair arms, clearing off fingerprints. Then, using the handkerchief over his hand, he dragged the easy chair back to its former position.

Had he touched anything else? No. He'd come in. He'd sat down. The wall. He'd been thrown against the wall. They probably wouldn't think to dust the walls, but they might. He used the handkerchief to go over the place where he'd been frisked.

He had no idea of what to do now, no idea of where to turn. His mind was spinning, wanting to shut itself down over the horror of Gene's suicide and the desperate situation that he was left with.

He scanned the room. Gene's car keys lay on the low-slung dresser—a way out of the police car. He grabbed the keys, having to step over the body to get to them. He didn't look at it, couldn't. Nothing else struck him so he turned and hurried to the door, vaulting the body a second time. He used the handkerchief to open the door, then looked carefully both ways before hanging out the DO NOT DISTURB sign and walked quickly across the parking lot, thankful that the icy ground kept him from running and making a spectacle of himself.

Melanie Patterson could tell something was wrong the moment Merchant walked out of room twenty-three and headed across the lot. His gait was professionally unhurried, his head held too erect. His pants legs, from the knees down, were wet. He climbed in beside her, in the cruiser's driver's seat, and stared straight out the windshield, at a concrete wall totally covered with gang graffiti.

"Gene's dead," he said, taking a long, slow breath.

"You didn't . . ."

"No. He killed himself. We've got to get out of here."

"We'll go to the room I got last night."

He wouldn't look at her. He kept staring straight ahead. He held up a ring of keys. "I've got his car keys. You drive it. I want to move this one down the street."

She climbed out of the cruiser and took the Lincoln, following Charlie as he drove a couple of erratic blocks and parked half on a sidewalk. His face was pale, drained of emotion, when he climbed out of the black and white. He carried the police riot gun with him when he got into the Lincoln's passenger seat.

He looked at her with defeated eyes. "Drive," he said.

She took them farther east, then north, getting on the beltway heading toward Baltimore. One lane was open, traffic moving slowly. He was silent—thinking or brooding—she didn't know which. Occasionally she'd turn to him. He sat, head held high, whatever pain that was tearing him apart locked inward. He'd taken BJ's best shots and was still on his feet, still moving. She'd never known anyone quite like Charlie Merchant, on the surface simple and direct, inside a seething ocean of conflicting thoughts and emotions. Yet he remained solid. Whatever faith drove him—truth, duty, or patriotism—was a sustaining faith. He'd lost everything that had meant anything to him, and his courage in the face of it was making her shake.

She reached out and put a hand on his leg. He covered it with his larger, callused hand, both of them taking sustenance from the simple contact, for truth to tell, what was coming next would be horrible for both of them. For Charles Merchant still had one lesson to learn about BJ, and only she could teach him. God help her, it was going to be the hardest thing she'd ever done.

Halfway to Baltimore, she pulled off the ramp and took the access road for half a mile. The motel, the Columbia Inn, was a small, no-frills, twenty-unit place tucked just off the beltway, where, presumably, secretaries and bosses could stop for little extracurriculars on the way home. The ultimate face time.

She pulled up to unit nine, on the side not facing the highway, and turned off the motor. "We're there," she said, and he looked up, taking the place in with a sweep of his eyes. Apparently satisfied, he held the riot gun close to his side and climbed out.

They walked silently to the door, Mel using her key, ushering him into a thirty-six-dollar-a-night paradise of particle board and sheetrock. Theft of fixtures and furniture was a bad problem with most motels, but not this one. Nobody would steal this furniture. She closed, deadbolted, and chained the door, then turned to Merchant, who had stretched out on the bed with an arm flung across his forehead. "Hell of a day," he said.

She looked at her watch. "It's after noon," she said. "We're running out of time."

He laughed and sat up on the bed, rubbing his eyes. "We're not only running out of time, we're running out of options."

She sat beside him. "You're a clever guy," she said. "You'll come up with something."

"You're the only one who seems to think so," he replied, putting an arm around her. She smiled, laying her head on his shoulder.

"I'm sorry about Tillotson. He's been on the edge ever since his wife died."

Merchant just nodded, then sat silently for a long minute. Finally, he said, "I'll tell you the truth, Mel. I'm not sure where to go from here. Every possible angle has been blocked off. I'm a fugitive. My family and friends are either dead or in jail. I'm flat out of answers."

"No, you're not," she said. "You're flat out of old answers, legal answers."

He took his hand off her shoulder and turned her a bit to face him. "What are you saying?"

She looked him full in the eyes, so deep, so caring. She had to look away. "I'm saying that it's time you got creative."

He tightened his lips, but his expression never changed. "You mean, walk over the line," he said.

She nodded. "Into BJ's territory. Somewhere inside you've always known that it would come to this. You've got to take him on his home ground."

"But his home ground is smoke and mirrors," Merchant said, "media hype and glad-handing. How am I supposed to deal with something like that?"

She smiled, quoting BJ. "Think big," she said. "Like he does."

Confusion filled his face and he looked at her with exasperation. "But I'm not that kind of man."

She had the answer in a word. "Change."

He hugged her close and was shaking his head as he pulled away. "To the world right now I'm either a fool or a traitor," he said. "Yet you can sit here and still believe in me."

"You haven't begun to tap your greatness," she said. "You're still trying to free yourself. Do it now. Show BJ what creative thought really is."

"You really think we've still got a chance?"

"I'm convinced of it. I have faith in you."

"But . . . why?"

The time had arrived and she knew it. Sometimes clarity of vision could be the greatest curse visited upon mankind. "Why do you think?" she said softly, taking his face in her hands and kissing him gently, lovingly, on the lips.

"Oh, my," he breathed quietly, and she could still feel the tension vibrating his whole body.

Their faces still close together, she whispered, "You think I spend my life throwing myself shamelessly at other men the way I do you? For a smart guy, you're sure dumb."

His eyes narrowed, his superego fighting for control "Mel, I . . ."

"Shut up," she said. "Come on, old man, even your wife has found herself a little extra on the side."

That seemed to do the trick. His eyes clearing of guilt immediately, Charlie grabbed her to him hard, all his frustration and his pain seeking release.

They tore at each other's clothes, throwing them everywhere, their mouths meeting hot and wet, tongues doing battle, as their hands explored each other's secret places. Mel gave herself over to it, her own passion long simmering. She'd wanted this man from the moment she'd laid eyes on him at BJ's party. She'd wanted his goodness, his humanity; not to take, but to share. To make herself feel clean again. She'd never loved anything in her entire life except for herself, but she loved this man. For this man she could give without taking, sacrifice without victory.

He entered her, their genitals hot, their emotions hotter. They were both nearly out of control with dammed up passion and frustration. Fear gave it an edge. Violent emotions increased the ardor. It wouldn't last long.

She rolled on top of him, pounding hard, their eyes meeting, locking. She heard screaming and realized that it was her own voice. Then he was screaming, too.

He came up off the bed, still holding her to him as his large hands grabbed her ass tight, locking them together as they collapsed in a sobbing heap on the bed, Mel surprised at how ragged her breath had become.

He tried to pull out of her, but she wouldn't let him, holding him to her, selfishly wanting just another minute of peace before the end. She drifted for a time, sailing over open seas, the breath of his loving whispers the wind in her sails. And for just a few minutes she lived the fantasy, feeling the fullness of real love and commitment and selfless giving.

And then, like the passage of the daylight, it was gone.

He rolled off her and sat up, his legs hanging over the edge of the bed. "God, Mel," he said. "I never knew it could be like that." He turned, leaning down to kiss her lips, her still-tender nipples. "You're a woman and a half."

"You're not so bad yourself, General," she said, smiling. She sat up and pulled the sheets up to her chin while she watched him dress, working hard to detach him from her mind and heart.

"You know," he said, "after this is all over, maybe we can get away, you and I, really far away. Forget everything."

"Whoa," she said. "Hold the phone there. While you're busy making plans, you might think about making them for yourself."

He turned to her, his eyes wary. "But, I thought that we . . . that I . . ."

"Look," she said. "You were down and needed someone. A little charity fuck is right up my alley, but don't go putting my name in the will."

"Charity fuck?" he said, hoarsely, his heart dying. "You mean, this didn't . . . mean anything to you."

"Sure it did," she said. "It was your last big lesson, hotshot." She pulled down the sheet and sat on the edge of the bed facing away from him so he wouldn't see her tears. "Had you going, didn't I? Mr. High and Mighty took the tumble with the call girl, right?"

"No," he said. "I can't believe . . . you were so . . . no. It was real!"

She forced a laugh. "Glad you bought in, because, Charlie, if you think I'm good, BJ is twice as good as me, twice as honest-sounding." She smiled. "Twice as heartless. If you want to be in the game with him, if you want to survive, you've got to take that on to yourself. Just like I did with you, BJ dials people in, scopes them out, finds their weaknesses, then exploits. This is not a polite game."

"No," he said quietly. "It's war."

"Charlie," she suddenly rasped, hand to her mouth, her other hand pointing past him.

He whirled to see two shadows on the curtain of the outside window, long cylinders jutting out from the softer human forms. Weapons!

His head darted to the riot gun on the night table just as a hand quietly tried the knob on the door. He grabbed the gun and dove across the bed, knocking Mel off, driving her to the floor.

He came up on his knees, sweeping out with his gun hand to smash the lamp, plunging them into near darkness.

Immediately, something hit the door, driving it inward, door frame cracking. Mel screamed. The door held. Merchant tensed on the gun, bringing it to firing position. They hit the door again, the frame breaking, the dead bolt holding. Mel screamed again.

Merchant's mind blossomed crystal clarity for the first time in a week. This was the exclamation point on Mel's sentence. This wasn't a drill. This wasn't a board game. It was war, the real thing. And to enter it he had to put his mind and heart in the place of war, a new kind of war waged with dollars and promises. And he finally, totally understood the stakes . . . life or death, right now. The old solider was the dead soldier.

Like Gene.

They hit the door again, door and frame splintering as a large, dark man charged through the space, firing an Uzi on full auto from the hip.

Charlie fought his mind for calm, aiming high even as the man got through the door. He pulled the trigger, the explosion deafening in the small room, Mel still screaming from the floor.

His shot took out the punk's face as he twisted wildly, screaming, to the floor, his finger locked on the Uzi's trigger as his arm swept wide, tearing up the front of the room and hitting the second man through the wall.

There were several seconds of clamorous, flashing activity, then dead silence. The second gunman eased around the door frame, his entire chest pumping blood. Charlie froze on the face . . . my God, it was the boy from the tape with Linda.

He fell into the room. "Ooh," he moaned weakly. "Help me. P-please . . . help."

Charlie stood, pumping up the gun again, making his way quickly to the door. People were gingerly moving out of their rooms to look. He turned to Mel, just coming off the floor. "Come on," he said.

"But, Charlie," she said, holding her arms out wide. She was still naked.

"Damnit, come on!" he said. "God knows how many more of them are out there. Grab a sheet and get your ass out here!"

She shut up and did as she was told, charging across the room to come up short at the two men on the floor and the carnage all around.

"M-Mel . . ." the boy was saying from the floor. "H-help me."

She looked up at Charlie. "We can't just . . . just . . ."

"Move your ass!" he said, no light of love shining in his eyes. "We'll call nine-eleven from the car."

They hurried into the Lincoln, the curious beginning to converge on the destroyed room. Charlie understood now completely. He wasn't going to eat the gun the way Tillotson had.

"Where are we going?" she asked as she shivered her way into the car with him.

"Back into the fire," he said, backing out of the snow-clogged lot, moving toward the beltway, toward Washington.

Mosquito Coast 2:17 P.M.

Breedlove sat perfectly still behind the wheel of the jeep, feeling the hot sun on his bare arms where it slanted through the palm tree branches, steam rising slowly from the ground, turning the jungle into a vibrant green, smoky daydream. The sweat rolled down from under his Yankee ball cap, etching small wet paths down his dust-encrusted face. Ten feet away Willie moved quietly through the foglike mist, knee deep in ferns, disappearing wraithlike in the shroud of white, only to emerge again, farther away.

"Here!" he called, examining the bark on one of the trees. "Right where you said it'd be."

Breed grunted, gearing the uncovered jeep to drive into the ferns near Willie. The man was smiling as he pointed to the machete gash in the palm tree, indicating they were going the right way.

"Good," Breedlove said as Willie hefted his bulk into the passenger side, the seat creaking beneath him. His Marine camouflage uniform was soaked through with sweat, Willie's smell like stale beer and urine. There were certainly things about his second in command that he'd not miss.

"I been thinkin'," Willie said as Breedlove geared them up again, heading in the direction of the small clearing where he'd hidden the bulldozer. "It don't make sense to me that Uncle would hire us to blow up so many of his own troops."

"Let me do the thinking, okay," Breedlove said, reaching out to cuff Willie on the shoulder. "I've gotten us this far, haven't I?"

"Yeah," Willie said, a huge fern leaf hitting him in the face as they plowed through a thick stand that had probably grown up since they'd hidden the dozer. "Somethin' else bothers me, too."

"Get it off your chest," Breed said. "Let's air it out."

"Okay," the big man said, turning his sweaty face to stare at Breed. "Did you kill Mulroy this mornin'?"

Breedlove hit the brakes, the jeep skidding on soft mud and unending undergrowth before coming to a stop. He turned angrily to Willie. "Are you accusing me of killing one of my own men?" he said loudly. "What the hell are you saying?"

"I know you two didn't get along, I just—"

"Zip it up, mister," Breed said, staring daggers. "I'd lay down my own life for any one of my people, Mulroy, you . . . anybody. We may not be regular army, but by God, we carry the same nobility, the same tradition. We're here doing a job for democracy. All we can depend upon out here in the bush is each other. If we can't do that, we're just animals, that's all. Just animals."

"Sorry," Willie said. "Guess I just been out here too long."

"Well, my friend, that we can remedy. Tomorrow at this time we'll be well out of it, celebrating a major blow for democracy." He reached out to start them off again, but noticed the shiny green tarp and shut down the engine instead. They had arrived.

"Come on, let's get it going," Breedlove said, the excitement, for the first time, really beginning to juice him when he saw the dozer. He was close now, so close he could taste it.

They jumped out of the jeep, fighting lush undergrowth as they tore the tarp off the bulldozer they'd used to dig their pit at camp. The blistering sun was already losing itself behind a fast-moving cover of black and gray clouds, the afternoon rain rapidly approaching. Breed would prefer getting everything finished before that happened.

The dozer was a medium-sized Cat painted in camouflage. Willie retrieved the two five-gallon gas cans out of the back of the jeep and filled the tank while Breed pulled out the ubiquitous aluminum steamer bag that traveled everywhere with him.

"Let's ride the dozer back together," he said, hoisting himself up to sit on the housing next to the driver's seat. "You drive."

Willie finished dumping the contents of the plastic can into the Cat, tossing the can into the bush. "What about the jeep?" he asked.

"Fuck it," Breed said. "We'll get it later."

Willie shrugged and grunted himself up into the driver's seat, starting the thing up to a cement mixer sound. They were vibrating wildly as they set off, Willie simply retracing the tracks and mowed bush of their three-mile drive out.

The sky had totally clouded over, the wind turning slightly chill. Breed looked up through the canopy of pine and palm branches and vine tangles to the sky above. "A man won't be able to breathe here tomorrow without croaking," he said. "Quite a weird thought."

"But what's the good?" Willie asked.

"The good is this, my friend," Breedlove said, "when those ducks go up tomorrow, the United States is going to have to come in here with everything they've got to take care of the fucking Companeros, and we're going to have to take care of the fucking Cubans at the same fucking time. We're finally going to get this hemisphere free of the damned reds. Think about that, Willie, you and I, single-handedly, taking care of communism in our hemisphere, in our lifetime. We'll lose some troops, sure, but it will be small potatoes compared to the hell we would have had to endure if the reds were allowed to begin to push up through Mexico and start flooding our borders with terrorists and Marxists. Do you understand what I'm saying here?"

"You're sayin' we done good," Willie said, smiling through crooked teeth, then nodding in satisfaction.

"Good?" Breed said, his right hand slowly moving down to idly scratch at his leg just above the top of his jungle boot. "We're heroes, man!"

"Rich heroes." Willie laughed, Breed slowly working his hand around his boot until he was just touching the handle of the K-bar knife he'd hidden there.

"Yes, sir," Breedlove said, his eyes now locked on the side of Willie's head as the man watched the trail before them. "They're going to talk about us like they talk about Lee Christmas and Douglas MacArthur. Willie Jones— legend."

"Yeah, I like that," Willie said. "Legend."

"Yeah," Breed said, jerking the K-bar out of the boot and jamming it into Willie's throat, punching all the way through to the other side.

The man stiffened in the seat, his face bloating up like a frog's as his hands went to his neck, his fingers getting cut up as they tore at the blade. He turned halfway to Breed, his eyes showing numbing fear as his mind comprehended what was happening to him. His mouth opened to a rush of deep red blood.

"You done good, Willie," Breed said, "but I really can't leave any loose ends behind. BJ taught me that."

He braced himself and brought up a foot, shoving hard against Willie, the man, close to death, already so weakened that he tumbled from the Cat without a sound to roll into the bush to die. Breedlove looked at his watch. Right on schedule. He smiled at the tattooed Puck on his arm. *What fools these mortals be.*

The sound brought him into camp, rock and roll music, too loud, his men laughing and yelling and dancing. He felt like Moses coming back from Mt. Sinai to the golden calf.

He drove up to the pit, Jamie, weaving drunkenly, a bottle of local whiskey in his hand. "Our fearless one has returned," he said, trying to hand the bottle up to Breed, who refused, staring hard at him.

"I thought I told you to break camp," he said.

Jamie shrugged, the skinny hippy, Merkle, walking up, stripped to the waist, a pair of shorts on his head. "Hey, Cap'n," he said. "Join the party."

"We'll party tomorrow night," Breedlove said.

"Hey," Jamie said. "Where's Willie?"

"I sent him ahead. Better that we don't all leave at the same time."

"But we had plans," Jamie said. "We were going off together."

"He'll meet you in San Miguel," Breed said.

Jamie frowned deeply. "We wasn't goin' to San Miguel."

"He didn't take the fucking money, did he?" Merkle asked, the man bringing a big, Bob Marley–size joint up to his lips and taking a hit.

Breed held up the bag. "Nope. Got it right here."

"When we gonna share up?" said Cactus, an Arizona Indian, from beside the pit. "Everybody's getting too close."

As if in answer to his question, a chopper passed

overhead several miles distant. It was time. His control was starting to slip away, the questions beginning. "We'll share up right now," he said, climbing down from the dozer, bringing the suitcase with him. "Gather round!"

They came charging up, dirty, smelly. Eight of them left. They looked at the suitcase with wide, greedy eyes that loomed brightly out of dirt-smeared, bearded faces. Hired guns all, their only dignity the surreal animal patriotism that held them together long enough to complete a task. Beyond that, they were worthless. Not in Breed's league at all. No sir, not the same kind of men at all.

He walked up near the entry to the pit, the ten-foot downslope that narrowed into their lead-roofed bunker. Opening the suitcase, he pretended to trip just at the entry, the money emptying out of the suitcase, tumbling in banded wads into the pit.

"Oops!" he said loudly, then, laughing, yelled, "Go for it!"

The men, whooping, jumped into the pit, scrambling for the lucre that had brought them into hell for a week. They were all down there, fighting over it, laughing. Breed leaned over to the Cat, pulling from it Mulroy's M-16 that he'd taken a liking to and set it on full auto.

He fired a two-second burst into the midst of the men in the pit, screams and angry shouts answering him. He grinned, teeth clenched, and fired again. They were locked in the pit, the only way out past him.

"Sorry fellers," he yelled over the screams, blowing Jamie's head off when he came, bloody and cursing, out of the hole. "Know that you died supporting a great and wonderful enterprise."

The screams had quieted to moans. He emptied the rest of the clip into the pit, then dumped the magazine and reloaded, emptying that, also. When he was done, there were no more moans.

He stood for a moment, the only sounds the music still blaring from the small radio set on a pine stump ten feet distant. He walked to the radio, smashing it with the stock of the M-16, then walked back to the pit.

He'd done it. He'd really done it. He'd changed the world and kept BJ's money. It was due north from here, and the small plane he had waiting at Puerto Castillo. From there, Mexico City, his gateway to the entire world.

He walked down the slope, stepping on bodies, and down into the pit, his smile getting larger as he moved. He laughed as it dawned on him that this was really all his. He bent, taking two stacks of bills out of the hands of the dead hippy, rolling the bloody corpse over to remove the stacks from the man's shirt.

He held up two handfuls of money. "Yes!" he yelled, kissing it, rubbing it all over himself, drinking in the smell of it—his reward for being better, smarter. He hurried to the bodies, one after another, stripping the dead, taking not only the cash, but anything else his former mates carried that he wanted. He couldn't move without walking on them.

"'Tis now the very witching time of night,'" he said softly as he continued going through the pockets of his dead fellows, their bodies twisted grotesquely in the horrid masquerade of sudden death. "'When churchyards yawn and hell itself breathes out contagion to this world: now could I drink hot blood, and do such bitter business as the day would quake to look on.'"

He finished quickly, stacking the money back into the suitcase and walking back up the slope into the coming fury of the storm. Wind raked the campsite, camp trash whipping around his feet. Laughing, he twirled a circle, arms outstretched. "Fuck you!" he yelled at the sky. "I kicked your ass, too!"

Still laughing, he climbed back aboard the bulldozer and started it up. Lowering the shovel, he began scooping up earth and trash, dumping it into the pit. Within ten minutes, the pit had been filled, the entire site stripped and jammed into the hole, leaving nothing but a clearing, which would soon enough cover itself over.

The remaining jeep was parked two hundred yards from the clearing. He drove the dozer to the place and climbed out with the suitcase. There was an old cattle trail about five miles from his position that he could pick up to get himself out of the jungle. He'd seen to it that the main action would be far to the south of him, so once he hit open country, he shouldn't have that much trouble. He'd need to change out of his jungle clothes and clean up, but he'd do that after clearing the territory. He had a room rented, full of clothes, in Raiti just for that purpose. From there, he'd take a ferry up to the Patuca River to the Caribbean, where he'd charter a deep-sea fishing boat to take him to Castillo. He might even get in some fishing along the way. By then, it would be way into the night. The nukes would probably go up at some point during the flight from Castillo to Mexico City. Maybe with some luck he'd be able to see the flashes from the air, like two more suns rising to the south. He smiled. Something to look forward to.

After placing the suitcase in the passenger seat of the open jeep, he got in, turning on the waterproof military band radio on the passenger floor to listen for troop movements and strengths. He started up the car, backed away from the dozer, then headed due north by the compass hanging from the rearview mirror.

With each minute he drove, skirting trees and mud holes, he put the morning farther and farther behind, leaving the past to die peacefully in the place where he didn't think about things. Instead, he thought about BJ.

Lightning crackled overhead, the darkening landscape strobing brightly for several seconds, then dimming again, the radio staticking loudly before resuming its chatter. When he got to Mexico City, he was going to call BJ and tell the man thanks for the extra mil. Then he was going to say, fuck you. Then he was going to call the FBI and tell them about BJ and about himself, for if he didn't expose it, nobody would ever know who did it and consequently have no one to thank. No. He'd accomplished something great and he'd be damned if he was going to allow it to go unsung. This was his ticket to history. To immortality.

The pain began in his eyes just as he skirted a long clump of tangled ferns to reach a natural clearing between stands of trees. The rain started then, too, whipping down hard, stinging.

His eyes were burning, both of them. He squinted the jeep into the turn, gunning it through the long, narrow clearing. He brought his left hand up to rub his eyes, realizing it was a mistake when his lips and tongue began burning, too.

His hands were burning, also, as he pulled them away from his face, his vision blurring, the pain like hot needles jammed into his eyes. He saw smoke rising from his hand. The money! That fucking BJ must have done something to it!

Agony tore through his burning eyes as he reached for the suitcase, the jeep lurching out of control to bang into a tree. He felt himself hurled through the air to slam against something hard, the pain in his body nothing compared to the fire that was searing into his brain. The suitcase had gone through the windshield with him, money scattered everywhere, smoldering in the driving rain.

He lay on the ground, burning, caustic acid searing away his face and fingerprints, his vision drowned in the fire of his eyes as he shook with the knowledge that his greatness was ultimately nothing more than food for the local predators.

Even that thought passed. All he wanted was escape, from the all-consuming, never-ending pain. In due course, he was granted his wish.

Arlington 2:23 P.M.

"I'm freezing!" Mel whispered urgently.

"Just hang on a minute," Merchant whispered back as he lay full on the snowdrift, picking up the corner of the sheet that covered them to stare down the street at the police car that sat parked in front of his house, fifty feet distant.

He turned to Mel, both of them squatting, the sheet completely covering them. She was frowning at him, and he couldn't blame her. Naked except for a red and black plaid flannel hunting shirt and rubber boots they'd found in Gene's truck, she was risking exposure of more than one kind. Her handbag was locked securely under her arm, the only thing she had grabbed from the motel.

"Look," he said, turning to her on his haunches. "We're

going to veer left. The cop is facing the other way and probably won't see us. We'll have a minute or two in the open, depending on how fast we move."

"What if there are other cops at the house?" she asked.

"I don't think there will be," he replied. "Not only is it the weekend, but this snow is crippling everything. It's working for us right now. I just don't think they can afford to commit anything else here today, which leaves us temporarily free. Don't think they'll really figure me to come back here. You ready?"

She hung her head, looking quite miserable. "Okay," she said, taking a deep breath. "Here goes nothing."

"Good girl. Now."

Still squatting, they began moving through the drifts toward the house, the snow thigh deep, well over Mel's boots. He could hear her teeth chattering as they moved as fast as they could given the conditions, an occasional "hurrrryyy" making its way through her vibrating lips.

Charlie, going first, tried to clear the snow out of the way for her, but it was futile. Pain crackled through his knees and legs, the deep bending they were doing taking its toll. He was out of shape.

His mind had cleared, though, to sharp focus. Mel's lesson had put everything into perspective for him, and he was thankful to her for that, though her methods put her, in his mind, in the enemy camp. She was antilife, just like BJ. She used people's trust and feelings against them. She'd hurt him more deeply than he'd ever admit. She'd done to him the same thing that BJ had done to Linda— punished her for being human. And wasn't that what he himself had done to Linda when he'd watched the tape? He found himself feeling sorry for the boy who'd died at the motel, and he found himself feeling like an idiot for letting his image of life stand in the way of truly living.

He stopped for a second, the woman bumping into him. Her legs were like ice. He turned slightly and began rubbing her thighs vigorously. They were like sculpted marble in his hands, perfectly formed.

He turned and peeked under the cover again. They were barely ten feet from the side of the house, the police car still sitting in its same spot, carbon monoxide smoke bleeding out of its exhaust.

He turned to her again. "Almost there," he said, the woman tightening her jaw and nodding. "Let's go."

They started out again, Merchant leaving a small peep-hole open in the front of the sheet. They reached the side of the house opposite the garage side within a minute.

"We can stand now," Merchant said as soon as they were out of sight of the police car. Neighbors might still see, but he was beginning to worry seriously about Mel's ability to handle much more cold.

They stood, still wrapped in the sheet, and hurried around the back of the house. The garage was a blackened pile of ash with a cinder-block foundation, his Cadillac still upside down in the neighbor's yard. They made it to the back door. Charlie reaching down behind the geraniums on the left side to get the key he kept hidden there.

He found it and got them inside, Mel shaking like a leaf, her body pale as death. Hypothermia. He grabbed her and threw her over his shoulder to get upstairs, the house a shambles all around him. She was heavy, the trip up wobbly, but he got her to the master bedroom, clothes strewn everywhere by the investigators. He peeled off the rest of her clothes and wrapped her in a blanket.

Then he turned the shower up hot and got her in there, watching closely as life slowly returned under the rush of steam. God, she was beautiful. He felt himself stirring with memories of the motel, but then other hotel memories crowded out the beauty of the moment. The sex had been like nothing he'd ever experienced, but he realized it was because he'd been working at it, too. He'd been giving.

Unknowingly, he'd compartmentalized his entire life into blocks of duty, even sex. He'd forgotten that the spontaneous, the uncontrollable, was for the living part, and that the duty was for the hard parts. Like war.

While she was still in the shower, he searched her purse, taking a small key from her ring and sticking it in his pocket. Then he got her out of the shower and began drying her off, Mel clinging to him the entire time, holding on like a child. He didn't understand the nature of that particular game, so he ignored it, just as he ignored the look of pain on her face when he pulled away from her and told her to take any of Linda's clothes she found on the floor. He changed into dry slacks and socks while she scrounged Linda's things.

"I'm going downstairs," he said as she began dressing. "Come down when you're finished here."

He went down, looking out the front window at the police car. His heart jumped when he saw a second car outside parked just in front of the first, but then the first car pulled away and he realized it was just shift change.

The house was a wreck as he made his way through it to the den. Apparently, the first investigators on the scene had gone through like a tornado, looking for anything obviously incriminating. Upon not finding anything, he opined, they'd decided to back off and wait for the fine-tooth boys from the government to come in and try to make two and two add up to five. The method of search had been to turn every drawer upside down and tear the stuffing out of all the furniture.

As he walked through the shambles, he was surprised at his own reaction. His house had been sacrosanct to him, the focus of his control of life. Seeing it practically destroyed, however, had a lightening effect on him. His control was gone, yet he still existed. It had meant nothing. It was just a messy house, no more, no less.

In the den he found several piles of junk on the floor. Apparently, they had started putting things in meaningful piles: electronic junk in one, official-looking papers in another, weapons in a third; but it had all gone to hell for them when they weren't finding anything special. One thing Charles Merchant could always say: He had absolutely nothing to hide. For whatever else his life was worth, Charlie lived it straight up and proper.

He found his overcoat in a pile of what was apparently suspicious-looking clothes. He put it on, sorely missed since their escape the night before, and snuck out to the shelter, still undiscovered, retrieving Mel's suitcase full of evidence to bring back into the den.

Now that he understood the game and the stakes, he was ready to make a move. This was the logical place for him to start, a planning session with his strengths and weaknesses laid out.

Waterloo had been dumped off the pool table to lie in

pieces on the floor. That was just fine. He'd have done the
same himself, for he had something else to put up there.

He went to the piles of suspicious papers and found his
map boxes. He rifled through the boxes until he came back
out with a graphed map of the world. Unfolding it, he laid
it out flat atop the pool table.

"A little tight," came a voice from the doorway, "but not
too bad."

He looked up to see Mel in jeans and a sweater that
Linda had had for years. Mel's larger breasts accounted for
the tightness, but all in all, she didn't look that much
better in it than his wife had. He wondered how Linda was
doing. He needed to find a way to get in touch with her.

"You're looking good," he told her, motioning her over
to the table. "You had me worried back there for a while."

She walked up and kissed him, but he didn't respond.
"I want to thank you for looking out for me," she said.

He nodded. "Knee jerk," he said, not meaning it to
sound so impersonal.

She turned quickly, walking to the table. "Looks like
the war has changed," she said, staring down at the map of
the world.

"Yeah," he said, "but not the substance of it. Gene told
me once that Napoleon lost at Waterloo because he was an
old soldier, not able to get himself up for one more combat.
I think Gene was describing himself as well as Napoleon.
I thought for a while he was describing me also."

She reached down into the mess of collapsed battlefield
and toy soldiers on the floor, picking out Napoleon
mounted on Desirée. She held it up. "The emperor also
lacked vision," she said.

He started. "That's what you said about BJ."

She nodded. "He had nothing, really, to fight for at
Waterloo," she said. "His day, his world, had already
passed. His military tactics had already redesigned the
way armies fought. Just look at Wellington's reverse slope
technique to counteract Napoleon's artillery. By Waterloo,
that was standard practice with all of France's enemies.
The great republic became a shattered dream when Napoleon realized that taking and governing were two different
things, his own relatives turning against him once he'd
made them heads of state. He wasn't a stupid man. He

undoubtedly had enough sense to see his day had already passed, and enough time to think about it in his previous exile."

Merchant took the piece from her and smiled down at it. "It has occurred to me," he said, "that when Napoleon returned from exile in Elba and had to face his own troops come to stop him, he was really hoping that they'd shoot him down then and get it over with. Instead, they screwed him by pledging their allegiance and becoming his new army." He set the piece down on his map, right on the spot occupied by Washington, D.C. "We'll let BJ be Napoleon for a while."

She reached into the pile again and came up with Wellington, handing it to him. "This will be you," she said. "We'll see how good your reverse slope is."

He set his own piece next to Napoleon's, then looked at the woman. "Get out your documentation," he said. "Let's get as much info as we can."

Mel got into her suitcase and began pulling out the chapbooks and lining them up in a row on the floor beside the table. "I didn't have much time," she said, "but I grabbed every name I could find that was familiar, hoping we'd have something we could use."

"Good enough." He walked to the files, kneeling to read them better. Each small case had a name fixed upon it in gold, stick-on letters. Ken Breedlove, Joann Durbin, Jerry Delany, Jack Braedman, Leonard Hurley, Weston and Mills (together), Charlie Merchant, Linda Merchant. Most of the names had pink pieces of paper taped beside them, with a date written on the paper. He reached out and touched one of the papers.

"Pink slips," Mel said. "If you look at the dates, I believe you'll find that these people died on that day."

"Except for this one," Merchant said, picking up Breedlove's. "It's got tomorrow's date on it, and the word 'sunrise.'"

They shared a long look, Charlie reaching down with shaky hands to pick up Joann Durbin's file. "Do you think . . . ?" he began, opening the file box to find a number of 8mm videotapes within. One had the date "Feb 4" written on it.

"I don't know," Mel replied, pulling an 8mm VCR out of

the suitcase and moving to the television to hook it up. Merchant looked and saw several more files in the suitcase.

"What are these?" he asked, reaching in to pull out June Chan's file.

"Those are mine," she said, a touch hard, and he put down the file as she got the TV turned on.

He picked up the February 4th tape and put it in the playback unit, turning it on. He saw blackness, then brilliant light. The bathroom at Dumbarton!

Joann was standing there, stark naked, staring at the camera that must have been mounted behind the mirror. His insides began shaking. Never having known her alive, he'd related to her perfection from a distance. But here she was, perfect, living, her eyes the match of Mel's. This time it didn't grab him the way it had before, perhaps because perfection was beginning to equal sterility to him.

The woman stared at the camera clinically, examining herself harshly. When she suddenly spoke, staring right through the screen, it made both of them jump.

"Even if you know, right now, what I'm doing," Joann said, looking directly at them, "it's too late to stop me."

Jesus. So much becomes clear. BJ's control was so complete, so all-consuming, that it must have seemed to Joann, just as it must have seemed to Gene, that suicide was the only real escape from it.

On screen, the woman turned away from the camera and spoke through the door to Braedman before turning back and smashing the razor on the sink and drawing the blade down her arms.

"Oh, God," Mel said, turning away from the rush of blood. But Merchant couldn't turn away. He was mesmerized by the tableau, the senseless death he'd been trying so very hard to understand.

The woman began writing on the mirror in her own blood, a message that Charlie would never forget. He watched her weaken, her eyes glaze with loss of blood, as she gradually lost control, slipping from the washstand to collapse on the floor, outside the view of the camera. Her death didn't horrify him this time, and it didn't make him sick. He took in the death, letting it stoke him up with hatred for the enemy. He would not give in to Ben James, and he would not let the man destroy the greatest country in the world.

War. Once he understood the nature of this confrontation, BJ held no more power over him. In war, a man puts everything on the line for the ideal. Charlie Merchant had nothing more to lose. He was a professional soldier on a suicide mission and would do anything it took, anything to achieve victory.

He turned off the tape. Mel had already given him enough, now, to clear Jack's name. He also now had the original (and he hoped only other) tape of Linda's infidelity. They were small, woefully inadequate victories; but they made him feel that at least he was a player. He'd entered the game in a big way.

He walked back to his battle map of the world and stared down at it. "Let's put it together," he said. "Let's make some assumptions." Sorting through the French soldiers at his feet, he fished out a piece, holding it up. "This is General Sault, Napoleon's Chief of Staff. He will be Ken Breedlove, the slippery mercenary. And let's say this whole thing started two weeks ago, in Poblado."

He set the piece on the board, the process of re-creation helping to set his mind to the possibilities. He sat a Hanoverian rifleman next to Breedlove to represent the Caribbean foreign minister who'd been assassinated two weeks previously. "Who shall you be?" he said, smiling at her. He bent to the pile. The second piece he'd ever painted, next to Napoleon, was someone not even involved in the conflict, but whose ghost was always present. He found it quickly in the scattered pile. "Bishop Talleyrand," he said, putting her piece between Napoleon and Wellington in D.C.

"I'm with you," she said, digging into the pile beside him.

When they were finished, the board was clustered with pieces. Charlie squatted, getting his eyes lined up at board level. He stared, silently, for several minutes, occasionally standing and moving around to a different part of the board.

Finally, he said, "I'm going to start with an assumption, but I think it'll fit." He stood, stretching. "Let's say that this scheme, in some form, had been initiated months ago, with the introduction of Delany to Joann, and with the eventual introduction of Breedlove to BJ. It probably had something to do with digging up money for the *libres*. Now, sometime later, some other things begin to happen. First, Braedman begins slipping in the polls. Why? He's been pushing a pro-defense stance in exchange for BJ's support for president, but it has come across as counterproductive. Braedman looks like old guard instead of new blood. BJ and Braedman square off, BJ stuck backing what looks like a loser. A lot of gears begin to mesh into place. BJ lets the relationship between Joann and Delany reach a kind of peak, then he hires the guy to take a plane to Houston and steal, legally, a couple of nukes."

He stopped talking and put up a finger. The figure of Delany, a bright blue Imperial Guardsman on horseback, was sitting on Alabama, the home offices of EquAir. He picked up the piece and moved it to Houston, Texas. "Meanwhile," Merchant said, "Breedlove, on orders, kills the Caribbean foreign minister."

He leaned over the map and knocked the minister over with his index finger. "Dead. And the next time we hear about Breedlove, he's been spotted . . . in the area of the Mosquito Coast." He moved the piece to the northwest corner of Caribbea.

He picked up Delany on horseback, along with two tiny cannons meant to represent the warheads, and moved them, also, to the Mosquito Coast. "Now bear with me," he said, picking up General Sault, Breedlove. "BJ then has Breedlove rendezvous with Delany and kill him, making it look like an accident or a shoot-down or whatever. The missiles are now officially lost at sea. But, actually, Breedlove has them hidden in the jungle."

He knocked over Delany and moved the cannons with Breedlove into the jungle. Then he moved the Sheila Traynor piece, a French rifleman, to Washington, setting it next to Gene Tillotson in the person of Jerome Bonaparte, the emperor's brother. "Gene starts feeding false data to the media via Sheila Traynor, a dumb fuck who doesn't know any better. BJ then tells Joann that he had her one and only love, Delany, killed."

"You think that BJ planned that part, too?" she asked,

Charlie realizing how sharp he was beginning to get now that the civility was gone.

"Sure he did. Somewhere in here it had to occur to him that this thing was too big and had too many people involved in it to stay secret for long. He's been methodically cleaning house of anyone connected with this in any way. He knew Joann's personality. Hell, he handpicked her for Jack. He convinced her that death was her only real option, same as he did with Gene."

He knocked over Joann's piece. "He had Weston and Mills kill Jack, then had them killed. So much for supporting a dog for president." He knocked over all three pieces, Braedman represented by a Prussian prisoner, Weston and Mills—French artillerymen. "He sent Hurley and Bignell to Germany"—he set the two pieces on Frankfurt, Bignell, a French infantryman; Hurley, Count Barclay de Tolly of Russia—"only to kill them." He knocked over both pieces. Jerome Bonaparte stood amid the carnage. Gene, whose sense of personal honor was more important to him than life itself. He knocked the piece over.

He rubbed his hands together. They were sweating. It was all beginning to make sense now, every bit of it falling into place. "Now," he said. "The vagaries of politics and the media begin to take over. These things are predictable. BJ counted on them."

Prussian Field Marshal Blucher and a contingent of his regular troops were standing on Cuba. He picked them up and moved them to Poblado. "The Cubans are on the move, trying to act tough, to fill in the role in Central America that the Russians have been abandoning. We start to act tough, everybody sick of the way we're getting pushed around." He moved to Tegucigalpa, knocking over Mark Jurgenson, Austrian Prince Schwarzenberg, with the Breedlove piece, then moving it back to the coast. "The ambassador's dead, and now we call in the Marines."

General Tucker was represented by Napoleon's Marshal Ney on horseback, his 822nd Airborne, the French cavalry. Merchant grabbed Ney, moving him to Washington, right next to BJ. "Tucker is called to glory by Macklin and Ben James, then he goes out to meet the enemy."

He picked up Tucker and his army and moved it to Honduras, pointing it toward Caribbea. "That brings us to

today," he said, standing back. He looked at the woman.
"What have we got?"

"A lot of dead people," she said, staring in horror at the
board. He looked down. She was right. A lot of board
pieces lay scattered over the world, a lot of death to keep
one secret.

"I see options," he said. "I think I see answers."

"What answers?" she asked, walking up to lean against
the table as he was doing, staring down at the map.

"What does BJ want out of all this?" he asked her.

She shrugged. "Basically, to keep working for the arms
industry. To continue being its sole representative. He
never thinks beyond day-to-day business."

"Okay, look," he said. "I'll show you how he can
accomplish that." He took the cannons from the coast and
put them on the Coco River, then he edged the opposing
armies in that direction.

"The American people have become convinced that the
Soviet Union has put offensive missiles into Caribbea.
What would happen if two nuclear missiles actually did
go off down there?"

She licked dry lips. "We'd blame the Communists," she
said.

"Sure we would. And we'd declare war on Caribbea,
and on Cuba. We'd tie ourselves up in jungles till way into
the twenty-first century. BJ's boys would all get more
business than they could handle."

"Would we go to war over this?" she asked.

"You kidding? By my estimate, we've got over twenty-
five thousand people in there. They've probably got about
the same. Hell, we declared war on Japan after three
thousand were killed at Pearl Harbor."

"This is . . . unbelievable," she said, slumping down
to her elbows.

"You think?" he said loudly. "It's weirder than that,
lady. Knowing BJ, he's got them as far along the river as he
can, using the water for transport and hiding. He'll tie 'em
up in trees to get the maximum scatter, then, if the wind's
right, he can do some *real* damage. Poblado's just two
hundred miles away to the southeast, and Tegucigalpa's
barely a hundred miles to the southwest, and all the major
population centers lie between." He took a long look at

her. "The prevailing wind is always from the northwest. With strong winds, your boss could probably kill over a million people."

With a heavy hand, he knocked over all the pieces in Caribbea. "And it all happens by daybreak tomorrow, according to Breedlove's pink slip."

She straightened, still looking quizzically at the board. "Have we got enough here to stop him?" she asked.

He shook his head. "Nope. No way."

"But you said there were options."

He nodded. "There are two that I can see." He looked at Washington. Five pieces still stood there: Napoleon, Wellington, Talleyrand, the French rifleman that represented Sheila Traynor, and President Macklin in the person of Napoleon's General Vandamme in a high-plumed helmet. He reached out and picked up the French rifleman and General Vandamme, putting the pieces in his pocket.

He looked at her. "I think it's time for us to split up," he said.

"You're not going to tell me the options," she said. "You don't trust me."

"You're out of it now," he said, avoiding her eyes. "You've done your part."

"You don't trust me," she said again.

"It isn't that I don't trust you," he said. "It's that I *can't* trust you, not now. Through this whole thing, BJ has known my every move, my every thought. For once, I've got him wondering. I can't lose that edge now. Having you on the loose in this city makes you a time bomb if you've got information. I have too much respect for BJ's wiles to think he won't catch you."

"And if he catches me," she said, "you figure I'll talk."

Finally he did look at her, staring hard. "If it's to your advantage," he said. "Yes, you'll talk."

"You've learned."

He nodded.

"It's all over with us, isn't it?"

"Was it ever on with us?" he asked.

She just stared sadly at him, biting back whatever she'd wanted to say.

"I just don't know that we're on the same side any-more," he said, looking at his watch. There was no time for this, no time at all. "Look, I'm going to have to go. Stay here if you want. I really don't think they'll come back in force until next week. At that point, you're on your own."

"I can't stick with you?" she said quietly.

"Not where I'm going," he said, moving to the chair to retrieve his heavy coat. He put it on, the woman watching his every move. Picking up the chapbooks on the floor, he emptied the 8mm tapes from them, sticking the tapes in his pocket.

"I don't guess we'll see each other again," she said as he picked up the sheet from the floor that they'd used to sneak in and wrapped it around himself.

"If we do," he said, "it probably won't be as friends. Good-bye, Mel. Thanks for opening my eyes."

With that he opened the door to the arctic air and hurried outside without a backward glance. Had he looked back, he would have seen Melanie Patterson, for the first time in her life, crying over a man.

Red Slipper Motel 4:20 P.M.

Merchant had gotten his first set of burglar's tools in Korea in 1950, back when the spy business was accomplished with legs instead of computers. He hadn't used them in years, but tooling open a door was something never forgotten once learned, like sex, like killing.

He moved slowly across the motel's parking lot, checking the surrounding area to make sure he wasn't being watched. The police car he'd abandoned had already been found, but apparently no one connected it up with the motel in any way, since the place looked as sleepy now as it had four hours ago.

He reached the orange door without seeing anyone, then used the number three pick on the lock, grading up to the number four before getting the door open. When it clicked in his hand, he took a deep breath and entered.

The smell of death was overpowering in the room, the metallic smell of blood enough to make his stomach lurch. Everything was just as he'd left it, including Gene, still lying facedown in a huge still-wet pool that had soaked the blue shag carpet a deep rust color, his chair still tipped over, the plastic Glock-17, encrusted with dried blood, still lying near the body.

He scanned the room, his mind calmer this time, analytical. Gene's uniform was hanging in the closet, his cap on the shelf above. On the small, low dresser where Charlie had gotten the car keys also lay the motel key and Gene's wallet. The wallet was the logical place to start.

He carefully stepped over the body to get to the wallet. He reached into his coat pocket and pulled out the Playtex gloves he'd picked up at a supermarket, putting them on. Only then did he pick up the wallet, opening it, searching.

Everyone with NSC membership would have emergency access, a way to get to the President no matter where you were or what you were doing. The codes would change, probably weekly, necessitating someone like Gene to carry the authorization around with him. He found it in the billfold part of the wallet, a piece of paper fixed with a series of geometrical drawings that Merchant recognized as a simple replacement code.

He removed the code from the wallet, took the motel pen, and played with it for several minutes, his mind intense, all-centered on his task, finally breaking the key letter down and solving it. He picked up the phone and dialed the local number he'd translated, a male voice answering on the first ring with the words "Authorization code please."

Merchant cleared his throat. "Authorization code: 2-Alpha, 3-Ralph, 9-Baker, 1734."

"Condition code?"

"Red."

"Access Level?"

"Access CIC, Priority One."

"Would you repeat please?" the voice said in surprise, as Charlie had just requested the Commander in Chief.

"Access CIC, Priority One," he repeated.

"Hold please."

He waited. This was a tough shot, but worth the try. As Commander in Chief, the President would be in a position to issue immediate orders for retreat if he chose, pulling the troops, at least, out of danger. Convincing him would be something else again.

The voice came back on the line, excited. "Please hold for the President," he said.

"Fine," Merchant said, the tension a physical thing in the room. He looked down at Gene's body. Maybe in death he could help in ways he never could or would when alive.

"This is Macklin," came a familiar voice. "To whom an I speaking?"

"Mr. President," Merchant said. "My name is Charles Merchant, I have—"

"I know that name," he said. "You were supposed to be arrested. Where are you? How did you get this number?"

"It's not important," Merchant said. "We need to talk quickly about a life-and-death matter."

"Mr. Merchant, we are in the midst of an extreme national emergency right now. How can you—"

"Ben James is getting ready to blow up Central America with the two Raytheon Bearcats he stole from you, Mr. President. You've got to stop him."

There was silence on the line for several long seconds. Finally, Macklin said, "Tell me about it."

Merchant outlined the action as far as he knew, using fact and his own assumptions interchangeably, playing it up. Macklin never spoke until he was finished. Then he said, "You've had nearly a whole day of freedom to think up a story, Colonel. Is this the best you can do?"

"Don't try and stonewall me on this, sir. My story makes sense. You know it does. You have to know that those missiles aren't sitting at the bottom of the Caribbean."

There was silence on the line for a moment. Then Macklin said, "What do you propose that I do about it?"

"Pull back the troops, first," Merchant said. "Warn the Caribbeans to do the same."

"Warn the Caribbeans?" Macklin said. "Have you forgotten that they're our enemy?"

"Ben James is the enemy, sir."

"No," Macklin said wearily. "He's just a catalyst. Look, you've seen the polls. The American people want us down there. They want us to avenge Mark's death and bring stability to the region."

"BJ talked them into it!" Merchant said loudly.

"But we don't now have time to talk them out of it."

"So what? You're the President. You can do what you want."

"Let's be frank, Mr. Merchant," Macklin said. "If I were to pull out now, the people in this country would take it as a sign of weakness. Nothing Americans like more than a tough president. My opponents would make political hay while I'd go down in history as the wimp who lost us Central America—"

"But, Mr. President," Merchant said, exasperated. "You're talking attitudes. I'm talking lives here, a lot of lives."

"If you're right," Macklin said, "and I'm saying 'if.' If you're right, the moment I pull out, the plans to blow up the bombs would go out the window. Nothing would happen. Then I'd really look like a fool. Better from my viewpoint to look at you as a fool and take my chances."

"Mr. President, hundreds of thousands of human lives may be hanging in the balance."

"Turn yourself in, Merchant," Macklin said. "Come back to the system."

"And make it easy for you? No. No, sir. Thank you just the same. So, what do you do now?"

Macklin didn't hesitate. "I forget that this phone call ever happened. What about you?"

"I'm going to try and save some lives."

"Well . . . good luck to both of us."

"Go to hell," Merchant said, hanging up on the man.

Macklin might be the Commander in Chief, but he was no soldier. If he were, he'd realize that the first rule in war is knowing who your enemies really are. It was going to get dicey now. He moved to the closet and took down Tillotson's full dress uniform. It took him five minutes to change into it, moving as quickly as he could. At this point, every moment would be precious.

There was a sheet of computer printout paper folded into the inner breast pocket. He pulled it out, not surprised to find that it was the missing sheet from the file on Ben James that Gene had given him. It detailed the unknown years of James's life. He'd been in federal prison in Leavenworth, serving two-to-ten on fourteen counts of mail fraud. God, a common garden-variety felon. This was the man Gene Tillotson had died for, a scam artist who was now running the biggest con of his life. Merchant wadded up the printout and stuffed it back in his pocket.

He moved to the television, hoping to hear about the progress of his manhunt, and to get anything new from Central America. When the set juiced, he was looking at another commercial for that damned woman newscaster. He reached into the clothes he'd just changed out of, pulling Macklin's and Traynor's pieces out of the pocket. He held up the French rifleman. A lot was going to depend on her from this point on. He hoped she wasn't as stupid as she seemed to act.

Going back into the wallet, he pulled out Gene's Visa gold card just to make sure it wasn't expired. He didn't need little hassles at this point. He stared at the card. It was drawn on a bank that he remembered from BJ's list of holdings, a noninterest card. Charlie smiled. He was going to use it to help readjust the reality that BJ had skewed.

He replaced the card, then stuck the wallet in his pocket, bundling his own clothes under his arm. He took the room key this time, not taking off the gloves until he'd gone back to the door.

The room had been cleaned before Merchant had shown up the first time. He figured the body was probably okay until the morning, since this wasn't the kind of establishment that usually turned down your bed at night and put a mint on the pillow.

The French rifleman and General Vandamme were rattling around in his pocket. He took out the figure representing the President, the general looking like a popinjay in his frilly green and purple jacket with the wide epaulets. He glared at it angrily as he walked to the car, then threw it as far as he could.

He climbed in and started the republican blue Lincoln, nosing it toward a shopping center he'd seen in the ride in. As he eased the big car through the slippery, snow-clogged streets, he picked up the car phone and called Cal Daniels's office, a number he'd gotten to know pretty well lately.

"Daniels and Lombard Associates," came the receptionist's practiced voice.

"I need to speak with Cal," Merchant said, hoping to sound familiar. "It's urgent."

"May I say who—"

"Life and death," Merchant interrupted. "Just say that." He could trust Cal, a lawyer's confidential relationship with his client sacrosanct to any attorney.

The woman put him on hold, the lawyer's voice, irritated, coming on within a minute. "Listen," he said. "I don't know who—"

"It's me," Merchant said, turning south onto Maryland Avenue. "We need to meet."

"Oh, my God . . . Charlie," the man said. "What the—"

"No time," Merchant said. "How's Linda?"

"Mad as a hornet with a burning nest," he said. "She can't believe the things they're saying about you."

"You've seen her?"

"Just phone talk," he said. "I'm going over there today. I'm covering Josh and Della now, too."

"Good. Can you meet me in . . ." He looked at his watch. "One hour?"

"Name the place."

"Jefferson Memorial . . . do you have a car phone?"

"Sure."

"Give me the number. When you get to the Memorial, stay in your car."

Merchant listened to the phone number, then repeated it to himself until he'd memorized it. Daniels wanted to talk, but got cut off for the trouble. There just wasn't time anymore.

The shopping center, a long row of similarly styled, upscale red-brick buildings, was located on the edge of an older residential area closer to the center of town. He pulled into the slot in front of an office supply store and killed the engine.

He went inside and made as much fuss as he possibly could buying a typewriter, then paying for it with Gene's Visa, acting drunk and belligerent the entire time so they'd remember the "crazy general."

He went back to the car and started back to the motel, once again on the phone, using New York information as a sounding board until locating Sheila Traynor's work phone. When he got the switchboard, he told the receptionist that "Froggy" was on the line for Sheila Traynor.

She was quickly located, coming on the line breathlessly. "Why didn't you use the private number?"

"I have to see you," he said low.

"I can barely hear you," she replied.

"I have to see you," he said again, softly.

"Where are you?" she asked. "You've never needed to see me before."

"I'm in Washington."

"Well, good luck. My flight for Honduras leaves JFK tonight at eight and I hear that Dulles is shut down with the weather."

He glanced at his watch. He had less than three and a half hours to get to New York, and the airport was shut down. "I'll meet you at the airport . . . hopefully by seven-thirty."

"What's this all about?" she asked, suspicious.

"The story of your lifetime," he answered, hanging up.

He shook his head as he pulled back into the Red Slipper parking lot. Yesterday he wouldn't have spit on the media. Today, they were his last hope. BJ used them. So could he.

He climbed out of the car with the typewriter under his arm, walking gingerly across the lot. Overhead, the skies were beginning to clear somewhat, several patches of blue evident amid the now pale gray sky.

He entered quickly, putting the gloves on again, anxious to get this part of it out of the way. The room and its ambience of death was becoming too familiar to him. Thin-king with the head-set of war, he looked at the body without emotion, then took the typewriter to the desk and cleared a space for it.

He left the receipt out in plain sight, then removed a piece of the onionskin paper that passed as motel stationery from the flimsy desk. He slid the paper into the typewriter and plugged the thing in. The letter he typed was direct and to the point. When he finished, he removed it from the typewriter and signed it with the motel Bic pen, imitating the signature on the driver's license in Gene's wallet.

Just to be on the safe side, he carried the pen and the

box the typewriter came in over to the corpse, using the right hand to touch everything, leaving fingerprints. Then he put the pen on the desk and the cover beside, leaving the note on the desktop.

He stood back, taking it all in with a practiced eye. Hopefully, by tomorrow, the steps he'd taken this afternoon would be important. He wondered if he'd be alive to appreciate it.

With a long breath, he moved to his friend's body and stared down at it. "I'm going to do this, Gene, and you're going to help me. It isn't for me and it isn't for you; it's for the country. I'm just sorry that it has to be this way.

"Wherever you are right now, I hope they keep your glass filled. Good-bye, old chum." With that, he turned from the corpse and put it out of his mind.

He moved to the door, taking off the gloves, wiping the handle inside and out before leaving. It was surprising how well Gene's uniform fit him. Had he not taken early retirement, it would have been his. Now he was going to get the chance to find out if he could handle the job. He looked at his watch. It was already five-fifteen and he still hadn't figured out how he was going to get to New York City in two hours and fifteen minutes.

He drove back into town, taking the snow emergency routes until he got into the heart of the city, from there he made the drive to the Tidal Basin past all of D.C.'s major monuments, setting once more in his head the concrete images of the country he loved so much. While others dedicated themselves to success and achievement, it had always seemed more important to Merchant to work for harmony and freedom, the body politic that Jefferson used to talk about—and not Jefferson Macklin, either. Perhaps that's why he wanted to meet Daniels at the Memorial, to reaffirm his sense of duty before the shrine of the man who had all but invented American democracy.

He pulled off Independence, onto Fifteenth where it circled the basin, passing the bushy skeletons of Washington's famous cherry trees as he made his way around to the entrance to the Memorial.

A long snow-filled drive led up to the Memorial itself. Usually, at any time of the day or night, the drive would be filled with the cars of tourists; but today it was deserted.

He didn't even see the usual FPS guards. He pulled up to where he figured the curb must be that fronted the circular structure of Tennessee marble.

He sat for a minute, vibrating, constantly rechecking his watch. "God, Cal, don't keep lawyer time on me," he whispered, then opened the door to step out into the cold. He had to move around.

Three tiers of steps with intervening terraces led up to the great portico, supported by twelve Ionic columns. A small area had been snow-cleared right up the middle of the steps. He walked up, past the columns and into the portico itself, its center dominated by the heroic statue of Jefferson sculpted by Rudolph Evans.

He stood silently alone in the open chamber, the wind howling through it, a sea of white visible to the horizon in all directions. He'd never been particularly religious, but the feeling of standing within this tribute, the still-fresh and electric words of America's mentor and elder statesman etched directly into the stone of the walls, was a nearly spiritual experience for him. He filled with renewed life, energy. Ben James was right in one respect. America was the land of possibilities. But the possibilities were for all, equally. Soldiers didn't fight for General Electric or North American Rockwell. They fought, and died, for their families, their friends, their lovers.

He took a ragged breath and looked straight up, into the great dome that covered the Memorial. Around the edge of the dome were written the words he had come here to see: "I have sworn before the altar of God, eternal hostility against every form of tyranny over the mind of man."

The mind of man. What were BJ's lies and creations but a kind of mental tyranny? There was truth, real truth, and upon it was based real freedom. Ben James was no less than the most cunning and insidious threat to that freedom the country had ever known.

He looked out the portico to see a big Chrysler fighting its way up the long drive. Cal. He took a long look around, trying to make the atmosphere in the Memorial a part of himself, then turned and hurried back down the long stairs to climb back into his car. He didn't want to meet Cal face-to-face.

His hands and face were numb with cold by the time he got back into his car. Cal was just pulling up, bringing his vehicle almost nose to nose with the Lincoln. The man waved to him from his car.

Merchant picked up the phone and dialed the number he'd committed to memory earlier, Daniels picking it up right away.

"Why are we doing this?" he asked.

"They're going to ask you if we met. You can tell them we spoke on the phone. I don't want you involved as an accessory."

"Are you wearing a uniform?"

"Don't worry 'bout it, Cal," Merchant said, "just listen to me. I've got a plan."

"I'm all ears," Daniels said. "And if you've got a plan for all this, I'm going to bring you into the firm and put you on retainer."

"First off, I'm real short on time," Merchant said, locking the phone between his shoulder and face to free up his hands. He began writing a note on the small pad he always carried. "I want you to do a couple of things for me. To begin with, tell Linda I'm sorry. Tell her . . . I love her."

"Easily handled."

"Next. Tell her she was right about being the quiet army wife. Tell her to start screaming as loud as she wants to, tell whoever'll listen all about the things that have happened over the last week. She probably believes it now. Go to the media, go—"

"Are you sure about this?" Cal said. "It's so unlike you."

"Just do it." He tore off the piece of paper on the notebook, smiling down at the little machine hooked up under the dash. "I don't suppose you have a fax machine in that car of yours, do you?"

"As a matter of fact . . ."

"Okay. Give me the number and I'll fax this press release over to you. When you get it, give it to Linda, tell her to release it if she wants to."

He got the number and stuck the note into the fax, using all the tools of an informational society to wire something a distance of ten feet.

"And, Cal," he said as he watched the paper disappear into the machine, "don't be low key on this. Whip it up, talk loud and long to whoever will listen to you. Can you do that?"

"I'm a lawyer, for God's sake," Cal replied. "Of course I can do it. But what about you? There's a manhunt going on for you right now, do you know that?"

"The less about me you know at this point, Cal, the better," Merchant said, then lowered his voice. "But listen, if I . . . if you never see me again, I . . . I didn't run or anything. Tell Linda. If you don't see me, it's because I'm dead."

"I can't tell Linda that!"

"You can and will. The worst thing in this world is wondering about missing loved ones. I may not come back from this one. What's happening with everyone else?"

Daniels took a breath. He was staring sadly from the other car, his face strained tight. "They've still got Bramley lost in the system under national security. Linda's being held now as a material witness and possible accessory. They may let her go after a time. Della was picked up and released for lack of evidence, and Josh is still waiting to be charged on Monday."

Merchant nodded. "Best I could hope for right now," he said. "Cal, buddy, I've got to go. I'm trusting you with a lot right now. Good luck."

"I'm afraid it's you who needs the luck," the man replied.

"Hold on a minute." Merchant reached into his over-coat pocket and pulled out the 8-mm tapes. He stepped out of the car and deposited them on top of a snow pile near Daniels's car. Then he got back into the Lincoln, picked up the phone, and spoke: "Take the tapes and hold on to them. Once Linda is out of jail, give them to her. She'll know what to do with them."

"Got you."

"Do it now. I want you out of here."

Daniels waved through the window and got out of his car, a pudgy little man in a snap-brimmed hat and fur-lined overcoat, a legal version of Truman Capote. He picked up the tapes, slipped once on the street to fall on his ass, then climbed back into his car and picked up the phone. "Not a word about the pratfall," he said.

"Cal, you're a good man," Merchant said. "I've always admired and respected you."

"Don't make this sound permanent," the man replied. "If you're too nice to me now, you won't be able to take it back later."

"My only prayer now, buddy, is that I get that chance. Good-bye."

"Good-bye, Charlie," the man said, Merchant hanging up right away and motioning through the windshield for the lawyer to leave. Daniels nodded and backed away from the scene. Within another minute, he'd rejoined the sparse traffic outside the circle.

Merchant sat for a moment. By his watch, it was 5:41. Everything depended upon getting to New York before that charter left. Then it hit him. For all intents and purposes at the moment he was a two-star general strapped tightly in the power loop. He had options still.

He picked up the phone again and dialed a number from heart that he'd used hundreds of times over the years, Air Material Command at Andrews.

"Andrews Air Force Base," came the male receptionist, Merchant clearing through the AMC headquarters.

He spoke as soon as they answered. "This is General Tillotson with DIA. I need to requisition a helicopter and pilot ASAP."

After going through the same authorization discussion he'd had to get the President, he was guaranteed a chopper, fueled and running, when he arrived at the airstrip. Life was so easy when you were in charge.

Cutting off Andrews, he called a D.C. cab, deciding the thing to do was to abandon the car here, as if Tillotson had parked it and taken a cab to the motel to avoid being spotted. Once again, he climbed out of the vehicle and paced.

When the cab arrived at six o'clock, Charles Merchant had approximately an hour and a half to get to New York and convince a half-baked reporter to help him try to save the country.

El Paraiso, Honduras 6 P.M.

General Tuck Tucker walked out onto the balcony of La
Casa de las Bonitas and watched the Huey land below in
the town square, raising a cloud of dust that sent citizens
and soldiers running and wrapped the barren, twilight
streets in a layer of hazy gauze. It got dark damned early
down here, too damned early. He'd counted on another
hour at least of daylight, nothing of his intelligence
informing him that by six it would, essentially, be night.

The dust cloud raised by the Huey drifted just below
his vantage point from the local whorehouse, his temporary command post. He would have liked to have chosen
another building, but this was the only two-story structure
in the city of five thousand. His men spread out below and
all around him—Task Force Thunder, eight thousand
strong, filling the meandering streets of rambling adobe
buildings and spilling into the surrounding fields of
just-planted tobacco, ruining most of the crop.

He was supposed to have been to the border by now, but
moving a large army presented a great many problems that
he'd long forgotten about. This part of Honduras was
enduring the rain right now, mechanized equipment
and sometimes entire companies of men getting bogged
down in the low ground. When the sun was out it
was blistering Caribbean sun, the troops wilting under
forced march conditions with forty-pound packs and
M-16s and combat helmets. Somehow, they'd come across
a problem with the mess, too. The food chain was continually behind the columns, unable to tear down and set up
fast enough to keep pace, which meant the task forces
themselves had to wait, literally, for their dinner to catch
up with them. That's what he was doing now. Waiting for
chow.

War is hell. A McDonald's franchise could clean up
here.

The problem, of course, was the circumstances. They
had no target, no objective, to hit. They were sent down as
a sign of strength, meant to deploy in a provocative
manner to tempt the Caribbeans to shoot first, the knock-

this-chip-off-my-shoulder approach to diplomacy. All low-intensity training situations had dealt in the world of the quick strike. This was TV warfare, as the sight of the reporters clustered around the pilots of the Huey verified. The purpose of this mission had as much to do with the people of the world clustered around their televisions as it did with border incursions. We were there, planting the flag, doing our propaganda business.

This had happened once before, when Reagan had called the National Guard down here for "exercises" when the Caribbeans had encroached the border in 1985. Nothing had happened. He hoped to God this wasn't another exercise in futility. It was time to let these people know that the United States of America was alive and well, and not taking any bullshit from anybody. It was bad enough that Task Force Tango, Lofton's SouthCom units, had gotten the choice position to the south, the closest to Poblado and the one most likely to encounter resistance, effectively chopping him off from the action. To go home totally unbloodied would be a travesty.

He heard footsteps behind and turned to see his aide, Major Balor, saluting through a layer of fine dust, a wide circle of sweat under his armpit dyeing his field shirt dark. "Sir. Distant perimeter watch has found something you might find interesting."

"Really, Dan," Tucker said, returning the salute. He was a man to whom the formalities meant something. "At ease. What is it?"

"A body, sir. In a field."

"Ours or theirs?"

"That's what they thought you might find interesting. They're not sure."

Tucker smiled. "I'm interested. Show me." He took one look out into the darkening sky, a thin band of pink dipping in and out of the distant mountain ranges, watching boiling black clouds in the far distance, their innards occasionally brightening with static electric charges. The air smelled wet. Moving at night was going to be tough enough. If it rained, his troops wouldn't be worth a nickel by the time they reached the enemy.

He followed Balor off the balcony, and through the

bedroom, red scarfs draping the night-table lamps, the brass bed rumpled and smelling of booze. The walls were covered with mirror tiles and *Playboy* centerfolds tacked up with pushpins. Hollow-eyed Carib women stared or leered at him through door spaces as he walked past a number of bedrooms before reaching the wooden stairs.

The parlor and bar that was the first floor of the place had been hurriedly turned into a communications center, Tucker stopping by the bar where the radio operator had filled its top with equipment, a huge set of headphones resting around his neck.

"What's the news, Corporal?" Tucker asked, walking behind the bar to "liberate" a bottle of Wild Turkey, handing it to Balor.

"General Lofton is still fifteen miles from the border," the shaved-headed man returned in a southern accent. "The Cubans and Companeros have arrived, however, and are deploying in companies along the border, mostly to the south of us."

"Thank you, son," Tucker said, running a hand through his crew-cut gray hair. He looked at Balor. "Fucking Lofton's sitting in the middle of the action. I wonder if I should turn the column and move south. If we march all night, we might be able to get there by the morning."

"SouthCom's not going to like that," Balor said. "Lofton would take gas if you turned the column without orders."

"Yeah, Danny . . . I know. Let's go check our dead man."

They walked through the parlor and its tacky bright-colored plastic furniture, the casa's madame watching them catlike from the couch, angry because her establishment had been commandeered, quiet because she was still hoping for some GI business.

They moved into semidarkness, the sky above so blue it was almost black. The streets outside were clogged with troops and mechanized equipment, tanks and armored personnel carriers moving east. The command post sat at a crossroads. To his right lay the town square and the Huey, to the left, screaming and horn blaring heralded a problem.

An old Indian, barefoot, was trying to lead his mule

across the street, the animal going nuts at the commotion all around it and squatting in the middle of the dusty road, blocking an entire column of MX1 tanks. A lieutenant stood alternately arguing with the old man and trying to pull the mule from his squat.

"Lieutenant!" Tucker called. "Get this column moving right now!"

"But, sir . . ." the man returned, opening his arms wide in confusion.

"Damn," Tucker whispered. "Do I have to do everything myself?"

He walked up to the mule and pulled out his sidearm, a 9mm Colt automatic. Putting it immediately to the mule's head he pulled the trigger to a loud pop, the animal wheezing like a concertina, then crashing to the road in the midst of a small dust cloud. "Now, move this column!" he yelled, walking away, the old man screaming and chasing after him.

He moved toward the chopper in the square, the old man following behind, cursing him in Spanish. He frowned at the man, wishing he were as easy to dispense as his mule was, then spoke to Balor. "Danny, get an interpreter and your paperwork and explain to the man that the U.S. government will requisition him another mule."

"Yes, sir," Balor said, angling the old man away from Tucker, who continued on to the Huey.

Reporters were clustered around the square, asking the pilot and gun crew about enemy activity. A company of riflemen had taken up near residence in the square, several of them sitting on the ledge of a long-dried-up stone fountain with a statue of the Virgin of Suyapa on top. "Sergeant!" he called to the most senior man he saw. "Take some men and cordon off the square. I want the reporters pushed back."

He arrived at the chopper as the reporters were being moved aside, protesting loudly. Fucking press. He'd just as soon shoot them, too.

A captain with the name Weathers stitched onto the breast of his flight suit and still wearing his helmet stood by the Huey's open bay, its M-60 loaded but pointing upward. "It's strange, sir," the man said, saluting. "Not sure what to make of it."

"Let's have a look," Tucker said, climbing into the open bay. A body lay covered with a tarp on the floor. The captain reached down and pulled off the cover to a young blond man, military haircut, dressed in fatigue pants and a T-shirt advertising something called a Motley Crue. He hadn't been shot, but the body had been broken up pretty well, though it didn't appear as if he'd been beaten. "Where'd you find him?"

"In the middle of a field about thirty miles east of here," he said.

"Show me," Tucker replied, reaching into his pocket and taking out a graphed map of the area.

He laid the map atop the body. "Right here," Weathers said, jabbing at the spot with an index finger. "Sector C-15, not far from where the Coco turns south and other boundaries begin to mark the border. What do you make of it, sir?"

"Mercenary," Tucker said. "But whose? Looks like he's been dead most of the day."

"For what's it worth," Weathers said, "we covered the same area extensively around daybreak this morning and saw nothing. Now, it's possible that we missed him on the first run, but judging from the body's condition, I just don't think so."

"I agree," Tucker said, Danny Balor moving up to join them in the bay, the press still arguing with their cordon, but at a distance of fifty feet. "I have to think that somebody's killed him, even though the body itself is unmarked. It'd be difficult to imagine him dying like this in a field."

"I used to jump before I moved up to staff," Balor said. "I've seen bodies that looked something like this, except worse, when their chutes didn't open."

"A fall?" Tucker said. "This gets more interesting by the minute." He looked at Balor. "Right off the top, how would you assess this?"

Balor squatted and stared at the body for a minute. "He fell . . . or was pushed from a high place and died from the fall. For whatever reason, the body was taken from the place of death and put into that field."

"So we would find it?" Tucker asked.

The man wiped a bead of sweat from his upper lip. "I have no idea."

Tucker straightened, stiff, and spoke to Weathers. "Have the body taken back to medical. Find somebody who can do an autopsy . . . and quickly. Don't let the reporters see it and don't report to anyone else but me, understood?"

"Yes, sir!"

"Come on, Major. We've got some planning to do."

Tucker and Balor climbed back out of the chopper, night having descended completely now, field lights brightening the square as chow lines began forming outside a commandeered café, the tank column now moving freely again, clanging past their position to form up south of the hamlet.

"Something happened on that river this morning," Tucker said, loud enough to get over the dull roar that continually surrounded them.

"Yes, sir."

"We also might as well face the fact that fucking Lofton, walking right down the Pan Am, is hiking to engage the enemy who's walking up the damned highway from the other side."

"Yes, sir."

"What would you think about chasing down this dead man, Major?"

Balor looked at him through squinted eyes. "Send the task force to the river?" he returned. "What if SouthCom needs us?"

"What if all that on the Pam American Highway is just a show, and the real action is going to take place closer to the river? After all, the initial incursions took place there."

"It's quite a chance, General."

Tucker smiled. "Is it?" he asked. "What happens if I turn the column east and head toward the river?"

Balor caught on slowly, the smile on his face widening by degrees as the plan sank in. "The Cubans would react to your movement as potentially hostile and probably send their own columns, possibly taking the action completely out of Lofton's hands."

"Bingo!" Tucker said happily. "Here's what we do. We radio SouthCom that there has been a possible skirmish with casualties near the river and that we are going to investigate. What can they say?"

Balor shrugged. "Bon voyage, I guess," he answered.

"Let's hurry them through chow, Major," Tucker said, feeling better already. "I want this column on the move by nineteen hundred hours. We may have just seized the initiative, and I can't wait."

Somewhere Over New York City 7:37 P.M.

Merchant stared out of the copilot window of the tandem-rotored Chinook helicopter at the empty expanse of Shea Stadium five hundred feet below, as the pilot, a nice kid named Aaron Chusid, radioed their position to Kennedy Control. The Chinook wasn't as fast as the Huey Cobra, but it was designed for all-weather usage and had made the trip just fine. The time had slipped away completely, though. They needed to bring it in and they needed to do it quickly.

"General," Chusid said. "Kennedy says that there's too much traffic right now and that we can't set her down for another twenty minutes."

"That's too late," Merchant said, plugging in his headset and speaking. "Control . . . this is General Gene Tillotson of the Defense Intelligence Agency. This flight is on a priority basis. We're dealing with a national emergency here! Over."

"I'm sorry, General," the weary controller's voice returned. "We're socked with all of our traffic plus all of Dulles's and National's. There's simply nowhere to put—"

"We're coming in now," Merchant said. "Clear us to the air charter hangars."

He put the mike back on the hot spur, then shut down the set. He looked at Chusid, so young to be a captain. "Take her in, boy," he said.

"Sir?"

"I said take her in. We'll spot charter visually once we get there. Stay on the treetops and don't worry about it."

"Yes, sir. You're giving the orders."

Merchant smiled. The kid had moxie. He took them down so low Merchant could see people eating dinner in the tract housing on the periphery of the airport. Then, the vast flat plain opened up before them, cut through with wide bands of runway all twinkling red and blue lights. A 747 roared several hundred feet beside them, landing with a squeal of tires and brakes as the chopper moved steadily toward the hangar area, the kid's hands locked on the stick, his eyes continually roving, searching for bogies. Merchant was glad the radio wasn't on to curse them as they went.

A series of air charter hangars loomed dark and foreboding before them. Near one of them, a 727 painted in camouflage was warming up on the runway, a fuel truck still topping off the tanks.

"There!" he said, pointing. "Take me down, then get the hell out of here before they send security around."

"Don't have to tell me twice, sir," Chusid replied with a sigh.

He brought them down a hundred feet from the fan jet, Merchant saluting and jumping out when they were a couple of feet above ground, Chusid angling steeply out of there as soon as Merchant hit ground.

Light spilled into pitch-blackness from the wide-open mouth of the hangar. Four vans fixed with the tri-colored NCC logo were parked just outside the hangar, two baggage carts being loaded from their open backs. He headed in that direction. A number of people milled around the vans drinking coffee. They were dressed for warmer temperatures and stood hunched over in the cold.

As he got closer, he recognized the woman, blond, dressed in jeans and a white sweatshirt and no coat. She stood talking to a man in a bright pink windbreaker and a slouch golf hat. At his approach, from twenty feet, she broke from the group and hurried in his direction. At ten feet she stopped, puzzled, and waited for him to come to her.

"You're not Froggy," she said, then stared hard at his nameplate over the breast pocket. "What's going on?"

"You've made a terrible mistake," he said as the van doors slammed one after the other, four times, followed by the loud creak of the wheels as the handlers guided the carts toward the jet, the words "El Tigre" written in bloodred on the plane's stabilizer.

"Why are you wearing General Tillotson's uniform?" she asked.

"Because I've been pretending to be Gene Tillotson," he answered simply.

"Why? Where is he?" Her voice dripped suspicion as the man in the golf hat started edging slowly in their direction.

"The why," he said, "is to right the terrible wrong that you've perpetrated. . . ." He lifted a hand and pointed past her at the golf hat. "No, sir. Don't come over here."

"The plane is getting ready to—"

"Please, sir. Stay back."

Traynor turned to watch the man retreat to the group. "What are you talking about?" she asked, high-pitched. "What terrible wrong."

"The news you released . . . about the missiles was wrong. There were no Russian missiles. General Tillotson planted that story with you because he figured you were green enough to bite without forcing too many questions."

She forced a laugh, loosening up. "Right," she said. "I'm supposed to listen to some . . . uniform thief, who shows up in the middle of the night, who—"

"I knew who Froggy was," he said.

"I want to talk to Tillotson," she said.

Charlie fixed her with hard eyes. "You can't. He's dead."

She searched his face, the cockiness leaving her own. "D-dead? When . . . how?" The color had drained totally out of her face. He'd made the point.

He took her arms and squeezed hard. "He stuck a Glock-17 into his mouth, pulled the trigger, and took the back of his head off. I was with him when he died. He killed himself with remorse for what he and you had done."

She shoved his arms from her and backed away slightly, shaking her head. "You're hitting me with too much here," she said, voice shaking.

"There's more," he said, "and you'd better listen. The missile story was planted so that the President would send troops to Caribbea. You remember the C-130 that went down?"

She nodded, eyes narrowed.

"It contained two nuclear bombs, which are now in the hands of Tillotson's cohort in Caribbea. They will be exploded tomorrow morning at sunrise, quite near the approaching armies."

"How could you know all this?"

"I worked it out," he answered. "Gene was my best friend. He confirmed the rest. He left a suicide note taking all the blame."

"Best friend," she said, then pointed at him. "You're Merchant . . . the spy, the missing spy!" She began walking away from him. "I'm getting ready to go get some help. You'll run if you know what's best for you."

"If you get on that plane," he said loudly after her, "you, and all those people over there, and most probably fifty thousand troops will be vaporized to nuclear dust at approximately seven A.M., Honduran time, tomorrow morning. Are you *that* sure I'm wrong?"

She took another few steps, then stopped walking. She came back. "Okay, you've got a little of my attention. Keep talking."

Behind him, he heard the jet engines kicking over, preparing for flight. Two men in gray overalls wheeled a steel flight of steps in the direction of the plane. He had already decided to leave Ben James out of it, keeping the message a lot simpler.

"Gene was afraid that the Pentagon was getting its budget cut too much. He thought that stirring up a little war might be a way to keep up the military spending. Can't say that he was much wrong in that thinking, either."

"Why come to me with this?"

"I just got it together this afternoon," he answered, a gust of wind tossing dust and papers past them, the woman's hair blowing into her face as she shivered. "There's no time to try and convince anyone that I'm right. It'll take too long. I've got to get to the source and stop it there."

"If you're right, and can't stop it, you'll blow up with the bombs."

He nodded. "I'm prepared for that possibility. You should be, too."

"You want me to take you to Honduras," she said, catching on. "What's in it for me?"

"I know that the truth means nothing to people like you," he said. "But besides performing a heroic act that may save thousands of lives, I do have more to offer. A right-out-front, exclusive story that will make people forget how you sold them lies. You may be able to not only save your ass here, but also come out on your feet. Just think about that, being right there for the final hours of the biggest political conspiracy of this century."

"If you're right," she said. "And if we don't all get blown to kingdom come first."

"I'm right," he replied.

She brought a hand up to her face, rubbing her temple. "I have to say that I don't want to believe you," she said.

"Lady," he replied. "I wouldn't have come to you if there was any other way. I'm warning you of your impending death here. I think you should listen."

"Mr. Merchant . . ."

"Call me Charlie."

Her eyes flashed and she folded her arms. Let me tell you about the truth, mister. That's the only thing I'm interested in right now and you're the first son of a bitch I've run into who doesn't think it's a dirty word. I have no idea of what you're talking about for the most part, but I heard the word missiles in there and missiles are what I'm interested in. I'll be damned if I'm going to sit around and eat shit and end up my life a bitter emphysema candidate like Joan."

"Who?"

"Never mind. You don't much like me, do you?"

"Not much," he said, then smiled at the fierce glint in her eyes. "But I'm beginning to respect you a bit."

"That's a start," she said, reaching out a hand that he shook. "Pleased to meet you, Colonel Merchant."

"Once we get down there," he said, "you've got to get me near Tucker."

She smiled. "It just so happens that we've already lined

up an exclusive interview with him when we arrive. But I haven't said you're going yet."

"Let's go!" somebody called from the vans, everybody moving in that direction.

"We've got an Army rep on the flight. How would we get you on board?"

"Switch me with somebody."

She turned and yelled to the man in the golf hat. "Hey, Mike! Hold on a minute, will you?" She turned back to Merchant. "Where'd he get the footage?"

Merchant smiled. "There're tons of file shit like that lying around. Being head of DIA gives you access to everything. Later, he gave you dummied-up films of the real missiles. It became self-generating."

"Sheila!" the golf hat called.

"A minute!" she screamed back. Then to Merchant. "Come on, convince me."

"Look in my face and tell me I'm a liar," he said. "Look inside of your own heart and face the real possibility of your own death . . . and your own failure when the suicide note is found tomorrow morning. You must set this thing to rights. Thousands upon thousands of lives depend on you."

"Jesus," she said. "Nothing's easy, is it?"

"Nothing worthwhile," he said.

"Okay, God damn it. I'll *earn* my fucking Emmy." She turned to the golf hat. "Come here, Mike. I'm going to let you off the hook."

The man approached. "We've got to go," he said.

"No," she replied, putting an arm around his shoulder. "I've got to go. You've got to move your ass back to one of those vans and change clothes with General Tillotson here."

"What?"

"By the way, meet Froggy," she said, winking at Merchant. "He's going down with me in your place. Hell, you didn't really want to go anyway."

"Merck will kill me."

"Not when he sees the story we squeeze out of this," she answered. "Come on, Mike. You were just going along to baby-sit me anyway. Is our government watchdog already on board?"

"Yeah," Baroni replied, looking uneasily at Merchant.

"This is a matter of extreme urgency," Merchant said to him. "Your country will be grateful."

The man sighed loudly. "My wife woulda left me over this trip anyway."

"Good," Merchant said. "I'm a little bigger than you, but I think it'll work okay. I'll need your passport." He grimaced at the pink jacket and golf hat. "Do all TV people dress like you?"

Baroni shook his head. "Only the ones with bad taste," he answered, then started walking to the van. "Let's get it over with."

They changed quickly, Merchant emerging with blue jeans three inches higher than his penny loafers and a hat designed for a sport he'd never played in his life. Baroni, it must be said, was a disgrace to the uniform.

Merchant walked quickly toward the 727, gray-suited ground crew waiting to take the up-ramp away. Sheila met him at the bottom of the ramp, stifling a smile at his appearance. She seemed excited, anxious almost. What had he plugged into here? His curse and his blessing seemed to be aggressive women, though he was beginning to learn how to sit back and enjoy it.

"Hurry," she said, leading him up the stairs. "The government guy is in the back. We'll just slide you up front and nobody will be any the wiser."

"At least until they check the passport in Tegucigalpa and see that I look nothing like Michael Baroni."

She smiled broadly. "We're going in with military clearance. Nobody's checking anything. Hell, this just might be fun."

"What—whistling to the gallows?"

She hooked an arm through his at the top of the steps, pulling herself closer. "We're going to bust this thing wide open, Charlie," she said, sounding like a cancer patient who'd just found she'd gone into remission. "I hope you're prepared to be famous, because if we survive the morning, you're going to be the most recognizable face in the entire country. I knew this was all tied up with those missiles."

They entered the plane, Merchant not sure if the woman really understood anything that he'd said and not sure that he understood anything that she'd said. It was going to be a hell of a night.

Pennsylvania Quarter 8:15 P.M.

Ben James watched his office television with a growing sense of outrage. The wife of that damned cop, Hurley, was on CCN screaming that her husband was killed by some sort of stupid government conspiracy and that he'd been working with Charles Merchant.

". . . was getting too close to the truth about Jack Braedman's death and they killed him," the woman was saying, "just like they're trying to get Colonel Merchant."

"What does this have to do with Senator Braedman?" an unseen reporter asked.

"He was murdered by the D.C. police," she said. "And my husband found out about it."

"Damn!" BJ picked up his Steuben Glass chunk paperweight and threw it angrily at the television, the thing crashing through the forty-inch screen to a fusillade of jumping sparks and gray-black smoke. Didn't the fucking press have anything better to do than report every stupid rumor that came along?

He pulled the phones up to his ears, touching June's pad.

"Yeah, boss?"

"Can't we do something about those CCN reports?" he growled. "We've got to squelch this shit now."

"No luck so far, boss. Probably too late. Their assignment editor is someone new who picked it up from the D.C. stringer, and the locals have already been picking it up all over the country. We're going to have to ride this one."

BJ's hands were clenched with rage, an ice pick of a headache beginning to form behind his eyes. "How about Merchant and Patterson? Anything on them?"

"Not since the motel shooting," she said. "They seem to have dropped off the face of the earth."

"No they haven't," he said, the darkness settling over

his brain. He hated to lose. It was like death to him. He wasn't going to blow this one in the eleventh hour because of that traitorous bitch. Where was the loyalty? What was happening to this country?

"Listen," he said low. "I want you jingling every bell, pushing every button. Merchant on his own isn't much, but with Mel . . . she's dangerous to us, June. We've got to find her. We've got to."

"Sure, boss. Listen . . . Pam Williams has just come in to the offices."

"Send her back."

He disconnected and creaked back in his desk chair, looking at his watch. Time was passing, too slowly, but it was passing. If he could only hold things together for another eleven hours or so, his worries would be over. Once the bombs went off, the country, and the world, would have other things to worry about. He took several deep breaths, trying to swallow the still-building headache. It would be okay. It would be. Things were too far along now to possibly stop.

A knock at the door. Pam. He buzzed her in, the woman entering wearing a leather jumpsuit, her hair pulled back in a French braid, her eye makeup, heavy on greens and blue, extending all the way to her ears. She walked up to BJ's side of the desk and leaned down, kissing him deeply.

"When do I get to stop dressing like the Bride of Frankenstein?" she asked, straightening to sit on the edge of his desk.

He smiled. "Very . . . very soon," he answered. "I know that Jeremy has been pretty rough duty—"

"Rough?" she said. "His idea of an intellectual discussion is talking about the relative merits of a slant six over a four-barrel carburetor. Give me a break. I'm going to need to fumigate my life after this."

"Well, I appreciate all you've done." He reached out and patted her leg. "You're a good actress. Didn't take you long to bring out his true stripe."

She shrugged, turning to stare at the smoke still bleeding from the office TV. "He was just a cheap hood, like you said. Grab. Grab. Grab. No plan, just strongarm. You're not really going to make him a partner, are you?"

He chuckled. "You got to know me better than that," he

said. "You just hang on for a couple more days and I'll take care of Mr. Bomar and give you a well-deserved rest."

She nodded broadly. "Next time, give me one of the Joint Chiefs or corporate guys, okay?"

He pointed a cocked finger at her, dropping his thumb like the hammer on a pistol. "Gotcha," he said.

She slid off the desk. "Oh, I almost forgot why numb nuts sent me over here," she said. "I'm supposed to pick up some of that coke you got from the Haitian ambassador."

"Oh, yeah," he said, straightening his chair and reaching into his top desk drawer. He pulled out a plastic bag containing a small amount of white powder.

"The guy should be a good connection," he said, handing her the bag. "He can bring it in in the diplomatic pouch, avoiding any kind of customs, and he makes a lot of trips back and forth."

"Okay," she said, dropping the bag into a small purse slung over her shoulder. "I'll pass it along."

"Try some of it with him." BJ smiled. "Let me know what you think."

"Will do," she said, bending for another kiss, BJ reaching out to fondle her ass.

She straightened again. "I'd better get back."

He nodded. "Hang in. It's almost over."

She rolled her eyes and waved, moving across the floor and out, the door clicking to lock behind her. He immediately brought up the headphones and buzzed June. "Anything yet?" he asked when she came on.

"No," she said. "We've checked all her usual haunts and had contact with everyone she knows, including her parents. She's disappeared completely. We'll keep—"

"Yeah, yeah," he said, disconnecting, the darkness settling over him again. He'd handled everything perfectly . . . except for Mel. He'd had a soft spot for her, his best pupil, and left her on active roster even when he'd known she'd been sneaking around on him. He should have pink-slipped her days ago, and now the lapse was coming back to haunt him. That's what emotion gets you, disloyalty and treason.

He stood, turning his hatred inward. He was surrounded by conspiracies. He should have been harder,

tougher. He walked away from his desk, moving to the
walls, his eyes roving the crammed full shelves of glass
figurines—solid translucence, a paradox. He moved along
the rows slowly, looking, until his eyes came to rest on the
five-inch-high glass elephant given to him by the minority
leader of the Senate.

He picked it off the shelf, its contours smooth and cool
to his hand. He could see his palm right through the solid
creature, the room light sliding in slick, eerie patterns
along its surface.

Cradling it gently, he walked back to the desk, staring at
it for a long moment to appreciate its uniqueness before
bringing it down hard on the edge of the desk, the elephant
shattering into several large pieces.

The creature's torso had broken in half at a jagged edge.
He picked the largest of the two pieces and set it on the
desktop.

"You dumb, dumb motherfucker," he said, and drew
his palm along the sharp edge of the glass, gashing himself
deeply, his blood rushing out of the wound to flow gently
over the surface of the glass, standing out boldly against it.
His hand was burning. He pulled it up to look at it,
clenching his teeth with the pain and smiling. A lesson. A
lesson here.

He bent to get his face closer to the bloody glass, then
picked it up, turning it this way and that, the ooze sliding
with his motions.

He held it up to the light, gleaming and glistening, as
the blood from his palm dripped all over his white suit.
And the darkness of his mind filled with beautiful color
and his rage calmed. Everything was going to be all right.
Despite Merchant. Despite Patterson. He had planned too
well to fail. Even that greedy asshole Breedlove had
probably figured that one out by now thanks to one of Doc
Jonah's variations on his famous acid peel.

He took off his paisley tie and idly began wrapping it
around his bleeding hand. He couldn't wait for the morning.

★ ★ ★ ★ ★ ★ ★ ★ ★ ★ ★ ★ ★ ★ ★ ★

FEBRUARY 10, SUNDAY

★ ★ ★ ★ ★ ★ ★ ★ ★ ★ ★ ★ ★ ★ ★ ★

■ NEWSBREAK ■

". . . please . . . just hold your questions until after I've read Mrs. Merchant's statement. It is direct and self-explanatory: 'To whom it may concern: I am a political prisoner being held against my will by the country of my birth. My husband, Colonel Charles Merchant, has been branded a traitor and is even now being hunted down like a common criminal. My husband is guilty of nothing except loving his country. He has uncovered a conspiracy within the military to force a war in Central America. The powers that be will have him silenced. But I am telling you here tonight that my husband is innocent of all charges against him, guilty of nothing except patriotism. God bless the United States, and God bless Charlie Merchant.'

"That's it, folks. I can only add that we are witnessing a great travesty of justice. I have known Colonel Merchant for twenty years and can honestly say that he is the most honest, forthright, and, yes, patriotic man it has ever been my good fortune to come in contact with. Charlie Merchant has made my life richer by knowing him. Such a man a traitor? I tell you no. No way on God's green earth. Questions?"

—quote from Cal Daniels
Nightline, February 9

". . . looks like that arctic front is finally beginning to budge a little bit. Believe it or not, Power City

residents, the forecast for tomorrow is sunny and
clear, with a high of thirty-seven and no north wind.
Sunbathing anyone?

"And finally, on the local front, a most bizarre
incident tonight at an upscale eatery. Two people
were found dead tonight in a rented Cadillac just
outside of Regardies Restaurant, local hangout for
those connected with money and power. A bag of
white powder that looked like cocaine was found on
the floor of the car. It later tested out as a caustic acid
highly reactive to water. The two had apparently
sniffed the substance up their noses thinking it
cocaine. The dead are identified as Jerry 'Jeremy'
Bomar, a small-time Chicago hoodlum, wanted by
the FBI on a succession of Rico statute complaints,
and a woman whose identity is being withheld
pending notification of next of kin. The ultimate
object lesson about knowing what goes into your
body."

> —WBAP Radio 900
> late news, February 9

Over Honduras 3:15 A.M.

Merchant sat on the floor of the Huey. Dark, inscrutable
jungle passed beneath the chopper's open bay beside him.
Traynor sat across from him, several techs jammed up all
around. The bay guns were both manned. A cameraman
was rolling tape on Sheila's orders, had been since they'd
boarded the 727 in New York, though he'd contributed
precious little on that leg of the trip, gratefully using the
flight time to catch some sleep during most of the five-
hour ride to Tegucigalpa.

"So Breedlove was connected up with Jerry Delany, the
pilot of the C-130?" she asked, voice vibrating with the
rattle of the chopper.

"They were both mercenaries working the same side of
the street," Merchant said to the camera's red light, be-

coming more comfortable with his reality re-creation the more he lived with it. "They'd known each other for years." He didn't know that for an exact fact, but it seemed logical.

The woman had been insistent upon the camera, and after Merchant had listened to her reasoning, he'd agreed completely. The events unfolding with them here were historical. The more activity that could be filmed, the more viewpoints, the better shot at the truth the world would have. It was a way for all of them to cover their asses, too. Not if they were wrong, but if they were right. Traynor's fear was one that Charlie had come to know—that the truth, without proper documentation, could be twisted and subverted into something else. They'd all committed to this. This was the record of that commitment.

"What are you going to say to General Tucker?" she asked.

He shook his head. "I don't know," he replied honestly. "I'm going to do what it takes to make him believe."

"What if he doesn't?"

"He has to. Though if we fail, we won't be around long enough to worry about it, will we?"

"Why are you doing it this way instead of taking it through channels?"

"The time element," he answered. "The wheels grind too slowly. The government could conference something like this to death. I just want to save the lives. We can all fight about it later."

"You're saying that the government's ineffective?"

"I'm saying that I don't have time to readjust everybody's thinking in time to stop the trouble. This way, I only have to convince two men—Tuck Tucker and the Caribbean commander."

"You're going to talk to the other side?"

He smiled. "How else?"

"We're going in!" one of the gunners said, Merchant leaning slightly out of the bay to get a look.

They were dipping into green hills, the chopper landing sites and storage on this side, the reverse slope, from the Caribbean positions—just like Wellington at Waterloo. It was raining here, a hard, steady downpour, the heat and humidity nearly overpowering to those just coming from the dead of winter.

They landed amid a small, self-contained encampment. Several choppers were tied down, portable floods brightening the landing area. There was an ammo dump, a small hospital, mess tents, and a repair area at the base of this hillside, the same setup repeated at the bases of the surrounding hills.

No sooner than they'd set down, a clipboard-carrying lieutenant in camouflage with rolled-up sleeves and an Air-Cav ball cap poked his head into the bay. "Which one of you is Miss Sheila Traynor?" he asked loudly.

Sheila, the only woman in the chopper, raised her hand.

"Miss Traynor," the man said, again loudly. "You will come with me, please, for your interview with General Tucker. You may bring one cameraman with you and take no more than ten minutes. We are facing a dangerous situation here."

"The sooner the better," Traynor said, standing and pointing at Charlie. "Be my cameraman."

They both jumped out of the chopper and into the hot rain, Merchant's appropriated penny loafers sinking totally in mud. He took the ridiculous pink jacket off, but left the golf cap to keep the rain out of his eyes. The camera, now wrapped in plastic, was passed out of the chopper to him and he tucked it up under his arm, following after the lieutenant who was already hurrying toward a waiting jeep.

Dark mountains covered with forest loomed steeply all around them, the rain a steady, dull roar. This was a no-man's-land, barely accessible, still uncontrolled. Black Carib Indians lived and worked these lands, hacking a living of beans out of the hillsides in much the same way their Mayan ancestors had. The sky crackled lightning overhead, strobing to life the lush green of untamed nature all around them.

They made their way through the small camp, most of the crew headed for coffee in the mess tent, and climbed into the jeep just on the other side of the egg of light. A road had been plowed right into the hillside, dozers parked nearby, and was now running dark mud.

Once they'd climbed into the back of the jeep, the lieutenant geared them into first and started the steep climb up the hillside, the jeep not wanting to grab hold of the shifting ground, constantly fishtailing. "I'm taking you up to our command post," he said loudly over his shoulder. "The enemy is digging in on the other side of the river."

"Defensive posture?" Merchant asked.

"Yes, sir. Same as us."

"How much of the force is here now," Merchant asked, the jeep sliding, nearly losing the road as it climbed at a forty-five-degree angle.

"About half, sir. General Lofton is controlling the area from the Pan Am Highway north."

"How many miles are we talking?"

"The border twists," the lieutenant said, beeping his horn, just barely avoiding another jeep that was sliding quickly down from the other direction. "But it looks like we're talking about a twenty-mile line from the edge of his position to here."

Merchant turned to Traynor. "A four-megaton explosion would vaporize everything in a twenty-five mile radius," he said.

Engine whining, throwing mud, they rounded the hill and entered the active front lines, Merchant's heart sinking at the immensity of it.

The ground flattened below them to fields of cotton and coffee that ran for a mile or two right up to the river. The Caribbean side of the river was the same as this side, cultivated flat land leading up to mountains.

Pinpoints of light filled the mountains on both sides of the river, troops digging in, as far as he could see in either direction. Below, on the flatland, he could see positions being taken up near the river and within dividing lines of trees that served as windbreaks. Tanks surrounded the few farmhouses on the flat ground, temporary command posts. Two formidable armies were lining up, both ready to defend their ground against invasion, both prepared to wage all-out war if necessary. It was frightening and exhilarating.

The road widened out somewhat, then dead-ended in a kind of parking lot near a dugout cave. The cave over-

looked the entire battlefield, and he could see Tucker
bustling around in its bright confines, giving and taking
messages from the communications van parked right beside the opening.

The lieutenant jumped from the vehicle, sloshing toward the command post.

Traynor turned to Merchant, a little of the excitement
gone out of her as she came upon the reality of war. "What
now?" she asked.

"We go and talk to Tuck," he said, handing her the
camera and following quickly behind the lieutenant.
Bright green moss hung thickly around the cave entrance.
The command post consisted of a large table with charts
and field telephones, another table with coffeepot and the
black box encoder that could put Tucker into instant
communication with the President. The general stood,
drinking coffee and paging through a small stack of
papers. He was stripped to his green T-shirt and fatigue
pants, his bronzed skin glistening with sweat as rain
dripped down the front of the cave like a small waterfall.

They moved into the fifteen-foot cave. "General," the
lieutenant said. "The newspeople are here."

"Look," Tucker said. "I told them I didn't—"

"Hi, Tuck," Merchant said, moving up near the man.

Tucker looked up with wide eyes, a smile playing
around his lips. He'd been too busy fighting a war to know
about Merchant's problems on the home front. "Charlie?
What the hell are you doing here?"

"It's a long story," Merchant said.

"Then we ain't got time for it right now," Tucker
replied, lips tight. "Want some coffee?"

"What's the situation?" Merchant asked, taking the
coffee.

"Well, this 'showing a presence' is for shit," Tuck said.
"Hell, everybody's out in the open. If we do fight, we're
going to take a shit pile of casualties." The man shook his
head. "But that ain't why you're here."

"How long have we known each other, Tuck?" Charlie
said.

"More than forty years, by my count," the man said,
"but don't tell anybody. They'll think we're old."

"If I told you that this discussion would be the most

important one you've ever had in your life, what would you say?"

Tucker narrowed his eyes, pudgy face straining. "What are you trying to tell me? Did the President send you?"

Merchant shook his head. "Give me fifteen minutes," he said.

Tucker looked at his watch. "Fifteen minutes," he said. "That's all we've got time for." He reached down under the desk and pulled out a bottle of Wild Turkey, pouring a shot in their coffee.

"By the way," Merchant said. "I'd like you to meet Sheila Traynor, one hell of a tough lady."

Tucker reached over and shook Traynor's hand. "Good to meet you," he said. "You're not a screamer, are you?"

"Depends on whose bed I'm in," she replied.

Tucker snorted, smiling. "Hope you like the show." Then he indicated the fold-up chairs. "Fifteen minutes," he said again.

Merchant sat and told him the story then, bringing it out with practiced ease, leaving off Ben James the way he'd been doing, and playing up Tillotson's role in the whole thing. He ended up with his phone call to the President and the man's telling him he wouldn't help.

When he finished, Tucker sat back in his chair, the breath wheezing out of him. "That's a lot of chaw to swallow," the man said. "Especially about Gene. I mean . . . oh, man. This is awful weird, Charlie."

"Are you saying I'm lying?" Merchant replied.

Tucker shook his head sadly. "Naw. You don't lie. Maybe you just went crazy, though. Nuts, you know?"

"Yeah, I might have," Merchant answered, taking a long drink of coffee. "But I didn't. And you know it, too."

"Fucking politicians," Tucker said, standing and walking to the mouth of the cave, watching through the curtain of rain the thousands upon thousands of lights. "Leave it up to them to send us all off to get killed down here without a second thought. You know, we found something interesting a few hours ago. The reason we're here now. Found a body in one of the fields down there, dead mercenary, no identification."

"Bait," Merchant said, "to lure you here."

"Think so?"

"They'd float the warheads down the river, then try and get as many troops as they could down here. The more dead, the better.

Tucker looked at the woman. "You leaked the missile story," he said.

She nodded and looked down. "Tillotson seemed like an unimpeachable source," she said.

Tucker took a long breath and returned to the table. "I'm a soldier, Charlie. All I can do is follow orders. If Gene did do what you say, I'm not sure that I think it's such a bad notion. You've seen what they've been doing to the military."

"I can't believe I just heard you say that," Merchant said, setting his cup down loudly. He stood, pacing. "The world is changing around us, Tuck. I know it's a scary world, one run by different principles than the ones we knew. But we've got to change with it, even if it means our own passing. If you want to kill yourself and do the country a favor, do it on your own time. I'll sit down here and die with you in the morning if you make me, but it's not the way I'd choose to go out."

"I don't know that I agree with you."

"Damnit!" Merchant moved to the cave mouth and pointed out. "And what about the men out there, the thousands who are going to die with the sunrise? Maybe they'd like a choice in all this. Maybe they'd like to think twice before dying to avoid a budget cut!"

Tucker jumped up, knocking the table over, maps scattering everywhere. "And what am I supposed to tell my officers? What am I supposed to tell the President? Should I say that I've decided that it's too dangerous to hold this ground and that I'm going to withdraw because something bad might happen?"

"No," Merchant said quietly, flaring around to stare at him. "You're going to go down on that river and find those fucking bombs and dismantle them!"

Tucker froze, staring at him, realizing for the first time that he did have an option here. Just at that second, the first explosion went up, followed quickly by many others.

They ran to the opening and looked out. Below them, the night was strobing in bright white fire, distant explosions pounding up and down the river, in the field, and along the windbreaks.

"Look like our discussion was moot," Tucker said, then turned to the encoder operator. "Tell the President we're under attack!"

Merchant stood watching as the night continued flaring around him, strangely enough, many charges going up on the Caribbean side also. Tucker turned back to the cave mouth and yelled to the man inside the communications van. "Get Major Balor up here!" he yelled. "Set up a chain of command. Scramble the choppers and put the 82nd on standby. This is it! Give me an open line to all unit commanders."

"This is President Macklin," came a mechanical voice through the encoder. "What is the situation?"

Tucker called back to the operator. "Tell him we're under attack and are preparing defense."

Merchant strained his eyes and ears into the distance, watching for muzzle flashes or cannon fire. Hueys began appearing overhead, moving in formation toward the river, searchlights angling wildly from their bottoms.

Tucker picked up a field telephone from the mess he'd dumped on the ground. "All units," he said. "This is General Tucker. Stand ready. Condition red. Prepare for frontal assault. Fire on my orders!"

"Wait," Merchant said.

The President's encoder voice screeched. "You will counterattack on my order!"

"Counterattack?" Tucker said, turning to stare at the encoder.

A major ran into the cave, explosions still flowering below, two of the farmhouses were in flames, tanks abandoning the area. "We're cranked, Tuck!" he called, saluting quickly. "Ready to go when you are!"

"Got it," Tucker said. "I want down in the middle of it!"

"No!" Merchant said, grabbing Tucker's arm as the man tried to leave the cave.

"Get your fucking hands off me!" Tucker yelled, the major pulling his sidearm and pointing it at Charlie.

"Would you listen to him!" Sheila yelled, Tucker whirling around to her, then pointing to the camera, its red light gleaming.

"Is that damned thing running?"

"Prepare for assault," came the mechanical voice. "What's happening there?"

"Listen!" Merchant screamed, shoving the major's gun hand aside. "Do you hear the whistle of incoming? Do you hear the rumble of distant guns or see muzzle flashes?"

"We need to go," the major said.

"What are you saying?" Tucker asked.

"Just look!" Merchant answered. "Look across the river. They're having as many problems as you are."

Tucker picked up field glasses from the encoder table and stared silently out.

"No one's firing," Merchant said. "Those things were planted same as the body to make sure you got here, to make sure you fight. Don't go down, not like this!"

Tucker stared at him for a long, silent minute, then picked up the field telephone. "This is Tucker. Do not fire. I repeat. Do not fire without confirmation from me. Out."

The explosions had subsided below, fires burning on both sides of the river, the figures of men silhouetted against the flames.

"Are you ready to go in?" came the encoder voice.

"General," came the voice of the radio operator from within the van. "We're gettin' some strange reports in here. Casualties are low, but men are reporting that the explosions are coming from beneath them. One went off under a tank tread."

Tucker jerked his head to stare at Charlie and the two men took each other's measure, Merchant knowing that Tucker wasn't the old soldier, ready to lose, either. "It's up to you and me, Tuck," Merchant said low. "Nobody else is going to do it or even understand it. You want glory? You want adventure? Let's go down into the snake pit."

Tucker smiled. "Screw the politicians," he whispered. He turned to the radio operator and said, "Raise the Caribbean commander."

"The Caribbean commander?" the operator called back from the blinking innards of the dark van.

"I don't stutter, son," the man said, smiling. "Raise the Caribbean commander, assure him that no one on this side of the river fired, and tell him we want to parlay."

"General Tucker," came the mechanical voice. "Are you there?"

Tucker turned to the encoder operator. "Tell the President that we are moving the encoder to a more secure location and that we'll get back to him when that is accomplished." He grinned. "Then cut it off and unplug the damned thing."

Merchant and Traynor shared a look. Now all they had to do was convince the enemy that they were telling the truth and find two hidden nuclear bombs in the three hours left until daylight. A cinch.

The radio operator called out, "The Caribbean commander has agreed to the meet," he said.

"Good," Tucker returned. "Where and when."

"Right now," the man said. "On the river."

Cuban and Companero troops lined the bank on the south side of the river, American and Honduran regulars, backed by a company of tanks, on the north. They were shadowy specters under the moonless night, flanked by the hulking silhouettes of palm and banana trees. The river was as wide as it got, maybe a hundred feet across, its progress lazy. Another half mile to the west it turned sharply, disappearing into the jungle and becoming Caribbea's alone. The hills sealed them in.

Now that the rain had stopped, Merchant was sweating profusely into Mike Baroni's clothes, his golf hat exchanged for a ball cap with SEAL stitched across its crown. He stood on the raft with Tucker and Sheila Traynor under the white flag, the only other passengers an NCC cameraman and the local owner of the raft, pressed into service, who poled them toward the middle of the soporific river. A barge, also poled, approached from the other side, also under the white flag. Two men stood ill at ease on the barge. They appeared to be involved in a heated discussion.

"Wonder what's going on over there?" Tucker asked.

"The one on the right's Cuban, isn't he?" Charlie said. "Hard to get a fix in the dark."

"Hope we won't need to get a damned interpreter," Tucker said, tucking in the tail of the field shirt he'd just put on. "What the hell time is it, anyway?"

"Getting on to five," Merchant said, not bothering to look at the watch he'd been looking at every minute for the last three hours. "We've got no time for this."

As the floats drew closer, everyone on both sides quieted, the only sounds the lapping of the water against the raft and the song of the wind in the trees. The darkness closed in on them and Merchant could feel the sweat trickling down his back. He watched the two men on the approaching barge. The Cuban was old, and in full Castro revolutionary dress uniform, his face slashed to a sneer. The other, the younger, was Carib dark and wore a field uniform, a single general's star on his red beret. No weapons were obvious. He worried about the older one. He seemed to carry himself imperiously.

"That older one looks like a real type A," Traynor whispered at that instant. "Watch out for him." She turned to the cameraman, twirling her finger for him to roll tape.

Tension was thick in the air, the sounds of weapons being brought to bear from both sides of the river more numerous and urgent the closer the vessels came to each other. Merchant looked straight up. The sky was beginning to lighten somewhat with the onset of morning.

He looked at the woman. "How's this for an exclusive?" he asked.

"It'll do," she said, her bulky shirt traded in for a GI T-shirt, which was clinging to her with sweat, her blond hair up in a bun, strands of it plastered to her cheek. "You sure know how to show a girl a good time."

The rafts bumped gently together. The Carib tossing a line to Tucker, the two men pulling the rafts tight together, then keeping the lines taut to hold them that way. There were several seconds of embarrassing silence, then the old man said in perfect English, "Why is that camera here? What sort of trick is this? Take it away immediately."

"No, sir," Tucker said softly, but with great authority. "We're recording this event of historical importance and want the truth of it to be seen. Unless you're not here with the same motives. . . ."

"This is my home . . . my country," said the Carib. "I have nothing to hide here. I do not fear your cameras."

The Cuban's eyes widened, but he said nothing. Tucker looked at him. "You must be General Gomez," he said.

"I've heard a lot about you. I'm General Tucker and this is Colonel Merchant."

"I am Antonio Gomez," the man replied, smiling slightly at the deference. He made a vague gesture in the direction of the Caribbean. "This is General Orosco. I must say at this moment that I do not condone this meeting without the approval of our governments."

"My . . . radio broke," General Orosco said, shrugging easily.

"Yeah, mind, too," Tucker returned.

"I've only just arrived," Gomez, looking well into his seventies, continued. "This meeting should not be taking place and I have come out here to demand that it be broken up."

"The bombs were blowing up beneath us," Orosco said, then picked up a small leather bag at his feet with his free hand, handing it across to Merchant. "And we found this."

Merchant looked in the bag. "Plastique explosive," he said, reaching in to bring something out. "And a timer. I told you."

"We had the same trouble," Tucker said. "Those bombs were planted to draw us here to fight."

Gomez snorted loudly. "And why would someone do that?"

Merchant gave them the short course, and when he was finished, the general laughed, shaking his head. "How stupid do you think we are?" he asked. "For a week you have been accusing our Caribbean friends of planting Russian missiles here. Now you say someone else is doing it, hoping no doubt that we'll simply leave your invasion force alone to perhaps plant your own missiles. No, senor. You are not dealing with ignorant peasants here. I have no idea of what your plan is, but I am here to see that it is not carried out. Once you return to your side of the river, a state of war once again exists between us. Anything you do on this river will be fired upon by our troops."

"What about the satchel bombs, General?" Tucker said. "Someone planted them."

"No, not someone," Gomez said, his wrinkled face twisted in distaste. "Anyone. Anyone from your side, anytime yesterday. I have confronted American treachery for more years than I care to admit. You are a devious

people, concerned with maintaining your bullying plea-
sures and imperialistic excesses at all costs. No, the
revolutionary spirit will not bend to your histrionics. You
must cease your threat to this region and withdraw immediately or there will be a great deal of bloodshed."

"General," Tucker said. "You're a goddamned fool. I'm
a fighting man same as you. Do you think for a minute that
I'd pull some stupid trick to avoid fighting you? Let me tell
you something. I think we should have run you and your
godless kind into the sea back in '45. Hell, I'd love to fight
your 'revolutionary forces' and show you what a real army
looks like."

The general smiled. "Ah, the true words of America,"
he said. "Finally."

Tucker balled up a fist and took a step forward. "You
Commie son of a—"

"Stop it!" Merchant said angrily. "Both of you. You let
this dissolve into petty ideology and nobody wins, everybody loses. It doesn't matter now, don't you understand
that?"

"Uh, Charlie," Tucker said low, his head inclined in the
direction of the camera. "This is all getting taped, you
know."

"Shut up, Tuck," Merchant said. "You always were a
hardheaded son of a bitch. I'm going to save our lives here
whether you help me or not."

"Yeah," Traynor said, a whisper. "Go, Charlie."

"This discussion has ended," the Cuban said, his voice
haughty. He turned to the poler. "Return us to shore."

Merchant looked at the Caribbean, Orosco. The man
still firmly held the line that joined the two rafts. He was
the key here, the link to survival. He stared hard at the
man. "They fight over your country like dogs over table
scraps," he said. "Is that what you want?"

"No," the man said immediately.

"Charlie . . ." Tucker said, a growl, Merchant ignoring
him as Tucker slipped back into the shadows, out of the
all-seeing eye of the camera, not man enough for the truth.

"It's your people who will die here," Merchant told
Orosco. "The Caribs in the hills, the fishermen on the
river, the tradesmen in the cities. They will all die, just as
surely as we stand here."

"Lies!" Gomez said angrily. "American lies."

"Truth," Merchant replied, "knows no nationality." He spoke directly to Gomez. "Why are you so afraid of my words? Are you that anxious to die?"

Orosco looked from Gomez to Merchant, his lips working soundlessly. "Give me a reason to believe you," he said at last.

Merchant slowly walked to the edge of the raft, within touching distance of Orosco, within staring distance of his shiny black eyes and slightly pockmarked face. "I'm telling you, General," he said, grabbing the man's eyes, holding them like a vise. "As one honorable man to another. There are two nuclear bombs planted somewhere on this river that will blow up with the rising sun if we don't do something. What the hell have you got to lose if I'm wrong or if I'm lying? A couple of hours. Are we so uncivilized that we can't postpone our mutual destruction for a couple of hours?"

"Truth is simple," Orosco said, "and I am a simple man." He turned to Gomez. "Only lies are complicated. I cannot speak for my Cuban ally, but my troops are yours to command."

"You fool!" Gomez spat, his face strained hard with anger and hatred. "This treachery will not take place. My men will blow you off the river."

Orosco turned to the man with quiet, contained fury. "I grow weary of you," he said low, controlled. "You try and stop me in my own country and you will be my enemy." He looked once again at Merchant. "Where do we begin?"

Charlie smiled, pointing upriver. "We've been drawn here so that the bombs' clout could be maximized effectively. I have to think that we'll find them planted in a tree somewhere upriver within a few miles."

They all followed his pointing finger. The jungle was tangled and dense all around them, the darkness making it worse. "You may be asking the impossible," Orosco said, looking up himself into the obviously lightening sky.

"No, sir," Merchant said. "I believe that you and I have already accomplished that." He reached a hand across the distance of the two rafts, Orosco smiling broadly and shaking it.

"Only one thing," Orosco said. "Your cameras. I think

that we should use them, perhaps broadcast live to show the world our cooperation should we fail."

Merchant looked at Tucker, the man shrugging broadly. "What can I say? If it works we'll all be heroes. If it doesn't, we're dead anyway. They can court-martial my body . . . if they can find it."

Merchant turned then to Traynor. "Sheila," he said. "This is your party, but I think for the search—"

She shook him off. "I've already got my exclusive," she said. "We'll let everybody in on the search. We're all betting our lives here."

"No," Gomez said quietly. "You are giving your lives away."

With that, he turned and yelled at the man with the pole to get them back to their side of the river.

Coco River Nearly Daybreak

Merchant sat in the prow of the motorboat beside the Navy SEAL demolition expert and a small stack of satchel bombs that had never gone off. Traynor, who'd apparently figured that sticking close to Merchant would be where the story was, sat on the bench seat behind, a cameraman rolling tape beside her. Both shores were alive with thousands of men, tramping through the bush, scanning the trees with searchlights and flares as tanks rolled through the underbrush, making the bank more accessible.

The sky had lightened to pale gray, Merchant's calculations giving them no more than thirty minutes at best to find the warheads. He looked at the demolitions man. "You think they've used the same kind of timer on the missiles?" he asked.

"I'd have to think so," he said, holding up one of the black digital timers. "It's simple and direct. Those missiles would have been transported without a trigger, so your boy had to have rigged something up himself, and I would go with something simple . . . like this."

"How do you dismantle it?"

The SEAL captain, dressed in wetsuit, took the two wires trailing out of the timer and held them apart. "These cables are weather thick," he said, "but easy to defuse. Don't pull on them, just cut through either of the lead wires so that the electrical connection cannot be completed." He took a small pair of wire cutters out of a tool case at his feet and handed them to Merchant. "This would do it," he said, snipping one of the leads to make his point.

Cameras lined the riverbank, the networks using mobile coverage to great effect, all of the TV people pooling their resources through a single director, who was making live cuts as the shots came up, broadcasting directly to the stations back home. There'd been no sign of General Gomez since the conclusion of the parlay.

Merchant looked up again into the sky, his heart racing. Tension got thicker on the riverbanks, the action more intense, the brighter the morning became. An edge of frantic hopelessness had begun to work its way into the proceedings that would only get worse as the minutes—

"We've found something!" someone yelled behind them, from the Honduran side of the river. "In the tree! In the tree!"

"Take us back!" Merchant yelled at the sergeant at the tiller. "Quickly!"

The engine whined loudly as the boat made a wide turn, slashing wake in all directions as the sergeant kicked up the engine to a high whine, banging them right up onto the riverbank near all the excitement.

Merchant and the SEAL jumped out of the boat onto dry land, looking up to see a warhead, three high-intensity lights focused on it, dangling precariously nearly a hundred feet up in the trees.

"We've got to get it down!" the SEAL yelled, Merchant looking to the tree itself, seeing the pulley rope wrapped around the trunk, holding the bomb aloft.

"Undo the rope!" Merchant yelled. "We've got to get that thing down here!"

The cameras began zeroing in on the area, as shouts brought the searchers closer to the action. Men with darkened faces and camouflage leaves in the netting of their helmets hurried to the rope, which was wrapped around the tree many times, and began laboriously trying to untie the knots.

Merchant ran to them. "Hurry!" he urged, wishing he could just reach out and pull that rope away from the tree.

"It's coming!" one of the men yelled after several agonizing minutes, a cheer rifling up and down the riverbank, testimony to the tension that had gripped them all. Even as his heart leapt at the sight of a line of men bracing themselves on the rope, his mind was burning with the thought of the other missile.

"There's no tension on the line," one of the men said, and Merchant looked up again, realizing that the rope was locked up in the pulley mechanism above.

"Get somebody up there to unlock the pulley!" he said, then turned and cupped his hands to his mouth. "We need climbers!"

He heard splashing from the other bank, and turned to see a number of men stripping out of their Companero uniforms and swimming toward him. The sky was bright enough now that the lights were being extinguished up and down the river.

Merchant was frantic as he watched the men swimming toward him. The time . . . the time. They reached the bank, stripped to their skivvies, three of them.

"We work the bananas," was all they said to him as they charged past and began scaling the tree like monkeys, holding themselves out at arm's length on the trunk and walking up the tree in a squat.

They moved quickly, more quickly than Merchant had thought possible, reaching the dizzying height in barely a minute. The first one to the top wrapped himself around the branch upside down and scooted across, slowly now, to the pulley.

"Get ready," Merchant told the troops holding on to the rope. "It's going to be heavy. Ready. . . ."

The man above reached out a hand and banged the lock mechanism of the pulley, the bomb coming down immediately, creaking loudly, nearly taking the rope out of the troops' hands. They stopped the rapid descent halfway down, the bomb now swinging wildly, the branch above cracking, but holding.

"Now, lower slowly . . . slowly."

The bomb inched down, maddeningly, as traces of pink showed up in the sky above. Merchant and the demolitions expert positioned themselves under the descent, Merchant's heart pounding louder the closer it got.

It was ten feet above. Then five.

"Easy . . . easy," he said, reaching up to steady the thing as it was lowered. "Stop!"

The men held firm, the bomb just above Merchant's head. The SEAL, taking a pair of cutters similar to the ones he had given Merchant, reached up without hesitation and cut both lead wires into the warhead, then reached out and pulled the magnetic timer off the side of the thing. His face was pale white. He handed the timer to Merchant and said, "Read it and weep."

Merchant looked down at the timer. It was under two minutes and counting down.

"Here! Here!" came shouts from the Caribbean side of the river, Merchant turning to see General Orosco pointing into the trees, searchlights pinpointing the spot.

It was the second bomb, and there was no time.

Merchant moved without thought, turning back to the boat and shoving it off the bank as he jumped in, Sheila Traynor and her cameraman still sitting there, filming everything.

The sergeant cranked up the motor and took them across the sixty-foot river span at top speed. "Get someone up in the tree!" Merchant screamed across at Orosco, who in turn ripped off his own shoes and socks and began climbing it himself.

As soon as the the boat bounced up on the Caribbean side of the shore, General Gomez and a contingent of men scrambled out of the underbrush, weapons pointed and ready.

"Prepare to fire!" Gomez said loudly, smiling as AK-47s were brought to bear. "I warned you of this, Colonel Merchant."

Merchant ignored Gomez, instead shouting to his troops. "That's a nuclear bomb hanging in that tree and it's just about to explode. If you stop us, everyone dies. If you're ready for that, then shoot me."

He walked toward the tree, grabbing a machete from a man clearing underbrush. There was no time to wait to untie the knots. "I need help on these ropes," he said, Caribbeans jumping to grab it above its wrapping.

"Fire!" Gomez shouted. "Fire at will!"

Nothing happened.

"Fire!" Gomez screamed, reaching for his sidearm. He pulled an automatic and aimed it at Merchant.

"Damn you!" Merchant screamed at him and began hacking away at the ropes on the tree, turning from the man.

The shot rang out hollowly, echoing up and down the morning river, everything stopping, Merchant waiting for the pain that didn't come. He turned to see Gomez, a look of stupefaction on his face, his hands trying futilely to hold back the rush of blood from a belly wound. One of his own men stood shaking wildly, ten feet away, smoke oozing from the barrel of his AK-47. And then the other Cubans fired at their commander, all of them in solidarity, Gomez falling heavily to splat on the riverbank.

"Got it!" Orosco yelled from where he straddled the branch so high above.

Merchant turned back to his work, cutting through the last of the bonds, the bomb dropping.

Three men were pulled up in the air, the rope whipping around the tree, slashing, dragging rapidly upward. Another man jumped on the rope and still the bomb lowered.

A fifth man leapt at the dangling rope and it wasn't going to be enough, Merchant grabbing an end to twist around the neck of the dead general, the body dangling in the air like a puppet on a string, dancing wildly. The bomb jerked to a halt thirty feet from the ground, Gomez doing in death what he would never have done while alive.

But the bomb was too high, maddeningly close, but out of reach. Merchant looked frantically around, spotting a Cuban tank fifteen feet away in the underbrush.

"Get that tank over here!" he ordered, then ran to the men on the line, only two of them with their feet on the ground. "Hang on . . . for God's sake!"

The tank rumbled into the clearing, Merchant jumping atop it, then atop the turret. Still not close enough. He looked at the cannon barrel. "Raise the gun!" he called, climbing on the cannon, straddling it, the cutters clamped tightly between his teeth.

They raised the barrel slowly, Merchant scooting out to its end and lying prone to keep from falling off. As the barrel got closer and closer to the bomb, Merchant began reaching, trying to claim it. He saw the timer. It had fifteen seconds left on it!

He kept straining toward it, trying to gain more height on the barrel, the Unitech logo, embossed on the trigger, mocking him. He pulled the cutters out of his mouth and reached again. Five seconds. Four . . . three . . .

He was ten seconds away from success when the timer ran out.

He tightened for the flash he knew he'd never see or feel, the warhead hissing loudly . . .

. . . then sputtering.

Then silence. In typical defense industry style, the damned thing had misfired.

The river was deathly quiet. Merchant, from his perch, looked all around, a smile beginning to crack his face, the smile turning to laughter. Loud, raucous laughter, echoing up and down the river. "A malfunction!" he screamed. "A malfunction!"

The river came alive. Deafening cheers and applause from thousands of troops drove the shore birds, screeching loudly, into the air as jungle animals bolted in fear.

Merchant turned from the barrel of the cannon and looked right at Traynor, who was crying and laughing at the same time from the turret, her cameraman grinding tape the whole time. "I'd like to call up the president of Unitech and thank him," Merchant said. "Then I want to cuss him out for shoddy workmanship." He laughed again. "Hell, the closest America gets to a real victory in half a century and it has to happen on a misfire." He shook his head. "What do you make of that?"

He slid back down the barrel, Traynor throwing herself into his arms and kissing him wildly all over his face, American and Communist troops dancing and singing all around the tank and all along the river.

"You did it, Charlie!" Traynor yelled to him above the noise. "You son of a bitch. You did it all by yourself."

"No, ma'am," he said, reaching into his pocket to bring out the toy soldier he'd carried all the way from Washington. He handed her the French rifleman. "This is you, lady. I couldn't have been here without you." He gave it to her, closing her hand over it. "Don't forget. Don't ever forget."

"Charlie," she said, crying, smiling. "Look around you. Nobody's ever going to be able to forget."

He looked. The clearing was filled with cameramen and newscasters, all of them rolling tape and doing stories, and to Charlie they were the most beautiful things he'd ever seen. The camera could be made to lie. But its real function was to tell the truth. And telling the truth was what they were doing now. The glorious, beautiful truth—that all life, all humanity, were one.

★ ★ ★ ★ ★ ★ ★ ★ ★ ★ ★ ★ ★ ★ ★

FEBRUARY 11,
MONDAY

★ ★ ★ ★ ★ ★ ★ ★ ★ ★ ★ ★ ★ ★ ★

◼◼◼◼ NEWSBREAK ◼◼◼◼

DIA CHIEF FOUND DEAD, LETTER CLEARS MERCHANT

Washington (AP)—The body of missing DIA head, General Eugene Tillotson, was found by a maid Sunday morning in an east-side motel, killed apparently by a self-inflicted gunshot wound. Police ruled the death a likely suicide. Tillotson had achieved national prominence just two days before when he accused Charles Merchant, former Army Intelligence head and hero of the Coco River, of conspiring to steal sensitive documents, resulting in the arrest of Merchant's wife, Linda, and a nationwide manhunt for Colonel Merchant himself. Linda Merchant was subsequently released and all contemplated charges dropped.

Acting head of D.C. homicide, Stan Grayson, at the scene said, "It appears that the general was eaten up with guilt after falsely accusing his best friend and took himself out. Things had just kind of spiraled out of control on him."

The text of an apparent suicide note found at the scene was released to news media this morning, despite the government's attempt to suppress it, and has been termed a political bombshell: "My greatest sin, perhaps, is that I love my country too much," the note read. "I loved her so much that I forgot that it is the wisdom of the people that makes a government work, not the other way around. Fearing the end of the military establishment that has kept this country strong, I conspired with a mercenary soldier, Ken Breedlove, to steal two nuclear missiles and blow them up in Caribbea, hoping that a resultant war would save Pentagon budget cuts. When my best friend discovered the plot, I accused him of treason to protect myself.

"I loved Charlie Merchant, just like I loved the military that I served for so long. That I've done them both a grave disservice is proof to me that I have outlived my usefulness as a contributing member of this wonderful country. I take full responsibility for everything that has occurred because of me and if you can't forgive me, at least try and understand.

"God bless America. I am so sorry."

The government has no comment on the incident except to term it "regrettable." Tillotson's chronic alcoholism is also listed as a contributing factor to the suicide.

—*Washington Post*
February 11

". . . and what can one say about the experience of a lifetime? I'd come down here to make myself famous, and came away grateful to have walked in the shadow of a great man. Charlie Merchant is a symbol to us all that simple human virtue is the most potent and important political theory to ever come along.

"More than anything else, Charlie Merchant shows us the possibilities. Through him, we've all gotten a little glimpse of how things could be. He is the true spirit of America, and he is on the ascendance. We've all seen the way. Our job now is to follow. This is Sheila Traynor reporting, with tears in my eyes, from somewhere in Honduras."

—NCC News
February 11

DEPARTMENT OF JUSTICE INTEROFFICE MEMO

TO: Securities Division, Prosecution
FROM: Office of the Director

Marc:

For God's sake, drop the insider charges against
Merchant's son! Do it first. Do it now. The last thing
we need is problems with *that* motherfucker. This
comes all the way from the Oval Office.

—Halpern

Pennsylvania Quarter 7:38 P.M.

Merchant hadn't worn a disguise since Linda had forced
him to go to a costume party back in 1972. He'd gone as a
French infantryman fighting with Washington's forces
during the War of Independence. The scuzzy false beard,
slouch hat, and inside-out overcoat he wore now weren't
nearly as sophisticated as his last outfit, but were every bit
as revolutionary in intent.

He crossed the wide foyer of the Quarter's hotel, heading for the elevators, reconnoitering the area through the
lenses of the big sunglasses he wore. He passed the open
doorway of the Hub Pub, the crowded lobby bar, pictures
of the action on the border juicing through a number of
TVs hanging from the ceiling. He smiled when he saw
himself.

The elevator foyer was empty when he arrived there. He
dug through his lining-side-out overcoat pocket and
pulled out the tiny elevator key he'd stolen from Mel's
purse when she'd been changing clothes at the house.

He moved quickly to the small private elevator and
used the key to get in. There was only one button to push,
the up arrow. He pushed it and took the ride up to BJ's
floor.

The hallway leading up to the LSI offices was dark and deserted. He took the walk casually, looking all around. He'd never been up here before, though he felt as if he knew the place. The double glass front doors were unlocked, opening into a waiting room sprouting green plants and tables full of magazines.

Past the foyer, the offices were dark, red and green lights blinking on a raised platform, Merchant smiling at what must be June Chan's famous tower. He felt as if he were visiting a neighborhood he used to live in as a kid. Everything was there, but seemed different.

When he'd called BJ's private number and asked to see James alone, he'd been promised privacy in the offices. The man was as good as his word at least. Following the directions he'd been given, he moved down the executive hallway that culminated with the security door at the end of the hall.

A buzzer was fixed beside the door. He rang it, the door clicking open immediately. He entered.

BJ sat on a straight-backed chair in the middle of the room, feeding videotape and a few papers into a trash can in front of him. The contents were burning, the video flames nearly red, licking out the top of the can, trickling smoke.

"Right on time," BJ said, smiling, then nodded toward Merchant and his disguise. "Very good, Charlie."

"Didn't want to be seen coming up here," Merchant said. "Burning evidence?"

BJ shrugged. "Just the last of this little adventure. The Tillotson tapes, stuff on Bignell . . . just cleanup. I hear you had a meeting with the President about me this afternoon. Hear you cut a deal."

Merchant nodded, taking off the fake beard and walking up to drop it into BJ's small fire. The hat followed, causing a lot of gray smoke. "The President was concerned," he said. "The President thought that you might be too close to the power to be exposed, how did he put it, 'for the good of the country.' So we cut a deal: I leave you out of things; he drops all charges against me and my family, plus gives Bramley a medal for blowing the whistle. There's a few rough edges, but I think it will smooth over."

"You learned well." BJ smiled. "I must be a good teacher."

"You were a damned good teacher," Merchant admitted. "And I whipped your ass."

"Did you?" BJ asked. "I still have my success in the House, the recision canceled. My tie-up deal in Central America didn't come off, but there'll be other chances to keep this country free and keep the military strong. I'm still doing fine, kicking ass. You win a few, lose a few. How's Mel, by the way?"

"I wouldn't know."

"You know, Charlie, I've just had a thought. You and I would make a great team. Now that you're a national hero, you should capitalize, run for office. I could back you to the sky. Together we could—"

"BJ," Charlie interrupted, taking off his overcoat and reversing it so that the proper side was out. "There's something I need to explain to you. You didn't exactly hear right about my talk with the President. We are, indeed, leaving you out of it. Completely. What I told the President was 'forget about BJ.'"

He put the coat back on and reached into the pocket, drawing out his .45. "You're the most dangerous man I've ever met, BJ," he said. "You can't be allowed to stay alive. You understand the system too well."

The man's eyes narrowed. "Go ahead," he said, smiling. "You know that everything that goes on in these offices is taped. You shoot me and spend the rest of your life in jail."

"One thing I learned years ago," Merchant said. "Is that people who hide cameras, never hide them in their own nest. No, BJ, there aren't any cameras."

The smile faded somewhat, then returned ruefully. "Well, Colonel Merchant," he said, "is this what you've reduced yourself to—disguises, assassinations? What happened to the truth, to justice? If you love this fucking system so much, arrest me, take me in. I'll be happy to let the courts decide my guilt or innocence."

"A week ago, I would have," Merchant said. "But I'm tainted now. I've played the same games you have and gotten dirty in the same ways."

"And you love it just like I do," BJ said. "Come on, Charlie. We're just alike. We love the juice, the thrill, controlling things. What a team we'd make. You can't shoot me. It's . . . not right."

"Oh, yeah," Merchant said. "You're the only one who's supposed to be allowed to break all the rules. I forgot. One of the nice things about war is that soldiers are never asked to decide complex issues of morality or ethics. They are only supposed to kill the enemy. And you are the most dangerous enemy I've ever faced."

"And what have I done? I'm a businessman, that's all. Just like all businessmen, I stake out my territory, then sell it. My territory just happens to be Congress. Think about it. I don't force anyone to do anything. Just like any businessman, I cut deals, take meetings, and try to maximize my potential in any way I can. I *am* America, the American dream in action where anyone from any walk of life can raise himself to the heights. Only in America, Charlie. Only in America. And you think I'm the only person who lies? Hell, look at you. You and the President have cooked up a lie, and you've made yourself a hero in the bargain. Let's see where your little contrivance leads, my friend. No, you're not any better than me."

"No, not any better, just different."

"Different, how?"

"I'm alive."

Merchant pulled the trigger, the gun coughing once, knocking BJ backward, chair and all falling over. He walked up to check. The man lay on his back, flopping like a fish, gasping, a gaping wound in his chest pumping out his life. He put another round through the man's head and ended it, winking in the direction of the FBI Building, visible through the patio door.

He took a long breath. Amazing how much trouble one hunk of flesh and blood could create. He put the gun back in his pocket and walked out of the office, not having touched anything.

BJ's penchant for privacy insured the perfection of Merchant's crime. There would be nothing physical to connect the two men to each other. In fact, now that BJ was dead, it would be as if he'd never existed at all. He was a paper man, and the paper had all been burned.

He walked back to the elevator and took it down to the lobby. BJ had suceeded on one level—he had corrupted

Merchant. Though things were all turned around now. When he'd been a saint, they'd hunted him down. Now that he was a cold-blooded killer, they honored him.

He stepped off the elevator and looked at his watch. Eight o'clock. Showtime. Looking like Charlie Merchant again, he strode purposefully toward the Hub Pub, smiling at all the surprised faces he saw as he came in.

They recognized him.

He walked into the middle of the busy room, looking around. He saw her at the corner table, nursing a glass of wine, her eyes staring at the tabletop. She looked beautiful, more beautiful than he'd ever remembered. He moved in that direction.

"Linda," he said, and she looked up at him, her eyes alight when she saw him smiling.

"Oh, Charlie," she said, standing, shaking. He took her in his arms and held her for a moment until the shaking stopped.

"It's going to be all right now," he whispered. "Everything's going to be all right."

She pulled away slightly, fear now in her eyes. "Is it?" she asked. "Is it?"

"Sit down," he said. "There's something I want to say to you."

They both sat, a cocktail waitress coming up to take his drink order.

"Scotch," he said. "Water back."

The woman started writing the order, then stopped, looking at him. "You're *him*, ain't you? That hero guy."

"Well, I . . ."

"Everybody!" she called loudly. "We got a real celebrity in here. Look! It's that guy from the TV!"

"Charlie Merchant!" somebody called, and the entire place broke out in cheers and applause, Merchant forced to stand and wave to them, acknowledging his fans. In the area of reality creation, he'd been quite successful for his first time out of the gate.

The woman ran off with the order, Linda and Charlie giggling behind their hands. They had too many years behind them to take any of it seriously.

"Listen to me," he told her when things had settled down. "I want you to know—"

"Wait," she said. "I have to get this out first. That boy I . . . I went to bed with. I was so confused, I . . . God help me, I wanted it, too, Charlie. I don't know what happened, I . . ."

"You got set up, that's all," he said, reaching out to take her hand. "You got set up by the best. Don't worry about it."

"You're not . . . angry?"

He smiled broadly. "I can't begin to tell you the turns that my life has taken in the last few days," he said. "No, I'm not angry. To be honest, I don't even blame you. After all the years I spent smothering you, I'm amazed and pleased that you did me the honor of showing up here at all tonight."

She shrugged. "But, Charlie . . . I love you. I realized when I was in jail that those terrible things they were saying about you weren't true. You are a good man. You have every right to be proud of the life you've led. I just . . . need more for myself right now. Your shadow is huge. I don't know that I can live under it anymore. I've been so unhappy."

"I honestly can't blame you," he said. "Linda, what I want you to know is that I've stopped making shadows and started living again. The wonder is in living, not in having lived. It's the only thing that matters. It takes an earthquake to move me, but by God, I've been moved. I'm so sorry for all the years I've held you back. If you're willing to give me another chance, I promise you that things will be far different from now on."

"I held myself back," she said, then looked at him quizzically. "No more army wife?"

"We've retired . . . with honors. Both of us. We'll make a game of it from now on. Expand out instead of closing in."

"Are you sure of this?" She smiled at him, catlike. "I've learned how to be a pretty pushy broad."

"The pushier, the better," he said, taking her face in his hands and kissing her. "Believe me. I love it."

"Uh . . . Mr. Merchant," came a voice behind him, Charlie turning to see the bartender standing there, holding his drink.

"Yes?"

The man leaned down. "The guy who owns this building," he said, putting the drink on the table, "Mr. James. He's a real patriot, like you. I know that he'd want you, and I want you, to have this drink on the house."

"Well, thank you," Merchant said, smiling wide. He was really going to enjoy the drink.

At that moment, all the televisions in the place began showing more pictures from the Honduran operation, then moving to a clip of the President holding a news conference.

"In my book," the President said, "Colonel Merchant is one of the great heroes of American history. This nation will never forget what he has done for all of us."

From that, they cut over to Charlie after attempting to dismantle the last bomb. He looked at the camera, smiled, and said, "What do you make of that?"

The place came apart with whoops and applause again, the bar patrons picking up a phrase that had already become legendary. "What do you make of that?" they called to him. "What do you make of that?"

He stood, holding his drink up and waving again to the crowd. He hoped he liked the new reality he'd created for himself, because it looked like he was going to be stuck with it. He smiled down at Linda then, the light in her eyes telling him all he'd ever need to know about truth.

LOBBYIST FOUND DEAD

Washington (AP)—Superlobbyist Ben James was found murdered this morning in the posh executive offices of Legislative Services, Inc., the business he had taken from a storefront consulting firm to a multibillion-dollar enterprise in just five years. James, 38, was shot at close range, execution style, in the chest and in the head with a large caliber weapon.

So far, the authorities have been unable to turn up a motive in the slaying. "There just aren't any clues," said D.C. police spokesman Howard McManus. "James was well liked by everyone, nothing was touched in the office, and he had five thousand dollars cash in his wallet at the time of his death. This is going to be a tough one."

James, a well-known name in Washington power circles, is generally credited with the concept of bringing PAC dollars together under a larger umbrella for more political clout. His accounts ranged everywhere from small dairy farmers in Wisconsin to the largest armaments manufacturers in the country. "This has been a terrible blow to everyone who knew BJ," said Melanie Patterson, speaking for LSI. "He was a man with no enemies, and had just enjoyed his greatest success with last week's antirecision vote in the House. We're all still in a state of shock."

Asked if James's death would mean the end of the largest lobbying firm in the world, Patterson said, "No. We've already reorganized. All our accounts are still in place. June Chan, BJ's executive secretary, and I will carry on the day-to-day operation of the business. BJ would have wanted it that way. We still guarantee satisfaction and we still deliver."

There are no suspects in the case at this time.

WHAT MAKES ROSEN RUN?

Anybody who knows anything about power politics was smirking over his grapefruit this morning with the announcement that demo-deluxe speaker of the House Phil Rosen has called a major news conference at the Capitol later this week. The speculation is rampant that Rosen will toss his yarmulke into the ring by announcing his candidacy for president. From this corner, that speculation looks a lot like certainty.

For many it makes no sense that an old-school liberal like Rosen could have a chance getting elected dogcatcher. After all, the country's gone conservative from sea to shining sea. Add to that

Rosen's devastating defeat on last week's recision vote, which effectively destroyed his power base, and you seem to have a man destined for the political trash heap. But look again, closer.

First off, the death of Jack Braedman left a sucking wound in the Democratic power structure. Braedman had been groomed from the get-go as next November's golden boy, toning down his liberal image to appeal to the masses. Nature abhors a vacuum, and Rosen's high profile could fill that void. Secondly, though he lost the recision vote, the events that occurred in Caribbea over the weekend proved that his head-above-water approach was thoughtful and correct. While everyone else in Congress was drowning in a sea of public opinion and false information, Rosen was calmly treading water, showing everyone the leadership qualities it takes to run a large and complex country like the United States. Last, and certainly not least, is Rosen's close connection to Charlie Merchant, America's first bona fide hero since Douglas MacArthur. We're talking men of character here, something this town hasn't seen for a long time, and they seem to get taller every time we see them. From my seat here at the Potomac junction, the air surrounding Phil Rosen smells sweet and pure. And in this era of serious pollutions, a breath of fresh oxygen may be just what this country needs.

—The Southwest Jewish Chronicle
February 25